HANS CHRISTIAN ANDERSEN TALES

Hans Christian Andersen Tales

Translation by Jean Hersholt
Translation of "The Tallow Candle" by Compass Languages

Word Cloud Classics

San Diego

Canterbury Classics
An imprint of Printers Row Publishing Group
10350 Barnes Canyon Road, Suite 100, San Diego, CA 92121
www.thunderbaybooks.com

Printers Row Publishing Group is a division of Readerlink Distribution Services, LLC. The Canterbury Classics and Word Cloud Classics names and logos are trademarks of Readerlink Distribution Services, LLC.

All correspondence concerning the content of this book should be addressed to Canterbury Classics, Editorial Department, at the above address.

Publisher: Peter Norton
Publishing Team: Lori Asbury, Ana Parker
Editorial Team: JoAnn Padgett, Melinda Allman, Traci Douglas
Production Team: Blake Mitchum, Rusty von Dyl, Lidija Tomas

Library of Congress Cataloging-in-Publication Data

Andersen, H. C. (Hans Christian), 1805-1875.
  [Tales. English]
  Hans Christian Andersen tales.
     pages cm -- (Word cloud classics)
  Summary: A collection of sixty-four fairy tales, including a translation by Compass Languages of "The Tallow Candle," written by Andersen early in his career but only recently discovered, and such classics as "Thumbelina" and "The Little Mermaid," as translated by Jean Hersholt.
  ISBN-13: 978-1-62686-259-3 (paperback)
  ISBN-10: 1-62686-259-1 (flexibound)
  1. Fairy tales--Denmark--Translations into English. 2. Children's stories, Danish--Translations into English. [1. Fairy tales. 2. Short stories.] I. Hersholt, Jean, 1886-1956 translator. II. Compass Languages. III. Title.
  PZ8.A54Hanm 2014
  839.813'6--dc23
                    2014008336

PRINTED IN CHINA
20 19 18 17 16 4 5 6 7 8

CONTENTS

PUBLISHER'S NOTE

In this volume, the years that appear after each story's title indicate the original date of the story's publication (in any language). Most were published by Andersen (in Danish) during his lifetime as serials in magazines, or as collected works.

Andersen's earliest story, "The Tallow Candle," lay unknown to scholars and the public for almost two centuries before it was discovered among papers donated to the Danish National Archives. Historians have confirmed it is Andersen's earliest known work, written in his teens before his true authorship began. We've indicated the date as the 1820s to give it chronological context, even though it was never officially published by Andersen.

THE TALLOW CANDLE (1820s)

There was sputtering and sizzling as the flames played under the pan. This was the tallow candle's cradle, and out of the warm cradle slipped the candle—perfectly shaped, all of a piece, shiny white and slender. It was formed in a way that made everyone who laid eyes on it believe that it must promise a bright and glorious future. Indeed, it was destined to keep that promise and fulfill their expectations.

The sheep—a pretty little sheep—was the candle's mother, and the melting pot was its father. From its mother, it had inherited its dazzlingly white body and an intuitive understanding of life; but from its father, it had acquired the desire for the blazing fire that would eventually reach its very core and "shine the light" for it in life.

That is how it had been made and how it cast itself, with the best and brightest of hopes, into life. Here it met an amazing number of fellow creatures with whom it had dealings, since it desired to get to know life and thus perhaps find the most suitable niche for itself. But the candle saw the world in too benevolent a light, while the world only cared about itself and not about the tallow candle at all. The world was unable to understand the true nature of the candle, so it tried to use it to its own advantage and handled the candle improperly. Black fingers made bigger and bigger spots on the white color of innocence, which little by little totally disappeared, to be covered with the filth of an outside world that had been far too harsh and come much closer than the candle could bear, since it had been unable to distinguish between the pure and the impure—but deep inside, it was still innocent and unspoiled.

That is when the false friends realized that they could not reach its innermost part. In anger, they threw away the candle, considering it a useless thing.

The outer black layer kept away everybody good—they were afraid of becoming contaminated by the black color, of getting spots on themselves, so they kept a distance.

Now, the poor tallow candle was lonely, abandoned, and at its wit's end. It felt cast off by what was good and discovered that it had been nothing but a blind tool used to advance what was bad. It felt so terribly

1

sad because it had lived its life without purpose—perhaps it had even tarnished some good things by its presence. It could not grasp why and to what end it had been created, why it was put on this Earth where it might destroy itself and even others.

More and more, increasingly deeply, it pondered the situation, but the more it thought, the greater its despondency, since it could not find anything good at all, no real meaning for itself—or see the purpose it had been given at birth. It was as if the black layer had also thrown a veil over its eyes.

That was when it met a small flame, a tinderbox. The tinderbox knew the light better than the tallow candle knew itself, for the tinderbox saw everything so clearly—right through the outer layer, and inside it found so much good. Therefore, it went closer, and bright hopes emerged in the candle. It lit up, and its heart melted.

The flame shone brightly—like a wedding torch of joy. Everything became bright and clear, and it showed the way for those in its company, its true friends—and helped by the light, they could now successfully seek truth.

The body, too, was strong enough to nurture and support the burning flame. Like the beginnings of new life, one round and plump drop after the other rolled down the candle, covering the filth of the past.

This was not only the bodily, but also the spiritual gain of the marriage.

The tallow candle had found its true place in life—and proved that a true light shone for a long time, spreading joy for itself and its fellow creatures.

THE TINDERBOX (1835)

There came a soldier marching down the high road—*one, two! one, two!* He had his knapsack on his back and his sword at his side as he came home from the wars. On the road, he met a witch, an ugly old witch, a witch whose lower lip dangled right down on her chest.

"Good evening, soldier," she said. "What a fine sword you've got there, and what a big knapsack. Aren't you every inch a soldier! And now you shall have money, as much as you please."

"That's very kind, you old witch," said the soldier.

"See that big tree." The witch pointed to one nearby them. "It's hollow to the roots. Climb to the top of the trunk, and you'll find a hole through which you can let yourself down deep under the tree. I'll tie a rope around your middle, so that when you call me, I can pull you up again."

"What would I do deep down under that tree?" the soldier wanted to know.

"Fetch money," the witch said. "Listen. When you touch bottom, you'll find yourself in a great hall. It is very bright there, because more than a hundred lamps are burning. By their light, you will see three doors. Each door has a key in it, so you can open them all.

"If you walk into the first room, you'll see a large chest in the middle of the floor. On it sits a dog, and his eyes are as big as saucers. But don't worry about that. I'll give you my blue-checked apron to spread out on the floor. Snatch up that dog, and set him on my apron. Then you can open the chest and take out as many pieces of money as you please. They are all copper.

"But if silver suits you better, then go into the next room. There sits a dog, and his eyes are as big as mill wheels. But don't you care about that. Set the dog on my apron while you line your pockets with silver.

"Maybe you'd rather have gold. You can, you know. You can have all the gold you can carry if you go into the third room. The only hitch is that there on the money-chest sits a dog, and each of his eyes is as big as the Round Tower of Copenhagen. That's the sort of dog he is. But never you mind how fierce he looks. Just set him on my apron and he'll do you no harm as you help yourself from the chest to all the gold you want."

"That suits me," said the soldier. "But what do you get out of all this, you old witch? I suppose that you want your share."

"No indeed," said the witch. "I don't want a penny of it. All I ask is for you to fetch me an old tinderbox that my grandmother forgot the last time she was down there."

"Good," said the soldier. "Tie the rope around me."

"Here it is," said the witch, "and here's my blue-checked apron."

The soldier climbed up to the hole in the tree and let himself slide through it, feet foremost down into the great hall where the hundreds of lamps were burning, just as the witch had said. Now he threw open the first door he came to. Ugh! There sat a dog glaring at him with eyes as big as saucers.

"You're a nice fellow," the soldier said, as he shifted him to the witch's apron and took all the coppers that his pockets would hold. He shut up the chest, set the dog back on it, and made for the second room. Alas and alack! There sat the dog with eyes as big as mill wheels.

"Don't you look at me like that." The soldier set him on the witch's apron. "You're apt to strain your eyesight." When he saw the chest brimful of silver, he threw away all his coppers and filled both his pockets and knapsack with silver alone. Then he went into the third room. Oh, what a horrible sight to see! The dog in there really did have eyes as big as the Round Tower, and when he rolled them, they spun like wheels.

"Good evening," the soldier said, and saluted, for such a dog he had never seen before. But on second glance, he thought to himself, "This won't do." So he lifted the dog down to the floor, and threw open the chest. What a sight! Here was gold and to spare. He could buy out all Copenhagen with it. He could buy all the cake-woman's sugar pigs, and all the tin soldiers, whips, and rocking horses there are in the world. Yes, *there* was really money!

In short order, the soldier got rid of all the silver coins he had stuffed in his pockets and knapsack, to put gold in their place. Yes sir, he crammed all his pockets, his knapsack, his cap, and his boots so full that he scarcely could walk. Now he was made of money. Putting the dog back on the chest, he banged out the door and called up through the hollow tree:

"Pull me up now, you old witch."

"Have you got the tinderbox?" asked the witch.

"Confound the tinderbox," the soldier shouted. "I clean forgot it."

When he fetched it, the witch hauled him up. There he stood on the high road again, with his pockets, boots, knapsack, and cap full of gold.

"What do you want with the tinderbox?" he asked the old witch.

"None of your business," she told him. "You've had your money, so hand over my tinderbox."

"Nonsense," said the soldier. "I'll take out my sword, and I'll cut your head off if you don't tell me at once what you want with it."

"I won't," the witch screamed at him.

So he cut her head off. There she lay! But he tied all his money in her apron, slung it over his shoulder, stuck the tinderbox in his pocket, and struck out for town.

It was a splendid town. He took the best rooms at the best inn, and ordered all the good things he liked to eat, for he was a rich man now because he had so much money. The servant who cleaned his boots may have thought them remarkably well worn for a man of such means, but that was before he went shopping. Next morning, he bought boots worthy of him, and the best clothes. Now that he had turned out to be such a fashionable gentleman, people told him all about the splendors of their town—all about their king, and what a pretty princess he had for a daughter.

"Where can I see her?" the soldier inquired.

"You can't see her at all," everyone said. "She lives in a great copper castle inside all sorts of walls and towers. Only the king can come in or go out of it, for it's been foretold that the princess will marry a common soldier. The king would much rather she didn't."

"I'd like to see her just the same," the soldier thought. But there was no way to manage it.

Now he lived a merry life. He went to the theater, drove about in the king's garden, and gave away money to poor people. This was to his credit, for he remembered from the old days what it feels like to go without a penny in your pocket. Now that he was wealthy and well dressed, he had all too many who called him their friend and a genuine gentleman. That pleased him.

But he spent money every day without making any, and wound up with only two coppers to his name. He had to quit his fine quarters to live in a garret, clean his own boots, and mend them himself with a darning needle. None of his friends came to see him, because there were too many stairs to climb.

One evening when he sat in the dark without even enough money to buy a candle, he suddenly remembered there was a candle end in the tinderbox that he had picked up when the witch sent him down the hollow tree. He got out the tinderbox, and the moment he struck sparks from the flint of it, his door burst open, and there stood a dog from down under the tree. It was the one with eyes as big as saucers.

"What," said the dog, "is my lord's command?"

"What's this?" said the soldier. "Have I got the sort of tinderbox that will get me whatever I want? Go get me some money," he ordered the dog. *Zip!* The dog was gone. *Zip!* He was back again, with a bag full of copper in his mouth.

Now the soldier knew what a remarkable tinderbox he had. Strike it once, and there was the dog from the chest of copper coins. Strike it twice, and here came the dog who had the silver. Three times brought the dog who guarded gold.

Back went the soldier to his comfortable quarters. Out strode the soldier in fashionable clothes. Immediately his friends knew him again, because they liked him so much.

Then the thought occurred to him, "Isn't it odd that no one ever gets to see the princess? They say she's very pretty, but what's the good of it as long as she stays locked up in that large copper castle with so many towers? Why can't I see her? Where's my tinderbox?" He struck a light and, *zip!* came the dog with eyes as big as saucers.

"It certainly is late," said the soldier. "Practically midnight. But I do want a glimpse of the princess, if only for a moment."

Out the door went the dog, and before the soldier could believe it, here came the dog with the princess on his back. She was sound asleep, and so pretty that everyone could see she was a princess. The soldier couldn't keep from kissing her, because he was every inch a soldier. Then the dog took the princess home.

Next morning when the king and queen were drinking their tea, the princess told them about the strange dream she'd had—all about a dog and a soldier. She'd ridden on the dog's back, and the soldier had kissed her.

"Now that was a fine story," said the queen. The next night, one of the old ladies of the court was under orders to sit by the princess's bed, and see whether this was a dream or something else altogether. The soldier was longing to see the pretty princess again, so the dog came by night to take her up and away as fast as he could run. But the old lady pulled on her storm boots and ran right after them. When she saw them disappear into a large house, she thought, "Now I know where it is," and drew a big cross on the door with a piece of chalk. Then she went home to bed, and before long the dog brought the princess home too. But when the dog saw that cross marked on the soldier's front door, he got himself a piece of chalk and cross-marked every door in the town.

This was a clever thing to do, because now the old lady couldn't tell the right door from all the wrong doors he had marked.

Early in the morning, along came the king and the queen, the old lady, and all the officers, to see where the princess had been.

"Here it is," said the king when he saw the first cross mark.

"No, my dear. There it is," said the queen, who was looking next door.

"Here's one, there's one, and yonder's another one!" said they all. Wherever they looked they saw chalk marks, so they gave up searching.

The queen, though, was an uncommonly clever woman, who could do more than ride in a coach. She took her big gold scissors, cut out a piece of silk, and made a neat little bag. She filled it with fine buckwheat flour and tied it onto the princess's back. Then she pricked a little hole in it so that the flour would sift out along the way, wherever the princess might go.

Again the dog came in the night, took the princess on his back, and ran with her to the soldier, who loved her so much that he would have been glad to be a prince just so he could make her his wife.

The dog didn't notice how the flour made a trail from the castle right up to the soldier's window, where he ran up the wall with the princess. So in the morning, it was all too plain to the king and queen just where their daughter had been.

They took the soldier, and they put him in prison. There he sat. It was dark, and it was dismal, and they told him, "Tomorrow is the day for you to hang." That didn't cheer him up any, and as for his tinderbox, he'd left it behind at the inn. In the morning he could see through his narrow little window how the people all hurried out of town to see him hanged. He heard the drums beat, and he saw the soldiers march. In the crowd of running people, he saw a shoemaker's boy in a leather apron and slippers. The boy galloped so fast that off flew one slipper, which hit the wall right where the soldier pressed his face to the iron bars.

"Hey there, you shoemaker's boy, there's no hurry," the soldier shouted. "Nothing can happen till I get there. But if you run to where I live and bring me my tinderbox, I'll give you four coppers. Put your best foot foremost."

The shoemaker's boy could use four coppers, so he rushed the tinderbox to the soldier, and—well, now we shall hear what happened!

Outside the town, a high gallows had been built. Around it stood soldiers and many hundred thousand people. The king and queen sat on a splendid throne, opposite the judge and the whole council. The soldier already stood upon the ladder, but just as they were about to put the rope around his neck, he said the custom was to grant a poor criminal one last small favor. He wanted to smoke a pipe of tobacco— the last he'd be smoking in this world.

The king couldn't refuse him, so the soldier struck fire from his tinderbox, once, twice, and a third time. *Zip!* There stood all the dogs, one with eyes as big as saucers, one with eyes as big as mill wheels, one with eyes as big as the Round Tower of Copenhagen.

"Help me. Save me from hanging!" said the soldier. Those dogs took the judges and all the council, some by the leg and some by the nose, and tossed them so high that they came down broken to bits.

"Don't!" cried the king, but the biggest dog took him and the queen too, and tossed them up after the others. Then the soldiers trembled, and the people shouted, "Soldier, be our king and marry the pretty princess."

So they put the soldier in the king's carriage. All three of his dogs danced in front of it, and shouted "Hurrah!" The boys whistled through their fingers, and the soldiers saluted. The princess came out of the copper castle to be queen, and that suited her exactly. The wedding lasted all of a week, and the three dogs sat at the table, with their eyes opened wider than ever before.

LITTLE CLAUS AND BIG CLAUS (1835)

In a village there lived two men who had the self-same name. Both were named Claus. But one of them owned four horses, and the other owned only one horse; so to distinguish between them, people called the man who had four horses Big Claus, and the man who had only one horse Little Claus. Now I'll tell you what happened to these two, for this is a true story.

The whole week through, Little Claus had to plow for Big Claus and lend him his only horse. In return, Big Claus lent him all four of his horses, but only for one day a week, and that had to be Sunday.

Each Sunday, how proudly Little Claus cracked his whip over all the five horses, which were as good as his own on that day. How brightly the sun shone. How merry were the church bells that rang in the steeple. How well dressed were all the people who passed him with hymnbooks tucked under their arms. And as they went their way to church, to hear the parson preach, how the people did stare to see Little Claus plowing with all five horses. This made him feel so proud that he would crack his whip and holler, "Get up, all my horses."

"You must not say that," Big Claus told him. "You know as well as I do that only one of those horses is yours." But no sooner did another bevy of churchgoers come by than Little Claus forgot he mustn't say it, and hollered, "Get up, all my horses."

"Don't you say that again," Big Claus told him. "If you do, I'll knock your horse down dead in his traces, and that will be the end of him."

"You won't catch me saying it again," Little Claus promised. But as soon as people came by, nodding to him and wishing him "Good morning," he was so pleased and so proud of how grand it looked to have five horses plowing his field, that he hollered again, "Get up, all my horses!"

"I'll get up your horse for you," Big Claus said, and he snatched up a tethering mallet, and he knocked Little Claus's one and only horse on the head so hard that it fell down dead.

"Now I haven't any horse at all," said Little Claus, and he began to cry. But by and by, he skinned his dead horse and hung the hide to dry in the wind. Then he crammed the dry skin in a sack, slung it up over his shoulder, and set out to sell it in the nearest town.

It was a long way to go, and he had to pass through a dark, dismal forest. Suddenly a terrible storm came up, and he lost his way. Before he could find it again, evening overtook him. The town was still a long way off, and he had come too far to get back home before night.

Not far from the road he saw a large farmhouse. The shutters were closed, but light showed through a crack at the top of the windows. "Maybe they'll let me spend the night here," Little Claus thought, as he went to the door and knocked.

The farmer's wife opened it, but when she heard what he wanted, she told him to go away. She said her husband wasn't home, and she wouldn't have any strangers in the house.

"Then I'll have to sleep outside," Little Claus decided, as she slammed the door in his face.

Near the farmhouse stood a large haystack, leading up to the thatched roof of a shed, which lay between it and the house. "That's where I'll sleep," said Little Claus when he noticed the thatch. "It will make a wonderful bed. All I hope is that the stork doesn't fly down and bite my legs." For a stork was actually standing guard on the roof where it had a nest.

So Little Claus climbed to the roof of the shed. As he turned over to make himself comfortable, he discovered that the farmhouse shutters didn't come quite to the top of the windows, and he could see over them. He could see into a room where a big table was spread with wine and roast meat and a delicious fish. The farmer's wife and the sexton were sitting there at the table, all by themselves. She kept helping him to wine, and he kept helping himself to fish. He must have loved fish.

"Oh, if only I could have some too," thought Little Claus. By craning his neck toward the window he caught sight of a great, appetizing cake. Why, they were feasting in there!

Just then he heard someone riding down the road to the house. It was the farmer coming home. He was an excellent man except for just one thing. He could not stand the sight of a sexton. If he so much as caught a glimpse of one, he would fly into a furious rage, which was the reason why the sexton had gone to see the farmer's wife while her husband was away from home, and the good woman could do no less than set before him all the good things to eat that she had in the house. When she heard the farmer coming, she trembled for the sexton, and begged him to creep into a big empty chest, which stood in one corner of the room. He lost no time about it, because he knew full well that her poor husband couldn't stand the sight of a sexton. The woman quickly set aside the wine and hid the good food in her oven, because if her husband had seen the feast, he would have asked questions hard to answer.

"Oh dear!" Up on the shed, Little Claus sighed to see all the good food disappearing.

"Who's up there?" the farmer peered at Little Claus. "Whatever are you doing up there? Come into the house with me." So Little Claus came down. He told the farmer how he had lost his way, and asked if he could have shelter for the night.

"Of course," said the farmer, "but first, let's have something to eat."

The farmer's wife received them well, laid the whole table, and set before them a big bowl of porridge. The farmer was hungry and ate it with a good appetite, but Little Claus was thinking about the good roast meat, that fish and that cake in the oven. Beside his feet under the table lay his sack with the horsehide, for as we know, he was on his way to sell it in the town. Not liking the porridge at all, Little Claus trod on the sack, and the dry hide gave a loud squeak.

"Sh!" Little Claus said to his sack, at the same time that he trod on it so hard that it squeaked even louder.

"What on Earth have you got in there?" said the farmer.

"Oh, just a conjuror," said Little Claus. "He tells me we don't have to eat porridge, because he has conjured up a whole oven-full of roast meat, fish, and cake for us."

"What do you say?" said the farmer. He made haste to open the oven, where he found all the good dishes. His wife had hidden them there, but he quite believed that they had been conjured up by the wizard in the sack. His wife didn't dare open her mouth as she helped them to their fill of meat, fish, and cake.

Then Little Claus trod upon the sack to make it squeak again.

"What does he say now?" asked the farmer.

"He says," Little Claus answered, "that there are three bottles of wine for us in the corner by the oven."

So the woman had to bring out the wine she had hidden. The farmer drank it till he grew merry, and wanted to get himself a conjuror just like the one Little Claus carried in his sack.

"Can he conjure up the devil?" the farmer wondered. "I'm in just the mood to meet him."

"Oh, yes," said Little Claus. "My conjuror can do anything I tell him. Can't you?" he asked and trod upon the sack till it squeaked. "Did you hear him answer? He said 'Yes.' He can conjure up the devil, but he's afraid we won't like the look of him."

"Oh, I'm not afraid. What's he like?"

"Well, he looks an awful lot like a sexton."

"Ho," said the farmer, "as ugly as that? I can't bear the sight of a sexton. But don't let that stop us. Now that I know it's just the devil, I shan't mind it so much. I'll face him, provided he doesn't come near me."

"Wait, while I talk with my conjuror." Little Claus trod on the sack and stooped down to listen.

"What does he say?"

"He says for you to go and open that big chest in the corner, and there you'll find the devil doubled up inside it. But you must hold fast to the lid, so he doesn't pop out."

"Will you help me hold it?" said the farmer. He went to the chest in which his wife had hidden the sexton—once frightened, now terrified. The farmer lifted the lid a little, and peeped in.

"Ho!" he sprang back. "I saw him, and he's the image of our sexton, a horrible sight!" After that, they needed another drink, and sat there drinking far into the night.

"You must sell me your conjuror," said the farmer. "You can fix your own price. I'd pay you a bushel of money right away."

"Oh, I couldn't do that," Little Claus said. "Just think how useful my conjuror is."

"But I'd so like to have him." The farmer kept begging to buy it.

"Well," said Little Claus at last, "you've been kind enough to give me a night's lodging, so I can't say no. You shall have my sack for a bushel of money, but it must be full to the brim."

"You shall have it," said the farmer. "But you must take that chest along with you, too. I won't have it in the house another hour. He might still be inside it. You never can tell."

So Little Claus sold his sack with the dried horsehide in it, and was paid a bushel of money, measured up to the brim. The farmer gave him a wheelbarrow, too, in which to wheel away the money and the chest.

"Fare you well," said Little Claus, and off he went with his money and his chest with the sexton in it. On the further side of the forest was a deep, wide river, where the current ran so strong that it was almost impossible to swim against it. A big new bridge had been built across the river, and when Little Claus came to the middle of it, he said, very loud so the sexton could hear him:

"Now what would I be doing with this silly chest? It's as heavy as stone, and I'm too tired to wheel it any further. So I'll throw it in the river, and if it drifts down to my house, well and good, but if it sinks, I haven't lost much." Then he tilted the chest a little, as if he were about to tip it into the river.

"Stop! Don't!" the sexton shouted inside. "Let me get out first."

"Oh," said Little Claus, pretending to be frightened, "is he still there? Then I'd better throw him into the river and drown him."

"Oh no, don't do that to me!" the sexton shouted. "I'd give a bushel of money to get out of this."

"Why, that's altogether different," said Little Claus, opening the chest. The sexton popped out at once, pushed the empty chest into the water, and hurried home to give Little Claus a bushel of money. What with the farmer's bushel and the sexton's bushel, Little Claus had his wheelbarrow quite full.

"I got a good price for my horse," he said when he got home and emptied all the money in a heap on the floor of his room. "How Big Claus will fret when he finds out that my one horse has made me so rich, but I won't tell him how I managed it." Then he sent a boy to borrow a bushel measure from Big Claus.

"Whatever would he want with it?" Big Claus wondered, and smeared pitch on the bottom of the bushel so that a little of what he measured would stick to it. And so it happened that when he got his measure back, he found three newly minted pieces of silver stuck to it.

"What's this?" Big Claus ran to see Little Claus. "Where did you get so much money?"

"Oh, that's what I got for the horsehide I sold last night."

"Heavens above! How the price of hides must have gone up." Big Claus ran home, took an ax, and knocked all four of his horses on the head. Then he ripped their hides off, and set out to town with them.

"Hides, hides! Who'll buy hides?" he bawled, up and down the streets. All the shoemakers and tanners came running to ask what their price was. "A bushel of money apiece," he told them.

"Are you crazy?" they asked. "Do you think we spend money by the bushel?"

"Hides, hides! Who'll buy hides?" he kept on shouting, and to those who asked how much, he said, "A bushel of money."

"He takes us for fools," they said. The shoemakers took their straps, and the tanners their leather aprons, and they beat Big Claus through the town.

"Hides, hides!" they mocked him. "We'll tan your hide for you if you don't get out of town." Big Claus had to run as fast as he could. He had never been beaten so badly.

"Little Claus will pay for this," he said when he got back home. "I'll kill him for it."

Now it so happened that Little Claus's old grandmother had just died. She had been as cross as could be—never a kind word did she have for him—but he was sorry to see her die. He put the dead woman in his own warm bed, just in case she came to life again, and let her lie there all night while he napped in a chair in the corner, as he had done so often before.

As he sat there in the night, the door opened, and in came Big Claus with an ax. He knew exactly where Little Claus's bed was, so he went straight to it and knocked the dead grandmother on the head, under the impression that she was Little Claus.

"There," he said, "You won't fool me again." Then he went home.

"What a wicked man," said Little Claus. "Why, he would have killed me. It's lucky for my grandmother that she was already dead, or he'd have been the death of her."

He dressed up his old grandmother in her Sunday best, borrowed a neighbor's horse, and hitched up his cart. On the back seat, he propped up his grandmother, wedged in so that the jolts would not topple her over, and away they went through the forest.

When the sun came up, they drew abreast of a large inn, where Little Claus halted and went in to get him some breakfast. The innkeeper was a wealthy man, and a good enough fellow in his way, but his temper was as fiery as if he were made of pepper and snuff.

"Good morning," he said to Little Claus. "You're up and dressed mighty early."

"Yes," said Little Claus. "I am bound for the town with my old grandmother, who is sitting out there in the cart. I can't get her to come in, but you might take her a glass of mead. You'll have to shout to make her hear you, for she's deaf as a post."

"I'll take it right out." The innkeeper poured a glass full of mead and took it to the dead grandmother, who sat stiffly on the cart.

"Your grandson sent you a glass of mead," said the innkeeper, but the dead woman said never a word. She just sat there.

"Don't you hear me?" the innkeeper shouted his loudest. "Here's a glass of mead from your grandson."

Time after time he shouted it, but she didn't budge. He flew into such a rage that he threw the glass in her face. The mead splashed all over her as she fell over backward, for she was just propped up, not tied in place.

"Confound it!" Little Claus rushed out the door and took the innkeeper by the throat. "You've gone and killed my grandmother. Look! There's a big hole in her forehead."

"Oh, what a calamity!" The innkeeper wrung his hands. "And all because of my fiery temper. Dear Little Claus, I'll give you a bushel of money, and I'll bury your grandmother as if she were my very own. But you must hush this thing up for me, or they'll chop off my head—how I'd hate it."

So it came about that Little Claus got another bushel of money, and the landlord buried the old grandmother as if she'd been his own.

Just as soon as Little Claus got home, he sent a boy to borrow a bushel measure from Big Claus.

"Little Claus wants to borrow it?" Big Claus asked. "Didn't I kill him? I'll go and see about that." So he himself took the measure over to Little Claus.

"Where did you get all that money?" he asked when he saw the height of the money pile.

"When you killed my grandmother instead of me," Little Claus told him, "I sold her for a bushel of money."

"Heavens above! That was indeed a good price," said Big Claus. He hurried home, took an ax, and knocked his old grandmother on the head. Then he put her in a cart, drove off to town, and asked the apothecary if he wanted to buy a dead body.

"Whose dead body?" asked the apothecary. "Where'd you get it?"

"It's my grandmother's dead body. I killed her for a bushel of money," Big Claus told him.

"Lord," said the apothecary. "Man, you must be crazy. Don't talk like that, or they'll chop off your head." Then he told him straight he had done a wicked deed, that he was a terrible fellow, and that the worst of punishments was much too good for him. Big Claus got frightened. He jumped in his cart, whipped up the horses, and drove home as fast as they would take him. The apothecary and everyone else thought he must be a madman, so they didn't stand in his way.

"I'll see that you pay for this," said Big Claus when he reached the high road. "Oh, won't I make you pay for this, Little Claus!" The moment he got home, he took the biggest sack he could find, went to see Little Claus, and said:

"You've deceived me again. First, I killed my four horses. Then I killed my old grandmother, and it's all your fault. But I'll make sure you don't make a fool of me again." Then he caught Little Claus and put him in the sack, slung it up over his back and told him, "Now I shall take you and drown you."

It was a long way to the river, and Little Claus was no light load. The road went by the church, and as they passed, they could hear the organ playing and the people singing very beautifully. Big Claus set down his sack just outside the church door. He thought the best thing for him to do was to go in to hear a hymn before he went any further. Little Claus was securely tied in the sack, and all the people were inside the church. So Big Claus went in too.

"Oh dear, oh dear!" Little Claus sighed in the sack. Twist and turn as he might, he could not loosen the knot. Then a white-haired old cattle drover came by, leaning heavily on his staff. The herd of bulls and cows he was driving bumped against the sack Little Claus was in and overturned it.

"Oh dear," Little Claus sighed, "I'm so young to be going to Heaven."

"While I," said the cattle drover, "am too old for this Earth, yet Heaven will not send for me."

"Open the sack!" Little Claus shouted. "Get in and take my place. You'll go straight to Heaven."

"That's where I want to be," said the drover, as he undid the sack. Little Claus jumped out at once. "You must look after my cattle," the old man said as he crawled in. As soon as Little Claus fastened the sack, he walked away from there with all the bulls and cows.

Presently, Big Claus came out of church. He took the sack on his back and found it light, for the old drover was no more than half as heavy as Little Claus.

"How light my burden is, all because I've been listening to a hymn," said Big Claus. He went on to the deep wide river, and threw the sack with the old cattle drover into the water.

"You'll never trick me again," Big Claus said, for he thought he had seen the last splash of Little Claus.

He started home, but when he came to the crossroads, he met Little Claus and all his cattle.

"Where did you come from?" Big Claus exclaimed. "Didn't I just drown you?"

"Yes," said Little Claus. "You threw me in the river half an hour ago."

"Then how did you come by such a fine herd of cattle?" Big Claus wanted to know.

"Oh, they're sea cattle," said Little Claus. "I'll tell you how I got them, because I'm obliged to you for drowning me. I'm a made man now. I can't begin to tell you how rich I am.

"But when I was in the sack, with the wind whistling in my ears as you dropped me off the bridge into the cold water, I was frightened enough. I went straight to the bottom, but it didn't hurt me because of all the fine soft grass down there. Someone opened the sack, and a beautiful maiden took my hand. Her clothes were white as snow, and she had a green wreath in her floating hair. She said, 'So you've come, Little Claus. Here's a herd of cattle for you, but they are just the beginning of my presents. A mile further up the road, another herd awaits you.'

"Then I saw that the river is a great highway for the people who live in the sea. Down on the bottom of the river, they walked and drove their cattle straight in from the sea to the land where the rivers end. The flowers down there are fragrant. The grass is fresh, and fish flit by as birds do up here. The people are fine, and so are the cattle that come grazing along the roadside."

"Then why are you back so soon?" Big Claus asked. "If it's all so beautiful, I'd have stayed there."

"Well," said Little Claus, "I'm being particularly clever. You remember I said the sea maiden told me to go one mile up the road and I'd find another herd of cattle. By 'road' she meant the river, for that's the only way she travels. But I know how the river turns and twists, and it seemed too roundabout a way of getting there. By coming up on land, I took a shortcut that saves me half a mile. So I get my cattle that much sooner."

"You *are* a lucky man," said Big Claus. "Do you think I would get me some cattle too if I went down to the bottom of the river?"

"Oh, I'm sure you would," said Little Claus. "Don't expect me to carry you there in a sack, because you're too heavy for me, but if you walk to the river and crawl into the sack, I'll throw you in with the greatest of pleasure."

"Thank you," said Big Claus, "but remember, if I don't get a herd of sea cattle down there, I'll give you a thrashing, believe me."

"Would you really?" said Little Claus.

As they came to the river, the thirsty cattle saw the water and rushed to drink it. Little Claus said, "See what a hurry they are in to get back to the bottom of the river."

"Help me get there first," Big Claus commanded, "or I'll give you that beating right now." He struggled into the big sack, which had been lying across the back of one of the cattle. "Put a stone in, or I'm afraid I shan't sink," said Big Claus.

"No fear of that," said Little Claus, but he put a big stone in the sack, tied it tightly, and pushed it into the river.

Splash! Up flew the water, and down to the bottom sank Big Claus.

"I'm afraid he won't find what I found!" said Little Claus as he herded all his cattle home.

THE PRINCESS ON THE PEA (1835)

Once there was a prince who wanted to marry a princess. Only a real one would do. So he traveled through all the world to find her, and everywhere things went wrong. There were princesses aplenty, but how was he to know whether they were real princesses? There was something not quite right about them all. So he came home again and was unhappy, because he did so want to have a real princess.

One evening, a terrible storm blew up. It lightninged and thundered and rained. It was really frightful! In the midst of it all came a knocking at the town gate. The old king went to open it.

Who should be standing outside but a princess, and what a sight she was in all that rain and wind. Water streamed from her hair down her clothes into her shoes, and ran out at the heels. Yet she claimed to be a real princess.

"We'll soon find that out," the old queen thought to herself. Without saying a word about it, she went to the bedchamber, stripped back the bedclothes, and put just one pea in the bottom of the bed. Then she took twenty mattresses and piled them on the pea. Then she took twenty eiderdown feather beds and piled them on the mattresses. Up on top of all these the princess was to spend the night.

In the morning they asked her, "Did you sleep well?"

"Oh!" said the princess. "No. I scarcely slept at all. Heaven knows what's in that bed. I lay on something so hard that I'm black and blue all over. It was simply terrible."

They could see she was a real princess and no question about it, now that she had felt one pea all the way through twenty mattresses and twenty more feather beds. Nobody but a princess could be so delicate. So the prince made haste to marry her, because he knew he had found a real princess.

As for the pea, they put it in the museum. There it's still to be seen, unless somebody has taken it.

There, that's a true story.

LITTLE IDA'S FLOWERS (1835)

My poor flowers are quite dead," said little Ida. "They were so pretty last evening, but now every leaf has withered and drooped. Why do they do that?" she asked the student who sat on the sofa.

She was very fond of him because he told such good stories and could cut such amusing figures out of paperhearts with dancing ladies inside them, flowers of all sorts, and castles with doors that you could open and close. He was a rollicking fellow.

"Why do my flowers look so ill today?" she asked him again, and showed him her withered bouquet.

"Don't you know what's the matter with them?" the student said. "They were at the ball last night, that's why they can scarcely hold up their heads."

"Flowers can't dance," said little Ida.

"Oh, indeed they can," said the student. "As soon as it gets dark and we go to sleep, they frolic about in a fine fashion. Almost every night, they give a ball."

"Can't children go to the ball?"

"Little daisies can go. So can lilies of the valley."

"Where do the prettiest flowers dance?" Ida asked.

"Haven't you often visited the beautiful flower garden just outside of town, around the castle where the king lives in the summertime? You remember—the place where swans swim close when you offer them bread crumbs. Believe me! That's where the prettiest flowers dance."

"Yesterday I was there with my mother," said Ida, "but there wasn't a leaf on the trees, or a flower left. Where are they? Last summer, I saw ever so many."

"They are inside the castle, of course," said the student. "Confidentially, just as soon as the king comes back to town with all of his court, the flowers run from the garden into the castle and enjoy themselves. You should see them. The two loveliest roses climb up on the throne, where they are the king and the queen. All the red coxcombs line up on either side, to stand and bow like grooms of the bedchamber. Then all the best-dressed flowers come, and the grand ball starts. The blue violets are the naval cadets. Their partners, whom they call 'Miss,' are hyacinths and crocuses. The tulips and tiger lilies are the old chaperones who see to it that the dancing is done well and that everyone behaves properly."

"But," said little Ida, "doesn't anybody punish the flowers for dancing in the king's own castle?"

"Nobody knows a thing about it," said the student. "To be sure, there's the old castle keeper, who is there to watch over things. Sometimes, he comes in the night with his enormous bunch of keys. But as soon as the flowers hear the keys jangle, they keep quiet, and hide, with only their heads peeking out from behind the curtains. Then the old castle keeper says, 'I smell flowers in here.' But he can't see any."

"What fun!" little Ida clapped her hands. "But couldn't I see the flowers either?"

"Oh easily," said the student. "The very next time you go there, remember to peep in the windows. There you will see them, as I did today. A tall yellow lily lay stretched on the sofa, pretending to be a lady-in-waiting."

"Can the flowers who live in the botanical gardens visit the castle? Can they go that far?"

"Why, certainly. They can fly all the way if it suits them. Haven't you seen lovely butterflies—white, yellow, and red ones? They almost look like flowers, and that's really what they used to be. They are flowers who have jumped up off their stems, high into the air. They beat the air with their petals, as though these were little wings, and so they manage to fly. If they behave themselves nicely, they get permission to fly all day long, instead of having to go home and sit on their stems. In time, their petals turn into real wings. You've seen them yourself. However, it's quite possible that the botanical garden flowers have never been to the king's castle and don't know anything about the fun that goes on there almost every night. Therefore, I'll tell you how to arrange a surprise for the botanical professor. You know the one I mean—he lives quite near here. Well, the next time you go to the garden, tell one of his flowers that they are having a great ball in the castle. One flower will tell the others, and off they'll fly. When the professor comes out in the garden, not one flower will he find, and where they've all gone, he will never be able to guess."

"How can a flower tell the others? You know flowers can't speak."

"They can't speak," the student agreed, "but they can signal. Haven't you noticed that whenever the breeze blows, the flowers nod to one another, and make signs with their leaves. Why, it's as plain as talk."

"Can the professor understand their signs?"

"Certainly he can. One morning, he came into his garden and saw a big stinging nettle leaf signaling to a glorious red carnation, 'You are so beautiful, and I love you so much.' But the professor didn't like that kind of thing, so he slapped the nettle's leaves, for they are its fingers. He was stung so badly that he hasn't laid hands on a stinging nettle since."

"Oh, how jolly!" little Ida laughed.

"How can anyone stuff a child's head with such nonsense?" said the prosy councillor, who had come to call and sit on the sofa too. He didn't like the student a bit. He always grumbled when he saw the student cut out those strange, amusing pictures—sometimes a man hanging from the gallows and holding a heart in his hand to show that he had stolen people's hearts away; sometimes an old witch riding a broomstick and balancing her husband on her nose. The councillor highly disapproved of those, and he would say as he said now, "How can anyone stuff a child's head with such nonsense—such stupid fantasy?"

But to little Ida, what the student told her about flowers was marvelously amusing, and she kept right on thinking about it. Her flowers couldn't hold their heads up, because they were tired out from dancing all night. Why, they must be ill. She took them to where she kept her toys on a nice little table, with a whole drawer full of pretty things. Her doll, Sophie, lay asleep in the doll's bed, but little Ida told her:

"Sophie, you'll really have to get up, and be satisfied to sleep in the drawer tonight, because my poor flowers are ill. Maybe, if I let them sleep in your bed tonight, they will get well again."

When she took the doll up, Sophie looked as cross as could be, and didn't say a word. She was sulky because she couldn't keep her own bed.

Ida put the flowers to bed, and tucked the little covers around them. She told them to be good and lie still, while she made them some tea, so that they would get well and be up and about tomorrow. She carefully drew the curtains around the little bed, so the morning sun would not shine in their faces.

All evening long, she kept thinking of what the student had said, before she climbed into bed herself. She peeped through the window curtains at the fine potted plants that belonged to her mother— hyacinths and tulips, too. She whispered very softly, "I know you are going to the ball tonight."

But the flowers pretended not to understand her. They didn't move a leaf. But little Ida knew all about them.

After she was in bed, she lay there for a long while thinking how pleasant it must be to see the flowers dance in the king's castle. "Were my flowers really there?" she wondered. Then she fell asleep. When she woke up again in the night, she had been dreaming of the flowers, and of the student, and of the prosy councillor who had scolded him and had said it was all silly nonsense. It was very still in the bedroom where Ida was. The night lamp glowed on the table, and Ida's mother and father were asleep.

"Are my flowers still asleep in Sophie's bed?" Ida wondered. "That's what I'd like to know."

She lifted herself a little higher on her pillow and looked toward the door that stood half open. In there were her flowers and all her toys. She listened, and it seemed to her that someone was playing the piano, very softly and more beautifully than she had ever heard it played.

"I'm perfectly sure that those flowers are all dancing," she said to herself. "Oh, my goodness, wouldn't I love to see them." But she did not dare get up, because that might awaken her father and mother.

"I do wish the flowers would come in here!" she thought. But they didn't. The music kept playing, and it sounded so lovely that she couldn't stay in bed another minute. She tiptoed to the door, and peeped into the next room. Oh, how funny—what a sight she saw there!

No night lamp burned in the next room, but it was well lighted just the same. The moonlight streamed through the window, upon the middle of the floor, and it was almost as bright as day. The hyacinths and the tulips lined up in two long rows across the floor. Not one was left by the window. The flowerpots stood there empty, while the flowers danced gracefully around the room, making a complete chain and holding each other by their long green leaves as they swung around.

At the piano sat a tall yellow lily. Little Ida remembered it from last summer, because the student had said, "Doesn't that lily look just like Miss Line?" Everyone had laughed at the time, but now little Ida noticed that there was a most striking resemblance. When the lily played, it had the very same mannerisms as the young lady, sometimes bending its long, yellow face to one side, sometimes to the other, and nodding in time with the lovely music.

No one suspected that little Ida was there. She saw a nimble blue crocus jump up on the table where her toys were, go straight to the doll's bed, and throw back the curtains. The sick flowers lay there, but they got up at once, and nodded down to the others that they also wanted to dance. The old chimney sweep doll, whose lower lip was broken, rose and made a bow to the pretty flowers. They looked quite themselves again as they jumped down to join the others and have a good time.

It seemed as if something clattered off the table. Little Ida looked and saw that the birch wand, that had been left over from Mardi Gras time was jumping down as if he thought he were a flower, too. The wand did cut quite a flowery figure with his paper rosettes and, to top him off, a little wax figure who had a broad trimmed hat just like the one that the councillor wore.

The wand skipped about on his three red wooden legs, and stamped them as hard as he could, for he was dancing the mazurka. The flowers could not dance it, because they were too light to stamp as he did.

All of a sudden, the wax figure grew tall and important. He whirled around to the paper flowers beside him and said, "How can anyone stuff a child's head with such nonsense—such stupid fantasy?" At that moment, he was a perfect image of the big-hatted councillor, just as sallow and quite as cross. But the paper flowers hit back. They struck his thin shanks until he crumpled up into a very small wax mannequin. The change was so ridiculous that little Ida could not keep from laughing.

Wherever the sceptered wand danced, the councillor had to dance too, whether he made himself tall and important or remained a little wax figure in a big black hat. The real flowers put in a kind word for him, especially those who had lain ill in the doll's bed, and the birch wand let him rest.

Just then, they heard a loud knocking in the drawer where Ida's doll, Sophie, lay with the other toys. The chimney sweep rushed to the edge of the table, lay flat on his stomach, and managed to pull the drawer out a little way. Sophie sat up and looked around her, most surprised.

"Why, they are having a ball!" she said. "Why hasn't somebody told me about it?"

"Won't you dance with me?" the chimney sweep asked her.

"A fine partner you'd be!" she said, and turned her back on him.

She sat on the edge of the drawer, hoping one of the flowers would ask her to dance, but not one of them did, She coughed, "Hm, hm, hm!" and still not one of them asked her. To make matters worse, the chimney sweep had gone off dancing by himself, which he did pretty well.

As none of the flowers paid the least attention to Sophie, she let herself tumble from the drawer to the floor with a bang. Now the flowers all came running to ask, "Did you hurt yourself?" They were very polite to her, especially those who had slept in her bed. But she wasn't hurt a bit. Ida's flowers thanked her for the use of her nice bed, and treated her well. They took her out in the middle of the floor, where the moon shone, and danced with her while all the other flowers made a circle around them. Sophie wasn't at all cross now. She said they might keep her bed. She didn't in the least mind sleeping in the drawer.

But the flowers said, "Thank you, no. We can't live long enough to keep your bed. Tomorrow we shall be dead. Tell little Ida to bury us in the garden, next to her canary bird's grave. Then we shall come up again next summer, more beautiful than ever."

"Oh, you mustn't die," Sophie said, and kissed all the flowers.

Then the drawing room door opened, and many more splendid flowers tripped in. Ida couldn't imagine where they had come from, unless—why, they must have come straight from the king's castle. First came two magnificent roses, wearing little gold crowns. These were the king and the queen. Then came charming gillyflowers and carnations, who greeted everybody. They brought the musicians along. Large poppies and peonies blew upon pea pods until they were red in the face. Blue hyacinths and little snowdrops tinkled their bells. It was such funny music. Many other flowers followed them, and they all danced together, blue violets with pink primroses, and daisies with the lilies of the valley.

All the flowers kissed one another, and that was very pretty to look at. When the time came to say good night, little Ida sneaked back to bed too, where she dreamed of all she had seen.

As soon as it was morning, she hurried to her little table to see if her flowers were still there. She threw back the curtain around the bed. Yes, they were there, but they were even more faded than yesterday. Sophie was lying in the drawer where Ida had put her. She looked quite sleepy.

"Do you remember what you were to tell me?" little Ida asked.

But Sophie just looked stupid, and didn't say one word.

"You are no good at all," Ida told her. "And to think how nice they were to you, and how all of them danced with you."

She opened a little pasteboard box, nicely decorated with pictures of birds, and laid the dead flowers in it.

"This will be your pretty coffin," she told them. "When my cousins from Norway come to visit us, they will help me bury you in the garden, so that you may come up again next summer and be more beautiful than ever."

Her Norwegian cousins were two pleasant boys named Jonas and Adolph. Their father had given them two new crossbows, which they brought with them for Ida to see. She told them how her poor flowers had died, and they got permission to hold a funeral. The boys marched first, with their crossbows on their shoulders. Little Ida followed, with her dead flowers in their nice box. In the garden, they dug a little grave. Ida first kissed the flowers, and then she closed the box and laid it in the earth. Adolph and Jonas shot their crossbows over the grave, for they had no guns or cannons.

THUMBELINA (1835)

There once was a woman who wanted so very much to have a tiny little child, but she did not know where to find one. So she went to an old witch, and she said:

"I have set my heart upon having a tiny little child. Please could you tell me where I can find one?"

"Why, that's easily done," said the witch. "Here's a grain of barley for you, but it isn't at all the sort of barley that farmers grow in their fields or that the chickens get to eat. Put it in a flower pot, and you'll see what you shall see."

"Oh, thank you!" the woman said. She gave the witch twelve pennies, and planted the barley seed as soon as she got home. It quickly grew into a fine large flower, which looked very much like a tulip. But the petals were folded tight, as though it were still a bud.

"This is such a pretty flower," said the woman. She kissed its lovely red and yellow petals, and just as she kissed it, the flower gave a loud *pop!* and flew open. It was a tulip, right enough, but on the green cushion in the middle of it sat a tiny girl. She was dainty and fair to see, but she was no taller than your thumb. So she was called Thumbelina.

A nicely polished walnut shell served as her cradle. Her mattress was made of the blue petals of violets, and a rose petal was pulled up to cover her. That was how she slept at night. In the daytime, she played on a table where the woman put a plate surrounded with a wreath of flowers. Their stems lay in the water, on which there floated a large tulip petal. Thumbelina used the petal as a boat, and with a pair of white horsehairs for oars, she could row clear across the plate—a charming sight. She could sing, too. Her voice was the softest and sweetest that anyone ever has heard.

One night as she lay in her cradle, a horrible toad hopped in through the window—one of the panes was broken. This big, ugly, slimy toad jumped right down on the table where Thumbelina was asleep under the red rose petal.

"Here's a perfect wife for my son!" the toad exclaimed. She seized upon the walnut shell in which Thumbelina lay asleep, and hopped off with it, out the window and into the garden. A big broad stream ran through it, with a muddy marsh along its banks, and here the toad lived with her son. Ugh! He was just like his mother, slimy and horrible. "Co-ax, co-ax, brek-ek-eke-kex," was all that he could say when he saw the graceful little girl in the walnut shell.

"Don't speak so loud, or you will wake her up," the old toad told him. "She might get away from us yet, for she is as light as a puff of swansdown. We must put her on one of the broad water lily leaves out in the stream. She is so small and light that it will be just like an island to her, and she can't run away from us while we are making our best room under the mud ready for you two to live in."

Many water lilies with broad green leaves grew in the stream, and it looked as if they were floating on the surface. The leaf that lay furthest from the bank was the largest of them all, and it was to this leaf that the old toad swam with the walnut shell that held Thumbelina.

The poor little thing woke up early next morning, and when she saw where she was, she began to cry bitterly. There was water all around the big green leaf, and there was no way at all for her to reach the shore. The old toad sat in the mud, decorating a room with green rushes and yellow water lilies, to have it looking its best for her new daughter-in-law. Then she and her ugly son swam out to the leaf on which Thumbelina was standing. They came for her pretty little bed, which they wanted to carry to the bridal chamber before they took her there.

The old toad curtsied deeply in the water before her, and said:

"Meet my son. He is to be your husband, and you will share a delightful home in the mud."

"Co-ax, co-ax, brek-ek-eke-kex," was all that her son could say.

Then they took the pretty little bed and swam away with it. Left all alone on the green leaf, Thumbelina sat down and cried. She did not want to live in the slimy toad's house, and she didn't want to have the toad's horrible son for her husband. The little fishes who swam in the water beneath her had seen the toad and heard what she had said. So up popped their heads to have a look at the little girl. No sooner had they seen her than they felt very sorry that anyone so pretty should have to go down to live with that hideous toad. No, that should never be! They gathered around the green stem that held the leaf where she was, and gnawed it in two with their teeth. Away went the leaf down the stream, and away went Thumbelina, far away where the toad could not catch her.

Thumbelina sailed past many a place, and when the little birds in the bushes saw her, they sang, "What a darling little girl." The leaf drifted further and further away with her, and so it was that Thumbelina became a traveler.

A lovely white butterfly kept fluttering around her, and at last alighted on the leaf, because he admired Thumbelina. She was a happy little girl again, now that the toad could not catch her. It was all very lovely as she floated along, and where the sun struck the water, it looked like shining gold. Thumbelina undid her sash, tied one end of it to the butterfly, and made the other end fast to the leaf. It went much faster now, and Thumbelina went much faster too, for of course she was standing on it.

Just then, a big May bug flew by and caught sight of her. Immediately, he fastened his claws around her slender waist and flew with her up into a tree. Away went the green leaf down the stream, and away went the butterfly with it, for he was tied to the leaf and could not get loose.

My goodness! How frightened little Thumbelina was when the May bug carried her up in the tree. But she was even more sorry for the nice white butterfly she had fastened to the leaf, because if he couldn't free himself, he would have to starve to death. But the May bug wasn't one to care about that. He sat her down on the largest green leaf of the tree, fed her honey from the flowers, and told her how pretty she was, considering that she didn't look the least like a May bug. After a while, all the other May bugs who lived in the tree came to pay them a call. As they stared at Thumbelina, the lady May bugs threw up their feelers and said:

"Why, she has only two legs—what a miserable sight!"

"She hasn't any feelers," one cried.

"She is pinched in at the waist—how shameful! She looks like a human being—how ugly she is!" said all of the female May bugs.

Yet Thumbelina was as pretty as ever. Even the May bug who had flown away with her knew that, but as every last one of them kept calling her ugly, he at length came to agree with them and would have nothing to do with her—she could go wherever she chose. They flew down out of the tree with her and left her on a daisy, where she sat and cried because she was so ugly that the May bugs wouldn't have anything to do with her.

Nevertheless, she was the loveliest little girl you can imagine, and as frail and fine as the petal of a rose.

All summer long, poor Thumbelina lived all alone in the woods. She wove herself a hammock of grass, and hung it under a big burdock leaf to keep off the rain. She took honey from the flowers for food, and drank the dew that she found on the leaves every morning. In this way, the summer and fall went by. Then came the winter, the long, cold winter. All the birds who had sung so sweetly for her flew away.

The trees and the flowers withered. The big burdock leaf under which she had lived shriveled up until nothing was left of it but a dry, yellow stalk. She was terribly cold, for her clothes had worn threadbare and she herself was so slender and frail. Poor Thumbelina, she would freeze to death! Snow began to fall, and every time a snowflake struck her it was as if she had been hit by a whole shovelful, for we are quite tall while she measured only an inch. She wrapped a withered leaf about her, but there was no warmth in it. She shivered with cold.

Near the edge of the woods where she now had arrived, was a large grain field, but the grain had been harvested long ago. Only the dry, bare stubble stuck out of the frozen ground. It was just as if she were lost in a vast forest, and oh, how she shivered with cold! Then she came to the door of a field mouse who had a little hole amid the stubble. There this mouse lived, warm and cozy, with a whole storeroom of grain, and a magnificent kitchen and pantry. Poor Thumbelina stood at the door, just like a beggar child, and pled for a little bit of barley, because she hadn't had anything to eat for two days past.

"Why, you poor little thing," said the field mouse, who turned out to be a kind-hearted old creature. "You must come into my warm room and share my dinner." She took such a fancy to Thumbelina that she said, "If you care to, you may stay with me all winter, but you must keep my room tidy, and tell me stories, for I am very fond of them." Thumbelina did as the kind old field mouse asked, and she had a very good time of it.

"Soon we shall have a visitor," the field mouse said. "Once every week, my neighbor comes to see me, and he is even better off than I am. His rooms are large, and he wears such a beautiful black velvet coat. If you could only get him for a husband, you would be well taken care of, but he can't see anything. You must tell him the very best stories you know."

Thumbelina did not like this suggestion. She would not even consider the neighbor, because he was a mole. He paid them a visit in his black velvet coat. The field mouse talked about how wealthy and wise he was, and how his home was more than twenty times larger than hers. But for all of his knowledge, he cared nothing at all for the sun and the flowers. He had nothing good to say for them, and had never laid eyes on them.

As Thumbelina had to sing for him, she sang, "May Bug, May Bug, Fly Away Home," and "The Monk Goes Afield." The mole fell in love with her sweet voice, but he didn't say anything about it yet, for he was a most discreet fellow.

He had just dug a long tunnel through the ground from his house to theirs, and the field mouse and Thumbelina were invited to use it whenever they pleased, though he warned them not to be alarmed by the dead bird that lay in this passage. It was a complete bird, with feather and beak. It must have died quite recently, when winter set in, and it was buried right in the middle of the tunnel.

The mole took in his mouth a torch of decayed wood. In the darkness, it glimmered like fire. He went ahead of them to light the way through the long, dark passage. When they came to where the dead bird lay, the mole put his broad nose to the ceiling and made a large hole through which daylight could fall. In the middle of the floor lay a dead swallow, with his lovely wings folded at his sides and his head tucked under his feathers. The poor bird must certainly have died of the cold. Thumbelina felt so sorry for him. She loved all the little birds who had sung and sweetly twittered to her all through the summer. But the mole gave the body a kick with his short stumps, and said, "Now he won't be chirping any more. What a wretched thing it is to be born a little bird. Thank goodness none of my children can be a bird, who has nothing but his 'chirp, chirp,' and must starve to death when winter comes along."

"Yes, you are so right, you sensible man," the field mouse agreed. "What good is all his chirp-chirping to a bird in the winter time, when he starves and freezes? But that's considered very grand, I imagine."

Thumbelina kept silent, but when the others turned their back on the bird, she bent over, smoothed aside the feathers that hid the bird's head, and kissed his closed eyes.

"Maybe it was he who sang so sweetly to me in the summertime," she thought to herself. "What pleasure he gave me, the dear, pretty bird."

The mole closed up the hole that let in the daylight, and then he took the ladies home. That night, Thumbelina could not sleep a wink, so she got up and wove a fine large coverlet out of hay. She took it to the dead bird and spread it over him, so that he would lie warm in the cold earth. She tucked him in with some soft thistledown that she had found in the field mouse's room.

"Good-bye, you pretty little bird," she said. "Good-bye, and thank you for your sweet songs last summer, when the trees were all green and the sun shone so warmly upon us." She laid her head on his breast, and it startled her to feel a soft thump, as if something were beating inside. This was the bird's heart. He was not dead—he was only numb with cold, and now that he had been warmed, he came to life again.

In the fall, all swallows fly off to warm countries, but if one of them starts too late, he gets so cold that he drops down as if he were dead, and lies where he fell. And then the cold snow covers him.

Thumbelina was so frightened that she trembled, for the bird was so big, so enormous compared to her own inch of height. But she mustered her courage, tucked the cotton wool down closer around the poor bird, brought the mint leaf that covered her own bed, and spread it over the bird's head.

The following night, she tiptoed out to him again. He was alive now, but so weak that he could barely open his eyes for a moment to look at Thumbelina, who stood beside him with the piece of touchwood that was her only lantern.

"Thank you, pretty little child," the sick swallow said. "I have been wonderfully warmed. Soon I shall get strong once more, and be able to fly again in the warm sunshine."

"Oh," she said, "it's cold outside, it's snowing, and freezing. You just stay in your warm bed, and I'll nurse you."

Then she brought him some water in the petal of a flower. The swallow drank, and told her how he had hurt one of his wings in a thorn bush, and for that reason couldn't fly as fast as the other swallows when they flew far, far away to the warm countries. Finally, he had dropped to the ground. That was all he remembered, and he had no idea how he came to be where she found him.

The swallow stayed there all through the winter, and Thumbelina was kind to him and tended him with loving care. She didn't say anything about this to the field mouse or to the mole, because they did not like the poor unfortunate swallow.

As soon as spring came and the sun warmed the earth, the swallow told Thumbelina it was time to say good-bye. She reopened the hole that the mole had made in the ceiling, and the sun shone in splendor upon them. The swallow asked Thumbelina to go with him. She could sit on his back as they flew away through the green woods. But Thumbelina knew that it would make the old field mouse feel badly if she left like that, so she said:

"No, I cannot go."

"Fare you well, fare you well, my good and pretty girl," said the swallow, as he flew into the sunshine. Tears came into Thumbelina's eyes as she watched him go, for she was so fond of the poor swallow.

"Chirp, chirp!" sang the bird, at he flew into the green woods.

Thumbelina felt very downcast. She was not permitted to go out in the warm sunshine. Moreover, the grain that was sown in the field above the field mouse's house grew so tall that, to a poor little girl who was only an inch high, it was like a dense forest.

"You must work on your trousseau this summer," the field mouse said, for their neighbor, that loathsome mole in his black velvet coat, had proposed to her. "You must have both woolens and linens, both bedding and wardrobe, when you become the mole's wife."

Thumbelina had to turn the spindle, and the field mouse hired four spiders to spin and weave for her day and night. The mole came to call every evening, and his favorite remark was that the sun, which now baked the earth as hard as a rock, would not be nearly so hot when summer was over. Yes, as soon as summer was past, he would be marrying Thumbelina. But she was not at all happy about it, because she didn't like the tedious mole the least bit. Every morning at sunrise and every evening at sunset, she would steal out the door. When the breeze blew the ears of grain apart, she could catch glimpses of the blue sky. She could dream about how bright and fair it was out of doors, and how she wished she would see her dear swallow again. But he did not come back, for doubtless he was far away, flying about in the lovely green woods.

When fall arrived, Thumbelina's whole trousseau was ready.

"Your wedding day is four weeks off," the field mouse told her. But Thumbelina cried and declared that she would not have the tedious mole for a husband.

"Fiddlesticks," said the field mouse. "Don't you be obstinate, or I'll bite you with my white teeth. Why, you're getting a superb husband. The queen herself hasn't a black velvet coat as fine as his. Both his kitchen and his cellar are well supplied. You ought to thank goodness that you are getting him."

Then came the wedding day. The mole had come to take Thumbelina home with him, where she would have to live deep underground and never go out in the warm sunshine again, because he disliked it so. The poor little girl felt very sad that she had to say good-bye to the glorious sun, which the field mouse had at least let her look out at through the doorway.

"Farewell, bright sun!" she said. With her arm stretched toward it, she walked a little way from the field mouse's home. The grain had been harvested, and only the dry stubble was left in the field. "Farewell, farewell!" she cried again, and flung her little arms around a small red flower that was still in bloom. "If you see my dear swallow, please give him my love."

"Chirp, chirp! Chirp, chirp!" She suddenly heard a twittering over her head. She looked up, and there was the swallow, just passing by. He was so glad to see Thumbelina, although, when she told him how she hated to marry the mole and live deep underground where the sun never shone, she could not hold back her tears.

"Now that the cold winter is coming," the swallow told her, "I shall fly far, far away to the warm countries. Won't you come along with me? You can ride on my back. Just tie yourself on with your sash, and away we'll fly, far from the ugly mole and his dark hole—far, far away, over the mountains to the warm countries where the sun shines so much fairer than here, to where it is always summer and there are always flowers. Please fly away with me, dear little Thumbelina, you who saved my life when I lay frozen in a dark hole in the earth."

"Yes, I will go with you!" said Thumbelina. She sat on his back, put her feet on his outstretched wings, and fastened her sash to one of his strongest feathers. Then the swallow soared into the air over forests and over lakes, high up over the great mountains that are always capped with snow. When Thumbelina felt cold in the chill air, she crept under the bird's warm feathers, with only her little head stuck out to watch all the wonderful sights below.

At length, they came to the warm countries. There the sun shone far more brightly than it ever does here, and the sky seemed twice as high. Along the ditches and hedgerows grew marvelous green and blue grapes. Lemons and oranges hung in the woods. The air smelled sweetly of myrtle and thyme. By the wayside, the loveliest children ran hither and thither, playing with the brightly colored butterflies.

But the swallow flew on still farther, and it became more and more beautiful. Under magnificent green trees, on the shore of a blue lake, there stood an ancient palace of dazzling white marble. The lofty pillars were wreathed with vines, and at the top of them, many swallows had made their nests. One nest belonged to the swallow who carried Thumbelina.

"This is my home," the swallow told her. "If you will choose one of those glorious flowers in bloom down below, I shall place you in it, and you will have all that your heart desires."

"That will be lovely," she cried, and clapped her tiny hands.

A great white marble pillar had fallen to the ground, where it lay in three broken pieces. Between these pieces grew the loveliest large white flowers. The swallow flew down with Thumbelina and put her on one of the large petals. How surprised she was to find in the center of the flower a little man, as shining and transparent as if he had been made of glass. On his head was the daintiest of little gold crowns, on his shoulders were the brightest shining wings, and he was not a bit bigger than Thumbelina. He was the spirit of the flower. In every flower there lived a small man or woman just like him, but he was the king over all of them.

"Oh, isn't he handsome?" Thumbelina said softly to the swallow. The king was somewhat afraid of the swallow, which seemed a very giant of a bird to anyone as small as he. But when he saw Thumbelina, he rejoiced, for she was the prettiest little girl he had ever laid eyes on. So he took off his golden crown and put it on her head. He asked if he might know her name, and he asked her to be his wife, which would make her queen over all the flowers. Here indeed was a different sort of husband from the toad's son and the mole with his black velvet coat. So she said "Yes" to this charming king. From all the flowers trooped little ladies and gentlemen delightful to behold. Every one of them brought Thumbelina a present, but the best gift of all was a pair of wings that had belonged to a large silver fly. When these were made fast to her back, she too could flit from flower to flower. Everyone rejoiced, as the swallow perched above them in his nest and sang his very best songs for them. He was sad, though, deep down in his heart, for he liked Thumbelina so much that he wanted never to part with her.

"You shall no longer be called Thumbelina," the flower spirit told her. "That name is too ugly for anyone as pretty as you are. We shall call you Maia."

"Good-bye, good-bye," said the swallow. He flew away again from the warm countries, back to faraway Denmark, where he had a little nest over the window of the man who can tell you fairy tales. To him, the bird sang, "Chirp, chirp! Chirp, chirp!" and that's how we heard the whole story.

THE NAUGHTY BOY (1835)

Once upon a time, there was an old poet—one of those good, honest old poets. One evening, as he was sitting quietly in his home, a terrible storm broke out—the rain poured down in torrents—but the old poet sat warm and cozy in his study, for a fire blazed brightly in his stove and roasting apples sizzled and hissed beside it.

"There won't be a dry stitch on anybody out in this rain," he told himself. You see, he was a very kindhearted old poet.

"Oh, please open the door for me! I'm so cold and wet!" cried a little child outside his house. Then it knocked at the door, while the rain poured down and the wind shook all the windows.

"Why, the poor little child!" cried the old poet as he hurried to open the door. Before him stood a naked little boy, with the water streaming down from his yellow hair! He was shivering, and would certainly have perished in the storm had he not been let in.

"You poor little fellow!" said the poet again, and took him by the hand. "Come in, and we'll soon have you warmed up! I shall give you some wine and a roasted apple, for you're such a pretty little boy."

And he really was pretty! His eyes sparkled like two bright stars, and his hair hung in lovely curls, even though the water was still streaming from it. He looked like a little angel, but he was pale with the cold and shivering in every limb. In his hand, he held a beautiful little bow-and-arrow set, but the bow had been ruined by the rain, and all the colors on the arrows had run together.

The old poet quickly sat down by the stove and took the little boy on his knee. He dried the child's hair, rubbed the blue little hands vigorously, and heated some sweet wine for him. And pretty soon the little boy felt better; the roses came back to his cheeks, and he jumped down from the old man's lap and danced around the old poet.

"You're a cheerful boy," laughed the old man. "What's your name?"

"My name is Cupid," was the reply. "Don't you know me? There lies my bow, and I can certainly shoot with it, too. Look, the storm is over, and the moon is shining!"

"Yes," the poet said, "but I'm afraid the rain has spoiled your bow."

"That would be a shame," replied the little boy as he looked the bow over carefully. "No, it's already dry again, and the string is good and tight. No damage done. I guess I'll try it." Then he fitted an arrow to his bow, aimed it, and shot the good old poet right through the heart!

"Do you see now that my bow is not spoiled?" he said laughingly, and ran out of the house. Wasn't he a naughty boy to shoot the good old poet who had been so kind to him, taken him into his warm room, and given him his delicious wine and his best apple?

The good poet lay on the floor and wept, because he really had been shot right through the heart. "What a naughty boy that Cupid is!" he cried. "I must warn all the good children, so that they will be careful and never play with him. Because he will certainly do them some harm!" So he warned all the good children, and they were very careful to keep away from that naughty Cupid.

But he is very clever, and he tricks them all the time. When the students are going home from the lectures, he runs beside them, with a black coat on and a book under his arm. They don't recognize him, but they take his arm, thinking he is a student, too, and then he sends his arrows into their hearts. And when the girls are in church to be confirmed, he is likely to catch them and shoot his darts into them. Yes, he is always after people!

In the theater, he sits up in the big chandelier, burning so brightly that people think he's a lamp, but they soon find out better. He runs about the king's garden and on the rampart, and once he even shot your father and mother right through the heart! Just ask them, and you'll hear what they say.

Yes, he's a bad boy, this Cupid—you had better never have anything to do with him, for he is after all of you. And what do you think? A long time ago, he even shot an arrow into your poor old grandmother! The wound has healed up, but she will never forget it.

Saucy Cupid! But now you know all about him, and what a naughty boy he is!

THE TRAVELING COMPANION (1835)

Poor John was greatly troubled, because his father was very ill and could not recover. Except for these two, there was no one in their small room. The lamp on the table had almost burned out, for it was quite late at night.

"You have been a good son, John," his dying father said, "and the Lord will help you along in the world." He looked at his son with earnest, gentle eyes, sighed deeply, and fell dead as if he were falling asleep.

John cried bitterly, for now he had no one in all the world, neither father nor mother, sister nor brother. Poor John! He knelt at the bedside, and kissed his dead father's hand. He cried many salty tears, until at last his eyes closed, and he fell asleep with his head resting against the hard bedstead.

Then he had a strange dream. He saw the sun and the moon bow down to him. He saw his father well again and strong, and heard him laughing as he always laughed when he was happy. A beautiful girl, with a crown of gold on her lovely long hair, stretched out her hand to John, and his father said, "See what a bride you have won. She is the loveliest girl in the world." Then he awoke, and all these fine things were gone. His father lay cold and dead on the bed, and there was no one with them. Poor John!

The following week, the dead man was buried. John walked close behind the coffin; he could no longer see his kind father, who had loved him so. He heard how they threw the earth down upon the coffin, and watched the last corner of it until a shovel of earth hid even that. He was so sad that he felt as if his heart were breaking in pieces. Then those around him sang a psalm that sounded so lovely that tears came to his eyes. He cried, and that did him good in his grief. The sun shone in its splendor down on the green trees, as if to say, "John, you must not be so unhappy. Look up and see how fair and blue the sky is. Your father is there, praying to the good Lord that things will always go well with you."

"I'll always be good," John said. "Then I shall go to join my father in Heaven. How happy we shall be to see each other again! How much I shall have to tell him, and how much he will have to show me and to teach me about the joys of Heaven, just as he used to teach me here on Earth. Oh, what joy that will be!"

He could see it all so clearly that he smiled, even though tears were rolling down his cheeks. The little birds up in the chestnut trees twittered, "Chirp, chirp! Chirp, chirp!" They were so happy and gay, for although they had attended a funeral, they knew very well that the dead man had gone to Heaven, where he now wore wings even larger and lovelier than theirs. They knew that he was happy now, because here on Earth he had been a good man, and this made them glad.

John saw them fly from the green trees far out into the world, and he felt a great desire to follow them. But first, he carved a large wooden cross to mark his father's grave. When he took it there in the evening, he found the grave neatly covered with sand and flowers. Strangers had done this, for they had loved the good man who now was dead.

Early the next morning, John packed his little bundle and tucked his whole inheritance into a money belt. All that he had was fifty dollars and a few pieces of silver, but with this, he meant to set off into the world. But first, he went to the churchyard, where he knelt and repeated the Lord's Prayer over his father's grave. Then he said, "Farewell, father dear! I'll always be good, so you may safely pray to our Lord that things will go well with me."

The fields through which he passed were full of lovely flowers that flourished in the sunshine and nodded in the breeze, as if to say, "Welcome to the green pastures! Isn't it nice here?" But John turned round for one more look at the old church where as a baby he had been baptized, and where he had gone with his father every Sunday to sing the hymns. High up, in one of the belfry windows, he saw the little church goblin with his pointed red cap, raising one arm to keep the sun out of his eyes. John nodded good-bye to him, and the little goblin waved his red cap, put his hand on his heart, and kissed his finger tips to him again and again, to show that he wished John well and hoped that he would have a good journey.

As John thought of all the splendid things he would see in the fine big world ahead of him, he walked on and on—farther away than he had ever gone before. He did not even know the towns through which he passed, nor the people whom he met. He was far away among strangers.

The first night, he slept under a haystack in the fields, for he had no other bed. But he thought it very comfortable, and the king himself could have no better. The whole field, the brook, the haystack, and the blue sky overhead, made a glorious bedroom. The green grass patterned with red and white flowers was his carpet. The elder bushes and hedges of wild roses were bouquets of flowers, and for his wash bowl he had the whole brook full of clear fresh water. The reeds nodded their heads to wish him both "Good night," and "Good morning." The moon was really a huge night lamp, high up in the blue ceiling where there was no danger of its setting fire to the bed curtains. John could sleep peacefully, and sleep he did, never once waking until the sun rose and all the little birds around him began singing, "Good morning! Good morning! Aren't you up yet?"

The church bells rang, for it was Sunday. People went to hear the preacher, and John went with them. As he sang a hymn and listened to God's Word, he felt just as if he were in the same old church where he had been baptized, and where he had sung the hymns with his father.

There were many, many graves in the churchyard, and some were overgrown with high grass. Then John thought of his own father's grave and of how it too would come to look like these, now that he could no longer weed and tend it. So he knelt down to weed out the high grass. He straightened the wooden crosses that had fallen, and replaced the wreaths that the wind had blown from the graves. "Perhaps," he thought, "someone will do the same for my father's grave, now that I cannot take care of it."

Outside the churchyard gate stood an old beggar, leaning on his crutch, and John gave him the few pieces of silver that he had. Happy and high-spirited, John went farther on—out into the wide world. Toward nightfall, the weather turned dreadfully stormy. John hurried along as—fast as he could to find shelter, but it soon grew dark. At last he came to a little church that stood very lonely upon a hill. Fortunately, the door was ajar, and he slipped inside to stay until the storm abated.

"I'll sit down here in the corner," he said, "for I am very tired and need a little rest." So he sat down, put his hands together, and said his evening prayer. Before he knew it, he was fast asleep and dreaming, while it thundered and lightninged outside.

When he woke up, it was midnight. The storm had passed, and the moon shone upon him through the window. In the middle of the church stood an open coffin and in it lay a dead man, awaiting burial. John was not at all frightened. His conscience was clear, and he was sure that the dead do not harm anyone. It is the living who do harm, and two such harmful living men stood beside the dead one, who had been put here in the church until he could be buried. They had a vile scheme to keep him from resting quietly in his coffin. They intended to throw his body out of the church—the helpless dead man's body.

Why do you want to do such a thing?" John asked. "It is a sin and a shame. In Heaven's name, let the man rest."

"Stuff and nonsense!" the two evil men exclaimed. "He cheated us. He owed us money that he could not pay, and now that he has cheated us by dying, we shall not get a penny of it. So we intend to revenge ourselves. Like a dog he shall lie outside the church door."

"I have only fifty dollars," John cried. "It is my whole inheritance, but I'll give it to you gladly if you will solemnly promise to let the poor dead man rest in peace. I can do without the money. I have my healthy, strong arms, and Heaven will always help me."

"Why, certainly," the villainous fellows agreed. "If you are willing to pay his debt, we won't lay a hand on him, you can count on that."

They took the money he gave them and went away roaring with laughter at his simplicity. John laid the body straight again in its coffin, folded its hands, and took his leave. He went away through the great forest, very well pleased.

All around him, wherever moonlight fell between the trees, he saw little elves playing merrily. They weren't disturbed when he came along because they knew he was a good and innocent fellow. It is only the wicked people who never are allowed to see the elves. Some of the elves were no taller than your finger, and their long yellow hair was done up with golden combs. Two by two, they seesawed on the big raindrops, which lay thick on the leaves and tall grass. Sometimes the drops rolled from under them, and then they tumbled down between the grass blades. The little mannequins would laugh and made a great to-do about it, for it was a very funny sight. They sang, and John knew all their pretty little songs, which had been taught him when he was a small boy.

Big spotted spiders, wearing silver crowns, were kept busy spinning long bridges and palaces from one bush to another, and as the tiny dewdrops formed on these webs, they sparkled like glass in the moonlight. All this went on until sunrise, when the little elves hid in the buds of flowers. Then the wind struck the bridges and palaces, which were swept away like cobwebs.

John had just come out of the forest, when behind him, a man's strong voice called out, "Ho there, comrade! Where are you bound?

"I'm bound for the wide world," John told him. "I have neither father nor mother. I am a poor boy, but I am sure the Lord will look after me."

"I am off to the wide world, too," the stranger said. "Shall we keep each other company?"

"Yes indeed," John replied. So they strode along together.

They got to like each other very much, for both of them were kindly. But John soon found that he was not nearly so wise as the stranger, who had seen most of the world, and knew how to tell about almost everything.

The sun was high in the heavens when they sat down under a big tree to eat their breakfast. Just then, an old woman came hobbling along. Oh! She was so old that she bent almost double and walked with a crutch. On her back was a load of firewood she had gotten from the forest. Her apron was tied up, and John could see these big bunches of fern fronds and willow switches sticking out. As she came near the two travelers, her foot slipped. She fell down, and screamed aloud, for the poor old woman had broken her leg.

John suggested that they carry the woman to her home right away, but the stranger opened up his knapsack and took out a little jar of salve, which he said would mend her leg completely and at once, so that she could walk straight home as well as if her leg had never been broken. But in return, he asked for the three bunches of switches that she carried in her apron.

"That's a very high price!" The old woman dubiously nodded her head. She did not want to give up the switches, but it was not very pleasant to lie there with a broken leg, so she let him have the three bunches. No sooner had he rubbed her with the salve than the old woman got to her feet and walked off much better than she had come—all this the salve could do. Obviously, it was not the sort of thing you can buy from the apothecary.

"What on Earth do you want with those bunches of switches?" John asked his companion.

"Oh, they are three nice bundles of herbs," he said. "They just happened to strike my fancy, because I'm an odd sort of fellow."

When they had gone on for quite a distance, John remarked, "See how dark the sky has grown. Those are dreadfully dense clouds."

"No," his comrade said, "those are not clouds. They are mountains—splendid high mountains, where you can get clear above the clouds into perfectly fresh air. It is glorious, believe me. Tomorrow we shall certainly be far up in the world."

But they were not so near as they seemed to be. It took a whole day to reach the mountains, where the dark forests rose right up to the skies, and where the boulders were almost as large as a whole town. To climb over all of them would be heavy going indeed, so John and his companion went to an inn to rest and strengthen themselves for tomorrow's journey.

Down in the big taproom at the inn were many people, because a showman was there with a puppet show. He had just set up his little theater, and the people sat there waiting to see the play. Down in front, a burly old butcher had taken a seat, the very best one too, and his big bulldog—how vicious it looked—sat beside him, with his eyes popping as wide as everyone else's.

Then the play started. It was a very pleasant play, all about a king and a queen who sat on a velvet throne. They wore gold crowns on their heads and long trains to their costumes, all of which they could very well afford. The prettiest little wooden dolls, with glass eyes and big mustaches, stood by to open and shut all the doors so that fresh air might come into the room. It was a very pleasant play, it wasn't sad at all. But just as the queen rose and swept across the stage—Heaven only knows what possessed the big bulldog to do it—as the fat butcher was not holding him, the dog made a jump right onto the stage, snatched up the queen by her slender waist, and crunched her until she cracked in pieces. It was quite tragic!

The poor showman was badly frightened, and quite upset about the queen, for she was his prettiest little puppet, and the ugly bulldog had bitten off her head. But after a while, when the audience had gone, the stranger who had come with John said that he could soon mend her. He produced his little jar, and rubbed the puppet with some of the ointment that had cured the poor old woman who had broken her leg. The moment the salve was applied to the puppet, she was as good as new—nay, better. She could even move by herself, and there was no longer any need to pull her strings. Except that she could not speak, the puppet was just like a live woman. The showman was delighted that he didn't have to pull strings for this puppet, who could dance by herself. None of the others could do that.

In the night, after everyone in the inn had gone to bed, someone was heard sighing so terribly, and the sighs went on for so long, that everybody got up to see who it could be. The showman went straight to his little theater, because the sighs seemed to come from there. All the wooden puppets were in a heap, with the king and his attendants mixed all together, and it was they who sighed so profoundly. They looked so pleading with their big glass eyes, and all of them wanted to be rubbed a little, just as the queen had been, so that they too would be able to move by themselves. The queen went down on her knees and held out her lovely golden crown as if to say: "Take even this from me, if you will only rub my king and his courtiers."

The poor showman felt so sorry for them that he could not keep back his tears. Immediately, he promised the traveling companion to give him all the money he would take in at the next performance, if only he would anoint four or five of the nicest puppets. But the traveling companion said he would not take any payment, except the big sword that hung at the showman's side. On receiving it, he anointed six of the puppets, who began to dance so well that all the girls, the real live girls who were watching, began to dance too. The coachman danced with the cook, and the waiter with the chambermaid. All the guests joined the dance, and the shovel and tongs did too, but these fell down as soon as they took their first step. It was a lively night indeed!

Next morning, John and his companion set off up the lofty mountainside and through the vast pine forests. They climbed so high that at last the church towers down below looked like little red berries among all that greenery. They could see in the distance, many and many a mile away, places where neither of them had ever been. Never before had John seen so many of the glories of this lovely world at once. The sun shone bright in the clear blue air, and along the mountainside he could also hear the hunters sounding their horns. It was all so fair and sweet that tears came into his eyes, and he could not help crying out, "Almighty God, I could kiss your footsteps in thankfulness for all the splendors that you have given us in this world."

His traveling companion also folded his hands and looked out over the woods and towns that lay before them in the warm sunlight. Just then, they heard a wonderful sound overhead. They looked up and saw a large white swan sweeping above them and singing as they had never before heard any bird sing. But the song became fainter and fainter, until the bird bowed his head and dropped slowly down dead at their feet—the lovely bird!

"Two such glorious wings!" said the traveling companion. "Wings so large and white as these are worth a good deal of money. I'll take them with me. You can see now what a good thing it was that I got a sword." With one stroke, he cut off both wings of the dead swan, for he wanted to keep them.

They journeyed many and many a mile over the mountains, until at last they saw a great town rise before them, with more than a hundred towers that shone like silver in the sun. In the midst of the town there was a magnificent marble palace, with a roof of red gold. That was where the king lived.

John and his companion did not want to enter the town at once. They stopped at a wayside inn outside the town to put on fresh clothes, for they wanted to look presentable when they walked through the streets. The innkeeper told them that the king was a good man who never harmed anyone. But as for his daughter—Heaven help us—she was a bad princess.

She was pretty enough. No one could be more lovely or more entertaining than she—but what good did that do? She was a wicked witch, who was responsible for many handsome princes' losing their lives. She had decreed that any man might come to woo her. Anybody might come, whether he were prince or beggar, it made no difference to her, but he must guess the answer to three questions that she asked him. If he knew the answers, she would marry him and he would be king over all the land when her father died. But if he could not guess the right answers, she either had him hanged or had his head chopped off. That was how bad and wicked the beautiful princess was.

The old king, her father, was terribly distressed about it, but he could not keep her from being so wicked, because he had once told her that he would never concern himself with her suitors—she could do as she liked with them. Whenever a prince had come to win the princess's hand by making three guesses, he had failed. Then he was either hanged or beheaded, for each suitor was warned beforehand, when he was still free to abandon his courtship. The old king was so distressed by all this trouble and grief that for one entire day every year, he and all his soldiers went down on their knees to pray that the princess might reform; but she never would. As a sign of mourning, old women who drank schnapps would dye it black before they quaffed it—so deeply did they mourn—and more than that they couldn't do.

"That abominable princess," John said, "ought to be flogged. It would be just the thing for her, and if I were the old king I'd have her whipped till her blood ran."

"Hurrah!" they heard people shout outside the inn. The princess was passing by, and she was so very beautiful that everyone who saw her forgot how wicked she was, and everyone shouted "Hurrah." Twelve lovely maidens, all dressed in white silk and carrying golden tulips, rode beside her on twelve coal-black horses. The princess herself rode a snow-white horse, decorated with diamonds and rubies. Her riding costume was of pure gold, and the whip that she carried looked like a ray of sunlight. The gold crown on her head twinkled like the stars of heaven, and her cloak was made from thousands of bright butterfly wings. But she herself was far lovelier than all these things.

When John first set eyes on her, his face turned red—as red as blood—and he could hardly speak a single word. The princess was the living image of the lovely girl with the golden crown, of whom he had dreamed on the night when his father died. He found the princess so fair that he could not help falling in love with her.

"Surely," he thought, "it can't be true that she is a wicked witch who has people hanged or beheaded when they can't guess what she asks them. Anyone at all may ask for her hand, even though he is the poorest beggar, so I really will go to the palace, for I cannot help doing it!"

Everyone told him he ought not to try it, lest he meet with the same fate that had befallen the others. His traveling companion also tried to persuade him not to go, but John felt sure he would succeed. He brushed his shoes and his coat, washed his face and his hands, and combed his handsome blond hair. Then, all alone, he went through the town to the palace.

"Come in," the old king said when John came knocking at his door. As John opened it, the old king advanced to meet him, wearing a dressing gown and a pair of embroidered slippers. He had his crown on his head, his scepter in one hand, and his orb in the other. "Just a minute," he said, tucking the orb under his arm so that he could offer a hand to John. But the moment he heard that John had come as a suitor, he fell to sobbing so hard that both the orb and scepter dropped to the floor, and he had to use his dressing gown to wipe his eyes. The poor old king!

"Don't try it!" he said. "You will fare badly like all the others. Come, let me show them to you."

Then he led John into the princess's pleasure garden, where he saw a fearful thing. From every tree hung three or four kings' sons who had been suitors of the princess but had not been able to answer the questions she put to them. The skeletons rattled so in every breeze that they terrified the little birds, who never dared come to the garden. All the flowers were tied to human bones, and human skulls grinned up from every flower pot. What a charming garden for a princess!

"There!" said the old king, "You see. It will happen to you as it happened to all these you see here. Please don't try it. You would make me awfully unhappy, for I take these things deeply to heart."

John kissed the good old king's hand, and said he was sure everything would go well, for he was infatuated with the princess's beauty. Just then, the princess and all of her ladies rode into the palace yard, so they went over to wish her good morning. She was lovely to look at, and when she held out her hand to John, he fell in love more deeply than ever. How could she be such a wicked witch as all the people called her?

The whole party went to the palace hall, where little pages served them jam and gingerbread. But the old king was so miserable that he couldn't eat anything at all. Besides, the gingerbread was too hard for his teeth.

It was arranged that John was to visit the palace again the following morning, when the judges and the full council would be assembled to hear how he made out with his answer. If he made out well, he would have to come back two more times, but as yet, no one had ever answered the first question, so they had forfeited their lives in the first attempt.

However, John was not at all afraid of his trial. Far from it! He was jubilant, and thought only of how lovely the princess was. He felt sure that help would come to him, though he didn't know how it would come, and he preferred not to think about it. He fairly danced along the road when he returned to the inn, where his comrade awaited him. John could not stop telling him how nicely the princess had treated him, and how lovely she was. He said that he could hardly wait for tomorrow to come, when he would go to the palace and try his luck in guessing. But his comrade shook his head, and was very sad.

"I am so fond of you," he said, "and we might have been comrades together for a long while to come, but now I am apt to lose you soon, poor, dear John! I feel like crying, but I won't spoil your happiness this evening, which is perhaps the last one we shall ever spend together. We shall be as merry as merry can be, and tomorrow, when you are gone, I'll have time enough for my tears."

Everyone in the town had heard at once that the princess had a new suitor, and therefore everyone grieved. The theater was closed; the women who sold cakes tied crepe around their sugar pigs; the king and the preachers knelt in the churches; and there was widespread lamentation. For they were all sure that John's fate would be no better than that of all those others.

Late that evening, the traveling companion made a large bowl of punch, and said to John, "Now we must be merry and drink to the health of the princess." But when John had drunk two glasses of the punch, he felt so sleepy that he couldn't hold his eyes open, and he fell sound asleep. His comrade quietly lifted him from the chair and put him to bed. As soon as it was entirely dark, he took the two large wings he had cut off the swan, and fastened them to his own shoulders. Then he put into his pocket the biggest bunch of switches that had been given him by the old woman who had fallen and broken her leg. He opened the window and flew straight over the house tops to the palace, where he sat down in a corner under the window that looked into the princess's bedroom.

All was quiet in the town until the clock struck a quarter to twelve. Then the window opened and the princess flew out of it, cloaked in white and wearing long black wings. She soared over the town to a high mountain, but the traveling companion had made himself invisible, so that she could not see him as he flew after her and lashed her so hard with his switch that he drew blood wherever he struck. Ah, how she fled through the air! The wind caught her cloak, which billowed out from her like a sail, and the moonlight shone through it.

"How it hails! How it hails!" the princess cried at each blow, but it was no more than she deserved.

At last she came to the mountain and knocked on it. With a thunderous rumbling, the mountainside opened, and the princess went in. No one saw the traveling companion go in after her, for he had made himself completely invisible. They went down a big, long passage where the walls were lighted in a peculiar fashion. Thousands of glittering spiders ran along the walls and gave off a fiery glow. Then they entered a vast hall, built of silver and gold. Red and blue blossoms the size of sunflowers covered the walls, but no one could pick them, for the stems were ugly poisonous snakes, and the flowers were flames darting out between their fangs. The ceiling was alive with glittering glowworms, and sky-blue bats that zapped their transparent wings. The place looked really terrible! A throne in the center of the floor was held up by four horse skeletons in a harness of fiery red spiders. The throne itself was of milk-colored glass, and its cushions consisted of little black mice biting each other's tails. The canopy above it was made of rose-red spider webs, speckled with charming little green flies that sparkled like emeralds.

On the throne sat an old sorcerer, with a crown on his hideous head and a scepter in his hand. He kissed the princess on her forehead, and made her sit with him on the costly throne as the music struck up. Big black grasshoppers played upon mouth harps, and the owl beat upon his own stomach, because he had no drum. It was a most fantastic concert! Many tiny goblins, with will-o'-the-wisps stuck in their little caps, capered around the hall. Nobody could see the traveling companion, who had placed himself behind the throne, where he could see and hear everything. The courtiers who now appeared seemed imposing and stately enough, but anyone with an observing eye could soon see what it all meant. They were mere cabbage heads stuck upon broomsticks, which the sorcerer had dressed in embroidered clothes and conjured into liveliness. But that didn't matter, for they were only needed to keep up appearances.

After the dance had gone on for a while, the princess told the sorcerer that she had a new suitor, and she asked what question she should put to him when he came to the palace tomorrow.

"Listen to me," said the sorcerer, "I'll tell you what; you must think of something commonplace, and then he will never guess what it is. Think of one of your shoes. He won't guess that. Then off with his head, and when you come tomorrow night, remember to fetch me his eyes, so that I may eat them."

The princess made a low curtsy, and promised not to forget about the eyes. The sorcerer opened the mountain for her, and she flew homeward. But the traveling companion flew behind her and thrashed her so hard with his switch that she bitterly complained of the fearful hailstorm, and made all the haste she could to get back through the open window of her bedroom. The traveling companion flew back to the inn, where John was still asleep. Taking off the wings, he tumbled into bed, for he had good reason to feel tired.

It was very early the next morning when John awoke. When his comrade arose, he told John of a very strange dream he had had about the princess and one of her shoes. He begged him to ask the princess if she didn't have one of her shoes in mind. This, of course, was what he had overheard the sorcerer say in the mountain, but he didn't tell John about that. He merely told him to be sure to guess that the princess had her shoe in mind.

"I may as well ask about that as anything else," John agreed. "Maybe your dream was true, for I have always thought that God would look after me. However, I'll be saying good-bye, because if I guess wrong, I shall never see you again."

They embraced, and John went straight through the town and up to the palace. The whole hall was packed with people. The judges sat in their armchairs, with eiderdown pillows behind their heads because they had so much to think about, and the old king stood there wiping his eyes with a white handkerchief. Then the princess entered. She was even lovelier than she was the day before, and she bowed to everyone in the most agreeable fashion. To John she held out her hand and wished him, "Good morning to you."

John was required to guess what she had in mind. She looked at him most charmingly until she heard him say the one word "shoe." Her face turned chalk-white, and she trembled from head to foot. But there was nothing she could do about it. His guess was right.

Merciful Heavens! How glad the old king was. He turned heels over head for joy, and everyone applauded both his performance and that of John, who had guessed rightly the first time.

The traveling companion beamed with delight when he heard how well things had gone. But John clasped his hands together and thanked God, who he was sure would help him through the two remaining trials. The following day he was to guess again.

That evening went by just like the previous one. As soon as John was asleep, his comrade flew behind the princess to the mountain and thrashed her even harder than before, for this time he had taken two scourges of switches. No one saw him, but he heard all that was said. The princess was to think of her glove, and he told this to John as if he had dreamed it.

Naturally, John had no trouble in guessing correctly, and there was unbounded rejoicing in the palace. The whole court turned heels over head as they had seen the king do on the first occasion. But the princess lay on her sofa, without a word to say. Now everything depended on John's answer to the third question. If it was right, he would get the lovely princess and inherit the whole kingdom after the old king died. But if he guessed wrong, he would forfeit his life, and the wizard would eat his beautiful blue eyes.

That evening John said his prayers, went to bed early, and fell serenely asleep. But his comrade tied the wings to his back, buckled the sword to his side, took all three scourges of switches, and flew off to the palace.

The night was pitch black. A gale blew so hard that it swept tiles from the roofs. In the garden where the skeletons dangled, the trees bent before the blast like reeds. Lightning flashed every moment, and thunder kept up one unbroken roar the whole night through. The window was flung open, and out flew the princess. She was deathly pale, but she laughed at the weather and thought it was not bad enough. Her white cloak lashed about in the wind like the sail of a ship, and the traveling companion thrashed her with his three switches until blood dripped to the ground. She could scarcely fly any farther, but at last she came to the mountain.

"How it hails and blows!" she said. "I have never been out in such weather."

"One may get too much of a good thing," the sorcerer agreed.

Now she told him how John had guessed right a second time, and if he succeeded again tomorrow, then he won, and never again could she come out to him in the mountains. Never again could she perform such tricks of magic as before, and therefore she felt very badly about it.

"He won't guess it this time," said the sorcerer. "I shall hit upon something that he will never guess unless he's a greater magician than I am. But first, let's have our fun.

He took the princess by both hands, and they danced around with all the little goblins and will-o'-the-wisps that were in the hall. The red spiders spun merrily up and down the walls, the fiery flowers seemed to throw off sparks, the owl beat the drum, the crickets piped, and the black grasshoppers played on mouth organs. It was an extremely lively ball.

After they had danced awhile, the princess had to start home, for fear that she might be missed at the castle. The sorcerer said he would go with her, to enjoy that much more of her company.

Away they flew through the storm, and the traveling companion wore out all three scourges on their backs. Never had the sorcerer felt such a hailstorm. As he said good-bye to the princess outside the palace, he whispered to her, "Think of my head."

But the traveling companion overheard it, and just at the moment when the princess slipped in through her window and the sorcerer was turning around, he caught him by his long black beard, and with the sword he cut the sorcerer's ugly head off, right at the shoulders, so that the sorcerer himself didn't even see it. He threw the body into the sea for the fishes to eat, but the head he only dipped in the water, wrapped it in his silk handkerchief, and took it back to the inn, where he lay down to sleep.

Next morning, he gave John the handkerchief but told him not to open it until the princess asked him to guess what she had thought about.

The hall was so full of people that they were packed together as closely as radishes tied together in a bundle. The judges sat in their chairs with the soft pillows. The old king had put on his new clothes, and his crown and scepter had been polished to look their best. But the princess was deathly pale, and she wore black, as if she were attending a funeral.

"Of what have I thought?" she asked John. He at once untied the handkerchief, and was quite frightened himself when he saw the sorcerer's hideous head roll out of it. Everyone there shuddered at this terrible sight, but the princess sat like stone, without a word to say. Finally, she got up and gave John her hand, for his guess was good. She looked no one in the face, but sighed and said:

"You are my master now. Our wedding will be held this evening."

"I like that!" the old king shouted. "This is as things should be."

All the people shouted "Hurrah!" The military band played in the streets, the bells rang out, and the cake women took the crepe off their sugar pigs, now that everyone was celebrating. Three entire oxen stuffed with ducks and chickens were roasted whole in the center of the market square, and everyone could cut himself a piece of them. The fountains spurted up the best of wine. Whoever bought a penny bun at the bakery got six large buns thrown in for good measure, and all the buns had raisins in them.

That evening, the entire town was illuminated. The soldiers fired their cannons, and the boys set off firecrackers. At the palace, there was eating and drinking, dancing and the clinking of glasses. All the lordly gentlemen and all the lovely ladies danced together. For a long way off, you could hear them sing:

> Here are many pretty girls, and don't they love to dance!
> See them hop and swing around whenever they've a chance.
> Dance! My pretty maid, anew, till the sole flies off your shoe.

But the princess was still a witch, and she had no love for John at all. His comrade kept this in mind, and gave him three feathers from the swan's wings, and a little bottle with a few drops of liquid in it. He said that John must put a large tub of water beside the princess's bed, and just as she was about to get in bed, he must give her a little push, so that she would tumble into the tub. There he must dip her three times, after he had thrown the feathers and the drops of liquid into the water. That would free her from the spell of sorcery, and make her love him dearly.

John did everything his companion had advised him to do, though the princess shrieked as he dipped her into the water, and struggled as he held her in the shape of a large black swan with flashing eyes. The second time, she came out of the water as a swan entirely white except for a black ring around its neck. John prayed hard, and as he forced the bird under the water once more, it changed into the beautiful princess. She was fairer than ever, and she thanked him with tears in her beautiful eyes for having set him free from the sorcerer's spell.

In the morning, the old king came with all his court, and congratulations lasted all through the day. Last of all came John's traveling companion; he had his stick in his hand and the knapsack on his back. John embraced him time and again, and said that he must not leave them. He must stay here with John, who owed all his happiness to him. But the traveling companion shook his head. Gently and kindly, he said:

"No, my time is now up. I have done no more than pay my debt to you. Do you remember the dead man whom the wicked men wanted to harm? You gave all that you had so that he might have rest in his grave. I am that dead man." And at once he disappeared.

The wedding celebration lasted a whole month. John and his princess loved each other dearly, and the old king lived on for many a happy day to let their little children ride astride his knee and play with his scepter. But it was John who was king over all the land.

THE LITTLE MERMAID (1837)

Far out in the ocean, the water is as blue as the petals of the loveliest cornflower, and as clear as the purest glass. But it is very deep, too. It goes down deeper than any anchor rope will go, and many, many steeples would have to be stacked one on top of another to reach from the bottom to the surface of the sea. It is down there that the sea folk live.

Now don't suppose that there are only bare white sands at the bottom of the sea. No indeed! The most marvelous trees and flowers grow down there, with such pliant stalks and leaves that the least stir in the water makes them move about as though they were alive. All sorts of fish, large and small, dart among the branches, just as birds flit through the trees up here. From the deepest spot in the ocean rises the palace of the sea king. Its walls are made of coral and its high pointed windows of the clearest amber, but the roof is made of mussel shells that open and shut with the tide. This is a wonderful sight to see, for every shell holds glistening pearls, any one of which would be the pride of a queen's crown.

The sea king down there had been a widower for years, and his old mother kept house for him. She was a clever woman, but very proud of her noble birth. Therefore, she flaunted twelve oysters on her tail while the other ladies of the court were only allowed to wear six. Except for this, she was an altogether praiseworthy person, particularly so because she was extremely fond of her granddaughters, the little sea princesses. They were six lovely girls, but the youngest was the most beautiful of them all. Her skin was as soft and tender as a rose petal, and her eyes were as blue as the deep sea, but like all the others, she had no feet. Her body ended in a fish tail.

The whole day long they used to play in the palace, down in the great halls where live flowers grew on the walls. Whenever the high amber windows were thrown open, the fish would swim in, just as swallows dart into our rooms when we open the windows. But these fish, now, would swim right up to the little princesses to eat out of their hands and let themselves be petted.

Outside the palace was a big garden, with flaming red and deep-blue trees. Their fruit glittered like gold, and their blossoms flamed like fire on their constantly waving stalks. The soil was very fine sand indeed, but as blue as burning brimstone. A strange blue veil lay over everything down there. You would have thought yourself aloft in the air with only the blue sky above and beneath you, rather than down at the bottom of the sea. When there was a dead calm, you could just see the sun, like a scarlet flower with light streaming from its calyx.

Each little princess had her own small garden plot, where she could dig and plant whatever she liked. One of them made her little flower bed in the shape of a whale, another thought it neater to shape hers like a little mermaid, but the youngest of them made hers as round as the sun, and there she grew only flowers that were as red as the sun itself. She was an unusual child, quiet and wistful, and when her sisters decorated their gardens with all kinds of odd things they had found in sunken ships, she would allow nothing in hers except flowers as red as the sun, and a pretty marble statue. This figure of a handsome boy, carved in pure white marble, had sunk down to the bottom of the sea from some ship that was wrecked. Beside the statue, she planted a rose-colored weeping willow tree, which thrived so well that its graceful branches shaded the statue and hung down to the blue sand, where their shadows took on a violet tint, and swayed as the branches swayed. It looked as if the roots and the tips of the branches were kissing each other in play.

Nothing gave the youngest princess such pleasure as to hear about the world of human beings up above them. Her old grandmother had to tell her all she knew about ships and cities, and of people and animals. What seemed nicest of all to her was that up on land, the flowers were fragrant, for those at the bottom of the sea had no scent. And she thought it was nice that the woods were green, and that the fish you saw among their branches could sing so loud and sweet that it was delightful to hear them. Her grandmother had to call the little birds "fish," or the princess would not have known what she was talking about, for she had never seen a bird.

"When you get to be fifteen," her grandmother said, "you will be allowed to rise up out of the ocean and sit on the rocks in the moonlight, to watch the great ships sailing by. You will see woods and towns, too."

Next year one of her sisters would be fifteen, but the others—well, since each was a whole year older than the next, the youngest still had five long years to wait until she could rise up from the water and see what our world was like. But each sister promised to tell the others about all that she saw and what she found most marvelous on her first day. Their grandmother had not told them half enough, and there were so many thing that they longed to know about.

The most eager of them all was the youngest, the very one who was so quiet and wistful. Many a night she stood by her open window and looked up through the dark blue water where the fish waved their fins and tails. She could just see the moon and stars. To be sure, their light was quite dim, but looked at through the water, they seemed much bigger than they appear to us. Whenever a cloudlike shadow swept across them, she knew that it was either a whale swimming overhead or a ship with many human beings aboard it. Little did they dream that a pretty young mermaid was down below, stretching her white arms up toward the keel of their ship.

The eldest princess had her fifteenth birthday, so now she received permission to rise up out of the water. When she got back, she had a hundred things to tell her sisters about, but the most marvelous thing of all, she said, was to lie on a sand bar in the moonlight, when the sea was calm, and to gaze at the large city on the shore, where the lights twinkled like hundreds of stars; to listen to music; to hear the chatter and clamor of carriages and people; to see so many church towers and spires; and to hear the ringing bells. Because she could not enter the city, that was just what she most dearly longed to do.

Oh, how intently the youngest sister listened. After this, whenever she stood at her open window at night and looked up through the dark blue waters, she thought of that great city with all of its clatter and clamor, and even fancied that in these depths she could hear the church bells ring.

The next year, her second sister had permission to rise up to the surface and swim wherever she pleased. She came up just at sunset, and she said that this spectacle was the most marvelous sight she had ever seen. The heavens had a golden glow, and as for the clouds—she could not find words to describe their beauty. Splashed with red and tinted with violet, they sailed over her head. But much faster than the sailing clouds were wild swans in a flock. Like a long white veil trailing above the sea, they flew toward the setting sun. She too swam toward it, but down it went, and all the rose-colored glow faded from the sea and sky.

The following year, her third sister ascended, and as she was the boldest of them all, she swam up a broad river that flowed into the ocean. She saw gloriously green, vine-colored hills. Palaces and manor houses could be glimpsed through the splendid woods. She heard all the birds sing, and the sun shone so brightly that often she had to dive under the water to cool her burning face. In a small cove, she found a whole school of mortal children, paddling about in the water quite naked. She wanted to play with them, but they took fright and ran away. Then along came a little black animal—it was a dog, but she had never seen a dog before. It barked at her so ferociously that she took fright herself, and fled to the open sea. But never could she forget the splendid woods, the green hills, and the nice children who could swim in the water although they didn't wear fish tails.

The fourth sister was not so venturesome. She stayed far out among the rough waves, which she said was a marvelous place. You could see all around you for miles and miles, and the heavens up above you were like a vast dome of glass. She had seen ships, but they were so far away that they looked like sea gulls. Playful dolphins had turned somersaults, and monstrous whales had spouted water through their nostrils so that it looked as if hundreds of fountains were playing all around them.

Now the fifth sister had her turn. Her birthday came in the wintertime, so she saw things that none of the others had seen. The sea was a deep green color, and enormous icebergs drifted about. Each one glistened like a pearl, she said, but they were more lofty than any church steeple built by man. They assumed the most fantastic shapes, and sparkled like diamonds. She had seated herself on the largest one, and all the ships that came sailing by sped away as soon as the frightened sailors saw her there with her long hair blowing in the wind.

In the late evening, clouds filled the sky. Thunder cracked and lightning darted across the heavens. Black waves lifted those great bergs of ice on high, where they flashed when the lightning struck.

On all the ships the sails were reefed, and there was fear and trembling. But quietly she sat there, upon her drifting iceberg, and watched the blue forked lightning strike the sea.

Each of the sisters took delight in the lovely new sights when she first rose up to the surface of the sea. But when they became grown-up girls who were allowed to go wherever they liked, they became indifferent to it. They would become homesick, and in a month, they said that there was no place like the bottom of the sea, where they felt so completely at home.

On many an evening, the older sisters would rise to the surface, arm in arm, all five in a row. They had beautiful voices, more charming than those of any mortal beings. When a storm was brewing, and they anticipated a shipwreck, they would swim before the ship and sing most seductively of how beautiful it was at the bottom of the ocean, trying to overcome the prejudice that the sailors had against coming down to them. But people could not understand their song, and mistook it for the voice of the storm. Nor was it for them to see the glories of the deep. When their ship went down, they were drowned, and it was as dead men that they reached the sea king's palace.

On the evenings when the mermaids rose through the water like this, arm in arm, their youngest sister stayed behind all alone, looking after them and wanting to weep. But a mermaid has no tears, and therefore she suffers so much more.

"Oh, how I do wish I were fifteen!" she said. "I know I shall love that world up there and all the people who live in it."

And at last she too came to be fifteen.

"Now I'll have you off my hands," said her grandmother, the old queen dowager. "Come, let me adorn you like your sisters." In the little maid's hair she put a wreath of white lilies, each petal of which was formed from half of a pearl. And the old queen let eight big oysters fasten themselves to the princess's tail, as a sign of her high rank.

"But that hurts!" said the little mermaid.

"You must put up with a good deal to keep up appearances," her grandmother said.

Oh, how gladly she would have shaken off all these decorations, and laid aside the cumbersome wreath! The red flowers in her garden were much more becoming to her, but she didn't dare to make any changes. "Good-bye," she said, and up she went through the water, as light and as sparkling as a bubble.

The sun had just gone down when her head rose above the surface, but the clouds still shone like gold and roses, and in the delicately tinted sky sparkled the clear gleam of the evening star. The air was mild and fresh and the sea unruffled. A great three-master lay in view with only one of all its sails set, for there was not even the whisper of a breeze, and the sailors idled about in the rigging and on the yards. There was music and singing on the ship, and as night came on, they lighted hundreds of such brightly colored lanterns that one might have thought the flags of all nations were swinging in the air.

The little mermaid swam right up to the window of the main cabin, and each time she rose with the swell, she could peep in through the clear glass panes at the crowd of brilliantly dressed people within. The handsomest of them all was a young prince with big dark eyes. He could not be more than sixteen years old. It was his birthday, and that was the reason for all the celebration. Up on deck, the sailors were dancing, and when the prince appeared among them, a hundred or more rockets flew through the air, making it as bright as day. These startled the little mermaid so badly that she ducked under the water. But she soon peeped up again, and then it seemed as if all the stars in the sky were falling around her. Never had she seen such fireworks. Great suns spun around, splendid fire-fish floated through the blue air, and all these things were mirrored in the crystal clear sea. It was so brilliantly bright that you could see every little rope of the ship, and the people could be seen distinctly. Oh, how handsome the young prince was! He laughed, and he smiled and shook people by the hand, while the music rang out in the perfect evening.

It got very late, but the little mermaid could not take her eyes off the ship and the handsome prince. The brightly colored lanterns were put out, no more rockets flew through the air, and no more cannons boomed. But there was a mutter and rumble deep down in the sea, and the swell kept bouncing her up so high that she could look into the cabin.

Now the ship began to sail. Canvas after canvas was spread in the wind, the waves rose high, great clouds gathered, and lightning flashed in the distance. Ah, they were in for a terrible storm, and the mariners made haste to reef the sails. The tall ship pitched and rolled as it sped through the angry sea. The waves rose up like towering black mountains, as if they would break over the masthead, but the swanlike ship plunged into the valleys between such waves and emerged to ride their lofty heights. To the little mermaid, this seemed good sport, but to the sailors, it was nothing of the sort. The ship creaked and labored, thick timbers gave way under the heavy blows, waves broke over the ship, the mainmast snapped in two like a reed, the ship listed over on its side, and water burst into the hold.

Now the little mermaid saw that people were in peril, and that she herself must take care to avoid the beams and wreckage tossed about by the sea. One moment, it would be black as pitch, and she couldn't see a thing. Next moment, the lightning would flash so brightly that she could distinguish every soul on board. Everyone was looking out for himself as best he could. She watched closely for the young prince, and when the ship split in two, she saw him sink down in the sea. At first, she was overjoyed that he would be with her, but then she recalled that human people could not live under the water, and he could only visit her father's palace as a dead man. No, he should not die! So she swam in among all the floating planks and beams, completely forgetting that they might crush her. She dived through the waves and rode their crests, until at length she reached the young prince, who was no longer able to swim in that raging sea. His arms and legs were exhausted, his beautiful eyes were closing, and he would have died if the little mermaid had not come to help him. She held his head above water, and let the waves take them wherever the waves went.

At daybreak, when the storm was over, not a trace of the ship was in view. The sun rose out of the waters, red and bright, and its beams seemed to bring the glow of life back to the cheeks of the prince, but his eyes remained closed. The mermaid kissed his high and shapely forehead. As she stroked his wet hair in place, it seemed to her that he looked like that marble statue in her little garden. She kissed him again and hoped that he would live.

She saw dry land rise before her in high blue mountains, topped with snow as glistening white as if a flock of swans were resting there. Down by the shore were splendid green woods, and in the foreground stood a church, or perhaps a convent; she didn't know which, but anyway it was a building. Orange and lemon trees grew in its garden, and tall palm trees grew beside the gateway. Here the sea formed a little harbor, quite calm and very deep. Fine white sand had been washed up below the cliffs. She swam there with the handsome prince, and stretched him out on the sand, taking special care to pillow his head up high in the warm sunlight.

The bells began to ring in the great white building, and a number of young girls came out into the garden. The little mermaid swam away behind some tall rocks that stuck out of the water. She covered her hair and her shoulders with foam so that no one could see her tiny face, and then she watched to see who would find the poor prince.

In a little while, one of the young girls came upon him. She seemed frightened, but only for a minute; then she called more people. The mermaid watched the prince regain consciousness, and smile at everyone around him. But he did not smile at her, for he did not even know that she had saved him. She felt very unhappy, and when they led him away to the big building, she dived sadly down into the water and returned to her father's palace.

She had always been quiet and wistful, and now she became much more so. Her sisters asked her what she had seen on her first visit up to the surface, but she would not tell them a thing.

Many evenings and many mornings, she revisited the spot where she had left the prince. She saw the fruit in the garden ripened and harvested, and she saw the snow on the high mountain melted away, but she did not see the prince, so each time she came home sadder than she had left. It was her one consolation to sit in her little garden and throw her arms about the beautiful marble statue that looked so much like the prince. But she took no care of her flowers now. They overgrew the paths until the place was a wilderness, and their long stalks and leaves became so entangled in the branches of the tree that it cast a gloomy shade.

Finally, she couldn't bear it any longer. She told her secret to one of her sisters. Immediately, all the other sisters heard about it. No one else knew, except a few more mermaids who told no one—except their most intimate friends. One of these friends knew who the prince was. She too had seen the birthday celebration on the ship. She knew where he came from and where his kingdom was.

"Come, little sister!" said the other princesses. Arm in arm, they rose from the water in a long row, right in front of where they knew the prince's palace stood. It was built of pale, glistening, golden stone with great marble staircases, one of which led down to the sea. Magnificent gilt domes rose above the roof, and between the pillars all around the building were marble statues that looked most lifelike. Through the clear glass of the lofty windows one could see into the splendid halls, with their costly silk hangings and tapestries and walls covered with paintings that were delightful to behold. In the center of the main hall a large fountain played its columns of spray up to the glass-domed roof, through which the sun shone down on the water and upon the lovely plants that grew in the big basin.

Now that she knew where he lived, many an evening and many a night she spent there in the sea. She swam much closer to shore than any of her sisters would dare venture, and she even went far up a narrow stream, under the splendid marble balcony that cast its long shadow in the water. Here she used to sit and watch the young prince when he thought himself quite alone in the bright moonlight.

On many evenings, she saw him sail out in his fine boat, with music playing and flags aflutter. She would peep out through the green rushes, and if the wind blew her long silver veil, anyone who saw it mistook it for a swan spreading its wings.

On many nights, she saw the fishermen come out to sea with their torches, and heard them tell about how kind the young prince was. This made her proud to think that it was she who had saved his life when he was buffeted about, half dead among the waves. And she thought of how softly his head had rested on her breast, and how tenderly she had kissed him, though he knew nothing of all this nor could he even dream of it.

Increasingly, she grew to like human beings, and more and more, she longed to live among them. Their world seemed so much wider than her own, for they could skim over the sea in ships, and mount up into the lofty peaks high over the clouds, and their lands stretched out in woods and fields farther than the eye could see. There was so much she wanted to know. Her sisters could not answer all her questions, so she asked her old grandmother, who knew about the "upper world," which was what she said was the right name for the countries above the sea.

"If men aren't drowned," the little mermaid asked, "do they live on forever? Don't they die, as we do down here in the sea?"

"Yes," the old lady said, "they too must die, and their lifetimes are even shorter than ours. We can live to be three hundred years old, but when we perish, we turn into mere foam on the sea, and haven't even a grave down here among our dear ones. We have no immortal soul, no life hereafter. We are like the green seaweed—once cut down, it never grows again. Human beings, on the contrary, have a soul that lives forever, long after their bodies have turned to clay. It rises through thin air, up to the shining stars. Just as we rise through the water to see the lands on Earth, so men rise up to beautiful places unknown, which we shall never see."

"Why weren't we given an immortal soul?" the little mermaid sadly asked. "I would gladly give up my three hundred years if I could be a human being only for a day, and later share in that heavenly realm."

"You must not think about that," said the old lady. "We fare much more happily and are much better off than the folk up there."

"Then I must also die and float as foam upon the sea, not hearing the music of the waves, and seeing neither the beautiful flowers nor the red sun! Can't I do anything at all to win an immortal soul?"

"No," her grandmother answered, "not unless a human being loved you so much that you meant more to him than his father and mother. If his every thought and his whole heart cleaved to you so that he would let a priest join his right hand to yours and would promise to be faithful here and throughout all eternity, then his soul would dwell in your body, and you would share in the happiness of mankind. He would give you a soul and yet keep his own. But that can never come to pass. The very thing that is your greatest beauty here in the sea—your fish tail—would be considered ugly on land. They have such poor taste that to be thought beautiful there you have to have two awkward props that they call legs."

The little mermaid sighed and looked unhappily at her fish tail.

"Come, let us be gay!" the old lady said. "Let us leap and bound throughout the three hundred years that we have to live. Surely that is time and to spare, and afterwards we shall be glad enough to rest in our graves. We are holding a court ball this evening."

This was a much more glorious affair than is ever to be seen on Earth. The walls and the ceiling of the great ballroom were made of massive but transparent glass. Many hundreds of huge rose-red and grass-green shells stood on each side in rows, with the blue flames that burned in each shell illuminating the whole room and shining through the walls so clearly that it was quite bright in the sea outside. You could see the countless fish, great and small, swimming toward the glass walls. On some of them, the scales gleamed purplish-red, while others were silver and gold. Across the floor of the hall ran a wide stream of water, and upon this the mermaids and mermen danced to their own entrancing songs. Such beautiful voices are not to be heard among the people who live on land. The little mermaid sang more sweetly than anyone else, and everyone applauded her. For a moment her heart was happy, because she knew she had the loveliest voice of all, in the sea or on the land. But her thoughts soon strayed to the world up above. She could not forget the charming prince, nor her sorrow that she did not have an immortal soul like his. Therefore, she stole out of her father's palace, and, while everything there was song and gladness, she sat sadly in her own little garden.

Then she heard a bugle call through the water, and she thought, "That must mean he is sailing up there, he whom I love more than my father or mother, he of whom I am always thinking, and in whose hands I would so willingly trust my lifelong happiness. I dare do anything to win him and to gain an immortal soul. While my sisters are dancing here, in my father's palace, I shall visit the sea witch of whom I have always been so afraid. Perhaps she will be able to advise me and help me."

The little mermaid set out from her garden toward the whirlpools that raged in front of the witch's dwelling. She had never gone that way before. No flowers grew there, nor any seaweed. Bare and gray, the sands extended to the whirlpools, where like roaring mill wheels the waters whirled and snatched everything within their reach down to the bottom of the sea. Between these tumultuous whirlpools, she had to thread her way to reach the witch's waters, and then for a long stretch, the only trail lay through a hot seething mire, which the witch called her peat marsh. Beyond it, her house lay in the middle of a weird forest, where all the trees and shrubs were polyps, half animal and half plant. They looked like hundred-headed snakes growing out of the soil. All their branches were long, slimy arms, with fingers like wriggling worms. They squirmed, joint by joint, from their roots to their outermost tentacles, and whatever they could lay hold of, they twined around and never let go. The little mermaid was terrified, and stopped at the edge of the forest. Her heart thumped with fear, and she nearly turned back, but then she remembered the prince and the souls that men have, and she summoned her courage. She bound her long flowing locks closely about her head so that the polyps could not catch hold of them, folded her arms across her breast, and darted through the water like a fish, in among the slimy polyps that stretched out their writhing arms and fingers to seize her. She saw that every one of them held something that it had caught with its hundreds of little tentacles, and to which it clung as with strong hoops of steel. The white bones of men who had perished at sea and sunk to these depths could be seen in the polyps' arms. Ships' rudders, and seamen's chests, and the skeletons of land animals had also fallen into their clutches, but the most ghastly sight of all was a little mermaid whom they had caught and strangled.

She reached a large muddy clearing in the forest, where big fat water snakes slithered about, showing their foul yellowish bellies. In the middle of this clearing was a house built of the bones of shipwrecked men, and there sat the sea witch, letting a toad eat out of her mouth just as we might feed sugar to a little canary bird. She called the ugly fat water snakes her little chickabiddies, and let them crawl and sprawl about on her spongy bosom.

"I know exactly what you want," said the sea witch. "It is very foolish of you, but just the same, you shall have your way, for it will bring you to grief, my proud princess. You want to get rid of your fish tail and have two props instead, so that you can walk about like a human creature, and have the young prince fall in love with you, and win him and an immortal soul besides." At this, the witch gave such a loud cackling laugh that the toad and the snakes were shaken to the ground, where they lay writhing.

"You are just in time," said the witch. "After the sun comes up tomorrow, a whole year would have to go by before I could be of any help to you. I shall compound you a draught, and before sunrise, you must swim to the shore with it, seat yourself on dry land, and drink the draught down. Then your tail will divide and shrink until it becomes what the people on Earth call a pair of shapely legs. But it will hurt; it will feel as if a sharp sword slashed through you. Everyone who sees you will say that you are the most graceful human being they have ever laid eyes on, for you will keep your gliding movement and no dancer will be able to tread as lightly as you. But every step you take will feel as if you were treading upon knife blades so sharp that blood must flow. I am willing to help you, but are you willing to suffer all this?"

"Yes," the little mermaid said in a trembling voice, as she thought of the prince and of gaining a human soul.

"Remember!" said the witch. "Once you have taken a human form, you can never be a mermaid again. You can never come back through the waters to your sisters, or to your father's palace. And if you do not win the love of the prince so completely that for your sake he forgets his father and mother, cleaves to you with his every thought and his whole heart, and lets the priest join your hands in marriage, then you will win no immortal soul. If he marries someone else, your heart will break on the very next morning, and you will become foam of the sea."

"I shall take that risk," said the little mermaid, but she turned as pale as death.

"Also, you will have to pay me," said the witch, "and it is no trifling price that I'm asking. You have the sweetest voice of anyone down here at the bottom of the sea, and while I don't doubt that you would like to captivate the prince with it, you must give this voice to me. I will take the very best thing that you have in return for my sovereign draught. I must pour my own blood in it to make the drink as sharp as a two-edged sword."

"But if you take my voice," said the little mermaid, "what will be left to me?"

"Your lovely form," the witch told her, "your gliding movements, and your eloquent eyes. With these, you can easily enchant a human heart. Well, have you lost your courage? Stick out your little tongue, and I shall cut it off. I'll have my price, and you shall have the potent draught."

"Go ahead," said the little mermaid.

The witch hung her caldron over the flames, to brew the draught. "Cleanliness is a good thing," she said, as she tied her snakes in a knot and scoured out the pot with them. Then she pricked herself in the chest and let her black blood splash into the caldron. Steam swirled up from it in such ghastly shapes that anyone would have been terrified by them. The witch constantly threw new ingredients into the caldron, and it started to boil with a sound like that of a crocodile shedding tears. When the draught was ready at last, it looked as clear as the purest water.

"There's your draught," said the witch. And she cut off the tongue of the little mermaid, who now was dumb and could neither sing nor talk.

"If the polyps should pounce on you when you walk back through my wood," the witch said, "just spill a drop of this brew upon them and their tentacles will break in a thousand pieces." But there was no need of that, for the polyps curled up in terror as soon as they saw the bright draught. It glittered in the little mermaid's hand as if it were a shining star. So she soon traversed the forest, the marsh, and the place of raging whirlpools.

She could see her father's palace. The lights had been snuffed out in the great ballroom, and doubtless everyone in the palace was asleep, but she dared not go near them, now that she was stricken dumb and was leaving her home forever. Her heart felt as if it would break with grief.

She tiptoed into the garden, took one flower from each of her sisters' little plots, blew a thousand kisses toward the palace, and then mounted up through the dark blue sea.

The sun had not yet risen when she saw the prince's palace. As she climbed his splendid marble staircase, the moon was shining clear. The little mermaid swallowed the bitter, fiery draught, and it was as if a two-edged sword struck through her frail body. She swooned away, and lay there as if she were dead. When the sun rose over the sea, she awoke and felt a flash of pain, but directly in front of her stood the handsome young prince, gazing at her with his coal-black eyes. Lowering her gaze, she saw that her fish tail was gone and that she had the loveliest pair of white legs any young maid could hope to have. But she was naked, so she clothed herself in her own long hair.

The prince asked who she was and how she came to be there. Her deep blue eyes looked at him tenderly but very sadly, for she could not speak. Then he took her hand and led her into his palace. Every footstep felt as if she were walking on the blades and points of sharp knives, just as the witch had foretold, but she gladly endured it. She moved as lightly as a bubble as she walked beside the prince. He and all who saw her marveled at the grace of her gliding walk.

Once clad in the rich silk and muslin garments that were provided for her, she was the loveliest person in all the palace, though she was dumb and could neither sing nor speak. Beautiful slaves attired in silk and cloth of gold came to sing before the prince and his royal parents. One of them sang more sweetly than all the others, and when the prince smiled at her and clapped his hands, the little mermaid felt very unhappy, for she knew that she herself used to sing much more sweetly.

"Oh," she thought, "if he only knew that I parted with my voice forever so that I could be near him."

Graceful slaves now began to dance to the most wonderful music. Then the little mermaid lifted her shapely white arms, rose up on the tips of her toes, and skimmed over the floor. No one had ever danced so well. Each movement set off her beauty to better and better advantage, and her eyes spoke more directly to the heart than any of the singing slaves could do.

She charmed everyone, and especially the prince, who called her his dear little foundling. She danced time and again, though every time she touched the floor she felt as if she were treading on sharp-edged steel. The prince said he would keep her with him always, and that she was to have a velvet pillow to sleep on outside his door.

He had a page's suit made for her, so that she could go with him on horseback. They would ride through the sweet-scented woods, where the green boughs brushed her shoulders and where the little birds sang among the fluttering leaves.

She climbed up high mountains with the prince, and though her tender feet bled so that all could see it, she only laughed and followed him on until they could see the clouds driving far below, like a flock of birds in flight to distant lands.

At home in the prince's palace, while the others slept at night, she would go down the broad marble steps to cool her burning feet in the cold sea water, and then she would recall those who lived beneath the sea. One night, her sisters came by, arm in arm, singing sadly as they breasted the waves. When she held out her hands toward them, they knew who she was, and told her how unhappy she had made them all. They came to see her every night after that, and once far, far out to sea, she saw her old grandmother, who had not been up to the surface this many a year. With her was the sea king, with his crown upon his head. They stretched out their hands to her, but they did not venture so near the land as her sisters had.

Day after day, she became more dear to the prince, who loved her as one would love a good little child, but he never thought of making her his queen. Yet she had to be his wife, or she would never have an immortal soul, and on the morning after his wedding, she would turn into foam on the waves.

"Don't you love me best of all?" the little mermaid's eyes seemed to question him, when he took her in his arms and kissed her lovely forehead.

"Yes, you are most dear to me," said the prince, "for you have the kindest heart. You love me more than anyone else does, and you look so much like a young girl I once saw but never shall find again. I was on a ship that was wrecked, and the waves cast me ashore near a holy temple, where many young girls performed the rituals. The youngest of them found me beside the sea and saved my life. Though I saw her no more than twice, she is the only person in all the world whom I could love. But you are so much like her that you almost replace the memory of her in my heart. She belongs to that holy temple; therefore, it is my good fortune that I have you. We shall never part."

"Alas, he doesn't know it was I who saved his life," the little mermaid thought. "I carried him over the sea to the garden where the temple stands. I hid behind the foam and watched to see if anyone would come. I saw the pretty maid he loves better than me." A sigh was the only sign of her deep distress, for a mermaid cannot cry. "He says that the other maid belongs to the holy temple. She will never come out into the world, so they will never see each other again. It is I who will care for him, love him, and give all my life to him."

Now rumors arose that the prince was to wed the beautiful daughter of a neighboring king, and that it was for this reason he was having such a superb ship made ready to sail. The rumor ran that the prince's real interest in visiting the neighboring kingdom was to see the king's daughter, and that he was to travel with a lordly retinue. The little mermaid shook her head and smiled, for she knew the prince's thoughts far better than anyone else did.

"I am forced to make this journey," he told her. "I must visit the beautiful princess, for this is my parents' wish, but they would not have me bring her home as my bride against my own will, and I can never love her. She does not resemble the lovely maiden in the temple, as you do, and if I were to choose a bride, I would sooner choose you, my dear mute foundling with those telling eyes of yours." And he kissed her on the mouth, fingered her long hair, and laid his head against her heart so that she came to dream of mortal happiness and an immortal soul.

"I trust you aren't afraid of the sea, my silent child," he said, as they went on board the magnificent vessel that was to carry them to the land of the neighboring king. And he told her stories of storms, of ships becalmed, of strange deep-sea fish, and of the wonders that divers have seen. She smiled at such stories, for no one knew about the bottom of the sea as well as she did.

In the clear moonlight, when everyone except the man at the helm was asleep, she sat on the side of the ship gazing down through the transparent water, and fancied she could catch glimpses of her father's palace. On the topmost tower stood her old grandmother, wearing her silver crown and looking up at the keel of the ship through the rushing waves. Then her sisters rose to the surface, looked at her sadly, and wrung their white hands. She smiled and waved, trying to let them know that all went well and that she was happy. But along came the cabin boy, and her sisters dived out of sight so quickly that the boy supposed the flash of white he had seen was merely foam on the sea.

Next morning, the ship came into the harbor of the neighboring king's glorious city. All the church bells chimed, and trumpets were sounded from all the high towers, while the soldiers lined up with flying banners and glittering bayonets. Every day had a new festivity, as one ball or levee followed another, but the princess was still to appear. They said she was being brought up in some faraway sacred temple, where she was learning every royal virtue. But she came at last.

The little mermaid was curious to see how beautiful this princess was, and she had to grant that a more exquisite figure she had never seen. The princess's skin was clear and fair, and behind the long, dark lashes, her deep blue eyes were smiling and devoted.

"It was you!" the prince cried. "You are the one who saved me when I lay like a dead man beside the sea." He clasped the blushing bride of his choice in his arms. "Oh, I am happier than a man should be!" he told his little mermaid. "My fondest dream—that which I never dared to hope—has come true. You will share in my great joy, for you love me more than anyone does."

The little mermaid kissed his hand and felt that her heart was beginning to break. For the morning after his wedding day would see her dead and turned to watery foam.

All the church bells rang out, and heralds rode through the streets to announce the wedding. Upon every altar, sweet-scented oils were burned in costly silver lamps. The priests swung their censers, the bride and the bridegroom joined their hands, and the bishop blessed their marriage. The little mermaid, clothed in silk and cloth of gold, held the bride's train, but she was deaf to the wedding march and blind to the holy ritual. Her thought turned on her last night upon Earth, and on all she had lost in this world.

That same evening, the bride and bridegroom went aboard the ship. Cannons thundered and banners waved. On the deck of the ship, a royal pavilion of purple and gold was set up and furnished with luxurious cushions. Here the wedded couple were to sleep on that calm, clear night. The sails swelled in the breeze, and the ship glided so lightly that it scarcely seemed to move over the quiet sea. All nightfall, brightly colored lanterns were lighted, and the mariners merrily danced on the deck. The little mermaid could not forget that first time she rose from the depths of the sea and looked on at such pomp and happiness. Light as a swallow pursued by his enemies, she joined in the whirling dance. Everyone cheered her, for never had she danced so wonderfully. Her tender feet felt as if they were pierced by daggers, but she did not feel it. Her heart suffered far greater pain. She knew that this was the last evening that she ever would see him for whom she had forsaken her home and family, for whom she had sacrificed her lovely voice and suffered such constant torment, while he knew nothing of all these things. It was the last night that she would breathe the same air with him, or look upon deep waters or the star fields of the blue sky. A never-ending night, without thought and without dreams, awaited her who had no soul and could not get one. The merrymaking lasted long after midnight, yet she laughed and danced on despite the thought of death she carried in her heart. The prince kissed his beautiful bride, and she toyed with his coal-black hair. Hand in hand, they went to rest in the magnificent pavilion.

A hush came over the ship. Only the helmsman remained on deck as the little mermaid leaned her white arms on the bulwarks and looked to the east to see the first red hint of daybreak, for she knew that the first flash of the sun would strike her dead. Then she saw her sisters rise up among the waves. They were as pale as she, and there was no sign of their lovely long hair that the breezes used to blow. It had all been cut off.

"We have given our hair to the witch," they said, "so that she would send you help, and save you from death tonight. She gave us a knife. Here it is. See the sharp blade! Before the sun rises, you must strike it into the prince's heart, and when his warm blood bathes your feet, they will grow together and become a fish tail. Then you will be a mermaid again, able to come back to us in the sea, and live out your three hundred years before you die and turn into dead salt sea foam. Make haste! He or you must die before sunrise. Our old grandmother is so grief-stricken that her white hair is falling fast, just as ours did under the witch's scissors. Kill the prince and come back to us. Hurry! Hurry! See that red glow in the heavens! In a few minutes the sun will rise and you must die." So saying, they gave a strange deep sigh and sank beneath the waves.

The little mermaid parted the purple curtains of the tent and saw the beautiful bride asleep with her head on the prince's breast. The mermaid bent down and kissed his shapely forehead. She looked at the sky, fast reddening for the break of day. She looked at the sharp knife, and again turned her eyes toward the prince, who in his sleep murmured the name of his bride. His thoughts were all for her, and the knife blade trembled in the mermaid's hand. But then she flung it from her, far out over the waves. Where it fell the waves were red, as if bubbles of blood seethed in the water. With eyes already glazing she looked once more at the prince, hurled herself over the bulwarks into the sea, and felt her body dissolve in foam.

The sun rose up from the waters. Its beams fell, warm and kindly, upon the chill sea foam, and the little mermaid did not feel the hand of death. In the bright sunlight overhead, she saw hundreds of fair ethereal beings. They were so transparent that through them she could see the ship's white sails and the red clouds in the sky. Their voices were sheer music, but so spiritlike that no human ear could detect the sound, just as no eye on Earth could see their forms. Without wings, they floated as light as the air itself. The little mermaid discovered that she was shaped like them, and that she was gradually rising up out of the foam.

"Who are you, toward whom I rise?" she asked, and her voice sounded like those above her, so spiritual that no music on Earth could match it.

"We are the daughters of the air," they answered. "A mermaid has no immortal soul, and can never get one unless she wins the love of a human being. Her eternal life must depend upon a power outside herself. The daughters of the air do not have an immortal soul either, but they can earn one by their good deeds. We fly to the south, where the hot poisonous air kills human beings unless we bring cool breezes. We carry the scent of flowers through the air, bringing freshness and healing balm wherever we go. When for three hundred years we have tried to do all the good that we can, we are given an immortal soul and a share in mankind's eternal bliss. You, poor little mermaid, have tried with your whole heart to do this too. Your suffering and your loyalty have raised you up into the realm of airy spirits, and now in the course of three hundred years, you may earn by your good deeds a soul that will never die."

The little mermaid lifted her clear bright eyes toward God's sun, and for the first time, her eyes were wet with tears.

On board the ship, all was astir and lively again. She saw the prince and his fair bride in search of her. Then they gazed sadly into the seething foam, as if they knew she had hurled herself into the waves. Unseen by them, she kissed the bride's forehead, smiled upon the prince, and rose up with the other daughters of the air to the rose-red clouds that sailed on high.

"This is the way that we shall rise to the Kingdom of God, after three hundred years have passed."

"We may get there even sooner," one spirit whispered. "Unseen, we fly into the homes of men, where there are children, and for every day on which we find a good child who pleases his parents and deserves their love, God shortens our days of trial. The child does not know when we float through his room, but when we smile at him in approval, one year is taken from our three hundred. But if we see a naughty, mischievous child, we must shed tears of sorrow, and each tear adds a day to the time of our trial."

THE EMPEROR'S
NEW CLOTHES (1837)

Many years ago, there was an emperor so exceedingly fond of new clothes that he spent all his money on being well dressed. He cared nothing about reviewing his soldiers, going to the theater, or going for a ride in his carriage, except to show off his new clothes. He had a coat for every hour of the day, and instead of saying, as one might, about any other ruler, "The king's in council," here they always said, "The emperor's in his dressing room."

In the great city where he lived, life was always gay. Every day, many strangers came to town, and among them one day came two swindlers. They let it be known they were weavers, and they said they could weave the most magnificent fabrics imaginable. Not only were their colors and patterns uncommonly fine, but clothes made of this cloth had a wonderful way of becoming invisible to anyone who was unfit for his office, or who was unusually stupid.

"Those would be just the clothes for me," thought the emperor. "If I wore them, I would be able to discover which men in my empire are unfit for their posts. And I could tell the wise men from the fools. Yes, I certainly must get some of the stuff woven for me right away." He paid the two swindlers a large sum of money to start work at once.

They set up two looms and pretended to weave, though there was nothing on the looms. All the finest silk and the purest old thread that they demanded went into their traveling bags, while they worked the empty looms far into the night.

"I'd like to know how those weavers are getting on with the cloth," the emperor thought, but he felt slightly uncomfortable when he remembered that those who were unfit for their position would not be able to see the fabric. It couldn't have been that he doubted himself, yet he thought he'd rather send someone else to see how things were going. The whole town knew about the cloth's peculiar power, and all were impatient to find out how stupid their neighbors were.

"I'll send my honest old minister to the weavers," the emperor decided. "He'll be the best one to tell me how the material looks, for he's a sensible man, and no one does his duty better."

So the honest old minister went to the room where the two swindlers sat working away at their empty looms.

"Heaven help me," he thought as his eyes flew wide open, "I can't see anything at all." But he did not say so.

Both the swindlers begged him to be so kind as to come near to approve the excellent pattern, the beautiful colors. They pointed to the empty looms, and the poor old minister stared as hard as he dared. He couldn't see anything, because there was nothing to see. "Heaven have mercy," he thought. "Can it be that I'm a fool? I'd have never guessed it, and not a soul must know. Am I unfit to be the minister? It would never do to let on that I can't see the cloth."

"Don't hesitate to tell us what you think of it," said one of the weavers.

"Oh, it's beautiful—it's enchanting." The old minister peered through his spectacles. "Such a pattern, what colors! I'll be sure to tell the emperor how delighted I am with it."

"We're pleased to hear that," the swindlers said. They proceeded to name all the colors and to explain the intricate pattern. The old minister paid the closest attention, so that he could tell it all to the emperor. And so he did.

The swindlers at once asked for more money, more silk and gold thread, to get on with the weaving. But it all went into their pockets. Not a thread went into the looms, though they worked at their weaving as hard as ever.

The emperor presently sent another trustworthy official to see how the work progressed and how soon it would be ready. The same thing happened to him that had happened to the minister. He looked and he looked, but as there was nothing to see in the looms, he couldn't see anything.

"Isn't it a beautiful piece of goods?" the swindlers asked him, as they displayed and described their imaginary pattern.

"I know I'm not stupid," the man thought, "so it must be that I'm unworthy of my good office. That's strange. I mustn't let anyone find it out, though." So he praised the material he did not see. He declared he was delighted with the beautiful colors and the exquisite pattern. To the emperor he said, "It held me spellbound."

All the town was talking of this splendid cloth, and the emperor wanted to see it for himself while it was still in the looms. Attended by a band of chosen men, among whom were his two old trusted officials—the ones who had been to the weavers—he set out to see the two swindlers. He found them weaving with might and main, but without a thread in their looms.

"Magnificent," said the two duped officials. "Just look, Your Majesty, what colors! What a design!" They pointed to the empty looms, each supposing that the others could see the stuff.

"What's this?" thought the emperor. "I can't see anything. This is terrible! Am I a fool? Am I unfit to be the emperor? What a thing to happen to me of all people!—Oh! It's *very* pretty," he said. "It has my highest approval." And he nodded approbation at the empty loom. Nothing could make him say that he couldn't see anything.

His whole retinue stared and stared. One saw no more than another, but they all joined the emperor in exclaiming, "Oh! It's *very* pretty," and they advised him to wear clothes made of this wonderful cloth especially for the great procession he was soon to lead. "Magnificent! Excellent! Unsurpassed!" were bandied from mouth to mouth, and everyone did his best to seem well pleased. The emperor gave each of the swindlers a cross to wear in his buttonhole, and the title of "Sir Weaver."

Before the procession, the swindlers sat up all night and burned more than six candles, to show how busy they were finishing the emperor's new clothes. They pretended to take the cloth off the loom. They made cuts in the air with huge scissors. And at last they said, "Now the emperor's new clothes are ready for him."

Then the emperor himself came with his noblest noblemen, and the swindlers each raised an arm as if they were holding something. They said, "These are the trousers, here's the coat, and this is the mantle," naming each garment. "All of them are as light as a spider web. One would almost think he had nothing on, but that's what makes them so fine."

"Exactly," all the noblemen agreed, though they could see nothing, for there was nothing to see.

"If Your Imperial Majesty will condescend to take your clothes off," said the swindlers, "we will help you on with your new ones here in front of the long mirror."

The emperor undressed, and the swindlers pretended to put his new clothes on him, one garment after another. They took him around the waist and seemed to be fastening something—that was his train—as the emperor turned round and round before the looking glass.

"How well Your Majesty's new clothes look. Aren't they becoming!" He heard on all sides, "That pattern, so perfect! Those colors, so suitable! It is a magnificent outfit."

Then the minister of public processions announced: "Your Majesty's canopy is waiting outside."

"Well, I'm supposed to be ready," the emperor said, and turned again for one last look in the mirror. "It is a remarkable fit, isn't it?" He seemed to regard his costume with the greatest interest.

The noblemen who were to carry his train stooped low and reached for the floor as if they were picking up his mantle. Then they pretended to lift and hold it high. They didn't dare admit they had nothing to hold.

So off went the emperor in procession under his splendid canopy. Everyone in the streets and the windows said, "Oh, how fine are the emperor's new clothes! Don't they fit him to perfection? And see his long train!" Nobody would confess that he couldn't see anything, for that would prove him either unfit for his position or a fool. No costume the emperor had worn before was ever such a complete success.

"But he hasn't got anything on," a little child said.

"Did you ever hear such innocent prattle?" said its father. And one person whispered to another what the child had said, "He hasn't anything on. A child says he hasn't anything on."

"But he hasn't got anything on!" the whole town cried out at last.

The emperor shivered, for he suspected they were right. But he thought, "This procession has got to go on." So he walked more proudly than ever, as his noblemen held high the train that wasn't there at all.

THE GALOSHES OF FORTUNE (1838)

I. A BEGINNING

It was in Copenhagen, in one of the houses on East Street, not far from King's Newmarket, that someone was giving a large party. For one must give a party once in a while, if one expects to be invited in return. Half of the guests were already at the card tables, and the rest were waiting to see what would come of their hostess's query:

"What can we think up now?"

Up to this point, their conversation had gotten along as best it might. Among other things, they had spoken of the Middle Ages. Some held that it was a time far better than our own. Indeed, Councillor of Justice Knap defended this opinion with such spirit that his hostess sided with him at once, and both of them loudly took exception to Oersted's article in the *Almanac*, which contrasted old times and new, and which favored our own period. The Councillor of Justice, however, held that the time of King Hans, about 1500 AD, was the noblest and happiest age.

While the conversation ran pro and con, interrupted only for a moment by the arrival of a newspaper, in which there was nothing worth reading, let us adjourn to the cloak room, where all the wraps, canes, umbrellas, and galoshes were collected together. Here sat two maids, a young one and an old one. You might have thought they had come in attendance upon some spinster or widow and were waiting to see their mistress home. However, a closer inspection would reveal that these were no ordinary serving women. Their hands were too well kept for that, their bearing and movements too graceful, and their clothes had a certain daring cut.

They were two fairies. The younger one, though not Dame Fortune herself, was an assistant to one of her ladies-in-waiting, and was used to deliver the more trifling gifts of Fortune. The older one looked quite grave. She was Dame Care, who always goes in her own sublime person to see to her errands herself, for then she knows that they are well done.

They were telling each other about where they had been that day. The assistant of Fortune had only attended to a few minor affairs, she said, such as saving a new bonnet from the rain, getting a civil greeting for an honest man from an exalted nincompoop, and such like matters. But her remaining errand was an extraordinary one.

"I must also tell you," she said, "that today is my birthday, and in honor of this, I have been entrusted to bring a pair of galoshes to mankind. These galoshes have this peculiarity: whoever puts them on will immediately find himself in whatever time, place, and condition of life that he prefers. His every wish in regard to time and place will instantly be granted, so for once, a man can find perfect happiness here below."

"Take my word for it," said Dame Care, "he will be most unhappy and will bless the moment when he can rid himself of those galoshes."

"How can you say such a thing?" the other woman exclaimed. "I shall leave them here beside the door, where someone will put them on by mistake and immediately be the happy one."

That ended their conversation.

II. WHAT HAPPENED TO THE COUNCILLOR OF JUSTICE

It was getting late when Councillor Knap decided to go home. Lost in thought about the good old days of King Hans, as fate would have it, he put on the galoshes of Fortune instead of his own and wore them out into East Street. But the power that lay in the galoshes took him back into the reign of King Hans, and as the streets were not paved in those days, his feet sank deep into the mud and the mire.

"Why, how deplorable!" the Councillor of Justice said. "The whole sidewalk is gone, and all the street lights are out."

As the moon had not yet risen high enough and the air was somewhat foggy, everything around him was dark and blurred. At the next corner, a lantern hung before an image of the Madonna, but for all the light it afforded him, it might as well not have been there. Only when he stood directly under it did he make out that painting of the mother and child.

"It's probably an art museum," he thought, "and they have forgotten to take in the sign."

Two people in medieval costumes passed by.

"How strange they looked!" he said. "They must have been to a masquerade."

Just then, the sound of drums and fifes came his way, and bright torches flared. The Councillor of Justice stopped and was startled to see an odd procession go past, led by a whole band of drummers who were dexterously drubbing away. These were followed by soldiers armed with long bows and crossbows. The chief personage of the procession was a churchman of rank. The astounded councillor asked what all this meant, and who the man might be.

"That is the Bishop of Seeland," he was told.

"What in the name of Heaven can have come over the bishop?" the Councillor of Justice wondered. He sighed and shook his head. "The bishop? Impossible."

Still pondering about it, without glancing to right or to left, he kept on down East Street and across Highbridge Square. The bridge that led from there to Palace Square was not to be found at all; at last, on the bank of the shallow stream, he saw a boat with two men in it.

"Would the gentleman want to be ferried over to the Holm?" they asked him.

"To the Holm?" blurted the councillor, who had not the faintest notion that he was living in another age. "I want to go to Christian's Harbor on Little Market Street."

The men gaped at him.

"Kindly tell me where the bridge is," he said. "It's disgraceful that all the street lamps are out, and besides, it's as muddy to walk here as in a swamp." But the more he talked with the boatmen, the less they understood each other. "I can't understand your jabbering Bornholm accent," he finally said, and angrily turned his back on them. But no bridge could he find. Even the fence was gone.

"What a scandalous state of affairs! What a way for things to look!" he said. Never had he been so disgruntled with his own age as he was this evening. "I think I'd better take a cab." But where were the cabs? There were none in sight. "I'll have to go back to King's Newmarket, where there is a cab stand, or I shall never reach Christian's Harbor."

So back he trudged to East Street, and had nearly walked the length of it when the moon rose.

"Good Heavens, what have they been building here?" he cried as he beheld the East Gate, which in the old days stood at the end of East

Street. In time, however, he found a gate through which he passed into what is now Newmarket. But all he saw there was a large meadow. A few bushes rose here and there, and the meadow was divided by a wide canal or stream. The few wretched wooden huts on the far shore belonged to Dutch sailors, so at that time the place was called Dutch Meadow.

"Either I'm seeing what is called Fata Morgana, or I'm drunk," the Councillor of Justice moaned. "What sort of place is this? Where am I?" He turned back, convinced that he must be a very ill man. As he walked through the street again, he paid more attention to the houses. Most of them were of wood, and many were thatched with straw.

"No, I don't feel myself at all," he complained. "I only took one glass of punch, but it doesn't agree with me. The idea of serving punch with hot salmon! I'll speak about it severely to our hostess—that agent's wife. Should I march straight back and tell her how I feel? No, that would be in bad taste, and besides, I doubt whether her household is still awake." He searched for the house, but wasn't able to find it.

"This is terrible!" he cried. "I don't even recognize East Street. There's not a shop to be seen; wretched old ramshackle huts are all I see, as if I were in Roskilde or Ringstedt. Oh, but I'm ill! There's no point in standing on ceremony, but where on Earth is the agent's house? This hut doesn't look remotely like it, but I can hear that the people inside are still awake. Ah, I'm indeed a very sick man."

He reached a half-open door, where light flickered through the crack. It was a tavern of that period—a sort of alehouse. The room had the look of a farmer's clay-floored kitchen in Holstein, and the people who sat there were sailors, citizens of Copenhagen, and a couple of scholars. Deep in conversation over their mugs, they paid little attention to the newcomer.

"Pardon me," the Councillor of Justice said to the landlady who came toward him, "but I am far from well. Would you send someone for a cab to take me to Christian's Harbor?"

The woman stared at him, shook her head, and addressed him in German. As the Councillor of Justice supposed that she could not speak Danish, he repeated his remarks in German. This, and the cut of his clothes, convinced the woman that he was a foreigner. She soon understood that he felt unwell, and fetched him a mug of water, decidedly brackish, for she drew it directly from the sea-level well outside. The councillor put his head in his hands, took a deep breath, and thought over all of the queer things that surrounded him.

"Is that tonight's number of *The Day*?" he remarked from force of habit, as he saw the woman putting away a large folded sheet.

Without quite understanding him, she handed him the paper. It was a woodcut, representing a meteor seen in the skies over Cologne.

"This is very old," said the councillor, who became quite enthusiastic about his discovery. "Where did you get this rare old print? It's most interesting, although of course the whole matter is a myth. In this day and age, such meteors are explained away as a manifestation of the northern lights, probably caused by electricity."

Those who sat near him heard the remark and looked at him in astonishment. One of them rose, respectfully doffed his hat, and said with the utmost gravity:

"Sir, you must be a great scholar."

"Not at all," replied the councillor. "I merely have a word or two to say about things that everyone should know."

"*Modestia* is an admirable virtue," the man declared. "In regard to your statement, I must say, *mihi secus videtur*, though I shall be happy to suspend my *judicium*."

"May I ask whom I have the pleasure of addressing?" the Councillor of Justice inquired.

"I am a bachelor of theology," the man told him in Latin.

This answer satisfied the Councillor of Justice, for the degree was in harmony with the fellow's way of dressing. "Obviously," he thought, "this is some old village schoolmaster, an odd character such as one still comes across now and then, up in Jutland."

"This is scarcely a *locus docendi*," the man continued, "but I entreat you to favor us with your conversation. You, of course, are well read in the classics?"

"Oh, more or less," the councillor agreed. "I like to read the standard old books, and the new ones too, except for those 'Every Day Stories' of which we have enough in reality."

"Every Day Stories?" our bachelor asked.

"Yes, I mean these modern novels."

"Oh," the man said with a smile. "Still they are very clever, and are popular with the court. King Hans is particularly fond of the *Romance of Iwain and Jawain*, which deals with King Arthur and his Knights of the Round Table. The king has been known to jest with his lords about it."

"Well," said the councillor, "one can't keep up with all the new books. I suppose it has just been published by Heiberg."

"No," the man said, "not by Heiberg, but by Gotfred von Ghemen."

"Indeed! What a fine old name for a literary man. Why, Gotfred von Ghemen was the first printer in Denmark."

"Yes," the man agreed, "he is our first and foremost printer."

Thus far, their conversation had flowed quite smoothly. Now one of the townsmen began to talk about the pestilence that had raged some years back, meaning the plague of 1484. The councillor understood him to mean the last epidemic of cholera, so they agreed well enough.

The freebooter's war of 1490 was so recent that it could not be passed over. The English raiders had taken ships from our harbor, they said, and the Councillor of Justice, who was well posted on the affair of 1801, manfully helped them to abuse the English.

After that, however, the talk floundered from one contradiction to another. The worthy bachelor was so completely unenlightened that the councillor's most commonplace remarks struck him as being too daring and too fantastic. They stared at each other, and when they reached an impasse, the bachelor broke into Latin, in the hope that he would be better understood, but that didn't help.

The landlady plucked at the councillor's sleeve and asked him, "How do you feel now?" This forcibly recalled to him all of those things that he had happily forgotten in the heat of his conversation.

"Merciful Heaven, where am I?" he wondered, and the thought made him dizzy.

"We will drink claret wine, and mead, and Bremen beer," one of the guests cried out, "and you shall drink with us."

Two girls came in, and one of them wore a cap of two colors. They filled the glasses and made curtsies. The councillor felt cold shivers up and down his spine. "What is all this? What is all this?" he groaned, but drink with them he must. They overwhelmed him with their kind intentions until he despaired, and when one man pronounced him drunk, he didn't doubt it in the least. All he asked was that they get him a *droschke*. Then they thought he was speaking in Russian.

Never before had he been in such low and vulgar company! "One would think that the country had lapsed back into barbarism," he told himself. "This is the most dreadful moment of my life."

Then it occurred to him to slip down under the table, crawl to the door, and try to sneak out, but just as he neared the threshold, his companions discovered him and tried to pull him out by his feet. However, by great good luck they pulled off his galoshes, and—with them—the whole enchantment.

The Councillor of Justice now distinctly saw a street lamp burning in front of a large building. He knew the building and the other buildings nearby. It was East Street as we all know it today. He lay on the pavement with his legs against a gate, and across the way, a night watchman sat fast asleep.

"Merciful heavens! Have I been lying here in the street dreaming?" the Councillor of Justice said. "To be sure, this is East Street. How blessedly bright and how colorful it looks. But what dreadful effect that one glass of punch must have had on me."

Two minutes later, he was seated in a cab, and well on his way to Christian's Harbor. As he recalled all the past terror and distress to which he had been subjected, he wholeheartedly approved of the present, our own happy age. With all its shortcomings, it was far preferable to that age into which he had recently stumbled. And that, thought the Councillor of Justice, was good common sense.

III. THE WATCHMAN'S ADVENTURE

"Why, I declare! There's a pair of galoshes," said the watchman. "They must belong to the lieutenant who lives up there on the top floor, for they are lying in front of the door." A light still burned upstairs, and the honest fellow was perfectly willing to ring the bell and return the overshoes. But he didn't want to disturb the other tenants in the house, so he didn't do it.

"It must be quite comfortable to wear a pair of such things," he said. "How soft the leather feels." They fitted his feet perfectly. "What a strange world we live in. The lieutenant might be resting easy in his soft bed, yet there he goes, pacing to and fro past his window. There's a happy man for you! He has no wife, and he has no child, and every night he goes to a party. Oh, if I were only in his place, what a happy man I would be."

Just as he expressed his wish, the galoshes transformed him into the lieutenant, body and soul, and there he stood in the room upstairs. Between his fingers, he held a sheet of pink paper on which the lieutenant had just written a poem. Who is there that has not at some time in his life felt poetic? If he writes down his thoughts while this mood is on him, poetry is apt to come of it. On the paper was written:

IF ONLY I WERE RICH

If only I were rich; I often said in prayer
When I was but a tiny lad without much care
If only I were rich, a soldier I would be
With uniform and sword, most handsomely;
At last an officer I was, my wish I got
But to be rich was not my lot;
But You, oh Lord, would always help.

I sat one eve, so happy, young and proud;
A darling child of seven kissed my mouth
For I was rich with fairy tales, you see
With money I was poor as poor can be,
But she was fond of tales I told
That made me rich, but—alas—not with gold;
But You, oh Lord, You know!

If only I were rich, is still my heavenly prayer.
My little girl of seven is now a lady fair;
She is so sweet, so clever and so good;
My heart's fair tale she never understood.
If only, as of yore, she still for me would care,
But I am poor and silent; I confess I do not dare.
It is Your will, oh Lord!

If only I were rich, in peace and comfort rest,
I would my sorrow to this paper never trust.
You, whom I love, if still you understand
then read this poem from my youth's far land,
Though best it be you never know my pain.
I am still poor, my future dark and vain,
But may, O Lord, You bless her!

Yes, a man in love writes many a poem that a man in his right mind does not print. A lieutenant, his love, and his lack of money—there's an eternal triangle for you, a broken life that can never be squared.

The lieutenant knew this all too well. He leaned his head against the window, and sighed, and said:

"The poor watchman down there in the street is a far happier man than I. He does not know what I call want. He has a home. He has a wife and children who weep with him in his sorrows and share in his joy. Ah, I would be happier if I could trade places with him, for he is much more fortunate than I am."

Instantly, the watchman was himself again. The galoshes had transformed him into the lieutenant, as we have seen. He was far less contented up there, and preferred to be just what he had been. So the watchman turned back into a watchman.

"I had a bad dream," he said. "Strangely enough, I fancied I was the lieutenant, and I didn't like it a bit. I missed my wife and our youngsters, who almost smother me with their kisses."

He sat down and fell to nodding again, unable to get the dream out of his head. The galoshes were still on his feet when he watched a star fall in the sky.

"There goes one," he muttered. "But there are so many, it will never be missed. I'd like to have a look at those trinkets at close range. I'd especially like to see the moon, which is not the sort of thing to get lost in one's hands. The student for whom my wife washes says that when we die, we fly about from star to star. There's not a word of truth in it. But it would be nice, just the same, if I could take a little jaunt through the skies. My body could stay here on the steps for all that I'd care."

Now there are certain things in the world that we ought to think about before we put them into words, and if we are wearing the galoshes of Fortune, it behooves us to think twice. Just listen to what happened to that watchman.

All of us know how fast steam can take us. We've either rushed along in a train or sped by steamship across the ocean. But all this is like the gait of a sloth, or pace of a snail, in comparison with the speed of light, which travels nineteen million times faster than the fastest race horse. Yet electricity moves even faster. Death is an electric shock to the heart, and the soul set free travels on electric wings. The sunlight takes eight minutes and some odd seconds to travel nearly one hundred million miles. On the wings of electricity, the soul can make the same journey in a few moments, and to a soul set free, the heavenly bodies are as close together as the houses of friends who live in the same town with us, or even in the same neighborhood. However, this electric shock strips us of our bodies forever, unless, like the watchman, we happen to be wearing the galoshes of Fortune.

In a few seconds the watchman took in his stride the 260,000 miles to the Moon. As we know, this satellite is made of much lighter material than the Earth, and is as soft as freshly fallen snow. The watchman landed in one of the numerous mountain rings that we all know from Doctor Maedler's large map of the moon. Within the ring was a great bowl, fully four miles deep. At the bottom of this bowl lay a town. We may get some idea of what it looked like by pouring the white of an egg into a glass of water. The town was made of stuff as soft as the egg albumen, and its form was similar, with translucent towers, cupolas, and terraces, all floating in thin air.

Over the watchman's head hung our Earth, like a huge dull red ball. Around him, he noticed crowds of beings who doubtless corresponded to men and women of the Earth, but their appearance was quite different from ours. They also had their own way of speaking, but no one could expect that the soul of a watchman would understand them. Nevertheless, he did understand the language of the people in the Moon very well. They were disputing about our Earth, and doubting whether it could be inhabited. The air on the Earth, they contended, must be too thick for any intelligent Moonman to live there. Only the Moon was inhabited, they agreed, for it was the original sphere on which the people of the Old World lived.

Now let us go back down to East Street, to see how the watchman's body was making out. Lifeless it lay, there on the steps. His morning star, that spiked club that watchmen carry, had fallen from his hands, and his eyes were turned toward the moon that his honest soul was exploring.

"What's the hour, watchman?" asked a passerby. But never an answer did he get. He gave the watchman a very slight tweak of the nose, and over he toppled. There lay the body at full length, stretched on the pavement. The man was dead. It gave the one who had tweaked him a terrible fright, for the watchman was dead, and dead he remained. His death was reported and investigated. As day broke, his body was taken to the hospital.

It would be a pretty pass if the soul should come back and in all probability look for its body in East Street, and fail to find it. Perhaps it would rush to the police station first, next to the Directory Office where it could advertise for lost articles, and last of all to the hospital. But we needn't worry. The soul by itself is clever enough. It's the body that makes it stupid.

As we said before, the watchman's body was taken to the hospital. They put it in a room to be washed, and naturally the galoshes were pulled off first of all. That brought the soul dashing back posthaste, and in a flash, the watchman came back to life. He swore it had been the most terrible night he had ever experienced, and he would never go through it again, no, not for two pennies. But it was over and done with. He was allowed to leave that same day, but the galoshes were left at the hospital.

IV. A GREAT MOMENT, AND A MOST EXTRAORDINARY JOURNEY

Everyone in Copenhagen knows what the entrance to Frederic's Hospital looks like, but as some of the people who read this story may not have been to Copenhagen, we must describe the building—briefly.

The hospital is fenced off from the street by a rather high railing of heavy iron bars, which are spaced far enough apart—at least so the story goes—for very thin interns to squeeze between them and pay little visits to the world outside. The part of the body they had most difficulty in squeezing through was the head. In this, as often happens in the world, small heads were the most successful. So much for our description.

One of the young interns, of whom it could be said that he had a great head only in a physical sense, had the night watch that evening. Outside, the rain poured down. But in spite of these difficulties, he was bent upon getting out for a quarter of an hour. There was no need for the doorman to know about it, he thought, if he could just manage to slip through the fence. There lay the galoshes that the watchman had forgotten, and while the intern had no idea that they were the galoshes of Fortune, he did know that they would stand him in good stead out in the rain. So he pulled them on. Now the question was whether he could squeeze between the bars, a trick that he had never tried before. There he stood, facing the fence.

"I wish to goodness I had my head through," he said, and though his head was much too large and thick for the space, it immediately slipped through quickly and with the greatest of ease. The galoshes saw to that. All he had to do now was to squeeze his body through after his head, but it wouldn't go. "Uff!" he panted, "I'm too fat. I thought my head would be the worst difficulty. No, I shall never get through."

He quickly attempted to pull his head back again, but it couldn't be done. He could move his neck easily, but that was all. First, his anger flared up. Then his spirits dropped down to zero. The galoshes of Fortune had gotten him in a terrible fix, and unluckily, it did not occur to him to wish his way out of it. No, instead of wishing, he struggled and strove, but he could not budge from the spot. The rain poured down; not a soul could be seen in the street; and he could not reach the bell by the gate. How could he ever get free? He was certain he would have to stay there till morning, and that they would have to send for a blacksmith to file through the iron bars. It would take time. All the boys in the school across the way would be up and shout, and the entire population of "Nyboder," where all the sailors lived, would turn out for the fun of seeing the man in a pillory. Why, he would draw a bigger crowd than the one that went to see the championship wrestling matches last year.

"Huff!" he panted, "the blood's rushing to my head. I'm going mad! Yes, I'm going mad! Oh, if I were only free again, and out of this fix, then I would be all right again."

This was what he ought to have said in the first place. No sooner had he said it than his head came free, and he dashed indoors, still bewildered by the fright that the galoshes of Fortune had given him. But don't think that this was the end of it. No! The worst was yet to come.

The night went by, and the next day passed, but nobody came for the galoshes. That evening, there was to be a performance at the little theater in Kannike Street. The house was packed, and in the audience was our friend, the intern, apparently none the worse for his adventure of the night before. He had again put on the galoshes. After all, no one had claimed them, and the streets were so muddy that he thought they would stand him in good stead.

At the theater a new sketch was presented. It was called "My Grandmother's Spectacles" and had to do with a pair of eyeglasses that enabled anyone who wore them to read the future from people's faces, just as a fortune-teller reads it from cards.

The idea occupied his mind very much. He would like to own such a pair of spectacles. Properly used, they might enable one to see into people's hearts. This, he thought, would be far more interesting than foresee what would happen next year. Future events would be known in due time, but no one would ever know the secrets that lie in people's hearts.

"Look at those ladies and gentlemen in the front row," he said to himself. "If I could see straight into their hearts, what stores of things—what great shops full of goods would I behold. And how my eyes would rove about those shops. In every feminine heart, no doubt I should find a complete millinery establishment. There sits one whose shop is empty, but a good cleaning would do it no harm. And of course some of the shops would be well stocked. Ah me," he sighed, "I know of one where all the goods are of the very best quality, and it would just suit me, but—alas and alack—there's a shopkeeper there already, and he's the only bad article in the whole shop. Many a one would say, 'Won't you walk in?' and I wish I could. I would pass like a nice little thought through their hearts."

The galoshes took him at his word. The intern shrank to almost nothing, and set out on a most extraordinary journey through the hearts of all the spectators in the first row. The first heart he entered was that of a lady, but at first, he mistook it for a room in the Orthopaedic Institute, or hospital, where the plaster casts of deformed limbs are hung upon the walls. The only difference was that at the hospital, those casts were made when the patients came in, while these casts that were kept in the heart were made as the good people departed. For every physical or mental fault of the friends she had lost had been carefully stored away.

He quickly passed on to another woman's heart, which seemed like a great holy cathedral. Over the high altar fluttered the white dove of innocence, and the intern would have gone down on his knees except that he had to hurry on to the next heart. However, he still heard the organ roll. And he felt that it had made a new and better man of him—a man not too unworthy to enter the next sanctuary. This was a poor garret where a mother lay ill, but through the windows the sun shone, warm and bright. Lovely roses bloomed in the little wooden flower box on the roof, and two bluebirds sang of happy childhood, while the sick woman prayed for a blessing on her daughter.

Next, the intern crawled on his hands and knees through an overcrowded butcher shop. There was meat, more meat, and meat alone, wherever he looked in this heart of a wealthy, respectable man, whose name you can find in the directory.

Next, he entered the heart of this man's wife, and an old tumbledown dovecote he found it. Her husband's portrait served as a mere weathervane, which was connected with the doors in such a way that they opened and closed as her husband turned round.

Then he found his way into a cabinet of mirrors such as is to be seen at Rosenborg Castle, though in this heart, the mirrors had the power of magnifying objects enormously. Like the Grand Lama of Tibet, the owner's insignificant ego sat in the middle of the floor, in admiring contemplation of his own greatness.

After this, he seemed to be crammed into a narrow case full of sharp needles. "This," he thought, "must certainly be an old maid's heart," but it was nothing of the sort. It was the heart of a very young officer who had been awarded several medals, and of whom everyone said, "Now there's a man of both intellect and heart."

Quite befuddled was the poor intern when he popped out of the heart of the last person in the front row. He could not get his thoughts in order, and he supposed that his strong imagination must have run away with him.

"Merciful heavens," he groaned, "I must be well on the road to the madhouse. And it's so outrageously hot in here that the blood is rushing to my head." Suddenly, he recalled what had happened the night before, when he had jammed his head between the bars of the hospital fence. "That must be what caused it," he decided. "I must do something before it is too late. A Russian bath might be the very thing. I wish I were on the top shelf right now."

No sooner said than there he lay on the top shelf of the steam bath. But he was fully dressed, down to his shoes and galoshes. He felt the hot drops of condensed steam fall upon him from the ceiling.

"Hey!" he cried, and jumped down to take a shower. The attendant cried out too when he caught sight of a fully dressed man in the steam room. However, the intern had enough sense to pull himself together and whisper, "I'm just doing this because of a bet."

But the first thing he did when he got back to his room was to put hot plasters on his neck and his back, to draw out the madness.

Next morning, he had a blistered back, and that was all he got out of the galoshes of Fortune.

V. THE TRANSFORMATION OF
THE COPYING CLERK

The watchman—you remember him—happened to remember those galoshes he had found, and that he must have been wearing them when they took his body to the hospital. He came by for them, and as neither the lieutenant nor anyone else in East Street laid claim to them, he turned them in at the police station.

"They look exactly like my own galoshes," one of the copying clerks at the police station said, as he set the ownerless galoshes down beside his own. "Not even a shoemaker could tell one pair from the other."

"Mr. Copying Clerk!" said a policeman, who brought him some papers.

The clerk turned around to talk with the policeman, and when he came back to the galoshes, he was uncertain whether the pair on the right or the pair on the left belonged to him.

"The wet ones must be mine," he thought, but he was mistaken, for they were the galoshes of Fortune. The police make their little mistakes, too.

So he pulled them on, pocketed some papers, and tucked some manuscripts under his arm to read and abstract when he got home. But as this happened to be Sunday morning, and the weather was fine, he thought, "A walk to Frederiksberg will be good for me." And off he went.

A quieter, more dependable fellow than this young man you seldom see. Let him take his little walk, by all means. It will do him a world of good after so much sitting. At first, he strode along without a wish in his head, so there was no occasion for the galoshes to show their magic power. On the avenue, he met an acquaintance of his, a young poet, who said he was setting out tomorrow on a summer excursion.

"What, off again so soon?" said the clerk. "What a free and happy fellow you are! You can fly away wherever you like, while the rest of us are chained by the leg."

"Chained only to a breadfruit tree," the poet reminded him. "You don't have to worry along from day to day, and when you get old, they will give you a pension."

"You are better off, just the same," the clerk said. "How agreeable it must be to sit and write poetry. Everyone pays you compliments, and you are your own master. Ah, you should see what it's like to devote your life to the trivial details of the courts."

The poet shook his head, and the clerk shook his, too. Each held to his own conviction, and they parted company.

"They are a queer race, these poets," thought the clerk. "I should like to try my hand at their trade—to turn poet myself. I'm sure I would never write such melancholy stuff as most of them do. What a splendid spring day this is, a day fit for a poet. The air is so unusually clear, the clouds so lovely, and the green grass so fragrant. For many a year, I have not felt as I feel just now."

Already, you could tell that he had turned poet. Not that there was anything you could put your finger on, for it is foolish to suppose that a poet differs greatly from other people, some of whom are far more poetic by nature than many a great and accepted poet. The chief difference is that a poet has a better memory for things of the spirit. He can hold fast to an emotion and an idea until they are firmly and clearly embodied in words, which is something that others cannot do. But for a matter-of-fact person to think in terms of poetry is noticeable enough, and it is this transformation that we can see in the clerk.

"What a glorious fragrance there is in the air!" he said. "It reminds me of Aunt Lone's violets. Ah me, I haven't thought of them since I was a little boy. The dear old girl! She used to live over there, behind the Exchange. She always had a spray or a few green shoots in water, no matter how severe the winter was. I'd smell those violets even when I was putting hot pennies against the frozen window pane to make peep holes. What a view that was—ships frozen tight in the canal, deserted by their crews, and a shrieking crow the only living creature aboard them. But when the springtime breezes blew, the scene turned lively again. There were shouts and laughter as the ice was sawed away. Freshly tarred and rigged, the ships sailed off for distant lands. I stayed here, and I must forever stay here, sitting in the police office where others come for their passports to foreign countries. Yes, that's my lot! Oh, yes!" he said, and heaved a sigh. Then he stopped abruptly.

"Great heavens! What's come over me. I never thought or felt like this before. It must be the spring air! It is as frightening as it is pleasant." He fumbled among the papers in his pockets.

"These will give me something else to think about," he said, as he glanced at the first page. *"Lady Sigbrith, An Original Tragedy in Five Acts,"* he read. "Why, what's this? It's in my own handwriting too. Have I written a tragedy? *The Intrigue on the Ramparts, or The Great Fast Day—a Vaudeville.* Where did that come from? Someone must have slipped it in my pocket. And here's a letter." It was from the board of directors of the theater, who rejected his plays, and the letter was anything but politely phrased.

"Hem, hem!" said the copying clerk as he sat down on a bench. His thoughts were lively and his heart sensitive. He plucked a flower at random, an ordinary little daisy. What the professor of botany requires several lectures to explain to us, this flower told in a moment. It told of the mystery birth, and of the power of the sunlight that opened those delicate leaves and gave them their fragrance. This made him think of the battle of life, which arouses emotions within us in similar fashion. Air and light are the flower's lovers, but light is her favorite. Toward it the flower is ever turning, and only when the light is gone does she fold her petals and sleep in the air's embrace.

"It is the light that makes me lovely," the flower said.

"But," the poet's voice whispered, "the air enables you to breathe."

Not far away, a boy was splashing in a muddy ditch with his stick. As the water flew up among the green branches, the clerk thought of the innumerable microscopic creatures in the splashing drops. For them to be splashed so high was as if we were to be tossed up into the clouds. As the clerk thought of these things, and of the great change that had come over him, he smiled and said:

"I must be asleep and dreaming. It's marvelous to be able to dream so naturally, and yet to know all along that this is a dream. I hope I can recall every bit of it tomorrow, when I wake up. I seem to feel unusually exhilarated. How clearly I understand things, and how wide awake I feel! But I know that if I recall my dream, it will only be a lot of nonsense, as has happened to me so often before. All those brilliant and clever remarks one makes and one hears in his dreams are like the gold pieces that goblins store underground. When one gets them, they are rich and shining, but seen in the daylight, they are nothing but rocks and dry leaves. Ah me," he sighed, as he sadly watched the singing birds flit merrily from branch to branch. "They are so much better off than I. Flying is a noble art, and lucky is he who is born with wings. Yes, if I could change into anything I liked, I would turn into a little lark."

In a trice, his coattails and sleeves grew together as wings, his clothes turned into feathers, and his galoshes became claws. He noticed the change clearly, and laughed to himself.

"Now," he said, "I know I am dreaming, but I never had a dream as silly as this one."

Up he flew, and sang among the branches, but there was no poetry in his song, for he was no longer a poet. Like anyone who does a thorough job of it, the galoshes could only do one thing at a time. When he wished to be a poet, a poet he became. Then he wanted to be a little bird, and in becoming one, he lost his previous character.

"This is most amusing," he said. "In the daytime, I sit in the police office, surrounded by the most matter-of-fact legal papers, but by night, I can dream that I'm a lark flying about in the Frederiksberg Garden. What fine material this would make for a popular comedy."

He flew down on the grass, twisting and turning his head, and pecking at the waving grass blades. In proportion to his own size, they seemed as large as the palm branches in North Africa. But this lasted only a moment. Then everything turned black, and it seemed as if some huge object had dropped over him. This was a big cap that a boy from Nyboder had thrown over the bird. A hand was thrust in. It laid hold of the copying clerk by his back and wing so tightly that it made him shriek. In his terror, he called out, "You impudent scoundrel! I am the copying clerk at the police office!" But this sounded like "Peep! peep!" to the boy, who thumped the bird on its beak and walked off with it.

On the avenue, this boy met with two other schoolboys. Socially, they were of the upper classes, though, properly ranked according to their merit, they were in the lowest class at school. They bought the bird for eight pennies, and in their hands the clerk came back to Copenhagen, to a family who lived in Gothers Street.

"It's a good thing I'm only dreaming this," said the clerk, "or I'd be furious. First I was a poet, and now I'm a lark. It must have been my poetic temperament that turned me into this little creature. It is a very sad state of affairs, especially when one falls into the hands of a couple of boys. But I wonder how it will all turn out."

The boys carried him into a luxuriously appointed room, where a stout, affable lady received them. She was not at all pleased with their common little field bird, as she called the lark, but she said that, for one day only, they could keep it in the empty cage near the window.

"Perhaps Polly will like it," she said, and smiled at the large parrot that swung proudly to and fro on the ring in his ornate brass cage. "It's Polly's birthday," she said, like a simpleton. "The little field bird wants to congratulate him."

Polly did not say a word, as proudly he swung back and forth. But a pretty canary bird who had been brought here last summer from his warm, sweet-scented homeland, began to sing at the top of his voice.

"Bawler!" the lady said, and threw a white handkerchief over his cage.

"Peep, peep. What a terrible snowstorm," the canary sighed, and with that sigh, he kept quiet.

The clerk, or, as the lady called him, the field bird, was put in a cage next to the canary's and not far from the parrot's. The only human words that the parrot could say, and which at times sounded quite comical, were, "Come now, let us be men." All the rest of his chatter made as little sense as the twittering of the canary. However, the clerk, who was now a bird himself, understood his companions perfectly.

"I used to fly beneath green palms and flowering almond trees," the canary bird sang. "With my brothers and sisters, I flew above beautiful flowers, and over the smooth sea where the plants that grow under water waved up at us. We used to meet many brilliant parrots, who told us the funniest stories—long ones and so many."

"Those were wild parrots!" said Polly. "Birds without any education. Come now, let us be men. Why don't you laugh? If the lady and all her guests laugh at my remark, so should you. To lack a sense of humor is a very bad thing. Come now, let us be men."

"Do you remember the pretty girls who danced in the tents spread beneath those flowering trees?" the canary sang. "Do you remember those delicious sweet fruits, and the cool juice of the wild plants?"

"Why, yes," said the parrot, "but I am much better off here, where I get the best of food and intimate treatment. I know that I am a clever bird, and that's enough for me. Come now, let us be men. You have the soul of a poet, as they call it, and I have sound knowledge and wit. You have genius, but no discretion. You burst into that shrill, spontaneous song of yours. That's why people cover you up. They don't ever treat me like that. No, I have cost them a lot, and, what is more imposing, my beak and my wits are sharp. Come now, let us be men."

"Oh, my warm flowery homeland!" said the canary. "I shall sing of your deep green trees and your quiet inlets, where the down-hanging branches kiss the clear mirror of the waters. I shall sing of my resplendent brothers and sisters, who rejoice as they hover over the cups of water in the cactus plants that thrive in the desert."

"Kindly stop your whimpering tunes," the parrot said. "Sing something to make us laugh. Laughter is a sign of the loftiest intellectual development. Can a dog or a horse laugh? No! They can cry, but as for laughter—that is given to mankind alone. Ho, ho, ho!" the parrot chuckled, and added his, "Come now, let us be men."

"You little grey bird of Denmark," the canary said to the lark, "have they made you a prisoner too? Although it must be very cold in your woods, you have your freedom there. Fly away! They have forgotten to close your cage. The door of the top is open. Fly! fly!"

Without pausing to think, the clerk did as he was told. In a jiffy, he was out of the cage. But just as he escaped from his prison, the half-open door leading into the next room began to creak. Stealthily, with green shining eyes, the house cat pounced in and gave chase to him. The canary fluttered in his cage. The parrot flapped his wings and called out, "Come now, let us be men." The dreadfully frightened clerk flew out of the window and away over the streets and houses, until at last he had to stop to rest.

That house across the street looked familiar. He flew in through one of its open windows. As he perched on the table, he found that he was in his own room.

"Come now, let us be men," he blurted out, in spontaneous mockery of the parrot. Instantly he resumed the body of the copying clerk, who sat there, perched on the table.

"How in the name of Heaven," he said, "do I happen to be sleeping here? And what a disturbing dream I've had—all nonsense from beginning to end."

VI. THE BEST THAT THE GALOSHES BROUGHT

Early the next morning, before the clerk was out of bed, someone tapped on his door. In walked his neighbor, a young theological student who lived on the same floor.

"Lend me your galoshes," he requested. "It is very wet in the garden, but the sun is shining so gloriously that I'd like to smoke a pipeful down there."

He pulled on the galoshes and went out into the garden, where there was one plum tree and a pear tree. But even a little garden like this one is a precious thing in Copenhagen.

It was only six o'clock. As the student walked up and down the path, he heard the horn of a stagecoach in the street.

"Oh, to travel, to travel!" he exclaimed, "that's the most pleasant thing in the world. It's the great goal of all my dreams. If only I could travel, I'm sure that this restlessness within me would be stilled. But it must be far, far away. How I should like to see beautiful Switzerland, to tour Italy, and—"

Fortunately the galoshes began to function at once, or he might have traveled entirely too much to suit him or to please us. Travel he did. He was high up in Switzerland, tightly packed in a diligence with eight other travelers. He had a pain in his head, his neck felt tired, and the blood had ceased to circulate in his legs. His feet were swollen, and his heavy boots hurt him. He was half-awake and half-asleep. In his right-hand pocket, he had his letter of credit, in his left-hand pocket, he had his passport, and sewn into a little bag inside his breast pocket, he had a few gold pieces. Every time he dozed off, he dreamed that he had lost one or another of these things. Starting feverishly awake, his first movement would be to trace with his hand a triangle from right to left, and up to his breast, to feel whether his treasures were still there.

Umbrellas, hats, and walking sticks swung in the net above him and almost spoiled the magnificent view. As he glanced out the window, his heart sang, as at least one poet has sung in Switzerland, these as yet unpublished words:

> This view is as fine as a view can be.
> Mount Blanc is sublime beyond a doubt,
> And the traveler's life is the life for me—
> But only as long as my money holds out.

Vast, severe, and somber was the whole landscape around him. The pine woods looked like patches of heather on the high cliffs, whose summits were lost in fog and cloud. Snow began to fall, and the cold wind blew.

"Ah," he sighed, "if only we were on the other side of the Alps, then it would be summer weather and I could get some money on my letter of credit. Worrying about my finances spoils all my enjoyment of Switzerland. Oh, if only I were on the other side."

And there he was on the other side, in the middle of Italy, between Florence and Rome. Before him lay Lake Thrasymene. In the evening light, it looked like a sheet of flaming gold among the dark blue hills. Here, where Hannibal beat Flaminius, the grape vines clung peacefully to each other with their green tendrils. Pretty little half-clothed children tended a herd of coal-black pigs under a fragrant clump of laurels by the roadside, and if we could paint the scene in its true colors, all would exclaim, "Glorious Italy!" But neither the student nor his companions in the stagecoach made any such exclamation.

Poisonous flies and gnats swarmed into the coach by the thousands. In vain, the travelers tried to beat them off with myrtle branches. The flies stung just the same. There was not a passenger whose face was not puffed and spotted with bites. The poor horses looked like carcasses. The flies made life miserable for them, and it only brought them a momentary relief when the coachman got down and scraped off swarms of the insects that settled upon them.

Once the sun went down, an icy chill fell upon everything. It wasn't at all pleasant. However, the hills and clouds took on that wonderful green tint, so clear and so shining. Yes, go and see for yourself. That is far better than to read about it. It was a lovely sight, and the travelers thought so too, but their stomachs were empty, their bodies exhausted, and every thought in their heads was directed toward a lodging for the night. But where would they lodge? They watched the road ahead far more attentively than they did the splendid view.

Their road ran through an olive grove, and the student could fancy that he was at home, passing through a wood of gnarled willow trees. And there stood a lonely inn. A band of crippled beggars were camping outside, and the liveliest among them looked like the eldest son of Famine who had just come of age. The rest either were blind, or so lame that they crawled about on their hands, or had withered arms and hands without any fingers. Here really was misery in rags.

"*Eccelenza, miserabili!*" they groaned, and stretched forth their crippled limbs. The hostess herself went barefoot. With uncombed hair and an unwashed blouse, she received her guests. The doors were hinged with string; half of the bricks of the floors had been put to other use; bats flew about the ceiling; and the smell—

"It were better to have supper in the stable," one traveler maintained. "There one at least knows what he is breathing."

The windows were opened to let a little fresh air come inside, but swifter than the air came those withered arms and that perpetual whine, "*Miserabili, eccellenza*." On the walls were many inscriptions, and half of them had little good to say for *la bella Italia*.

Supper was served. Supper was a watery soup flavored with pepper and rancid oil. This same oil was the better part of the salad. Dubious eggs and roasted cockscombs were the best dishes, and even the wine was distasteful. It was a frightful collation.

That night, the trunks were piled against the door, and one of the travelers mounted guard while the others slept. The student stood the first guard mount. How close it was in there! The heat was overpowering, the gnats droned and stabbed, and outside, the *miserabili* whined in their dreams.

"Traveling," said the student, "would be all very well if one had no body. Oh, if only the body could rest while the spirit flies on without it. Wherever I go, there is some lack that I feel in my heart. There is always something better than the present that I desire. Yes, something better—the best of all, but what is it, and where shall I find it? Down deep in my heart, I know what I want. I want to reach a happy goal, the happiest goal of all."

As soon as the words were said, he found himself back in his home. Long white curtains draped the windows, and in the middle of the floor, a black coffin stood. In this he lay, sleeping the quiet sleep of death. His wish was fulfilled—his body was at rest, and his spirit was free to travel. "Call no man happy until he rests in his grave," said Solon, and here his words proved true again.

Every corpse is a sphinx of immortality. The sphinx in this black casket that confronts us could say no more than the living man had written two days before:

> Stern Death, your silence has aroused my fears.
> Shall not my soul up Jacob's ladder pass,
> Or shall your stone weight me throughout the years,
> And I rise only in the graveyard grass?

> Our deepest grief escapes the world's sad eye!
> You who are lonely to the very last,
> A heavier burden on your heart must lie
> Than all the earth upon your coffin cast!

Two figures moved about the room. We know them both. Those two who bent over the dead man were Dame Care and Fortune's minion.

"Now," said Care, "you can see what happiness your galoshes have brought mankind."

"They have at least brought everlasting rest to him who here lies sleeping," said Fortune's minion.

"Oh, no!" said Care. "He went of his own free will. He was not called away. His spiritual power was not strong enough to undertake the glorious tasks for which he is destined. I shall do him a favor."

She took the galoshes from his feet. Then the sleep of death was ended, and the student awakened to life again. Care vanished, and she took the galoshes along with her, for she probably regarded them as her own property.

THE STEADFAST TIN SOLDIER (1838)

There were once five-and-twenty tin soldiers. They were all brothers, born of the same old tin spoon. They shouldered their muskets and looked straight ahead of them, splendid in their uniforms, all red and blue.

The very first thing in the world that they heard was, "Tin soldiers!" A small boy shouted it and clapped his hands as the lid was lifted off their box on his birthday. He immediately set them up on the table.

All the soldiers looked exactly alike except one. He looked a little different as he had been cast last of all. The tin was short, so he had only one leg. But there he stood, as steady on one leg as any of the other soldiers on their two. But just you see, he'll be the remarkable one.

On the table with the soldiers were many other playthings, and one that no eye could miss was a marvelous castle of cardboard. It had little windows through which you could look right inside it. And in front of the castle were miniature trees around a little mirror supposed to represent a lake. The wax swans that swam on its surface were reflected in the mirror. All this was very pretty, but prettiest of all was the little lady who stood in the open doorway of the castle. Though she was a paper doll, she wore a dress of the fluffiest gauze. A tiny blue ribbon went over her shoulder for a scarf, and in the middle of it shone a spangle that was as big as her face. The little lady held out both her arms, as a ballet dancer does, and one leg was lifted so high behind her that the tin soldier couldn't see it at all, and he supposed she must have only one leg, as he did.

"That would be a wife for me," he thought. "But maybe she's too grand. She lives in a castle. I have only a box, with four-and-twenty roommates to share it. That's no place for her. But I must try to make her acquaintance." Still as stiff as when he stood at attention, he lay down on the table behind a snuffbox, where he could admire the dainty little dancer who kept standing on one leg without ever losing her balance.

When the evening came, the other tin soldiers were put away in their box, and the people of the house went to bed. Now the toys began to play among themselves at visits, and battles, and at giving balls. The tin soldiers rattled about in their box, for they wanted to play too, but they could not get the lid open. The nutcracker turned somersaults, and the slate pencil squeaked out jokes on the slate. The toys made such a noise that they woke up the canary bird, who made them a speech, all in verse. The only two who stayed still were the tin soldier and the little dancer. Without ever swerving from the tip of one toe, she held out her arms to him, and the tin soldier was just as steadfast on his one leg. Not once did he take his eyes off her.

Then the clock struck twelve and—clack!—up popped the lid of the snuffbox. But there was no snuff in it, no—out bounced a little black bogey, a jack-in-the-box.

"Tin soldier," he said. "Will you please keep your eyes to yourself?" The tin soldier pretended not to hear.

The bogey said, "Just you wait till tomorrow."

But when morning came, and the children got up, the soldier was set on the window ledge. And whether the bogey did it, or there was a gust of wind, all of a sudden, the window flew open, and the soldier pitched out headlong from the third floor. He fell at breathtaking speed and landed cap first, with his bayonet buried between the paving stones and his one leg stuck straight in the air. The housemaid and the little boy ran down to look for him, and, though they nearly stepped on the tin soldier, they walked right past without seeing him. If the soldier had called, "Here I am!" they would surely have found him, but he thought it contemptible to raise an uproar while he was wearing his uniform.

Soon, it began to rain. The drops fell faster and faster, until they came down by the bucketful. As soon as the rain let up, along came two young rapscallions.

"Hi, look!" one of them said, "There's a tin soldier. Let's send him sailing."

They made a boat out of newspaper, put the tin soldier in the middle of it, and away he went down the gutter with the two young rapscallions running beside him and clapping their hands. High heavens! How the waves splashed, and how fast the water ran down the gutter. Don't forget that it had just been raining by the bucketful. The paper boat pitched, and tossed, and sometimes it whirled about so rapidly that it made the soldier's head spin. But he stood as steady as ever. Never once flinching, he kept his eyes front and carried his gun shoulder-high. Suddenly, the boat rushed under a long plank where the gutter was boarded over. It was as dark as the soldier's own box.

"Where can I be going?" the soldier wondered. "This must be that black bogey's revenge. Ah! If only I had the little lady with me, it could be twice as dark here for all that I would care."

Out popped a great water rat who lived under the gutter plank.

"Have you a passport?" said the rat. "Hand it over."

The soldier kept quiet and held his musket tighter. On rushed the boat, and the rat came right after it, gnashing his teeth as he called to the sticks and straws:

"Halt him! Stop him! He didn't pay his toll. He hasn't shown his passport." But the current ran stronger and stronger. The soldier could see daylight ahead where the board ended, but he also heard a roar that would frighten the bravest of us. Hold on! Right at the end of that gutter plank, the water poured into the great canal. It was as dangerous to him as a waterfall would be to us.

He was so near it he could not possibly stop. The boat plunged into the whirlpool. The poor tin soldier stood as staunch as he could, and no one can say that he so much as blinked an eye. Thrice and again the boat spun around. It filled to the top—and was bound to sink. The water was up to his neck, and still the boat went down, deeper, deeper, deeper, and the paper got soft and limp. Then the water rushed over his head.

He thought of the pretty little dancer whom he'd never see again, and in his ears rang an old, old song:

> Farewell, farewell, O warrior brave,
> Nobody can from Death thee save.

And now the paper boat broke beneath him, and the soldier sank right through. And just at that moment, he was swallowed by a most enormous fish.

My! How dark it was inside that fish. It was darker than under the gutter plank, and it was so cramped, but the tin soldier still was staunch. He lay there full length, soldier fashion, with musket to shoulder.

Then the fish flopped and floundered in a most unaccountable way. Finally, it was perfectly still, and after a while, something struck through him like a flash of lightning. The tin soldier saw daylight again, and he heard a voice say, "The Tin Soldier!" The fish had been caught, carried to market, bought, and brought to a kitchen where the cook cut him open with her big knife.

She picked the soldier up bodily between her two fingers, and carried him off upstairs. Everyone wanted to see this remarkable traveler who had traveled about in a fish's stomach, but the tin soldier took no pride in it. They put him on the table and—lo and behold, what curious things can happen in this world—there he was, back in the same room as before. He saw the same children, the same toys were on the table, and there was the same fine castle with the pretty little dancer. She still balanced on one leg, with the other raised high. She too was steadfast. That touched the soldier so deeply that he would have cried tin tears, only soldiers never cry. He looked at her, and she looked at him, and never a word was said. Just as things were going so nicely for them, one of the little boys snatched up the tin soldier and threw him into the stove. He did it for no reason at all. That black bogey in the snuffbox must have put him up to it.

The tin soldier stood there dressed in flames. He felt a terrible heat, but whether it came from the flames, or from his love he didn't know. He'd lost his splendid colors, maybe from his hard journey, maybe from grief, nobody can say.

He looked at the little lady, and she looked at him, and he felt himself melting. But still he stood steadfast, with his musket held trim on his shoulder.

Then the door blew open. A puff of wind struck the dancer. She flew like a sylph, straight into the fire with the soldier, blazed up in a flash, and was gone. The tin soldier melted, all in a lump. The next day, when a servant took up the ashes, she found him in the shape of a little tin heart. But of the pretty dancer, nothing was left except her spangle, and it was burned as black as a coal.

THE WILD SWANS (1838)

Far, far away where the swallows fly when we have winter, there lived a king who had eleven sons and one daughter, Elisa. The eleven brothers, princes all, each went to school with a star at his breast and a sword at his side. They wrote with pencils of diamond upon golden slates, and could say their lesson by heart just as easily as they could read it from the book. You could tell at a glance how princely they were. Their sister, Elisa, sat on a little footstool of flawless glass. She had a picture book that had cost half a kingdom. Oh, the children had a very fine time, but it did not last forever.

Their father, who was king over the whole country, married a wicked queen, who did not treat his poor children at all well. They found that out the very first day. There was feasting throughout the palace, and the children played at entertaining guests. But instead of letting them have all the cakes and baked apples that they used to get, their new stepmother gave them only some sand in a teacup, and told them to make believe that it was a special treat.

The following week, the queen sent little Elisa to live in the country with some peasants. And before long, she had made the king believe so many falsehoods about the poor princes that he took no further interest in them.

"Fly out into the world and make your own living," the wicked queen told them. "Fly away like big birds without a voice."

But she did not harm the princes as much as she meant to, for they turned into eleven magnificent white swans. With a weird cry, they flew out of the palace window, across the park into the woods.

It was so early in the morning that their sister, Elisa, was still asleep when they flew over the peasant hut where she was staying. They hovered over the roofs, craning and twisting their long necks and flapping their wings, but nobody saw them or heard them. They were forced to fly on, high up near the clouds and far away into the wide world. They came down in a vast, dark forest that stretched down to the shores of the sea.

Poor little Elisa stayed in the peasant hut, and played with a green leaf, for she had no other toy. She made a little hole in the leaf and looked through it at the sun. Through it, she seemed to see her brothers' bright eyes, and whenever the warm sunlight touched her cheek, it reminded her of all their kisses.

One day passed like all the others. When the wind stirred the hedge roses outside the hut, it whispered to them, "Who could be prettier than you?" But the roses shook their heads and answered, "Elisa!" And on Sunday, when the old woman sat in the doorway reading the psalms, the wind fluttered through the pages and said to the book, "Who could be more saintly than you?" "Elisa," the book testified. What it and the roses said was perfectly true.

Elisa was to go back home when she became fifteen, but as soon as the queen saw what a beautiful princess she was, the queen felt spiteful and full of hatred toward her. She would not have hesitated to turn her into a wild swan, like her brothers, but she did not dare to do it just yet, because the king wanted to see his daughter.

In the early morning, the queen went to the bathing place, which was made of white marble, furnished with soft cushions, and carpeted with the most splendid rugs. She took three toads, kissed them, and said to the first:

"Squat on Elisa's head when she bathes, so that she will become as torpid as you are." To the second she said, "Squat on her forehead, so that she will become as ugly as you are, and her father won't recognize her." And to the third, she whispered, "Lie against her heart, so that she will be cursed and tormented by evil desires.

Thereupon the queen dropped the three toads into the clear water, which at once turned a greenish color. She called Elisa, made her undress, and told her to enter the bath. When Elisa went down into the water, one toad fastened himself to her hair, another to her forehead, and the third against her heart. But she did not seem to be aware of them, and when she stood up, three red poppies floated on the water. If the toads had not been poisonous, and had not been kissed by the witch, they would have been turned into red roses. But at least they had been turned into flowers, by the mere touch of her head and heart. She was too innocent and good for witchcraft to have power over her.

When the evil queen realized this, she rubbed Elisa with walnut stain that turned her dark brown, smeared her beautiful face with a vile ointment, and tousled her lovely hair. No one could have recognized the beautiful Elisa, and when her father saw her, he was shocked. He said that this could not be his daughter. No one knew her except the watchdog and the swallows, and they were humble creatures who had nothing to say.

Poor Elisa cried and thought of her eleven brothers, who were all away. Heavy-hearted, she stole away from the palace and wandered all day long over fields and marshes, till she came to the vast forest. She had no idea where to turn. All she felt was her sorrow and her longing to be with her brothers. Like herself, they must have been driven out into the world, and she set her heart upon finding them. She had been in the forest only a little while when night came on, and as she had strayed from any sign of a path, she said her prayers and lay down on the soft moss, with her head pillowed against a stump. All was quiet, the air was so mild, and hundreds of fireflies glittered like a green fire in the grass and moss. When she lightly brushed against a single branch, the shining insects showered about her like falling stars.

She dreamed of her brothers all night long. They were children again, playing together, writing with their diamond pencils on their golden slates, and looking at her wonderful picture book that had cost half a kingdom. But they no longer scribbled sums and exercises as they used to do. No, they set down their bold deeds and all that they had seen or heard. Everything in the picture book came alive. The birds sang, and the people strolled out of the book to talk with Elisa and her brothers, but whenever she turned a page, they immediately jumped back into place, to keep the pictures in order.

When she awoke, the sun was already high. She could not see it plainly, for the tall trees spread their tangled branches above her, but the rays played above like a shimmering golden gauze. There was a delightful fragrance of green foliage, and the birds came near enough to have perched on her shoulder. She heard the water splashing from many large springs, which all flowed into a pool with the most beautiful sandy bottom. Although it was hemmed in by a wall of thick bushes, there was one place where the deer had made a path wide enough for Elisa to reach the water. The pool was so clear that if the wind had not stirred the limbs and bushes, she might have supposed they were painted on the bottom of the pool. For each leaf was clearly reflected, whether the sun shone upon it or whether it grew in the shade.

When Elisa saw her own face, she was horrified to find it so brown and ugly. But as soon as she wet her slender hand and rubbed her brow and her eyes, her fair skin showed again. Then she laid aside her clothes and plunged into the fresh water. In all the world, there was no king's daughter as lovely as Elisa. When she had dressed herself and plaited her long hair, she went to the sparkling spring and drank from the hollow of her hand. She wandered deeper into the woods without knowing whither she went. She thought of her brothers, and she thought of the good Lord, who she knew would not forsake her. He lets the wild crab apples grow to feed the hungry, and he led her footsteps to a tree with its branches bent down by the weight of their fruit. Here she had her lunch. After she put props under the heavy limbs, she went on into the depths of the forest. It was so quiet that she heard her own footsteps and every dry leaf that rustled underfoot. Not a bird was in sight, not a ray of the sun could get through the big heavy branches, and the tall trees grew so close together that when she looked straight ahead, it seemed as if a solid fence of lofty palings imprisoned her. She had never known such solitude.

The night came on, pitch black. Not one firefly glittered among the leaves as she despondently lay down to sleep. Then it seemed to her that the branches parted overhead and the Lord looked kindly down upon her, and little angels peeped out from above His head and behind Him.

When she awoke the next morning, she did not know whether she had dreamed this, or whether it had really happened.

A few steps farther on, she met an old woman who had a basket of berries and gave some of them to her. Elisa asked if she had seen eleven princes riding through the forest.

"No," the old woman said. "But yesterday I saw eleven swans who wore golden crowns. They were swimming in the river not far from here."

She led Elisa a little way to the top of a hill that sloped down to a winding river. The trees on either bank stretched their long leafy branches toward each other, and where the stream was too wide for them to grow across it, they had torn their roots from the earth and leaned out over the water until their branches met. Elisa told the old woman good-bye and followed the river down to where it flowed into the great open sea.

Before the young girl lay the whole beautiful sea, but not a sail nor a single boat was in sight. How could she go on? She looked at the countless pebbles on the beach, and saw how round the water had worn them. Glass, iron ore, stones, all that had been washed up, had been shaped by the water that was so much softer than even her tender hand.

"It rolls on tirelessly, and that is the way it makes such hard things smooth," she said. "I shall be just as untiring. Thank you for your lesson, you clear rolling waves. My heart tells me that someday you will carry me to my beloved brothers."

Among the wet seaweed, she found eleven white swan feathers, which she collected in a sheaf. There were still drops of water on them, but whether these were spray or tears, no one could say. It was very lonely along the shore, but she did not mind, for the sea was constantly changing. Indeed, it showed more changes in a few hours than an inland lake does in a whole year. When the sky was black with threatening clouds, it was as if the sea seemed to say, "I can look threatening too." Then the wind would blow, and the waves would raise their white crests. But when the wind died down and the clouds were red, the sea would look like a rose petal.

Sometimes it showed white, and sometimes green, but however calm it might seem, there was always a gentle lapping along the shore, where the waters rose and fell like the chest of a child asleep.

Just at sunset, Elisa saw eleven white swans, with golden crowns on their heads, fly toward the shore. As they flew, one behind another, they looked like a white ribbon floating in the air. Elisa climbed up and hid behind a bush on the steep bank. The swans came down near her and flapped their magnificent white wings.

As soon as the sun went down beyond the sea, the swans threw off their feathers, and there stood eleven handsome princes. They were her brothers, and, although they were greatly altered, she knew in her heart that she could not be mistaken. She cried aloud and rushed into their arms, calling them each by name. The princes were so happy to see their little sister. And they knew her at once, for all that she had grown tall and lovely. They laughed, and they cried, and they soon realized how cruelly their stepmother had treated them all.

"We brothers," said the eldest, "are forced to fly about disguised as wild swans as long as the sun is in the heavens, but when it goes down, we take back our human form. So at sunset, we must always look about us for some firm foothold, because if ever we were flying among the clouds at sunset we would be dashed down to the earth.

"We do not live on this coast. Beyond the sea, there is another land as fair as this, but it lies far away, and we must cross the vast ocean to reach it. Along our course, there is not one island where we can pass the night, except one little rock that rises from the middle of the sea. It is barely big enough to hold us, however close together we stand, and if there is a rough sea, the waves wash over us. But still we thank God for it.

"In our human forms, we rest there during the night, and without it, we could never come back to our own dear homeland. It takes two of the longest days of the year for our journey. We are allowed to come back to our native land only once a year, and we do not dare to stay longer than eleven days. As we fly over this forest, we can see the palace where our father lives and where we were born. We can see the high tower of the church where our mother lies buried. And here we feel that even the trees and bushes are akin to us. Here the wild horses gallop across the moors as we saw them in our childhood, and the charcoal-burner sings the same old songs to which we used to dance when we were children. This is our homeland. It draws us to it, and here, dear sister, we have found you again. We may stay two days longer, and then we must fly across the sea to a land that is fair enough, but not our own. How shall we take you with us? For we have neither ship nor boat."

"How shall I set you free?" their sister asked, and they talked on for most of the night, sparing only a few hours for sleep.

In the morning, Elisa was awakened by the rustling of swans' wings overhead. Her brothers, once more enchanted, wheeled above her in great circles until they were out of sight. One of them, her youngest brother, stayed with her and rested his head on her breast while she stroked his wings. They spent the whole day together, and toward evening, the others returned. As soon as the sun went down, they resumed their own shape.

"Tomorrow," said one of her brothers, "we must fly away, and we dare not return until a whole year has passed. But we cannot leave you like this. Have you courage enough to come with us? My arm is strong enough to carry you through the forest, so surely the wings of us all should be strong enough to bear you across the sea."

"Yes, take me with you," said Elisa.

They spent the entire night making a net of pliant willow bark and tough rushes. They made it large and strong. Elisa lay down upon it, and when the sun rose and her brothers again became wild swans, they lifted the net in their bills and flew high up toward the clouds with their beloved sister, who still was fast asleep. As the sun shone straight into her face, one of the swans flew over her head so as to shade her with his wide wings.

They were far from the shore when she awoke. Elisa thought she must still be dreaming, so strange did it seem to be carried through the air, high over the sea. Beside her lay a branch full of beautiful ripe berries and a bundle of sweet-tasting roots. Her youngest brother had gathered them and put them there for her. She gave him a grateful smile. She knew he must be the one who flew over her head to protect her eyes from the sun.

They were so high that the first ship they sighted looked like a gull floating on the water. A cloud rolled up behind them, as big as a mountain. Upon it, Elisa saw gigantic shadows of herself and of the eleven swans. It was the most splendid picture she had ever seen, but as the sun rose higher, the clouds grew small, and the shadow picture of their flight disappeared.

All day, they flew like arrows whipping through the air, yet, because they had their sister to carry, they flew more slowly than on their former journeys. Night was drawing near, and a storm was rising. In terror, Elisa watched the sinking sun, for the lonely rock was nowhere in sight. It seemed to her that the swans beat their wings in the air more desperately. Alas, it was because of her that they could not fly fast enough. So soon as the sun went down they would turn into men, and all of them would pitch down into the sea and drown. She prayed to God from the depths of her heart, but still no rock could be seen. Black clouds gathered, and great gusts told of the storm to come. The threatening clouds came on as one tremendous wave that rolled down toward them like a mass of lead, and flash upon flash of lightning followed them. Then the sun touched the rim of the sea. Elisa's heart beat madly as the swans shot down so fast that she thought they were falling, but they checked their downward swoop. Half of the sun was below the sea when she first saw the little rock below them. It looked no larger than the head of a seal jutting out of the water. The sun sank very fast. Now it was no bigger than a star, but her foot touched solid ground. Then the sun went out like the last spark on a piece of burning paper. She saw her brothers stand about her, arm in arm, and there was only just room enough for all of them. The waves beat upon the rock and washed over them in a shower of spray. The heavens were lit by constant flashes, and bolt upon bolt of thunder crashed. But the sister and brothers clasped each other's hands and sang a psalm, which comforted them and gave them courage.

At dawn, the air was clear and still. As soon as the sun came up, the swans flew off with Elisa, and they left the rock behind. The waves still tossed, and from the height where they soared, it looked as if the white flecks of foam against the dark green waves were millions of white swans swimming upon the waters.

When the sun rose higher, Elisa saw before her a mountainous land, half floating in the air. Its peaks were capped with sparkling ice, and in the middle rose a castle that was a mile long, with one bold colonnade perched upon another. Down below, palm trees swayed and brilliant flowers bloomed as big as mill wheels. She asked if this was the land for which they were bound, but the swans shook their heads. What she saw was the gorgeous and ever-changing palace of Fata Morgana. No mortal being could venture to enter it. As Elisa stared at it, before her eyes the mountains, palms, and palace faded away, and in their place rose twenty splendid churches, all alike, with lofty towers and pointed windows. She thought she heard the organ peal, but it was the roll of the ocean she heard. When she came close to the churches, they turned into a fleet of ships sailing beneath her, but when she looked down, it was only a sea mist drifting over the water.

Scene after scene shifted before her eyes until she saw at last the real country whither they went. Mountains rose before her beautifully blue, wooded with cedars and studded with cities and palaces. Long before sunset, she was sitting on a mountainside, in front of a large cave carpeted over with green creepers so delicate that they looked like embroidery.

"We shall see what you'll dream of here tonight," her youngest brother said, as he showed her where she was to sleep.

"I only wish I could dream how to set you free," she said.

This thought so completely absorbed her, and she prayed so earnestly for the Lord to help her that even in her sleep she kept on praying. It seemed to her that she was flying aloft to the Fata Morgana palace of clouds. The fairy who came out to meet her was fair and shining, yet she closely resembled the old woman who gave her the berries in the forest and told her of the swans who wore golden crowns on their heads.

"Your brothers can be set free," she said, "but have you the courage and tenacity to do it? The sea water that changes the shape of rough stones is indeed softer than your delicate hands, but it cannot feel the pain that your fingers will feel. It has no heart, so it cannot suffer the anguish and heartache that you will have to endure. Do you see this stinging nettle in my hand? Many such nettles grow around the cave where you sleep. Only those and the ones that grow upon graves in the churchyards may be used—remember that! Those you must gather, although they will burn your hands to blisters. Crush the nettles with your feet and you will have flax, which you must spin and weave into eleven shirts of mail with long sleeves. Once you throw these over the eleven wild swans, the spell over them is broken. But keep this well in mind! From the moment you undertake this task until it is done, even though it lasts for years, you must not speak. The first word you say will strike your brothers' hearts like a deadly knife. Their lives are at the mercy of your tongue. Now, remember what I told you!"

She touched Elisa's hand with nettles that burned like fire and awakened her. It was broad daylight, and close at hand where she had been sleeping grew a nettle like those of which she had dreamed. She thanked God upon her knees, and left the cave to begin her task.

With her soft hands, she took hold of the dreadful nettles that seared like fire. Great blisters rose on her hands and arms, but she endured it gladly in the hope that she could free her beloved brothers. She crushed each nettle with her bare feet, and spun the green flax.

When her brothers returned at sunset, it alarmed them that she did not speak. They feared this was some new spell cast by their wicked stepmother, but when they saw her hands, they understood that she labored to save them. The youngest one wept, and wherever his tears touched Elisa, she felt no more pain, and the burning blisters healed.

She toiled throughout the night, for she could not rest until she had delivered her beloved brothers from the enchantment. Throughout the next day, while the swans were gone, she sat all alone, but never had the time sped so quickly. One shirt was made, and she set to work on the second one.

Then she heard the blast of a hunting horn on the mountainside. It frightened her, for the sound came nearer until she could hear the hounds bark. Terror-stricken, she ran into the cave, bundled together the nettles she had gathered and woven, and sat down on this bundle.

Immediately, a big dog came bounding from the thicket, followed by another, and still another, all barking loudly as they ran to and fro. In a very few minutes, all the huntsmen stood in front of the cave. The most handsome of these was the king of the land, and he came up to Elisa. Never before had he seen a girl so beautiful. "My lovely child," he said, "how do you come to be here?"

Elisa shook her head, for she did not dare to speak. Her brothers' deliverance and their very lives depended upon it, and she hid her hands under her apron to keep the king from seeing how much she suffered.

"Come with me," he told her. "You cannot stay here. If you are as good as you are fair, I shall clothe you in silk and velvet, set a golden crown upon your head, and give you my finest palace to live in." Then he lifted her up on his horse. When she wept and wrung her hands, the king told her, "My only wish is to make you happy. Someday you will thank me for doing this." Off through the mountains he spurred, holding her before him on his horse as his huntsmen galloped behind them.

At sundown, his splendid city with all its towers and domes lay before them. The king led her into his palace, where great fountains played in the high marble halls and where both walls and ceilings were adorned with paintings. But she took no notice of any of these things. She could only weep and grieve. Indifferently, she let the women dress her in royal garments, weave strings of pearls in her hair, and draw soft gloves over her blistered fingers.

She was so dazzlingly beautiful in all this splendor that the whole court bowed even deeper than before. And the king chose her for his bride, although the archbishop shook his head and whispered that this lovely maid of the woods must be a witch who had blinded their eyes and stolen the king's heart.

But the king would not listen to him. He commanded that music be played, the costliest dishes be served, and the prettiest girls dance for her. She was shown through sweet-scented gardens and into magnificent halls, but nothing could make her lips smile or her eyes sparkle. Sorrow had set its seal upon them. At length, the king opened the door to a little chamber adjoining her bedroom. It was covered with splendid green embroideries, and looked just like the cave in which he had found her. On the floor lay the bundle of flax she had spun from the nettles, and from the ceiling hung the shirt she had already finished. One of the huntsmen had brought these with him as curiosities.

"Here you may dream that you are back in your old home," the king told her. "Here is the work that you were doing there, and surrounded by all your splendor here, it may amuse you to think of those times."

When Elisa saw these things that were so precious to her, a smile trembled on her lips, and the blood rushed back to her cheeks. The hope that she could free her brothers returned to her, and she kissed the king's hand. He pressed her to his heart and commanded that all the church bells peal to announce their wedding. The beautiful mute girl from the forest was to be the country's queen.

The archbishop whispered evil words in the king's ear, but they did not reach his heart. The wedding was to take place. The archbishop himself had to place the crown on her head. Out of spite, he forced the tight circlet so low on her forehead that it hurt her. But a heavier band encircled her heart, and the sorrow she felt for her brothers kept her from feeling any hurt of the flesh. Her lips were mute, for one single word would mean death to her brothers, but her eyes shone with love for the kind and handsome king who did his best to please her. Every day, she grew fonder and fonder of him in her heart. Oh, if only she could confide in him, and tell him what grieved her. But mute she must remain, and finish her task in silence. So at night she would steal away from his side into her little chamber that resembled the cave, and there she wove one shirt after another, but when she set to work on the seventh, there was not enough flax left to finish it.

She knew that the nettles she must use grew in the churchyard, but she had to gather them herself. How could she go there?

"Oh, what is the pain in my fingers compared with the anguish I feel in my heart!" she thought. "I must take the risk, and the good Lord will not desert me."

As terrified as if she were doing some evil thing, she tiptoed down into the moonlit garden, through the long alleys, and down the deserted streets to the churchyard. There, she saw a group of vampires sitting in a circle on one of the large gravestones. These hideous ghouls took off their ragged clothes as they were about to bathe. With skinny fingers, they clawed open the new graves. Greedily, they snatched out the bodies and ate the flesh from them. Elisa had to pass close to them, and they fixed their vile eyes upon her, but she said a prayer, picked the stinging nettles, and carried them back to the palace.

Only one man saw her—the archbishop. He was awake while others slept. Now he had proof of what he had suspected. There was something wrong with the queen. She was a witch, and that was how she had duped the king and all his people.

In the confessional, he told the king what he had seen and what he feared. As the bitter words spewed from his mouth, the images of the saints shook their heads, as much as to say, "He lies. Elisa is innocent." The archbishop, however, had a different explanation for this. He said they were testifying against her, and shaking their heads at her wickedness.

Two big tears rolled down the king's cheeks as he went home with suspicion in his heart. That night, he pretended to be asleep, but no restful sleep touched his eyes. He watched Elisa get out of bed. Every night, he watched her get up, and each time, he followed her quietly and saw her disappear into her private little room. Day after day, his frown deepened. Elisa saw it and could not understand why this should be, but it made her anxious and added to the grief her heart already felt for her brothers. Her hot tears fell down upon her queenly robes of purple velvet. There they flashed like diamonds, and all who saw this splendor wished that they were queen.

Meanwhile, she had almost completed her task. Only one shirt was lacking, but again she ran out of flax. Not a single nettle was left. Once more, for the last time, she must go to the churchyard and pluck a few more handfuls. She thought with fear of the lonely walk and the ghastly vampires, but her will was as strong as her faith in God.

She went upon her mission, but the king and his archbishop followed her. They saw her disappear through the iron gates of the churchyard, and when they came in after her, they saw vampires sitting on a gravestone, just as Elisa had seen them.

The king turned away, for he thought Elisa was among them— Elisa, whose head had rested against his heart that very evening.

"Let the people judge her," he said. And the people did judge her. They condemned her to die by fire.

She was led from her splendid royal halls to a dungeon, dark and damp, where the wind whistled in between the window bars. Instead of silks and velvets, they gave her for a pillow the bundle of nettles she had gathered, and for her coverlet the harsh, burning shirts of mail she had woven. But they could have given her nothing that pleased her more.

She set to work again, and prayed. Outside, the boys in the street sang jeering songs about her, and not one soul came to comfort her with a kind word.

But toward evening, she heard the rustle of a swan's wings close to her window. It was her youngest brother who had found her at last. She sobbed for joy. Though she knew that this night was all too apt to be her last, the task was almost done, and her brothers were near her.

The archbishop came to stay with her during her last hours on Earth, for this much he had promised the king. But she shook her head, and by her expression and gestures begged him to leave. This was the last night she had to finish her task, or it would all go for naught—all her pain, and her tears, and her sleepless nights. The archbishop went away, saying cruel things against her. But poor Elisa knew her own innocence, and she kept on with her task.

The little mice ran about the floor, and brought nettles to her feet, trying to help her all they could. And a thrush perched near the bars of her window to sing the whole night through, as merrily as he could, so that she would keep up her courage.

It was still in the early dawn, an hour before sunrise, when the eleven brothers reached the palace gates and demanded to see the king. This, they were told, was impossible. It was still night. The king was asleep and could not be disturbed. They begged and threatened so loudly that the guard turned out, and even the king came running to find what the trouble was. But at that instant the sun rose, and the eleven brothers vanished. Eleven swans were seen flying over the palace.

All the townsmen went flocking out through the town gates, for they wanted to see the witch burned. A decrepit old horse pulled the cart in which Elisa sat. They had dressed her in coarse sackcloth, and all her lovely long hair hung loose around her beautiful head. Her cheeks were deathly pale, and her lips moved in silent prayer as her fingers twisted the green flax. Even on her way to death, she did not stop her still unfinished work. Ten shirts lay at her feet, and she worked away on the eleventh. "See how the witch mumbles," the mob scoffed at her.

"That's no psalm book in her hands. No, there she sits, nursing her filthy sorcery. Snatch it away from her, and tear it to bits!"

The crowd of people closed in to destroy all her work, but before they could reach her, eleven white swans flew down and made a ring around the cart with their flapping wings. The mob drew back in terror.

"It is a sign from Heaven. She must be innocent," many people whispered. But no one dared say it aloud.

As the executioner seized her arm, she made haste to throw the eleven shirts over the swans, who instantly became eleven handsome princes. But the youngest brother still had a swan's wing in place of one arm, where a sleeve was missing from his shirt. Elisa had not quite been able to finish it.

"Now," she cried, "I may speak! I am innocent."

All the people who saw what had happened bowed down to her as they would before a saint. But the strain, the anguish, and the suffering had been too much for her to bear, and she fell into her brothers' arms as if all life had gone out of her.

"She is innocent indeed!" said her eldest brother, and he told them all that had happened. And while he spoke, the scent of a million roses filled the air, for every piece of wood that they had piled up to burn her had taken root and grown branches. There stood a great high hedge, covered with red and fragrant roses. At the very top, a single pure white flower shone like a star. The king plucked it and put it on Elisa's breast. And she awoke, with peace and happiness in her heart.

All the church bells began to ring of their own accord, and the air was filled with birds. Back to the palace went a bridal procession such as no king had ever enjoyed before.

THE GARDEN OF PARADISE (1839)

There was once a king's son; no one had so many beautiful books as he. In them, he could read of everything that had ever happened in this world, and he could see it all pictured in fine illustrations. He could find out about every race of people and every country, but there was not a single word about where to find the Garden of Paradise, and this, just this, was the very thing that he thought most about.

When he was still very young and was about to start his schooling, his grandmother had told him that each flower in the Garden of

Paradise was made of the sweetest cake, and that the pistils were bottles full of finest wine. On one sort of flower, she told, history was written, on another geography, or multiplication tables, so that one only had to eat cake to know one's lesson, and the more one ate, the more history, geography, or arithmetic one would know.

At the time he believed her, but when the boy grew older and more learned and much wiser, he knew that the glories of the Garden of Paradise must be of a very different sort.

"Oh, why did Eve have to pick fruit from the Tree of Knowledge, and why did Adam eat what was forbidden him? Now if it had only been I, that would never have happened, and sin would never have come into the world." He said it then, and when he was seventeen, he said it still. The Garden of Paradise was always in his thoughts.

He went walking in the woods one day. He walked alone, for this was his favorite amusement. Evening came on, the clouds gathered, and the rain poured down as if the sky were all one big floodgate from which the water plunged. It was as dark as it would be at night in the deepest well. He kept slipping on the wet grass, and tripping over the stones that stuck out of the rocky soil. Everything was soaking wet, and at length, the poor prince didn't have a dry stitch to his back. He had to scramble over great boulders where the water trickled from the wet moss. He had almost fainted, when he heard a strange puffing and saw a huge cave ahead of him. It was brightly lit, for inside the cave burned a fire so large that it could have roasted a stag. And this was actually being done. A magnificent deer, antlers and all, had been stuck on a spit, and was being slowly turned between the rough-hewn trunks of two pine trees. An elderly woman, so burly and strong that she might have been taken for a man in disguise, sat by the fire and threw log after log upon it.

"You can come nearer," she said. "Sit down by the fire and let your clothes dry."

"There's an awful draft here," the prince remarked, as he seated himself on the ground.

"It will be still worse when my sons get home," the woman told him. "You are in the cave of the winds, and my sons are the four winds of the world. Do I make myself clear?"

"Where are your sons?" the prince asked.

"Such a stupid question is hard to answer," the woman told him. "My sons go their own ways, playing ball with the clouds in that great hall." And she pointed up toward the sky.

"Really!" said the prince. "I notice that you have a rather forceful way of speaking, and are not as gentle as the women I usually see around me."

"I suppose they have nothing better to do. I have to be harsh to control those sons of mine. I manage to do it, for all that they are an obstinate lot. See the four sacks that hang there on the wall! They dread those as much as you used to dread the switch that was kept behind the mirror for you. I can fold the boys right up, let me tell you, and pop them straight into the bag. We don't mince matters. There they stay. They aren't allowed to roam around again until I see fit to let them. But here comes one of them."

It was the North Wind who came hurtling in, with a cold blast of snowflakes that swirled about him and great hailstones that rattled on the floor. He was wearing a bearskin coat and trousers; a sealskin cap was pulled over his ears; long icicles hung from his beard; and hailstone after hailstone fell from the collar of his coat.

"Don't go right up to the fire so quickly," the prince warned him. "Your face and hands might get frostbite."

"Frostbite!" the North Wind laughed his loudest. "Frostbite! Why, frost is my chief delight. But what sort of 'longleg' are you? How do you come to be in the cave of the winds?"

"He is my guest," the old woman intervened. "And if that explanation doesn't suit you, into the sack you go. Do I make myself clear?"

She made herself clear enough. The North Wind now talked of whence he had come, and where he had traveled for almost a month.

"I come from the Arctic Sea," he told them. "I have been on Bear Island with the Russian walrus hunters. I lay beside the helm and slept as they sailed from the North Cape. When I awoke from time to time, the storm bird circled about my knees. There's an odd bird for you! He gives a quick flap of his wings, and then holds them perfectly still and rushes along at full speed."

"Don't be so long-winded," his mother told him. "So you came to Bear Island?"

"It's a wonderful place! There's a dancing floor for you, as flat as a platter! The surface of the island is all half-melted snow, little patches of moss, and outcropping rocks. Scattered about are the bones of whales and polar bears, colored a moldy green, and looking like the arms and legs of some giant.

"You'd have thought that the sun never shone there. I blew the fog away a bit, so that the house could be seen. It was a hut built of wreckage and covered with walrus skins, the fleshy side turned outward, and smeared with reds and greens. A lovely polar bear sat growling on the roof of it.

"I went to the shore and looked at birds' nests, and when I saw the featherless nestlings shrieking, with their beaks wide open, I blew down into their thousand throats. That taught them to shut their mouths. Further along, great walruses were wallowing about like monstrous maggots, with pigs' heads, and tusks a yard long."

"How well you do tell a story, my son," the old woman said. "My mouth waters when I hear you!"

"The hunt began. The harpoon was hurled into the walrus' breast, and a streaming blood stream spurted across the ice like a fountain. This reminded me of my own sport. I blew my sailing ships, those towering icebergs, against the boats until their timbers cracked. Ho! How the crew whistled and shouted. But I outwhistled them all. Overboard on the ice they had to throw their dead walruses, their tackle, and even their sea chests. I shrouded them in snow and let them drift south with their broken boats and their booty alongside, for a taste of the open sea. They won't ever come back to Bear Island."

"That was a wicked thing to do," said the mother of the winds.

"I'll let others tell of my good deeds," he said. "But here comes my brother from the west. I like him best of all. He has a seafaring air about him, and carries a refreshing touch of coolness wherever he goes."

"Is that little Zephyr?" the prince asked.

"Of course it's Zephyr," the old woman replied, "but he's not little. He was a nice boy once, but that was years ago."

He looked like a savage, except that he wore a broad-rimmed hat to shield his face. In his hand he carried a mahogany bludgeon, cut in the mahogany forests of America. Nothing less would do!

"Where have you come from?" his mother asked.

"I come from the forest wilderness," he said, "where the thorny vines make a fence between every tree, where the water snake lurks in the wet grass, and where people seem unnecessary."

"What were you doing there?"

"I gazed into the deepest of rivers and saw how it rushed through the rapids and threw up a cloud of spray large enough to hold the rainbow. I saw a wild buffalo wading in the river, but it swept him away. He swam with a flock of wild ducks that flew up when the river went over a waterfall. But the buffalo had to plunge down it. That amused me so much that I blew up a storm, which broke age-old trees into splinters."

"Haven't you done anything else?" the old woman asked him.

"I turned somersaults across the plains, stroked the wild horses, and shook coconuts down from the palm trees. Yes indeed, I have tales worth telling, but one shouldn't tell all he knows. Isn't that right, old lady?" Then he gave her such a kiss that it nearly knocked her over backward. He was certainly a wild young fellow.

Then the South Wind arrived, in a turban and a Bedouin's billowing robe.

"It's dreadfully cold in here," he cried, and threw more wood on the fire. "I can tell that the North Wind got here before me."

"It's hot enough to roast a polar bear here," the North Wind protested.

"You are a polar bear yourself," the South Wind said.

"Do you want to be put into the sack?" the old woman asked. "Sit down on that stone over there and tell me where you have been."

"In Africa, dear Mother," said he. "I have been hunting the lion with Hottentots in Kaffirland. What fine grass grows there on the plains. It is as green as an olive. There danced the gnu, and the ostrich raced with me, but I am fleeter than he is. I went into the desert where the yellow sand is like the bottom of the sea. I met with a caravan, where they were killing their last camel to get drinking water, but it was little enough they got. The sun blazed overhead and the sand scorched underfoot. The desert was unending.

"I rolled in the fine loose sand and whirled it aloft in great columns. What a dance that was! You ought to have seen how despondently the dromedaries hunched up, and how the trader pulled his burnoose over his head. He threw himself down before me as he would before Allah, his god. Now they are buried, with a pyramid of sand rising over them all. When someday I blow it away, the sun will bleach their bones white, and travelers will see that men have been there before them. Otherwise, no one would believe it, there in the desert."

"So you have done nothing but wickedness!" cried his mother. "Into the sack with you!" And before he was aware of it, she picked the South

Wind up bodily and thrust him into the bag. He thrashed about on the floor until she sat down on the sack. That kept him quiet.

"Those are boisterous sons you have," said the prince.

"Indeed they are," she agreed, "but I know how to keep them in order. Here comes the fourth one."

This was the East Wind. He was dressed as a Chinaman.

"So that's where you've been!" said his mother. "I thought you had gone to the Garden of Paradise."

"I won't fly there until tomorrow," the East Wind said. "Tomorrow it will be exactly a hundred years since I was there. I am just home from China, where I danced around the porcelain tower until all the bells jangled. Officials of state were being whipped through the streets. Bamboo sticks were broken across their shoulders, though they were people of importance, from the first to the ninth degree. They howled, 'Thank you so much, my father and protector,' but they didn't mean it. And I went about clanging the bells and sang, 'Tsing, tsang, tsu!'"

"You are too saucy," the old woman told him. "It's a lucky thing that you'll be off to the Garden of Paradise tomorrow, for it always has a good influence on you. Remember to drink deep out of the fountain of wisdom and bring back a little bottleful for me."

"I'll do that," said the East Wind. "But why have you popped my brother from the south into the sack? Let's have him out. He must tell me about the phoenix bird, because the princess in the Garden of Paradise always asks me about that bird when I drop in on her every hundred years. Open up my sack, like my own sweet mother, and I'll give you two pockets full of tea as green and fresh as it was when I picked it off the bush."

"Well—for the sake of the tea, and because you are my pet, I'll open the sack."

She opened it up, and the South Wind crawled out. But he looked very glum, because the prince, who was a stranger, had seen him humbled.

"Here's a palm-leaf fan for the princess," the South Wind said. "It was given to me by the old phoenix, who was the only one of his kind in the world. On it he scratched with his beak a history of the hundred years that he lived, so she can read it herself. I watched the phoenix bird set fire to her nest, and sat there while she burned to death, just like a

Hindu widow. What a crackling there was of dry twigs, what smoke, and what a smell of smoldering! Finally it all burst into flames, and the old phoenix was reduced to ashes, but her egg lay white-hot in the blaze. With a great bang it broke open, and the young phoenix flew out of it. Now he is the ruler over all the birds, and he is the only phoenix bird in all the world. As his greetings to the princess, he thrust a hole in the palm leaf I am giving you."

"Let's have a bite to eat," said the mother of the winds.

As they sat down to eat the roast stag, the prince took a place beside the East Wind, and they soon became fast friends.

"Tell me," said the prince, "who is this princess you've been talking so much about, and just where is the Garden of Eden?"

"Ah, ha!" said the East Wind. "Would you like to go there? Then fly with me tomorrow. I must warn you, though, no man has been there since Adam and Eve. You have read about them in the Bible?"

"Surely," the prince said.

"After they were driven out, the Garden of Paradise sank deep into the earth, but it kept its warm sunlight, its refreshing air, and all of its glories. The queen of the fairies lives there on the Island of the Blessed, where death never comes and where there is everlasting happiness. Sit on my back tomorrow, and I shall take you with me. I think it can be managed. But now let's stop talking, for I want to sleep."

And then they all went to sleep. When the prince awoke the next morning, it came as no small surprise to find himself high over the clouds. He was seated on the back of the East Wind, who carefully held him safe. They were so far up in the sky that all the woods, fields, rivers, and lakes looked as if they were printed on a map spread beneath them.

"Good morning," said the East Wind. "You might just as well sleep a little longer. There's nothing very interesting in this flat land beneath us, unless you care to count churches. They stand out like chalk marks upon the green board."

What he called "the green board" was all the fields and pastures.

"It was not very polite of me to leave without bidding your mother and brothers farewell," the prince said.

"That's excusable, when you leave in your sleep," the East Wind told him, as they flew on faster than ever.

One could hear it in the tree tops. All the leaves and branches rustled as they swept over the forest, and when they crossed over lakes or over seas, the waves rose high, and tall ships bent low to the water as if they were drifting swans.

As darkness gathered that evening, it was pleasant to see the great cities with their lights twinkling here and spreading there, just as when you burn a piece of paper and the sparks fly one after another. At this sight, the prince clapped his hands in delight, but the East Wind advised him to stop it and hold on tight, or he might fall and find himself stuck upon a church steeple.

The eagle in the dark forest flew lightly, but the East Wind flew more lightly still. The Cossack on his pony sped swiftly across the steppes, but the prince sped still more swiftly.

"Now," said the East Wind, "you can view the Himalayas, the highest mountains in Asia. And soon we shall reach the Garden of Paradise."

They turned southward, where the air was sweet with flowers and spice. Figs and pomegranates grew wild, and on untended vines grew red and blue clusters of grapes. They came down here, and both of them stretched out on the soft grass, where flowers nodded in the breeze as if to say: "Welcome back."

"Are we now in the Garden of Paradise?" the prince asked.

"Oh, no!" said the East Wind. "But we shall come to it soon. Do you see that rocky cliff, and the big cave, where the vines hang in a wide curtain of greenery? That's the way we go. Wrap your coat well about you. Here the sun is scorching hot, but a few steps and it is as cold as ice. The bird that flies at the mouth of the cave has one wing in summery and the other in wintry air."

"So this is the way to the Garden of Paradise," said the prince, as they entered the cave.

Brr-r-r! How frosty it was there, but not for long. The East Wind spread his wings, and they shone like the brighest flames. But what a cave that was! Huge masses of rock, from which water was trickling, hung in fantastic shapes above them. Sometimes the cave was so narrow that they had to crawl on their hands and knees, sometimes so vast that it seemed that they were under the open sky. The cave resembled a series of funeral chapels, with mute organ pipes and banners turned to stone.

"We are going to the Garden of Paradise through the gates of death, are we not?" the prince asked.

The East Wind answered not a word, but pointed to a lovely blue light that shone ahead of them. The masses of stone over their heads grew more and more misty, and at last they looked up at a clear white cloud in the moonlight. The air became delightfully clement, as fresh as it is in the hills, and as sweetly scented as it is among the roses that bloom in the valley.

The river that flowed there was clear as the air itself, and the fish in it were like silver and gold. Purple eels that at every turn threw off blue sparks frolicked about in the water, and the large leaves of the aquatic flowers gleamed in all of the rainbow's colors. The flowers themselves were like a bright orange flame, which fed on the water just as a lamplight is fed by oil.

A strong marble bridge, made so delicately and artistically that it looked as if it consisted of lace and glass pearls, led across the water to the Island of the Blessed, where the Garden of Paradise bloomed.

The East Wind swept the prince up in his arms and carried him across to the island, where the petals and leaves sang all the lovely old songs of his childhood, but far, far sweeter than any human voice could sing. Were these palm trees that grew there, or immense water plants? Such vast and verdant trees the prince had never seen before. The most marvelous climbing vines hung in garlands such as are to be seen only in old illuminated church books, painted in gold and bright colors in the margins or twined about the initial letters. Here was the oddest assortment of birds, flowers, and twisting vines.

On the grass nearby, with their brilliantly starred tails spread wide was a flock of peacocks. Or so they seemed, but when the prince touched them, he found that these were not birds. They were plants. They were large burdock leaves that were as resplendent as a peacock's train. Lions and tigers leaped about, as lithe as cats, in the green shrubbery that the olive blossoms made so fragrant. The lions and tigers were quite tame, for the wild wood pigeon, which glistened like a lovely pearl, brushed the lion's mane with her wings, and the timid antelopes stood by and tossed their heads as if they would like to join in their play.

Then the fairy of the garden came to meet them. Her garments were as bright as the sun, and her face was as cheerful as that of a happy mother who is well pleased with her child. She was so young and lovely, and the other pretty maidens who followed her each wore a shining star in their hair. When the East Wind gave her the palm-leaf message from the phoenix, her eyes sparkled with pleasure.

She took the prince by his hand and led him into her palace, where the walls had the color of a perfect tulip petal held up to the sun. The ceiling was made of one great shining flower, and the longer one looked up, the deeper did the cup of it seem to be. The prince went to the window. As he glanced out through one of the panes, he saw the Tree of Knowledge, with the serpent, and Adam and Eve standing under it.

"Weren't they driven out?" he asked.

The fairy smilingly explained to him that Time had glazed a picture in each pane, but that these were not the usual sort of pictures. No, they had life in them. The leaves quivered on the trees, and the people came and went as in a mirror.

He looked through another pane and there was Jacob's dream, with the ladder that went up to Heaven, and the great angels climbing up and down. Yes, all that ever there was in the world lived on, and moved across these panes of glass. Only Time could glaze such artistic paintings so well.

The fairy smiled and led him on into a vast and lofty hall with walls that seemed transparent. On the walls were portraits, each fairer than the one before. These were millions of blessed souls, a happy choir that sang in perfect harmony. The uppermost faces appeared to be smaller than the tiniest rosebud drawn as a single dot in a picture. In the center of the hall grew a large tree, with luxuriantly hanging branches. Golden apples large and small hung like oranges among the leaves. This was the Tree of Knowledge, of which Adam and Eve had tasted. A sparkling red drop of dew hung from each leaf, as if the tree were weeping tears of blood.

"Now let us get into the boat," the fairy proposed. "There we will have some refreshments on the heaving water. Though the rocking boat stays in one place, we shall see all the lands in the world glide by."

It was marvelous how the whole shore moved. Now the high snow-capped Alps went past, with their clouds and dark evergreen trees. The Alpine horn was heard, deep and melancholy, and the shepherds yodeled gaily in the valley. But soon the boat was overhung by the long arching branches of banana trees. Jet-black swans went swimming by, and the queerest animals and plants were to be seen along the banks. This was New Holland and the fifth quarter of the globe that glided past, with its blue hills in the distance. They heard the songs of the priests and saw the savages dance to the sound of drums and trumpets of bone. The cloud-tipped pyramids of Egypt, the fallen columns, and sphinxes half buried in the sands, swept by. The northern lights blazed over the glaciers around the pole in a display of fireworks that no one could imitate. The prince saw a hundred times more than we can tell, and he was completely happy.

"May I always stay here?" he asked.

"That is up to you," the fairy told him. "Unless, as Adam did, you let yourself be tempted and do what is forbidden, you may stay here always."

"I won't touch the fruit on the Tree of Knowledge," the prince declared. "Here are thousands of other fruits that are just as attractive."

"Look into your heart, and, if you have not strength enough, go back with the East Wind who brought you here. He is leaving soon, and will not return for a hundred years, which you will spend as quickly here as if they were a hundred hours.

"But that is a long time to resist the temptation to sin. When I leave you every evening, I shall have to call, 'Come with me,' and hold out my hands to you. But you must stay behind. Do not follow me, or your desire will grow with every step. You will come into the hall where the Tree of Knowledge grows. I sleep under the arch of its sweet-smelling branches. If you lean over me, I shall have to smile, but if you kiss me on the mouth, this paradise will vanish deep into the earth, and you will lose it. The cutting winds of the wasteland will blow about you, the cold rain will drip from your hair, and sorrow and toil will be your destiny."

"I shall stay," the prince said.

The East Wind kissed his forehead. "Be strong," he said, "and in a hundred years we shall meet here again. Farewell! Farewell!" Then the East Wind spread his tremendous wings that flashed like lightning seen at harvest time or like the northern lights in the winter cold.

"Farewell! Farewell!" the leaves and trees echoed the sound, as the storks and the pelicans flew with him to the end of the garden in lines that were like ribbons streaming through the air.

"Now we will start our dances," the fairy said. "When I have danced the last dance with you at sundown, you will see me hold out my hands to you, and hear me call, 'come with me.' But do not come.

Every evening for a hundred years, I shall have to repeat this. Every time that you resist, your strength will grow, and at last you will not even think of yielding to temptation. This evening is the first time, so take warning!"

And the fairy led him into a large hall of white, transparent lilies. The yellow stamens of each flower formed a small golden harp that vibrated to the music of strings and flutes. The loveliest maidens, floating and slender, came dancing by, clad in such airy gauze that one could see how perfectly shaped they were. They sang of the happiness of life—they who would never die—and they sang that the Garden of Paradise would forever bloom.

The sun went down. The sky turned to shining gold, and in its light, the lilies took on the color of the loveliest roses. The prince drank the sparkling wine that the maidens offered him and felt happier than he had ever been. He watched the background of the hall thrown open, and the Tree of Knowledge standing in a splendor that blinded his eyes. The song from the tree was as soft and lovely as his dear mother's voice, and it was as if she were saying, "My child, my dearest child."

The fairy then held out her hands to him and called most sweetly:

"Follow me! Oh, follow me!"

Forgetting his promise—forgetting everything, on the very first evening that she held out her hands and smiled—he ran toward her. The fragrant air around him became even more sweet, the music of the harps sounded even more lovely, and it seemed as though the millions of happy faces in the hall where the tree grew nodded to him and sang, "One must know all there is to know, for man is the lord of the Earth." And it seemed to him that the drops that fell from the Tree of Knowledge were no longer tears of blood, but red and shining stars.

"Follow me! Follow me!" the quivering voice still called, and at every step that the prince took his cheeks flushed warmer and his pulse beat faster.

"I cannot help it," he said. "This is no sin. It cannot be wicked to follow beauty and happiness. I must see her sleeping. No harm will be done if only I keep myself from kissing her. And I will not kiss her, for I am strong. I have a determined will."

The fairy threw off her bright robe, parted the boughs, and was instantly hidden within them.

"I have not sinned yet," said the prince, "and I shall not!"

He pushed the branches aside. There she lay, already asleep. Lovely as only the fairy of the Garden of Paradise can be, she smiled in her sleep, but as he leaned over her, he saw tears trembling between her lashes.

"Do you weep for me?" he whispered. "Do not weep, my splendid maiden. Not until now have I known the bliss of paradise. It runs through my veins and through all my thoughts. I feel the strength of an angel, and the strength of eternal life in my mortal body. Let eternal night come over me. One moment such as this is worth it all." He kissed away the tears from her eyes, and then his lips had touched her mouth.

Thunder roared, louder and more terrible than any thunder ever heard before, and everything crashed! The lovely fairy and the blossoming paradise dropped away, deeper and deeper. The prince saw it disappear into the dark night. Like a small shining star, it twinkled in the distance. A deathly chill shook his body. He closed his eyes, and for a long time, he lay as if he were dead.

The cold rain fell in his face, and the cutting wind blew about his head. Consciousness returned to him.

"What have I done?" he gasped. "Like Adam, I have sinned—sinned so unforgivably that paradise has dropped away, deep in the earth."

He opened his eyes and he still saw the star far away, the star that twinkled like the Paradise he had lost-it was the morning star in the sky. He rose and found himself in the forest, not far from the cave of the winds. The mother of the winds sat beside him. She looked at him angrily and raised her finger.

"The very first evening!" she said. "I thought that was the way it would be. If you were my son, into the sack you would certainly go."

"Indeed he shall go there!" said Death, a vigorous old man with a scythe in his hand and long black wings. "Yes, he shall be put in a coffin, but not quite yet. Now I shall only mark him. For a while I'll let him walk the Earth to atone for his sins and grow better. But I'll be back someday. Someday, when he least expects me, I shall put him in a black coffin, lift it on my head, and fly upward to the star. There too blooms the Garden of Paradise, and if he is a good and pious man, he will be allowed to enter it. But if his thoughts are bad and his heart is still full of sin, he will sink down deeper with his coffin than Paradise sank. Only once in a thousand years shall I go to see whether he must sink still lower, or may reach the star—that bright star away up there."

THE FLYING TRUNK (1839)

There once was a merchant so wealthy that he could have paved a whole street with silver and still have had enough left over to pave a little alley. But he did nothing of the sort. He knew better ways of using his money than that. If he parted with pennies, they came back to him as crowns. That's the sort of merchant he was—and then he died.

Now his son got all the money, and he led a merry life, went to masquerades every night, made paper dolls out of banknotes, and played ducks and drakes at the lake with gold pieces instead of pebbles. This makes the money go, and his inheritance was soon gone. At last, he had only four pennies, and only a pair of slippers and a dressing gown to wear.

Now his former friends didn't care for him anymore, as he could no longer appear in public with them, but one of them was so good as to send him an old trunk, with the hint that he pack and be off. This was all very well, but he had nothing to pack, so he sat himself in it.

It was no ordinary trunk. Press on the lock, and it would fly. And that's just what it did. *Whisk!* It flew up the chimney, and over the clouds, and away through the skies. The bottom of it was so creaky that he feared he would fall through it, and what a fine somersault he would have made then! Good gracious! But at long last, he came down safely, in the land of the Turks. He hid his trunk under some dry leaves in the woods and set off toward the nearest town. He could do so very well, for the Turks all wear dressing gowns and slippers, just as he did.

When he passed a nurse with a child, he said, "Hello, Turkish nurse. Tell me, what's that great big palace at the edge of town? The one that has its windows up so high."

"That's where the Sultan's daughter lives," said the nurse. "It has been foretold that she will be unhappy when she falls in love, so no one is ever permitted to visit her except in the presence of her mother and father."

"Thank you," said the merchant's son. Back he went to the woods, sat in his trunk, and whisked off to the roof of the palace. From there, he climbed in at the princess's window.

She lay fast asleep on a sofa, and she looked so lovely that the merchant's son couldn't help kissing her. She woke up and was terribly frightened, but he told her he was a Turkish prophet who had sailed through the air just to see her. This pleased her very much.

As they sat there side by side, he told her stories about her eyes. He said they were beautifully dark, deep lakes in which her thoughts went swimming by like mermaids. He told her about her forehead, which he compared to a snow-covered mountainside with its many wonderful halls and pictures. Then he told her about the stork, which brings lovely little children from over the sea. Oh, they were such pretty stories! Then he asked her to marry him, and the princess said yes, right away.

"But you must come on Saturday," she told him, "when my mother and father will be here to have tea with me. They will be so proud when I tell them I am going to marry a prophet. But be sure you have a really pretty tale to tell them, for both my parents love stories. My mother likes them to be elevating and moral, but my father likes them merry, to make him laugh."

"I shall bring no other wedding present than a fairy tale," he told her, and so they parted. But first, the princess made him a present of a gold saber all covered with gold pieces, and this came in very handy.

He flew away, bought himself a new dressing gown, and went to the woods to invent a fairy tale. That wasn't so easy. However, he had it ready promptly on Saturday. The Sultan, his wife, and the whole court awaited him at the princess's tea party. They gave him a splendid reception.

"Won't you tell us a story?" said the Sultan's wife. "One that is instructive and thoughtful."

"One that will make us laugh, too," said the Sultan.

"To be sure," he said, and started his story. Now listen closely.

"There once was a bundle of matches, and they were particularly proud of their lofty ancestry. Their family tree—that is to say, the great pine tree of which they were little splinters—had been a great old tree in the forest. As the matches lay on the kitchen shelf, they talked of their younger days to the tinderbox and an old iron pot beside them.

"'When we were a part of the green branches,' they said, 'then we really were on a green branch! Every morning and evening, we were served the diamond tea that is called dew drops. We had sunshine all day long, and the little birds had to tell us stories. It was plain to see that we were wealthy, for while the other trees' garments lasted only the summer, our family could afford to wear green clothes all the year round. But then the woodcutters came, there was a big revolution, and our family was broken up. The chief support of our family got a place as the mainmast of a fine ship, that could sail around the world if need be. The other branches were scattered in different directions, and now our task is to bring light to the lower classes. That's the reason we distinguished people came to this kitchen.'

"'My lot has been quite different,' said the iron pot, who stood next to the matches. 'From the moment I came into this world, I've known little but cooking and scouring, day in, day out. I look after the solid and substantial part, and am in fact the most important thing in the house. My only amusement comes when dinner is over. Then, clean and tidy, I take my place here to have a sound conversation with my associates. But except for the watering pot, who now and then makes excursions into the yard, we always live indoors. Our only source of news is the market basket, and he speaks most alarmingly about the government and the people. Why, just the other day, an old conservative pot was so upset that he fell down and burst. That basket is a liberal, I tell you!'

"'You talk too much,' the tinderbox flashed sparks from his flint. 'Let's have a pleasant evening.'

"'Yes, let's talk about who among us is most aristocratic,' said the matches.

"'No. I don't like to talk about myself,' said the earthenware crock. 'Let's have some entertainment this evening. I'll begin. I'll tell you the sort of things we already know. That won't tax our imaginations, and it is so amusing. By the Baltic sea, by the beech trees of Denmark—'

"'That's a very pretty beginning,' the plates chattered. 'That's just the kind of story we like.'

"'There I passed my youth in a quiet home, where they polished the furniture, and swept the floor, and hung up fresh curtains every fourteenth day!'

"'How well you tell a story!' said the broom. 'You can hear right away that it's a woman who tells it. There's not a speck of dirt in it.'

"'Yes, one feels that,' said the water pail, and made a happy little jump so the water splashed on the floor.

"'The crock went on with her story, and the end was as good as the beginning.

"All the plates clattered for joy. The broom made a wreath of parsley to crown the crock, because she knew how that would annoy the others. And the broom thought, 'If I crown her tonight, she will crown me tomorrow.'

"'Now I'll do a dance,' said the fire tongs, and dance she did. Yes, good heavens, how she could kick one of her legs up in the air! The old chair cover in the corner split to see it. 'Will you crown me too?' said the tongs, so they gave her a wreath.

"'What a common mob,' said the matches.

"The teapot was asked to sing, but she had a cold in her throat. She said nothing short of boiling water could make her sing, but that was sheer affectation. She wished to sing only for the ladies and gentlemen in the drawing room.

"On the window sill was an old quill pen that the servant used. There was nothing remarkable about him except that he had been dipped too deep in the ink, but in that difference he took pride.

"'The teapot can sing or not, as she pleases,' he declared. 'In a cage, outside my window, there's a nightingale who will sing for us. He hasn't practiced for the occasion, but tonight we won't be too critical.'

"'I find it highly improper,' said the teakettle, who was the official kitchen singer, and a half-sister of the teapot. 'Why should we listen to a foreign bird? Is that patriotic? Let the market basket make the decision.'

"'I am most annoyed,' said the market basket. 'I am more annoyed than anyone can imagine. Is this any way to spend an evening? Wouldn't it be better to call the house to order? Everyone take his appointed place, and I shall run the whole game. That will be something quite different.'

"'Yes. Let us all make a noise,' they clamored.

"Just then, the servant opened the door, and they stood stock-still. Not one had a word to say. But there was not a pot among them who did not know what he could do, and how well qualified he was. 'If I had wanted to,' each one thought, 'we could have a gay evening. No question about it!'

"The servant girl took the matches and struck a light with them. My stars, how they sputtered and flared!

"'Now,' they thought, 'everyone can see we are the first. How brilliant we are! What a light we spread.' Then they burned out."

"That was a delightful story," said the Sultan's wife. "I felt myself right in the kitchen with the matches. My dear prophet, thou shalt certainly marry our daughter."

"Yes, indeed," said the Sultan. "Thou shalt marry her on Monday." They said "Thou" to him now, for he was soon to be one of the family.

So the wedding day was set, and on the evening that preceded it, the whole city was gay with lights. Cookies and cakes were thrown among the people. The boys in the street stood on tiptoe. They shouted, "Hurrah!" and whistled through their fingers. It was all so grand.

"I suppose I really ought to do something too," said the merchant's son. So he bought firecrackers and rockets and fireworks of every sort, loaded his trunk with them, and flew over the town.

Pop! went the crackers, and *swoosh!* went the rockets. The Turks jumped so high that their slippers flopped over their ears. Such shooting stars they never had seen. Now they could understand that it was the prophet of the Turks himself who was to marry their princess.

As soon as the merchant's son came down in the woods, he thought, "I'll go straight to the town to hear what sort of impression I made." It was the natural thing to do.

Oh, what stories they told! Every last man he asked had his own version, but all agreed it had been fine. Very fine!

"I saw the prophet himself," said one. "His eyes shone like stars, and his beard foamed like water."

"He was wrapped in a fiery cloak," said another. "The heads of beautiful angels peeped out of the folds of it."

Yes, he heard wonderful things, and his wedding was to be on the following day. He went back to the woods to rest in his trunk—but what had become of it? The trunk was burned! A spark from the fireworks had set it on fire, and now the trunk was burned to ashes. He couldn't fly anymore. He had no way to reach his bride. She waited for him on the roof, all day long. Most likely, she is waiting there still. But he wanders through the world, telling tales that are not half so merry as that one he told about the matches.

THE STORKS (1839)

On the roof of the last house in a little village was a stork's nest. The mother stork sat in it with her four young ones, who stuck out their heads with their little black beaks. (You see, their beaks had not yet turned red as they would in time.) And a little way off, all alone on the ridge of the roof, stood Father Stork, very upright and stiff. He was really a sentry on guard, but, so that he would not be entirely idle, he had drawn up one leg. My, how grand he looked, standing there on one leg! So still you might have thought he was carved from wood!

"It must look pretty fine for my wife to have a sentry standing by her nest!" he thought. "People don't know I'm her husband; they'll think I'm a servant, ordered to stand here on guard. It looks very smart, I must say."

So he went on, standing on one leg.

A crowd of children were playing down in the street, and as soon as they saw the storks, one of the boldest boys, followed by the others, began to sing the old song about storks. They sang it just as their leader remembered it:

> Stork, stork, long-legged stork,
> Off to your wife you'd better fly.
> She's waiting for you in the nest,
> Rocking four young ones to rest.
> The first he will be hanged,
> The second will be stabbed,
> The third he will be burned,
> And the fourth will be slapped!

"Just listen to what they are saying!" cried the little stork children. "They say we're going to be hanged and burned!"

"Don't pay any attention to that," replied the mother stork crossly. "Don't listen to them, and then it won't make any difference."

But the boys went on singing and pointing mockingly at the storks with their fingers. Only one boy, whose name was Peter, said it was a shame to make fun of the birds, and he wouldn't join the others.

The mother stork tried to comfort her children. "Don't let that bother you at all," she said. "Look how quietly your father is standing, and only on one leg, too!"

"But we're very much frightened!" insisted the young storks, and they drew their heads far back into the nest.

Next day, when the children came out to play and saw the storks, they began their song again:

> The first he will be hanged,
> The second will be burned!

"Are we really going to be hanged and burned?" asked the young storks.

"No, certainly not," replied their mother. "You're going to learn to fly! I'll teach you. Then we'll fly out over the meadows and visit the frogs; they'll bow down to us in the water and sing, 'Co-ax! Co-ax!' and then we'll eat them up. That'll be a lot of fun!"

"And then what?" asked the young storks.

"Then the storks from all over the country will assemble for the autumn maneuvers," their mother continued. "And it is of great importance that you know how to fly well then, for if you can't, the general will stab you dead with his beak; so when I start to teach you, pay attention and learn well."

"Oh, then we'll be stabbed, just the way the boys say! And listen, there they go, saying it again!"

"Never mind them; pay attention to me," said Mother Stork. "After the big maneuvers, we'll fly away to the warm countries, oh, so far away from here, over mountains and forests. We'll get to Egypt, where they have four-cornered houses of stone that come up to a point higher than the clouds. They call them pyramids, and they're even older than a stork could imagine. They have a river there too, that runs out of its banks, and turns the whole land to mud! We walk about in that mud, eating frogs."

"Oh!" cried the young storks.

"Yes, indeed. It's wonderful there. You don't do anything but eat all day long. And while we're so comfortable there, back here, there isn't a green leaf left on the trees, and it's so cold that the clouds freeze to pieces and fall down in little white rags."

She meant snow of course, but she didn't know any other way to explain it to the young ones.

"And do the naughty boys freeze to pieces, too?" asked the young storks.

"No, they don't quite do that," their mother replied. "But they come pretty close to it, and have to sit moping in a dark room. But we, on the other hand, fly about in foreign lands among the flowers and in the warm sunshine."

Some time passed, and the young storks grew large enough so that they could stand up in the nest and look at the wide world around them. Every day, Father Stork brought them beautiful frogs and delicious little snakes and all sorts of dainties that storks like. And how they laughed when he did tricks to amuse them! He would lay his head entirely back on his tail, and clap his beak as if it were a rattle. And then he would tell them stories, all about the marshes that they would see someday.

At last one day, Mother Stork led them all out onto the ridge of the roof.

"Now," she said, "it's time for you to learn to fly." Oh, how they wobbled and how they tottered, trying to balance themselves with their wings, and nearly falling off the roof!

"Watch me now," their mother called. "Hold your head like this! Move your legs like that! One, two! One, two! That'll help you get somewhere in the world!"

Then she flew a little way from the roof, and the young ones made a clumsy attempt to follow. Bumps! There they lay, for their bodies were still too heavy.

"I don't want to fly," complained the youngest one, creeping back into the nest. "I don't care about going to the warm countries at all!"

"Oh, so you want to freeze to death here when the winter comes, do you?" demanded his mother. "You want the boys to come and hang you and beat you and burn you, do you? All right, I'll call them!"

"Oh, no! Don't do that!" cried the little stork, and hopped out on the ridge again with the others.

By the third day, they could fly a little, and so they thought they could soar and hover in the air without moving their wings, but—when they tried it—bumps!—down they fell! They soon found they had to move their wings to keep up in the air.

That same day, the boys came back and began their song again:

Stork, stork, long-legged stork!

"Shall we fly down and pick their eyes out?" asked the young storks eagerly.

"Certainly not," replied their mother promptly. "Let them alone. Pay attention to me. That's much more important. One, two, three! Now we fly around to the right. One, two, three! Now to the left around the chimney. That was very good. That last flap of the wings was so perfect that you can fly with me tomorrow to the marshes. Several very nice stork families go there with their young ones, and I want to show them that mine are much the nicest. Don't forget to strut about; that looks very well and makes you seem important."

"But can't we take revenge on those rude boys first?" asked the young storks.

"Oh, let them scream as much as they like," replied their mother. "You'll fly with the clouds, and way off to the land of the pyramids while they'll be freezing. There won't be a green leaf or a sweet apple here then."

"But we *will* have our revenge!" the young storks whispered to each other, and went on practicing their flying.

Now, among the boys down there in the street, the worst of all was the boy who had begun the teasing song. He was a very little boy, hardly more than six years old, but the young storks thought he was at least a hundred, for he was much bigger than Mother and Father Stork, and how could they know how old children and grown-ups can be?

The young storks made up their minds to take revenge upon this boy, because he was the first to start the song, and he always kept on. As they grew bigger, they were determined to do something about it. At last, to keep them quiet, their mother had to promise them that they would be revenged, but they were not to learn about it until the day before they left the country.

"First, we'll have to see how you behave at the big maneuvers," she warned them. "If you don't do well, so that the general has to stab you with his beak, the boys will be right, at least in that way. We'll see."

"Yes, you'll see," replied the young ones, and my! How they worked! They practiced every day, until they could fly so neatly and lightly that it was a pleasure to watch them.

At last the autumn came on, and all the storks began to assemble before flying away to the warm countries to get away from the winter up here. What a review that was! All of the young storks had to fly over forests and villages to show how well they had learned, for they had a very long journey before them. And the young storks did so well that their report cards were marked, "Remarkably well, with frogs and snakes!" That was the highest mark, and meant that they could eat frogs and snakes as a prize. And that is what they did!

"Now we will have our revenge!" they cried to their mother.

"Yes," their mother agreed. "What I have thought of will be just the right thing to do. I know the pond where all the little human babies lie until the storks come to take them to their parents. The pretty little babies lie in that pond, dreaming more sweetly than they ever dream afterwards. All parents want a little baby, and every child wants a little sister or brother. Now, we'll go to that pond and bring a little baby sister or brother for each of the children who didn't sing that wicked song or make fun of us. But those that did won't get any."

"But that naughty, ugly boy who began the song?" demanded the young storks. "What shall we do with him?"

"In that pond," said his mother slowly, "there is a little baby that has dreamed itself to death; we'll bring that to him. And then he'll cry because we've brought him a little dead brother. But don't forget that good little boy who said it was a shame to make fun of us! We'll take him both a brother *and* a sister! And since his name is Peter, you shall all be called Peter, too!"

It was done just the way she said. And all the young storks were named Peter, and all storks are called Peter to this very day.

THE BUCKWHEAT (1841)

When after a thunderstorm you pass by a field in which buckwheat is growing, you will very often notice that the buckwheat appears quite blackened and singed as if a fire had swept over it. The farmer will tell you, "It got that from lightning." But why and how did it happen?

I'll tell you the story as the sparrow told it to me, and he heard it from an old willow tree that stands beside a buckwheat field. And who could possibly know better than that old willow tree, for he still stands there? He is such a respectable and dignified tree, but is old and crippled, with grass and brambles growing out of a cleft in his middle. He bends forward, with his branches hanging down to the ground as if they were long green hair.

In the fields around the tree, corn was growing, and rye and barley, and oats—oh, very fine oats, which when ripe looked like a whole flock of little yellow canary birds sitting on sprays. The corn stood so prosperous in its field, and the fuller an ear was, the deeper it bent in pious humility.

But just opposite the old willow tree there was also a field of buckwheat. And the buckwheat didn't bend like the rest of the grain, but strutted very proudly and stiffly. "I'm as rich as any old corn," he said. "And besides, I'm lots handsomer; my flowers are as beautiful as the apple blossoms; it's a pleasure to look at me and my family. Do you know anybody more splendid than we are, you old willow tree?"

And the willow tree nodded his head, just as if he were saying, "Yes, certainly I do."

But the buckwheat puffed himself up with foolish pride and said, "That stupid tree's so old he has grass growing out of his stomach!"

Suddenly, a terrible storm broke out, and all the field flowers folded their petals and bowed their delicate heads while the storm passed over them, but the buckwheat strutted with arrogance.

"Bend your head down the way we do!" cried the flowers.

"I don't need to!" replied the buckwheat.

"Bend your head!" the other crops all cried. "The Angel of Storm is flying down on us! He has wings that reach from the clouds right down to Earth, and he'll break you in two before you can cry for mercy!"

"Yes, but I certainly won't bend," replied the buckwheat defiantly.

"Shut up your flowers and bend your leaves," the old willow tree called. "And whatever you do, don't look up at the lightning when the cloud bursts! Even human beings don't dare do that, for in the lightning, one can look into God's Heaven itself, and that sight will strike even human beings blind! So if we, who are so much less worthy than they, dared to do it, what would happen to us!"

"Now I'll certainly look straight up into Heaven itself!" And he did so with pride and haughtiness. So vivid was the lightning that it seemed as if the whole world were on fire.

When the storm finally passed, the flowers and crops stood again in the clear, sweet air, refreshed by the rain; but the buckwheat was blasted coal-black by the lightning, and he was now a dead, useless weed on the field. Then the willow tree waved his branches in the breeze, and great drops of water fell from his green leaves just as if he was crying. "Why are you weeping?" the sparrows asked him. "Everything is so wonderful here. Look how the sun shines, see how the clouds sail across the sky. Can't you smell the fragrance of the flowers and the bushes? Why do you weep, old willow tree?"

Then the willow tree told them of the pride and the haughtiness of the buckwheat, and of the punishment that he had to suffer.

And I who tell you this story have heard it from the sparrows. One evening when I asked them for a tale, they told it to me.

OLE LUKOIE (1841)

There's no one on Earth who knows so many stories as Ole Lukoie—he certainly can tell them!

When night comes on and children still sit in good order around the table or on their little stools, Ole Lukoie arrives. He comes upstairs quietly, for he walks in his socks. Softly he opens the door, and *flick!* He sprinkles sweet milk in the children's eyes—just a tiny bit, but always enough to keep their eyes closed so they won't see him. He tiptoes behind them and breathes softly on their necks, and this makes their heads hang heavy. Oh yes! But it doesn't hurt them, for Ole Lukoie loves children and only wants them to be quiet, and that they are only when they have been put to bed. He wants them to be quiet so that he can tell them stories.

As soon as the children fall asleep, Ole Lukoie sits down on the bed beside them. He is well dressed. His coat is made of silk, but it would be impossible to say what color it is because it gleams red, or green, or blue, as he turns about. Under each arm, he carries an umbrella. One has pictures on it, and that one he opens up over good children. Then they dream the most beautiful stories all night long. The other is just a plain umbrella with nothing on it at all, and that one he opens over naughty children. Then they sleep restlessly, and when they wake up in the morning, they have had no dreams at all.

Now you shall hear how for a whole week, Lukoie came every evening to a little boy named Hjalmar, and what he told him. There are seven of these stories, because there are seven days to a week.

MONDAY

"Now listen," Ole Lukoie said, as soon as he got Hjalmar to bed that evening. "First, let's put things to rights."

Then all the flowers in the flower pots grew to be big trees, arching their long branches under the ceiling and along the walls until the room became a beautiful bower. The limbs were loaded with flowers, each more lovely than any rose, and their fragrance was so sweet that if you wanted to eat it—it was sweeter than jam. The fruit gleamed like gold, and besides, there were dumplings bursting with currants. It was all so splendid!

Suddenly, a dreadful howl came from the table drawer where Hjalmar kept his schoolbooks.

"What can the matter be?" said Ole Lukoie, as he went to the table and opened the drawer. It was the slate, which was throwing a fit and was ready to fall to pieces because there was a mistake in the sum that had been worked on it. The slate pencil tugged and jumped at the end of its string as if it were a little dog. It wanted to correct the sum, but it could not.

Another lamentation came from Hjalmar's copybook. Oh, it was dreadful to listen to. On each page, the capital letters stood one under the other, each with its little letter beside it. This was the copy. Next to these were the letters which Hjalmar had written. Though they thought they looked just like the first ones, they tumbled all over the lines on which they were supposed to stand.

"See, this is how you should hold yourselves," said the copy. "Look, slanting like this, with a bold stroke."

"Oh, how glad we would be to do that!" Hjalmar's letters replied, "but we can't. We are so weak."

"Then you must take medicine," Ole Lukoie told them.

"Oh, no!" they cried, and stood up so straight that it was a pleasure to see them.

"Now we can't tell any stories," said Ole Lukoie. "I must give them their exercises. One, two! One, two!" He put the letters through their paces until they stood straight, more graceful than any copy could stand. But when Ole Lukoie left, and Hjalmar looked at them in the morning, they were just as miserable as ever.

TUESDAY

As soon as Hjalmar was in bed, Ole Lukoie touched all the furniture in the room with his little magic sprinkler, and immediately everything began to talk. Everything talked about itself except the spittoon, which kept silent. It was annoyed that they should be so conceited as to talk only about themselves and think only about themselves, without paying the least attention to it, sitting so humbly in the corner and letting everyone spit at it.

Over the chest of drawers hung a large painting in a gilt frame. It was a landscape in which one could see tall old trees, flowers in the grass, and a large lake from which a river flowed away through the woods, past many castles, far out to the open sea. Ole Lukoie touched the painting with his magic sprinkler, and the birds in it began to sing, the branches stirred on the trees, and the clouds billowed along. You could see their shadows sweep across the landscape.

Then Ole Lukoie lifted little Hjalmar up to the frame and put the boy's feet into the picture, right in the tall grass, and there he stood. The sun shone down on him through the branches of the trees as he ran to the water and got into a little boat that was there. It was painted red and white, and its sails shone like silver. Six swans, each with a golden crown around its neck and a bright blue star upon its forehead, drew the boat through the deep woods, where the trees whispered of robbers and witches, and the flowers spoke about the dainty little elves, and about all that the butterflies had told them.

Splendid fish with scales like gold and silver swam after the boat. Sometimes they gave a leap—so that it said "splash" in the water. Birds red and blue, large and small, flew after the boat in two long lines. The gnats danced, and the cockchafers went *boom, boom!* They all wanted to go with Hjalmar, and every one of them had a story to tell.

What a magnificent voyage that was! Sometimes the forest was deep and dark, and sometimes like the loveliest garden full of sun and flowers. There were palaces of marble and glass, and on the balconies stood princesses. Hjalmar knew them well. They were all little girls with whom he had played. Each of them stretched out her hand, and each held out the prettiest sugar pig that ever a cake woman sold. Hjalmar grasped each sugar pig as he went by, and the princess held fast, so that each got a piece of it. The princess got the smaller piece, and Hjalmar got the larger one. Little princes stood guard at each palace. They saluted with their swords and caused raisins and tin soldiers to shower down. You could tell that they were princes indeed.

Sometimes Hjalmar sailed through the forests, sometimes through great halls, or straight through a town. He also came through the town where his nurse lived, she who had carried him in her arms when he was a very small boy and had always been fond of him. She bowed and waved, and sang the pretty song which she had made up herself and sent to Hjalmar:

> I think of you as often,
> Hjalmar, my little dear,
> As I've kissed your lips so soft, and
> Your cheeks and your eyes so clear.

I heard your first laughter and weeping,
And too soon I heard your good-byes.
May God have you in his keeping,
My angel from the skies.

All the birds sang too, and the flowers danced on their stalks, and the old trees nodded, just as if Ole Lukoie were telling stories to *them*.

WEDNESDAY

How the rain came down outdoors! Hjalmar could hear it in his sleep, and when Ole Lukoie opened the window, the water had risen up to the window sill. There was a real lake outside, and a fine ship lay close to the house.

"If you will sail with me, little Hjalmar," said Ole Lukoie, "you can voyage to distant lands tonight and be back again by morning."

Immediately, Hjalmar stood in his Sunday clothes aboard this splendid ship. And immediately, the weather turned glorious as they sailed through the streets and rounded the church. Now everything was a great wild sea. They sailed until land was far out of sight, and they saw a flock of storks who also came from home and wanted to travel to warmer climes. These storks flew in line, one behind the other, and they had already flown a long, long way. One of them was so weary that his wings could scarcely carry him on. He was the very last in the line, and soon he was left a long way behind the others. Finally, he sank with outstretched wings, lower and lower. He made a few more feeble strokes with his wings, but it was no use. Now he touched the ship's rigging with his feet, slid down the sail, and landed, *bang!* upon the deck.

The cabin boy caught him and put him in the chicken coop with the hens, ducks, and turkeys. The poor stork stood among them most dejected.

"Funny looking fellow!" said all the hens. The turkey gobbler puffed himself as big as ever he could, and asked the stork who he was. The ducks backed off and told each other, "He's a quack! He's a quack!"

Now the stork tried to tell them about the heat of Africa; about the pyramids; and about the ostrich, how it runs across the desert like a wild horse. But the ducks did not understand him. They said to each other, "Don't we all agree that he's a fool?"

"Yes, to be sure, he's a fool," the turkey gobbler gobbled, as the stork kept silent and thought of his Africa.

"What beautiful thin legs you've got," said the turkey gobbler. "What do they cost a yard?"

"Quack, quack, quack!" The ducks all laughed, but the stork pretended not to hear them.

"You can laugh too," the gobbler told him, "for that was a mighty witty remark, or was it too deep for you? No indeed, he isn't very bright, so let's keep on being clever ourselves."

The hens cackled, the ducks went, "Quick, quack! quick, quack!" and it was dreadful to see how they made fun of him among themselves. But Hjalmar opened the back door of the chicken coop and called to the stork. He hopped out on the deck. He was rested now, and he seemed to nod to Hjalmar to thank him. Then he spread his wings and flew away to the warm countries. But the hens clucked, and the ducks quacked, and the turkey gobbler's face turned fiery red.

"Tomorrow, we'll make soup out of you," said Hjalmar. With these words, he woke up in his own little bed. It was a marvelous journey that Ole Lukoie had taken him on during the night.

THURSDAY

"I tell you what," Ole Lukoie said. "Don't be afraid if I show you a little mouse." He held out a hand with the quaint little creature in it. "It has come to ask you to a wedding. There are two little mice here who are to enter into the state of marriage this very night. They live under the floor of your mother's pantry, which is supposed to be the most charming quarters."

"How can I get through that little mouse hole in the floor?" Hjalmar asked.

"Leave that to me," said Ole Lukoie. "I'll make you small enough." Then he touched Hjalmar with his magic sprinkler. He immediately became shorter and shorter, until at last he was only as tall as your finger. "Now you may borrow the tin soldier's uniform. I think it will just fit you, and uniforms always look well when one is at a party."

"Oh, don't they!" said Hjalmar. Instantly he was dressed like the finest tin soldier.

"If you will be so kind as to sit in your mother's thimble," the mouse said, "I shall consider it an honor to pull you along."

"Will you really go to all that trouble, young lady?" Hjalmar cried.

And in this fashion, off they drove to the mouse's wedding. First, they went down a long passage under the floor boards. It was just high enough for them to drive through in the thimble, and the whole passage was lighted with touchwood.

"Doesn't it smell delightful here?" said the mouse. "This whole road has been greased with bacon rinds, and there's nothing better than that."

Now they came to the wedding hall. On the right stood all the little lady mice, whispering and giggling as if they were making fun of each other. On the left stood all the gentlemen mice, twirling their mustaches with their forepaws. The bridegroom and his bride stood in a hollow cheese rind in the center of the floor, and kissed like mad, in plain view of all the guests. But of course, they were engaged, and were to be married immediately.

More and more guests kept crowding in. The mice were nearly trampling each other to death, and the bridal couple had posted themselves in the doorway, so no one could come or leave. Like the passage, this whole hall had been greased with bacon rind, and that was the complete banquet. However, for the dessert, a pea was brought in, on which a little mouse of the family had bitten the name of the bridal couple, that is to say, the first letter of the name. This was a most unusual touch.

All the mice said it was a charming wedding and that the conversation was perfect. And then Hjalmar drove home again. He had been in very high society, for all that he had been obliged to make himself very small to fit in the tin soldier's uniform.

FRIDAY

"It's astonishing how many older people are anxious to get hold of me," said Ole Lukoie. "Especially those whose consciences are bothering them. 'Good little Ole,' they say to me, 'we can't close our eyes. We lie awake all night, facing our wicked deeds that sit on the edge of our beds like ugly little fiends and soak us in hot perspiration. Won't you come and turn them out so that we can have a good night's sleep?' At that, they sigh very deeply. 'We will be glad to pay you for it. Good night, Ole. The money lies on the window sill.' But I don't do things for pay," said Ole Lukoie.

"What are we going to have tonight?" little Hjalmar asked.

"I don't know whether you'd like to go to a wedding again tonight, but it's quite different from the one last night. Your sister's big doll, who looks like a man and is named Herman, is to be married to the doll called Bertha. It's Bertha's birthday, too, so there'll be no end to the presents."

"Yes, I know," Hjalmar told him. "Whenever the dolls need new clothes, my sister either lets them have a birthday or hold a wedding. It must have happened a hundred times already."

"Yes, but tonight is the hundred and first wedding, and, with one hundred and one, things come to an end. That's why it's to be so splendid. Oh, look!"

Hjalmar looked over at the table. There he saw a little pasteboard house with the windows alight, and all the tin soldiers presenting arms in front of it. The bridal couple sat on the floor and leaned against the table leg. They looked thoughtful, and with good reason. Ole Lukoie, rigged out in grandmother's black petticoat, married them off. When the ceremony was over, all the furniture in the room sang the following fine song, which the pencil had written. It went to the tune of the soldier's tattoo:

> Let us lift up our voices as high as the sun,
> In honor of those who today are made one.
> Although neither knows quite what they've done,
> And neither one quite knows who's been won,
> Oh, wood and leather go well together,
> So let's lift up our voices as high as the sun.

Then they were given presents, but they had refused to take any food at all, because they planned to live on love.

"Shall we go to a summer resort, or take a voyage?" the bridegroom asked. They consulted the swallow, who was such a traveler, and the old setting hen who had raised five broods of chicks. The swallow told them about the lovely warm countries where grapes hang in great ripe bunches, where the air is soft, and where the mountains have wonderful colors that they don't have here.

"But they haven't got our green cabbage," the hen said. "I was in the country with all my chickens one summer, and there was a sand pit in which we could scratch all day. We also had access to a garden where cabbages grew. Oh, how green they were! I can't imagine anything lovelier."

"But one cabbage looks just like another," said the swallow, "and then we so often have bad weather. It is cold here—it freezes."

"That's good for the cabbage," said the hen. "Besides, it's quite warm at times. Didn't we have a hot summer four years ago? For five whole weeks, it was so hot that one could scarcely breathe. Then too, we don't have all those poisonous creatures that infest the warm countries, and we don't have robbers. Anyone who doesn't think ours is the most beautiful country is a rascal. Why, he doesn't deserve to live here!" The hen burst into tears. "I have done my share of traveling. I once made a twelve-mile trip in a coop, and there's no pleasure at all in traveling."

"Isn't the hen a sensible woman!" said Bertha, the doll. "I don't fancy traveling in the mountains because first you go up, and then you go down. No, we will move out by the sand pit and take our walks in the cabbage patch."

That settled the matter.

SATURDAY

"Shall we have some stories?" little Hjalmar asked, as soon as Ole Lukoie had put him to bed.

"There's no time for any tonight," Ole told him, as he spread his best umbrella over the boy. "Just look at these Chinamen."

The whole umbrella looked like a large Chinese bowl, with blue trees and arched bridges on which little Chinamen stood nodding their heads.

"We must have all the world spruced up by tomorrow morning," said Ole. "It's a holiday because it is Sunday. I must go to church steeples to see that the little church goblins are polishing the bells so that they will sound their best. I must go out into the fields to see whether the wind is blowing the dust off of the leaves and grass, and my biggest job of all will be to take down all the stars and shine them. I put them in my apron, but first, each star must be numbered and the hole from which it comes must be numbered the same, so that they go back in their proper places, or they wouldn't stick. Then we would have too many falling stars, for one after another would come tumbling down."

"Oh, I say, Mr Lukoie," said an old portrait that hung on the wall of Hjalmar's bedroom. "I am Hjalmar's great-grandfather. I thank you for telling the boy your stories, but you mustn't put wrong ideas in his head. The stars can't be taken down and polished. The stars are worlds too, just like Earth, and that's the beauty of them."

"My thanks, you old great-grandfather," said Ole Lukoie. "I thank you, indeed! You are the head of the family, you are the oldest of the ancestors, but I am older than you are. I am an old heathen. The Greeks and the Romans called me their god of dreams. I have been to the nobles' homes, and still go there. I know how to behave with all people, great and small. Now you may tell stories yourself." Ole Lukoie tucked his umbrella under his arm and took himself off.

"Well! It seems one can't even express an opinion these days," the old portrait grumbled. And Hjalmar woke up.

SUNDAY

"Good evening," said Ole Lukoie.

Hjalmar nodded, and ran to turn his great-grandfather's portrait to the wall so that it wouldn't interrupt them, as it had the night before.

"Now," he said, "you must tell stories; about the five peas who lived in a pod, about the rooster's foot-track that courted the hen's foot-track, and about the darning needle who gave herself such airs because she thought she was a sewing needle."

"That would be too much of a good thing," said Ole Lukoie. "You know that I would rather show you things. I shall show you my own brother. He too is named Ole Lukoie, but he comes only once to anyone. When he comes, he takes people for a ride on his horse and tells them stories. He only knows two. One is more beautiful than anyone on Earth can imagine, and the other is horrible beyond description." Then Ole Lukoie lifted little Hjalmar up to the window. "There," he said, "you can see my brother, the other Ole Lukoie. He is also called Death. You can see that he doesn't look nearly as bad as they make him out to be in the picture books, where he is only bones and knuckles. No, his coat is embroidered with silver. It is the magnificent uniform of a hussar, and a cloak of black velvet floats behind him and billows over his horse. See how he gallops along."

And Hjalmar saw how the other Ole Lukoie rode off on his horse with young folk as well as old people. He took some up before him, and some behind, but first, he always asked them:

"What conduct is marked on your report card?" They all said, "Good," but he said, "Indeed. Let me see for myself." Then they had to show him the card. All those who were marked "very good" or "excellent," he put on his horse in front of him, and told them a lovely story. But those who were marked "below average" or "bad" had to ride behind him, and he told them a frightful tale. They shivered and wept, and tried to jump down off the horse. But this they couldn't do. They had immediately grown fast to it.

"Why, Death is the most beautiful Ole Lukoie," Hjalmar exclaimed. "I'm not afraid of him."

"You needn't be," Ole Lukoie told him, "only be sure that you have a good report card."

"There now, that's instructive," great-grandfather's portrait muttered. "It certainly helps to speak one's mind." He was completely satisfied.

You see, that's the story of Ole Lukoie. Tonight, he himself can tell you some more.

THE SWINEHERD (1841)

Once there was a poor prince. He had a kingdom; it was very tiny. Still, it was large enough to marry upon, and on marriage his heart was set.

Now it was certainly rather bold of him to say, "Will you have me?" to the emperor's own daughter. But he did, for his name was famous, and far and near there were hundreds of princesses who would have said, "Yes!" and "Thank you!" too. But what did the emperor's daughter say? Well, we'll soon find out.

A rose tree grew over the grave of the prince's father. It was such a beautiful tree. It bloomed only once in five long years, and then it bore but a single flower. Oh, that was a rose indeed! The fragrance of it would make a man forget all of his sorrows and his cares. The prince had a nightingale, too. It sang as if all the sweet songs of the world were in its little throat. The nightingale and the rose were to be gifts to the princess. So they were sent to her in two large silver cases.

The emperor ordered the cases carried before him to the great hall where the princess was playing at "visitors," with her maids-in-waiting. They seldom did anything else. As soon as the princess saw that the large cases contained presents, she clapped her hands in glee. "Oh," she said, "I do hope I get a little pussycat." She opened a casket, and there was the splendid rose.

"Oh, how pretty it is," said all the maids-in-waiting.

"It's more than pretty," said the emperor. "It's superb."

But the princess poked it with her finger, and she almost started to cry. "Oh, fie! Papa," she said, "it isn't artificial. It is natural."

"Oh, fie," said all her maids-in-waiting, "it's only natural."

"Well," said the emperor, "before we fret and pout, let's see what's in the other case." He opened it, and out came the nightingale, which sang so sweetly that for a little while no one could think of a single thing to say against it.

"*Superbe!*" "*Charmant!*" said the maids-in-waiting with their smattering of French, each one speaking it worse than the next.

"How the bird does remind me of our lamented empress' music box," said one old courtier. "It has just the same tone, and the very same way of trilling."

The emperor wept like a child. "Ah, me," he said.

"Bird?" said the princess. "You mean to say it's real?"

"A real live bird," the men who had brought it assured her.

"Then let it fly and begone," said the princess, who refused to hear a word about the prince, much less to see him.

But it was not so easy to discourage him. He darkened his face both brown and black, pulled his hat down over his eyes, and knocked at the door.

"Hello, Emperor," he said. "How do you do? Can you give me some work about the palace?"

"Well," said the emperor, "people are always looking for jobs, but let me see. I do need somebody to tend the pigs, because we've got so many of them."

So the prince was appointed "Imperial Pig Tender." He was given a wretched little room down by the pigsties, and there he had to live. All day long, he sat and worked, as busy as could be, and by evening, he had made a neat little kettle with bells all around the brim of it. When the kettle boiled, the bells would tinkle and play the old tune:

Oh, dear Augustin,
All is lost, lost, lost.

But that was the least of it. If anyone put his finger in the steam from this kettle, he could immediately smell whatever there was for dinner in any cooking pot in town. No rose was ever like this!

Now the princess happened to be passing by with all of her maids-in-waiting. When she heard the tune, she stopped and looked pleased, for she too knew how to play "Oh, dear Augustin." It was the only tune she did know, and she played it with one finger.

"Why, that's the very same tune I play. Isn't the swineherd highly accomplished? I say," she ordered, "go and ask him the price of the instrument."

So one of the maids had to go in among the pigsties, but she put on her overshoes first.

"What will you take for the kettle?" she asked.

"I'll take ten kisses from the princess," said the swineherd.

"Oo, for goodness' sakes!" said the maid.

"And I won't take less," said the swineherd.

"Well, what does he say?" the princess wanted to know.

"I can't tell you," said the maid. "He's too horrible."

"Then whisper it close to my ear." She listened to what the maid had to whisper. "Oo, isn't he naughty!" said the princess and walked right away from there. But she had not gone very far when she heard the pretty bells play again:

Oh, dear Augustin,
All is lost, lost, lost.

"I say," the princess ordered, "ask him if he will take his ten kisses from my maids-in-waiting."

"No, I thank you," said the swineherd. "Ten kisses from the princess, or I keep my kettle."

"Now isn't that disgusting!" said the princess. "At least stand around me so that no one can see."

So her maids stood around her and spread their skirts wide, while the swineherd took his ten kisses. Then the kettle was hers.

And then the fun started. Never was a kettle kept so busy. They boiled it from morning till night. From the chamberlain's banquet to the cobbler's breakfast, they knew all that was cooked in town. The maids-in-waiting danced about and clapped their hands.

"We know who's having sweet soup and pancakes. We know who's having porridge and cutlets. Isn't it interesting?"

"Most interesting," said the head lady of the bedchamber.

"Now, after all, I'm the emperor's daughter," the princess reminded them. "Don't you tell how I got it."

"Goodness gracious, no!" said they all.

But the swineherd—that's the prince, for nobody knew he wasn't a real swineherd—was busy as he could be. This time, he made a rattle. Swing it around, and it would play all the waltzes, jigs, and dance tunes that have been heard since the beginning of time.

"Why it's *superbe*!" said the princess as she came by. "I never did hear better music. I say, go and ask him the price of that instrument. But mind you—no more kissing!"

"He wants a hundred kisses from the princess," said the maid-in-waiting who had been in to ask him.

"I believe he's out of his mind," said the princess, and she walked right away from there. But she had not gone very far when she said, "After all, I'm the emperor's daughter, and it's my duty to encourage the arts. Tell him he can have ten kisses, as he did yesterday, but he must collect the rest from my maids-in-waiting."

"Oh, but we wouldn't like that," said the maids.

"Fiddlesticks," said the princess, "If he can kiss me, he certainly can kiss you. Remember, I'm the one who gives you board and wages." So the maid had to go back to the swineherd.

"A hundred kisses from the princess," the swineherd told her, "or let each keep his own."

"Stand around me," said the princess, and all her maids-in-waiting stood in a circle to hide her while the swineherd began to collect.

"What can have drawn such a crowd near the pigsties?" the emperor wondered, as he looked down from his balcony. He rubbed his eyes, and he put on his spectacles. "Bless my soul if those maids-in-waiting aren't up to mischief again. I'd better go see what they are up to now."

He pulled his easy slippers up over his heels, though ordinarily he just shoved his feet in them and let them flap. Then, my! How much faster he went. As soon as he came near the pens, he took very soft steps. The maids-in-waiting were so busy counting kisses, to see that everything went fair and that he didn't get too many or too few, that they didn't notice the emperor behind them. He stood on his tiptoes.

"Such naughtiness!" he said when he saw them kissing, and he boxed their ears with his slipper just as the swineherd was taking his eighty-sixth kiss.

"Be off with you!" the emperor said in a rage. And both the princess and the swineherd were turned out of his empire. And there she stood crying. The swineherd scolded, and the rain came down in torrents.

"Poor little me," said the princess. "If only I had married the famous prince! Oh, how unlucky I am!"

The swineherd slipped behind a tree, wiped the brown and black off his face, threw off his ragged clothes, and showed himself in such princely garments that the princess could not keep from curtsying.

"I have only contempt for you," he told her. "You turned down a prince's honest offer, and you didn't appreciate the rose or the nightingale, but you were all too ready to kiss a swineherd for a tinkling toy to amuse you. You are properly punished."

Then the prince went home to his kingdom, and shut and barred the door. The princess could stay outside and sing to her heart's content:

Oh, dear Augustin,
All is lost, lost, lost.

THE NIGHTINGALE (1843)

The emperor of China is a Chinaman, as you most likely know, and everyone around him is a Chinaman, too. It's been a great many years since this story happened in China, but that's all the more reason for telling it before it gets forgotten.

The emperor's palace was the wonder of the world. It was made entirely of fine porcelain, extremely expensive but so delicate that you could touch it only with the greatest of care. In the garden, the rarest flowers bloomed, and to the prettiest ones were tied little silver bells that tinkled so that no one could pass by without noticing them. Yes, all things were arranged according to plan in the emperor's garden, though how far and wide it extended not even the gardener knew. If you walked on and on, you came to a fine forest where the trees were tall and the lakes were deep. The forest ran down to the deep blue sea, so close that tall ships could sail under the branches of the trees. In these trees a nightingale lived. His song was so ravishing that even the poor fisherman, who had much else to do, stopped to listen on the nights when he went out to cast his nets, and heard the nightingale.

"How beautiful that is," he said, but he had his work to attend to, and he would forget the bird's song. But the next night, when he heard the song he would again say, "How beautiful."

From all the countries in the world, travelers came to the city of the emperor. They admired the city. They admired the palace and its garden, but when they heard the nightingale, they said, "That is the best of all."

And the travelers told of it when they came home, and men of learning wrote many books about the town, about the palace, and about the garden. But they did not forget the nightingale. They praised him highest of all, and those who were poets wrote magnificent poems about the nightingale who lived in the forest by the deep sea.

These books went all the world over, and some of them came even to the emperor of China. He sat in his golden chair and read, nodding his head in delight over such glowing descriptions of his city, and palace, and garden. *But the nightingale is the best of all*. He read it in print.

"What's this?" the emperor exclaimed. "I don't know of any nightingale. Can there be such a bird in my empire—in my own garden—and I not know it? To think that I should have to learn of it out of a book."

Thereupon, he called his lord-in-waiting, who was so exalted that when anyone of lower rank dared speak to him, or ask him a question, he only answered, "P," which means nothing at all.

"They say there's a most remarkable bird called the nightingale," said the emperor. "They say it's the best thing in all my empire. Why haven't I been told about it?"

"I've never heard the name mentioned," said the lord-in-waiting. "He hasn't been presented at court."

"I command that he appear before me this evening, and sing," said the emperor. "The whole world knows my possessions better than I do!"

"I never heard of him before," said the lord-in-waiting. "But I shall look for him. I'll find him."

But where? The Lord-in-Waiting ran upstairs and downstairs, through all the rooms and corridors, but no one he met with had ever heard tell of the nightingale. So the lord-in-waiting ran back to the emperor, and said it must be a story invented by those who write books. "Your Imperial Majesty would scarcely believe how much of what is written is fiction, if not downright black art."

"But the book I read was sent me by the mighty Emperor of Japan," said the emperor. "Therefore, it can't be a pack of lies. I must hear this nightingale. I insist upon his being here this evening. He has my high imperial favor, and if he is not forthcoming I will have the whole court punched in the stomach, directly after supper."

"Tsing-pe!" said the lord-in-waiting, and off he scurried up the stairs, through all the rooms and corridors. And half the court ran with him, for no one wanted to be punched in the stomach after supper.

There was much questioning as to the whereabouts of this remarkable nightingale, who was so well known everywhere in the world except at home. At last, they found a poor little kitchen girl, who said:

"The nightingale? I know him well. Yes, indeed, he can sing. Every evening, I get leave to carry scraps from table to my sick mother. She lives down by the shore. When I start back, I am tired, and rest in the woods. Then I hear the nightingale sing. It brings tears to my eyes. It's as if my mother were kissing me."

"Little kitchen girl," said the lord-in-waiting, "I'll have you appointed scullion for life. I'll even get permission for you to watch the emperor dine, if you'll take us to the nightingale who is commanded to appear at court this evening."

So they went into the forest where the nightingale usually sang. Half the court went along. On the way to the forest, a cow began to moo.

"Oh," cried a courtier, "that must be it. What a powerful voice for a creature so small. I'm sure I've heard her sing before."

"No, that's the cow," said the little kitchen girl. "We still have a long way to go."

Then the frogs in the marsh began to croak.

"Glorious!" said the Chinese court person. "Now I hear it—like church bells ringing."

"No, that's the frogs," said the little kitchen girl. "But I think we shall hear him soon."

Then the nightingale sang.

"That's it," said the little kitchen girl. "Listen, listen! And yonder he sits." She pointed to a little gray bird high up in the branches.

"Is it possible?" cried the lord-in-waiting. "Well, I never would have thought he looked like that, so unassuming. But he has probably turned pale at seeing so many important people around him."

"Little nightingale," the kitchen girl called to him, "our gracious emperor wants to hear you sing."

"With the greatest of pleasure," answered the nightingale, and burst into song.

"Very similar to the sound of glass bells," said the lord-in-waiting. "Just see his little throat, how busily it throbs. I'm astounded that we have never heard him before. I'm sure he'll be a great success at court."

"Shall I sing to the emperor again?" asked the nightingale, for he thought that the emperor was present.

"My good little nightingale," said the lord-in-waiting, "I have the honor to command your presence at a court function this evening, where you'll delight His Majesty the Emperor with your charming song."

"My song sounds best in the woods," said the nightingale, but he went with them willingly when he heard it was the emperor's wish.

The palace had been especially polished for the occasion. The porcelain walls and floors shone in the rays of many gold lamps. The flowers with tinkling bells on them had been brought into the halls, and there was such a commotion of coming and going that all the bells chimed away until you could scarcely hear yourself talk.

In the middle of the great throne room, where the emperor sat, there was a golden perch for the nightingale. The whole court was there, and they let the little kitchen girl stand behind the door, now that she had been appointed "Imperial Pot-Walloper." Everyone was dressed in his best, and all stared at the little gray bird to which the emperor graciously nodded.

And the nightingale sang so sweetly that tears came into the emperor's eyes and rolled down his cheeks. Then the nightingale sang still more sweetly, and it was the emperor's heart that melted. The emperor was so touched that he wanted his own golden slipper hung round the nightingale's neck, but the nightingale declined it with thanks. He had already been amply rewarded.

"I have seen tears in the emperor's eyes," he said. "Nothing could surpass that. An emperor's tears are strangely powerful. I have my reward." And he sang again, gloriously.

"It's the most charming coquetry we ever heard," said the ladies-in-waiting. And they took water in their mouths so they could gurgle when anyone spoke to them, hoping to rival the nightingale. Even the lackeys and chambermaids said they were satisfied, which was saying a great deal, for they were the hardest to please. Unquestionably, the nightingale was a success. He was to stay at court and have his own cage. He had permission to go for a walk twice a day, and once a night. Twelve footmen attended him, each one holding tight to a ribbon tied to the bird's leg. There wasn't much fun in such outings.

The whole town talked about the marvelous bird, and if two people met, one could scarcely say "night" before the other said "gale," and then they would sigh in unison, with no need for words. Eleven pork-butchers' children were named "nightingale," but not one could sing.

One day, the emperor received a large package labeled "The Nightingale."

"This must be another book about my celebrated bird," he said. But it was not a book. In the box was a work of art, an artificial nightingale most like the real one except that it was encrusted with diamonds, rubies, and sapphires. When it was wound, the artificial bird could sing one of the nightingale's songs while it wagged its glittering gold and silver tail. Round its neck hung a ribbon inscribed: "The Emperor of Japan's nightingale is a poor thing compared with that of the Emperor of China."

"Isn't that nice?" everyone said, and the man who had brought the contraption was immediately promoted to be "Imperial-Nightingale-Fetcher-in-Chief."

"Now let's have them sing together. What a duet that will be," said the courtiers.

So they had to sing together, but it didn't turn out so well, for the real nightingale sang whatever came into his head while the imitation bird sang by rote.

"That's not the newcomer's fault," said the music master. "He keeps perfect time, just as I have taught him."

Then they had the imitation bird sing by itself. It met with the same success as the real nightingale, and besides, it was much prettier to see, all sparkling like bracelets and breastpins. Three and thirty times it sang the selfsame song without tiring. The courtiers would gladly have heard it again, but the emperor said the real nightingale should now have his turn. Where was he? No one had noticed him flying out the open window, back to his home in the green forest.

"But what made him do that?" said the emperor.

All the courtiers slandered the nightingale, whom they called a most ungrateful wretch. "Luckily, we have the best bird," they said, and made the imitation one sing again. That was the thirty-fourth time they had heard the same tune, but they didn't quite know it by heart because it was a difficult piece. And the music master praised the artificial bird beyond measure. Yes, he said that the contraption was much better than the real nightingale, not only in its dress and its many beautiful diamonds, but also in its mechanical interior.

"You see, ladies and gentlemen, and above all Your Imperial Majesty, with a real nightingale, one never knows what to expect, but with this artificial bird, everything goes according to plan. Nothing is left to chance. I can explain it and take it to pieces, and show how the mechanical wheels are arranged, how they go around, and how one follows after another."

"Those are our sentiments exactly," said they all, and the music master was commanded to have the bird give a public concert next Sunday. The emperor said that his people should hear it. And hear it they did, with as much pleasure as if they had all gotten tipsy on tea, Chinese fashion. Everyone said, "Oh," and held up the finger we call "lickpot," and nodded his head. But the poor fishermen who had heard the real nightingale said, "This is very pretty, very nearly the real thing, but not quite. I can't imagine what's lacking."

The real nightingale had been banished from the land. In its place, the artificial bird sat on a cushion beside the emperor's bed. All its gold and jeweled presents lay about it, and its title was now "Grand Imperial Singer-of-the-Emperor-to-Sleep." In rank, it stood first from the left, for the emperor gave preeminence to the left side because of the heart. Even an emperor's heart is on the left.

The music master wrote a twenty-five-volume book about the artificial bird. It was learned, long-winded, and full of hard Chinese words, yet everybody said they read and understood it, lest they show themselves stupid and would then have been punched in their stomachs.

After a year the emperor, his court, and all the other Chinamen knew every twitter of the artificial song by heart. They liked it all the better now that they could sing it themselves. Which they did. The street urchins sang, "Zizizi! kluk, kluk, kluk," and the emperor sang it, too. That's how popular it was.

But one night, while the artificial bird was singing his best by the emperor's bed, something inside the bird broke with a twang. *Whir-r-r*, all the wheels ran down, and the music stopped. Out of bed jumped the emperor and sent for his own physician, but what could he do? Then he sent for a watchmaker, who conferred, and investigated, and patched up the bird after a fashion. But the watchmaker said that the bird must be spared too much exertion, for the cogs were badly worn, and if he replaced them, it would spoil the tune. This was terrible. Only once a year could they let the bird sing, and that was almost too much for it. But the music master made a little speech full of hard Chinese words that meant that the bird was as good as it ever was. So that made it as good as ever.

Five years passed by, and a real sorrow befell the whole country. The Chinamen loved their emperor, and now he fell ill. Ill unto death, it was said. A new emperor was chosen in readiness. People stood in the palace street and asked the lord-in-waiting how it went with their emperor.

"P," said he, and shook his head.

Cold and pale lay the emperor in his great magnificent bed. All the courtiers thought he was dead, and went to do homage to the new emperor. The lackeys went off to trade gossip, and the chambermaids gave a coffee party because it was such a special occasion. Deep mats were laid in all the rooms and passageways to muffle each footstep. It was quiet in the palace, dead quiet. But the emperor was not yet dead. Stiff and pale he lay, in his magnificent bed with the long velvet curtains and the heavy gold tassels. High in the wall was an open window, through which moonlight fell on the emperor and his artificial bird.

The poor emperor could hardly breathe. It was as if something were sitting on his chest. Opening his eyes he saw it was Death who sat there, wearing the emperor's crown, handling the emperor's gold sword, and carrying the emperor's silk banner. Among the folds of the great velvet curtains there were strangely familiar faces. Some were horrible, others gentle and kind. They were the emperor's deeds, good and bad, who came back to him now that Death sat on his heart.

"Don't you remember—?" they whispered one after the other. "Don't you remember—?" And they told him of things that made the cold sweat run on his forehead.

"No, I will not remember!" said the emperor. "Music, music, sound the great drum of China, lest I hear what they say!" But they went on whispering, and Death nodded, Chinese fashion, at every word.

"Music, music!" the emperor called. "Sing, my precious little golden bird, sing! I have given you gold and precious presents. I have hung my golden slipper around your neck. Sing, I pray you, sing!"

But the bird stood silent. There was no one to wind it, nothing to make it sing. Death kept staring through his great hollow eyes, and it was quiet, deadly quiet.

Suddenly, through the window came a burst of song. It was the little live nightingale who sat outside on a spray. He had heard of the emperor's plight and had come to sing of comfort and hope. As he sang, the phantoms grew pale, and still more pale, and the blood flowed quicker and quicker through the emperor's feeble body. Even Death listened, and said, "Go on, little nightingale, go on!"

"But," said the little nightingale, "will you give back that sword, that banner, that emperor's crown?"

And Death gave back these treasures for a song. The nightingale sang on. It sang of the quiet churchyard where white roses grow, where the elder flowers make the air sweet, and where the grass is always green, wet with the tears of those who are still alive. Death longed for his garden. Out through the windows drifted a cold gray mist, as Death departed.

"Thank you, thank you!" the emperor said. "Little bird from Heaven, I know you of old. I banished you once from my land, and yet you have sung away the evil faces from my bed, and Death from my heart. How can I repay you?"

"You have already rewarded me," said the nightingale. "I brought tears to your eyes when first I sang for you. To the heart of a singer, those are more precious than any precious stone. But sleep now, and grow fresh and strong while I sing." He sang on until the emperor fell into a sound, refreshing sleep, a sweet and soothing slumber.

The sun was shining in his window when the emperor awoke, restored and well. Not one of his servants had returned to him, for they thought him dead, but the nightingale still sang.

"You must stay with me always," said the emperor. "Sing to me only when you please. I shall break the artificial bird into a thousand pieces."

"No," said the nightingale. "It did its best. Keep it near you. I cannot build my nest here, or live in a palace, so let me come as I will. Then

I shall sit on the spray by your window, and sing things that will make you happy and thoughtful too. I'll sing about those who are gay, and those who are sorrowful. My songs will tell you of all the good and evil that you do not see. A little singing bird flies far and wide, to the fisherman's hut, to the farmer's home, and to many other places a long way off from you and your court. I love your heart better than I do your crown, and yet the crown has been blessed too. I will come and sing to you, if you will promise me one thing."

"All that I have is yours," cried the emperor, who stood in his imperial robes, which he had put on himself, and held his heavy gold sword to his heart.

"One thing only," the nightingale asked. "You must not let anyone know that you have a little bird who tells you everything; then all will go even better." And away he flew.

The servants came in to look after their dead emperor—and there they stood. And the emperor said, "Good morning."

THE UGLY DUCKLING (1843)

It was so beautiful out on the country, it was summer—the wheat fields were golden, the oats were green, and down among the green meadows, the hay was stacked. There the stork minced about on his red legs, clacking away in Egyptian, which was the language his mother had taught him. Round about the field and meadowlands rose vast forests in which deep lakes lay hidden. Yes, it was indeed lovely out there in the country.

In the midst of the sunshine, there stood an old manor house that had a deep moat around it. From the walls of the manor right down to the water's edge great burdock leaves grew, and there were some so tall that little children could stand upright beneath the biggest of them. In this wilderness of leaves, which was as dense as the forests itself, a duck sat on her nest, hatching her ducklings. She was becoming somewhat weary, because sitting is such a dull business and scarcely anyone came to see her. The other ducks would much rather swim in the moat than waddle out and squat under the burdock leaf to gossip with her.

But at last, the eggshells began to crack, one after another. "Peep, peep!" said the little things, as they came to life and poked out their heads.

"Quack, quack!" said the duck, and quick as quick can be they all waddled out to have a look at the green world under the leaves. Their mother let them look as much as they pleased, because green is good for the eyes.

"How wide the world is," said all the young ducks, for they certainly had much more room now than they had when they were in their eggshells.

"Do you think this is the whole world?" their mother asked. "Why, it extends on and on, clear across to the other side of the garden and right on into the parson's field, though that is further than I have ever been. I do hope you are all hatched," she said as she got up. "No, not quite all. The biggest egg still lies here. How much longer is this going to take? I am really rather tired of it all," she said, but she settled back on her nest.

"Well, how goes it?" asked an old duck who came to pay her a call.

"It takes a long time with that one egg," said the duck on the nest. "It won't crack, but look at the others. They are the cutest little ducklings I've ever seen. They look exactly like their father, the wretch! He hasn't come to see me at all."

"Let's have a look at the egg that won't crack," the old duck said. "It's a turkey egg, and you can take my word for it. I was fooled like that once myself. What trouble and care I had with those turkey children, for I may as well tell you, they are afraid of the water. I simply could not get them into it. I quacked and snapped at them, but it wasn't a bit of use. Let me see the egg. Certainly, it's a turkey egg. Let it lie, and go teach your other children to swim."

"Oh, I'll sit a little longer. I've been at it so long already that I may as well sit here half the summer."

"Suit yourself," said the old duck, and away she waddled.

At last, the big egg did crack. "Peep," said the young one, and out he tumbled, but he was so big and ugly.

The duck took a look at him. "That's a frightfully big duckling," she said. "He doesn't look the least like the others. Can he really be a turkey baby? Well, well! I'll soon find out. Into the water he shall go, even if I have to shove him in myself."

Next day, the weather was perfectly splendid, and the sun shone down on all the green burdock leaves. The mother duck led her whole family down to the moat. Splash! She took to the water. "Quack,

quack," said she, and one duckling after another plunged in. The water went over their heads, but they came up in a flash, and floated to perfection. Their legs worked automatically, and they were all there in the water. Even the big, ugly gray one was swimming along.

"Why, that's no turkey," she said. "See how nicely he uses his legs, and how straight he holds himself. He's my very own son after all, and quite good-looking if you look at him properly. Quack, quack come with me. I'll lead you out into the world and introduce you to the duck yard. But keep close to me so that you won't get stepped on, and watch out for the cat!"

Thus they sallied into the duck yard, where all was in an uproar because two families were fighting over the head of an eel. But the cat got it, after all.

"You see, that's the way of the world." The mother duck licked her bill because she wanted the eel's head for herself. "Stir your legs. Bustle about, and mind that you bend your necks to that old duck over there. She's the noblest of us all, and has Spanish blood in her. That's why she's so fat. See that red rag around her leg? That's a wonderful thing, and the highest distinction a duck can get. It shows that they don't want to lose her, and that she's to have special attention from man and beast. Shake yourselves! Don't turn your toes in. A well-bred duckling turns his toes way out, just as his father and mother do—this way. So then! Now duck your necks and say quack!"

They did as she told them, but the other ducks around them looked on and said right out loud, "See here! Must we have this brood too, just as if there weren't enough of us already? And—fie! what an ugly-looking fellow that duckling is! We won't stand for him." One duck charged up and bit his neck.

"Let him alone," his mother said. "He isn't doing any harm."

"Possibly not," said the duck who bit him, "but he's too big and strange, and therefore he needs a good whacking."

"What nice-looking children you have, Mother," said the old duck with the rag around her leg. "They are all pretty except that one. He didn't come out so well. It's a pity you can't hatch him again."

"That can't be managed, your ladyship," said the mother. "He isn't so handsome, but he's as good as can be, and he swims just as well as the rest, or, I should say, even a little better than they do. I hope his looks will improve with age, and after a while, he won't seem so big. He took

too long in the egg, and that's why his figure isn't all that it should be."
She pinched his neck and preened his feathers. "Moreover, he's a drake,
so it won't matter so much. I think he will be quite strong, and I'm sure
he will amount to something."

"The other ducklings are pretty enough," said the old duck. "Now
make yourselves right at home, and if you find an eel's head, you may
bring it to me."

So they felt quite at home. But the poor duckling who had been
the last one out of his egg, and who looked so ugly, was pecked
and pushed about and made fun of by the ducks and the chickens as
well. "He's too big," said they all. The turkey gobbler, who thought
himself an emperor because he was born wearing spurs, puffed up
like a ship under full sail and bore down upon him, gobbling and
gobbling until he was red in the face. The poor duckling did not know
where he dared stand or where he dared walk. He was so sad because
he was so desperately ugly, and because he was the laughing stock of
the whole barnyard.

So it went on the first day, and after that, things went from bad to
worse. The poor duckling was chased and buffeted about by everyone.
Even his own brothers and sisters abused him. "Oh," they would
always say, "how we wish the cat would catch you, you ugly thing."
And his mother said, "How I do wish you were miles away." The ducks
nipped him, and the hens pecked him, and the girl who fed them kicked
him with her foot.

So he ran away and he flew over the fence. The little birds in the
bushes darted up in a fright. "That's because I'm so ugly," he thought,
and closed his eyes, but he ran on just the same until he reached the
great marsh where the wild ducks lived. There he lay all night long,
weary and disheartened.

When morning came, the wild ducks flew up to have a look at their
new companion. "What sort of creature are you?" they asked, as the
duckling turned in all directions, bowing his best to them all. "You are
terribly ugly," they told him, "but that's nothing to us so long as you
don't marry into our family."

Poor duckling! Marriage certainly had never entered his mind. All
he wanted was for them to let him lie among the reeds and drink a little
water from the marsh.

There he stayed for two whole days. Then he met two wild geese, or rather wild ganders—for they were males. They had not been out of the shell very long, and that's what made them so sure of themselves.

"Say there, comrade," they said, "you're so ugly that we have taken a fancy to you. Come with us and be a bird of passage. In another marsh nearby, there are some fetching wild geese, all nice young ladies who know how to quack. You are so ugly that you'll completely turn their heads."

Bing! Bang! Shots rang in the air, and these two ganders fell dead among the reeds. The water was red with their blood. *Bing! Bang!* the shots rang, and as whole flocks of wild geese flew up from the reeds, another volley crashed. A great hunt was in progress. The hunters lay under cover all around the marsh, and some even perched on branches of trees that overhung the reeds. Blue smoke rose like clouds from the shade of the trees and drifted far out over the water.

The bird dogs came *splash, splash!* through the swamp, bending down the reeds and the rushes on every side. This gave the poor duckling such a fright that he twisted his head about to hide it under his wing. But at that very moment, a fearfully big dog appeared right beside him. His tongue lolled out of his mouth, and his wicked eyes glared horribly. He opened his wide jaws, flashed his sharp teeth, and— *splash, splash*—on he went without touching the duckling.

"Thank heavens," he sighed, "I'm so ugly that the dog won't even bother to bite me."

He lay perfectly still while the bullets splattered through the reeds as shot after shot was fired. It was late in the day before things became quiet again, and even then, the poor duckling didn't dare move. He waited several hours before he ventured to look about him, and then he scurried away from that marsh as fast as he could go. He ran across field and meadows. The wind was so strong that he had to struggle to keep his feet.

Late in the evening, he came to a miserable little hovel, so ramshackle that it did not know which way to tumble, and that was the only reason it still stood. The wind struck the duckling so hard that the poor little fellow had to sit down on his tail to withstand it. The storm blew stronger and stronger, but the duckling noticed that one hinge had come loose and the door hung so crooked that he could squeeze through the crack into the room, and that's just what he did.

Here lived an old woman with her cat and her hen. The cat, whom she called "Sonny," could arch his back, purr, and even make sparks, though for that you had to stroke his fur the wrong way. The hen had short little legs, so she was called "Chickey Shortleg." She laid good eggs, and the old woman loved her as if she had been her own child.

In the morning, they were quick to notice the strange duckling. The cat began to purr, and the hen began to cluck.

"What on Earth!" The old woman looked around, but she was shortsighted, and she mistook the duckling for a fat duck that had lost its way. "That was a good catch," she said. "Now I shall have duck eggs—unless it's a drake. We must try it out." So the duckling was tried out for three weeks, but not one egg did he lay.

In this house, the cat was master and the hen was mistress. They always said, "We and the world," for they thought themselves half of the world, and much the better half at that. The duckling thought that there might be more than one way of thinking, but the hen would not hear of it.

"Can you lay eggs?" she asked.

"No."

"Then be so good as to hold your tongue."

The cat asked, "Can you arch your back, purr, or make sparks?"

"No."

"Then keep your opinion to yourself when sensible people are talking."

The duckling sat in a corner, feeling most despondent. Then he remembered the fresh air and the sunlight. Such a desire to go swimming on the water possessed him that he could not help telling the hen about it.

"What on Earth has come over you?" the hen cried. "You haven't a thing to do, and that's why you get such silly notions. Lay us an egg, or learn to purr, and you'll get over it."

"But it's so refreshing to float on the water," said the duckling, "so refreshing to feel it rise over your head as you dive to the bottom."

"Yes, it must be a great pleasure!" said the hen. "I think you must have gone crazy. Ask the cat, who's the wisest fellow I know, whether he likes to swim or dive down in the water. Of myself, I say nothing. But ask the old woman, our mistress. There's no one on Earth wiser than she is. Do you imagine she wants to go swimming and feel the water rise over her head?"

"You don't understand me," said the duckling.

"Well, if we don't, who would? Surely you don't think you are cleverer than the cat and the old woman—to say nothing of myself. Don't be so conceited, child. Just thank your Maker for all the kindness we have shown you. Didn't you get into this snug room, and fall in with people who can tell you what's what? But you are such a numbskull that it's no pleasure to have you around. Believe me, I tell you this for your own good. I say unpleasant truths, but that's the only way you can know who are your friends. Be sure now that you lay some eggs. See to it that you learn to purr or to make sparks."

"I think I'd better go out into the wide world," said the duckling.

"Suit yourself," said the hen.

So off went the duckling. He swam on the water, and dived down in it, but still he was slighted by every living creature because of his ugliness.

Autumn came on. The leaves in the forest turned yellow and brown. The wind took them and whirled them about. The heavens looked cold as the low clouds hung heavy with snow and hail. Perched on the fence, the raven screamed, "Caw, caw!" and trembled with cold. It made one shiver to think of it. Pity the poor little duckling!

One evening, just as the sun was setting in splendor, a great flock of large, handsome birds appeared out of the reeds. The duckling had never seen birds so beautiful. They were dazzling white, with long graceful necks. They were swans. They uttered a very strange cry as they unfurled their magnificent wings to fly from this cold land, away to warmer countries and to open waters. They went up so high, so very high, that the ugly little duckling felt a strange uneasiness come over him as he watched them. He went around and round in the water, like a wheel. He craned his neck to follow their course, and gave a cry so shrill and strange that he frightened himself. Oh! He could not forget them—those splendid, happy birds. When he could no longer see them he dived to the very bottom and when he came up again, he was quite beside himself. He did not know what birds they were or whither they were bound, yet he loved them more than anything he had ever loved before. It was not that he envied them, for how could he ever dare dream of wanting their marvelous beauty for himself? He would have been grateful if only the ducks would have tolerated him—the poor ugly creature.

The winter grew cold—so bitterly cold that the duckling had to swim to and fro in the water to keep it from freezing over. But every night, the hole in which he swam kept getting smaller and smaller. Then it froze so hard that the duckling had to paddle continuously to keep the crackling ice from closing in upon him. At last, too tired to move, he was frozen fast in the ice.

Early that morning a farmer came by, and when he saw how things were, he went out on the pond, broke away the ice with his wooden shoe, and carried the duckling home to his wife. There the duckling revived, but when the children wished to play with him, he thought they meant to hurt him. Terrified, he fluttered into the milk pail, splashing the whole room with milk. The woman shrieked and threw up her hands as he flew into the butter tub, and then in and out of the meal barrel. Imagine what he looked like now! The woman screamed and lashed out at him with the fire tongs. The children tumbled over each other as they tried to catch him, and they laughed and they shouted. Luckily the door was open, and the duckling escaped through it into the bushes, where he lay down in the newly fallen snow, as if in a daze.

But it would be too sad to tell of all the hardships and wretchedness he had to endure during this cruel winter. When the warm sun shone once more, the duckling was still alive among the reeds of the marsh. The larks began to sing again. It was beautiful springtime.

Then, quite suddenly, he lifted his wings. They swept through the air much more strongly than before, and their powerful strokes carried him far. Before he quite knew what was happening, he found himself in a great garden where apple trees bloomed. The lilacs filled the air with sweet scent and hung in clusters from long, green branches that bent over a winding stream. Oh, but it was lovely here in the freshness of spring!

From the thicket before him came three lovely white swans. They ruffled their feathers and swam lightly in the stream. The duckling recognized these noble creatures, and a strange feeling of sadness came upon him.

"I shall fly near these royal birds, and they will peck me to bits because I, who am so very ugly, dare to go near them. But I don't care. Better be killed by them than to be nipped by the ducks, pecked by the hens, kicked about by the hen-yard girl, or suffer such misery in winter."

So he flew into the water and swam toward the splendid swans. They saw him and swept down upon him with their rustling feathers raised. "Kill me!" said the poor creature, and he bowed his head down over the water to wait for death. But what did he see there, mirrored in the clear stream? He beheld his own image, and it was no longer the reflection of a clumsy, dirty, gray bird, ugly and offensive. He himself was a swan! Being born in a duck yard does not matter, if only you are hatched from a swan's egg.

He felt quite glad that he had come through so much trouble and misfortune, for now he had a fuller understanding of his own good fortune and of beauty when he met with it. The great swans swam all around him and stroked him with their bills.

Several little children came into the garden to throw grain and bits of bread upon the water. The smallest child cried, "Here's a new one," and the others rejoiced, "Yes, a new one has come." They clapped their hands, danced around, and ran to bring their father and mother.

And they threw bread and cake upon the water, while they all agreed, "The new one is the most handsome of all. He's so young and so good-looking." The old swans bowed in his honor.

Then he felt very bashful, and tucked his head under his wing. He did not know what this was all about. He felt so very happy, but he wasn't at all proud, for a good heart never grows proud. He thought about how he had been persecuted and scorned, and now he heard them all call him the most beautiful of all beautiful birds. The lilacs dipped their clusters into the stream before him, and the sun shone so warm and so heartening. He rustled his feathers and held his slender neck high, as he cried out with a full heart: "I never dreamed there could be so much happiness, when I was the ugly duckling."

THE SWEETHEARTS; OR, THE TOP AND THE BALL (1843)

A top and a ball were lying together in a drawer among a lot of other toys. The top said to the ball, "Since we live in the same drawer, we ought to be sweethearts."

But the ball, which was covered with a morocco leather and thought as much of itself as any fine lady, would not even answer such a proposal.

The next day, the little boy to whom the top belonged took it out, painted it red and yellow, and drove a brass nail into it; so that the top looked very elegant when it was spinning around.

"Look at me!" it said to the ball. "What do you think? Shall we be sweethearts now? We are just made for each other! You bounce, and I dance. None could be happier than we two."

"That's what you think!" said the ball. "You evidently don't realize that my father and my mother were a pair of morocco slippers, and that I have a cork in my body!"

"Yes, but I am made of mahogany!" said the top. "The mayor himself turned me on his own lathe and had a lot of fun doing it."

"Am I supposed to believe that?" said the ball.

"May I never be whipped again if I'm lying!" answered the top.

"You speak very well for yourself, but I'm afraid it's impossible. I'm almost engaged to a swallow. Whenever I bounce up in the air, it puts its head out of its nest and says, 'Will you be mine? Will you be mine?' And to myself, I've always said 'Yes.' But I promise I shall never forget you."

"That will do me a lot of good," said the top, and that ended their conversation right then and there!

The next day, the ball was taken out, and the top saw her flying high up into the air, just like a bird, so high that you could hardly see her. And every time she came back, she bounced up again, as soon as she touched the ground. That was either because she was longing for the swallow or because she had cork in her body. At the ninth bounce, the ball disappeared; the boy looked and looked, but it was gone. The top sighed "I know where she is: She's in the swallow's nest and has married the swallow."

The more the top thought of this, the more infatuated he became with the ball. Just because he couldn't have her, his love for her increased, but, alas! She was in love with somebody else. The top danced and spun, and in his thoughts, the ball became more and more beautiful.

Many years went by—it was now an old love affair. The top was no longer young. But one day, he was gilded all over; never had he looked so beautiful. He was now a golden top, and he leaped and spun till he hummed. This certainly was something. But suddenly he jumped too high, and disappeared! They looked and looked, even down in the cellar, but he was not to be found. Where was he? He had jumped into the dustbin, where all sorts of rubbish was lying—old cabbage stalks, dust, dirt, and gravel that had fallen down through the gutter.

"What a place to land in! Here my gilding will soon disappear. And what kind of riffraff am I with?" he mumbled, as he glared at a long, scrawny-looking cabbage stalk and at a strange round thing that looked like an apple. But it wasn't an apple—it was an old ball that for years had been lying in the roof gutter and was soaked through with water.

"Thank goodness! At last I have an equal to talk to!" said the ball, looking at the golden top. "I want you to know that I am made of morocco leather, sewn by maiden hands, and that I have a cork in my body; but no one will think so now! I almost married a swallow, but I landed in the roof gutter instead, and there I have been for the last five years, soaked! That's a long time, believe me, for a young lady."

But the top said nothing. He thought of his old sweetheart, and the more he listened, the more certain he felt it was she. Just then the housemaid came to throw some rubbish in the dustbin.

"Why," she cried, "here's the golden top!"

And the top was carried back into the living room and admired by everybody. But the ball was never heard of again. The top never spoke a word about his old sweetheart, for love vanishes when one's sweetheart has been soaking in a roof gutter for five years. Yes, you don't even recognize her when you meet her in a dustbin.

THE FIR TREE (1844)

Out in the woods stood such a pretty little fir tree. It grew in a good place, where it had plenty of sun and plenty of fresh air. Around it stood many tall comrades, both fir trees and pines.

The little fir tree was in a headlong hurry to grow up. It didn't care a thing for the warm sunshine, or the fresh air, and it took no interest in the peasant children who ran about chattering when they came to pick strawberries or raspberries. Often when the children had picked their pails full, or had gathered long strings of berries threaded on straws, they would sit down to rest near the little fir. "Oh, isn't it a nice little tree?" they would say. "It's the baby of the woods." The little tree didn't like their remarks at all.

Next year, it shot up a long joint of new growth, and the following year, another joint, still longer. You can always tell how old a fir tree is by counting the number of joints it has.

"I wish I were a grown-up tree, like my comrades," the little tree sighed. "Then I could stretch out my branches and see from my top what the world is like. The birds would make me their nesting place, and when the wind blew, I could bow back and forth with all the great trees."

It took no pleasure in the sunshine, nor in the birds. The glowing clouds that sailed overhead at sunrise and sunset meant nothing to it.

In winter, when the snow lay sparkling on the ground, a hare would often come hopping along and jump right over the little tree. Oh, how irritating that was! That happened for two winters, but when the third winter came, the tree was so tall that the hare had to turn aside and hop around it.

"Oh, to grow, grow! To get older and taller," the little tree thought. "That is the most wonderful thing in this world."

In the autumn, woodcutters came and cut down a few of the largest trees. This happened every year. The young fir was no longer a baby tree, and it trembled to see how those stately great trees crashed to the ground, how their limbs were lopped off, and how lean they looked as the naked trunks were loaded into carts. It could hardly recognize the trees it had known when the horses pulled them out of the woods.

Where were they going? What would become of them?

In the springtime, when swallows and storks came back, the tree asked them, "Do you know where the other trees went? Have you met them?"

The swallows knew nothing about it, but the stork looked thoughtful and nodded his head. "Yes, I think I met them," he said. "On my way from Egypt, I met many new ships, and some had tall, stately masts. They may well have been the trees you mean, for I remember the smell of fir. They wanted to be remembered to you."

"Oh, I wish I were old enough to travel on the sea. Please tell me what it really is, and how it looks."

"That would take too long to tell," said the stork, and off he strode.

"Rejoice in your youth," said the sunbeams. "Take pride in your growing strength and in the stir of life within you."

And the wind kissed the tree, and the dew wept over it, for the tree was young and without understanding.

When Christmas came near, many young trees were cut down. Some were not even as old or as tall as this fir tree of ours, who was in such a hurry and fret to go traveling. These young trees, which were always the handsomest ones, had their branches left on them when they were loaded on carts and the horses drew them out of the woods.

"Where can they be going?" the fir tree wondered. "They are no taller than I am. One was really much smaller than I am. And why are they allowed to keep all their branches? "Where can they be going?"

"We know! We know!" the sparrows chirped. "We have been to town and peeped in the windows. We know where they are going. The greatest splendor and glory you can imagine awaits them. We've peeped through windows. We've seen them planted right in the middle of a warm room and decked out with the most splendid things—gold apples, good gingerbread, gay toys, and many hundreds of candles."

"And then?" asked the fir tree, trembling in every twig. "And then? What happens then?"

"We saw nothing more. And never have we seen anything that could match it."

"I wonder if I was created for such a glorious future?" The fir tree rejoiced. "Why, that is better than to cross the sea. I'm tormented with longing. Oh, if Christmas would only come! I'm just as tall and grown-up as the trees they chose last year. How I wish I were already in the cart, on my way to the warm room where there's so much splendor and glory. Then—then something even better, something still more important is bound to happen, or why should they deck me so fine? Yes, there must be something still grander! But what? Oh, how I long: I don't know what's the matter with me."

"Enjoy us while you may," the air and sunlight told him. "Rejoice in the days of your youth, out here in the open."

But the tree did not rejoice at all. It just grew. It grew and was green both winter and summer—dark evergreen. People who passed it said, "There's a beautiful tree!" And when Christmas time came again, they cut it down first. The ax struck deep into its marrow. The tree sighed as it fell to the ground. It felt faint with pain. Instead of the happiness it had expected, the tree was sorry to leave the home where it had grown up. It knew that never again would it see its dear old comrades, the little bushes and the flowers about it—and perhaps not even the birds. The departure was anything but pleasant.

The tree did not get over it until all the trees were unloaded in the yard, and it heard a man say, "That's a splendid one. That's the tree for us." Then two servants came in fine livery, and carried the fir tree into a big splendid drawing room. Portraits were hung all around the walls. On either side of the white porcelain stove stood great Chinese vases with lions on their lids. There were easy chairs, silk-covered sofas, and long tables strewn with picture books and with toys that were worth a mint of money, or so the children said.

The fir tree was planted in a large tub filled with sand, but no one could see that it was a tub because it was wrapped in a gay green cloth and set on a many-colored carpet. How the tree quivered! What would come next? The servants and even the young ladies helped it on with its fine decorations. From its branches, they hung little nets cut out of colored paper, and each net was filled with candies. Gilded apples and walnuts hung in clusters as if they grew there, and a hundred little white, blue, and even red candles were fastened to its twigs. Among its green branches swayed dolls that it took to be real living people, for the tree had never seen their like before. And up at its very top was set a large gold tinsel star. It was splendid, I tell you, splendid beyond all words!

"Tonight," they all said, "ah, tonight how the tree will shine!"

"Oh," thought the tree, "if tonight would only come! If only the candles were lit! And after that, what happens then? Will the trees come trooping out of the woods to see me? Will the sparrows flock to the windows? Shall I take root here, and stand in fine ornaments all winter and summer long?"

That was how much it knew about it. All its longing had gone to its bark and set it to arching, which is as bad for a tree as a headache is for us.

Now the candles were lighted. What dazzling splendor! What a blaze of light! The tree quivered, so in every bough a candle set one of its twigs ablaze. It hurt terribly.

"Mercy me!" cried every young lady, and the fire was quickly put out. The tree no longer dared rustle a twig—it was awful! Wouldn't it be terrible if it were to drop one of its ornaments? Its own brilliance dazzled it.

Suddenly, the folding doors were thrown back, and a whole flock of children burst in as if they would overturn the tree completely. Their elders marched in after them, more sedately. For a moment, but only for a moment, the young ones were stricken speechless. Then they shouted till the rafters rang. They danced about the tree and plucked off one present after another.

"What are they up to?" the tree wondered. "What will happen next?"

As the candles burned down to the bark, they were snuffed out, one by one, and then the children had permission to plunder the tree. They went about it in such earnest that the branches crackled, and, if the tree had not been tied to the ceiling by the gold star at top, it would have tumbled headlong.

The children danced about with their splendid playthings. No one looked at the tree now, except an old nurse who peered in among the branches, but this was only to make sure that not an apple or fig had been overlooked.

"Tell us a story! Tell us a story!" the children clamored, as they towed a fat little man to the tree. He sat down beneath it and said, "Here we are in the woods, and it will do the tree a lot of good to listen to our story. Mind you, I'll tell only one. Which will you have, the story of Ivedy-Avedy, or the one about Humpty-Dumpty who tumbled downstairs, yet ascended the throne and married the princess?"

"Ivedy-Avedy," cried some. "Humpty-Dumpty," cried the others. And there was a great hullabaloo. Only the fir tree held its peace, though it thought to itself, "Am I to be left out of this? Isn't there anything I can do?" For all the fun of the evening had centered upon it, and it had played its part well.

The fat little man told them all about Humpty-Dumpty, who tumbled downstairs, yet ascended the throne and married the princess. And the children clapped and shouted, "Tell us another one! Tell us another one!" For they wanted to hear about Ivedy-Avedy too, but after Humpty-Dumpty, the storytelling stopped. The fir tree stood very still as it pondered how the birds in the woods had never told it a story to equal this.

"Humpty-Dumpty tumbled downstairs, yet he married the princess. Imagine! That must be how things happen in the world. You never can tell. Maybe I'll tumble downstairs and marry a princess too," thought the fir tree, who believed every word of the story because such a nice man had told it.

The tree looked forward to the following day, when they would deck it again with fruit and toys, candles and gold. "Tomorrow I shall not quiver," it decided. "I'll enjoy my splendor to the full. Tomorrow I shall hear about Humpty-Dumpty again, and perhaps about Ivedy-Avedy too." All night long, the tree stood silent as it dreamed its dreams, and next morning, the butler and the maid came in with their dusters.

"Now my splendor will be renewed," the fir tree thought. But they dragged it upstairs to the garret, and there they left it in a dark corner where no daylight ever came. "What's the meaning of this?" the tree wondered. "What am I going to do here? What stories shall I hear?" It leaned against the wall, lost in dreams. It had plenty of time for dreaming, as the days and the nights went by. Nobody came to the garret. And when at last someone did come, it was only to put many big boxes away in the corner. The tree was quite hidden. One might think it had been entirely forgotten.

"It's still winter outside," the tree thought. "The earth is too hard and covered with snow for them to plant me now. I must have been put here for shelter until springtime comes. How thoughtful of them! How good people are! Only, I wish it weren't so dark here, and so very, very lonely. There's not even a little hare. It was so friendly out in the woods when the snow was on the ground and the hare came hopping along. Yes, he was friendly even when he jumped right over me, though I did not think so then. Here it's all so terribly lonely."

"Squeak, squeak!" said a little mouse just then. He crept across the floor, and another one followed him. They sniffed the fir tree and rustled in and out among its branches.

"It is fearfully cold," one of them said. "Except for that, it would be very nice here, wouldn't it, you old fir tree?"

"I'm not at all old," said the fir tree. "Many trees are much older than I am."

"Where did you come from?" the mice asked him. "And what do you know?" They were most inquisitive creatures.

"Tell us about the most beautiful place in the world. Have you been there? Were you ever in the larder, where there are cheeses on shelves and hams that hang from the rafters? It's the place where you can dance upon tallow candles—where you can dart in thin and squeeze out fat."

"I know nothing of that place," said the tree. "But I know the woods where the sun shines and the little birds sing." Then it told them about its youth. The little mice had never heard the like of it. They listened very intently, and said, "My! How much you have seen! And how happy it must have made you."

"I?" the fir tree thought about it. "Yes, those days were rather amusing." And it went on to tell them about Christmas Eve, when it was decked out with candies and candles.

"Oh," said the little mice, "how lucky you have been, you old fir tree!"

"I am not at all old," it insisted. "I came out of the woods just this winter, and I'm really in the prime of life, though at the moment, my growth is suspended."

"How nicely you tell things," said the mice. The next night they came with four other mice to hear what the tree had to say. The more it talked, the more clearly it recalled things, and it thought, "Those were happy times. But they may still come back—they may come back again. Humpty-Dumpty fell downstairs, and yet he married the princess. Maybe the same thing will happen to me." It thought about a charming little birch tree that grew out in the woods. To the fir tree, she was a real and lovely princess.

"Who is Humpty-Dumpty?" the mice asked it. So the fir tree told them the whole story, for it could remember it word by word. The little mice were ready to jump to the top of the tree for joy. The next night, many more mice came to see the fir tree, and on Sunday, two rats paid it a call, but they said that the story was not very amusing. This made the little mice so sad that they began to find it not so very interesting either.

"Is that the only story you know?" the rats asked.

"Only that one," the tree answered. "I heard it on the happiest evening of my life, but I did not know then how happy I was."

"It's a very silly story. Don't you know one that tells about bacon and candles? Can't you tell us a good larder story?"

"No," said the tree.

"Then good-bye, and we won't be back," the rats said, and went away.

At last, the little mice took to staying away, too. The tree sighed, "Oh, wasn't it pleasant when those gay little mice sat around and listened to all that I had to say? Now that, too, is past and gone. But I will take good care to enjoy myself, once they let me out of here."

When would that be? Well, it came to pass on a morning when people came up to clean out the garret. The boxes were moved, the tree was pulled out and thrown—thrown hard—on the floor. But a servant dragged it at once to the stairway, where there was daylight again.

"Now my life will start all over," the tree thought. It felt the fresh air and the first sunbeam strike it as if it came out into the courtyard. This all happened so quickly, and there was so much going around it, that the tree forgot to give even a glance at itself. The courtyard adjoined a garden, where flowers were blooming. Great masses of fragrant roses hung over the picket fence. The linden trees were in blossom, and between them, the swallows skimmed past, calling, "Tilira-lira-lee, my love's come back to me." But it was not the fir tree of whom they spoke.

"Now I shall live again," it rejoiced, and tried to stretch out its branches. Alas, they were withered, and brown, and brittle. It was tossed into a corner, among weeds and nettles. But the gold star that was still tied to its top sparkled bravely in the sunlight.

Several of the merry children, who had danced around the tree and taken such pleasure in it at Christmas, were playing in the courtyard. One of the youngest seized upon it and tore off the tinsel star.

"Look what is still hanging on that ugly old Christmas tree," the child said, and stamped upon the branches until they cracked beneath his shoes.

The tree saw the beautiful flowers blooming freshly in the garden. It saw itself, and wished that they had left it in the darkest corner of the garret. It thought of its own young days in the deep woods, and of the merry Christmas Eve, and of the little mice who had been so pleased when it told them the story of Humpty-Dumpty.

"My days are over and past," said the poor tree. "Why didn't I enjoy them while I could? Now they are gone—all gone."

A servant came and chopped the tree into little pieces. These heaped together quite high. The wood blazed beautifully under the big copper kettle, and the fir tree moaned so deeply that each groan sounded like a muffled shot. That's why the children who were playing nearby ran to make a circle around the flames, staring into the fire and crying, "Pif! Paf!" But as each groans burst from it, the tree thought of a bright summer day in the woods, or a starlit winter night. It thought of Christmas Eve and thought of Humpty-Dumpty, which was the only story it ever heard and knew how to tell. And so the tree was burned completely away.

The children played on in the courtyard. The youngest child wore on his breast the gold star that had topped the tree on its happiest night of all. But that was no more, and the tree was no more, and there's no more to my story. No more, nothing more. All stories come to an end.

THE SNOW QUEEN (1844)

A TALE IN SEVEN STORIES

FIRST STORY
WHICH HAS TO DO WITH A MIRROR
AND ITS FRAGMENTS

Now then! We will begin. When the story is done, you shall know a great deal more than you do know.

He was a terribly bad hobgoblin, a goblin of the very wickedest sort, and, in fact, he was the devil himself. One day, the devil was in a very good humor because he had just finished a mirror that had this peculiar power: Everything good and beautiful that was reflected in it seemed to dwindle to almost nothing at all, while everything that was worthless and ugly became most conspicuous and even uglier than ever. In this mirror, the loveliest landscapes looked like boiled spinach, and the very best people became hideous, or stood on their heads and had no stomachs. Their faces were distorted beyond any recognition, and if a person had a freckle, it was sure to spread until it covered both nose and mouth.

"That's very funny!" said the devil. If a good, pious thought passed through anyone's mind, it showed in the mirror as a carnal grin, and the devil laughed aloud at his ingenious invention.

All those who went to the hobgoblin's school—for he had a school of his own—told everyone that a miracle had come to pass. Now, they asserted, for the very first time you could see how the world and its people really looked. They scurried about with the mirror until there was not a person alive nor a land on Earth that had not been distorted.

Then they wanted to fly up to Heaven itself, to scoff at the angels and our Lord. The higher they flew with the mirror, the wider it grinned. They could hardly manage to hold it. Higher they flew, and higher still, nearer to Heaven and the angels. Then the grinning mirror trembled with such violence that it slipped from their hands and fell to the earth, where it shattered into hundreds of millions of billions of bits, or perhaps even more. And now it caused more trouble than it did before it was broken, because some of the fragments were smaller than a grain of sand, and these went flying throughout the wide world. Once they got in people's eyes, they would stay there. These bits of glass distorted everything the people saw and made them see only the bad side of things, for every little bit of glass kept the same power that the whole mirror had possessed.

A few people even got a glass splinter in their hearts, and that was a terrible thing, for it turned their hearts into lumps of ice. Some of the fragments were so large that they were used as window panes—but not the kind of window through which you should look at your friends. Other pieces were made into spectacles, and evil things came to pass when people put them on to see clearly and to see justice done. The fiend was so tickled by it all that he laughed till his sides were sore. But fine bits of the glass are still flying through the air, and now you shall hear what happened.

SECOND STORY

A Little Boy and a Little Girl

In the big city, it was so crowded with houses and people that few found room for even a small garden, and most people had to be content with a flowerpot, but two poor children who lived there managed to have a garden that was a little bigger than a flowerpot. These children were not brother and sister, but they loved each other just as much as if they had been. Their parents lived close to one another in the garrets of two adjoining houses. Where the roofs met and where the rain gutter ran between the two houses, their two small windows faced each other. One had only to step across the rain gutter to go from window to window.

In these windows, the parents had a large box in which they planted vegetables for their use, and a little rosebush too. Each box had a bush, which thrived to perfection. Then it occurred to the parents to put these boxes across the gutter, where they very nearly reached from one window to the other and looked exactly like two walls of flowers. The pea plants hung down over the boxes, and the rosebushes threw out long sprays that framed the windows and bent over toward each other. It was almost like a little triumphal arch of greenery and flowers. The boxes were very high, and the children knew that they were not to climb about on them, but they were often allowed to take their little stools out on the roof under the roses, where they had a wonderful time playing together.

Winter, of course, put an end to this pleasure. The windows often frosted over completely. But they would heat copper pennies on the stove and press these hot coins against the frost-coated glass. Then they had the finest of peepholes, as round as a ring, and behind them appeared a bright, friendly eye, one at each window—it was the little boy and the little girl who peeped out. His name was Kay and hers was Gerda. With one skip, they could join each other in summer, but to visit together in the wintertime, they had to go all the way downstairs in one house and climb all the way upstairs in the other. Outside, the snow was whirling.

"See the white bees swarming," the old grandmother said.

"Do they have a queen bee, too?" the little boy asked, for he knew that real bees have one.

"Yes, indeed they do," the grandmother said. "She flies in the thick of the swarm. She is the biggest bee of all, and can never stay quietly on the earth, but goes back again to the dark clouds. Many a wintry night, she flies through the streets and peers in through the windows. Then they freeze over in a strange fashion, as if they were covered with flowers."

"Oh yes, we've seen that," both the children said, and so they knew it was true.

"Can the Snow Queen come in here?" the little girl asked.

"Well, let her come!" cried the boy. "I would put her on the hot stove and melt her."

But Grandmother stroked his head, and told them other stories.

That evening when little Kay was at home and half ready for bed, he climbed on the chair by the window and looked out through the little peephole. A few snowflakes were falling, and the largest flake of all alighted on the edge of one of the flower boxes. This flake grew bigger and bigger, until at last it turned into a woman who was dressed in the finest white gauze that looked as if it had been made from millions of star-shaped flakes. She was beautiful and she was graceful, but she was ice-shining, glittering ice. She was alive, for all that, and her eyes sparkled like two bright stars, but in them there was neither rest nor peace. She nodded toward the window and beckoned with her hand. The little boy was frightened, and as he jumped down from the chair, it seemed to him that a huge bird flew past the window.

The next day was clear and cold. Then the snow thawed, and springtime came. The sun shone, the green grass sprouted, swallows made their nests, windows were thrown open, and once again the children played in their little roof garden, high up in the rain gutter on top of the house.

That summer, the roses bloomed their splendid best. The little girl had learned a hymn in which there was a line about roses that reminded her of their own flowers. She sang it to the little boy, and he sang it with her:

> Where roses bloom so sweetly in the vale,
> There shall you find the Christ Child, without fail.

The children held each other by the hand, kissed the roses, looked up at the Lord's clear sunshine, and spoke to it as if the Christ Child were there. What glorious summer days those were, and how beautiful it was out under those fragrant rosebushes that seemed as if they would never stop blooming.

Kay and Gerda were looking at a picture book of birds and beasts one day, and it was then—just as the clock in the church tower was striking five—that Kay cried:

"Oh! Something hurt my heart. And now I've got something in my eye."

The little girl put her arm around his neck, and he blinked his eye. No, she couldn't see anything in it.

"I think it's gone," he said. But it was not gone. It was one of those splinters of glass from the magic mirror. You remember that goblin's mirror—the one that made everything great and good that was reflected in it appear small and ugly, but that magnified all evil things until each blemish loomed large. Poor Kay! A fragment had pierced his heart as well, and soon it would turn into a lump of ice. The pain had stopped, but the glass was still there.

"Why should you be crying?" he asked. "It makes you look so ugly. There's nothing the matter with me." And suddenly, he took it into his head to say:

"Ugh! That rose is all worm-eaten. And look, this one is crooked. And these roses, they are just as ugly as they can be. They look like the boxes they grow in." He gave the boxes a kick and broke off both of the roses.

"Kay! What are you doing?" the little girl cried. When he saw how it upset her, he broke off another rose and then leaped home through his own window, leaving dear little Gerda all alone.

Afterwards, when she brought out her picture book, he said it was fit only for babes in the cradle. And whenever Grandmother told stories, he always broke in with a "but—." If he could manage it, he would steal behind her, perch a pair of spectacles on his nose, and imitate her. He did this so cleverly that it made everybody laugh, and before long, he could mimic the walk and the talk of everyone who lived on that street. Everything that was odd or ugly about them, Kay could mimic so well that people said, "That boy has surely got a good head on him!" But it was the glass in his eye and the glass in his heart that made him tease even little Gerda, who loved him with all her soul.

Now his games were very different from what they used to be. They became more sensible. When the snow was flying about one wintry day, he brought a large magnifying glass out of doors and spread the tail of his blue coat to let the snowflakes fall on it.

"Now look through the glass," he told Gerda. Each snowflake seemed much larger and looked like a magnificent flower or a ten-pointed star. It was marvelous to look at.

"Look, how artistic!" said Kay. "They are much more interesting to look at than real flowers, for they are absolutely perfect. There isn't a flaw in them, until they start melting."

A little while later, Kay came down with his big gloves on his hands and his sled on his back. Right in Gerda's ear he bawled out, "I've been given permission to play in the big square where the other boys are!" and away he ran.

In the square, some of the more adventuresome boys would tie their little sleds on behind the farmer's carts, to be pulled along for quite a distance. It was wonderful sport. While the fun was at its height, a big sleigh drove up. It was painted entirely white, and the driver wore a white, shaggy fur cloak and a white, shaggy cap. As the sleigh drove twice around the square, Kay quickly hooked his little sled behind it, and down the street they went, faster and faster. The driver turned around in a friendly fashion and nodded to Kay, just as if they were old acquaintances. Every time Kay started to unfasten his little sleigh, its driver nodded again, and Kay held on, even when they drove right out through the town gate.

Then the snow began to fall so fast that the boy could not see his hands in front of him as they sped on. He suddenly let go the slack of the rope in his hands in order to get loose from the big sleigh, but it did no good. His little sled was tied on securely, and they went like the wind. He gave a loud shout, but nobody heard him. The snow whirled, and the sleigh flew along. Every now and then it gave a jump, as if it were clearing hedges and ditches. The boy was terror-stricken. He tried to say his prayers, but all he could remember was his multiplication tables.

The snowflakes got bigger and bigger, until they looked like big white hens. All of a sudden, the curtain of snow parted, and the big sleigh stopped, and the driver stood up. The fur coat and the cap were made of snow, and it was a woman, tall and slender and blinding white—she was the Snow Queen herself.

"We have made good time," she said. "Is it possible that you tremble from cold? Crawl under my bear coat." She took him up in the sleigh beside her, and as she wrapped the fur about him, he felt as if he were sinking into a snowdrift.

"Are you still cold?" she asked, and kissed him on the forehead. *Brr-r-r*. That kiss was colder than ice. He felt it right down to his heart, half of which was already an icy lump. He felt as if he were dying, but only for a moment. Then he felt quite comfortable and no longer noticed the cold.

"My sled! Don't forget my sled!" It was the only thing he thought of. They tied it to one of the white hens, which flew along after them with the sled on its back. The Snow Queen kissed Kay once more, and then he forgot little Gerda, and Grandmother, and all the others at home.

"You won't get any more kisses now," she said, "or else I should kiss you to death." Kay looked at her. She was so beautiful! A cleverer and prettier face he could not imagine. She no longer seemed to be made of ice, as she had seemed when she sat outside his window and beckoned to him. In his eyes, she was perfect, and she was not at all afraid. He told her how he could do mental arithmetic even with fractions, and that he knew the size and population of all the countries. She kept on smiling, and he began to be afraid that he did not know as much as he thought he did. He looked up at the great big space overhead, as she flew with him high up on the black clouds, while the storm whistled and roared as if it were singing old ballads.

They flew over forests and lakes, over many a land and sea. Below them, the wind blew cold, wolves howled, and black crows screamed as they skimmed across the glittering snow. But up above, the moon shone bright and large, and on it Kay fixed his eyes throughout that long, long winter night. By day, he slept at the feet of the Snow Queen.

THIRD STORY
The Flower Garden of the Woman
Skilled in Magic

How did little Gerda get along when Kay did not come back? Where could he be? Nobody knew. Nobody could give them any news of him. All that the boys could say was that they had seen him hitch his little sled to a fine big sleigh, which had driven down the street and out through the town gate. Nobody knew what had become of Kay. Many tears were shed, and little Gerda sobbed hardest of all. People said that he was dead—that he must have been drowned in the river not far from town. Ah, how gloomy those long winter days were!

But spring and its warm sunshine came at last.

"Kay is dead and gone," little Gerda said.

"I don't believe it," said the sunshine.

"He's dead and gone," she said to the swallows.

"We don't believe it," they sang. Finally, little Gerda began to disbelieve it too. One morning, she said to herself:

"I'll put on my new red shoes, the ones Kay has never seen, and I'll go down by the river to ask about him."

It was very early in the morning. She kissed her old grandmother, who was still asleep, put on her red shoes, and all by herself, she hurried out through the town gate and down to the river.

"Is it true that you have taken my own little playmate? I'll give you my red shoes if you will bring him back to me."

It seemed to her that the waves nodded very strangely. So she took off her red shoes, which were her dearest possession, and threw them into the river. But they fell near the shore, and the little waves washed them right back to her. It seemed that the river could not take her dearest possession, because it did not have little Kay. However, she was afraid that she had not thrown them far enough, so she clambered into a boat that lay among the reeds, walked to the end of it, and threw her shoes out into the water again. But the boat was not tied, and her movements made it drift away from the bank. She realized this and tried to get ashore, but by the time she reached the other end of the boat, it was already more than a yard from the bank, and was fast gaining speed.

Little Gerda was so frightened that she began to cry, and no one was there to hear her except the sparrows. They could not carry her to land, but they flew along the shore twittering, "We are here! Here we are!" as if to comfort her. The boat drifted swiftly down the stream, and Gerda sat there quite still, in her stocking feet. Her little red shoes floated along behind, but they could not catch up with her because the boat was gathering headway. It was very pretty on both sides of the river, where the flowers were lovely, the trees were old, and the hillsides afforded pasture for cattle and sheep. But not one single person did Gerda see.

"Perhaps the river will take me to little Kay," she thought, and that made her feel more cheerful. She stood up and watched the lovely green banks for hour after hour.

Then she came to a large cherry orchard, in which there was a little house with strange red and blue windows. It had a thatched roof, and outside it stood two wooden soldiers, who presented arms to everyone who sailed past.

Gerda thought they were alive, and called out to them, but of course, they did not answer her. She drifted quite close to them as the current drove the boat toward the bank. Gerda called even louder, and an old, old woman came out of the house. She leaned on a crooked stick; she had on a big sun hat, and on it were painted the most glorious flowers.

"You poor little child!" the old woman exclaimed. "However did you get lost on this big swift river, and however did you drift so far into the great wide world?" The old woman waded right into the water, caught hold of the boat with her crooked stick, pulled it in to shore, and lifted little Gerda out of it.

Gerda was very glad to be on dry land again, but she felt a little afraid of this strange old woman, who said to her:

"Come and tell me who you are, and how you got here." Gerda told her all about it. The woman shook her head and said, "Hmm, hmm!" And when Gerda had told her everything and asked if she hadn't seen little Kay, the woman said he had not yet come by, but that he might be along any day now. And she told Gerda not to take it so to heart, but to taste her cherries and to look at her flowers. These were more beautiful than any picture book, and each one had a story to tell. Then she led Gerda by the hand into her little house, and the old woman locked the door.

The windows were placed high up on the walls, and through their red, blue, and yellow panes, the sunlight streamed in a strange mixture of all the colors there are. But on the table were the most delicious cherries, and Gerda, who was no longer afraid, ate as many as she liked. While she was eating them, the old woman combed her hair with a golden comb. Gerda's pretty hair fell in shining yellow ringlets on either side of a friendly little face that was as round and blooming as a rose.

"I've so often wished for a dear little girl like you," the old woman told her. "Now you'll see how well the two of us will get along." While her hair was being combed, Gerda gradually forgot all about Kay, for the old woman was skilled in magic. But she was not a wicked witch. She only dabbled in magic to amuse herself, but she wanted very much to keep little Gerda. So she went out into her garden and pointed her crooked stick at all the rosebushes. In the full bloom of their beauty, all of them sank down into the black earth, without leaving a single trace behind. The old woman was afraid that if Gerda saw them they would remind her so strongly of her own roses, and of little Kay, that she would run away again.

Then Gerda was led into the flower garden. How fragrant and lovely it was! Every known flower of every season was there in full bloom. No picture book was ever so pretty and gay. Gerda jumped for joy, and played in the garden until the sun went down behind the tall cherry trees. Then she was tucked into a beautiful bed, under a red silk coverlet quilted with blue violets. There she slept, and there she dreamed as gloriously as any queen on her wedding day.

The next morning, she again went out into the warm sunshine to play with the flowers—and this she did for many a day. Gerda knew every flower by heart, and, plentiful though they were, she always felt that there was one missing, but which one she didn't quite know. One day, she sat looking at the old woman's sun hat, and the prettiest of all the flowers painted on it was a rose. The old woman had forgotten this rose on her hat when she made the real roses disappear in the earth. But that's just the sort of thing that happens when one doesn't stop to think.

"Why aren't there any roses here?" said Gerda. She rushed out among the flower beds, and she looked and she looked, but there wasn't a rose to be seen. Then she sat down and cried. But her hot tears fell on the very spot where a rosebush had sunk into the ground, and when her warm tears moistened the earth, the bush sprang up again, as full of blossoms as when it disappeared. Gerda hugged it, and kissed the roses. She remembered her own pretty roses, and thought of little Kay.

"Oh, how long I have been delayed," the little girl said. "I should have been looking for Kay. Don't you know where he is?" she asked the roses. "Do you think that he is dead and gone?"

"He isn't dead," the roses told her. "We have been down in the Earth where the dead people are, but Kay is not there."

"Thank you," said little Gerda, who went to all the other flowers, put her lips near them, and asked, "Do you know where little Kay is?"

But every flower stood in the sun and dreamed its own fairy tale, or its story. Though Gerda listened to many, many of them, not one of the flowers knew anything about Kay.

What did the tiger lily say?

"Do you hear the drum? *Boom, boom!* It was only two notes, always *boom, boom!* Hear the women wail. Hear the priests chant. The Hindu woman in her long red robe stands on the funeral pyre. The flames rise around her and her dead husband, but the Hindu woman is thinking of that living man in the crowd around them. She is thinking of him whose eyes are burning hotter than the flames— of him whose fiery glances have pierced her heart more deeply than these flames that soon will burn her body to ashes. Can the flame of the heart die in the flame of the funeral pyre?"

"I don't understand that at all," little Gerda said.

"That's my fairy tale," said the lily.

What did the trumpet flower say?

"An ancient castle rises high from a narrow path in the mountains. The thick ivy grows leaf upon leaf where it climbs to the balcony. There stands a beautiful maiden. She leans out over the balustrade to look down the path. No rose on its stem is as graceful as she, nor is any apple blossom in the breeze so light. Hear the rustle of her silk gown, sighing, 'Will he never come?'"

"Do you mean Kay?" little Gerda asked.

"I am talking about my story, my own dream," the trumpet flower replied.

What did the little snowdrop say?

"Between the trees, a board hangs by two ropes. It is a swing. Two pretty little girls, with frocks as white as snow and long green ribbons fluttering from their hats, are swinging. Their brother, who is bigger than they are, stands behind them on the swing, with his arms around the ropes to hold himself. In one hand, he has a little cup, and in the other, a clay pipe. He is blowing soap bubbles, and as the swing flies, the bubbles float off in all their changing colors. The last bubble is still clinging to the bowl of his pipe and fluttering in the air as the swing sweeps to and fro. A little black dog, light as a bubble, is standing on his hind legs and trying to get up in the swing. But it does not stop. High and low the swing flies, until the dog loses his balance, barks, and loses his temper. They tease him, and the bubble bursts. A swinging board pictured in a bubble before it broke—that is my story."

"It may be a very pretty story, but you told it very sadly, and you didn't mention Kay at all."

What did the hyacinths say?

"There were three sisters, quite transparent and very fair. One wore a red dress, the second wore a blue one, and the third went all in white. Hand in hand, they danced in the clear moonlight, beside a calm lake. They were not elfin folk. They were human beings. The air was sweet, and the sisters disappeared into the forest. The fragrance of the air grew sweeter. Three coffins, in which lie the three sisters, glide out of the forest and across the lake. The fireflies hover about them like little flickering lights. Are the dancing sisters sleeping, or are they dead? The fragrance of the flowers says they are dead, and the evening bell tolls for their funeral."

"You are making me very unhappy," little Gerda said. "Your fragrance is so strong that I cannot help thinking of those dead sisters.

Oh, could little Kay really be dead? The roses have been down under the ground, and they say no."

"Ding, dong," tolled the hyacinth bells. "We do not toll for little Kay. We do not know him. We are simply singing our song—the only song we know."

And Gerda went on to the buttercup that shone among its glossy green leaves.

"You are like a bright little sun," said Gerda. "Tell me, do you know where I can find my playmate?"

And the buttercup shone brightly as it looked up at Gerda. But what sort of song would a buttercup sing? It certainly wouldn't be about Kay.

"In a small courtyard, God's sun was shining brightly on the very first day of spring. Its beams glanced along the white wall of the house next door, and close by grew the first yellow flowers of spring, shining like gold in the warm sunlight. An old grandmother was sitting outside in her chair. Her granddaughter, a poor but very pretty maidservant, had just come home for a little visit. She kissed her grandmother, and there was gold, a heart full of gold, in that kiss. Gold on her lips, gold in her dreams, and gold above in the morning beams. There, I've told you my little story," said the buttercup.

"Oh, my poor old grandmother," said Gerda. "She will miss me so. She must be grieving for me as much as she did for little Kay. But I'll soon go home again, and I'll bring Kay with me. There's no use asking the flowers about him. They don't know anything except their own songs, and they haven't any news for me."

Then she tucked up her little skirts so that she could run away faster, but the narcissus tapped against her leg as she was jumping over it. So she stopped and leaned over the tall flower.

"Perhaps you have something to tell me," she said.

What did the narcissus say?

"I can see myself! I can see myself! Oh, how sweet is my own fragrance! Up in the narrow garret, there is a little dancer, half dressed. First she stands on one leg. Then she stands on both, and kicks her heels at the whole world. She is an illusion of the stage. She pours water from the teapot over a piece of cloth she is holding—it is her bodice. Cleanliness is such a virtue! Her white dress hangs from a hook. It too has been washed in the teapot, and dried on the roof. She puts it on and ties a saffron scarf around her neck to make the dress seem whiter.

Point your toes! See how straight she balances on that single stem. I can see myself! I can see myself!"

"I'm not interested," said Gerda. "What a thing to tell me about!"

She ran to the end of the garden, and though the gate was fastened, she worked the rusty latch until it gave way and the gate flew open. Little Gerda scampered out into the wide world in her bare feet. She looked back three times, but nobody came after her. At last, she could run no farther, and she sat down to rest on a big stone, and when she looked up, she saw that summer had gone by and it was late in the fall. She could never have guessed it inside the beautiful garden where the sun was always shining and the flowers of every season were always in full bloom.

"Gracious! How long I've dallied," Gerda said. "Fall is already here. I can't rest any longer."

She got up to run on, but how footsore and tired she was! And how cold and bleak everything around her looked! The long leaves of the willow tree had turned quite yellow, and damp puffs of mist dropped from them like drops of water. One leaf after another fell to the ground. Only the blackthorn still bore fruit, and its fruit was so sour that it set your teeth on edge.

Oh, how dreary and gray the wide world looked.

FOURTH STORY
THE PRINCE AND THE PRINCESS

The next time that Gerda was forced to rest, a big crow came hopping across the snow in front of her. For a long time, he had been watching her and cocking his head to one side, and now he said, "Caw, caw! Good caw day!" He could not say it any better, but he felt kindly inclined toward the little girl, and asked her where she was going in the great wide world, all alone. Gerda understood him when he said "alone," and she knew its meaning all too well. She told the crow the whole story of her life, and asked if he hadn't seen Kay. The crow gravely nodded his head and cawed, "Maybe I have, maybe I have!"

"What! do you really think you have?" the little girl cried, and almost hugged the crow to death as she kissed him.

"Gently, gently!" said the crow. "I think that it may have been little Kay that I saw, but if it was, then he has forgotten you for the princess."

"Does he live with a princess?" Gerda asked.

"Yes. Listen!" said the crow. "But it is so hard for me to speak your language. If you understand crow talk, I can tell you much more easily."

"I don't know that language," said Gerda. "My grandmother knows it just as well as she knows baby talk, and I do wish I had learned it."

"No matter," said the crow. "I'll tell you as well as I can, though that won't be any too good." And he told her all that he knew.

"In the kingdom where we are now, there is a princess who is uncommonly clever, and no wonder. She has read all the newspapers in the world and forgotten them again—that's how clever she is. Well, not long ago she was sitting on her throne. That's by no means as much fun as people suppose, so she fell to humming an old tune, and the refrain of it happened to run:

Why, oh, why, shouldn't I get married?

"'Why, that's an idea!' said she. And she made up her mind to marry as soon as she could find the sort of husband who could give a good answer when anyone spoke to him, instead of one of those fellows who merely stand around looking impressive, for that is so tiresome. She had the drums drubbed to call together all her ladies-in-waiting, and when they heard what she had in mind, they were delighted.

"'Oh, we like that!' they said. 'We were just thinking the very same thing.'

"Believe me," said the crow, "every word I tell you is true. I have a tame ladylove who has the run of the palace, and I had the whole story straight from her." Of course his ladylove was also a crow, for birds of a feather will flock together.

"The newspapers immediately came out with a border of hearts and the initials of the princess, and you could read an announcement that any presentable young man might go to the palace and talk with her. The one who spoke best and who seemed most at home in the palace would be chosen by the princess as her husband.

"Yes, yes," said the crow, "believe me, that's as true as it is that here I sit. Men flocked to the palace, and there was much crowding and crushing, but on neither the first nor the second day was anyone chosen. Out in the street, they were all glib talkers, but after they entered the palace gate where the guardsmen were stationed in their silver-braided uniforms, and after they climbed up the staircase lined with footmen in gold-embroidered livery, they arrived in the brilliantly lighted reception halls without a word to say. And when they stood in front of the princess on her throne, the best they could do was to echo the last word of her remarks, and she didn't care to hear it repeated.

"It was just as if everyone in the throne room had his stomach filled with snuff and had fallen asleep; for as soon as they were back in the streets, there was no stopping their talk.

"The line of candidates extended all the way from the town gates to the palace. I saw them myself," said the crow. "They got hungry and they got thirsty, but from the palace they got nothing—not even a glass of lukewarm water. To be sure, some of the clever candidates had brought sandwiches with them, but they did not share them with their neighbors. Each man thought, 'Just let him look hungry, then the princess won't take him!'"

"But Kay, little Kay," Gerda interrupted, "when did he come? Was he among those people?"

"Give me time, give me time! We are just coming to him. On the third day, a little person, with neither horse nor carriage, strode boldly up to the palace. His eyes sparkled the way yours do, and he had handsome long hair, but his clothes were poor."

"Oh, that was Kay!" Gerda said, and clapped her hands in glee. "Now I've found him."

"He had a little knapsack on his back," the crow told her.

"No, that must have been his sled," said Gerda. "He was carrying it when he went away."

"Maybe so," the crow said. "I didn't look at it carefully. But my tame ladylove told me that when he went through the palace gates and saw the guardsmen in silver, and on the staircase the footmen in gold, he wasn't at all taken aback. He nodded and he said to them:

"'It must be very tiresome to stand on the stairs. I'd rather go inside.'

"The halls were brilliantly lighted. Ministers of state and privy councillors were walking about barefooted, carrying golden trays in front of them. It was enough to make anyone feel solemn, and his boots creaked dreadfully, but he wasn't a bit afraid."

"That certainly must have been Kay," said Gerda. "I know he was wearing new boots. I heard them creaking in Grandmother's room."

"Oh, they creaked all right," said the crow. "But it was little enough he cared as he walked straight to the princess, who was sitting on a pearl as big as a spinning wheel. All the ladies-in-waiting with their attendants and their attendants' attendants, and all the lords-in-waiting with their gentlemen and their gentlemen's men, each of whom had his page with him, were standing there, and the nearer they stood to the door, the more arrogant they looked. The gentlemen's men's pages, who always wore slippers, were almost too arrogant to look, as they stood at the threshold."

"That must have been terrible!" little Gerda exclaimed. "And yet Kay won the princess?"

"If I weren't a crow, I would have married her myself, for all that I'm engaged to another. They say he spoke as well as I do when I speak my crow language. Or so my tame ladylove tells me. He was dashing and handsome, and he was not there to court the princess but to hear her wisdom. This he liked, and she liked him."

"Of course it was Kay," said Gerda. "He was so clever that he could do mental arithmetic even with fractions. Oh, please take me to the palace."

"That's easy enough to say," said the crow, "but how can we manage it? I'll talk it over with my tame ladylove, and she may be able to suggest something, but I must warn you that a little girl like you will never be admitted."

"Oh, yes, I shall," said Gerda. "When Kay hears about me, he will come out to fetch me at once."

"Wait for me beside that stile," the crow said. He wagged his head, and off he flew.

Darkness had set in when he got back.

"Caw, caw!" he said. "My ladylove sends you her best wishes, and here's a little loaf of bread for you. She found it in the kitchen, where they have all the bread they need, and you must be hungry. You simply can't get into the palace with those bare feet. The guardsmen in silver and the footmen in gold would never permit it. But don't you cry. We'll find a way. My ladylove knows of a little back staircase that leads up to the bedroom, and she knows where they keep the key to it."

Then they went into the garden and down the wide promenade where the leaves were falling one by one. When one by one the lights went out in the palace, the crow led little Gerda to the back door, which stood ajar.

Oh, how her heart did beat with fear and longing. It was just as if she were about to do something wrong, yet she only wanted to make sure that this really was little Kay. Yes, truly it must be Kay, she thought, as she recalled his sparkling eyes and his long hair. She remembered exactly how he looked when he used to smile at her as they sat under the roses at home. Wouldn't he be glad to see her! Wouldn't he be interested in hearing how far she had come to find him and how sad they had all been when he didn't come home. She was so frightened, and yet so happy.

Now they were on the stairway. A little lamp was burning on a cupboard, and there stood the tame crow, cocking her head to look at Gerda, who made the curtsy that her grandmother had taught her.

"My fiancé has told me many charming things about you, dear young lady," she said. "Your biography, as one might say, is very touching. Kindly take the lamp, and I shall lead the way. We shall keep straight ahead, where we aren't apt to run into anyone."

"It seems to me that someone is on the stairs behind us," said Gerda. Things brushed past, and from the shadows on the wall, they seemed to be horses with spindly legs and waving manes. And there were shadows of huntsmen, ladies and gentlemen, on horseback.

"Those are only dreams," said the crow. "They come to take the thoughts of their royal masters off to the chase. That's just as well, for it will give you a good opportunity to see them while they sleep. But I trust that when you rise to high position and power, you will show a grateful heart."

"Tut tut! You've no need to say that," said the forest crow.

Now they entered the first room. It was hung with rose-colored satin, embroidered with flowers. The dream shadows were flitting by so fast that Gerda could not see the lords and ladies. Hall after magnificent hall quite bewildered her, until at last they reached the royal bedroom.

The ceiling of it was like the top of a huge palm tree, with leaves of glass, costly glass. In the middle of the room two beds hung from a massive stem of gold. Each of them looked like a lily. One bed was white, and there lay the princess. The other was red, and there Gerda hoped to find little Kay. She bent one of the scarlet petals and saw the nape of a little brown neck. Surely this must be Kay. She called his name aloud and held the lamp near him. The dreams on horseback pranced into the room again, as he awoke—and turned his head—and it was not little Kay at all.

The prince only resembled Kay about the neck, but he was young and handsome. The princess peeked out of her lily-white bed and asked what had happened. Little Gerda cried and told them all about herself and about all that the crows had done for her.

"Poor little thing," the prince and the princess said. They praised the crows and said they weren't the least bit angry with them, but not to do it again. Furthermore, they should have a reward.

"Would you rather fly about without any responsibilities," said the princess, "or would you care to be appointed court crows for life, with rights to all scraps from the kitchen?"

Both the crows bowed low and begged for permanent office, for they thought of their future and said it was better to provide for their "old age," as they called it.

The prince got up and let Gerda have his bed. It was the utmost that he could do. She clasped her little hands and thought, "How nice the people and the birds are." She closed her eyes, fell peacefully asleep, and all the dreams came flying back again. They looked like angels, and they drew a little sled on which Kay sat. He nodded to her, but this was only in a dream, so it all disappeared when she woke up.

The next day, she was dressed from her head to her heels in silk and in velvet, too. They asked her to stay at the palace and have a nice time there, but instead, she begged them to let her have a little carriage, a little horse, and a pair of little boots, so that she could drive out into the wide world to find Kay.

They gave her a pair of boots and also a muff. They dressed her as nicely as could be, and when she was ready to go, there at the gate stood a brand new carriage of pure gold. On it the coat of arms of the prince and the princess glistened like a star.

The coachman, the footman, and the postilions—for postilions there were—all wore golden crowns. The prince and the princess themselves helped her into the carriage and wished her Godspeed. The forest crow, who was now a married man, accompanied her for the first three miles, and sat beside Gerda, for it upset him to ride backward. The other crow stood beside the gate and waved her wings. She did not accompany them because she was suffering from a headache, brought on by eating too much in her new position. Inside, the carriage was lined with sugared cookies, and the seats were filled with fruit and gingerbread.

"Fare you well, fare you well," called the prince and princess. Little Gerda cried and the crow cried too, for the first few miles. Then the crow said good-bye, and that was the saddest leave-taking of all. He flew up into a tree and waved his big black wings as long as he could see the carriage, which flashed as brightly as the sun.

FIFTH STORY
THE LITTLE ROBBER GIRL

The carriage rolled on into a dark forest. Like a blazing torch, it shone in the eyes of some robbers. They could not bear it.

"That's gold! That's gold!" they cried. They sprang forward, seized the horses, killed the little postilions, the coachman, and the footman, and dragged little Gerda out of the carriage.

"How plump and how tender she looks, just as if she'd been fattened on nuts!" cried the old robber woman, who had a long bristly beard and long eyebrows that hung down over her eyes. "She looks like a fat little lamb. What a dainty dish she will be!" As she said this, she drew out her knife, a dreadful, flashing thing.

"Ouch!" the old woman howled. At just that moment, her own little daughter had bitten her ear. The little girl, whom she carried on her back, was a wild and reckless creature. "You beasty brat!" her mother exclaimed, but it kept her from using that knife on Gerda.

"She shall play with me," said the little robber girl. "She must give me her muff and that pretty dress she wears, and sleep with me in my bed." And she again gave her mother such a bite that the woman hopped and whirled around in pain. All the robbers laughed, and shouted:

"See how she dances with her brat."

"I want to ride in the carriage," the little robber girl said, and ride she did, for she was too spoiled and headstrong for words. She and Gerda climbed into the carriage, and away they drove over stumps and stones, into the depths of the forest. The little robber girl was no taller than Gerda, but she was stronger and much broader in the shoulders. Her skin was brown and her eyes coal-black—almost sad in their expression. She put her arms around Gerda, and said:

"They shan't kill you unless I get angry with you. I think you must be a princess."

"No, I'm not," said little Gerda. And she told about all that had happened to her, and how much she cared for little Kay. The robber girl looked at her gravely, gave a little nod of approval, and told her:

"Even if I should get angry with you, they shan't kill you, because I'll do it myself!" Then she dried Gerda's eyes, and stuck her own hands into Gerda's soft, warm muff.

The carriage stopped at last, in the courtyard of a robber's castle. The walls of it were cracked from bottom to top. Crows and ravens flew out of every loophole, and bulldogs huge enough to devour a man jumped high in the air. But they did not bark, for that was forbidden.

In the middle of the stone-paved, smoky old hall, a big fire was burning. The smoke of it drifted up to the ceiling, where it had to find its own way out. Soup was boiling in a big caldron, and hares and rabbits were roasting on the spit.

"Tonight, you shall sleep with me and all my little animals," the robber girl said. After they had something to eat and drink, they went over to a corner that was strewn with rugs and straw. On sticks and perches around the bedding roosted nearly a hundred pigeons. They seemed to be asleep, but they stirred just a little when the two little girls came near them.

"They are all mine," said the little robber girl. She seized the one that was nearest to her, held it by the legs, and shook it until it flapped its wings. "Kiss it," she cried, and thrust the bird in Gerda's face. "Those two are the wild rascals," she said, pointing high up the wall to a hole barred with wooden sticks. "Rascals of the woods they are, and they would fly away in a minute if they were not locked up."

"And here is my old sweetheart, Bae," she said, pulling at the horns of a reindeer that was tethered by a shiny copper ring around his neck. "We have to keep a sharp eye on him, or he would run away from us, too. Every single night, I tickle his neck with my knife blade, for he is afraid of that." From a hole in the wall, she pulled a long knife and rubbed it against the reindeer's neck. After the poor animal had kicked up its heels, the robber girl laughed and pulled Gerda down into the bed with her.

"Are you going to keep that knife in bed with you?" Gerda asked, and looked at it, a little frightened.

"I always sleep with my knife," the little robber girl said. "You never can tell what may happen. But let's hear again what you told me before about little Kay, and about why you are wandering through the wide world."

Gerda told the story all over again, while the wild pigeons cooed in their cage overhead and the tame pigeons slept. The little robber girl clasped one arm around Gerda's neck, gripped her knife in the other hand, fell asleep, and snored so that one could hear her. But Gerda could not close her eyes at all. She did not know whether she was to live or whether she was to die. The robbers sat around their fire, singing and drinking, and the old robber woman was turning somersaults. It was a terrible sight for a little girl to see.

Then the wood pigeons said, "Coo, coo. We have seen little Kay. A white hen was carrying his sled, and Kay sat in the Snow Queen's sleigh. They swooped low, over the trees where we lay in our nest. The Snow Queen blew upon us, and all the young pigeons died except us. Coo, coo."

"What is that you are saying up there?" cried Gerda. "Where was the Snow Queen going? Do you know anything about it?"

"She was probably bound for Lapland, where they always have snow and ice. Why don't you ask the reindeer who is tethered beside you?"

"Yes, there is ice and snow in that glorious land," the reindeer told her. "You can prance about freely across those great, glittering fields. The Snow Queen has her summer tent there, but her stronghold is a castle up nearer the North Pole, on the island called Spitzbergen."

"Oh, Kay, little Kay," Gerda sighed.

"Lie still," said the robber girl, "or I'll stick my knife in your stomach."

In the morning, Gerda told her all that the wood pigeons had said. The little robber girl looked quite thoughtful. She nodded her head and exclaimed, "Leave it to me! Leave it to me.

"Do you know where Lapland is?" she asked the reindeer.

"Who knows it better than I?" the reindeer said, and his eyes sparkled. "There I was born, there I was bred, and there I kicked my heels in freedom, across the fields of snow."

"Listen!" the robber girl said to Gerda. "As you see, all the men are away. Mother is still here, and here she'll stay, but before the morning is over, she will drink out of that big bottle, and then she usually dozes off for a nap. As soon as that happens, I will do you a good turn."

She jumped out of bed, rushed over and threw her arms around her mother's neck, pulled at her beard bristles, and said, "Good morning, my dear nanny goat." Her mother thumped her nose until it was red and blue, but all that was done out of pure love.

As soon as the mother had tipped up the bottle and dozed off to sleep, the little robber girl ran to the reindeer and said, "I have a good notion to keep you here and tickle you with my sharp knife. You are so funny when I do, but never mind that. I'll untie your rope and help you find your way outside, so that you can run back to Lapland. But you must put your best leg forward and carry this little girl to the Snow Queen's palace, where her playmate is. I suppose you heard what she told me, for she spoke so loud, and you were eavesdropping."

The reindeer was so happy that he bounded into the air. The robber girl hoisted little Gerda on his back, carefully tied her in place, and even gave her a little pillow to sit on. "I don't do things half way," she said. "Here, take back your fur boots, for it's going to be bitter cold. I'll keep your muff, because it's such a pretty one. But your fingers mustn't get cold. Here are my mother's big mittens, which will come right up to your elbows. Pull them on. Now your hands look just like my ugly mother's big paws."

And Gerda shed happy tears.

"I don't care to see you blubbering," said the little robber girl. "You ought to look pleased now. Here, take these two loaves of bread and this ham along, so that you won't starve."

When these provisions were tied on the back of the reindeer, the little robber girl opened the door and called in all the big dogs. Then she cut the tether with her knife and said to the reindeer, "Now run, but see that you take good care of the little girl."

Gerda waved her big mittens to the little robber girl and said good-bye. Then the reindeer bounded away, over stumps and stones, straight through the great forest, over swamps and across the plains, as fast as he could run. The wolves howled, the ravens shrieked, and *ker-shew, ker-shew!* The red streaks of light ripped through the heavens, with a noise that sounded like sneezing.

"Those are my old northern lights," said the reindeer. "See how they flash." And on he ran, faster than ever, by night and day. The loaves were eaten and the whole ham was eaten—and there they were in Lapland.

SIXTH STORY

The Lapp Woman and the Finn Woman

They stopped in front of the little hut, and a makeshift dwelling it was. The roof of it almost touched the ground, and the doorway was so low that the family had to lie on their stomachs to crawl in it or out of it. No one was at home except an old Lapp woman, who was cooking fish over a whale-oil lamp. The reindeer told her Gerda's whole story, but first he told his own, which he thought was much more important. Besides, Gerda was so cold that she couldn't say a thing.

"Oh, you poor creatures," the Lapp woman said, "you've still got such a long way to go. Why, you will have to travel hundreds of miles into the Finmark. For it's there that the Snow Queen is taking a country vacation and burning her blue fireworks every evening. I'll jot down a message on a dried codfish, for I haven't any paper. I want you to take it to the Finn woman who lives up there. She will be able to tell you more about it than I can."

As soon as Gerda had thawed out and had had something to eat and drink, the Lapp woman wrote a few words on a dried codfish, told Gerda to take good care of it, and tied her again on the back of the reindeer. Off he ran, and all night long, the skies crackled and swished as the most beautiful northern lights flashed over their heads. At last, they came to the Finmark and knocked at the Finn woman's chimney, for she hadn't a sign of a door. It was so hot inside that the Finn woman went about almost naked. She was small and terribly dowdy, but she at once helped little Gerda off with her mittens and boots and loosened her clothes. Otherwise the heat would have wilted her. Then the woman put a piece of ice on the reindeer's head and read what was written on the codfish. She read it three times and when she knew it by heart, she put the fish into the kettle of soup, for they might as well eat it. She never wasted anything.

The reindeer told her his own story first, and then little Gerda's. The Finn woman winked a knowing eye, but she didn't say anything.

"You are such a wise woman," said the reindeer, "I know that you can tie all the winds of the world together with a bit of cotton thread. If the sailor unties one knot, he gets a favorable wind. If he unties another, he gets a stiff gale, while if he unties the third and fourth knots, such a tempest rages that it flattens the trees in the forest. Won't you give this little girl something to drink that will make her as strong as twelve men, so that she may overpower the Snow Queen?"

"Twelve strong men," the Finn woman sniffed. "Much good that would be."

She went to the shelf, took down a big rolled-up skin, and unrolled it. On this skin strange characters were written, and the Finn woman read them until the sweat rolled down her forehead.

The reindeer again begged her to help Gerda, and little Gerda looked at her with such tearful, imploring eyes that the woman began winking again. She took the reindeer aside in a corner, and while she was putting another piece of ice on his head, she whispered to him:

"Little Kay is indeed with the Snow Queen, and everything there just suits him fine. He thinks it is the best place in all the world, but that's because he has a splinter of glass in his heart and a small piece of it in his eye. Unless these can be gotten out, he will never be human again, and the Snow Queen will hold him in her power."

"But can't you fix little Gerda something to drink that will give her more power than all those things?"

"No power that I could give could be as great as that which she already has. Don't you see how men and beasts are compelled to serve her, and how far she has come in the wide world since she started out in her naked feet? We mustn't tell her about this power. Strength lies in her heart, because she is such a sweet, innocent child. If she herself cannot reach the Snow Queen and rid little Kay of those pieces of glass, then there's no help that we can give her. The Snow Queen's garden lies about eight miles from here. You may carry the little girl there and put her down by the big bush covered with red berries that grows on the snow. Then don't you stand there gossiping, but hurry to get back here."

The Finn woman lifted little Gerda onto the reindeer, and he galloped away as fast as he could.

"Oh!" cried Gerda, "I forgot my boots and I forgot my mittens." She soon felt the need of them in that knifelike cold, but the reindeer did not dare to stop. He galloped on until they came to the big bush that was covered with red berries. Here he set Gerda down and kissed her on the mouth, while big shining tears ran down his face. Then he ran back as fast as he could. Little Gerda stood there without boots and without mittens, right in the middle of icy Finmark.

She ran as fast as ever she could. A whole regiment of snowflakes swirled toward her, but they did not fall from the sky, for there was not a cloud up there, and the northern lights were ablaze.

The flakes skirmished along the ground, and the nearer they came, the larger they grew. Gerda remembered how large and strange they had appeared when she looked at them under the magnifying glass. But here, they were much more monstrous and terrifying. They were alive. They were the Snow Queen's advance guard, and their shapes were most strange. Some looked like ugly, overgrown porcupines. Some were like a knot of snakes that stuck out their heads in every direction, and others were like fat little bears with every hair abristle. All of them were glistening white, for all were living snowflakes.

It was so cold that as little Gerda said the Lord's Prayer, she could see her breath freezing in front of her mouth, like a cloud of smoke. It grew thicker and thicker, and took the shape of little angels that grew bigger and bigger the moment they touched the ground. All of them had helmets on their heads, and they carried shields and lances in their hands. Rank upon rank, they increased, and when Gerda had finished her prayer, she was surrounded by a legion of angels. They struck the dread snowflakes with their lances and shivered them into a thousand pieces. Little Gerda walked on, unmolested and cheerful. The angels rubbed her hands and feet to make them warmer, and she trotted briskly along to the Snow Queen's palace.

But now, let us see how little Kay was getting on. Little Gerda was furthest from his mind, and he hadn't the slightest idea that she was just outside the palace.

SEVENTH STORY
What Happened in the Snow Queen's Palace and What Came of It

The walls of the palace were driven snow. The windows and doors were the knife-edged wind. There were more than a hundred halls, shaped as the snow had drifted, and the largest of these extended for many a mile. All were lighted by the flare of the northern lights. All of the halls were so immense and so empty, so brilliant and so glacial! There was never a touch of gaiety in them; never so much as a little dance for the polar bears, at which the storm blast could have served for music, and the polar bears could have waddled about on their hind legs to show off their best manners. There was never a little party with such games as blind-bear's buff or hide the paw-kerchief for the cubs, nor even a little afternoon coffee over which the white fox vixens could gossip. Empty, vast, and frigid were the Snow Queen's halls. The northern lights flared with such regularity that you could time exactly when they would be at the highest and lowest. In the middle of the vast, empty hall of snow was a frozen lake. It was cracked into a thousand pieces, but each piece was shaped so exactly like the others that it seemed a work of wonderful craftsmanship. The Snow Queen sat in the exact center of it when she was at home, and she spoke of this as sitting on her "Mirror of Reason." She said this mirror was the only one of its kind, and the best thing in all the world.

Little Kay was blue, yes, almost black, with the cold. But he did not feel it, because the Snow Queen had kissed away his icy tremblings, and his heart itself had almost turned to ice.

He was shifting some sharp, flat pieces of ice to and fro, trying to fit them into every possible pattern, for he wanted to make something with them. It was like the Chinese puzzle game that we play at home, juggling little flat pieces of wood about into special designs. Kay was cleverly arranging his pieces in the game of ice-cold reason. To him, the patterns were highly remarkable and of the utmost importance, for the chip of glass in his eye made him see them that way. He arranged his pieces to spell out many words; but he could never find the way to make the one word he was so eager to form. The word was "Eternity." The Snow Queen had said to him, "If you can puzzle that out, you shall be your own master, and I'll give you the whole world and a new pair of skates." But he could not puzzle it out.

"Now I am going to make a flying trip to the warm countries," the Snow Queen told him. "I want to go and take a look into the black caldrons." She meant the volcanos of Etna and Vesuvius. "I must whiten them up a bit. They need it, and it will be such a relief after all those yellow lemons and purple grapes."

And away she flew. Kay sat all alone in that endless, empty, frigid hall and puzzled over the pieces of ice until he almost cracked his skull. He sat so stiff and still that one might have thought he was frozen to death.

All of a sudden, little Gerda walked up to the palace through the great gate that was a knife-edged wind. But Gerda said her evening prayer. The wind was lulled to rest, and the little girl came on into the vast, cold, empty hall. Then she saw Kay. She recognized him at once, and ran to throw her arms around him. She held him close and cried, "Kay, dearest little Kay! I've found you at last!"

But he sat still, and stiff, and cold. Gerda shed hot tears, and when they fell upon him, they went straight to his heart. They melted the lump of ice and burned away the splinter of glass in it. He looked up at her, and she sang:

> Where roses bloom so sweetly in the vale,
> There shall you find the Christ Child, without fail.

Kay burst into tears. He cried so freely that the little piece of glass in his eye was washed right out. "Gerda!" He knew her, and cried out in his happiness, "My sweet little Gerda, where have you been so long? And where have I been?" He looked around him and said, "How cold it is here! How enormous and empty!" He held fast to Gerda, who laughed until happy tears rolled down her cheeks. Their bliss was so heavenly that even the bits of glass danced about them and shared in their happiness. When the pieces grew tired, they dropped into a pattern that made the very word that the Snow Queen had told Kay he must find before he became his own master and received the whole world and a new pair of skates.

Gerda kissed his cheeks, and they turned pink again. She kissed his eyes, and they sparkled like hers. She kissed his hands and feet, and he became strong and well. The Snow Queen might come home now whenever she pleased, for there stood the order for Kay's release, written in letters of shining ice.

Hand in hand, Kay and Gerda strolled out of that enormous palace. They talked about Grandmother, and about the roses on their roof. Wherever they went, the wind died down and the sun shone out. When they came to the bush that was covered with red berries, the reindeer was waiting to meet them. He had brought along a young reindeer mate who had warm milk for the children to drink, and who kissed them on the mouth. Then these reindeer carried Gerda and Kay first to the Finn woman. They warmed themselves in her hot room, and when she had given them directions for their journey home, they rode on to the Lapp woman. She had made them new clothes, and was ready to take them along in her sleigh.

Side by side, the reindeer ran with them to the limits of the north country, where the first green buds were to be seen. Here they said good-bye to the two reindeer and to the Lapp woman. "Farewell," they all said.

Now the first little birds began to chirp, and there were green buds all around them in the forest. Through the woods came riding a young girl on a magnificent horse that Gerda recognized, for it had once been harnessed to the golden carriage. The girl wore a bright red cap on her head and a pair of pistols in her belt. She was the little robber girl, who had grown tired of staying at home and who was setting out on a journey to the north country. If she didn't like it there, why, the world was wide, and there were many other places where she could go. She recognized Gerda at once, and Gerda knew her too. It was a happy meeting.

"You're a fine one for gadding about," she told little Kay. "I'd just like to know whether you deserve to have someone running to the end of the Earth for your sake."

But Gerda patted her cheek and asked her about the prince and the princess.

"They are traveling in foreign lands," the girl told her.

"And the crow?"

"Oh, the crow is dead," she answered. "His tame ladylove is now a widow, and she wears a bit of black wool wrapped around her leg. She takes great pity on herself, but that's all stuff and nonsense. Now tell me what has happened to you and how you caught up with Kay."

Gerda and Kay told her their story.

"*Snip snap snurre*, *basse lurre*," said the robber girl. "So everything came out all right." She shook them by the hand and promised that if ever she passed through their town, she would come to see them. And then she rode away.

Kay and Gerda held each other by the hand. And as they walked along, they had wonderful spring weather. The land was green and strewn with flowers, church bells rang, and they saw the high steeples of a big town. It was the one where they used to live. They walked straight to Grandmother's house, and up the stairs, and into the room, where everything was just as it was when they left it. And the clock said *tick-tock*, and its hands were telling the time. But the moment they came in the door, they noticed one change. They were grown-up now.

The roses on the roof looked in at the open window, and their two little stools were still out there. Kay and Gerda sat down on them, and held each other by the hand. Both of them had forgotten the icy, empty splendor of the Snow Queen's palace as completely as if it were some bad dream. Grandmother sat in God's good sunshine, reading to them from her Bible:

"Except ye become as little children, ye shall not enter into the Kingdom of Heaven."

Kay and Gerda looked into each other's eyes, and at last they understood the meaning of their old hymn:

> Where roses bloom so sweetly in the vale,
> There shall you find the Christ Child, without fail.

And they sat there, grown-up, but children—still children at heart. And it was summer—warm, glorious summer.

THE ELF MOUND (1845)

Several lizards darted briskly in and out of the cracks of a hollow tree. They understood each other perfectly, for they all spoke lizard language.

"My! How it rumbles and buzzes in the old elf mound," said one lizard. "It rumbles and bumbles so that I haven't had a wink of sleep for the past two nights. I might as well have a toothache, for that also prevents me from sleeping."

"There's something afoot," said another lizard. "Until the cock crowed for dawn, they had the mound propped up on four red poles to give it a thoroughgoing airing. And the elf maidens are learning to stamp out some new dances. Something is surely afoot."

"Yes, I was just talking about it with an earthworm I know," said a third lizard. "He came straight from the mound, where he has been nosing around night and day. He overheard a good deal. For he can't see, poor thing, but he knows his way around and makes an uncommonly good eavesdropper. They expect company in the elf mound, distinguished visitors, but the earthworm wouldn't say who they are. Or maybe he didn't know. All the will-o'-the-wisps have been told to parade with their torches, as they are called, and all of the flat silver and gold plate with which the hill is well stocked is being polished and put out in the moonlight."

"Who *can* the visitors be?" the lizards all wanted to know. "What in the world is going on? Listen to the hustle! Listen to the bustle!"

Just at that moment, the elf mound opened, and an old-maid elf minced out of it. The woman had no back, but otherwise she was quite properly dressed, with her amber jewelry in the shape of a heart. She kept house for her distant cousin, the old king of the elves, and she was very spry in the legs. *Trip, trot,* away she went. How she hurried and scurried off to see the night raven down in the marsh.

"You are hereby invited to the elf mound, this very night," she told him. "But may I ask you to do us a great favor first? Please deliver the other invitations for us. As you have no place of your own where you can entertain, you must make yourself generally useful. We shall have some very distinguished visitors—goblins of rank, let me tell you. So the old elf king wants to make the best impression he can."

"Who is being invited?" the night raven asked.

"Oh, everybody may come to the big ball—even ordinary mortals if they talk in their sleep or can do anything else that we can do. But at the banquet, the company must be strictly select. Only the very best people are invited to it. I've threshed that out thoroughly with the elf king, because I insist we should not even invite ghosts. First of all, we must invite the Old Man of the Sea and his daughters. I suppose they won't like to venture out on dry land, but we can at least give them a comfortable wet stone to sit on, or something better, and I don't think they'll refuse this time. Then we must have all the old trolls of the first degree, with tails. We must ask the old man of the stream, and the brownies, and I believe we should ask the grave-pig, the bone-horse, and the church dwarf, though they live under churches and, properly speaking, belong to the clergy, who are not our sort of people at all. Still, that is their vocation, and they are closely related to us, and often come to call."

"*Cra!*" said the night raven as he flew to summon the guests.

On their mound, the elf maidens had already begun to dance, and they danced with long scarves made of mist and moonlight. To those who care for scarf dancing, it was most attractive.

The large central hall of the elf mound had been especially prepared for this great night. The floor was washed with moonlight, and the walls were polished with witch wax, which made them glisten like the petals of a tulip. The kitchen abounded with skewered frogs, snakeskins stuffed with small children's fingers, fungus salad made of mushroom seed, wet mouse noses, and hemlock. There was beer of the swamp witch's brewing and sparkling salpeter champagne from graveyard vaults. All very substantial! Rusty nails and ground glass from church windows were among the delicacies.

The old elf king had his gold crown polished with powdered slate pencil. It was a prize pupil's slate pencil, and a prize pupil's slate pencil is not so easy for an elf king to obtain. The curtains in the bedroom were freshly starched with snail slime. Oh, how they did hustle and bustle.

"Now we shall burn horsehair and pig's bristles for incense, and my duty is done," said the housekeeper.

"Dear Papa Elf," said his youngest daughter, "will you tell me now who the guests of honor are to be?"

"Well," he said, "it's high time that I told you. I have made a match for two of my daughters. Two of you must be ready to get married without fail. The venerable goblin chief of Norway, who lives in the old Dovrefjeld Mountains, and possesses a gold mine and crag castles and strongholds much better than people can imagine, is on his way here with his two sons, and each son wants a wife. The old goblin chief is a real Norwegian, honest and true, straightforward and merry. I have known him for many a year, and we drank to our lasting friendship when he came here to get his wife. She's dead now, but she was the daughter of the king of the chalk cliffs at Möen. I used to tell him that he got married on the chalk, as if he had bought his wife on credit. How I look forward to seeing him again. His sons, they say, are rough and rowdy. But they'll improve when they get older. It's up to you to polish them."

"How soon will they come?" one of his daughters asked.

"That depends on the wind and the weather," he said. "They are thrifty travelers—they will come by ship when they have a chance. I wanted them to travel overland by way of Sweden, but the old gentleman wouldn't hear of it. He doesn't keep up with the times, and I don't like that."

Just then, two will-o'-the-wisps came tumbling in, one faster than the other, and therefore he got there first. Both of them were shouting:

"Here they come, here they come!"

"Hand me my crown. Let me stand where the moon shines most brightly," the elf king said.

His daughters lifted their long scarves and curtsied low to the ground.

There came the venerable goblin chief from the Dovrefjeld, crowned with sparkling icicles and polished fir cones, muffled in his bearskin coat, and wearing his sledge boots. His sons dressed quite differently, with their throats uncovered and without suspenders. They were husky fellows.

"Is that a hill?" The smallest of the two brothers pointed his finger at the elf mound. In Norway, we would call it a hole."

"Son!" cried the old goblin chief. "Hills come up, and holes go down. Have you no eyes in your head?"

The only thing that amazed them, they said, was the language that people spoke here. Why, they could actually understand it.

"Don't make such tomfools of yourselves," said their father, "or people will think you ignoramuses."

They entered the elf mound, where all the best people were gathered, though they assembled so fast that they seemed swept in by the wind. Nevertheless, the arrangements were delightfully convenient for everybody. The Old Man of the Sea and his daughters were seated at the table in large casks of water, which they said made them feel right at home. Everybody had good table manners except the two young Norwegian goblins, who put their feet on the table as if anything they did were all right.

"Take your feet out of your plates," said the old goblin chief, and they obeyed, but not right away. They had brought fir cones in their pockets to tickle the ladies sitting next to them. To make themselves comfortable, they pulled off their boots and gave them to the ladies to hold. However, their father, the old Dovre goblin, conducted himself quite differently. He talked well of the proud crags of Norway, and of waterfalls rushing down in a cloud of spray, with a roar like thunder and the sound of an organ. He told how the salmon leap up through the waterfall when they hear the nixies twang away on golden harps. He described bracing winter nights on which the sleigh bells chime and boys with flaming torches skim over polished ice so clear that one can see the startled fish swish away underfoot. Yes, he had a way of talking that made you both hear and see the sawmill sawing and the boys and girls as they sang and danced the Norwegian Hallinge dance. Hurrah! In the wink of an eye, the goblin chief gave the old maid elf such a kiss that it smacked, though they weren't in the least related.

Then the elf maidens must do their dances, first the ordinary dances and then the dance where they stamped their feet, which set them off to perfection. Then they did a really complicated one called, "A Dance to End Dancing." Keep us and save us, how light they were on their feet. Whose leg was whose? Which were arms and which were legs? They whipped through the air like shavings at a planing mill. The girls twirled so fast that it made the bone-horse's head spin, and he staggered away from the table.

"Whir-r-r," said the goblin chief. "The girls are lively enough, but what can they do besides dancing like mad, spinning like tops, and making the bone-horse dizzy?"

"I'll show you what they can do," the elf king boasted. He called his youngest daughter. She was as thin and fair as moonlight. She was the most dainty of all the sisters, and when she took a white wand in her mouth, it vanished away. That was what she could do. But the goblin chief said this was an art he wouldn't like his wife to possess, and he didn't think his sons would either.

The second daughter could walk alongside herself as if she had a shadow, which is something that trolls don't possess. The third was a very different sort of girl. She had studied brewing with the swamp witch, and she was a good hand at seasoning alder stumps with glowworms.

"Now this one would make a good housewife," said the goblin chief, winking instead of drinking to her, for he wanted to keep his wits clear.

The fourth daughter played upon a tall, golden harp. As soon as she fingered the first string, everyone kicked up his left leg, for all of the troll tribe are left-legged. And as soon as she fingered the second string, everyone had to do just as she said.

"What a dangerous woman," said the goblin chief. His sons were very bored, and they strolled out of the elf mound as their father asked, "What can the next daughter do?"

"I have learned to like Norwegians," she told him. "I'll never marry unless I can live in Norway."

But her youngest sister whispered in the old goblin's ear, "She only says that because of the old Norwegian saying that even though the world should fall, the rocks of Norway would still stand tall; that's why she wants to go there. She's afraid to die."

"Hee, hee," said the goblin, "somebody let the cat out of the bag. Now for the seventh and last."

"The sixth comes before the seventh," said the elf king, who was more careful with his arithmetic. But the sixth daughter would not come forward.

"I can only tell the truth," she said, "so nobody likes me, and I have enough to do to sew upon my shroud."

Now came the seventh and last daughter. What could she do? She could tell tales, as many as ever she pleased.

"Here are my five fingers," said the old goblin. "Tell me a story for each of them."

The elf maiden took him by the wrist, and he chuckled till he almost choked. When she came to the fourth finger, which wore a gold ring just as if it knew that weddings were in the air, the old goblin said, "Hold it fast, for I give you my hand. I'll take you to wife myself."

The elf maiden said that the stories of Guldbrand, the fourth finger, and of little Peter Playfellow, the fifth finger, remained to be told.

"Ah, we shall save those until winter," said the old goblin chief. "Then you shall tell me about the fir tree and the birch, of the ghost presents and of the creaking frost. You will be our teller of tales, for none of us has the knack of it. We shall sit in my great stone castle where the pine logs blaze, and we shall drink our mead out of the golden horns of old Norwegian kings. I have two that Water Goblin washed into my hand. And while we sit there side by side, Sir Garbo will come to call, and he will sing you the mountain maidens' song. How merry we then shall be! The salmon will leap in the waterfall and beat against our stone walls, but he'll never get in to where we sit so snug. Ah, I tell you, it is good to live in glorious old Norway. But where have the boys gone?"

Where indeed? They were charging through the fields, blowing out the will-o'-the-wisps who were coming so modestly for their torchlight parade.

"Is that a way to behave?" said the goblin chief. "I have chosen a stepmother for you, so come and choose wives of your own."

But his sons said they preferred speeches and drink to matrimony. So they made speeches, and they drank healths, and turned their glasses bottom side up to show how empty they were. Then they took off their coats, and lay down on the table to sleep, for they had no manners. But the old goblin danced around the room with his young bride, and changed his boots for hers, which was much more fashionable than merely exchanging rings.

"There's that cock crowing!" the old maid housekeeper of the elves warned them. "Now we must close the shutters to keep the sun from burning us."

So they closed the mound. But outside, the lizards darted around the hollow tree, and one said to the other: "Oh, how we liked that old Norwegian goblin chief!"

"I preferred his jolly sons," said the earthworm, but then he had no eyes in his head, poor thing.

THE RED SHOES (1845)

There was once a little girl, very nice and very pretty, but so poor that she had to go barefooted all summer. And in winter, she had to wear thick wooden shoes that chafed her ankles until they were red, oh, as red as could be.

In the middle of the village lived Old Mother Shoemaker. She took some old scraps of red cloth and did her best to make them into a little pair of shoes. They were a bit clumsy, but well meant, for she intended to give them to the little girl. Karen was the little girl's name.

The first time Karen wore her new red shoes was on the very day when her mother was buried. Of course, they were not right for mourning, but they were all she had, so she put them on and walked barelegged after the plain wicker coffin.

Just then a large old carriage came by, with a large old lady inside it. She looked at the little girl and took pity upon her. And she went to the parson and said: "Give the little girl to me, and I shall take good care of her."

Karen was sure that this happened because she wore red shoes, but the old lady said the shoes were hideous, and ordered them burned. Karen was given proper new clothes. She was taught to read, and she was taught to sew. People said she was pretty, but her mirror told her, "You are more than pretty. You are beautiful."

It happened that the queen came traveling through the country with her little daughter, who was a princess. Karen went with all the people who flocked to see them at the castle. The little princess, all dressed in white, came to the window to let them admire her. She didn't wear a train, and she didn't wear a gold crown, but she did wear a pair of splendid red morocco shoes. Of course, they were much nicer than the ones Old Mother Shoemaker had put together for little Karen, but there's nothing in the world like a pair of red shoes!

When Karen was old enough to be confirmed, new clothes were made for her, and she was to have new shoes. They went to the house of a thriving shoemaker to have him take the measure of her little feet. In his shop were big glass cases, filled with the prettiest shoes and the shiniest boots. They looked most attractive, but, as the old lady did not see very well, they did not attract her. Among the shoes there was a pair of red leather ones that were just like those the princess had worn. How perfect they were! The shoemaker said he had made them for the daughter of a count, but that they did not quite fit her.

"They must be patent leather to shine so," said the old lady.

"Yes, indeed they shine," said Karen. As the shoes fitted Karen, the old lady bought them, but she had no idea they were red. If she had known that, she would never have let Karen wear them to confirmation, which is just what Karen did.

Every eye was turned toward her feet. When she walked up the aisle to the chancel of the church, it seemed to her as if even those portraits of bygone ministers and their wives, in starched ruffs and long black gowns—even they fixed their eyes upon her red shoes. She could think of nothing else, even when the pastor laid his hands upon her head and spoke of her holy baptism, and her covenant with God, and her duty as a Christian. The solemn organ rolled, the children sang sweetly, and the old choir leader sang too, but Karen thought of nothing except her red shoes.

Before the afternoon was over, the old lady had heard from everyone in the parish that the shoes were red. She told Karen it was naughty to wear red shoes to church. Highly improper! In the future, she was always to wear black shoes to church, even though they were her old ones.

Next Sunday, there was holy communion. Karen looked at her black shoes. She looked at her red ones. She kept looking at her red ones until she put them on.

It was a fair, sunny day. Karen and the old lady took the path through the cornfield, where it was rather dusty. At the church door, they met an old soldier, who stood with a crutch and wore a long, curious beard. It was more reddish than white. In fact, it was quite red. He bowed down to the ground and asked the old lady if he might dust her shoes. Karen put out her little foot too.

"Oh, what beautiful shoes for dancing," the soldier said. "Never come off when you dance," he told the shoes, as he tapped the sole of each of them with his hand.

The old lady gave the soldier a penny, and went on into the church with Karen. All the people there stared at Karen's red shoes, and all the portraits stared, too. When Karen knelt at the altar rail, and even when the chalice came to her lips, she could think only of her red shoes. It was as if they kept floating around in the chalice, and she forgot to sing the psalm. She forgot to say the Lord's Prayer.

Then church was over, and the old lady got into her carriage. Karen was lifting her foot to step in after her when the old soldier said, "Oh, what beautiful shoes for dancing!"

Karen couldn't resist taking a few dancing steps, and once she began, her feet kept on dancing. It was as if the shoes controlled her. She danced round the corner of the church—she simply could not help it. The coachman had to run after her, catch her, and lift her into the carriage. But even there, her feet went on dancing so that she gave the good old lady a terrible kicking. Only when she took her shoes off did her legs quiet down. When they got home the shoes were put away in a cupboard, but Karen would still go and look at them.

Shortly afterward the old lady was taken ill, and it was said she could not recover. She required constant care and faithful nursing, and for this she depended on Karen. But a great ball was being given in the town, and Karen was invited. She looked at the old lady, who could not live in any case. She looked at the red shoes, for she thought there was no harm in looking. She put them on, for she thought there was no harm in that either. But then she went to the ball and began dancing. When she tried to turn to the right, the shoes turned to the left. When she wanted to dance up the ballroom, her shoes danced down. They danced down the stairs, into the street, and out through the gate of the town. Dance she did, and dance she must, straight into the dark woods.

Suddenly, something shone through the trees, and she thought it was the moon, but it turned out to be the red-bearded soldier. He nodded and said, "Oh, what beautiful shoes for dancing."

She was terribly frightened, and tried to take off her shoes. She tore off her stockings, but the shoes had grown fast to her feet. And dance she did, for dance she must, over fields and valleys, in the rain and in the sun, by day and night. It was most dreadful by night. She danced over an unfenced graveyard, but the dead did not join her dance. They had better things to do. She tried to sit on a pauper's grave, where the bitter fennel grew, but there was no rest or peace for her there. And when she danced toward the open doors of the church, she saw it guarded by an angel with long white robes and wings that reached from his shoulders down to the ground. His face was grave and stern, and in his hand he held a broad, shining sword.

"Dance you shall!" he told her. "Dance in your red shoes until you are pale and cold, and your flesh shrivels down to the skeleton. Dance you shall from door to door, and wherever there are children proud and vain, you must knock at the door till they hear you, and are afraid of you. Dance you shall. Dance always."

"Have mercy upon me!" screamed Karen. But she did not hear the angel answer. Her shoes swept her out through the gate, and across the fields, along highways and byways, forever and always dancing.

One morning, she danced by a door she knew well. There was the sound of a hymn, and a coffin was carried out covered with flowers. Then she knew the old lady was dead. She was all alone in the world now, and cursed by the angel of God.

Dance she did and dance she must, through the dark night. Her shoes took her through thorn and briar that scratched her until she bled. She danced across the wastelands until she came to a lonely little house. She knew that this was where the executioner lived, and she tapped with her finger on his window pane.

"Come out!" she called. "Come out! I can't come in, for I am dancing."

The executioner said, "You don't seem to know who I am. I strike off the heads of bad people, and I feel my ax beginning to quiver."

"Don't strike off my head, for then I could not repent of my sins," said Karen. "But strike off my feet with the red shoes on them."

She confessed her sin, and the executioner struck off her feet with the red shoes on them. The shoes danced away with her little feet, over the fields into the deep forest. But he made wooden feet and a pair of crutches for her. He taught her a hymn that prisoners sing when they are sorry for what they have done. She kissed his hand that held the ax, and went back across the wasteland.

"Now I have suffered enough for those red shoes," she said. "I shall go and be seen again in the church." She hobbled to church as fast as she could, but when she got there, the red shoes danced in front of her, and she was frightened and turned back.

All week long she was sorry, and cried many bitter tears. But when Sunday came again, she said, "Now I have suffered and cried enough. I think I must be as good as many who sit in church and hold their heads high." She started out unafraid, but the moment she came to the church gate, she saw her red shoes dancing before her. More frightened than ever, she turned away, and with all her heart, she really repented.

She went to the pastor's house and begged him to give her work as a servant. She promised to work hard, and do all that she could. Wages did not matter, if only she could have a roof over her head and be with good people. The pastor's wife took pity on her, and gave her work at the parsonage. Karen was faithful and serious. She sat quietly in the evening and listened to every word when the pastor read the Bible aloud. The children were devoted to her, but when they spoke of frills and furbelows and of being as beautiful as a queen, she would shake her head.

When they went to church next Sunday, they asked her to go too, but with tears in her eyes, she looked at her crutches, and shook her head. The others went to hear the word of God, but she went to her lonely little room, which was just big enough to hold her bed and one chair. She sat with her hymnal in her hands, and as she read it with a contrite heart, she heard the organ roll. The wind carried the sound from the church to her window. Her face was wet with tears as she lifted it up, and said, "Help me, O Lord!"

Then the sun shone bright, and the white-robed angel stood before her. He was the same angel she had seen that night at the door of the church. But he no longer held a sharp sword. In his hand was a green branch, covered with roses. He touched the ceiling with it. There was a golden star where it touched, and the ceiling rose high. He touched the walls, and they opened wide. She saw the deep-toned organ. She saw the portraits of ministers and their wives. She saw the congregation sit in flower-decked pews and sing from their hymnals. Either the church had come to the poor girl in her narrow little room, or it was she who had been brought to the church. She sat in the pew with the pastor's family. When they had finished the hymn, they looked up and nodded to her.

"It was right for you to come, little Karen," they said.

"It was God's own mercy," she told them.

The organ sounded, and the children in the choir sang, softly and beautifully. Clear sunlight streamed warm through the window, right down to the pew where Karen sat. She was so filled with the light of it, and with joy and with peace, that her heart broke. Her soul traveled along the shaft of sunlight to Heaven, where no one questioned her about the red shoes.

THE JUMPERS (1845)

Once upon a time, a flea, a grasshopper, and a jumping goose wanted to see which one could jump the highest, so they invited the whole world, and even a few others, to come to a festival to watch the test. They were three famous jumpers indeed, and they all met together in a big room.

"I'll give my daughter to the one who jumps the highest," said the king. "It seems so stingy to have these fellows jump for nothing."

The flea was the first to be introduced. He had such beautiful manners and bowed right and left, for he had noble blood in him, and besides, he was accustomed to move in human society, and that makes a great difference.

The grasshopper was next. He was certainly heavier than the flea, but he was equally well mannered, and wore a green uniform, which was his by right of birth. He explained that he belonged to a very ancient Egyptian family and that everyone thought a great deal of him in the country where he was then living. They had brought him in out of the fields and put him in a three-storied card house, all made of picture cards with the colored side inwards.

The doors and windows were cut out of the body of the Queen of Hearts.

"I sing so extremely well," he explained, "that sixteen native grasshoppers who have been singing since childhood and still haven't any house of cards to live in grew even thinner with jealousy than they were before when they heard about me."

So both the flea and the grasshopper had now explained who they were, and they felt sure they were quite good enough to marry the princess.

The jumping goose didn't say anything, but the company decided that meant he was thinking a great deal, and when the court dog sniffed at him, he reported that the jumping goose was certainly of good family. The old councillor, who had received three decorations to keep him quiet, declared that he knew that the jumping goose was gifted with magic power; you could tell by his back if the winter would be severe or mild, and that was more than you could say even for the man who writes the almanac.

"I'm not saying anything," the king remarked, "but I have my opinion of these things."

Now it was time for the trial. The flea jumped first, and he went so high that nobody could see him. So they all said he hadn't jumped at all, but had only been pretending. And that was a cheap thing to do.

The grasshopper only jumped half as high as the flea, but he jumped right into the king's face! And the king said it was disgusting.

The jumping goose stood still for a long time, lost in thought, and people began to wonder if he could jump at all.

"I hope he isn't sick," said the court dog, and gave him another sniff. Then suddenly, plop! The jumping goose jumped sideways right into the lap of the princess, who was sitting on a little golden stool nearby.

At once the king said, "To jump up to my daughter is the highest jump that can be made. But it takes brains to get an idea like that, and the jumping goose has shown that he does have brains. He is a pretty clever fellow."

And that's how the jumping goose won the princess.

"I don't care a bit," said the flea. "I jumped the highest. She can have that old goosebone, with his stick and his wax. In this world, real merit is very seldom rewarded. A fine physique is what people look at nowadays."

So the flea went away to fight in foreign service, and it is said that he was killed.

The grasshopper settled down in a ditch and pondered over the way of the world, and he too said, "Yes, a good physique is everything. A good physique is everything." Then he chirped his own sad little song, from which I've taken this story. The story may just possibly not be true, even if it is printed here in black and white.

THE SHEPHERDESS AND THE CHIMNEY SWEEP (1845)

Have you ever seen a very old chest, black with age and covered with outlandish carved ornaments and curling leaves? Well, in a certain parlor, there was just such a chest, handed down from some great-grandmother. Carved all up and down it ran tulips and roses— odd-looking flourishes—and from fanciful thickets, little stags stuck out their antlered heads.

Right in the middle of the chest, a whole man was carved. He made you laugh to look at him grinning away, though one couldn't call his grinning laughing. He had hind legs like a goat's, a little horn on his forehead, and a long beard. All his children called him "General Headquarters-Hindquarters-Gives-Orders-Front-and-Rear-Sergeant-Billygoat-Legs." It was a difficult name to pronounce, and not many people get to be called by it, but he must have been very important, or why should anyone have taken trouble to carve him at all?

However, there he stood, forever eyeing a delightful little china shepherdess on the tabletop under the mirror. The little shepherdess wore golden shoes and looped up her gown fetchingly with a red rose. Her hat was gold, and even her crook was gold. She was simply charming!

Close by her stood a little chimney sweep, as black as coal, but made of porcelain, too. He was as clean and tidy as anyone can be, because you see he was only an ornamental chimney sweep. If the china makers had wanted to, they could just as easily have turned him out as a prince, for he had a jaunty way of holding his ladder, and his cheeks were as pink as a girl's. That was a mistake, don't you think? He should have been dabbed with a pinch or two of soot.

He and the shepherdess stood quite close together. They had both been put on the table where they stood, and, having been placed there, they had become engaged because they suited each other exactly. Both were young, both were made of the same porcelain, and neither could stand a shock.

Near them stood another figure, three times as big as they were. It was an old Chinaman who could nod his head. He too was made of porcelain, and he said he was the little shepherdess's grandfather.

But he couldn't prove it. Nevertheless, he claimed that this gave him authority over her, and when General Headquarters-Hindquarters-Gives-Orders-Front-and-Rear-Sergeant-Billygoat-Legs asked for her hand in marriage, the old Chinaman had nodded consent.

"There's a husband for you!" the old Chinaman told the shepherdess. "A husband who, I am inclined to believe, is made of mahogany. He can make you Mrs. General Headquarters-Hindquarters-Gives-Orders-Front-and-Rear-Sergeant-Billygoat-Legs. He has the whole chest full of silver, and who knows what else he's got hidden away in his secret drawers?"

"But I don't want to go and live in the dark chest," said the little shepherdess. "I have heard people say he's got eleven china wives in there already."

"Then you will make twelve," said the Chinaman. "Tonight, as soon as the old chest commences to creak, I'll marry you off to him, as sure as I'm a Chinaman." Then he nodded off to sleep. The little shepherdess cried and looked at her true love, the porcelain chimney sweep.

"Please let's run away into the big, wide world," she begged him, "for we can't stay here."

"I'll do just what you want me to," the little chimney sweep told her. "Let's run away right now. I feel sure I can support you by chimney sweeping."

"I wish we were safely down off this table," she said. "I'll never be happy until we are out in the big, wide world."

He told her not to worry, and showed her how to drop her little feet over the table edge and how to step from one gilded leaf to another down the carved leg of the table. He set up his ladder to help her, and down they came safely to the floor. But when they glanced at the old chest, they saw a great commotion. All the carved stags were craning their necks, tossing their antlers, and turning their heads. General Headquarters-Hindquarters-Gives-Orders-Front-and-Rear-Sergeant-Billygoat-Legs jumped high in the air and shouted to the old Chinaman, "They're running away! They're running away!"

This frightened them so that they jumped quickly into a drawer of the window seat. Here they found three or four decks of cards, not quite complete, and a little puppet theater, which was set up as well as it was possible to do. A play was in progress, and all the diamond queens, heart queens, club queens, and spade queens sat in front row and fanned themselves with the tulips they held in their hands. Behind them the knaves lined up, showing that they had heads both at the top and at the bottom, as face cards do have. The play was all about two people who were not allowed to marry, and it made the shepherdess cry because it was so like her own story.

"I can't bear to see any more," she said. "I must get out of this drawer at once." But when they got back to the floor and looked up at the table, they saw the old Chinaman was wide awake now. Not only his head, but his whole body rocked forward. The lower part of his body was one solid piece, you see.

"The old Chinaman's coming!" cried the little shepherdess, who was so upset that she fell down on her porcelain knees.

"I have an idea," said the chimney sweeper. "We'll hide in the potpourri vase in the corner. There we can rest upon rose petals and lavender, and when he finds us, we can throw salt in his eyes."

"It's no use," she said. "Besides, I know the potpourri vase was once the old Chainman's sweetheart, and where there used to be love, a little affection is sure to remain. No, there's nothing for us to do but to run away into the big wide world."

"Are you really so brave that you'd go into the wide world with me?" asked the chimney sweep. "Have you thought about how big it is, and that we can never come back here?"

"I have," she said.

The chimney sweep looked her straight in the face and said, "My way lies up through the chimney. Are you really so brave that you'll come with me into the stove, and crawl through the stovepipe? It will take us to the chimney. Once we get there, I'll know what to do. We shall climb so high that they'll never catch us, and at the very top, there's an opening into the big wide world."

He led her to the stove door.

"It looks very black in there," she said. But she let him lead her through the stove and through the stovepipe, where it was pitch-black night.

"Now we've come to the chimney," he said. "And see! See how the bright star shines over our heads."

A real star, high up in the heavens, shone down as if it wished to show them the way. They clambered and scuffled, for it was hard climbing and terribly steep—way, way up high! But he lifted her up, held her safe, and found the best places for her little porcelain feet. At last, they reached the top of the chimney, where they sat down. For they were so tired, and no wonder!

Overhead was the starry sky, and spread before them were all the housetops in the town. They looked out on the big wide world. The poor shepherdess had never thought it would be like that. She flung her little head against the chimney sweep and sobbed so many tears that the gilt washed off her sash.

"This is too much," she said. "I can't bear it. The wide world is too big. Oh! If I only were back on my table under the mirror. I'll never be happy until I stand there again, just as before. I followed you faithfully out into the world, and if you love me the least bit you'll take me right home."

The chimney sweep tried to persuade her that it wasn't sensible to go back. He talked to her about the old Chinaman, and of General Headquarters-Hindquarters-Gives-Orders-Front-and-Rear-Sergeant-Billygoat-Legs, but she sobbed so hard and kissed her chimney sweep so much that he had to do as she said, though he thought it was the wrong thing to do.

So back down the chimney they climbed with great difficulty, and they crawled through the wretched stovepipe into the dark stove. Here they listened behind the door to find out what was happening in the room. Everything seemed quiet, so they opened the door and—oh, what a pity! There on the floor lay the Chinaman, in three pieces. When he had come running after them, he tumbled off the table and smashed. His whole back had come off in one piece, and his head had rolled into the corner. General Headquarters-Hindquarters-Gives-Orders-Front-and-Rear-Sergeant-Billygoat-Legs was standing where he always stood, looking thoughtful.

"Oh, dear," said the little shepherdess, "poor old Grandfather is all broken up, and it's entirely our fault. I shall never live through it." She wrung her delicate hands.

"He can be patched," said the chimney sweep. "He can be riveted. Don't be so upset about him. A little glue for his back and a strong rivet in his neck, and he will be just as good as new, and just as disagreeable as he was before."

"Will he, really?" she asked, as they climbed back to their old place on the table.

"Here we are," said the chimney sweep. "Back where we started from. We could have saved ourselves a lot of trouble."

"Now if only old Grandfather were mended," said the little shepherdess. "Is mending terribly expensive?"

He was mended well enough. The family had his back glued together, and a strong rivet put through his neck. That made him as good as new, except that never again could he nod his head.

"It seems to me that you have grown haughty since your fall, though I don't see why you should be proud of it," General Headquarters-Hindquarters-Gives-Orders-Front-and-Rear-Sergeant-Billygoat-Legs complained. "Am I to have her, or am I not?"

The chimney sweep and the little shepherdess looked so pleadingly at the old Chinaman, for they were deathly afraid he would nod. But he didn't. He couldn't. And neither did he care to tell anyone that, forever and a day, he'd have to wear a rivet in his neck.

So the little porcelain people remained together. They thanked goodness for the rivet in Grandfather's neck, and they kept on loving each other until the day they broke.

THE BELL (1845)

In the narrow streets of the big town, toward evening when the sun was setting and the clouds shone like gold on the chimney tops, people would hear a strange sound like that of a church bell. But they heard it only for a few moments before it was lost in the rumble of city carriages and the voices of the multitudes, for such noises are very distracting. "Now the evening bell is ringing," people used to say. "The sun is setting."

People who were outside the town, where the houses were more scattered, with little gardens or fields between them, could see the evening sky in even more splendor and hear the bell more distinctly. It was as if the tones came from some church, buried in the silent and fragrant depths of the forest, and people looked solemnly in that direction.

A long time passed, and people began to say to each other, "I wonder if there really is a church out there in the woods? That bell has a mysterious, sweet tone. Let's go out there and see what it looks like."

So the rich people drove out, and the poor people walked out, but to all of them, it seemed a very long way. When they reached a grove of willows on the outskirts of the woods, they sat down and looked up into the branches and imagined they were really in the heart of the forest. The town confectioner came out and set up his tent there, and then another confectioner came, and he hung a bell right above his tent; but the bell had no clapper and was all tarred over as a protection against the rain.

When the people went home again, they said it had all been very romantic, much more fun than a tea party. Three people even said that they had gone right through the forest to the far side and had still heard the strange sound of the bell, only then it seemed to be coming from the direction of town.

One of these even wrote a poem about the bell and compared its tones to those of a mother singing to a beloved child—no melody could be sweeter than the tones of that bell.

The emperor of the country heard about the bell and issued a solemn proclamation promising that whoever discovered the source of the lovely sounds would receive the title of "Bell Ringer to the World," even if there were not really a bell there at all.

Of course, a great many people went to the woods now to try to gain that fine title, but only one of them came back with some kind of an explanation. No one had been deep enough into the forest—neither had he, for that matter—but just the same, he said the sound was made by a very large owl in an old hollow tree, a wise owl that continually knocked its head against the trunk of the tree. He wasn't quite sure whether the sound came from the bird's head or from the hollow trunk, but still, he was appointed "Public Bell Ringer Number One," and every year, he wrote a little treatise about the remarkable old owl. No one was much the wiser for it.

Now on a certain confirmation day, the minister had preached a very beautiful and moving sermon; the children who were confirmed were deeply touched by it. It was a tremendously important day in their lives, for on this day, they were leaving childhood behind and becoming grown-up persons. Their infant souls would take wing into the bodies of adults. It was a glorious, sunny day, and after the confirmation the children walked together out of the town, and from the depths of the woods, the strange tolling of the bell came with a mysterious clear sweetness.

At once, all the children decided to go into the woods and find the bell. All except three, that is to say. The first of these three just had to go home and try on a new ball dress for that forthcoming ball was the very reason she had been confirmed at this time; otherwise, she would have had to wait until next year's ceremony. The second was a poor boy who had borrowed his confirmation coat and boots from the landlord's son and had to give them back by a certain hour. And the third said he never went to a strange place without his parents; he had always been a dutiful child and would continue to be good, even though he was confirmed now. The others made fun of him for this, which was very wrong of them indeed.

So these three dropped out while the others started off into the woods. The sun shone, the birds sang, and the children sang, too, walking along hand in hand. They had not yet received any responsibilities or high position in life—all were equal in the eyes of God on that confirmation day.

But soon two of the smallest grew tired and returned to town; two other little girls sat down to make wreaths and so did not go any farther. The rest went on until they reached the willows where the confectioner had his tent, and then they said, "Well, here we are! You see, the bell doesn't really exist at all; it's just something people imagine!"

And then suddenly, the sound of the bell came from the depths of the woods, so sweet and solemn that four or five of the young people decided to follow it still farther. The underbrush was so thick and close that their advance was most difficult. Woodruff and anemone grew almost too high; convolvuluses and blackberry brambles hung in long garlands from tree to tree, where the nightingale sang and the sunbeams played through the leaves. It was so lovely and peaceful, but it was a bad place for the girls, because they would get their dresses torn on the brambles.

There were large boulders overgrown with many-colored mosses, and a fresh spring bubbled forth among them with a strange little gurgling sound. "Cluck, cluck," it said.

"I wonder if that can be the bell," one of the children thought, lying down to listen to it. "I'd better look into this." So he remained there, and the others went on without him.

They came to a little hut, all made of branches and tree bark. Its roof was covered with roses, and over it a wild apple tree was bending as if it would shower its blessings down on the little house. The long sprays of the apple tree clustered around the gable, and on that there hung a little bell!

Could that be the one they had heard? Yes, they all—except for one boy—agreed it must be. This one boy said it was much too small and delicate to be heard so far away, and besides, its tones were very different from those that moved human hearts so strangely. The boy who spoke was a king's son, so the other children said, "Of course he thinks he knows a lot more than anybody else."

So the king's son went on alone, and as he proceeded deeper into the woods, his heart was filled more and more with the solitude of the forest. He could still hear the little bell that had satisfied the others, and when the wind was from the right direction, he could even hear the voices of the people around the confectioner's tent, singing while they were having their tea.

But above all rose the peeling of that mysterious bell. Now it sounded as if an organ were being played with it, and the tones came from the left-hand side, where the heart is.

Suddenly there was a rustling in the bushes, and a little boy stood before the king's son. He was wearing wooden shoes and such a short jacket that the sleeves did not cover his long wrists. They knew each other at once, for this was the poor boy who had had to go back to return the coat and boots to the landlord's son. This done, he had changed again into his shabby clothes and wooden shoes and come into the woods, for the bell sounded so loudly and so deeply that he had to follow its call.

"Then let's go on together," suggested the king's son.

But the poor boy in his wooden shoes was very shy, pulled at his short sleeves, and said he was afraid he could not walk as fast as the king's son; besides, he was sure the sound of the bell came from the right, because that side looked much more beautiful.

"Then I guess we can't go together," said the king's son, nodding his head to the poor boy, who went in the direction he thought best, which took him into the thickest and darkest part of the forest. The thorns tore his shabby clothes and scratched his face, hands, and feet until they bled.

The king's son received some scratches too, but the sun shone on his path. And he is the one we will follow, for he was a bright young lad.

"I will and must find that bell," he said, "even if I have to go to the end of the world!"

High in the trees above him, ugly monkeys sat and grinned and showed their teeth. "Let's throw things at him!" they said to each other. "Let's thrash him, 'cause he's the son of a king."

But he went on unwearied, and went farther and farther into the woods, where the most wonderful flowers were growing. There were lilies white as stars, with blood-red stamens; there were light-blue tulips that gleamed in the breeze, and apple trees with their fruit shining like big soap bubbles. Imagine how those trees sparkled in the sunlight! Around the beautiful rolling green meadows where the deer played grew massive oaks and beeches; and wherever one of the trees had a crack in the bark, mosses and long tendrils were growing out of it. In some of the meadows were quiet lakes, where beautiful white swans swam and beat the air gently with their wings. The king's son often stopped to listen, for the tones of the bell sometimes seemed to come from the depths of these lakes; then again, he felt sure that the notes were coming from farther away in the forest.

Slowly the sun set, and the clouds turned a fiery red; a stillness, a deep stillness, settled over the forest. The boy fell on his knees, sang his evening hymn, and said to himself, "I'll never find what I'm seeking now. The sun is setting, and the night is coming—the dark night. But perhaps I can catch one more glimpse of the round red sun before it disappears below the horizon. I'll climb up on those rocks; they rise up as high as the tallest trees!" Seizing the roots and creepers, he slowly made his way up the slippery stones, where the water snakes writhed and the toads and frogs seemed to be barking at him. Yet he reached the summit just as the sun was going down. Oh, what a wonderful sight!

The sea, the great, the beautiful sea, rolling its long waves against the shore, lay stretched out before him, and the sun stood like a large shining altar, where ocean and heaven met; the whole world seemed to melt together in glowing colors. The forest sang, the sea sang, and the heart of the boy sang, too. Nature was a vast, holy church, where the trees and drifting clouds were the pillars; flowers and grass made the velvet carpet, and Heaven itself was the great dome. Up there, the red colors faded as the sun sank into the ocean, but then millions of stars sprang out, like millions of diamond lamps, and the king's son spread out his arms in joy toward the heavens, the sun, and the forest.

At that moment, from the right-hand path, there appeared the poor boy with the short sleeves and the wooden shoes. He had come there as quickly and by following his own path. Joyfully they ran toward each other, and held each other by the hand in the great tabernacle of Nature and Poetry, while above them sounded the invisible, holy bell. The blessed spirits floated around them and lifted up their voices in a joyful hallelujah.

THE DARNING NEEDLE (1845)

Once upon a time, there was a darning needle who imagined she was so fine that she really was a sewing needle.

"Be careful and hold me tightly!" she warned the fingers that picked her up. "Don't drop me! If I fall on the floor, you may never find me again; that's how fine I am!"

"That's what you think!" replied the fingers, and squeezed her around the waist.

"Look, here I come with my train!" said the darning needle, and she drew a long thread behind her, but there was no knot in the thread.

The fingers aimed the needle straight at the cook's slipper, where the upper leather had burst and had to be sewed together.

"My! What vulgar work!" sniffed the darning needle. "I'll never get through! Look out! I'm breaking! I'm breaking in two." And just then, she did break. "I told you so," she said. "I'm much too delicate!"

"Well, she's no good now," thought the fingers, but they had to hold onto her all the same. For the cook dropped a little sealing wax on the end of the needle to make a head, and then she pinned her kerchief together with it in front.

"Look! Now I'm a breastpin," said the needle. "I knew perfectly well I'd be honored. If you are something, you always amount to something."

Then she laughed, but it was inwardly, because no one can ever really see a darning needle laugh. There she sat on the cook's bosom, proud as if she were in a state coach, and looked all around her.

"May I be permitted to inquire if you're made of gold?" she very politely asked a little pin near her. "You look pretty, and you have a head of your own, but it's rather small. You must be careful to grow bigger. Not everyone can have sealing wax on one end like me!"

Then the darning needle drew herself up so proudly that she fell right out of the kerchief into the sink, at the very moment the cook was rinsing it out.

"Looks now as if we are off on a journey," she said to herself. "Let's hope I don't get lost." But she really was lost down the drain.

"I'm too fine for this world," she observed calmly as she lay in the gutter outside. "But I know who I am, and that's always a satisfaction." So the darning needle was still proud, and she never lost her good humor. She watched the many strange things floating above her—chips and straws and pieces of old newspapers.

"Look at them sail!" she said to herself. "They don't know what's down below them! Here I sit! I can sting! Look at that stick go, thinking of nothing in the world but himself—a stick! And that's exactly what he is! And there's a straw floating by; look at him twist and look how he turns! You'd better not think so much about yourself up there! You'll run into the curb! There goes a newspaper. Everybody has forgotten what was written on it, but still it spreads itself out, while I sit quietly down here below. I know who I am, and I shall never forget it!"

One day, the darning needle saw something beside her that glittered splendidly in the sunbeams. It was only a bit of broken bottle, but because the darning needle was quite sure it was something valuable like a diamond, she spoke to it, introducing herself as a breastpin.

"I suppose you're a diamond?" she asked.

"Yes, something like that," was the reply.

Then, since each thought the other was very important, they began talking about the world and how conceited everyone was.

"I used to live in a lady's case," said the darning needle. "And this lady was a cook. On each hand, she had five fingers, and you never saw anything so conceited as those five fingers! And yet they were only there so that they could hold me, take me out of my case, and put me back into it."

"Did they shine?" asked the bit of bottle glass.

"Shine? Not at all," said the darning needle. "They were arrogant. There were five brothers, all belonging to the Finger family, and they kept close together, although they were all of different lengths. The one on the outside, Thumbling, who walked out in front of the others, was short and fat and had only one joint in his back, so he could only make a single bow. But he insisted that if he were cut off a person's hand, that person could not be a soldier. Lickpot, the second one, pushed himself into sweet and sour, and pointed at the sun and the moon, and it was he who pressed on the pen when they wrote. Longman, the third, looked over the heads of the others. Guldbrand was the fourth—he always wore a golden belt around his waist. And little Peter Playfellow didn't do anything at all, and was very proud of it. They did nothing but brag all the time; that's why I went down the sink."

"And now we just sit here and glitter," said the bit of broken bottle. But just then, a flood of water came rushing down the gutter so that it overflowed and swept the bottle glass away.

"See now! He's been promoted," remarked the darning needle, "but I'm still here. I'm too fine for that sort of thing. But that's my pride, and that is very commendable!" So she sat up straight, lost in many big thoughts. "I almost think I was born a sunbeam, I'm so fine; besides, the sunbeams always seem to be trying to get to me, under the water. I'm so fine that even my mother can't find me. If I had my old eye, the one that broke off, I think I might cry about that. But no! I think I wouldn't cry anyway; it's not at all refined to cry."

One day, some street boys were grubbing in the gutter, looking for coins and things of that sort. It was filthy work, but they were having a wonderful time.

"Ouch!" one cried as he pricked himself on the darning needle. "You're a pretty sharp fellow!"

"I'm not a fellow; I'm a young lady," replied the darning needle. But of course, they couldn't hear her.

Her sealing wax had come off, and she had turned black; but black always makes you look more slender, and she was sure she was even finer than before.

"Look!" cried the boys. "Here comes an eggshell sailing along," And they stuck the darning needle fast into the shell.

"White walls, and I am black myself!" cried the darning needle. "That's very becoming! People can really see me now! I only hope I'm not seasick; that would surely break me!" But she wasn't seasick, and she did not break. "It's a very good protection against seasickness to have a steel stomach and to remember that one is a little finer than ordinary human beings. Oh, yes! I'm all right. The finer you are, the more you can bear."

"Crack!" went the eggshell at that moment, for a heavily loaded wagon ran over it.

"Goodness, I'm being crushed!" cried the darning needle. "I'm going to get really seasick now! I'm breaking! I'm breaking!" But she didn't break, though the wagon went over her; she lay at full length along the cobblestones, and there we'll leave her.

THE LITTLE MATCH GIRL (1845)

It was so terribly cold. Snow was falling, and it was almost dark. Evening came on, the last evening of the year. In the cold and gloom, a poor little girl, bareheaded and barefoot, was walking through the streets. Of course, when she had left her house she'd had slippers on, but what good had they been? They were very big slippers, way too big for her, for they belonged to her mother. The little girl had lost them running across the road, where two carriages had rattled by terribly fast. One slipper she'd not been able to find again, and a boy had run off with the other, saying he could use it very well as a cradle someday when he had children of his own. And so the little girl walked on her naked feet, which were quite red and blue with the cold. In an old apron, she carried several packages of matches, and she held a box of them in her hand. No one had bought any from her all day long, and no one had given her a cent.

Shivering with cold and hunger, she crept along, a picture of misery, poor little girl! The snowflakes fell on her long fair hair, which hung in pretty curls over her neck. In all the windows, lights were shining, and there was a wonderful smell of roast goose, for it was New Year's Eve. Yes, she thought of that!

In a corner formed by two houses, one of which projected farther out into the street than the other, she sat down and drew up her little feet under her. She was getting colder and colder, but did not dare to go home, for she had sold no matches, nor earned a single cent, and her father would surely beat her. Besides, it was cold at home, for they had nothing over them but a roof through which the wind whistled even though the biggest cracks had been stuffed with straw and rags.

Her hands were almost dead with cold. Oh, how much one little match might warm her! If she could only take one from the box and rub it against the wall and warm her hands. She drew one out. *R-r-ratch!*

How it sputtered and burned! It made a warm, bright flame, like a little candle, as she held her hands over it; but it gave a strange light! It really seemed to the little girl as if she were sitting before a great iron stove with shining brass knobs and a brass cover. How wonderfully the fire burned! How comfortable it was! The youngster stretched out her feet to warm them too; then the little flame went out, the stove vanished, and she had only the remains of the burnt match in her hand.

She struck another match against the wall. It burned brightly, and when the light fell upon the wall, it became transparent like a thin veil, and she could see through it into a room. On the table a snow-white cloth was spread, and on it stood a shining dinner service. The roast goose steamed gloriously, stuffed with apples and prunes. And what was still better, the goose jumped down from the dish and waddled along the floor with a knife and fork in its breast, right over to the little girl. Then the match went out, and she could see only the thick, cold wall. She lighted another match. Then she was sitting under the most beautiful Christmas tree. It was much larger and much more beautiful than the one she had seen last Christmas through the glass door at the rich merchant's home. Thousands of candles burned on the green branches, and colored pictures like those in the printshops looked down at her. The little girl reached both her hands toward them. Then the match went out. But the Christmas lights mounted higher. She saw them now as bright stars in the sky. One of them fell down, forming a long line of fire.

"Now someone is dying," thought the little girl, for her old grandmother, the only person who had loved her and who was now dead, had told her that when a star fell down, a soul went up to God.

She rubbed another match against the wall. It became bright again, and in the glow, the old grandmother stood clear and shining, kind and lovely.

"Grandmother!" cried the child. "Oh, take me with you! I know you will disappear when the match is burned out. You will vanish like the warm stove, the wonderful roast goose, and the beautiful big Christmas tree!"

And she quickly struck the whole bundle of matches, for she wished to keep her grandmother with her. And the matches burned with such a glow that it became brighter than daylight. Grandmother had never been so grand and beautiful. She took the little girl in her arms, and both of them flew in brightness and joy above Earth, very, very high, and up there was neither cold, nor hunger, nor fear—they were with God.

But in the corner, leaning against the wall, sat the little girl with red cheeks and smiling mouth, frozen to death on the last evening of the old year. The New Year's sun rose upon a little pathetic figure. The child sat there, stiff and cold, holding the matches, of which one bundle was almost burned.

"She wanted to warm herself," the people said. No one imagined what beautiful things she had seen, and how happily she had gone with her old grandmother into the bright New Year.

THE SHADOW (1847)

It is in the hot countries that the sun burns down in earnest, turning the people there a deep mahogany-brown. In the hottest countries of all, they are seared into negroes, but it was not quite that hot in this country to which a man of learning had come from the colder north. He expected to go about there just as he had at home, but he soon discovered that this was a mistake. He and other sensible souls had to stay inside. The shutters were drawn, and the doors were closed all day long. It looked just as if everyone were asleep or away from home. The narrow street of high houses where he lived was so situated that from morning till night the sun beat down on it—unbearably!

To this young and clever scholar from the colder north, it felt as if he were sitting in a blazing hot oven. It exhausted him so that he became very thin, and even his shadow shrank much smaller than it had been at home. Only in the evenings, after sundown, did the man and his shadow begin to recover.

This was really a joy to see. As soon as a candle was brought into the room, the shadow had to stretch itself to get its strength back. It stretched up to the wall, yes, even along the ceiling, so tall did it grow. To stretch himself, the scholar went out on the balcony. As soon as the stars came out in the beautifully clear sky, he felt as if he had come back to life.

In warm countries, each window has a balcony, and on all the balconies up and down the street, people came out to breathe the fresh air that one needs, even if one is already a fine mahogany-brown. Both up above and down below, things became lively. Tailors, shoemakers— everybody—moved out in the street. Chairs and tables were brought out, and candles were lighted, yes, candles by the thousand. One man talked, another sang, people strolled about, carriages drove by, and donkeys trotted along, *ting-a-ling-a-ling,* for their harness had bells on it. There were church bells ringing, hymn singing, and funeral processions. There were boys in the street firing off Roman candles. Oh yes, it was lively as lively can be down in that street.

Only one house was quiet—the one directly across from where the scholarly stranger lived. Yet someone lived there, for flowers on the balcony grew and thrived under that hot sun, which they could not have done unless they were watered. So someone must be watering them, and there must be people in the house. Along in the evening, as a matter of fact, the door across the street was opened. But it was dark inside, at least in the front room. From somewhere in the house, farther back, came the sound of music. The scholarly stranger thought the music was marvelous, but it is quite possible that he only imagined this, for out there in the warm countries, he thought everything was marvelous—except the sun. The stranger's landlord said that he didn't know who had rented the house across the street. No one was ever to be seen over there, and as for the music, he found it extremely tiresome. He said:

"It's just as if somebody sits there practicing a piece that's beyond him—always the selfsame piece. 'I'll play it right yet,' he probably says, but he doesn't, no matter how long he tries."

One night, the stranger woke up. He slept with the windows to his balcony open, and as the breeze blew his curtain aside, he fancied that a marvelous radiance came from the balcony across the street. The colors of all the flowers were as brilliant as flames. In their midst stood a maiden, slender and lovely. It seemed as if a radiance came from her, too. It actually hurt his eyes, but that was because he had opened them too wide in his sudden awakening.

One leap, and he was out of bed. Without a sound, he looked out through his curtains, but the maiden was gone. The flowers were no longer radiant, though they bloomed as fresh and fair as usual. The door was ajar, and through it came music so lovely and soft that one could really feel very romantic about it. It was like magic. But who lived there? What entrance did they use? Facing the street, the lower floor of the house was a row of shops, and people couldn't run through them all the time.

On another evening, the stranger sat out on his balcony. The candle burned in the room behind him, so naturally, his shadow was cast on the wall across the street. Yes, there it sat among the flowers, and when the stranger moved, it moved with him.

"I believe my shadow is the only living thing to be seen over there," the scholar thought to himself. "See how he makes himself at home among the flowers. The door stands ajar, and if my shadow were clever, he'd step in, have a look around, and come back to tell me what he had seen."

"Yes," he said as a joke, "you ought to make yourself useful. Kindly step inside. Well, aren't you going?" He nodded to the shadow, and the shadow nodded back. "Run along now, but be sure to come back."

The stranger rose, and his shadow across the street rose with him. The stranger turned around, and his shadow turned, too. If anyone had been watching closely, he would have seen the shadow enter the half-open balcony door in the house across the way at the same instant that the stranger returned to his room and the curtain fell behind him.

Next morning, when the scholar went out to take his coffee and read the newspapers, he said, "What's this?" as he came out in the sunshine. "I haven't any shadow! So it really did go away last night, and it stayed away. Isn't that annoying?"

What annoyed him most was not so much the loss of his shadow, but the knowledge that there was already a story about a man without a shadow. All the people at home knew that story. If he went back and told them his story, they would say he was just imitating the old one. He did not care to be called unoriginal, so he decided to say nothing about it, which was the most sensible thing to do.

That evening, he again went out on the balcony. He had placed the candle directly behind him, because he knew that a shadow always likes to use its master as a screen, but he could not coax it forth. He made himself short and he made himself tall, but there was no shadow. It didn't come forth. He hemmed and he hawed, but it was no use.

This was very vexing, but in the hot countries, everything grows most rapidly, and in a week or so, he noticed with great satisfaction that when he went out in the sunshine, a new shadow was growing at his feet. The root must have been left with him. In three weeks' time, he had a very presentable shadow, and as he started north again, it grew longer and longer, until it got so long and large that half of it would have been quite sufficient.

The learned man went home and wrote books about those things in the world that are true, that are good, and that are beautiful.

The days went by, and the years went past, many, many years, in fact. Then one evening when he was sitting in his room, he heard a soft tapping at his door. "Come in," said he, but no one came in. He opened the door and was confronted by a man so extremely thin that it gave him a strange feeling. However, the man was faultlessly dressed and looked like a person of distinction.

"With whom do I have the honor of speaking?" the scholar asked.

"Ah," said the distinguished visitor, "I thought you wouldn't recognize me, now that I've put real flesh on my body and wear clothes. I don't suppose you ever expected to see me in such fine condition. Don't you know your old shadow? You must have thought I'd never come back. Things have gone remarkably well with me since I was last with you. I've thrived in every way, and if I have to buy my freedom, I can." He rattled a bunch of valuable charms that hung from his watch, and fingered the massive gold chain he wore around his neck. Ho! How his fingers flashed with diamond rings—and all this jewelry was real.

"No, I can't get over it!" said the scholar. "What *does* it all mean?"

"Nothing ordinary, you may be sure," said the shadow. "But you are no ordinary person, and I, as you know, have followed in your footsteps from childhood. As soon as you thought me sufficiently experienced to strike out in the world for myself, I went my way. I have been immeasurably successful. But I felt a sort of longing to see you again before you die, as I suppose you must, and I wanted to see this country again. You know how one loves his native land. I know that you have got hold of another shadow. Do I owe anything to either of you? Be kind enough to let me know."

"Well! Is it really you?" said the scholar. "Why, this is most extraordinary! I would never have imagined that one's own shadow could come back in human form."

"Just tell me what I owe," said the shadow, "because I don't like to be in debt to anyone."

"How can you talk that way?" said the student. "What debt could there be? Feel perfectly free. I am tremendously pleased to hear of your good luck! Sit down, my old friend, and tell me a bit about how it all happened, and about what you saw in that house across the street from us in the warm country."

"Yes, I'll tell you all about it," the shadow said, as he sat down. "But you must promise that if you meet me anywhere, you won't tell a soul in town about my having been your shadow. I intend to become engaged, for I can easily support a family."

"Don't you worry," said the scholar. "I won't tell anyone who you really are. I give you my hand on it. I promise, and a man is as good as his word."

"And a word is as good as its—shadow," the shadow said, for he couldn't put it any other way.

It was really remarkable how much of a man he had become, dressed all in black, with the finest cloth, patent-leather shoes, and an opera hat that could be pressed perfectly flat until it was only brim and top, not to mention those things we already know about—those seals, that gold chain, and the diamond rings. The shadow was well dressed indeed, and it was just this that made him appear human.

"Now I'll tell you," said the shadow, grinding his patent-leather shoes on the arm of the scholar's new shadow, which lay at his feet like a poodle dog. This was arrogance, perhaps, or possibly he was trying to make the new shadow stick to his own feet. The shadow on the floor lay quiet and still, and listened its best, so that it might learn how to get free and work its way up to be its own master.

"Do you know who lived in the house across the street from us?" the old shadow asked. "She was the most lovely of all creatures—she was Poetry herself. I lived there for three weeks, and it was as if I had lived there three thousand years, reading all that has ever been written. That's what I said, and it's the truth! I have seen it all, and I know everything."

"Poetry!" the scholar cried. "Yes, to be sure, she often lives as a hermit in the large cities. Poetry! Yes, I saw her myself, for one brief moment, but my eyes were heavy with sleep. She stood on the balcony, as radiant as the northern lights. Tell me! Tell me! You were on the balcony. You went through the doorway, and then—"

"Then I was in the anteroom," said the shadow. "It was the room you were always staring at from across the way. There were no candles there, and the room was in twilight. But door upon door stood open in a whole series of brilliantly lit halls and reception rooms. That blaze of lights would have struck me dead had I gone as far as the room where the maiden was, but I was careful—I took my time, as one should."

"And then what did you see, my old friend?" the scholar asked.

"I saw everything, and I shall tell everything to you, but—it's not that I'm proud—but as I am a free man and well educated, not to mention my high standing and my considerable fortune, I do wish you wouldn't call me your old friend."

"I beg your pardon!" said the scholar. "It's an old habit, and hard to change. You are perfectly right, my dear sir, and I'll remember it. But now, my dear sir, tell me of all that you saw."

"All?" said the shadow, "for I saw it all, and I know everything."

"How did the innermost rooms look?" the scholar asked. "Was it like a green forest? Was it like a holy temple? Were the rooms like the starry skies seen from some high mountain?"

"Everything was there," said the shadow. "I didn't quite go inside. I stayed in the dark anteroom, but my place there was perfect. I saw everything, and I know everything. I have been in the antechamber at the court of Poetry."

"But what did you see? Did the gods of old march through the halls? Did the old heroes fight there? Did fair children play there and tell their dreams?"

"I was there, I tell you, so you must understand that I saw all that there was to be seen. Had you come over, it would not have made a man of you, as it did of me. Also, I learned to understand my inner self, what is born in me, and the relationship between me and Poetry. Yes, when I was with you, I did not think of such things, but you must remember how wonderfully I always expanded at sunrise and sunset. And in the moonlight, I almost seemed more real than you. Then I did not understand myself, but in that anteroom, I came to know my true nature. I was a man! I came out completely changed. But you were no longer in the warm country. Being a man, I was ashamed to be seen as I was. I lacked shoes, clothes, and all the surface veneer that makes a man.

"I went into hiding—this is confidential, and you must not write it in any of your books. I went into hiding under the skirts of the cake-woman. Little she knew of what she concealed. Not until evening did I venture out. I ran through the streets in the moonlight and stretched myself tall against the walls. It's such a pleasant way of scratching one's back. Up I ran and down I ran, peeping into the highest windows, into drawing rooms, and into garrets. I peered in where no one else could peer. I saw what no one else could see, or should see. Taken all in all, it's a wicked world. I would not care to be a man if it were not considered the fashionable thing to be. I saw the most incredible behavior among men and women, fathers and mothers, and among those 'perfectly darling' children. I saw what nobody knows but everybody would like to know, and that is what wickedness goes on next door. If I had written it in a newspaper, oh, how widely it would have been read! But instead, I wrote to the people directly concerned, and there was the most terrible consternation in every town to which I came. They were so afraid of me, and yet so remarkably fond of me. The professors appointed me a professor, and the tailor made me new clothes—my wardrobe is most complete. The master of the mint coined new money for me, the women called me such a handsome man; and so I became the man I am. Now I must bid you good-bye. Here's my card. I live on the sunny side of the street, and I am always at home on rainy days." The shadow took his leave.

"How extraordinary," said the scholar.

The days passed. The years went by. And the shadow called again. "How goes it?" he asked.

"Alack," said the scholar, "I still write about the true, the good, and the beautiful, but nobody cares to read about such things. I feel quite despondent, for I take it deeply to heart."

"I don't," said the shadow. "I am getting fat, as one should. You don't know the ways of the world, and that's why your health suffers. You ought to travel. I'm taking a trip this summer. Will you come with me? I'd like to have a traveling companion. Will you come along as my shadow? It would be a great pleasure to have you along, and I'll pay all the expenses."

"No, that's a bit too much," said the scholar.

"It depends on how you look at it," said the shadow. "It will do you a lot of good to travel. Will you be my shadow? The trip won't cost you a thing."

"This has gone much too far!" said the scholar.

"Well, that's the way the world goes," the shadow told him, "and that's the way it will keep on going." And away he went.

The learned man was not at all well. Sorrow and trouble pursued him, and what he had to say about the good, the true, and the beautiful appealed to most people about as much as roses appeal to a cow. Finally, he grew quite ill.

"You really look like a shadow," people told him, and he trembled at the thought.

"You must visit a watering place," said the shadow, who came to see him again. "There's no question about it. I'll take you with me, for old friendship's sake. I'll pay for the trip, and you can write about it, as well as doing your best to amuse me along the way. I need to go to a watering place too, because my beard isn't growing as it should. That's a sort of disease too, and one can't get along without a beard. Now do be reasonable and accept my proposal. We shall travel just like friends!"

So off they started. The shadow was master now, and the master was the shadow. They drove together, rode together, and walked together, side by side, before or behind each other, according to the way the sun fell. The shadow was careful to take the place of the master, and the scholar didn't much care, for he had an innocent heart, besides being most affable and friendly.

One day, he said to the shadow, "As we are now fellow-travelers and have grown up together, shall we not call each other by our first names, the way good companions should? It is much more intimate."

"That's a splendid idea!" said the shadow, who was now the real master. "What you say is most open-hearted and friendly. I shall be just as friendly and open-hearted with you. As a scholar, you are perfectly well aware how strange is man's nature. Some men cannot bear the touch of gray paper. It sickens them. Others quail if they hear a nail scratched across a pane of glass. For my part, I am affected in just that way when I hear you call me by my first name. I feel myself ground down to the earth, as I was in my first position with you. You understand. It's a matter of sensitivity, not pride. I cannot let you call me by my first name, but I shall be glad to call you by yours, as a compromise." So thereafter, the shadow called his one-time master by his first name.

"It has gone too far," the scholar thought, "when I must call him by his last name while he calls me by my first!" But he had to put up with it.

At last, they came to the watering place. Among the many people was a lovely princess. Her malady was that she saw things too clearly, which can be most upsetting. For instance, she immediately saw that the newcomer was a very different sort of person from all the others.

"He has come here to make his beard grow, they say. But I see the real reason. He can't cast a shadow."

Her curiosity was aroused, and on the promenade she addressed this stranger directly. Being a king's daughter, she did not have to stand upon ceremony, so she said to him straight:

"Your trouble is that you can't cast a shadow."

"Your Royal Highness must have improved considerably," the shadow replied. "I know your malady is that you see too clearly, but you are improving. As it happens, I do have a most unusual shadow. Don't you see that figure who always accompanies me? Other people have a common shadow, but I do not care for what is common to all. Just as we often allow our servants better fabrics for their liveries than we wear ourselves, so I have had my shadow decked out as a man. Why, you see, I have even outfitted him with a shadow of his own. It is expensive, I grant you, but I like to have something uncommon."

"My!" the princess thought. "Can I really be cured? This is the foremost watering place in the world, and in these days, water has come to have wonderful medicinal powers. But I shan't leave just as the place is becoming amusing. I have taken a liking to this stranger. I only hope his beard won't grow, for then he would leave us."

That evening, the princess and the shadow danced together in the great ballroom. She was light, but he was lighter still. Never had she danced with such a partner. She told him what country she came from, and he knew it well. He had been there, but it was during her absence. He had looked through every window, high or low. He had seen this, and he had seen that. So he could answer the princess and suggest things that astounded her. She was convinced that he must be the wisest man in all the world. His knowledge impressed her so deeply that while they were dancing, she fell in love with him. The shadow could tell, for her eyes transfixed him, through and through. They danced again, and she came very near telling him she loved him, but it wouldn't do to be rash. She had to think of her country, and her throne, and the many people over whom she would reign.

"He is a clever man," she said to herself, "and that is a good thing. He dances charmingly, and that is good too. But is his knowledge more than superficial? That's just as important, so I must examine him."

Tactfully, she began asking him the most difficult questions, which she herself could not have answered. The shadow made a wry face.

"You can't answer me?" said the princess.

"I knew all that in my childhood," said the shadow. "Why, I believe that my shadow over there by the door can answer you."

"Your shadow!" said the princess. "That would be remarkable indeed!"

"I can't say for certain," said the shadow, "but I'm inclined to think so, because he has followed me about and listened to me for so many years. Yes, I am inclined to believe so. But your Royal Highness must permit me to tell you that he is quite proud of being able to pass for a man, so if he is to be in the right frame of mind to answer your questions he must be treated just as if he were human."

"I like that!" said the princess.

So she went to the scholar in the doorway and spoke with him about the sun and the moon, and about people, what they are inside, and what they seem to be on the surface. He answered her wisely and well.

"What a man that must be, to have such a wise shadow!" she thought. "It will be a godsend to my people and to my country if I choose him for my consort. That's just what I'll do!"

The princess and the shadow came to an understanding, but no one was to know about it until she returned to her own kingdom.

"No one. Not even my shadow!" said the shadow. And he had his own private reason for this.

Finally they came to the country that the princess ruled when she was at home.

"Listen, my good friend," the shadow said the scholar, "I am now as happy and strong as one can be, so I'll do something very special for you. You shall live with me in my palace, drive with me in my royal carriage, and have a hundred thousand dollars a year. However, you must let yourself be called a shadow by everybody. You must not ever say that you have been a man, and once a year, while I sit on the balcony in the sunshine, you must lie at my feet as shadows do. For I tell you I am going to marry the princess, and the wedding is to take place this very evening."

"No! That's going too far," said the scholar. "I will *not*. I won't do it. That would be betraying the whole country and the princess too. I'll tell them everything—that I am the man, and you are the shadow merely dressed as a man."

"No one would believe it," said the shadow. "Be reasonable, or I'll call the sentry."

"I'll go straight to the princess," said the scholar.

"But I will go first," said the shadow, "and you shall go to prison."

And to prison he went, for the sentries obeyed the one who, they knew, was to marry the princess.

"Why, you're trembling," the princess said, as the shadow entered her room. "What has happened? You mustn't fall ill this evening, just as we are about to be married."

"I have been through the most dreadful experience that could happen to anyone," said the shadow. "Just imagine! Of course a poor shadow's head can't stand very much. But imagine! My shadow has gone mad. He takes himself for a man, and—imagine it! He takes *me* for his shadow."

"How terrible!" said the princess. "He's locked up, I hope!"

"Oh, of course. I'm afraid he will never recover."

"Poor shadow," said the princess. "He is very unhappy. It would really be a charitable act to relieve him of the little bit of life he has left. And, after thinking it over carefully, my opinion is that it will be necessary to put him out of the way."

"That's certainly hard, for he was a faithful servant," said the shadow. He managed to sigh.

"You have a noble soul," the princess told him.

The whole city was brilliantly lit that evening. The cannons boomed, and the soldiers presented arms. That was the sort of wedding it was! The princess and the shadow stepped out on the balcony to show themselves and be cheered, again and again.

The scholar heard nothing of all this, for they had already done away with him.

THE OLD HOUSE (1847)

Somewhere in the street stood an old, old house; it was almost 300 years old, as you could tell from the date cut into the great beam. Tulips and hopbines and also whole verses of poetry were carved into the wood as people used to do in those days, and over every window, a mocking face was cut into the beam. The second story hung way out over the ground floor, and right under the eaves was a leaden spout with a dragon's head. Rain water was supposed to run out of the dragon's mouth, but it came from his belly instead, for there was a hole in it.

All of the other houses in the street were so neat and modern, with large windowpanes and smooth walls, that you could easily tell they would have nothing to do with the old house. They evidently thought, "How long do you suppose that decrepit old thing is going to stand there, making an eyesore of our street? And that bay window stands so far out we can't see from our windows what's happening in that direction. Those front steps are as broad as those of a palace, and as high as those that go up to a church tower! The iron railings—they look like the door to an old family vault! And those dreadful brass rails on them! It makes one feel ashamed!"

Across the street were other neat and modern houses, and they thought the same way. But at the window in the house directly opposite sat a little boy with bright shining eyes and fresh rosy cheeks. And he liked the old house best of all those on the street, whether by sunshine or by moonlight.

When he looked across at the wall where the mortar had fallen out, he could imagine the strangest pictures. He could see the street as it was in the old days; he could see soldiers with halberds, and the houses with their steps and projecting windows and pointed gables, and rainspouts in the shapes of dragons and serpents. Yes, to him, that was indeed a house worth looking at!

An old man lived over there—an old man who wore old-fashioned plush breeches and a coat with big brass buttons, and a wig that you could plainly tell was a real one. Every morning, an old male servant came to put the rooms in order and do the marketing, but aside from that, the old man in the plush breeches lived all alone in his old house. Sometimes he came to the window and looked out, and the little boy waved to him, and the old man waved back, and so they became acquaintances and then friends. Of course, they had never spoken to each other, but that really made no difference.

One day, the little boy heard his parents say, "The old man over there is very well-to-do, but he's terribly lonely!"

Next Sunday, the little boy wrapped a small object in a piece of paper, went downstairs to his doorway, and, when the old servant who did the marketing came by, said to him, "Look, sir, will you please give this to the old gentleman across the way? I have two tin soldiers; this is one of them, and I want him to have it 'cause I know he's terribly lonely."

The old servant looked very pleased as he nodded, and took the tin soldier across to the house. And later, he brought back a message inviting the little boy to come over and pay a visit. Happily, the little boy asked his parents' permission, then went across to the old house.

The brass knobs on the railings shone brighter than ever—one would think they had been especially polished in honor of his visit. And the little trumpeters carved in tulips on the doorway seemed to puff out their cheeks and blow with all their might, "Tratteratra! The boy approaches! Tratteratra!" Then the door opened.

The whole hallway was hung with old portraits of knights in armor and ladies in silken gowns, and the armor seemed to rattle and the silken gowns rustle! Then there was a flight of stairs that went a long way up and a little way down, and then the little boy came out on a balcony. It was very dilapidated, with grass and leaves growing out of holes and long crevices, for the whole balcony outside, the yard, and the walls were so overgrown that it looked like a garden. But still, it was just a balcony. There were old flowerpots with faces and donkey's ears, and flowers growing out of them just as they pleased. One of the pots was almost brimming over with carnations—that is, with the green part; shoot grew by shoot, and each seemed to say quite distinctly, "The air has blessed me, and the sun has kissed me and promised me a little flower on Sunday! A little flower on Sunday!"

Now the little boy entered a room where the walls were covered with pigskin and printed with golden flowers.

"Gilding fades fast;
But pigskin will last,"

said the walls.

There were heavily carved easy chairs there, with high backs and arms on both sides. "Sit down! Sit down!" they cried. "Oh, how I creak! I know I'll get the gout, like the old cupboard! Oh!"

And at last, the little boy came into the room where the bay window was, and there sat the old man.

"I thank you for the tin soldier, my young friend," he said. "And I thank you again because you came over to see me."

"Thanks! Thanks!" or perhaps "Creak! Creak!" sounded from all the furniture. And there was so much of it in the room that the pieces seemed to crowd in each other's way, trying to get a look at the little boy.

In the middle of the wall hung a painting of a beautiful lady, young and happy, but dressed as in olden times, with clothes that stood out stiffly and with powdered hair. She neither said, "Thanks!" nor "Creak!" but just looked with mild eyes at the little boy. He promptly asked, "Where did she come from?"

"From the secondhand dealer down the street," said the old man, "where there are so many pictures. No one knows or cares anything about them, for all the people are buried. That lady has been dead and gone these fifty years, but I knew her in the old days."

In a glass frame beneath the portrait there hung a bouquet of withered flowers; they, too, must have been fifty years old—at least they looked it.

The pendulum of the great clock slowly swung to and fro, and the hands slowly turned, and everything in the room slowly became still older, but they didn't notice it.

"My mother and daddy say," said the little boy, "that you're terribly lonely."

"Oh," he answered, "the old thoughts, with what they may bring with them, come to see me, and now you come, too! I'm really very happy."

Then he took a picture book down from the shelf. There were long processions and strange coaches such as one never sees nowadays, soldiers who looked like the Knave of Clubs, and tradesmen with waving banners. The tailors had a banner that showed a pair of shears held by two lions; and the shoemakers had on theirs not a boot, but an eagle with two heads, for shoemakers must have everything in pairs. What a wonderful picture book that was!

And the old man went into the next room to fetch jam, apples, and nuts. Yes, the old house was a wonderful place. "I can't bear this any longer," cried the tin soldier, who was sitting on a chest of drawers. "It's so lonely and sad here! Anyone who has been in a family circle as I have can't get used to this sort of life. I can't bear it any longer! The days are so long, and the evenings are still longer! Things here aren't the way they were over at your house, where your father and mother spoke so pleasantly, and you and the other nice children made such delightful, happy noises. How lonely this old man is! Do you think he ever gets a kiss? Do you think he ever gets a kindly look or a Christmas tree? He'll get nothing but a funeral—I simply can't stand it any longer!"

"You mustn't let it make you so sad," said the little boy. "I think it's fun here, and then all the old memories, with what they may bring with them, come to visit here."

"Yes," said the tin soldier, "but I can't see them, because I don't know them. I tell you, I can't stand it!"

"But you must!" replied the little boy firmly.

Then the old man came back with his face all smiling, and with the most delicious jam and apples and nuts! So the little boy forgot about the tin soldier.

He went home, happy and pleased, and days and weeks passed, while nods and waves were exchanged to the old house and from the old house. Then he went over to call again.

Again the carved trumpeters seemed to blow, "Tratteratra! The little boy approaches! Tratteratra!" And the swords and armor on the knight paintings rattled, and the silken gowns rustled; the pigskin spoke, and the old chairs had rheumatism in their backs—"Ouch!" It was just like the first time, for in that house, one day or hour was just like another.

"I can't bear it!" wailed the tin soldier. "I've been shedding tin tears—it's too sad here! I'd rather go to the wars, and lose arms and legs; at least that would be a change! I just can't stand it! Now I know what it's like to have a visit from one's old memories and what they may bring with them. One of mine came to see me, and let me tell you, that isn't a very pleasant experience! I nearly jumped down from this chest!

"Because I saw you all over there so clearly, as if you really were right here! It was again that Sunday morning that you surely remember; all you children stood before the table and sang your hymns, just as you do every Sunday. You looked so devout, with your hands folded together; and your father and mother were just as pious. Then the door was opened, and little Sister Mary was put in the room. She really shouldn't have been there because she's less than two years old, and always tries to dance when she hears any kind of music or singing. She began to dance then, but she couldn't keep time—the music was too slow. First she stood on one leg and bent her head forward, and then she stood on the other leg and bent her head again—but it wouldn't do. You all stood together and looked very serious, although it was difficult to keep from laughing, but I did laugh to myself so hard I fell off the table and got a bump that I still have! It was very wrong of me to laugh. But it all comes back to me now in thought, and everything that I've seen all my life; these are the old memories, and what they may bring with them!

"Tell me, do you still sing on Sundays? Tell me about little Mary! And how is my comrade, the other tin soldier, doing? I imagine he's happy enough! Oh, I can't stand it anymore!"

"You were given away as a present," said the little boy firmly. "And you must stay here! Can't you understand that?"

Now the old man brought in a drawer in which there were many treasures—balm boxes and coin boxes and large, gilded, old playing cards, such as one never sees anymore. Several drawers were opened, and then the piano was opened; landscapes were painted on the inside of its lid, and it was so squeaky when the old man played it! Then he hummed a little song.

"She used to sing that," he said softly as he nodded up at the portrait he had bought from the secondhand dealer. And the old man's eyes shone brightly.

"I'm going to the wars! I tell you, I'm going to the wars!" the tin soldier shouted as loudly as he could; then, he threw himself off the chest right down to the floor.

What had become of him? The old man searched, and the little boy searched, but he was gone; they couldn't find him.

"I'll find him," said the old man, but he never did; the flooring was open and full of holes, and the tin soldier had fallen into one of the many cracks in the floor and lay there as if in an open grave.

And that day passed, and the little boy went home. A week passed, and several more weeks passed.

The windows of his home were frosted over, and the little boy had to breathe hard on one to make a peephole over to the old house. Then he saw that the snow had drifted into all the carving and inscriptions and up over the steps, just as if there were no one there. And there wasn't, really. For the old man was dead!

That evening, a hearse drove up before the door, and the old man's coffin was borne into it; he was going out into the country now, to lie in his grave. And so he was driven away, but there was no one to follow him, for all the old man's friends were dead. There was only the little boy who blew a kiss to the coffin as it was driven away.

A few days later, the old house was sold at auction, and from his window, the little boy watched them carry away the old knights and their ladies, and the long-eared flowerpots, the old chairs, and the old cupboards; some pieces landed here, and others landed there; the portrait that had come from the secondhand dealer went back to the secondhand dealer again, and there it hung, for no one knew the lady anymore, and no one cared about the old picture.

In the spring, the house was torn down, for everybody said it was nothing but a ruin. One could see from the street right into the room with the pigskin hangings, which were slashed and torn; and the green foliage about the balcony hung wild among the falling beams. The site was cleared.

"Good riddance," said the neighboring houses.

Then a fine house was built there, with large windows and smooth white walls; but in front of it, where the old house used to stand, a little garden was laid out, with a wild grapevine running up the wall of the neighboring house. Before the garden was a large railing with an iron gate; it looked quite splendid, and many people stopped to peer in. Scores of sparrows fluttered in the vines and chattered away to each other as fast as they could, but they didn't talk about the old house, for they couldn't remember it. So many years had passed.

Yes, many years had passed, and the little boy had grown up now to be a fine man; yes, an able man, and a great joy to his old parents. He had just been married, and, with his pretty little wife, came to live in the new house where the garden was.

He was standing beside her in the garden while she planted a wild flower she was so fond of. She bedded it in the ground with her little hand and pressed the earth around it with her fingers. Ouch, what was that! She had pricked herself. There was something there, pointed straight up in the soft dirt.

Yes, it was—just imagine, the little tin soldier! The same one that had been lost in the old man's room. He had tumbled and tossed about among the gravel and the timber and at last had lain for years in the ground.

The young wife wiped the dirt off the soldier, first with a green leaf and then with her delicate handkerchief, which had such a delightful scent that it woke the soldier up from his trance.

"Let me see him," said the young man. Then he laughed and shook his head. "No, it couldn't be he, but he certainly reminds me of a tin soldier I had when I was a little boy." Then he told her all about the old house and the old man and the tin soldier that had been sent over to keep him company because he was so terribly lonely. He told it just as it had happened, and the tears came into the eyes of his young wife—tears of pity for the old house and the old man.

"It might just possibly be the same tin soldier," she said gently. "I'll keep it, and remember everything you've told me. But you must show me the old man's grave."

"But I don't know where it is," he replied. "Nobody knows. All his friends were dead, and there was no one to take care of it. I was then just a little boy."

"How terribly lonely he must have been!" she murmured.

"Terribly lonely!" repeated the tin soldier. "But it's wonderful not to be forgotten!"

"Wonderful!" cried something else close by, but only the tin soldier saw that it was a scrap of the pigskin hanging. It had lost all of its gilding and looked like a piece of wet clay, but it still had its opinion, and gave it:

> Gilding fades fast;
> But pigskin will last!

But the tin soldier didn't really believe it.

THE DROP OF WATER (1847)

Of course, you must know what a microscope is, that round magnifying glass that makes everything look hundreds of times larger than it really is. If you take it and hold it close to your eye and look at a single drop of ditchwater, you'll see thousands of strange little creatures, such as you couldn't imagine living in a drop of water. But they are really there. They look almost like a plateful of shrimp, all jumping and crowding against each other, and they are so ferocious, they tear off each other's arm and legs; yet in their own way, they are happy and merry.

Now, once there was an old man whom his neighbors called Krible-Krable, for that was his name. He always tried to make the best of everything, and if he couldn't do it any other way, he would try magic.

One day, he sat with his eye glued to his microscope, peering at a drop of water taken from a puddle in the ditch. My! How it crawled and squirmed! All those thousands of little imps leaping and springing about, devouring each other, or pulling each other to pieces.

"This is too hideous for words!" said the old Krible-Krable. "There must be some way to make them live in peace and quiet and each mind his own business." But though he thought and thought, he couldn't find the answer. So he decided to use magic. "At least I can give them a color," he said, "so I can see them better." And then he let fall into the water a tiny drop of something that looked like red wine, but was really witches' blood, the very finest kind, and worth two pennies. Instantly, the strange little creatures became red all over, and the drop of water now looked like a whole town full of naked wild men.

"What have you got there?" asked another old magician, who had no name at all, which made him very distinguished.

"If you can guess what it is," replied Krible-Krable, "I'll give it to you. But it's not very easy to find out if one doesn't know."

So the nameless magician peered down through the microscope. The scene before his eyes really resembled a town where all the inhabitants ran about without clothing. What a terrible sight it was! But it was still more horrible to see them kick and cuff, and struggle and fight, and pull and bite at each other. All those on the bottom were struggling to get to the top, and those on the top were being pushed to the bottom. "Look! Look!" the creatures seemed to be crying. "His leg is longer than mine! Bah! Off with it! And here's one with a little lump behind his ear! An innocent little lump, but it hurts him, and it'll hurt him more!" And they hacked at it and tore at him and devoured him, all because of the little lump.

But one sat very quiet and still, all by itself, like a modest maiden, wishing for nothing but peace and quiet. But the others couldn't stand for that—they pulled her out, beat her, cut her, and ate her.

"This is extremely amusing!" said the magician.

"Yes, but what do you think it is?" asked Krible-Krable. "Can you find out?"

"Why, that's easy to see," answered the magician. "Of course, it is Copenhagen, or some other large city. I can't tell which, for they all look alike. But it's certainly some large city."

"It's a drop of ditchwater!" said Krible-Krable.

THE HAPPY FAMILY (1847)

The biggest leaf we have in this country is certainly the burdock leaf. If you hold one in front of your little stomach, it's just like a real apron; and in rainy weather, if you lay it on your head, it does almost as well as an umbrella. It's really amazingly large. Now, a burdock never grows alone; no, when you see one, you'll always see others around it. It's a splendid sight; and all this splendor is nothing more than food for snails—the big white snails that the fine people in olden days used to have made into fricassees. When they had eaten them, they would smack their lips and say, "My! How good that is!" For somehow, they had the idea that the snails tasted delicious. You see, these snails lived on the burdock leaves, and that's why the burdock was first grown.

There was a certain old manor house where the people didn't eat snails anymore. The snails had almost died out, but the burdock hadn't. These grew and grew on all the walks and flower beds—they couldn't be stopped—until the whole place was a forest of burdocks. Here and there stood an apple or a plum tree, but except for that, people wouldn't have thought there had ever been a garden there. Everywhere was burdock, and among the burdocks lived the last two incredibly old snails!

They themselves didn't know how old they were, but they could remember very clearly that once there had been a great many more of them, that they had descended from a prominent foreign family, and they knew perfectly well that the whole forest had been planted just for them and their family.

They had never been away from home, but they did know that somewhere there was something called a manor house, and that there you were boiled until you turned black, and were laid on a silver dish; but what happened afterwards they hadn't the least idea. Furthermore, they couldn't imagine what it would be like to be boiled and laid on a silver dish, but everyone said it must be very wonderful and a great distinction. Neither the cockchafer nor the toad nor the earthworm, whom they asked about it, could give them any information. None of their families had ever been boiled or laid on silver dishes.

So the old white snails knew they were by far the most important people in the world. The forest was there just for their sake, and the manor house existed just so that they could be boiled and laid on silver dishes!

The two old snails led a quiet and happy life, and since they were childless, they had adopted a little orphan snail, which they were bringing up as their own child. He wouldn't grow very large, for he was only a common snail; but the two old snails—and especially the mother snail—thought it was easy to see how well he was growing. And she begged the father snail to touch the little snail's shell, if he couldn't see it, and so he felt it and found that she was right.

One day, it rained very hard.

"Just listen to it drum on the burdock leaves!" cried Father Snail. "Rum-dum-dum! Rum-dum-dum!"

"Drops are also coming down here!" said the mother. "It's coming straight down the stalks, and it'll be wet down here before you know it. I'm certainly glad we have our own good houses and the little one has his own. We're better off than any other creatures; it's quite plain that we're the most important people in the world. We have our own houses from our very birth, and the burdock forest has been planted just for us. I wonder how far it extends, and what lies beyond it."

"There can't be anything beyond," said Father Snail, "that's any better than we have here. I have nothing in the world to wish for."

"Well, I have," said the mother. "I'd like to be taken to the manor house and boiled and laid on a silver dish. All our ancestors had that done to them, and, believe me, it must be something quite uncommon!"

"Maybe the manor house has fallen to pieces," suggested Father Snail. "Or perhaps the burdock forest has grown over it, so that the people can't get out at all. Don't be in such a hurry—but then you're always hurrying so. And the little one is beginning to do the same thing. Why, he's been creeping up that stalk for three days. It really makes my head dizzy to watch him go!"

"Don't scold him," said Mother Snail. "He crawls very carefully. He'll bring us much joy, and we old folk don't have anything else to live for. But have you ever thought where we can find a wife for him? Don't you think there might be some more of our kind of people farther back in the burdock woods?"

"I suppose there may be black snails back there," said the old man.

"Black snails without houses! Much too vulgar! And they're conceited, anyway. But let's ask the ants to find out for us; they're always running around as if they had important business. They're sure to know of a wife for our little snail."

"Certainly, I know a very beautiful bride," said one of the ants. "But I don't think she'd do, because she's a queen!"

"That doesn't matter," said Mother Snail emphatically. "Does she have a house?"

"She has a castle!" replied the ant. "The most beautiful ant's castle, with seven hundred corridors!"

"Thank you very much," said Mother Snail, "but our boy shall not go into an anthill! If you don't know of anything better, we'll ask the white gnats to find out for us. They flit around in the rain and sunshine, and they know this forest inside and out."

"We have just the wife for him," said the gnats. "A hundred man-steps from here, a little snail with a house is sitting on a gooseberry bush. She is all alone in the world, and quite old enough to marry. It's only a hundred man-steps from here!"

"Fine, but she must come to him," said the old couple. "Our child has a whole burdock forest, and she has only a bush."

And so the gnats had the little maiden snail come over. It took her eight days to get there, but that was the wonderful part of it—for it showed she had the right sort of dignity.

And then they had a fine wedding! Six glowworms lit up the place as well as they could, but aside from that, it was a very quiet ceremony, for the old people did not care for feasting or merriment. A charming speech was made by Mother Snail, but Father Snail couldn't say a word; he was too deeply moved. And so she gave the young couple the whole burdock forest for a dowry, and repeated what she had always said—that it was the finest place in the world, and that the young people, if they lived honorably and had many children, would someday be taken with their young ones to the manor house, to be boiled black and laid on a silver dish. And when Mother Snail's speech was finished, the old people crept into their houses and never came out again, for they went to sleep.

Now the young couple ruled the forest and did have many children. But since none of them were ever boiled and laid in silver dishes, they decided that the manor house must have fallen into ruins and that all the people in the world had died out. And since nobody contradicted them, I think they must have been right. So the rain beat on the burdock leaves, to play the drum for them, and the sun shone, to color the forest for them; and they were very happy. The whole family was happy—extremely happy, indeed they were.

THE STORY OF A MOTHER (1847)

A mother sat by her little child. She was so sad, so afraid he would die. The child's face was pallid. His little eyes were shut. His breath came faintly now, and then heavily as if he were sighing, and the mother looked more sadly at the dear little soul.

There came a knocking at the door, and a poor old man hobbled into the house. He was wrapped in a thick horseblanket. It kept him warm, and he needed it to keep out the wintry cold, for outside the world was covered with snow and ice, and the wind cut like a knife.

As the child was resting quietly for a moment, and the old man was shivering from the cold, the mother put a little mug of beer to warm on the stove for him. The old man rocked the cradle, and the mother sat down near it to watch her sick child, who labored to draw each breath. She lifted his little hand, and asked:

"You don't think I shall lose him, do you? Would the good Lord take him from me?"

The old man was Death himself. He jerked his head strangely, in a way that might mean yes or might mean no. The mother bowed her head and tears ran down her cheeks. Her head was heavy.

For three days and three nights, she had not closed her eyes. Now she dozed off to sleep, but only a moment. Something startled her and she awoke, shuddering in the cold.

"What was that?" she said, looking everywhere about the room. But the old man had gone and her little child had gone. Death had taken the child away. The old clock in the corner whirred and whirred. Its heavy lead weight dropped down to the floor with a thud. *Bong*! The clock stopped. The poor mother rushed wildly out of the house, calling for her child.

Out there in the snow sat a woman, dressed in long black garments. "Death," she said, "has been in your house. I just saw him hurrying away with your child in his arms. He goes faster than the wind. And he never brings back what he has taken away."

"Tell me which way he went," said the mother. "Only tell me the way, and I will find him."

"I know the way," said the woman in black, "but before I tell you, you must sing to me all those songs you used to sing to your child. I am Night. I love lullabies, and I hear them often. When you sang them, I saw your tears."

"I shall sing them again—you shall hear them all," said the mother, "but do not stop me now. I must catch him. I must hurry to find my child."

Night kept silent and still, while the mother wrung her hands, and sang, and wept. She sang many songs, but the tears that she shed were many, many more. At last Night said to her, "Go to the right. Go into the dark pine woods. I saw Death go there with your child."

Deep into the woods, the mother came to a crossroad, where she was at a loss which way to go. At the crossroad grew a blackthorn bush, without leaf or flower, for it was wintertime and its branches were glazed with ice.

"Did you see Death go by with my little child?"

"Yes," said the blackthorn bush. "But I shall not tell you which way he went unless you warm me against your heart. I am freezing to death. I am stiff with ice."

She pressed the blackthorn bush against her heart to warm it, and the thorns stabbed so deep into her flesh that great drops of red blood flowed. So warm was the mother's heart that the blackthorn bush blossomed and put forth green leaves on that dark winter's night. And it told her the way to go.

Then she came to a large lake, where there was neither sailboat nor rowboat. The ice on the lake was too thin to hold her weight, and yet not open or shallow enough for her to wade. But across the lake she must go if ever she was to find her child. She stooped down to drink the lake dry, and that of course was impossible for any human being, but the poor woman thought that maybe a miracle would happen.

"No, that would never do," the lake objected. "Let us make a bargain between us. I collect pearls, and your two eyes are the clearest I've ever seen. If you will cry them out for me, I shall carry you over to the great greenhouse where Death lives and tends his trees and flowers. Each one of them is a human life."

"Oh, what would I not give for my child," said the crying mother, and she wept till her eyes dropped down to the bottom of the lake and became two precious pearls. The lake took her up as if in a swing and swept her to the farther shore.

Here stood the strangest house that ever was. It rambled for many a mile. One wouldn't know whether it was a cavernous, forested mountain, or whether it was made of wood. But the poor mother could not see this, for she had cried out her eyes.

"Where shall I find Death, who took my child from me?" she cried.

"He has not come back yet," said the old woman who took care of the great greenhouse while Death was away. "How did you find your way here? Who helped you?"

"The Lord helped me," she said. "He is merciful, and so must you be. Where can I find my child?"

"I don't know him," said the old woman, "and you can't see to find him. But many flowers and trees have withered away in the night, and Death will be along soon to transplant them. Every human being, you know, has his tree or his flower of life, depending on what sort of person he is. These look like other plants, but they have a heart that beats. A child's heart beats, too. You know the beat of your own child's heart. Listen and you may hear it. But what will you give me if I tell you what else you must do?"

"I have nothing left," the poor mother said, "but I will go to the ends of the Earth for you."

"I have nothing to do there," said the old woman, "but you can give me your long black hair. You know how beautiful it is, and I like it. I'll give you my white hair for it. White hair is better than none."

"Is that all you ask?" said the mother. "I will gladly give it to you." And she gave her beautiful long black tresses in exchange for the old woman's white hair.

Then they went into Death's great greenhouse, where flowers and trees were strangely intertwined. In one place, delicate hyacinths were kept under glass bells, and around them, great hardy peonies flourished. There were water plants too, some thriving where the stalks of others were choked by twisting water snakes or gnawed away by black crayfish. Tall palm trees grew there, and plane trees, and oaks. There grew parsley and sweet-smelling thyme. Every tree or flower went by the name of one particular person, for each was the life of someone still living in China, in Greenland, or in some other part of the world. There were big trees stunted by the small pots that their roots filled to bursting, and elsewhere grew languid little flowers that came to nothing, for all the care that was lavished upon them and for all the rich earth and the mossy carpet where they grew. The sad, blind mother bent over the tiniest plants and listened to the beat of their human hearts, and among so many millions, she knew her own child's heartbeat.

"This is it," she cried, groping for a little blue crocus, which had wilted and dropped to one side.

"Don't touch that flower," the old woman said. "Stay here. Death will be along any minute now, and you may keep him from pulling it up. Threaten him that, if he does, you will pull up other plants. That will frighten him, for he has to account for them to the Lord. Not one may be uprooted until God says so."

Suddenly an icy wind blew through the place, and the blind mother felt Death come near.

"How did you find your way here?" he asked her. "How did you ever get here before me?"

"I am a mother," she said.

Then Death stretched out his long hand toward the wilted little flower, but she held her hands tightly around it, in terror lest he touch a single leaf. Death breathed upon her hands, and his breath was colder than the coldest wind. Her hands fell, powerless.

"You have no power to resist me," Death told her.

"But our Lord has," she said.

"I only do his will," said Death, "I am his gardener. I take his flowers and trees and plant them again in the great Paradise gardens, in the unknown land. But how they thrive, and of their life there, I dare not speak."

"Give me back my child," the mother wept and implored him. Suddenly, she grasped a beautiful flower in each hand, and as she clutched them, she called to Death: "I shall tear out your flowers by the roots, for I am desperate."

"Do not touch them!" Death told her. "You say you are desperate, yet you would drive another mother to the same despair."

"Another mother!" The blind woman's hands let go the flowers.

"Behold," said Death, "you have your eyes again. I saw them shining as I crossed the lake, and fished them up, but I did not know they were yours. They are clearer than before. Take them and look deep into this well. I shall tell you the names of the flowers you were about to uproot, and you shall see the whole future of those human lives that you would have destroyed and disturbed."

She looked into the well, and it made her glad to see how one life became a blessing to the world, for it was so kind and happy. Then she saw the other life, which held only sorrow, poverty, fear, and woe.

"Both are the will of God," said Death.

"Which one is condemned to misery, and which is the happy one?" she asked.

"That I shall not tell you," Death said. "But I tell you this. One of the flowers belongs to your own child. One life that you saw was your child's fate, your own child's future."

Then the mother shrieked in terror, "Which was my child? Tell me! Save my innocent child. Spare him such wretchedness. Better that he be taken from me. Take him to God's kingdom. Forget my tears. Forget the prayers I have said and the things I have done."

"I do not understand," Death said. "Will you take your own child back, or shall I take him off to a land unknown to you?"

Then the mother wrung her hands, fell on her knees, and prayed to God:

"Do not hear me when I pray against your will. It is best. Do not listen, do not listen!" And she bowed her head, as Death took her child to the unknown land.

THE SHIRT COLLAR (1847)

There was once a perfect gentleman whose whole household goods consisted of one bootjack and a comb. But he also had one of the most remarkable shirt collars in the world. I'll tell you a story about it.

When the shirt collar had passed his prime, he turned his thoughts to marriage. In the fullness of time, he went to the wash, and there he met with a garter.

"My!" said the collar, "Anyone so slender, so tender, so neat and nice as you are, I never did see. May I know your name?"

"No," said the garter. "I won't tell you."

"Then at least tell me where you live?" asked the collar.

But the garter was so modest that she couldn't bring herself to answer such an embarrassing question.

"I believe you are a girdle," said the collar. "A sort of underneath girdle. And I dare say you're as useful as you are beautiful, my pretty little dear."

"I forbid you to speak to me," said the garter. "I'm sure I haven't given you the slightest encouragement."

"Your beauty is every encouragement," said the collar.

"Kindly keep away from me," said the garter. "You look too masculine."

"Oh, I'm a perfect gentleman," said the collar. "I've a bootjack and a comb to prove it."

This wasn't true at all, for they belonged to his master, but he liked to boast.

"Please don't come so close," said the garter. "I'm not used to such behavior."

"Prude!" the collar called her as they took him from the washtub. They starched him, hung him over a chair back in the sun, and then stretched him out on an ironing board. There he met with a sadiron.

"My dear lady," said the collar, "you adorable widow woman, the closer you come, the warmer I feel. I'm a changed collar since I met you, without a wrinkle left in me. You burn clear through me. Oh, won't you be mine?"

"Rag!" said the sadiron, as she flattened him out, for she went her way like a railway engine pulling cars down a track. "Rag!" was what she said.

The collar was the worse for wear at the edges, so the scissors were called to trim him.

"Oh," said the collar, "you must be a ballet dancer. How straight you stretch your legs out. Such a graceful performance! No one can do that like you."

"I'm well aware of it," said the scissors.

"You deserve to be no less than a countess," said the collar. "All I have to offer is my perfect gentleman, bootjack and comb. Oh, if only I had an earldom."

"I do believe he's daring to propose," said the scissors. She cut him so furiously that he never recovered.

"Now I shall have to ask the comb," said the collar. "My dear, how remarkably well you've kept your teeth. Have you ever thought of getting engaged?"

"Why, of course," said the comb. "I am engaged—to the bootjack."

"Engaged!" the collar exclaimed. Now that there was no one left for him to court, the collar pretended that he had never meant to marry.

Time passed, and the collar went his way to the bin in a paper mill, where the rags kept company according to rank, the fine rags in one bin, the coarse in another, just as it is in the world. They all gossiped aplenty, but the collar chattered the most, for he was an awful braggart.

"I've had sweethearts by the dozen," he told them. "Ladies never would leave me alone, and you can't blame them; for I was such a perfect gentleman, stiff with starch, and with a bootjack and comb to spare. You should have seen me then. You should have seen me unbend.

"I'll never forget my first love—such a charming little girdle, so slender and tender. She threw herself into a tub of water, all for the love of me. Then there was the widow, glowing to get me, but I jilted her and let her cool off. And there was the ballet dancer, whose mark I bear to this day. What a fiery creature she was! And even my comb fell so hard in love with me that she lost all her teeth when I left her. Yes, indeed, I have plenty on my conscience. But the garter—I mean the girdle—who drowned herself in the wash tub, is the one I feel most badly about. Oh, I have a black record, and it's high time I turned into spotless white paper."

And that's exactly what happened. All the rags were made into paper, and the collar became the page you see, the very paper on which this story is printed. That was because he boasted so outrageously about things that never had happened. So let's be careful to behave we better than he did, for you never can tell. Someday we may end up in the ragbag and be made into white paper on which the whole story of our life is printed in full detail. Then we'd have to turn tattletale on ourselves, just as the shirt collar has done.

THERE IS A DIFFERENCE (1851)

It was in the month of May. The wind was still cold, but spring had come, said the trees and the bushes, the fields and the meadows. Everywhere, flowers were budding into blossom; even the hedges were alive with them. Here spring spoke about herself; it spoke from a little apple tree, from which hung a single branch so fresh and blooming, and fairly weighed down by a glorious mass of rosy buds just ready to open.

Now this branch knew how lovely it was, for that knowledge lies in the leaf as well as in the flesh, so it wasn't a bit surprised when one day a grand carriage stopped in the road beside it, and the young countess in the carriage said that this apple branch was the most beautiful she had ever seen—it was spring itself in its loveliest form. So she broke off the apple branch and carried it in her own dainty hand, shading it from the sun with her silk parasol, as they drove on to her castle, in which there were lofty halls and beautifully decorated rooms. Fleecy-white curtains fluttered at its open windows, and there were many shining, transparent vases full of beautiful flowers. In one of these vases, which looked as if it were carved of new-fallen snow, she placed the apple branch, among fresh green beech leaves—a lovely sight indeed.

And so it happened that the apple branch grew proud, and that's quite human.

All sorts of people passed through the rooms, and, according to their rank, expressed their admiration in different ways; some said too much, some said too little, and some said nothing at all. And the apple branch began to realize that there were differences in people as well as in plants.

"Some are used for nourishment, some are for ornament, and some you could very well do without," thought the apple branch.

From its position at the open window, the apple branch could look down over the gardens and meadows below, and consider the differences among the flowers and plants beneath. Some were rich, some were poor, and some were very poor.

"Miserable, rejected plants," said the apple branch. "There is a difference, indeed! It's quite proper and just that distinctions should be made. Yet how unhappy they must feel, if indeed a creature like that is capable of feeling anything, as I and my equals do. But it must be that way; otherwise, everybody would be treated as though they were just alike."

And the apple branch looked down with especial pity on one kind of flower that grew everywhere in meadows and ditches. They were much too common ever to be gathered into bouquets; they could be found between the paving stones; they shot up like the rankest and most worthless of weeds. They were dandelions, but people have given them the ugly name, "the devil's milk pails."

"Poor wretched outcasts," said the apple branch. "I suppose you can't help being as common as you are, and having such a vulgar name! It's the same with plants as with men—there must be a difference."

"A difference?" repeated the sunbeam, as it kissed the apple branch; but it kissed the golden "devil's milk pails," too. And all the other sunbeams did the same, kissing all the flowers equally, poor as well as rich.

The apple branch had never thought about our Lord's infinite love for everything that lives and moves in him, had never thought how much that is good and beautiful can lie hidden but still not be forgotten; and that, too, was human.

But the sunbeam, the ray of light, knew better. "You don't see very clearly; you are not very farsighted. Who are these outcast flowers that you pity so much?"

"Those devil's milk pails down there," replied the apple branch. "Nobody ever ties them up in bouquets; they're trodden under foot, because there are too many of them. And when they go to seed, they fly about along the road like little bits of wool and hang on people's clothes. They're just weeds! I suppose there must be weeds, too, but I'm certainly happy and grateful that I'm not like one of them!"

Now a whole flock of children ran out into the meadow to play. The youngest of them was so tiny that he had to be carried by the others. When they set him down in the grass among the golden blossoms, he laughed and gurgled with joy, kicked his little legs, rolled over and over, and plucked only the yellow dandelions. These he kissed in innocent delight.

The bigger children broke off the flowers of the dandelions and joined the hollow stalks link by link into chains. First, they would make one for a necklace, then a longer one to hang across the shoulders and around the waist, and finally one to go around their heads; it was a beautiful wreath of splendid green links and chains.

But the biggest of the children carefully gathered the stalks that had gone to seed, those loose, aerial, woolly blossoms, those wonderfully perfect balls of dainty white plumes, and held them to their lips, trying to blow away all the white feathers with one breath. Granny had told them that whoever could do that would receive new clothes before the year was out. The poor, despised dandelion was considered quite a prophet on such occasions.

"Now do you see?" asked the sunbeam. "Do you see its beauty and power?"

"Oh, it's all right—for children," replied the apple branch.

Now an old woman came into the meadow. She stooped and dug up the roots of the dandelion with a blunt knife that had lost its handle. Some of the roots she would roast instead of coffee berries; others she would sell to the apothecary to be used as drugs.

"Beauty is something higher than this," said the apple branch. "Only the chosen few can really be allowed into the kingdom of the beautiful; there's as much difference between plants as between men."

Then the sunbeam spoke of the infinite love of the Creator for all his creatures, for everything that has life, and of the equal distribution of all things in time and eternity.

"That's just your opinion," replied the apple branch.

Now some people came into the room, and among them was the young countess who had placed the apple branch in the transparent vase. She was carrying a flower—or whatever it was—that was protected by three or four large leaves around it like a cap, so that no breath of air or gust of wind could injure it. She carried it more carefully and tenderly than she had the apple branch when she had brought it to the castle. Very gently, she removed the leaves, and then the apple branch could see what she carried. It was a delicate, feathery crown of starry seeds borne by the despised dandelion!

This was what she had plucked so carefully and carried so tenderly, so that no single one of the loose, dainty, feathered arrows that rounded out its downy form should be blown away. There it was, whole and perfect. With delight, she admired the beautiful form, the airy lightness, the marvelous mechanism of a thing that was destined so soon to be scattered by the wind.

"Look how wonderfully beautiful our Lord made this!" she cried. "I'll paint it, together with the apple branch. Everybody thinks it is so extremely beautiful, but this poor flower is lovely, too; it has received as much from our Lord in another way. They are very different, yet both are children in the kingdom of the beautiful!"

The sunbeam kissed the poor dandelion, and then kissed the blooming apple branch, whose petals seemed to blush a deeper red.

IT'S QUITE TRUE! (1852)

It's a dreadful story!" said a hen, and she said it in a part of town, too, where it had not taken place. "It's a dreadful story to happen in a henhouse. I'm afraid to sleep alone tonight; it's a good thing there are many of us on the perch!" And then she told a story that made the feathers of the other hens stand on end and the rooster's comb fall. It's quite true!

But we will begin at the beginning and tell what had happened in a henhouse at the other end of town.

The sun went down, and the hens flew up. One of them was a white-feathered and short-limbed hen who laid her eggs according to the regulations and who was a respectable hen in every way. As she settled herself on the perch, she plucked herself with her beak, and a tiny feather came out.

"There it goes," she said. "No doubt the more I pluck, the more beautiful I will get." But she said it only in fun, for she was considered the jolliest among the hens, although, as we've said before, most respectable. Then she fell asleep.

There was darkness all around, and the hens sat closely together. But the hen that sat closest to the white hen was not asleep; she had heard and had not heard, as one should do in this world, if one wishes to live in peace. But still, she couldn't resist telling it to her nearest neighbor.

"Did you hear what was said? Well, I don't want to mention any names, but there is a hen here who intends to pluck out all her feathers just to make herself look well. If I were a rooster, I would despise her."

Right above the hens lived a mother owl with a father owl and all her little owls. They had sharp ears in that family, and they all heard every word that their neighbor hen had said. They all rolled their eyes, and the mother owl flapped her wings and said; "Don't listen to it. But I suppose you all heard what was said. *I* heard it with my own ears, and one must hear a great deal before they fall off. One of the hens has so completely forgotten what is becoming conduct to a hen that she plucks out all her feathers, while the rooster watches her."

"Little pitchers have long ears," said the father owl. "Children shouldn't hear such talk."

"I must tell it to the owl across the road," said the mother owl. "She is such a respectable owl!" And away flew Mamma.

"Hoo-whoo! Hoo-whoo!" they both hooted to the pigeons in the pigeon house across the road. "Have you heard it? Have you heard it? Hoo-whoo! There is a hen who has plucked out all her feathers just to please the rooster. She must be freezing to death; that is, if she isn't dead already. Hoo-whoo! Hoo-whoo!"

"Where? Where?" cooed the pigeons.

"In the yard across the way. I have as good as seen it myself. It is almost not a proper story to tell, but it's quite true!"

"True, true, every word of it," said the pigeons, and cooed down into their poultry yard. "There is a hen, and some say there are two hens, who have plucked out all their feathers in order to look different from the rest and to attract the attention of the rooster."

"Wake up! Wake up!" crowed the rooster, and flew up on the fence. He was still half asleep, but he crowed just the same. "Three hens have died of a broken heart, all for the sake of a rooster, and they have plucked all their feathers out! It's a dreadful story, but I will not keep it to myself. Tell it everywhere!"

"Tell it everywhere!" shrieked the bats; and the hens clucked and the roosters crowed. "Tell it everywhere!"

And so the story traveled from henhouse to henhouse until at last it was carried back to the very same place from where it had really started.

"There are five hens," now ran the tale, "who all have plucked out all their feathers to show which of them had lost the most weight through unhappy love for their rooster. And then they pecked at each other till they bled and all five dropped dead, to the shame and disgrace of their families, and to the great loss of their owner."

And the hen who had lost the little loose feather naturally didn't recognize her own story; and as she was a respectable hen, she said, "I despise such hens, but there are many of that kind! Such stories should not be hushed up, and I'll do my best to get the story into the newspapers. Then it will be known all over the country; that will serve those hens right, and their families, too." And it got to the newspapers, and it was printed. And it is quite true. One little feather may grow till it becomes five hens.

A GOOD HUMOR (1852)

From my father I have inherited that most worthy of bequests—a cheerful temper. And who was my father? Well, that really has nothing to do with a good humor. He was thrifty and lively, fat and round; in fact, his exterior and interior were both at variance with his office.

And what was his office, his position in the community? Why, if the answer to that question were written and printed at the very beginning of a book, most people would lay the book down as soon as they opened it, saying, "There is something dismal about it. I don't want anything like this."

And yet my father was neither a hangman nor a headsman. On the contrary, his office often brought him into contact with the most honorable men of the state, and he was certainly entitled to be there; he had to be ahead of them, even ahead of bishops and princes of the royal blood, for, to tell the truth, he was the driver of a hearse!

Now you know it! But I must add that when one saw my father sitting high up on the carriage of death, dressed in his long black mantle and crepe-bordered, three-cornered hat, his face as round and smiling as the sun, one could not think of sorrow and graves, for that face said, "Never mind, it's going to be much better than you think."

You see, then, that from him I have my good humor and also the habit of frequently visiting the churchyard; and that is rather amusing, if one goes there in a cheerful temper. Oh, yes, I also subscribe to the *Advertiser,* just as he used to do.

I am not exactly young, and I have neither wife, nor children, nor library to divert me. But, as I have told you, I read the *Advertiser*—that's all I need; it was my father's favorite newspaper, and it's mine, too. It is a most useful paper, and contains everything a person ought to know.

From it I learn who is preaching in the churches and who preaches in the new books; I know where I may obtain houses, servants, clothes, and food; I know who is selling out and who is buying up. Then, too, I learn of so many deeds of charity, and I read so many innocent verses, which are quite free of any offense, and of marriages desired. Yes, it is all so natural and simple. One can live very happily, and be happily buried, if one reads the *Advertiser*—and then when death comes about, one has such a lot of paper that one can rest softly on it, if one doesn't care to rest on wood shavings. The churchyard and the *Advertiser* were as always the things that most elevated my mind.

Everyone is free, of course, to read the *Advertiser,* but if anybody would like to share my walks in the churchyard, let him join me someday when the sun is shining and the trees are green.

Then let us ramble together among the old graves; each one is like a closed book with the cover toward you, so you can read the title that tells you what the book contains and yet says nothing at all. But from my father, and through my own experiences, I know all about it. I have written it all in a book for my own especial benefit and instruction; there is something written about most of them.

Now we are in the churchyard.

Behind this white-painted trellis, where once grew a rosebush—it is dead now, but a stray bit of evergreen from the next grave stretches a long green finger across the sod, as if to make up for the loss—there rests a man who was singularly unhappy. Yet you would not have called him unfortunate; he had sufficient income and never suffered any great calamity. His unhappiness was of his own making; as we say it, he took everything, especially his "art," too much to heart. Thus, if he spent an evening at the theater, he nearly went out of his mind if the machinist had put too strong a light into each cheek of the moon, or if canvases representing the sky were hanging in front of the scene instead of behind, or if a palm tree appeared in a local landscape, cacti on the Tyrolean plains, or beech trees in the high mountains of Norway. What does it matter; who cares! It is only a play intended for amusement. The audience was sure to be wrong, sometimes applauding too much and sometimes too little. "Look, that is wet wood tonight," he said. "It won't burn!" And when he turned around to see what kind of people were there, he found them laughing in the wrong places. All this annoyed and pained him. He was a miserable man, and now he is in his grave.

Here rests, on the other hand, a very fortunate man—I mean to say he was a man of extremely noble birth. In fact, that constituted his good fortune, for had he not been highborn he would never have amounted to anything. But, then, everything is so wisely arranged, and that is a pleasure to know. His coats were embroidered in front and in back, very much like a fine, embroidered bellpull in a room, for behind the handsome, gaudy bellpull is always a good, strong, plain cord that really does all the work. And this man had his good, stout cord behind him, which now does the work behind a new embroidered bellpull. That's the way it is; everything is so wisely arranged that it is very easy to keep one's good humor.

Over here there rests—now, this is really sad!—a man who for sixty-seven years worried and wracked his brains to hit upon a great idea. For the sake of this idea he lived alone all his days, and when at last he had convinced himself that he had succeeded, he was so overcome that he died of joy at having found it—before he even had time to announce it to the world—so nobody ever heard about his great idea. I can almost fancy that he has no rest in his grave, because of that great idea which no one but himself has enjoyed or ever can enjoy. For suppose this was an idea that could be explained successfully only at breakfast time; and everyone knows that ghosts can walk only at midnight. And if this ghost should appear among his friends at that appointed hour, his idea would be an utter failure. No one would laugh, for jesting comes unseasonably at midnight, and so the unhappy ghost would return to the grave with his great idea. It is really very sad.

Here lies a lady who was a miser. During her lifetime she often arose at night and mewed, so that the neighbors would imagine she kept a cat, which she was too stingy to do.

And here is a young lady of good family. She always insisted upon singing in society, and when she sang, "*Mi manca la voce!*" that was the only truth she ever spoke.

Here rests another young girl, of a very different nature. Alas! When the bird of the heart begins to sing, too often will Reason stop up her ears. Lovely maiden, she was to be married; but that's an everyday story—may she rest in peace!

Here lies a widow who had the sweetness of the swan on her lips and the gall of the owl in her heart. She went from one family to another, feeding upon the faults of her neighbors.

Now, this is a family vault; every member of that family lived in the sublime faith that whatever the world and the newspapers said must indeed be true. If the young son of that house came home from school and announced, "This is how I heard it—," his news, whatever it might be, was received without question, because he belonged to the family. And certain it is that if the cock of that family had decided to crow at midnight, the whole family would have insisted that morning had dawned, even if the watchman and all the clocks of the town announced it was midnight.

The great Goethe concluded his *Faust* with the words, "It may be continued"; and thus will I conclude our walk in the churchyard.

I go there often, for whenever one of my friends or unfriends, gives me to understand that he wishes to be as one dead to me, I go there, find a spot of green turf, and dedicate it to him or her, whomever I wish to bury. In this way I have buried many of my acquaintances. There they lie, powerless to harm me, until the time when they may return to life, better and wiser than before. I write down in my book their life and history, as seen from my point of view. Everybody ought to do so!

You shouldn't be upset if your friends do something foolish; bury them at once, keep your good humor, and read the *Advertiser*, for this paper is written by the people, although their pens are sometimes wrongly guided.

When at last I myself and the story of my life are to be bound in the grave, then write upon it the epitaph:

A GOOD HUMOR!

This is my story.

HEARTACHE (1852)

The story we have for you here is really divided into two parts. The first part could be omitted, but it gives us some preliminary information which is useful.

We were staying at a manor house in the country, and it happened that the owner was absent for a day or so. Meanwhile a lady with a pug dog arrived from the next town; come, she explained, to dispose of the shares in her tannery. She had her certificates with her, and we advised her to seal them in an envelope and to write on it the address of the proprietor of the estate, "General War Commissary, Knight," etc.

She listened to us, took up the pen, then hesitated, and begged us to repeat the address slowly. We complied and she wrote, but in the middle of the "General War—" she stopped, sighed, and said, "I'm only a woman!" While she wrote, she had placed her Puggie on the floor, and he was growling, for the dog had come with her for pleasure and health's sake, and a visitor shouldn't be placed on the floor. He was characterized outwardly by a snub nose and a fleshy back.

"He doesn't bite," said the woman. "He hasn't any teeth. He's like one of the family, faithful and grouchy; but the latter is the fault of my grandchildren for teasing him. They play wedding, and want to make him the bridesmaid, and that's too strenuous for the poor old fellow."

Then she delivered her certificates and took Puggie up in her arms. And that's the first part of the story, which could have been omitted.

Puggie died! That's the second part.

About a week later we arrived in the town and put up at the inn. Our windows looked out into the tannery yard, which was divided into two parts by a wooden fence; in one section were hides and skin caps, raw and tanned. Here was all the equipment for carrying on a tanning business, and it belonged to the widow. Puggie had died that morning and was to be buried in this section of the yard. The widow's grandchildren (that is, the tanner's widow's, for Puggie had never married) covered the grave—a grave so beautiful it must have been quite pleasant to lie there.

The grave was bordered with broken flowerpots and strewn over with sand; at its head they had stuck up a small beer bottle with the neck upward, and that wasn't at all symbolic.

The children danced around the grave, and then the oldest of the boys, a practical youngster of seven, proposed that there should be an exhibition of Puggie's grave for everybody living in the street. The price of admission would be one trouser button; that was something every boy would be sure to have and which he also could give to the little girls. This suggestion was adopted by acclamation.

And all the children from the street, and even from the little lane behind, came, and each gave a button. Many were seen that afternoon going about with one suspender, but then they had seen Puggie's grave, and that sight was worth it.

But outside the tannery yard, close to the entrance, stood a ragged little girl, very beautiful, with the prettiest curly hair, and eyes so clear and blue that it was a pleasure to look into them. She didn't say a word, nor did she cry, but every time the gate was opened she looked into the yard as long as she could. She had no button, as she knew very well, so she had to stand sorrowfully outside, until all the others had seen the grave and everyone had left. Then she sat down, put her little brown hands before her eyes, and burst into tears, for she alone hadn't seen Puggie's grave. It was a heartache as great as any grown-up can experience.

We saw this from above—and seen from above, this, like many of our own and others' griefs could, made us smile! That's the story, and anyone who doesn't understand it can go and buy a share in the widow's tannery.

EVERYTHING IN ITS PROPER PLACE (1852)

It was over a hundred years ago. By the great lake behind the wood there stood an old mansion. Round about it circled a deep ditch, with bulrushes, reeds, and grasses growing in it. Close by the bridge, near the entrance gate, an old willow tree bent over the reeds.

From the narrow lane came the sound of horns and the trampling of horses, and therefore the little girl who tended the geese hastened to drive her charges away from the bridge before the hunting party came galloping up. They approached with such speed that she was obliged to climb up onto one of the high cornerstones of the bridge, to avoid being run down. She was still little more than a child, pretty and slender, with a gentle expression in her face and lovely bright eyes. But the baron took no note of this; as he galloped past her, he reversed the whip in his hand, and in rough play gave her such a blow in the chest with the butt end that she fell backward into the ditch.

"Everything in its proper place!" he cried. "Into the mud with you!" And he laughed loudly, for this was intended to be funny, and the rest of the company joined in his mirth. They shouted and clamored, while the hunting dogs barked even more loudly than before. It was indeed: "Rich birds come rushing."

But goodness knows how rich he was. The poor goose girl, in falling, managed to seize one of the drooping branches of the willow tree and hang from it over the muddy water. As soon as the company and the dogs had disappeared through the castle gate, she tried to climb up again, but the branch broke off at the top, and she would have fallen into the reeds if, at that moment, a strong hand had not caught her from above. It was a peddler who from a little distance away had seen what had happened and had hurried up to give aid.

"Everything in its proper place," he said, mocking the baron, and pulled her up to the dry ground. He put the tree branch back to the place from which it had broken, but "everything in its place" cannot always be managed, and so he thrust it into the soft ground. "Grow if you can, until you can furnish a good flute for them up yonder," he said. It would have given him great pleasure to see the baron and his companions well thrashed.

And then the peddler made his way to the mansion, but did not go into the main hall; he was much too humble for that! He went instead to the servants' quarters, and the men and maids looked over his stock of goods and bargained with him. From above, where the guests were at table, was heard a sound of roaring and screaming that was intended for song; that was the best they could do! There was loud laughter, mingled with the barking and yapping of dogs, for there was riotous feasting up there. Wine and strong old ale foamed in jugs and glasses, and the dogs ate with their masters, and some of them, after having their snouts wiped with their ears, were kissed by them.

The peddler was told to come upstairs with his wares, but it was only to make fun of him. The wine had mounted into their heads and the sense had flown out. They insisted that the peddler drink with them, but, so that he would have to drink quickly, they poured his beer into a stocking. This was considered a great joke and caused more gales of laughter. And then entire farms, complete with oxen and peasants, were staked on a single card, and lost and won.

"Everything in its proper place," said the peddler thankfully when he had finally escaped from what he called "the Sodom and Gomorrah up there." "The open road is my proper place," he said. "I didn't feel at all happy up there."

And the little goose girl nodded kindly to him as he walked by the pasture gate.

Days passed and weeks passed; and the willow branch that the peddler had thrust into the ground beside the water ditch remained fresh and green and even put forth new shoots. The little goose girl saw that it must have taken root, and she was very happy about it; this was her tree, she thought.

Yes, the tree flourished, but everything else at the mansion went to seed, what with feasting and gambling. For these two are like wheels, upon which no man can stand securely.

Scarcely six years had passed before the baron left the mansion, a beggar, with bag and stick in hand; and the mansion itself was bought by a rich merchant. And the purchaser was the very peddler who had once been mocked at in the great hall and forced to drink beer from a stocking! Honesty and industry are good winds to speed a vessel, and now the peddler was the master of the mansion. But from that moment card playing was not permitted there any more.

"That is bad reading," he said. "When the Devil saw a Bible for the first time, he wanted something to counteract it, and so he invented card playing."

The new owner took himself a wife, and who do you suppose she was but the pretty little goose girl, who had always been so faithful and good! In her new clothes she looked as beautiful and fine as if she had been of high birth. How did all this happen? Well, that is too long a story to tell you in these busy times, but it really did happen, and the most important part of the story is still to come.

It was pleasant and cheerful to live in the old mansion. The mother managed the household affairs, and the father superintended the estate, and blessings seemed to rain down on the home. For where there is rectitude, prosperity is sure to follow. The old house was cleaned and repainted; ditches were cleared, and new fruit trees were planted. The floors were as polished as a draughtboard, and everything wore a bright cheerful look.

In the large hall the lady sat in the winter evenings, with all her maids spinning woolen and linen yarn, and every Sunday evening there was a reading from the Bible by the Councillor of Justice himself. In his old age the peddler had achieved this title. There were children, and as they grew up they received the best possible education, although all were not equally gifted—just as it is in all families.

But the willow branch outside had grown to be a big splendid tree, which stood free and undisturbed. "That is our family tree," the old people said. And they explained to all the children, even those who were not very bright, that the tree was to be honored and respected.

So a hundred years rolled by.

Now it was our own time. The lake had grown into a marsh, and the old mansion had almost disappeared. A long narrow pool of water near the remains of a stone wall was all that was left of the deep ditch; yet here still stood a magnificent old willow tree with drooping branches. It was the family tree, and it showed how beautiful a tree may be if left to itself. To be sure, the main trunk was split from root to crown, and storms had given it a little twist, but it still stood firmly. From every cleft and crack into which the winds had carried soil, grasses and flowers had sprung forth, especially near the top, where the great branches separated. There a sort of a small hanging garden had been formed of wild raspberries and chickweed, and even a little serviceberry tree had taken root and stood slender and graceful in the midst of the old tree, which reflected itself in the dark water when the wind had driven all the duckweed into a corner of the pool. A narrow path, which led across the fields, passed close by the old tree.

High on the hill near the forest, with a splendid view in every direction, stood the new mansion, large and magnificent, the glass of its windows so clear and transparent that there seemed to be no panes there at all. The stately flight of steps that led up to the entrance looked like a bower covered with roses and broad-leaved plants. The lawn was as freshly and vividly green as if each separate blade of grass were washed mornings and evenings. In the great hall hung valuable pictures; there were silken chairs and sofas so airy and graceful that they seemed almost ready to walk on their own legs; there were tables with polished marble tops, and books bound in rich morocco and gold. Yes, they were really wealthy people who lived here; they were people of position; here lived the baron and his family.

Everything here fitted with everything else. The motto of the house was still "Everything in its proper place." So all the pictures that at one time had hung with honor and glory in the former mansion were now relegated to the passage that led to the servants' hall, for they were considered nothing but old junk; especially two old portraits, one of a man in a pink coat and a wig, the other of a lady with powdered, high-dressed hair and a rose held in her hand, and each surrounded by a large wreath of willow branches. These two old pictures were marred by many holes, for the baron's children were fond of using the two old people as targets for their crossbows. They were the portraits of the Councillor of Justice and his lady, from whom the whole family descended.

"But they didn't really belong to our family," said one of the young barons. "He was a peddler, and she was a goose girl! They weren't like Papa and Mamma!"

The pictures were judged to be worthless junk, and as the motto was "Everything in its proper place," Great-grandmother and Great-grandfather were hung in the passage that led to the servants' hall.

Now, the son of the village pastor was the tutor at the mansion. One day he was out walking with his pupils, the young barons and their older sister, who had just been confirmed. They followed the path toward the old willow, and as they strolled along, the young girl gathered some field flowers and bound them together—"Everything in its proper place"—and the flowers became a beautiful bouquet. At the same time she heard every word that was spoken, for she liked to listen to the clergyman's son talk of the power of nature and the great men and women of history. She had a good, sweet temper, with true nobility of soul and mind, and a heart that appreciated all that God had created.

They stopped at the old willow tree, where the youngster boy insisted on having a flute made for him, as had been cut for him from other willow branches before; and the pastor's son therefore broke off a branch.

"Oh, don't," cried the young baroness, but it was already too late. "That is our famous old tree," she explained, "and I love it dearly. They laugh at me at home for it, but I don't care. There's an old tale attached to this tree."

Then she told them all the story about the tree, about the old mansion, and the peddler and the goose girl who had met for the first time on this very spot and had afterward founded the noble family to which these young people belonged.

"They didn't want to be knighted, the grand old people!" she said. "They kept their motto, 'Everything in its proper place,' and so they thought it would be out of place for them to buy a title. It was their son—my grandfather—who was made a baron. They say he was very learned, a great favorite with princes and princesses, and was present at all their festivals. The others at home love him the best, but I don't know—there seems to be something about that first pair that draws my heart to them. How comfortable and patriarchal it must have been in the old mansion then, with the mistress sitting at her spinning wheel among all her maids, and the old master reading aloud from the Bible!"

"They must have been wonderful people, sensible people," said the pastor's son.

Then the conversation turned naturally toward noblemen and commoners. The young man hardly seemed to belong to the lower classes, so well did he understand and speak of the purpose and meaning of nobility.

"It is good fortune," he said, "to belong to a family that has distinguished itself. In your own blood there is then, so to speak, a spur that urges you on to make progress in everything that is good. It's gratifying to bear the name of a family that is a card of admission to the highest circles. Nobility means something great and noble; it is a gold coin that has been stamped to show its worth. It is a modern belief, and many poets, of course, agree with it, that all of nobility must be bad and stupid, and that the lower you go among poor people, the more wisdom and virtue do you find. But that isn't my opinion, for I think it's entirely foolish, entirely false. There are many beautiful and kindly traits found in the upper classes. I could give you many examples; here's one my mother told me once.

"She was visiting a noble family in town, where I think my grandmother had nursed the lady of the house. The old nobleman and my mother were together in his apartments when he noticed an old woman come limping into the courtyard on crutches. She used to come there every Sunday, to receive a little gift.

"'Ah! There is the poor old lady!' said the nobleman. 'Walking is so hard for her!' And before my mother understood what he meant, the seventy-year-old excellency was out of the room and down the stairs, carrying his gift to the old woman, to spare her the difficult walk.

"Now that was only a little thing, but like the widow's mite it has a sound that echoes to the depths of the human heart. Those are the things that poets ought to sing about, especially in these times, for it does good; it soothes and reconciles mankind. But when a person, just because he is of noble birth and has a pedigree, stands on his hind legs and neighs in the street like an Arabian horse, and, when a commoner has been in the rooms, sneers, 'Something out of the street has been in here!'—that is nobility in decay and just a mask—a mask such as Thespis created. People are glad to see one like that satirized."

That was the way the pastor's son spoke. It was a rather long speech, but while talking he had finished carving the flute.

That night there was a great party at the mansion, with many guests from about the neighborhood and from the capital. The main hall was full of people; some of the ladies were dressed tastefully, while others showed no taste at all. The clergymen of the neighborhood remained gathered respectfully in a corner, looking as if they were conducting a burial service there. But it was a party of pleasure; only the pleasure hadn't begun yet.

There was to be a great concert, so the little baron brought in his new willow flute. But neither he nor his father could get a note from it, so they decided it was worthless. There were chamber music and song, both of the sort that pleases the performers most—yet quite charming.

Suddenly a certain cavalier—his father's son and nothing else—spoke to the tutor. "Are you a musician?" he demanded. "You play the flute and make it, too! That's genius! That should command, and receive, the place of honor! Heaven knows, I try to follow the times. You have to do that, you know. Come, you will enchant us all with the little instrument, won't you?"

Then he handed the tutor the flute made from the old willow down by the pool and announced loudly that the tutor was about to favor them with a solo on that instrument.

Now, it was easy to tell that they only wanted to make fun of him, so the tutor refused, though he could really play well. But they crowded around him and insisted so strongly that at last he put the flute to his lips.

That was a strange flute! A tone was heard, as sustained as the whistle of a steam engine, yes, and much stronger; it echoed over the courtyard, garden, and wood, and miles away into the country. And with that note there came a rushing wind that seemed to roar, "Everything in its proper place!"

And then Papa flew, as if carried by the wind, straight out of the great hall and into the shepherd's cottage, while the shepherd was blown—not into the main hall, for there he could not come—no, up into the servants' room, among the haughty lackeys strutting in their silk stockings. The proud servants were almost paralyzed at the very thought that such a common person would dare to sit at table with them!

But in the great hall the young baroness flew to the upper end of the table, where she was worthy to sit; the pastor's son found himself next to her, and there they both sat as if they were a newly married couple. A gentle old count of one of the most ancient families in the country remained unmoved in his honorable place, for the flute was just, as everyone ought to be. But the witty cavalier who was nothing more than the son of his father, and who had caused the flute playing, flew head over heels into the poultry house—and he was not alone.

For a whole mile around the countryside the sound of the flute could be heard, and remarkable things happened. The family of a rich merchant, driving along in their coach and four, was blown completely out of the carriage and could not even find a place on the back of it. Two wealthy peasants who in our times had grown too high for their own cornfields were tumbled back into the ditch.

Yes, that was indeed a dangerous flute. But luckily it burst after that first note, and that was a fortunate thing for everybody, for then it was put back into the owner's pocket. "Everything in its proper place."

The next day no one spoke of what had happened; and that is where we get the expression, "To pocket the flute." Everything was back in its former state, except for the two old portraits of the merchant and the goose girl. They had been blown up onto the wall of the drawing room; and when one of the well-known experts said they had been painted by an old master, they were left there, and carefully restored. Nobody knew before that they were worth anything, and how could they have known? Now they hung in the place of honor. "Everything in its proper place."

And it will come to that. Eternity is long—even longer than this story.

THE GOBLIN AND THE GROCER (1852)

There was a student, who lived in the garret and didn't own anything. There was also a grocer, who kept shop on the ground floor and owned the whole house. The household goblin stuck to the grocer, because every Christmas Eve it was the grocer who could afford him a bowl of porridge with a big pat of butter in it. So the goblin stayed in the grocery shop, and that was very educational.

One evening the student came in by the back door to buy some candles and cheese. He had no one to send, and that's why he came himself. He got what he came for, paid for it, and the grocer and his wife nodded, "Good evening." There was a woman who could do more than just nod, for she had an unusual gift of speech. The student nodded too, but while he was reading something on the piece of paper which was wrapped around his cheese, he suddenly stopped. It was a page torn out of an old book that ought never to have been put to this purpose, an old book full of poetry.

"There's more of it," the grocer told him. "I gave an old woman a few coffee beans for it. If you will give me eight pennies, you shall have the rest."

"If you please," said the student, "let me have the book instead of the cheese. There's no harm in my having plain bread and butter for supper, but it would be sinful to tear the book to pieces. You're a fine man, a practical man, but you know no more about poetry than that tub does."

Now this was a rude way to talk, especially to the tub. The grocer laughed and the student laughed. After all, it was said only as a joke, but the goblin was angry that anyone should dare say such a thing to a grocer, a man who owned the whole house, a man who sold the best butter.

That night, when the shop was shut and everyone in bed except the student, the goblin borrowed the long tongue of the grocer's wife, who had no use for it while she slept. And any object on which he laid this tongue became as glib a chatterbox as the grocer's wife herself. Only one object could use the tongue at a time, and that was a blessing, for otherwise they would all have spoken at once. First the goblin laid the tongue on the tub in which old newspapers were kept.

"Is it really true," asked the goblin, "that you don't know anything about poetry?"

"Of course, I know all about poetry," said the tub. "It's the stuff they stick at the end of a newspaper column when they've nothing better to print, and which is sometimes cut out. I dare say I've got more poetry in me than the student has, and I'm only a small tub compared to the grocer."

Then the goblin put the tongue on the coffee mill—how it did chatter away. He put it on the butter cask and on the cashbox, he put it on everything around the shop, until it was back upon the tub again. To the same question everyone gave the same answer as the tub, and the opinion of the majority must be respected.

"Oh, won't I light into that student," said the goblin, as he tiptoed up the back stairs to the garret where the student lived. A candle still burned there, and by peeping through the keyhole the goblin could see that the student was reading the tattered old book he had brought upstairs with him.

But how bright the room was! From the book a clear shaft of light rose, expanding into a stem and a tremendous tree which spread its branching rays above the student. Each leaf on the tree was evergreen, and every flower was the face of a fair lady, some with dark and sparkling eyes, some with eyes of the clearest blue. Every fruit on the tree shone like a star, and the room was filled with song.

Never before had the little goblin imagined such splendor. Never before had he seen or heard anything like it. He stood there on tiptoe, peeping and peering till the light went out. But even after the student blew out his lamp and went to bed, the little fellow stayed to listen outside the door. For the song went on, soft but still more splendid, a beautiful cradle song lulling the student to sleep.

"No place can compare with this," the goblin exclaimed. "I never expected it. I've a good notion to come and live with the student." But he stopped to think, and he reasoned, and he weighed it, and he sighed, "The student has no porridge to give me."

So he tiptoed away, back to the shop, and high time too. The tub had almost worn out the tongue of the grocer's wife. All that was right-side-up in the tub had been said, and it was just turning over to say all the rest that was in it, when the goblin got back and returned the tongue to its rightful owner. But forever afterward the whole shop, from the cashbox right down to the kindling wood, took all their ideas from the tub. Their respect for it was so great and their confidence so complete that, whenever the grocer read the art and theatrical reviews in the evening paper, they all thought the opinions came out of the tub.

But the little goblin was no longer content to sit listening to all the knowledge and wisdom down there. No! As soon as the light shone again in the garret, he felt as if a great anchor rope drew him up there to peep through the keyhole. And he felt the great feeling that we feel when watching the ever-rolling ocean as a storm passes over it. And he started to cry, for no reason that he knew, but these were tears that left him strong and glad. How glorious it would be to sit with the student under the tree of light! He couldn't do that. He was content with the keyhole. There he stood on the cold landing, with wintry blasts blowing full upon him from the trapdoor to the roof. It was cold, so cold, but the little fellow didn't feel it until the light went out and the song gave way to the whistle of the wind. Ugh! He shivered and shook as he crept down to his own corner, where it was warm and snug. And when Christmas came round—when he saw that bowl of porridge and the big pat of butter in it—why then it was the grocer whose goblin he was.

But one midnight, the goblin was awakened by a hullabaloo of banging on the shutters. People outside knocked their hardest on the windows, and the watchman blasted away on his horn, for there was a house on fire. The whole street was red in the light of it. Was it the grocer's house? Was it the next house? Where? Everybody was terrified! The grocer's wife was so panicky that she took off her gold earrings and put them in her pocket to save them. The grocer ran to get his stocks and bonds, and the servant for the silk mantilla she had scrimped so hard to buy. Everyone wanted to rescue what he treasured most, and so did the little goblin. With a leap and a bound he was upstairs and into the garret. The student stood calmly at his window, watching the fire, which was in the neighbor's house. The goblin snatched the wonderful book from the table, tucked it in his red cap, and held it high in both hands. The treasure of the house was saved! Off to the roof he ran. Up to the top of the chimney he jumped. There he sat, in the light of the burning house across the street, clutching with both hands the cap which held his treasure.

Now he knew for certain to which master his heart belonged. But when they put the fire out, and he had time to think about it, he wasn't so sure.

"I'll simply have to divide myself between them," he decided. "I can't give up the grocer, because of my porridge."

And this was all quite human. Off to the grocer all of us go for our porridge.

THOUSANDS OF YEARS
FROM NOW (1853)

Yes, thousands of years from now, men will fly on wings of steam through the air, across the ocean. The young inhabitants of America will visit old Europe. They will come to see the monuments and the great cities, which will then lie in ruins, just as we in our time make pilgrimages to the ruined splendors of southern Asia. Thousands of years from now they will come!

The Thames, the Danube, and the Rhine still roll in their valleys, Mont Blanc still stands firm with its snowy summit, the northern lights still glitter over the lands of the North, but generation after generation has become dust. Mighty names of today are forgotten—as forgotten as those who already slumber under the hill where the rich corn merchant sits and gazes out across his flat and waving cornfields.

"To Europe!" cry the young sons of America. "To the land of our ancestors, that glorious land of memory and legends! To Europe!"

The ship of the air comes. It is crowded with passengers, for this is a much faster crossing than by sea. The electromagnetic wire under the ocean has already cabled the number of the aerial travelers. Already Europe is in sight—the coast of Ireland. But the passengers are still asleep and will not be called until they are over England. It is there that they still take their first step onto the soil of Europe, in the land of Shakespeare, as the intellectual call it, or the land of politics and land of machines, as it is called by others.

Here they stay a whole day! That is all the time this busy generation can give to the whole of England and Scotland. Then they rush on, through the tunnel under the English Channel, to France, the country of Charlemagne and Napoleon. The learned among them speak of Molière and the classic and romantic school of remote antiquity; others applaud the names of heroes, poets, and scientists whom our time does not yet know, but who will in afterdays be born in that crater of Europe, Paris.

Now the steamboat of the air crosses the country whence Columbus set sail, where Cortez was born, and where Calderón sang his dramas in resounding verse. Beautiful, black-eyed women still live in those blooming valleys, and the ancient songs tell of the Cid and the Alhambra.

Then through the air, across the sea, to Italy, where once stood old, eternal Rome. It has vanished! The Campagna is a desert; a solitary ruined wall is shown as the remains of St. Peter's, and there is even doubt that this ruin is authentic.

On to Greece, to spend a night in the hotel at the top of Mount Olympus, just so they can say that they have been there. Then to the Bosporus, for a few hours' rest and to see the spot where Byzantium stood; and where legends tell of the harems of the Turks, poor fishermen are now spreading their nets.

Over the ruins of the mighty cities of the Danube, cities that we in our days know not yet; and on the rich sites of some of those that time shall yet bring forth, the air travelers sometimes descend, only to depart again quickly.

Down below lies Germany, which was once covered with a massive network of railways and canals. Germany, where Luther spoke, and

Goethe sang, and Mozart once held the scepter of music! Great names of science and art now shine there—names still unknown to us. One day's stopover for Germany, and one for the other—the country of Oersted and Linnaeus, and for Norway, land of old heroes and young Norwegians. Iceland is visited on the journey home; the geysers burst forth no more, the volcano Hecla is extinct, but that great island is still fixed in the foaming sea, mighty monument of legend and poetry.

"There is really a great deal to be seen in Europe," says the young American proudly. "And we've seen it in eight days; and it is quite possible, as the great traveler" (and here he names one of his contemporaries) "tells us in his famous book, *How to See All Europe in Eight Days.*"

CLUMSY HANS (1855)

Out in the country there was an old mansion where an old squire lived with his two sons, who were so witty that they thought themselves too clever for words. They decided to go out and propose to the king's daughter, which they were at liberty to do, for she had announced publicly that she would take for a husband the man who had the most to say for himself.

The two brothers made their preparations for eight days beforehand. That was all the time they had, but it was enough, for they had many accomplishments, and everyone knows how useful they can be. One of them knew the whole Latin dictionary by heart and the town's newspaper for three years—so well that he could repeat it backward or forward. The other had learned all the articles of law and knew what every alderman must know; consequently, he was sure he could talk of governmental affairs, and besides this he could embroider suspenders, for he was very gentle and also clever with his fingers.

"I shall win the princess!" they both said, as their father gave each one of them a beautiful horse. The one who had memorized the dictionary and the newspapers had a coal-black horse, while the one who knew all about governmental affairs and could embroider had a milk-white one. Then they smeared the corners of their mouths with cod-liver oil, to make them more glib.

All the servants assembled in the courtyard to watch them mount their horses, but just then the third brother came up; for there were really three, although nobody paid much attention to the third, because he was not so learned as the other two. In fact, everybody called him "Clumsy Hans."

"Where are you going in all your Sunday clothes?" he asked.

"To the king's court, to woo the princess. Haven't you heard what the king's drummer is proclaiming all over the country?" Then they told him about it.

"Gracious," said Clumsy Hans, "I guess I'll go, too!" But his brothers only burst out laughing at him as they rode away.

"Father," shouted Clumsy Hans, "Let me have a horse. I feel like getting married, too. If she takes me, she takes me; and if she doesn't take me, I'll take her, anyway."

"That's a lot of nonsense!" replied his father. "You'll get no horse from me. Why, you don't know how to talk properly. Now, your brothers are intelligent men."

"If I can't have a horse I'll take the billy goat," said Clumsy Hans. "He belongs to me, and he can carry me very well." So he mounted the billy goat, dug his heels into its sides, and galloped off down the highway.

"Alley-oop! What a ride! Here I come!" shouted Clumsy Hans, singing so loud that his voice was heard far away.

But his two brothers rode quietly on ahead of him. They were not speaking a word to each other, for they were thinking about all the clever speeches they would have to make, and of course these had to be carefully prepared and memorized beforehand.

"Halloo!" cried Clumsy Hans. "Here I come! Look what I found on the road!" Then he showed them a dead crow he had picked up.

"Clumsy!" said the brothers. "What are you going to do with that?"

"Why, I am going to give it to the princess!"

"Yes, you do that," they said as they rode on laughing.

"Halloo, here I come again! Just look what I've found this time! You don't find things like this in the road every day!" So the brothers turned around to see what it was this time.

"Clumsy!" they said. "That's just an old wooden shoe, and the upper part's broken off, anyway. Is the princess going to have that, too?"

"She certainly is," replied Hans, and the brothers again laughed and rode on far in advance of him.

"Halloo! Here I am again," shouted Clumsy Hans. "Now this is getting better and better! This is really something!"

"Well, what have you found this time?" asked the brothers.

"Oh, I can't really tell you," Clumsy Hans said. "How pleased the princess will be!"

"Uh!" said the brothers. "Why, it's nothing but mud out of the ditch!"

"Yes, of course," said Clumsy Hans, "but the very finest sort of mud. Look, it runs right through your fingers." Then he filled his pockets with it.

But his brothers galloped on ahead as fast as they could, and so they arrived at the town gate a full hour ahead of Hans. At the gate each suitor was given a numbered ticket, and as fast as they arrived they were arranged in rows, six to a row, packed together so tightly that they could not even move their arms. That was a wise plan, for otherwise they could have cut each other's backs to pieces, just because one stood in front of another. All the inhabitants of the town stood around the castle, peering in through the windows to watch the princess receive her suitors; but as each young man came into the room, he became tongue-tied.

"No good!" said the princess. "Take him away!"

Now came the brother who had memorized the dictionary, but he had completely forgotten it while standing in line. The floor creaked under his footsteps, and the ceiling was made of mirrors so that he could see himself standing on his head; and at each window stood three clerks and an alderman, writing down every word that was spoken, so that it immediately could be printed in the newspapers and sold for two pennies on the street corners.

It was a terrible ordeal, and besides there were such fires in the stoves that the pipe was red-hot.

"It's terribly hot in here," said the suitor.

"That's because my father is roasting chickens today," said the princess.

"Baa!" There he stood. He was not ready for a speech of this kind and hadn't a word to say, just when he wanted to say something extremely witty. "Baa!"

"No good!" said the princess. "Take him away!" And consequently he had to leave.

Now the second brother approached.

"It's dreadfully warm here," he said.

"Yes, we're roasting chickens today," replied the princess.

"What—what did you—uh—what?" he stammered, and all the clerks carefully wrote down, "What—what did you—uh—what?"

"No good," said the princess again. "Out with him!"

Now it was Clumsy Hans' turn, and he rode his billy goat right into the hall.

"Terribly hot in here," he said.

"I'm roasting young chickens," replied the princess.

"Why, that's fine!" said Clumsy Hans. "Then I suppose I can get my crow roasted?"

"That you can," said the princess. "But have you anything to roast it in? I haven't any pots or pans."

"But I have," replied Clumsy Hans. "Here's a cooking pot with a tin handle!" Then he pulled out the old wooden shoe and put the crow right into it.

"Why, that's enough for a whole meal!" said the princess. "But where do we get the sauce from?"

"I have that in my pocket," replied Clumsy Hans. "In fact, I have so much I can afford to spill some of it." Then he poured a little of the mud from his pocket.

"I like that!" said the princess. "You have an answer for everything, and you know how to speak. I'll take you for my husband. But do you know that everything we've said and are saying is written down and will be published in the paper tomorrow? Look over there, and you'll see in each window three clerks and an old alderman, and that alderman is the worst of all; he doesn't understand anything!"

She said this only to frighten him, but all the clerks chuckled with delight and spurted blots of ink on the floor.

"Oh, so these are the gentlemen!" said Clumsy Hans. "Then I must give the alderman the best thing I have." Then he turned out his pockets and threw the wet mud in the face of the alderman.

"Cleverly done!" said the princess. "I could never have done that, but I'll learn in time!"

So Clumsy Hans was made a king, with a wife and a crown, and sat on a throne. And we had this story straight from the alderman's newspaper—but that is one you can't always depend upon.

SOUP FROM A SAUSAGE PEG (1858)

I. SOUP FROM A SAUSAGE PEG

That was a perfectly delightful dinner yesterday," one old female mouse told another, who had not attended the feast. "I sat number twenty-one from the old mouse king, which wasn't at all bad. Would you like to hear the menu? The courses were exceedingly well arranged—mouldy bread, bacon rind, tallow candle, and sausage, and then the same dishes all over again, from start to finish, so it was as good as two banquets. There was such a pleasant atmosphere, and such good humor, that it was like a family gathering. Not a scrap was left except the pegs at the ends of the sausages.

"The conversation turned to these wooden pegs, and the expression 'soup from a sausage peg,' came up. Everybody had heard it, but nobody had ever tasted such a soup, much less knew how to make it. We drank a fine toast to the health of whoever invented the soup, and we said he deserved to be appointed manager of the poorhouse. Wasn't that witty? And the old mouse king rose and promised that the young maiden mouse who could make this soup should be his queen. He gave them a year and a day to learn how."

"That wasn't so bad, after all," said the other mouse. "But how do you make this soup?"

"Yes, how do you make it? That's exactly what all the female mice are asking—the young ones and the old maids, too. Every last one of them wants to be the queen, but they don't want to bestir themselves and go out in the wide world to learn how to make soup, as they certainly would have to do. Not everyone has the courage to leave her family and her own snug corner. Out in the world one doesn't come upon cheese parings or smell bacon every day. No indeed. One must endure hunger, yes, and perhaps be eaten alive by the cat."

Very likely this was what frightened most of them from venturing out in the wide world to find the secret of the soup. Only four mice declared themselves ready to go. They were young and willing, but poor. Each would go to one of the four corners of the world, and then let fortune decide among them. All four took sausage pegs with them as a reminder of their purpose. These were to be their pilgrim staffs.

It was the beginning of May when they set out, and they did not return until May of the following year. But only three of them returned. The fourth did not report, and there was no news about her, though the day for the contest had come.

"Yes, something always goes wrong on even the most pleasant occasions," the mouse king observed. But he commanded that all the mice for many miles around should be invited.

They gathered in the kitchen, and the three travelers lined up in a row by themselves. For the fourth, who was missing, they placed a sausage peg-shrouded in crepe. No one dared to express an opinion until the three travelers had made their reports, and the mouse king had rendered his decision. Now we shall hear.

II. WHAT THE FIRST LITTLE MOUSE HAD SEEN AND HEARD ON HER TRAVELS

"When I went out into the wide world," the little mouse said, "I thought, as many others do when they are my age, that I knew everything. But such was not the case. It takes days and years to know everything. I immediately set out to sea. I went on a northbound ship, for I had heard that ships' cooks must know how to manage. But it isn't so hard to manage at sea when you have an abundance of bacon, and whole barrels of salt meat and mouldy flour. You live like a lord, but you don't learn to make soup from a sausage peg. We sailed many days and we sailed many nights. The boat rolled dreadfylly, and we got many a drenching. When we reached port at last, I left the ship. That was far up in the north country.

"It's a strange thing to leave one's chimney corner, sail away in a ship which is a sort of corner too, and then suddenly find oneself in a foreign land, hundreds of miles away. There were vast and trackless forests of birch and pine. They smelled so strong that I didn't like it! The fragrance of the wild herbs was so spiced it made me sneeze and think of sausages.

"There, too, were broad lakes of water which was perfectly clear when you came close to it, though from a distance it looked as black as ink. White swans rested on the lakes, and they were so still that at first I thought they were flecks of foam. But when I saw them fly, and I saw them walk, I knew at once that they were members of the duck family—I could tell by the way they waddled. One can't disown his relatives! I kept to my own kind. I went with the field and forest mice, although they knew little enough of anything, and nothing at all of cookery, which was the very thing, I had traveled so far to find out about. That it was possible to think soup could be made from a sausage peg startled them so that the information was immediately bandied throughout the vast forest. But that there could be any solution to such a problem they thought was utterly impossible, and little did I expect that there, before the night was over, I should be initiated into the making of it.

"It was midsummer. The mice said that this was why the woods and the herbs were redolent, and the waters so clear and yet so dark blue in contrast with the whiteness of the swans. At the edge of the forest, between three or four houses they had raised a pole as high as a ship's mainmast. Garlands and ribbons fluttered from the peak of it. It was a maypole. Young men and maidens danced around it and sang at the top of their voices, while the fiddler played them a tune. They were merry in the sunset and merry in the moonlight, but I had no part in it, for what would a little mouse be doing at a forest dance? So I sat in the soft moss, and held tight to my sausage peg. The moonlight fell particularly bright on one spot, where there was a tree. This spot was carpeted with moss so soft that I dare say it was as fine as the mouse king's fur, but its color was green and it was a blessing to the eyes.

"All of a sudden there appeared a few of the most enchanting little folk, no taller than my knee. They resembled human beings, except that they were better proportioned. 'Elves' was what they called themselves. They went dressed very fine, in clothes made of flower petals trimmed with the wings of flies and gnats. It wasn't at all bad looking. They seemed in search of something, but I didn't know what it could be until a couple of them came up to me. Then their leader pointed to my sausage peg and said:

"'That's just what we need. It's pointed. It's perfect!' The more he looked at my sausage peg, the happier it made him.

"'You can borrow it,' I told him, 'but not keep it.'

"'Not keep it,' all of them promised, as they took the sausage peg that I gave them and danced away with it to the place where the soft moss grew. They wanted to have a maypole of their own, and mine seemed made to order for them. Then they decorated it. Yes, what a sight it was!

"Small spiders spun gold thread around it. They draped it with streamers and banners so fine and bleached so snowy white in the moonlight that they dazzled my eyes. They took the color from a butterfly's wing and splashed it about on my sausage peg until it seemed blooming with flowers and sparkling with diamonds. I scarcely knew it, for in all the world there is no match to the maypole they had made of it.

"Now the real party of elves appeared, in great numbers. Not a stitch did they wear, yet it couldn't have been more refined. I was invited to look on, but from a distance, because I was too big for them.

"Then the music struck up, and such music! It seemed as if a thousand bells of glass were ringing. It was so rich and full that I thought it was the swans who were singing. Yes, I even thought I heard the cuckoos, and blackbirds, until it was as if the whole forest had joined in the chorus. Children's voices, bell tones, and birds' songs, all seemed to keep tune in the loveliest melody, yet it all came from the elves' maypole. It was a whole chime of bells—yet it was my sausage peg. I would never have imagined so much could have been done with it, but that depends altogether upon who gets hold of it. I was deeply touched. From sheer pleasure, I wept as much as a little mouse can weep.

"The night was all too short, but the nights in the far north are not any longer at that time of the year. As dawn broke, and the morning breeze rippled the mirrored surface of the lake, the fine-spun streamers and banners were blown away. The billowing garlands of spider web, the suspension bridges from leaf to leaf, the balustrades and whatever else they are called, blew away like nothing at all. Six elves brought back my sausage peg, and asked if I wished for anything they could give me. So I begged them to tell me how to make soup from a sausage peg.

"The chief elf smiled, and said, 'How do we do it? Why, you have just seen it. I'm sure you scarcely knew your sausage peg.'

"'To you, it's only a trick of speech,' I said. I told him honestly what I traveled in search of, and what importance was attached to it here at home. 'What good,' said I, 'does it do our mouse king or our great kingdom for me to witness all this merrymaking? I can't just wave my sausage peg and say, "See the peg. Here comes the soup." This sort of dish is good only after all the guests at the table have had their fill.'

"Then the chief elf dipped his little finger in the blue cup of a violet, and told me:

"'Watch this. I shall anoint your pilgrim's staff. When you come home again to the mouse king's palace, you need only touch his warm heart with it, and the staff will immediately be covered with violets, even in the coldest wintertime. So I should say I have given you something to take home with you, and a little more for good measure.'"

Before the little mouse said what this "little more" was, she held out her stick to the king's heart. Really and truly, it became covered with the most beautiful bouquet of flowers, and their fragrance was so strong that the mouse king ordered the mice who stood nearest the fire to singe their tails. He wanted a smell of something burning to overcome the scent of violets, which was not the kind of perfume that he liked.

"What was that 'little more for good measure'?" he asked.

"Oh yes," said the little mouse. "I think it is what they call an effect." She turned the stick around and, behold! there was not a flower to be seen on the bare sausage peg in her hand. She flourished it like a music baton. "'Violets are to see, and smell, and touch,' the elf told me. So something must be done for us to hear and taste."

The little mouse began to beat time, and music was heard. It was not the elfin music of the forest. No, it was such as can be heard in the kitchen. There was the bubbling sound of boiling and stewing. It came all at once, as though the wind rushed through every chimney funnel and every pot and kettle boiled over. The fire shovel clanged upon the copper kettle, and then all at once the sound died down. One heard the whisper of the teakettle's song, so sweet to hear and so low they could scarcely tell when it began or left off. The little pot simmered and the big pot boiled, and neither kept time with the other. It was as if there were no reason left in the pots. And the little mouse flourished her baton even more fiercely. The pots seethed, bubbled, and boiled over. The wind whistled and roared down the chimney. *Puff!* It rose so tremendously that the little mouse at length lost hold of her stick.

"That was thick soup," said the mouse king. "Is it ready to be served?"

"That's all there is to it." The little mouse curtsied.

"All?" said the mouse king. "Then we had better hear what the next has to tell us."

III. WHAT THE SECOND LITTLE MOUSE
HAD TO TELL

"I was born in the palace library," said the second mouse. "I and other members of my family have never known the luxury of visiting a dining room, much less a pantry. Only on my journey and here today have I seen a kitchen. In the library, we often went hungry indeed, but we got a great deal of knowledge. The news of the royal reward offered for making soup from a sausage peg finally reached us. It was my grandmother who promptly ferreted out a manuscript, which of course she could not read, but from which she has heard the following passage read: 'If one is a poet, one can make soup out of a sausage peg.'

"She asked me if I were a poet. I told her I was entirely innocent in such matters, but she insisted that I must go forth and manage to be one. I asked how to do it, for that was as hard for me to learn as it was to find out how to make the soup. But my grandmother had heard a good many books read, and she told me that three things were essential: 'Understanding, imagination, and feeling—if you can manage to get these into you, you'll be a poet, and this business of the sausage peg will come to you by nature.'

"So off I went, marching westward, out into the wide world to become a poet.

"I knew that understanding comes first in everything, because the other two virtues aren't half as well thought of, so I set off in search of understanding at once. Yes, but where does it live? 'Go to the ant and be wise,' said the great King of the Jews. I learned that in the library. So I did not rest until I came to a big ant hill. There I posted myself on watch, to learn wisdom.

"The ants are a very respectable race. They understand things thoroughly. With them everything is like a well-worked problem in arithmetic that comes out right. Work and lay eggs, they say, for you must both live your life and provide for the future. So that is just what they do. They are divided into clean ants and those who do the dirty work. Each one is numbered according to his rank, and the ant queen is number *one*. What she thinks is the only right way to think, for she contains all wisdom, and it was most important for me to learn this from her. But she talked so cleverly that it seemed like nonsense to me.

"She asserted that her ant hill was the highest thing in all the world, though quite close to it grew a tree which was obviously higher. It was so very much higher that there was no denying it, and consequently, it was never mentioned. One evening, an ant got lost in the tree. She climbed up the trunk, not to the very top but higher than any ant had climbed before. When she came home and told of finding something even more lofty than the ant hill, the other ants considered that she had insulted the whole community. She was muzzled and comdemned to solitary confinement for life. Shortly afterward, another ant climbed the tree, making the same journey and the same discovery. But this ant reported it with suitable caution and diffidence, as they say. Besides, she was one of the upper-class ants—one of the clean ones. So they believed her, and when she died, they gave her an eggshell momument, to show their love of science."

The little mouse went on to say, "I saw the ants continually running to and fro with eggs on their backs. One of them dropped hers, and tried to pick it up again, but she couldn't manage it. Two others came to help her with all their power. But when they came near dropping their own eggs in the attempt, they at once stopped helping, for each must first think of himself. The queen ant said that they had displayed both heart and understanding.

"'These two virtues,' she said, 'raise ants above all other creatures of reason. Understanding must and shall always come first, and I have more of it than anyone else.' With this, she reared up on her hind legs so that all could be sure who she was. I was sure who she was, and I ate her. 'Go to the ant and be wise'—and I had swallowed the queen.

"I now went over to the tree I mentioned. It was an oak, with a mighty trunk and far-flung branches, for it was very old. I knew that a living spirit must live in it, a dryad, as she is called, who is born when the tree is born and dies when it dies. I had heard of this in the library, and now I saw such a tree with such an oak maiden. She shrieked frightfully when she saw me so near her, for like other women, she is terribly afraid of mice. But she had more reason to fear me than the others have, because I might have gnawed through the bark of the tree on which her life depended. I spoke to her in a cordial, friendly fashion, and told her she had nothing to fear.

"She took me up in her slender hand, and when I told her why I had come out into the wide world she promised that perhaps that very evening I should find one of the two virtues for which I still searched. She told me that Fantasy was her very good friend, that he was as beautiful as the god of love, and that he often rested under the leafy boughs of the tree, which would then rustle even more softly over these two. He called her his dryad, she said, and the tree his tree, for the magnificent gnarled oak just suited him. He liked its roots which went down so deep and steadfast in the earth, and the trunk which rose so high in the clear air that it felt the pelting snow, the driving wind, and the warm sun as they ought to be felt.

"'Yes,' the dryad talked on, 'the birds up aloft there sing and tell of distant lands. On the single dead branch the stork has built a nest which is very picturesque, and he tells me about the land where the pyramids are. Fantasy loves to hear all this, but it is not enough for him. I too must tell him of my life in the forest, from the time when I was small and the tree so tiny that a nettle could shade it, until now when the tree is so tall and strong. Sit down under the sweet thyme, and watch closely. When Fantasy comes I shall manage to pinch his wings and pull out a little feather. Take it. A poet can get no better gift—and it will be all you need.'

"When Fantasy came, the feather was plucked and I took it," said the little mouse. "I soaked it in water until it was soft. Still it was hard to swallow, but I nibbled it down at last. It's no easy matter to become a poet, with all the things one must cram inside oneself.

"Now I had both understanding and imagination, and they taught me that the third virtue was to be found in the library. For a great man once said and wrote that there are romances whose only purpose is to relieve people of their superfluous tears, and that these romances are like sponges, sopping up the emotions. I remembered that a few of these old books had always looked especially tasty. They had been thumbed quite greasy. They must have absorbed an enormous lot of tears.

"I returned to the library and devoured a whole novel—that is to say, the soft and the essential part; but the crust—that is, the binding, I left. When I had digested this, and another one too, I felt fluttery inside. I ate still a third and there I was, a poet. That is what I told myself, and that is what I told everyone else. I had headache, stomach aches—I can't remember all the different aches.

"Now I began to recall all the stories that could be made to apply to a sausage peg. Many pegs came to mind—the ant queen must have had magnificent understanding. I remembered the story about a man who would take a white peg out of his mouth to make both himself and the peg invisible. I thought of old beer with a peg stuck in it, of peg legs, and 'round pegs in square holes,' and 'the peg to one's coffin.' All my thoughts ran on pegs. When one is a poet—as I am, for I have worked like mad to become one—one can turn all of these subjects into poems. So every day, I shall be able to entertain your majesty with another peg, another story—yes that's my soup."

"Let's hear what the third one has to say," the king commanded.

"Squeak, squeak!" they heard at the kitchen door, and the fourth little mouse—the one they had given up for dead—whizzed in like an arrow and upset the crepe-covered sausage peg. She had been running night and day, and when she saw her chance, she had traveled by rail on the freight train. Even so, she was almost too late. She pushed forward, looking the worse for wear. She had lost her sausage peg but not her tongue, for she immediately took over the conservation as if everybody had been waiting to hear her, and her alone, and as if nothing else mattered in the world. She spoke at once, and she spoke in full. She appeared so suddenly that no one had time to check her or her speech until she was through. So let's hear her.

IV. WHAT THE FOURTH MOUSE, WHO SPOKE BEFORE THE THIRD, HAD TO SAY

"I went at once to the largest town," she said. "I don't recall the name of it. I have such a bad memory for names. From the railway station I was carried with some confiscated goods to the courthouse, and from there I ran to see the jailor. He was talking about his prisoners, and especially about one who had spoken rashly. One word led to another. About these words, other words had been spoken, read and recorded.

"'The whole business is soup from a sausage peg,' said the jailor, 'but it is a soup that may cost him his head.'

"This gave me such an interest in the prisoner," the little mouse went on to say, "that I watched my chance, and darted into his cell. For there is always some mouse hole behind every locked door. The prisoner looked pale. He had a big beard and big, brilliant eyes. His lamp smoked up the cell, but the walls were so black that they couldn't get any blacker, and the prisoner whiled away the time by scratching drawings and verses in white on this black background. I didn't read them, but I believe he found it dull there, for I was a welcome guest. He tempted me out with crumbs, and whistling, and pet words. He was glad to see me, won my confidence, and we became fast friends. We shared his bread and water, and he treated me to cheese and sausage, so I lived well. However, I would say that it was chiefly for his good company that I stayed with him. He let me run up his hand and arm into his sleeve, and climb in his beard. He called me his little friend, and I really liked him, for friendship is a two-sided thing. I forgot my mission in the wide world and I forgot my sausage peg. It is lying there still in a crack in the floor. I wanted to stay with him, for if I had gone away the poor prisoner wouldn't have had a friend in the world. That would not be right, so I stayed. But he did not stay. He spoke to me sadly for the last time, gave me a double ration of bread and cheese, and blew me a parting kiss. Then he went away and he never came back. I don't know what became of him.

"'Soup from a sausage peg,' the jailor had said, so I went to see him. But he was not to be trusted. He took me up in his hand, right enough, but he popped me into a cage, a treadmill, a terrible machine in which you run around and around without going anywhere. And, besides, people laugh at you.

"The jailor's grandchild was a charming little girl, with curls that shone like gold, such sparkling eyes, and such merry lips.

"'Why, you poor little mouse,' she said, as she peeped into my ugly old cage. She drew back the iron bolt, and out I jumped to the window sill, and from there to the rain spout. I was free, free! That was all I thought of, and not of the purpose of my journey.

"It was almost dark. Night was coming on when I established myself in an old tower already inhabited by a watchman and an owl. I didn't trust either of them, and the owl least of all. It is like the cat, and has the unforgivable vice of eating mice. But one can be mistaken, as I was, for this old owl was most worthy and knowing. She knew more than the watchman, and as much as I did. The young owls were always making a fuss about everything. 'Don't try to make soup out of a sausage peg,' she told them, and she had such tender affection for her own family that those were the hardest word she would say.

"Her behavior gave me such confidence in her that from the crevice where I hid, I called out, 'Squeak!' My trust in her pleased her so that she promised to take me under her protection. No animal would be allowed to molest me, and she would save me for the wintertime when food ran short.

"She was wise in every way. The watchman, she told me, can only hoot with the horn that hangs by his side. 'He is vastly puffed up about it,' she declared, 'and thinks he's an owl in a tower. It sounds so big, but it is very little—all soup from a sausage peg.'

"I begged her to give me the recipe for this soup, but she explained to me that, '"Soup from a sausage peg" is only a human expression. It means different things, and everybody thinks his meaning is the right one, but the real meaning is nothing at all.'

"'Nothing at all?' I squeaked. That was a blow! Truth isn't always pleasant, but 'Truth above all else.' The old owl said so, too. Now that I thought about it, I clearly saw that if I brought back what was 'above all else,' I would be bringing something much better than soup from a sausage peg. So I hurried back, to be home in time and to bring back the best thing of all, something above everything else, which is the *truth*. We mice are an enlightened people, and the mouse king is the most enlightened of us all. He is capable of making me his queen for the sake of truth."

"Your truth is false!" said the mouse who had not yet had her say. "I can make the soup, and I intend to do so."

V. HOW THE SOUP WAS MADE

"I didn't go traveling," the third mouse informed them. "I stayed at home, and that's the right thing to do. There's no need to travel. One can get everything just as well here, so I stayed at home. I have not learned what I know from fabulous creatures, or swallowed it whole, or taken an owl's word for it. I found it out from my own meditation. Kindly put a kettle brimful of water on the fire! Now stir up the fire until the water boils up and boils over. Now throw the peg in! And now will the mouse king kindly dip his tail in the scalding water, to stir it. The longer he stirs it, the stronger the soup will be. There's no expense—it needs no other ingredients. Just stir it around."

"Can't someone else stir it?" the mouse king asked.

"No," she told him. "The necessary touch can be given only by the mouse king's tail."

The water bubbled and boiled as the mouse king stood close to the kettle. It was almost dangerous. He held out his tail, as mice do in a dairy when they skim a pan of milk and lick the cream from their tails. But no sooner did the hot steam strike his tail than away he jumped.

"Naturally, you are my queen," he declared. "The soup can wait until our golden anniversary. That will give the poor people among my subjects something to which they can look forward, with pleasure—and a long pleasure."

And then the wedding was held. But as the mice returned home, some of them said that it could scarcely be called soup from a sausage peg. Soup from a mouse tail was more like it. This or that of what had been told was quite good, they admitted, but the whole thing could have been done very differently.

"Now I would have said this, and that, and the other thing." So said the critics, who are so wise after a thing is done. But the story was told around the world. Various opinions were held of it but they didn't do the story itself any harm. So it's well to remember that for all things great and small, as well as in regard to soup from a sausage peg, don't expect any thanks.

THE OLD OAK TREE'S LAST DREAM (1858)

In the woods, on a high bank near the open seashore, there stood such a very old oak tree. It was exactly 365 years old, but this long span of years seemed to the tree scarcely longer than as many days do to people like us. A tree's life is not the same as a man's. We are awake during the day, and sleep at night, and we have our dreams.

It is different with a tree; it is awake throughout three seasons, and not until winter comes does it go to sleep. Winter is its time for sleeping; that is its night after the long day which we call spring, summer, and autumn.

Many a warm summer day the mayflies danced around its crown, lived happily and felt fortunate as they flitted about; and if one of the tiny creatures rested from its blissful play for a moment on a large oak leaf, the tree always said, "Poor little insect! Your whole life is but one day long! How sad!"

"Sad?" the little mayfly always answered. "What do you mean by that? Everything is so bright and warm and beautiful, and I am so happy!"

"But only for one day, and then all is over."

"Over?" said the mayfly. "What does over mean? Is it also over for you?"

"No, I shall live perhaps thousands of your days, and a day for me lasts a whole year. That is something so long you can't even figure it out."

"No, I don't understand you at all. You have thousands of my days to live, but I have thousands of moments in which to be happy and joyous. Will all the beauty of this world die when you die?"

"No," said the tree. "It will probably last longer, infinitely longer, than I am able to imagine."

"Well, then, we each have an equally long lifetime, only we figure differently."

And so the mayfly danced and glided in the air, with its fine, artistic wings of veil and velvet, rejoicing in the warm air that was so perfumed with delicious scents from the clover field and the wild roses, elders, and honeysuckles of the hedges, not ot speak of the bluebells, cowslip, and wild thyme; the fragrance was so strong that the tiny insect felt a little intoxicated from it. The day was long and beautiful, full of happiness and sweet experiences, and by sunset, the little May fly was pleasantly weary from all the excitement. Its dainty wings would no longer support it; very gently it glided down onto the cool, rocking blades of grass, nodded its head as a mayfly can, and fell into a very peaceful slumber; it was dead.

"Poor little mayfly," said the Oak; "that was really too short a life!"

And every summer day was repeated the same dance, the same question, the same answer, and the same peaceful falling asleep; it happened through many generations of mayflies, and all of them were lighthearted and happy.

The Oak stood wide awake through its spring morning, its summer noon, and autumn evening; soon now it would be sleeping time, the tree's night, for winter was coming. Already the winds were singing, "Good night! Good night! There falls a leaf; there falls a leaf! We plucked it, we plucked it! See that you go to sleep! We will sing you to sleep, we will rock you to sleep! Surely it will do your old limbs good. They crackle from pure contentment. Sleep sweetly, sleeep sweetly! This is your 365th night, but you are really only a yearling! Sleep sweetly! The skies are sprinkling snow; it will spread a warm coverlet over your feet. Sleep sweetly and have pleasant dreams!"

And now the great Oak stood stripped of its foliage, ready to rest throughout the long winter, and in its sleep to dream of something that had happened to it, just as men dream.

The tree had once been very small; yes, an acorn had been its cradle. According to human calculation, it was now in its fourth century; it was the tallest and mightiest tree in the forest; its crown towered high above all the other trees and could be seen far out at sea, where it served as a landmark to ships. The Oak had never thought of how many eyes sought it out from the watery distance. High up in its green crown, the wood doves had built their nests, and there the cuckoo made its voice heard; and in the autumn, when its leaves looked like hammered-out copper plates, the birds of passage rested awhile there before flying on across the seas. But now it was winter; the tree was leafless, and the bowed and gnarled branches showed their dark outlines; crows and jackdaws came to gossip about the hard times that were beginning and how difficult it was to find food in the winter.

It was just at the holy Christmastime that the Oak dreamed its most beautiful dream—and this we shall hear.

The tree had a distinct feeling that it was a holiday season. It seemed to hear all the church bells ringing round about, and at that the day was mild and warm, like a lovely summer day. The Oak spread its mighty crown; sunbeams flickered among the leaves and branches, and the air was filled with the fragrance of herbs and blossoms. Colored butterflies played tag, and the mayflies danced, which was the only way they could show their happiness. All that the tree had encountered and witnessed through the many years passed by as if in a holiday procession.

Knights and ladies of bygone days, with feathers in their caps and hawks on their wrists, rode gaily through the forest; dogs barked, and the hunting horn sounded. The tree saw hostile soldiers, in shining armor and gaily colored garments, with spears and halberds, pitching their tents and then striking them again; the watchfire blazed, and they sang and then slept under the tree's protecting boughs. It saw lovers meet in quiet happiness there in the moonlight and carve their names, or their initials, on the gray-green bark. At one time, many years before, a guitar and an Aeolian harp had been hung up in the Oak's boughs by carefree traveling youths; now they hung there again, and now once more their lovely music sounded. The wood doves cooed, as if they were trying to express what the tree felt, and the cuckoo announced many more summer days it had to live.

Then it seemed that a new and stronger current of life flowed through the Oak, down into its smallest roots, up into its highest twigs, even out into the leaves! The tree felt that it was stretching; it could feel how life and warmth stirred down in the earth about its roots; it felt the strength increase and that it was growing taller and taller. The trunk shot up; there was no rest for the tree; it grew more and more; its crown became fuller; it spread and towered. And as the tree grew, its strength grew also, as did its ardent yearning to reach higher and higher toward the bright, warm sun.

Already it was high above the clouds, which drifted far below it, like a troop of dark migratory birds or like flocks of white swans.

And every leaf of the tree could see as if it had eyes; the stars became visible to them by daylight, large and bright, all shining, like very clear, mild eyes. They reminded the Oak of dear, kindly eyes it had known, the eyes of children, the eyes of lovers, who had met beneath the tree.

It was a blessed moment, so full of joy! And yet in all its joy, the Oak felt a longing, a great desire that all the other trees below, all the bushes, plants, and flowers of the forest, might be lifted up with it to share in its glory and gladness. Amid all its dream of splendor, the mighty Oak could not be fully happy without all the others, small and great, sharing in it, and this yearning thrilled through boughs and leaves as fervently, as strongly, as it would within a human heart.

The crown of the tree bowed and looked back, as if it sought someting it had missed. Then it felt the thyme and soon the still stronger scent of honeysuckle and violet, and imagined it could hear the cuckoo talking to itself.

Yes, and now the green tops of the forest peeped up through the clouds. The Oak saw that the other trees below were growing and lifting themselves up as it had; bushes and plants rose high into the air, some even tearing themselves loose from their roots, to soar up all the faster. The birch grew the most rapidly; like a white flash of lightning its slender stem shot up, its boughs waving like green gauze and banners. The whole forest, even the feathery brown reeds, grew high into the sky; the birds followed and sang, and on the grass that waved to and fro like long, green silken ribbons, the grasshopper sat, and drummed with his wings against his lean legs. The cockchafers hummed and the bees buzzed and every bird sang to the best of its ability; song and happiness were everywhere, right up into Heaven.

"But the little red flower by the water—that should come along!" said the Oak tree. "And the bluebell flower, and the little daisy!" Yes, the Oak wanted to have them all with it.

"We are here! We are with you!" they sang and rang out.

"But the pretty anemones of last summer—and the mass of lilies of the valley of the year before that—and the wild crabapple tree that bloomed so beautifully—and all the beauties of the forest, throughout the many years—if only they had lived on and remained till now, then they also could have been with us!"

"We are here! We are with you!" they sang and rang out, even higher up; it seemed that they had ascended before the others.

"No, this is too wonderful to be true!" rejoiced the Oak. "I have them all with me; small and great, not one is forgotten! How can all this blessedness be conceivable and possible?"

"In the kingdom of God, all things are conceivable and possible," came the mighty answer.

And the tree, which continued to grow, felt its very roots loosening themselves from the earth. "This is the best of all," it said. "Now no bonds shall hold me; I can soar upward to the heights of glory and light! And my loved ones are all with me, small and great—all with me!"

"All!"

That was the dream of the Oak tree, and while it dreamed on that holy Christmas Eve, a mighty storm was sweeping over land and sea. The ocean piled its heavy billows onto the shore; the tree cracked, groaned, and was torn up by the roots, at the very moment when it was dreaming that its roots were freeing themselves from the earth. It fell. Its 365 years were now as a day is to the mayfly.

Christmas morning, when the sun rose, the storm was past. All the church bells rang, while from every chimney, even the smallest one, on the peasant's hut, the blue smoke curled upward, like sacrificial steam rising from the altars of the ancient Druids. The sea became more and more calm, and aboard a big vessel that had weathered the storm of the night before, all flags were hoisted now in greeting to the Yuletide. "The tree is gone—the old oak tree that was our landmark!" said the sailors. "It must have fallen during the storm last night. What can ever replace it? Nothing!"

That was the tree's eulogy, brief but sincere. There it lay, stretched out on the carpet of snow near the shore, while over it sounded the hymn sung on the ship, sung in thanksgiving for the joy of Christmas, for the bliss of the human soul's salvation through Christ, for the gift of eternal life:

> Sing loud, sweet angel, on Christmas morn.
> Hallelujah! Christ the Savior is born.
> In joy receive His blessing.
> Hallelujah! Hallelujah!

Thus sounded the old hymn, and everyone aboard the ship felt himself lifted heavenward by the hymn, and by prayer, even as the old tree had lifted itself in its last, most beautiful dream that Christmas Eve.

THE MARSH KING'S DAUGHTER (1858)

The storks tell many, many stories to their young ones, all about the bogs and marshes. In general, each story is suited to the age and sense of the little storks. While the youngest ones are satisfied with, "Kribble-krabble, plurry-murry," and think it a very fine story, the older ones demand something with more sense to it, or at least something about the family.

Of the two oldest stories which have been handed down among the storks, we all know the one about Moses, who was put by his mother on the banks of the Nile, where a king's daughter found him. How well she brought him up, how he became a great man, and how no one knows where he lies buried, are things that we all have heard.

The other tale is not widely known, perhaps because it is almost a family story. This tale has been handed down from one mother stork to another for a thousand years, and each succeeding storyteller has told it better and better, and now we shall tell it best of all.

The first pair of storks who told this tale and who themselves played a part in it, had their summer home on the roof of the Viking's wooden castle up by the Wild Marsh in Vendsyssel. If we must be precise about our knowledge, this is in the country of Hjorring, high up near Skagen in Jutland. There is still a big marsh there, which we can read about in the official reports of that district. It is said that the place once lay under the sea, but the land has risen somewhat and is now a wilderness extending for many a mile. One is surrounded on all sides by marshy meadows, quagmires, and peat bogs, overgrown by cloud berries and stunted trees. Dank mists almost always hang over the place, and about seventy years ago, wolves still made their homes there. Well may it be called the Wild Marsh. Think how desolate it was, and how much swamp and water there must have been among all those marshes and ponds a thousand years ago! Yet in most matters, it must have looked then as it looks now. The reeds grew just as high, and had the same long leaves and feathery tips of a purplish-brown tint that they have now. Birch trees grew there with the same white bark and the same airily dangling leaves. As for the living creatures, the flies have not changed the cut of their gauzy apparel, and the favorite colors of the storks were white trimmed with black, and long red stockings.

However, people dressed very differently from the fashion of today. But if any of them—thrall or huntsman, it mattered not—set foot in the quagmire, they fared the same a thousand years ago as they would fare today. In they would fall, and down they would sink to him whom they call the Marsh King, who rules below throughout the entire marsh land. They also call him King of the Quicksands, but we like the name Marsh King better, and that was what the storks called him. Little or nothing is known about his rule, but perhaps that is just as well.

Near the marsh and close to the Liim Fjord, lay wooden castle of the Vikings, three stories high from its watertight stone cellars to the tower on its roof. The storks had built their nest on this roof, and there the mother stork sat hatching her eggs. She was certain they would be hatched.

One evening, the father stork stayed out rather late, and when he got home, he looked ruffled and flurried.

"I have something simply dreadful to tell you," he said to the mother stork.

"Then you had better keep it to yourself," she told him. "Remember, I am hatching eggs! If you frighten me, it might have a very bad effect on them."

"But I must tell you," he insisted. "The daughter of our Egyptian host has come here. She has ventured to take this long journey, and— she's lost!"

"She who comes of fairy stock? Speak up. You know that I must not be kept in suspense while I'm on my eggs."

"It's this way, Mother. Just as you told me, she must have believed the doctor's advice. She believed that the swamp flowers up here would cure her sick father, and she has flown here in the guise of a swan, together with two other princesses who put on swan plumage and fly north every year, to take the baths that keep them young. She has come, and she is lost."

"You make your story too long-winded," the mother stork protested. "My eggs are apt to catch cold. I can't bear such suspense at a time like this."

"I have been keeping my eyes open," said the father stork, "and this evening I went among the reeds where the quagmire will barely support me. There I saw three swans flying my way. There was something about their flight that warned me, 'See here! These are not real swans. These creatures are merely disguised in swan feathers!' You know as well as I do, Mother, that one feels instinctly whether a thing is true or false."

"To be sure, I do," said she. "But tell me about the princess. I am tired of hearing about swan feathers."

"Well," the father stork said, "as you know, in the middle of the marsh, there is a sort of pool. You can catch a glimpse of it from here if you will rise up a trifle. There, between the reeds and the green scum of the pool, a large alder stump juts up. On it the three swans alighted, flapped their wings and looked about them. One of them threw off her swan plumage and immediately I could see that she was the princess from our home in Egypt. There she sat with no other cloak than her own long hair. I heard her ask the others to take good care of her swan feathers, while she dived down in the water to pluck the swamp flower which she fancied she saw there. They nodded, and held their heads high as they picked up her empty plumage.

"'What are they going to do with it?' I wondered, and she must have wondered, too. Our answer came soon enough, for they flew up in the air with her feather garment.

"'Dive away,' they cried. 'Never more shall you fly about as a swan. Never more shall you see the land of Egypt. You may have your swamp forever.' They tore her swan guise into a hundred pieces, so that feathers whirled around like a flurry of snow. Then away they flew, those two deceitful princesses."

"Why, that's dreadful," the mother stork said. "I can't bear to listen. Tell me what happened next."

"The princess sobbed and lamented. Her tears sprinkled down on the alder stump, and the stump moved, for it was the Marsh King himself, who lives under the quagmire. I saw the stump turn, and this was no longer a tree stump that stretched out its two muddy, branchlike arms toward the poor girl. She was so frightened that she jumped out on the green scum which cannot bear my weight, much less hers. She was instantly swallowed up, and it was the alder stump, which plunged in after her, that dragged her down. Big black bubbles rose, and these were the last traces of them. She is now buried in the Wild Marsh, and never will she get back home to Egypt with the flowers she came to find. Mother, you could not have endured the sights I saw."

"You ought not to tell me such a tale at a time like this. Our eggs may be the worse for it. The princess can look out for herself. Someone will surely help her. Now if it had been I, or you, or any of our family, it would have been all over with us."

"I shall look out for her, every day," said the father stork, and he did so.

A long time went by, but one day, he saw a green stalk shooting up from the bottom of the pool. When it came to the surface, it grew a leaf, which got broader and broader, and then a bud appeared. As the stork was flying by one morning, the bud opened in the strong sunbeams, and in the center of it lay a beautiful child, a baby girl who looked as fresh as if she had just come from her bath. So closely did the baby resemble the princess from Egypt that the stork thought it was she, who had become a child again. But when he considered the matter, he decided that this child who lay in the cup of a water lily must be the daughter of the princess and the Marsh King.

"She cannot remain there," the stork said to himself, "yet my nest is already overcrowded. But I have an idea. The Viking's wife hasn't any children, although she is always wishing for a little one. I'm often held responsible for bringing children, and this time I shall really bring one. I shall fly with this baby to the Viking's wife. What joy there will be."

The stork picked up the little girl, flew with her to the log castle, pecked a hole with his beak in the piece of bladder that served as a window pane, and laid the baby in the arms of the Viking woman.

Then he flew home to his wife and told her all about it. The baby storks listened attentively, for they were old enough now to be curious.

"Just think! The princess is not dead," he told them. "She sent her little one up to me, and I have found a good home for it."

"I told you to start with that it would come out all right," said the mother stork. "Turn your thoughts now to your own children. It is almost time for us to start on our long journey. I am beginning to tingle under my wings. The cuckoo and the nightingale have flown already, and I heard the quail saying that we shall soon have a favorable wind. Our young ones will do us credit on the flight, or I don't know my own children."

How pleased the Viking's wife was when she awoke in the morning and found the lovely child in her arms. She kissed it and caressed it, but it screamed frightfully and thrashed about with its little arms and legs. There was no pleasing it until at last it cried itself to sleep, and as it lay there, it was one of the loveliest little creatures that anyone ever saw. The Viking's wife was so overjoyed that she felt light-headed as well as light-hearted. She turned quite hopeful about everything, and felt sure that her husband and all his men might return as unexpectedly as the little one had come to her. So she set herself and her entire household to work, in order to have everything in readiness. The long, colored tapestry on which she and her handmaidens had embroidered figures of their gods—Odin, Thor, and Freya, as they were called—were hung in place. The thralls were set to scouring and polishing the old shields that decorated the walls; cushions were laid on the benches; and dry logs were stacked on the fireplace in the middle of the hall, so that the pile might be lighted at a moment's notice. The Viking's wife worked so hard that she was tired out, and slept soundly when evening came.

Along toward morning she awoke, and was greatly alarmed to find no trace of her little child. She sprang up, lighted a splinter of pine wood, and searched the room. To her astonishment, she found at the foot of her bed not the beautiful child, but a big, ugly frog. She was so appalled that she took up a heavy stick to kill the creature, but it looked at her with such strange, sad eyes that she could not strike. As she renewed her search, the frog gave a faint, pitiful croak. She sprang from the bed to the window, and threw open the shutter. The light of the rising sun streamed in and fell upon that big frog on the bed. It seemed as if the creature's wide mouth contracted into small, red lips.

The frog legs unbent as the most exquisitely shaped limbs, and it was her lovely little child that lay there, and not that ugly frog.

"What's all this?" she exclaimed. "Have I had a nightmare? This is my pretty little elf lying here." She kissed it and pressed it affectionately to her heart, but it struggled and tried to bite, like the kitten of a wild cat.

Neither that day nor the next did her Viking husband come home. Though he was on his way, the winds were against him. They were blowing southward to speed the storks. A fair wind for one is a foul wind for another.

In the course of a few days and nights, it became plain to the Viking's wife how things were with the little child. It was under the influence of some terrible spell of sorcery. By day it was as lovely as a fairy child, but it had a wicked temper. At night, on the contrary, it was an ugly frog, quiet and pathetic, with sorrowful eyes. Here were two natures that changed about both inwardly and outwardly. This was because the little girl whom the stork had brought had by day her mother's appearance, together with her father's temper. But at night, she showed her kinship with him in her outward form, while her mother's mind and heart inwardly became hers. Who would be able to release her from this powerful spell of sorcery that lay upon her? The Viking's wife felt most anxious and distressed about it, yet her heart went out to the poor little thing.

She knew that when her husband came home she would not dare tell him of this strange state of affairs, for he would certainly follow the custom of those times and expose the poor child on the high road, to let anyone take it who would. The Viking's good-natured wife had not the heart to do this, so she determined that he should only see the child in the daytime.

At daybreak one morning, the wings of storks were heard beating over the roof. During the night, more than a hundred pairs of storks had rested there, and now they flew up to make their way to the south.

"Every man ready," was their watchword. "Let the wives and children make ready, too."

"How light we feel!" clacked the little storks. "We tingle and itch right down to our toes, as if we were full of live frogs. How fine it feels to be traveling to far-off lands."

"Keep close in one flock," cried their father and mother. "Don't clack your beaks so much, it's bad for your chest."

And away they went.

At that very instant, the blast of a horn rang over the heath, to give notice that the Viking had landed with all of his men. They came home with rich booty from the Gaelic coast, where, as in Britain, the terrified people sang, "Deliver us from the wild Northmen."

What a lively bustle now struck this Viking's castle near the Wild Marsh! A cask of mead was rolled out into the hall, the pile of wood was lighted, and horses were slaughtered. What a feast they were going to have! Priests sprinkled the horses' warm blood over the thralls as a blood offering. The fires crackled, the smoke rolled up to the roof, and soot dropped down from the beams, but they were used to that. Guests were invited and were given handsome presents. Old grudges and double-dealings were forgotten. They all drank deep and threw the gnawed bones in each other's faces, but that was a sign of good humor. The skald, a sort of minstrel but at the same time a fighting man who had been with them and knew what he sang about, trolled them a song, in which he told of all their valiant deeds in battle, and all their wonderful adventures. After each verse came the same refrain:

> Fortunes perish, friends die, one dies oneself,
> But a glorious name never dies!

Then they all banged their shields, and rattled on the table with their knives or the knucklebones, making a terrific noise.

The Viking's wife sat on the bench that ran across this public banquet hall. She wore a silken dress with gold bracelets and big amber beads. She was in her finest attire, and the skald included her in his song. He spoke of the golden treasure which she had brought her rich husband. This husband of hers rejoiced in the lovely child whom he had seen only by day, in all its charming beauty. The savage temper that went with her daytime beauty rather pleased him, and he said that she might grow up to be a stalwart soldier maid, able to hold her own—the sort who would not flinch if a skilled hand, in fun, took a sharp sword and cut off her eyebrows for practice.

The mead cask was emptied, a full one was rolled in, and it too was drunk dry. These were folk who could hold a great deal. They were familiar with the old proverb to the effect that, "The cattle know when to quit their pasture, but a fool never knows the measure of his stomach."

Yes, they all knew it quite well, but people often know the right thing and do the wrong thing. They also knew that, "One wears out his welcome when he sits too long in another man's house," but they stayed on, for all that. Meat and mead are such good things, and they were a jovial crew. That night the thralls slept on the warm ashes, dipped their fingers into the fat drippings, and licked them. Oh yes, those were glorious days.

The Vikings ventured forth on one more raid that year, though the storms of autumn were beginning to blow. The Viking and his men went to the coast of Britain—"just across the water," he said—and his wife stayed at home with her little girl. It soon came about that the foster mother cared more for the poor frog with its sad eyes and pathetic croaking, than for the little beauty who scratched and bit everyone who came near her.

The raw, dank mist of fall invaded the woods and thickets. "Gnaw-worms," they called it, for it gnawed the leaves from the trees. "Pluck-feathers," as they called the snow, fell in flurry upon flurry, for winter was closing in. Sparrows took over the stork nest and gossiped about the absent owners, as tenants will. The two storks and all their young ones—where were they now?

The storks were now in the land of Egypt, where the sun shone as warm as it does upon us on a fine summer day. Tamarind and acacia trees bloomed in profusion, and the glittering crescent of Mohammed topped the domes of all the mosques. On the slender minarets many a pair of storks rested after their long journey. Whole flocks of them nested together on the columns of ancient temples and the ruined arches of forgotten cities. The date palm lifted its high screen of branches, like a parasol in the sun. The gray-white pyramids were sharply outlined against the clear air of the desert, where the ostrich knew he could use his legs and the lion crouched to gaze with big solemn eyes at the marble sphinx half buried in the sand. The waters of the Nile had receded, and the delta was alive with frogs. The storks considered this the finest sight in all the land, and the young storks found it hard to believe their own eyes. Yes, everything was wonderful.

"See! It is always like this in our southern home," their mother told them. And their little bellies tingled at the spectacle.

"Do we see any more?" they asked. "Shall we travel on into the country?"

"There is nothing else worth seeing," their mother said. "Beyond this fertile delta lie the deep forests, where the trees are so interwoven by thorny creepers that only the elephant can trample a path through them with his huge, heavy feet. The snakes there are too big for us to eat, and the lizards too nimble for us to catch. And, if you go out in the desert, the slightest breeze will blow your eyes full of sand, while a storm would bury you under the dunes. No, it is best here, where there are plenty of frogs and locusts. Here I stop, and here you stay."

So they stayed. In nests atop the slender minarets the old storks rested, yet kept quite busy smoothing their feathers and sharpening their bills against their red stockings. From time to time, they would stretch their necks, bow very solemnly, and hold up their heads with such high foreheads, fine feathers, and wise brown eyes. The young maiden storks strolled solemnly through the wet reeds, making eyes at the other young storks and scraping acquaintances. At every third step they would gulp down a frog, or pause to dangle a small snake in their bills. They were under the impression that this became them immensely and besides, it tasted so good.

The young bachelor storks picked many a squabble, buffeted each other with their wings, and even stabbed at each other with their sharp bills till blood was shed. Yes, and then this young stork would get engaged, and that young stork would get engaged. Maidens and bachelors would pair off, for that was their only object in life. They built nests of their own and squabbled anew, for in the hot countries everyone is hotheaded. But it was very pleasant there, particularly so for the old storks, who thought that their children could do no wrong. The sun shone every day, there was plenty to eat, and they had nothing to do but enjoy themselves.

However, in the splendid palace of their Egyptian host, as they called him, there was no enjoyment. This wealthy and powerful lord lay on his couch, as stiff and stark as a mummy. In the great hall, which was as colorful as the inside of a tulip, he was surrounded by his kinsmen and servants. Though he was not quite dead, he could hardly be said to be alive. The healing flower from the northern marshes, which she who had loved him best had gone to seek, would never reach him. His lovely young daughter, who had flown over land and sea in the guise of a swan, would never come home from the far North.

"She is dead and gone," the two other swan princesses reported, when they returned. They concocted the following yarn, which they told:

"We three were flying together through the air, when a huntsman shot an arrow at us, and it struck our companion, our young friend. Like a dying swan, she sang her farewell song as she slowly dropped down to a lake in the forest. There on the shore we buried her, under a drooping birch tree. But we avenged her. We bound coals of fire to the wings of a swallow that nested under the thatched eaves of the huntsman's cottage. The roof blazed up, the cottage burst into flames, and the huntsman was burned to death. The flames were reflected across the lake, under the drooping birch tree where she lies, earth of this Earth. Never, alas! shall she return to the land of Egypt."

They both wept. But when the father stork heard their tale he rattled his bill, and said, "All lies and invention! I should dearly love to drive my bill right through their breasts."

"And most likely break it," said the mother stork. "A nice sight you'd be then. Think first of yourself, and then of your family. Never mind about outsiders."

"Nevertheless, I shall perch on the open cupola tomorrow, when all the wise and learned folk come to confer about the sick man. Perhaps they will hit upon something nearer the truth."

The wise men assembled and talked loud and long, but neither could the stork make sense out of what they had to say, nor did any good come of it to the sick man or to his daughter in the Wild Marsh. Yet we may as well hear what they had to say, for we have to listen to a lot in this world.

Perhaps it will be well to hear what had gone on before down there in Egypt. Then we shall know the whole story, or at least as much of it as the father stork knew.

"Love brings life. The greatest love brings the greatest life. Only through love may life be brought back to him." This doctrine the learned men had stated before, and they now said they had stated it wisely and well.

"It is a beautiful thought," the father stork quickly agreed.

"I don't quite understand it," said the mother stork. "That's its fault though, not mine. But no matter. I have other things to think about."

The learned men talked on about all the different kinds of love: the love of sweethearts, the love between parents and their children, plants' love of the light, and the love that makes seeds grow when the sun's rays kiss the earth. Their talk was so elaborate and learned that the father stork found it impossible to follow, much less repeat. However, their discussion made him quite thoughtful. All the next day he stood on one leg, with his eyes half closed, and thought, and thought. So much learning lay heavy upon him.

But one thing he understood clearly. Both the people of high degree and the humble folk had said from the bottom of their hearts that for this man to be sick, without hope of recovery, was a disaster to thousands, yes, to the whole nation, and that it would bring joy and happiness to everyone if he recovered.

"But where does the flower grow that can heal him?" they asked. For the answer they looked to their scholarly manuscripts, to the twinkling stars, to the wind, and to the weather. They searched through all the bypaths of knowledge, but all their wisdom and knowledge resolved down to the doctrine: "Love brings life—it can bring back a father's life," and although they said rather more than they understood, they accepted it, and wrote it down as a prescription. "Love brings life." Well and good, but how was this precept to be applied? That was their stumbling block.

However, they had at last agreed that help must come from the princess, who loved her father with all her heart. And they had devised a way in which she could help him. It was more than a year ago that they had sent the princess into the desert, just when the new moon was setting, to visit the marble sphinx. At the base of the sphinx she had to scrape away the sand from a doorway and follow a long passage which led to the middle of a great pyramid where one of the mightiest kings of old lay wrapped as a mummy in the midst of his glory and treasure. There she leaned over the corpse to have it revealed to her where she might find life and health for her father. When she had done all this, she had a dream in which she learned that in the Danes' land there was a deep marsh—the very spot was described to her. Here, beneath the water, she would feel a lotus flower touch her breast, and when that flower was brought home to her father it would cure him. So, in the guise of a swan she had flown from the land of Egypt to the Wild Marsh.

All this was known to the father and mother stork, and now we too are better informed. Furthermore, we know that the Marsh King dragged her down, and that those at home thought her dead and gone. Only the wisest among them said, as the stork mother had put it, "She can look out for herself." They waited to see what would come to pass, for they knew nothing better they could do.

"I believe I shall make off with those swan feathers of the faithless princesses," said the father stork. "Then they will fly no more to do mischief in the Wild Marsh. I'll hide the two sets of feathers up North, until we find a use for them."

"Where would you keep them?" the mother stork asked.

"In our nest by the Wild Marsh," he said. "I and our sons will take turns carrying them when we go back. If they prove too much of a burden, there are many places along the way where we can hide them until our next flight. One set of swan feathers would be enough for the princess, but two will be better. In that northern land it's well to have plenty of wraps."

"You will get no thanks for it," she told him, "but please yourself. You are the master, and except at hatching time, I have nothing to say."

Meanwhile, in the Viking's castle near the Wild Marsh, toward which the storks came flying, now that it was spring, the little girl had been given a name. She was called Helga, but this name was too mild for the violent temper that this lovely girl possessed. Month by month her temper grew worse. As the years went by and the storks traveled to and fro, to the banks of the Nile in the fall, and back to the Wild Marsh in the springtime, the child grew to be a big girl. Before anyone would have thought it, she was a lovely young lady of sixteen. The shell was fair to see but the kernel was rough and harsh—harsher than most, even in that wild and cruel age.

She took delight in splashing her hands about in the blood of horses slaughtered as an offering to the gods. In savage sport, she would bite off the head of the black cock that the priest was about to sacrifice, and in dead earnest she said to her foster father:

"If your foe were to come with ropes and pull down the roof over your head, I would not wake you if I could. I would not even hear the house fall, for my ears still tingle from that time you boxed them, years ago—yes, you! I'll never forget it."

But the Viking did not believe she was serious. Like everyone else, he was beguiled by her beauty, and he did not know the change that came over Helga's body and soul.

She would ride an unsaddled horse at full gallop, as though she were part of her steed, nor would she dismount even though he fought with his teeth against the other wild horses. And many a time she would dive off the cliff into the sea, with all of her clothes on, and swim out to meet the Viking as his boat neared home. To string her bow, she cut off the longest lock of her beautiful hair, and plaited it into a string. "Self-made is well made," said she.

The Viking's wife had a strong and determined will, in keeping with the age, but with her daughter she was weak and fearful, for she knew that an evil spell lay on that dreadful child.

Out of sheer malice, as it seemed, when Helga saw her foster mother stand on the balcony or come into the courtyard, she would sit on the edge of the well, throw up her hands, and let herself tumble into that deep, narrow hole. Froglike, she would dive in and clamber out. Like a wet cat, she would run to the main hall, dripping such a stream of water that the green leaves strewn on the floor were floating in it.

However, there was one thing that held Helga in check—and that was evening. As she came on, she grew quiet and thoughtful. She would obey and accept advice. Some inner force seemed to make her more like her real mother. When the sun went down and the usual change took place in her appearance and character, she sat quiet and sad, shriveled up in the shape of a frog. Now that she had grown so much larger than a frog, the change was still more hideous. She looked like a miserable dwarf, with the head and webbed fingers of a frog. There was something so very pitiful in her eyes, and she had no voice. All she could utter was a hollow croak, like a child who sobs in her dreams. The Viking's wife would take this creature on her lap. Forgetting the ugly form as she looked into those sad eyes, she would often say, "I almost wish that you would never change from being my poor dumb-stricken frog child. For you are more frightful when I see you cloaked in beauty."

Then she would write out runes against illness and witchcraft and throw them over the wretched girl, but it was little good they did.

"One can hardly believe that she was once so tiny that she lay in the cup of a water lily," said the father stork. "She has grown up and is the living image of her Egyptian mother, whom we'll never see again. She did not look out for herself as well as you and those wise men predicted she would. Year in, year out, I've flown to and fro across the Wild Marsh, but never a sign have I seen of her. Yes, I may as well tell you that year after year, when I flew on ahead to make our nest ready and put things in order, I spent whole nights flying over the pool as if I were an owl or a bat, but to no avail. Nor have we found a use for the two sets of swan feathers, which I and our sons took so much trouble to bring all the way from the banks of the Nile. It took us three trips to get them here. For years now they have lain at the bottom of our nest. If perchance a fire broke out and this wooden castle burned down, they would be gone."

"And our good nest would be gone too," the mother stork reminded him. "But you care less for that than you do for your swan feathers and your swamp princess. Sometime you ought to go down in the mire with her and stay there for good. You are a poor father to your children, just as I've been telling you ever since I hatched our first brood. All I hope is that neither we nor our young ones get an arrow shot under our wings by that wild Viking brat. She doesn't know what she is doing. I wish she would realize that this has been our home much longer than it has been hers. We have always been punctilious about paying our rent every year with a feather, an egg, and a young one, according to custom. But do you think that, when she is around, I dare venture down into the yard, as I used to, and as I still do in Egypt, where I am everyone's crony and they let me peer into every pot and kettle? No, I sit up here vexing myself about her—the wench!—and about you, too. You should have left her in the water lily, and that would have been the end of her."

"You aren't as hardhearted as you sound," said the father stork. "I know you better than you know yourself." Up he hopped, twice he beat with his wings, and stretching his legs behind him, off he flew, sailing away without moving his wings until he had gone some distance. Then he took a powerful stroke. The sunlight gleamed on his white feathers. His neck and head were stretched forward. There were speed and swing in his flight.

"After all, he's the handsomest fellow of all," said the mother stork, "but you won't catch me telling him so."

Early that fall the Viking came home with his booty and captives. Among the prisoners was a young Christian priest, one of those who preached against the northern gods. Of late there had been much talk in hall and bower about the new faith that was spreading up from the south, and for which St. Ansgarius had won converts as far north as Hedeby on the Slie. Even young Helga had heard of this faith in the White Christ, who so loved mankind that he had given his life to save them. But as far as she was concerned, as the saying goes, such talk had come in one ear and gone out the other. Love was a meaningless word to her except during those hours when, behind closed doors, she sat shriveled up as a frog. But the Viking's wife had heard the talk, and she felt strangely moved by the stories that were told about the son of the one true God.

Back from their raid, the Vikings told about glorious temples of costly hewn stone, raised in honor of him whose message is one of love. They had brought home with them two massive vessels, artistically wrought in gold, and from these came the scent of strange spices. They were censers, which the Christian priests swung before altars where blood never flowed, but instead the bread and wine were changed into the body and blood of him who had given himself for generations yet unborn.

Bound hand and foot with strips of bark, the young priest was cast into the deep cellars of the Viking's castle. The Viking's wife said that he was as beautiful as the god Balder, and she was sorry for him, but young Helga proposed to have a cord drawn through his feet and tied to the tails of wild oxen.

"Then," she exclaimed, "I would loose the dogs on him. Ho, for the chase through mud and mire! That would be fun to see, and it would be even more fun to chase him."

But this was not the death that the Viking had in mind for this enemy and mocker of the high gods. Instead, he planned to sacrifice the priest on the blood stone in their grove. It would be the first human sacrifice that had ever been offered there.

Young Helga begged her father to let her sprinkle the blood of the victim upon the idols and over the people. When one of the many large, ferocious dogs that hung about the house came within reach while she was sharpening her gleaming knife, she buried the blade in his side, "Just to test its edge," she said.

The Viking's wife looked in distress at this savage, ill-natured girl, and when night came and the beauty of body and soul changed places in the daughter, the mother spoke of the deep sorrow that lay in her heart. The ugly frog with the body of a monster gazed up at her with its sad brown eyes. It seemed to listen, and to understand her as a human being would.

"Never once, even to my husband, have I let fall a word of the two-edged misery you have brought upon me," said the Viking's wife. "My heart is filled with more sorrow for you than I would have thought it could hold, so great is a mother's love. But love never entered into your feelings. Your heart is like a lump of mud, dank and cold. From whence came you into my house?"

The miserable form trembled strangely, as if these words had touched some hidden connection between its soul and it hideous body. Great tears came into those eyes.

"Your time of disaster will come," said the Viking's wife, "and it will be a disastrous time for me, too. Better would it have been to have exposed you beside the highway when you were young, and to have let the cold of the night lull you into the sleep of death." The Viking's wife wept bitter tears. In anger and distress, she passed between the curtains of hides that hung from a beam and divided the chamber.

The shriveled-up frog crouched in a corner. The dead quiet was broken at intervals by her half-stifled sighs. It was as if in pain a new life had been born in her heart. She took a step forward, listened, stepped forward again, and took hold of the heavy bar of the door with her awkward hands. Softly she unbarred the door. Silently she lifted the latch. She picked up the lamp that flickered in the hall outside, and it seemed that some great purpose had given her strength. She drew back the iron bolt from the well-secured cellar door, and stole down to the prisoner. He was sleeping as she touched him with her cold, clammy hand. When he awoke and saw the hideous monster beside him, he shuddered as if he had seen an evil specter. She drew her knife, severed his bonds, and beckoned for him to follow her.

He uttered holy names and made the sign of the Cross. As the creature remained unchanged, he said, in the words of the Bible:

"'Blessed is he that considereth the poor. The Lord will deliver him in time of trouble.' Who are you, that in guise of an animal are so gentle and merciful?"

The frog beckoned for him to follow her. She led him behind sheltering curtains and down a long passage to the stable, where she pointed to a horse. When he mounted it, she jumped up in front ot him, clinging fast to the horse's mane. The prisoner understood her, and speedily they rode out on the open heath by a path he could never have found.

He ignored her ugly shape, for he knew that the grace and kindness of God could take strange forms. When he prayed and sang hymns, she trembled. Was it the power of song and prayer that affected her, or was she shivering at the chill approach of dawn? What had come over her?

She rose up, trying to stop the horse so that she could dismount, but the Christian priest held her with all his might, and chanted a psalm in the hope that it might have power to break the spell which held her in the shape of a hideous frog.

The horse dashed on, more wildly than ever. The skies turned red, and the first ray of the sun broke through the clouds. In that first flash of sunlight she changed. She became the lovely maiden with the cruel, fiendish temper. The priest was alarmed to find himself holding a fair maid in his arms. He checked the horse, and sprang off it, thinking he faced some new trick of the devil. Young Helga sprang down too, and the child's smock that she wore was so short that it came only to her knee. From the belt of it she snatched her sharp knife, and attacked the startled priest.

"Let me get at you," she screamed. "Let me get at you and plunge my knife in your heart. You are as pale as straw, you beardless slave!"

She closed with him, and fiercely they struggled together, but an unseen power seemed to strengthen the Christian priest. He held her fast, and the old oak tree under which they stood helped him, for it entangled her feet in its projecting roots. With clear water from a nearby spring, the priest sprinkled her neck and face, commanding the unclean spirit to leave her, and blessing her with the sign of the Cross in Christian fashion. But the waters of baptism have no power unless faith wells from within.

Even so, against the evil that struggled within her, he had opposed a power more mighty than his own human strength. Her arms dropped to her sides, as she gazed in pale-faced astonishment at this man whom she took for a mighty magician, skilled in sorcery and in the secret arts. Those were magic runes he had repeated, and mystic signs he had traced in the air. She would not have flinched had he shaken a keen knife or a sharp ax in her face, but she flinched now as he made the sign of the Cross over her head and heart. She sat like a tame bird, with her head drooped upon her breast.

Gently he spoke to her of the great kindness she had shown him during the night, when she had come in the guise of a hideous frog to sever his bonds and to lead him out into light and life again. He said she was bound by stronger bonds than those which had bound him, but that he would lead her out of darkness to eternal life. He would take her to the holy Ansgarius at Hedeby, and there in the Christian city, the spell that had power over her would be broken. But he would not let her sit before him on the horse, even though she wished it. He dared not.

"You must sit behind me on the horse, not in front of me," he said, "for your enchanted beauty has a power that comes of evil, and I fear it. Yet, with the help of the Lord, I shall win through to victory."

He knelt and prayed devoutly and sincerely. It seemed as if the quiet wood became a church, consecrated by his prayers. The birds began to sing as if they belonged to the new congregation. The wild mint smelled sweet, as if to replace incense and ambergris, and the young priest recited these words from the Bible:

"To give light to them that sit in darkness, and in the shadow of death; to guide our feet into the ways of peace."

While he spoke of the life everlasting, the horse that had carried them in wild career stood quietly by and pulled at the tall bramble bushes until the ripe juicy berries fell into Helga's hand, offering themselves for her refreshment.

Patiently, she let herself be lifted on horseback, and sat there like one in a trance, neither quite awake nor quite asleep. The priest tied two green branches in the shape of a cross, and held it high as they rode through the woods. The shrubs grew thicker and thicker, until at last they rode along in a pathless wilderness.

Bushes of the wild sloe blocked their way so that they had to ride around these thickets. The springs flowed no longer into little streams but into standing ponds, and they had to ride around these, too. But the cool breezes of the forest refreshed and strengthened them, and there was no less strength in the words of faith and Christian love that the young priest found to say, because of his great desire to lead this poor lost soul back to light and life.

They say that raindrops will wear a hollow in the hardest stone, and that the waves of the sea will in time wear the roughest stones smooth and round. Thus did the dew of mercy, which fell on Helga, soften that which was hard, and smooth that which was rough in her nature. Not that any change could yet be seen, or that she knew she was changing, any more than the seed in the ground is aware that the rain and the warm sun will cause it to grow and burst into flower.

When a mother's song unconsciously impresses itself on her child's memory, he babbles the words after her without understanding, but in time, they assume order in his mind and become meaningful to him. Even so, God's healing word began to impress itself on Helga's heart.

They rode out of the wilderness, crossed a heath, and rode on through another pathless forest. There, toward evening, they met with a robber band.

"Where did you kidnap this beautiful wench?" the robbers shouted. They stopped the horse and dragged the two riders from its back.

The priest was surrounded, and he was unarmed except for the knife he had taken from Helga, but with this he now tried to defend her. As one of the robbers swung his ax, the priest sprang aside to avoid the blow, which fell instead on the neck of the horse. Blood spurted forth, and the animal fell to the ground. Startled out of the deep trance in which she had ridden all day, Helga sprang forward and threw herself over the dying horse. The priest stood by to shield and defend her, but one of the robbers raised his iron hammer and brought it down on the priest's head so hard that he bashed it in. Brains and blood spattered about as the priest fell down dead.

The robbers seized little Helga by her white arms, but it was sundown, and as the sun's last beam vanished, she turned back into a frog. The greenish white mouth took up half her face, her arms turned spindly and slimy, and her hands turned into broad, webbed fans. In terror and amazement, the robbers let go of this hideous creature. Froglike she hopped as high as her head and bounded into the thicket. The robbers felt sure this was one of Loki's evil tricks, or some such secret black magic, so they fled from the place in terror.

The full moon rose. It shone in all its splendor as poor frog-shaped Helga crept out of the thicket and crouched beside the slain priest and the slaughtered horse. She stared at them with eyes that seemed to weep, and she gave a sob like the sound of a child about to burst into tears. She threw herself on first one and then the other. She fetched them water in her large hands, which could hold a great deal because of the webbed skin, and poured it over them, but dead they were and dead they would remain. At last, she realized this. Wild animals would come soon and devour their bodies. But no, that must not be!

She dug into the ground as well as she could, trying to make for them a grave as deep as possible. But she had nothing to dig with except the branch of her tree and her own two hands. The webs between her fingers were torn by her labors until they bled, and she made so little headway that she saw the task was beyond her. Then she brought clear water to wash the dead man's face, which she covered with fresh green leaves. She brought large branches to cover him, and scattered dry leaves between them. Then she brought the heaviest stones she could carry, piled them over the body, and filled in the cracks with moss. Now she thought the mound would be strong and safe, but the difficult task had taken her all night long. The sun came up, and there stood young Helga in all her beauty, with blood on her hands and for the first time maidenly tears on her flushed cheeks.

During this transformation, it seemed as if two natures were contending within her. She trembled, and looked about her as if she had just awakened from a nightmare. She took hold of the slender branch of a tree for support. Presently she climbed like a cat to the topmost branches of this tree, and clung there. Like a frightened squirrel, she stayed there the whole day through, in the deep solitude of the forest where all is dead still, as they say.

Dead still! Why, butterflies fluttered all about in play or strife. At the ant hills nearby, hundreds of busy little workmen hurried in and out. The air was filled with countless dancing gnats, swarms of buzzing flies, ladybugs, dragonflies with golden wings, and other winged creatures. Earthworms crawled up from the moist earth, and moles came out. Oh, except for all these, the people might be right when they call the forest "dead still."

No one paid any attention to little Helga except the jays that flew screeching to the tree top where she perched. Bold and curious, they hopped about her in the branches, but there was a look in her eyes that soon put them to flight. They could not make her out, any more than she could understand herself. When evening came on, the setting sun gave warning that it was time for her to change, and it aroused her to activity again. She had no sooner climbed down than the last beam of the sun faded out, and once more she sat there, a shriveled frog with the torn webbed skin covering her hands.

But now her eyes shone with a new beauty that in her lovely form they had not possessed. They were gentle, tender, maidenly eyes. And though they looked out through the mask of a frog, they reflected the deep feelings of a human heart. They brimmed over with tears— precious drops that lightened her heart.

Beside the grave mound lay the Cross of green boughs that had been tied together with bark string, the last work of him who lay buried there. Helga picked it up, and the thought came to her to plant it between the stones that covered the man and the horse. Memory of the priest brought fresh tears to her eyes, and with a full heart she made cross marks in the earth around the grave, as a fence that would guard it well. When with both hands she made the sign of the Cross, the webbed membrane fell from her fingers like a torn glove. She washed her hands at the forest spring, and gazed in amazement at their delicate whiteness. Again, in the air she made the holy sign between herself and the dead man. Her lips trembled, her tongue moved and the name she had heard the priest mention so often during their ride through the woods rose to her lips. She uttered the name of the savior.

The frog's skin fell from her. Once more she was a lovely maiden. But her head hung heavy. She was much in need of rest, and she fell asleep.

However, she did not sleep for long. She awoke at midnight and saw before her the dead horse, prancing and full of life. A shining light came from his eyes and from the wound in his neck. Beside him stood the martyred Christian priest, "more beautiful than Balder," the Viking woman had truly said, for he stood in a flash of flame.

There was such an air of gravity and of righteous justice in the penetrating glance of his great, kind eyes that she felt as if he were looking into every corner of her heart. Little Helga trembled under his gaze, and her memories stirred within her as though this were Judgment Day. Every kindness that had been done her and each loving word spoken to her, were fresh in her mind. Now she understood how it had been love that sustained her through those days of trial, during which all creatures made of dust and spirit, soul and clay, must wrestle and strive. She realized that she had only obeyed the impulse of her inclinations. She had not saved herself. Everything had been given to her, and Providence had guided her. Now, in humility and shame, she bent before him who could read every thought in her heart, and at that moment she felt the pure light of the Holy Spirit enter her soul.

"Daughter of the marsh," the priest said, "out of the earth and the marsh you came, and from this earth you shall rise again. The light in you that is not of the sun but of God, shall return to its source, remembering the body in which it has lain. No soul shall be lost. Things temporal are full of emptiness, but things eternal are the source of life. I come from the land of the dead. Someday, you too shall pass through the deep valley to the shining mountain tops, where compassion and perfection dwell. I cannot lead you to receive Christian baptism at Hedeby, for you must first break the watery veil that covers the deep marsh and bring out of its depths the living source of your birth and your being. You must perform a blessed act before you may be blessed."

He lifted her on the horse and put in her hand a golden censer, like the ones she had seen in the Viking's castle. From it rose a sweet incense, and the wound in the martyr's forehead shone like a diadem. He took the cross from the grave and raised it high as they rose swiftly through the air, over the rustling woods and over the mounds where the heroes of old are buried, each astride his dead war horse. These mighty warriors rose and rode up to the top of the mounds. Golden crowns shone on their foreheads in the moonlight, and their cloaks billowed behind them in the night wind. The dragon on guard over his treasure also lifted his head and watched them pass. Goblins peered up from their hills and hollows, where they swarmed to and fro with red, blue, and green lights as numerous as the sparks of burning paper.

Away over the forest and heath, river and swamp, they hastened until they circled over the Wild Marsh. The priest held aloft the cross, which shone like gold. From his lips fell holy prayers. Little Helga joined in the hymns that he sang, as a child follows its mother's song. She swung the censer, and it gave forth a churchly incense so miraculously fragrant that the reeds and sedges burst into bloom, every seed in the depths sent forth stalks, and all things flourished that had a spark of life within them. Water lilies spread over the surface of the pool like a carpet patterned with flowers, and on this carpet a young and beautiful woman lay asleep. Helga thought this was her own reflection, mirrored in the unruffled water. But what she saw was her mother, the princess from the land of the Nile, who had become the Marsh King's wife.

The martyred priest commanded that the sleeper be lifted up on horseback. Under this new burden, the horse sank down as though his body were an empty, wind-blown shroud. But the sign of the Cross lent strength to the spectral horse, and he carried all three riders back to solid earth.

Then crowed the cock in the Viking's castle, and the spectral figures became a part of the mist that drove before the wind. But the Egyptian princess and her daughter were left there, face to face.

"Is this myself I see, reflected in the deep waters?" cried the mother.

"Is this myself I see, mirrored on the bright surface?" the daughter exclaimed. As they approached one another and met in a heart-to-heart embrace, the mother's heart beat faster, and it was the mother who understood.

"My child! My heart's own flower, my lotus from beneath the waters." She threw her arms about the child and wept. For little Helga, these tears were a fresh baptism of life and love.

"I flew hither in the guise of a swan," Helga's mother told her. "Here I stripped off that plumage and fell into the quagmire. The deep morass closed over me like a wall, and I felt a strong current—a strange power—drag me deeper and deeper. I felt sleep weigh down my eyelids. I slumbered and dreamed. I dreamed that I stood again in the Egyptian pyramid, yet the swaying alder stump that had frightened me so on the surface of the morass stood ever before me. As I watched the check marks in its bark, they took on bright colors and turned into hieroglyphics. I was looking at the casket of a mummy. It burst open, and from it stepped that monarch of a thousand years ago. His mummy was pitch black, a shining, slimy black, like the wood snail or like the mud of the swamp. Whether it was the Marsh King or that mummy of the pyramid, I know not. He threw his arms around me, and I felt that I would die. When I came back to consciousness, I felt something warm over my heart, and there nestled a little bird, twittering and fluttering its wings. From my heart it flew into the heavy darkness overhead, but a long, green strand still bound it to me. I heard and understood its plaintive song, 'To freedom, to the sunlight, to our Father!' Then I remembered my own father, in the sunflooded land of my birth, my life, and my love. I loosed the strand and let the little bird fly home to my father. From that moment, I have known no other dreams. I have slept, long and deep, until this hour when wondrous sounds and incense woke me and set me free."

What had become of that green strand between the mother's heart and the heart and the bird's wing? Where did it flutter now? What had become of it? Only the stork had ever seen it. That strand was the green stalk, and the bow at the end of it was the bright flower that had cradled the child, who was grown in beauty and now rested once more on her mother's heart.

As they stood there in each other's arms, the stork circled over their heads. Away he flew to his nest for the two sets of swan feathers that he had stored there for so many years. He dropped these sets of feathers upon the mother and daughter, and, once the plumage had covered them, they rose from the ground as two white swans.

"Let's have a chat," said the father stork, "for now we can understand one another, even though different birds have different beaks. It's the luckiest thing in the world that I found you tonight. Tomorrow we shall be on our way, Mother, the young ones, and I, all flying south. Yes, you well may stare. I am your old friend from the banks of the Nile, and Mother is too. Her heart is softer than her beak. She always did say the princess could look out for herself, but I and our sons brought these sets of swan feathers up here. Why, how happy this makes me, and how lucky it is that I am still here. At daybreak we shall set out, with a great company of storks. We shall fly in the vanguard, and if you follow us closely you can't miss your way. The young ones and I will keep an eye on you, too."

"And the lotus flower which I was to fetch," said the Egyptian princess, "now flies beside me in the guise of a swan. I bring with me the flower that touched my heart, and the riddle has been solved. Home we go!"

But Helga said she could not leave the land of the Danes until she had once more seen her good foster mother, the Viking's wife. Helga vividly recalled every fond moment spent with her, every kind word, and even every tear she had caused the foster mother to shed. At that moment she almost felt that she loved her foster mother best of all.

"Yes, we must go to the Viking's castle," said the father stork. "Mother and the young ones are waiting for me there. How their eyes will pop and their beaks will rattle! Mother is no great one for talking. She's a bit curt and dry, but she means very well. Now I must make a great to-do so that they will know we are coming."

So the father stork rattled his beak as he and the swans flew home to the Viking's castle.

Everyone there lay sound asleep. The Viking's wife had gone to bed late that night because she was so worried about Helga, who had been missing ever since the Christian priest disappeared three days ago. She must have helped him escape, for it was her horse that was gone from the stable. But what power could have brought this about? The Viking's wife thought of all the miracles she had heard were performed by the White Christ and by those who had the faith to follow Him. Her troubled thoughts gave way to dreams. She dreamed that she lay there, on her bed, still awake, still lost in thought while darkness reigned outside. A storm blew up. To the east and to the west she heard the high seas roll—waves of the North Sea and waves of the Kattegat. The great snake, which in the depth of the ocean coils around Earth, was in convulsions of terror. It was the twilight of the gods, Ragnarok, as the heathens called Judgment Day, when all would perish, even their highest gods. The war horn sounded, and over the rainbow bridge the gods rode, clad in steel, to fight their last great fight. The winged Valkyries charged on before them, and dead heroes marched behind. The whole firmament blazed with the northern lights, yet darkness conquered in the end. It was an awful hour.

Beside the terror-stricken dreamer, little Helga seemed to crouch on the floor, in the ugly frog's shape. She shuddered, and crept close to her foster mother, who took the creature up in her lap and, hideous though it was, lovingly caressed it. The air resounded with the clashing of swords and clubs, and the rattle of arrows like a hailstorm upon the roof. The hour had come when Heaven and Earth would perish, the stars would fall, and everything be swallowed up by Surtur's sea of fire. Yet she knew there would be a new Heaven and a new Earth. The grain would grow in waving fields where the sea now rolled over the golden sands.

Then the god whose name could not yet be spoken would reign at last, and to him would come Balder, so mild and loving, raised up from the kingdom of the dead. He came, and the Viking's wife saw him clearly. She knew his face, which was that of the captive Christian priest. "The White Christ," she cried aloud, and as she spoke that name she kissed the ugly brow of her frog child. Off fell the frog skin, and it was Helga who stood before her in radiant beauty, gentle as she had never been before, and with beaming eyes. She kissed her foster mother's hands, and blessed her for all the loving kindness that had been lavished upon her in those days of bitter trials and sorrow. She thanked the Viking's wife for the thoughts she had nurtured in her, and for calling upon the name which she repeated—the White Christ. And little Helga arose in the shape of a white, mighty swan. With the rushing sound of a flock of birds of passage taking flight, she spread her powerful wings.

The Viking's wife awakened to hear this very same noise overhead. She knew it was about time for the storks to fly south, and that they must be what she heard. She wanted to see them once more and bid them good luck for their journey, so she got up and went out on her balcony. There, on the roofs of all the outbuildings she saw stork upon stork, and all round the castle bands of storks whirled in widening circles above the high trees. Directly in front of her, beside the well where Helga had so often sat and frightened her with wild behavior, two white swans were sitting. They looked up at her with such expressive eyes that it recalled her dream, which still seemed to her almost real. She thought of Helga in the guise of a swan. She thought of the Christian priest, and suddenly her heart felt glad. The swans waved their wings and bowed their necks to her as if in greeting. The Viking's wife held out her arms as if she understood, and thinking of many things, she smiled at them through her tears.

Then, with a great clattering of beaks and flapping of wings, the storks all started south.

"We won't wait for those swans," said the mother stork. "If they want to go with us they had better come now. We can't dillydally here until the plovers start. It is nicer to travel as we do in a family group, instead of like the finches and partridges, among whom the males and females fly in separate flocks. I call that downright scandalous. And what kind of strokes do those swans call those that they are making?"

"Oh, everyone has his own way of flying," the father stork said. "Swans fly in a slantwise line, cranes in a triangle, and the plovers in snakelike curves."

"Don't talk about snakes while we are flying up here," said the mother stork. "It will put greedy thoughts in the young ones' heads at a time when they can't be appeased."

"Are those the high mountains of which I have heard?" Helga asked as she flew along in the swan plumage.

"There are thunder clouds, billowing below us," her mother told her.

"And what are the white clouds that rise to such heights?" Helga asked.

"Those heights that you see are the mountains that are always capped with snow," her mother said, as they flew over the Alps, out over the blue Mediterranean.

"African sands! Egyptian strands!" In the upper air through which her swan wings soared, the daughter of the Nile rejoiced when she spied once more the yellow wave-washed coast of her native country. The storks spied it too, and they quickened their flight.

"I can sniff the Nile mud and the juicy frogs," the mother stork cried. "What an appetizing feeling! Yes, there you shall have fine eating and things to see—marabou storks, ibises, and cranes. They are all cousins of ours, but not nearly so handsome as we. They are vain creatures, especially the ibises. The Egyptians stuff them with spices and make mummies of them, and this has quite turned their heads. As for me, I would rather be stuffed with live frogs, and so would you, and so you shall be. Better to have your mouth well stuffed when you are alive than have such a to-do made over you when you are dead. That's the only way I feel about it, and I am always right."

"The storks have come back," said the people in the magnificent home on the banks of the Nile where, on a leopard skin spread over soft cushions in the lofty hall, the master lay between life and death, waiting and hoping for the lotus flower from the deep marshes in the far north. His kinsmen and servants were standing beside his couch, when into the room flew two magnificent white swans who had come with the storks. They doffed their glistening swan feathers, and there stood two lovely women who resembled each other as closely as two drops of water. They bent over the pale, feeble old man, and threw back their long hair. When little Helga leaned above her grandfather, the color returned to his cheeks, light to his eyes, and life to his stiffened limbs. Hale and hearty, the old man rose. His daughter and granddaughter threw their arms around him, as if they were joyously greeting him on the morning after a long and trying dream.

Great was the rejoicing in that house, and in the stork's nest, too, though the storks rejoiced chiefly because of the good food and the abundance of frogs. While the learned men sketchily scribbled down the story of the two princesses, and of the healing flower that had brought such a blessing to that household and throughout all the land, in their own way the parent storks told the story to their children, but not until all of them were full, or they would have had better things to do than listen to stories.

"Now you will become a somebody at last," the mother stork whispered. "It's the least we can expect."

"Oh, what would I become?" said the father stork. "What have I done? Nothing much."

"You have done more than all the others put together. Except for you and our young ones, the two princesses would never have seen Egypt again, nor would the old man have been healed. You will assuredly become a somebody. At the very least, they will give you the title of doctor, and our young ones will inherit it, and their little ones after them. Why, at least to my eyes, you already have the look of an Egyptian doctor."

The wise and learned men propounded the basic principle, as they called it, on which the whole matter rested. "Love brings life," was their doctrine, and this they explained in different ways. "The warm sunbeam was the Egyptian princess. She descended unto the Marsh King, and from their meeting, the flower arose."

"I can't quite repeat the exact words," said the father stork, who had been listening on the roof and wanted to tell his family all about it. "What they said was so incomprehensibly wise that they were given titles and presents too. Even the chief cook was rewarded, no doubt for his soup."

"And what was your reward?" the mother stork wanted to know. "It was not right for them to pass over the most important one in the whole affair, which is just what you are. The learned men did nought but wag their tongues. However, I have no doubt that your turn will come."

Late that night, when the happy household lay peacefully asleep, there was one person left awake. This was not the father stork, who, like a drowsy sentry, stood in his nest on one leg. No, this wide-awake person was little Helga. She leaned over the rail of her balcony and looked up through the clear air at the great shining stars. They were larger and more lustrous than she had ever seen them in the North, but they were the same stars. She thought of the Viking's wife near the Wild Marsh, of her gentle eyes, and of the tears which she had shed over her poor frog child, who now was standing in the splendor of the clear starlight and the wonderful spring air by the waters of the Nile. She thought of the love that filled the heathen woman's heart, the love she had shown that wretched creature who was hateful in her human form and dreadful to see or touch in her animal shape. She looked at the shining stars and was reminded of the glory that had gleamed on the brow of the martyred priest when he flew with her over moor and forest. She recalled the tone of his voice. She recalled those words he had said, when they rode together and she sat like an evil spirit—those words that had to do with that high source of the greatest love that encompasses all mankind throughout all the generations.

Yes, what had she not received, won, gained! Night and day, Helga was absorbed in contemplating her happiness. She regarded it like a child who turns so quickly from the giver to all those wonderful gifts. Her happy thoughts ran on to the even greater happiness that could lie ahead, and would lie ahead. On and on she thought, until she so lost herself in dreams of future bliss that she forgot the giver of all good things. It was the wanton pride of her youth that led her on into the pitfall. Her eyes were bright with pride when a sudden noise in the yard below recalled her straying thoughts. She saw two large ostriches rushing about in narrow circles, and never before had she seen this animal, this huge, fat, and awkward bird. The wings looked as if they had been roughly handled. When she asked why this was, for the first time she heard the legend that Egyptians tell about the ostrich.

Once, they said, the ostriches were a race of glorious and beautiful birds with wings both wide and strong. One evening the other large birds of the forest said to the ostrich, "Brother, shall we fly to the river tomorrow, God willing, and quench our thirst?"

"Yes," the ostrich answered, "so I will." At dawn, away they flew. First they flew aloft toward the sun, which is the eye of God. Higher and higher the ostrich flew, far ahead of all the other birds. In his pride he flew straight toward the light, vaunting his own strength and paying no heed to him from whom strength comes. "God willing," he did not say.

Then, suddenly the avenging angel drew aside the veil from the flaming seas of the sun, and in an instant the wings of that proud bird was burned away, and he wretchedly tumbled to Earth. Never since that day has the ostrich or any of his family been able to rise in the air. He can only flee timidly along the ground and run about in circles. He is a warning to us that in all human thoughts and deeds we should say, "God willing."

Helga bowed her head in thoughts. As the ostrich rushed about, she observed how timorous he was and what vain pride he took in the size of the shadow he cast on the white, sunlit wall.

She devoted herself to more serious thoughts. A happy life had been given her, but what was to come of it? Great things, "God willing."

When, in the early spring, the storks made ready to fly north again, Helga took the golden bracelet from her arm and scratched her name upon it. She beckoned to the father stork, slipped the golden band around his neck, and told him to take it to the Viking's wife, as a sign that her adopted daughter was alive, and happy, and had not forgotten her.

"It's a heavy thing to carry," the father stork thought, as he wore it around his neck. "But gold and honor are not to be tossed away on the highroad. The people up there will indeed be saying that the stork brings luck."

"You lay gold and I lay eggs," the mother stork told him, "although you lay only once, while I lay every year. Neither of us gets any thanks for it, which is most discouraging."

"One knows when he's done his duty," the father stork said.

"But you can't hang such knowledge up for all to admire," she said. "Neither will it bring you a favorable wind nor a full meal." Then away they flew.

The little nightingale who sang in the tamarind tree would also be flying north soon. Helga had often heard him singing up near the Wild Marsh. She decided to use him as a messenger, for she had learned the language of the birds when she flew in the guise of a swan, and as she had often talked with the storks and swallows she knew the little nightingale would understand her. She begged him to fly to the beech forest in Jutland, where she had built the tomb of stone and branches. She begged him to tell all the little birds there to guard the grave, and to sing there often. The nightingale flew away—and time went flying by.

That fall, the eagle that perched on the pyramid saw a magnificent caravan of camels, richly laden and accompanied by armed men. These men were splendidly robed and were mounted on prancing Arab horses as white as shining silver, with quivering pink nostrils and big flowing manes that swept down to their slender legs. A royal prince of Arabia, handsome as a prince should be, came as an honored guest to the palace where the storks' nest now stood empty. The nest-owners had been away in the far North, but they would soon return. They did return, on the very evening when the festive celebration was at its height.

It was the wedding that was being celebrated, and the bride was lovely Helga, jeweled and robed in silk. The bridegroom was the young Arabian prince. They sat at the head of the table, between Helga's mother and grandfather. But Helga was not watching the bridegroom's handsome bronzed face, round which his black beard curled. Nor was she looking into the dark, fiery eyes that he fixed upon her. She was staring out at a bright, glistening star that shone down from the sky.

Then there was a rush of wings through the air, and the storks came back. Tired though they were, and badly as they needed rest after their journey, the two old parent storks flew straight to the veranda railing. They knew of the marriage feast, and at the frontier they had already heard news that Helga had commanded their pictures to be painted on the walls, for truly they were a part of her life story.

"That certainly was very nice and thoughtful," said the father stork.

"It was little enough," the mother stork told him. "She could hardly do less."

When Helga saw them, she rose from the table and went out on the veranda to stroke their backs. The old storks bowed their heads, while the youngest of their children looked on and appreciated the honor bestowed on them.

Helga looked up at the bright star, which grew yet more brilliant and clear. Between her and the star hovered a form even purer than the air, and therefore visible through it. As it floated down quite near her, she saw that it was the martyred priest. He too came to her wedding feast—came from the Kingdom of Heaven.

"The splendor and happiness up there," he said, "surpass all that is known on Earth."

More humbly and fervently than she had ever yet prayed, Helga asked that for one brief moment she might be allowed to go there and cast a single glance into the bright Kingdom of Heaven. Then he raised her up in splendor and glory, through a stream of melody and thoughts. The sound and the brightness were not only around her but within her soul as well. They lay beyond all words.

"We must go back, or you will be missed," the martyred priest said to her.

"Only one more glance," she begged. "Only one brief moment more."

"We must go back to Earth, for all your guests are leaving."

"Only one more look! The last!"

Then Helga stood again on the veranda, but all the torches had been extinguished, and the banquet hall was dark. The storks were gone. No guests were to be seen, and no bridegroom. All had vanished in those three brief moments.

A great fear fell upon her. She wandered through the huge, empty hall into the next room, where foreign soldiers lay asleep. She opened the side door that led into her own bedroom. When she thought she had entered it, she found herself in the garden, but it wasn't the garden she knew. Red gleamed the sky, for it was the break of day. Only three moments in Heaven, and a long time had passed on Earth.

She saw the storks and called to them in their own language. The father stork turned his head, listened and came down to her.

"You speak our language," he admitted. "What is your wish, strange woman, and why do you come here?"

"But it is I—Helga. Do you not know me? Only three moments ago we were talking together over there on the veranda."

"You are mistaken," the stork said. "You must have dreamed it."

"No, no!" she said, and reminded him of the Viking's castle, of the Wild Marsh, and of the journey hither.

Then the father stork blinked his eyes. "Why, that is a very old story that my great-great-grandmother told me," he said. "Truly, there once was a princess in Egypt who came from the land of the Danes. But she disappeared on the night of her wedding, hundreds of years ago, and never was seen again. You may read about it yourself, there on the monument in the garden. Swans and storks are carved upon it, and at the top is your own figure, sculptured in white marble."

And this was true. Little Helga saw it, understood it, and dropped upon her knees.

The sun shone brightly in all its splendor. As in the old days when at the first touch of sunlight the frog's skin fell away to reveal a beautiful maiden, so now, in that baptism by the sun a form of heavenly beauty, clearer and purer than the air itself, rose as a bright beam to join the Father. The body crumbled to dust, and only a wilted lotus flower lay where she had knelt.

"Well," said the father stork. "That's a new ending to the story. I hadn't expected it, but I liked it quite well."

"How will the young ones like it?" the mother stork wondered.

"Ah," said the father stork, "that certainly is the most important thing, after all."

PEN AND INKSTAND (1859)

In a poet's study, somebody made a remark as he looked at the inkstand that was standing on the table: "It's strange what can come out of that inkstand! I wonder what the next thing will be. Yes, it's strange!"

"That it is!" said the Inkstand. "It's unbelievable, that's what I have always said." The Inkstand was speaking to the Pen and to everything else on the table that could hear it. "It's really amazing what comes out of me! Almost incredible! I actually don't know myself what will come next when that person starts to dip into me. One drop from me is enough for half a piece of paper, and what may not be on it then? I am something quite remarkable. All the works of this poet come from me. These living characters, whom people think they recognize, these deep emotions, that gay humor, the charming descriptions of nature—I don't understand those myself, because I don't know anything about nature—all of that is in me. From me have come out, and still come out, that host of lovely maidens and brave knights on snorting steeds. The fact is, I assure you, I don't know anything about them myself."

"You are right about that," said the Pen. "You have very few ideas, and don't bother about thinking much at all. If you did take the trouble to think, you would understand that nothing comes out of you except a liquid. You just supply me with the means of putting down on paper what I have in me; that's what I write with. It's the pen that does the writing. Nobody doubts that, and most people know as much about poetry as an old inkstand!"

"You haven't had much experience," retorted the Inkstand. "You've hardly been in service a week, and already you're half worn out. Do you imagine you're the poet? Why, you're only a servant; I have had a great many like you before you came, some from the goose family and some of English make. I'm familiar with both quill pens and steel pens. Yes, I've had a great many in my service, and I'll have many more when the man who goes through the motions for me comes to write down what he gets from me. I'd be much interested in knowing what will be the next thing he gets from me."

"Inkpot!" cried the Pen.

Late that evening the Poet came home. He had been at a concert, had heard a splendid violinist, and was quite thrilled with his marvelous performance. From his instrument he had drawn a golden river of melody. Sometimes it had sounded like the gentle murmur of rippling water drops, wonderful pearl-like tones, sometimes like a chorus of twittering birds, sometimes like a tempest tearing through mighty forests of pine. The Poet had fancied he heard his own heart weep, but in tones as sweet as the gentle voice of a woman. It seemed as if the music came not only from the strings of the violin, but from its sounding board, its pegs, its very bridge. It was amazing! The selection had been extremely difficult, but it had seemed as if the bow were wandering over the strings merely in play. The performance was so easy that an ignorant listener might have thought he could do it himself. The violin seemed to sound, and the bow to play, of their own accord, and one forgot the master who directed them, giving them life and soul. Yes, the master was forgotten, but the Poet remembered him. He repeated his name and wrote down his thoughts.

"How foolish it would be for the violin and bow to boast of their achievements! And yet we human beings often do so. Poets, artists, scientists, generals—we are all proud of ourselves, and yet we're only instruments in the hands of our Lord! To him alone be the glory! We have nothing to be arrogant about."

Yes, that is what the Poet wrote down, and he titled his essay "The Master and the Instruments."

"That ought to hold you, madam," said the Pen, when the two were alone again. "Did you hear him read aloud what I had written?"

"Yes, I heard what I gave you to write," said the Inkstand. "It was meant for you and your conceit. It's strange that you can't tell when anyone is making fun of you. I gave you a pretty sharp cut there; surely I must know my own satire!"

"Inkpot!" said the Pen.

"Scribble-stick!" said the Inkstand.

They were both satisfied with their answers, and it is a great comfort to feel that one has made a witty reply—one sleeps better afterward. So they both went to sleep.

But the Poet didn't sleep. His thoughts rushed forth like the violin's tones, falling like pearls, sweeping on like a storm through the forest.

He understood the sentiments of his own heart; he caught a ray of the light from the everlasting Master.

To him alone be the glory!

THE BUTTERFLY (1860)

The Butterfly wanted a sweetheart, and naturally he wanted one of the prettiest of the dear little flowers. He looked at each of them; there they all sat on their stalks as quiet and modest as little maidens ought to sit before they are engaged; but there were so many to choose from that it would be quite difficult to decide. So the Butterfly flew down to the Daisy, whom the French call "Marguerite." They know she can tell fortunes. This is the way it's done: the lovers pluck off the little petals one by one, asking questions about each other, "Does he love me from the heart? A little? A lot? Or loves he not at all?"—or something like that; everyone asks in his own language. So the Butterfly also came to ask, but he wouldn't bite off the leaves; instead he kissed each one in turn, thinking that kindness is the best policy.

"Sweet Miss Marguerite Daisy," he said, "you're the wisest woman of all the flowers—you can tell fortunes! Tell me, should I choose this one or that one? Which one am I to have? When you have told me, I can fly straight to her and propose."

But Marguerite answered not a word. She resented his calling her "a woman," for she was unmarried and quite young. He put his question a second time, and then a third time, and when he still couldn't get a word out of her, he gave up and flew away to begin his wooing.

It was early spring; the snowdrops and crocuses were growing in abundance. "They're really very charming," said the Butterfly. "Neat little schoolgirls, but a bit too sweet." For, like all very young men, he preferred older girls. So he flew to the anemones, but they were a bit too bitter for his taste. The violets were a little too sentimental, the tulips much too gay, the lilies too middle class, the linden blossoms too small, and, besides, there were too many in their family. He admitted the apple blossoms looked like roses, but if they opened one day and the wind blew they fell to pieces the very next; surely such a marriage would be far too brief. He liked the sweet pea best of all; she was red and white, dainty and delicate, and belonged to that class of domestic girl who is pretty yet useful in the kitchen. He was about to propose to her when he noticed a pea pod hanging nearby, with a withered flower clinging to it. "Who's that?" he asked.

"It's my sister," said the pea flower.

"Oh, so that's how you'll look later on!" This frightened the Butterfly, and away he flew.

Honeysuckles hung over the hedges; there were plenty of those girls, long-faced and with yellow complexions. No, he didn't like that kind at all. Yes, but what *did* he like? You ask him!

Spring passed and summer passed; then autumn came, and he was still no nearer making up his mind. Now the flowers wore beautiful, colorful dresses, but what good did that do? The fresh, fragrant youth had passed, and it is fragrance the heart needs as one grows older; and of course dahlias and hollysocks have no particular fragrance. So the Butterfly went to see the mint.

"It's not exactly a flower—or rather it's all flower, fragrant from root to top, with sweet scent in every leaf. Yes, she's the one I want!" So at last he proposed to her.

But the mint stood stiff and silent, and at last said, "Friendship, if you like, but nothing else. I'm old, and you're old, too. It would be all right to live for each other, but marriage—no! Don't let's make fools of ourselves in our old age!"

And so the Butterfly did not find a sweetheart at all. He had hesitated too long, and one shouldn't do that! The Butterfly became an old bachelor, as we call it.

Now it was a windy and wet late autumn; the wind blew cold down the backs of the poor trembling old willows. And that made them creak all over. When the weather is like that it isn't pleasant to fly about in summer clothing, outside. But the Butterfly was not flying out-of-doors; he had happened to fly into a room where there was a fire in the stove and the air was as warm as summer. Here he could at least keep alive. "But just to keep alive isn't enough," he said. "To live you must have sunshine and freedom and a little flower to love!"

And he flew against the windowpane, was noticed by people, admired, and set on a needle to be stored in a butterfly collection. This was the most they could do for him.

"Now I'm sitting on a stalk, just like the flowers," said the Butterfly. "It isn't very much fun; it's just like being married, you're bound up so tightly!" He comforted himself with this reflection.

"A poor consolation, after all," said the pot plants in the room.

"But you can't take the opinion of pot plants," thought the Butterfly. "They converse too much with human beings!"

THE BEETLE (1861)

The emperor's horse was shod with gold—a golden shoe on each of its feet.

And why was he getting golden shoes?

He was a magnificent-looking animal, with slender legs, intelligent eyes, and a mane that hung down his neck like a soft veil of silk. He had carried his master through the smoke and flame of battle and heard the bullets sing and whistle around him; he had kicked and bitten those about him and done his share of the fighting whenever the enemy advanced; he had leaped, carrying his master on his back, over the enemy's fallen horse and had saved the emperor's red-gold crown, saved the life of the emperor, which was much more valuable than the red gold; and that's why the emperor's horse had golden shoes, a golden shoe on each of his feet.

And the Beetle came creeping out.

"First the big ones," he said, "and then the little ones; but size isn't the only thing that does it." Then he stretched out his thin legs.

"And what do you want?" demanded the Blacksmith.

"Golden shoes," replied the Beetle.

"Why, you must be crazy!" said the Blacksmith. "Do you want golden shoes, too?"

"Golden shoes," said the Beetle. "I'm just as good as that great creature that is waited on, currycombed, and brushed, and served with food and drink. Don't I belong to the imperial stable, too?"

"But *why* does the horse have golden shoes?" asked the Blacksmith. "Don't you understand that?"

"Understand? I understand that it is a personal insult to me," said the Beetle. "It's just done to annoy me, so I'm going out into the world."

"Get out of here!" said the Blacksmith.

"What a rude person!" said the Beetle as he left the stable. He flew a little way and presently found himself in a beautiful flower garden, all fragrant with roses and lavender.

"Isn't it lovely here?" asked one of the little Ladybirds that were flying about, with black spots on their red shieldlike wings. "How sweet it smells here and how beautiful it is!"

"I'm used to much better things," said the Beetle. "Do you call *this* beautiful? Why, there isn't so much as a manure pile here!"

Then he went on and got into the shadow of a large Gillyflower. A Caterpillar was crawling along on it.

"How beautiful the world is!" said the Caterpillar. "The sun is so warm, and everything is so pleasant! And when my time comes and I must die, as people call it, I'll wake up again, and I'll be a butterfly!"

"What conceit!" said the Beetle. "*You* fly about like a butterfly, indeed! I'm from the stable of the emperor, and no one there, not even the emperor's favorite horse—who wears my castoff golden shoes—has any idea like that! Get wings! Fly! Why, I can fly already!" and then the Beetle flew away. "I don't really want to be annoyed, and yet I am annoyed."

Soon afterward he settled on a large lawn. Here he lay quietly for a while, and then he fell asleep.

My goodness! The rain came down in buckets! The noise woke up the Beetle, and he wanted to get down into the earth at once, but he couldn't. He tumbled over; sometimes he was swimming on his stomach, sometimes on his back, and it was out of the question to try to fly; would he ever escape from there with his life? So he just lay where he was and remained lying there.

When the rain had let up a little, and the Beetle had blinked the water from his eyes, he saw something gleaming white. It was linen that had been put out there to bleach; he managed to make his way to it and creep into a fold of the damp cloth. Certainly this place wasn't as comfortable as the warm stable, but there was nothing better, and so he stayed there for a whole day and a whole night, while the rain stayed, too. The next morning he crept out, very much annoyed with the weather.

Two frogs were sitting on the linen, their bright eyes shining with pleasure.

"What wonderful weather this is!" one of them said. "How refreshing! And this linen holds the water together so perfectly! My hind legs are tickling as if I were going to swim."

"I'd like to know," said the other frog, "whether the swallow, who flies so far in her many trips to foreign countries, ever finds a better climate than ours. Such a storm, and such a downpour! You really might think you were lying in a wet ditch. Anybody that doesn't enjoy this weather certainly doesn't love his native country!"

"Have you ever been in the emperor's stable?" asked the Beetle. "The dampness there is both warm and refreshing. That's what I am used to; that's the climate for me; but one can't take it along on a journey. Isn't there a nice hotbed here in the garden, where persons of rank, like me, can find a place to live and make himself at home?"

But the frogs either didn't or wouldn't understand him.

"I never ask a question twice," said the Beetle, after he had already asked three times without getting any answer.

He went on a little farther and bumped against a piece of broken pottery. It certainly shouldn't have been lying there, but since it was it gave good shelter. Several families of Earwigs lived here, and they didn't need very much room; but they liked company. The females were full of the most devoted mother love, and so each one considered her own child the most beautiful and clever of all.

"Our son has become engaged!" said one mother. "The sweet, innocent baby! His greatest ambition is to creep someday into a clergyman's ear! He's such a lovely boy. And being engaged will keep him out of mischief. What joy for a mother!"

"Our son," said another mother, "had hardly crept from the egg before he got into mischief. He's so full of life and spirits he'll run his horns off! What joy that is for a mother! Isn't that true, Mr. Beetle?" for she had recognized the stranger by his shape.

"You're both quite right," said the Beetle; so they invited him to walk in—that is, to come as far as he could under the broken flowerpot.

"Now you ought to see *my* little earwig!" observed a third mother, and a fourth. "They're such lovely children, and so amusing! They never behave badly, except when they have a stomachache, but that happens pretty often at their age."

Then each mother spoke of her own youngster, and the youngsters joined in the conversation, and used the little forks in their tails to pull the Beetle's mustache.

"The little scamps, they're always up to something!" said the mothers, beaming with maternal love. But the Beetle was bored by all this, and so he asked how far it was to the nearest hotbed.

"Oh, that's way out in the world, on the other side of the ditch," said an Earwig. "I hope none of my children ever goes that far—it would be the death of me."

"Just the same *I'll* try to go that far," said the Beetle, and then he went off without taking any formal leave, for that's considered the politest thing to do. And by the ditch he met several of his kind—all Beetles.

"We live here," they said. "And we're very cozy here, too. May we invite you to step down into this rich soil? The journey must have tired you out."

"Indeed it has," said the Beetle. "I've been lying on linen out in the rain, and cleanliness tires me very much. I also have rheumatism in my wing joints, from standing in a draft under a broken flowerpot. It's really very relaxing to be among one's own kind again."

"Perhaps you come from the hotbed?" asked the oldest of them.

"Oh, I come from a much higher place," said the Beetle. "I come from the emperor's stable, where I was born with golden shoes on! I'm traveling on a secret mission. You mustn't ask me any questions, for I won't tell you anything."

And so the Beetle stepped down into the rich soil. There sat three young lady Beetles, and they tittered because they didn't know what to say.

"They are not engaged yet," said their mother, and then the young lady Beetles tittered again, this time from embarrassment.

"I have never seen greater beauties even in the emperor's stables!" said the traveling Beetle.

"Now don't you spoil my daughters," said the mother, "and please don't speak to them unless you have serious intentions. But of course your intentions are honorable, and so I give you my blessing!"

"Hurrah!" cried all the other Beetles at once, and so the Beetle was engaged. First the engagement, then the wedding; there was nothing to wait for.

The following day passed pleasantly, and the next was fair enough, but by the third day it was time to think of food for the wife and perhaps for children.

"I've let them put something over on me," he said, "and now the only thing to do is put something over on them in return."

And that he did. Away he went, away all day, and away all night, while his wife was left a widow.

The other Beetles said that they had taken nothing more than a complete tramp into the family and now his wife was left a burden on their hands.

"Well, then, she shall be unmarried again," said her mother, "and sit here among my unmarried daughters. Shame on that disgusting rascal who deserted her!"

Meanwhile the Beetle had been traveling on and had sailed across the ditch on a cabbage leaf. That morning two persons came by, and when they saw the Beetle they picked him up, turned him over and over, and both looked very learned—especially one of them, a boy.

"Allah sees the black beetle in the black stone and in the black mountain," he said. "Isn't that in the Koran?" Then he translated the Beetle's name into Latin and discoursed upon its nature and family history. The older scholar was opposed to carrying him home, saying they had just as good a specimen there. This, the Beetle thought, was a very rude thing to say; consequently he suddenly flew out of the speaker's hand. As his wings were dry now, he flew a considerable distance and reached a greenhouse, where he found a sash of the glass roof partly open, so, with the greatest of ease, he slipped in and buried himself in the manure.

"It's very comfortable here," he remarked.

Soon he feel asleep and dreamed that the emperor's horse had fallen down and that Mr. Beetle had been given its golden shoes, with the promise that he should have two more.

It was all very charming. And when the Beetle woke up he crept out and looked around him. What splendor there was in the greenhouse! Great palm trees were growing high, and the sun made them look transparent. And beneath them what a riot of green, and blooming flowers, red as fire, yellow as amber, or white as freshly fallen snow!

"What magnificent plants! How delicious they'll taste when they're nice and decayed!" said the Beetle. "This is a splendid larder! I am sure some of my relatives live here; I'll just see if I can find anyone fit to associate with. I'm proud, and I'm proud of being that way."

So he thought of the dream he had had about the dying horse and the golden shoes he had won. But suddenly a hand seized the Beetle and squeezed him and turned him over and over.

The gardener's little son and his playmate had come to the greenhouse and, seeing the Beetle, had decided to have some fun with him. First he was wrapped in a vine leaf and then shoved down into a warm trousers pocket. He squirmed and wriggled, but he got a good squeezing from the boy's hand. The boy went rapidly toward the great lake at the bottom of the garden. Here they put the Beetle in an old broken wooden shoe, with the top part missing. A little stick was placed upright for a mast, and to this the Beetle was bound with a woolen thread. Now he was a skipper and had to sail away.

The lake was very large, and to the Beetle it seemed a vast ocean; he was so amazed at its size that he fell over on his back and kicked out with all his legs.

The wooden shoe sailed away. The current bore it along, but whenever it went too far from shore one of the boys would roll up his trousers, go in after it, and bring it back. However, just as it sailed merrily out to sea again, the boys were called away, and quite sharply, too, so that they ran away from the lake, leaving the wooden shoe to its fate. It drifted away from the shore, farther and farther out; it was a terrible situation for the Beetle; he couldn't fly, for he was bound tightly to the mast.

Then a Fly paid him a visit.

"What beautiful weather we're having!" said the Fly. "I'll rest here; I can take a sun bath here. You're certainly having a nice time of it!"

"You don't know what you're talking about," replied the Beetle. "Can't you see I'm tied up?"

"I'm not a prisoner," said the Fly, and promptly flew away.

"Well, now I guess I know the world," the Beetle said. "And it's a mean place. I'm the only honest person in it. First, they won't give me my golden shoes, then I have to lie on wet linen and stand in a draft, and as a climax they hitch a wife to me. Then, when I made a quick move out into the world, and found out how people live, and how I ought to live, one of these human puppies comes and ties me up and leaves me to the mercy of the wild ocean, while the emperor's horse prances about proudly in golden shoes. That's what annoys me more than anything else! But you mustn't expect sympathy in this world! My career has been very interesting, but what's the good of that, if nobody knows about it? The world doesn't deserve to know about it, for it should have given me golden shoes when the emperor's horse was shod and I stretched out my feet to be shod, too. If they'd given me golden shoes I'd have been an honor to the stable. Now the stable has lost me, and the world has lost me! It's all over!"

But it wasn't all over yet. Some young girls came rowing up in a boat.

"There's an old wooden shoe sailing along over there!" said one of them.

"And there's a little animal tied fast in it!" said another.

Their boat came quite close to the wooden shoe, and they fished him out of the water. One of the girls took out a tiny pair of scissors and cut the woolen thread without hurting the Beetle; and when she stepped on shore she placed him down on the grass.

"Crawl, crawl, fly, fly away if you can!" she said. "Freedom is a precious thing!"

And the Beetle flew straight through the open window of a large building, and there he sank down, tired and exhausted, in the long, fine, soft mane of the emperor's favorite horse, which was standing in the stable where he and the Beetle lived. He clung fast to the mane and sat there a little while until he had collected himself.

"Here I am sitting on the emperor's favorite horse! Yes, sitting on him as his rider! But what am I saying? Oh, yes, now it's clear to me; yes, it's a good idea and quite right. Why did the horse get golden shoes, the blacksmith asked me. Now I know the answer. They were given to the horse on *my* account!"

That put the Beetle in good spirits again.

"Traveling broadens the mind," he said.

The sun's rays streamed in on him and shone very brightly.

"On the whole, the world isn't so bad, after all!" said the Beetle. "But you must know how to take it!"

The world was wonderful, because the emperor's favorite horse had golden shoes and because the Beetle was its rider.

"Now I am going down to the other beetles and tell them about all the pleasures I have enjoyed on my trip abroad, and I am going to say that now I'm going to stay at home until the horse has worn out his golden shoes."

WHAT THE OLD MAN DOES IS ALWAYS RIGHT (1861)

Now I'm going to tell you a story that I heard when I was a little fellow and that I like better and better the more I think of it. For it's the same with stories as with many people; the older they grow, the nicer they grow, and that is delightful.

You have been out in the country, of course. There you must have seen a really old farmhouse with a thatched roof, where moss and weeds have planted themselves; a stork's nest decorates the chimney (you can never do without the stork); the walls are slanting; the windows are low (in fact, only one of them was made to open); the baking oven sticks out like a fat little stomach; and an elder bush leans over the gate, where you can see a tiny pond with a duck or ducklings under a gnarled willow tree. Yes, and then, of course, there's a watchdog which barks at everybody and everything.

Well, there was a farmhouse just like that out in the country, and in it there lived two people, a farmer and his wife. They had few enough possessions, but still there was one they could do without, and that was a horse, which grazed along the ditch beside the highway. The old farmer used it to ride to town and lent it to his neighbors, receiving some slight services from them in return, but still it would be much more profitable to sell the horse, or at least exchange it for something that would be more useful to them.

But which should they do, sell or trade?

"You'll know what's best, Father," said the wife. "It's market day. Come on, ride off to town, and get money for the horse, or make a good bargain with it. Whatever you do is always right; so be off for the market!"

So she tied on his neckerchief—for that was something she understood much better than he—tied it with a double bow, and made him look quite dashing. She brushed his hat with the palm of her hand, and she kissed him on the mouth, and then off he went, riding the horse that was to be either sold or bartered. Of course, he would know the right thing to do.

The sun was scorching, and there was not a cloud in the sky. The road was dusty and crowded with people on their way to market, some in wagons, some on horseback, and some on their own two legs. Yes, it was a fierce sun, with no shade all the way.

Now a man came along, driving a cow, as pretty a cow as you could wish to see. "I'm sure she must give grand milk," thought the peasant. "It would be a pretty good bargain if I got her. Hey, you with the cow!" he said. "Let's have a little talk. Look here, I believe a horse costs more than a cow, but it doesn't matter to me, since I have more use for a cow. Shall we make a swap?"

"Fair enough," said the man with the cow; and so they swapped.

Now the farmer might just as well have turned home again, for he had finished his business. But he had planned to go to market, so to market he would go, if only to look on; hence, with his cow, he continued on his way. He walked fast, and so did the cow, and pretty soon they overtook a man who was leading a sheep; it was a fine-looking sheep, in good condition and well clothed with wool.

"I certainly would like to have that," thought the peasant. "It would find plenty of grazing beside our ditch, and in the winter we could keep it in our own room. It would really be much more sensible for us to be keeping a sheep rather than a cow. Shall we trade?"

Yes, the sheep's owner was quite willing, so the exchange was made, and now the farmer went on along the highway with his sheep. Near a road gate he met a man with a big goose under his arm.

"Well, you've got a fine heavy fellow there!" said the farmer. "It's got plenty of feathers and fat! How nice it would be to have it tied up near our little pond, and, besides, it would be something for Mother to save the scraps for. She has often said, 'If we only had a goose.' Now she can have one—and she shall, too! Will you swap? I'll give you my sheep for your goose, and my thanks, too."

The other had no objection, so they swapped, and the farmer got the goose. By now he was close to the town; the road was getting more and more crowded, people and cattle pushing past him, thronging in the road, in the ditch, and right up to the toll keeper's potato patch, where his one hen was tied up, in case it should lose its head in a panic and get lost. It was a bobtailed hen that winked with one eye and looked in good condition.

"Cluck, cluck," it said; what it meant by that, I wouldn't know; but what the peasant thought when he saw it was this, "She's the prettiest hen I've ever seen—much prettier than any of our parson's brood hens. I would certainly like to have her. A hen can always find a grain of corn, and she can almost provide for herself. I almost think it would be a good idea to take her instead of the goose. Shall we trade?" he asked.

"Trade?" said the other. "Well, not a bad idea!" And so they traded. The toll keeper got the goose, and the farmer got the hen.

He had completed a good deal of business since he started for town; it was hot, and he was tired. What he needed was a drink and a bite to eat.

He had reached an inn and was ready to enter, when the innkeeper's helper met him in the doorway, carrying a sackful of something.

"What have you got there?" asked the farmer.

"Rotten apples," was the answer. "A whole sackful for the pigs."

"What a lot! Wouldn't Mother like to see so many! Why, last year we had only one single apple on the old tree by the peat shed. That apple was to be kept, and it stood on the chest of drawers till it burst. 'That is always a sign of prosperity,' Mother said. Here she could see plenty of prosperity! Yes, I only wish she could have it!"

"Well, what'll you give me for them?" asked the innkeeper's helper.

"Give for them? Why, I'll give you my hen!" So he turned over the hen, took the apples, and went into the inn, straight up to the bar; he set his sack upright against the stove, without noticing that there was a fire in it. There were a number of strangers present, horse dealers, cattle dealers, and two Englishmen so rich that their pockets were bursting with gold coins. They were fond of making bets, as Englishmen in stories always are.

"Suss! Suss! Suss!" What was that noise at the stove? It was the apples beginning to roast!

"What's that?" everybody said, and they soon found out. They were hearing the whole story of the horse that had been traded first for a cow and finally for a sack of rotten apples.

"Well, you'll get a good beating from your old woman when you go home!" said the Englishmen. "You're in for a rough time."

"I'll get kisses, not cuffs," said the farmer. "Mother will say, 'Whatever the old man does is right.'"

"Shall we bet on it?" said the Englishmen. "We have gold by the barrel! A hundred pounds sterling to a hundred-pound weight?"

"Let's say a bushelful," replied the peasant. "I can only bet my bushel of apples, and throw in myself and the old woman, but I think that'll be more than full measure."

"That's a bet!" the Englishmen cried, and the bet was made! So the innkeeper's cart was brought out, the Englishmen got into it, the farmer got into it, the rotten apples got into it, and away they went to the old man's cottage.

"Good evening, Mother."

"Same to you, Father."

"Well, I've made the bargain."

"Yes, you know how to do business," said the wife, and gave him a big hug, forgetting both the sack and the strangers.

"I traded the horse for a cow."

"Thank God for the milk!" said the wife. "Now we can have milk, butter, and cheese on our table! What a splendid swap!"

"Yes, but I swapped the cow for a sheep."

"That's still better!" cried the wife. "You're always so thoughtful. We have plenty of grass for a sheep. But now we'll have sheep's milk, and sheep's cheese, and woolen stockings, yes, and a woolen nightgown, too. A cow couldn't give us that; she loses all her hairs. But you're always such a thoughtful husband."

"But then I exchanged the sheep for a goose."

"What! Will we really have goose for Michaelmas this year, dear Father? You always think of what would please me, and that was a beautiful thought! We can tie up the goose, and it'll grow even fatter for Michaelmas Day."

"But I traded the goose for a hen," continued the peasant.

"A hen? Well, that was a fine trade!" replied his wife. "A hen will lay eggs and sit on them and we'll have chickens. Imagine, a chicken yard! Just the thing I've always wanted most!"

"Yes, but I exchanged the hen for a sack of rotten apples."

"Then I must certainly give you a kiss!" said the wife. "Thank you, my own husband. And now I have something to tell you. When you had gone I decided I'd get a fine dinner ready for you—omelet with chives. Now I had the eggs all right, but no chives. So I went over to the schoolmaster's, because I know they have chives; but that sweet woman is so stingy she wanted something in return. What could I give her? Nothing grows in our garden, not even a rotten apple; I didn't even have that for her. But now I can give her ten or even a whole sackful! Isn't it funny, Father!" she said, and kissed him right on his mouth.

"I like that!" cried both the Englishmen. "Always downhill, but always happy. That alone is worth the money!" So they were quite content to pay the bushelful of gold pieces to the peasant, who had got kisses instead of cuffs for his bargains.

Yes, it always pays when the wife believes and admits that her husband is the wisest man in the world and that whatever he does is right.

Well, this is the story. I heard it when I was a youngster, and now you've heard it, too, so you know that what the old man does is always right.

THE SNOW MAN (1861)

It's so bitterly cold that my whole body crackles!" said the Snow Man. "This wind can really blow life into you! And how that glaring thing up there glares at me!" He meant the sun; it was just setting. "She won't make *me* blink; I'll hold onto the pieces."

"The pieces" were two large triangular pieces of tile, which he had for eyes. His mouth was part of an old rake, hence he had teeth. He had been born amid the triumphant shouts of the boys and welcomed by the jingling of sleigh bells and the cracking of whips from the passing sleighs.

The sun went down, and the full moon rose, big and round, bright and beautiful, in the clear blue sky.

"Here she comes again from the other side," said the Snow Man, for he thought it was the sun showing itself again. "Ah, I've cured her of staring, all right. Now let her hang up there and shine so that I can see myself. If I only knew how to move from this place—I'd like so much to move! If I could, I'd slide along there on the ice, the way I see the boys slide, but I don't know how to run."

"Away! Away!" barked the old Watchdog. He was quite hoarse from the time when he was a house dog lying under the stove. "The sun will teach you how to run. I saw your predecessor last winter, and before that *his* predecessor. Away! Away! And away they all go!"

"I don't understand you, friend," said the Snow Man. "Is that thing up there going to teach me to run?" He meant the moon. "Why, she was running the last time I saw her a little while ago, and now she comes sneaking back from the other side."

"You don't know anything at all," replied the Watchdog. "But then, of course, you've just been put together. The one you are looking at now is called the moon, and the one who went away was the sun. She will come again tomorrow, and she will teach you to run down into the ditch. We're going to have a change of weather soon; I can feel it in my left hind leg; I have a pain in it. The weather's going to change."

"I don't understand him," said the Snow Man to himself, "but I have a feeling he's talking about something unpleasant. The one that stared at me and went away, whom he called the sun, is no friend of mine either, I can feel that."

"Away! Away!" barked the Watchdog, and then he walked around three times and crept into his kennel to sleep.

The weather really did change. Early next morning a thick, damp mist lay over the whole countryside. At dawn a wind rose; it was icy cold. The frost set in hard, but when the sun rose, what a beautiful sight it was! The trees and bushes were covered with hoarfrost and looked like a forest of white coral, while every twig seemed smothered with glittering white flowers. The enormously many delicate branches that are concealed by the leaves in summer now appeared, every single one of them, and made a gleaming white lacework, so snowy white that a white radiance seemed to spring from every bough. The birch waved in the wind as if it had life, like the rest of the trees in the summer. It was all wonderfully beautiful. And when the sun came out, how it all glittered and sparkled, as if everything had been strewn with diamond dust, and big diamonds had been sprinkled on the snowy carpet of the Earth; or one could also imagine that countless little lights were gleaming, brighter even than the snow itself.

"It's wonderfully beautiful!" said a young girl, who had come out into the garden with a young man. They stopped near the Snow Man and gazed at the flashing trees. "Summer can't show us a lovelier sight!" she said, and her eyes sparkled with delight.

"And we can't have a fellow like this in the summertime, either," the young man agreed, as he pointed to the Snow Man. "He's splendid."

The young girl laughed, nodded to the Snow Man, and then danced over the snow with her friend—over snow that crackled under their feet as though they were walking on starch.

"Who were those two?" asked the Snow Man of the Watchdog. "You've been around this yard longer than I have. Do you know them?"

"Of course I know them," said the Watchdog. "She pets me, and he once threw me a meat bone. I don't bite those two."

"But what are they supposed to be?" asked the Snow Man. "Sweethearts!" replied the Watchdog. "They'll go to move into the same kennel someday and gnaw the same bone together. Away! Away!"

"But are they as important as you and I?" asked the Snow Man.

"Why, they are members of the master's family," said the Watchdog. "People certainly don't know very much if they were only born yesterday; I can tell that from you. Now I have age and knowledge. I know everybody here in the house, and I know a time when I didn't have to stand out here in the cold, fastened to a chain. Away! Away!"

"The cold is lovely," said the Snow Man. "But tell me, tell me. Only don't rattle that chain; it makes me shiver inside when you do that."

"Away! Away!" barked the Watchdog. "They used to tell me I was a pretty little puppy, when I lay in a velvet-covered chair up in the master's house, or sat in the mistress' lap. They used to kiss me on the nose and wipe my paws with an embroidered handkerchief.

"They called me 'the handsomest' and 'little puppsy-wuppsy.' But then I grew too big for them to keep, so they gave me away to the housekeeper. That's how I came to live down in the basement. You can look down into it from where you're standing; you can look right into the room where I was master, for that was what I was to the housekeeper. Of course, the place was inferior to that upstairs, but I was more comfortable there and wasn't constantly grabbed and pulled about by the children as I had been upstairs. I had just as good food as ever, and much more of it. I had my own cushion, and then there was a stove, which is the finest thing in the world at this time of year. I crept right in under it, so that I was out of the way. Ah, I still dream of that stove sometimes. Away! Away!"

"Does a stove look so beautiful?" asked the Snow Man. "Does it look like me?"

"It's just the opposite of you. It's as black as coal and has a long neck and a brass stomach. It eats firewood, so that fire spurts from its mouth. You must keep beside it or underneath it; it's very comfortable there. You must be able to see it through the window from where you're standing."

Then the Snow Man looked, and he really saw a brightly polished thing with a brass stomach and fire glowing from the lower part of it. A very strange feeling swept over the Snow Man; he didn't know what it meant, and couldn't understand it, but all people who aren't snowmen know that feeling.

"Why did you leave her?" asked the Snow Man, for it seemed to him that the stove must be a female. "How could you leave a place like that?"

"I was compelled to," replied the Watchdog. "They turned me outside and chained me up here. You see, I had bitten the youngest of the master's children in the leg, because he had kicked away a bone I was gnawing. 'A bone for a bone,' I always say. They didn't like that at all, and from that time I've been chained out here and have lost my voice. Don't you hear how hoarse I am? Away! Away! And that was the end of that!"

But the Snow Man wasn't listening to him any longer. He kept peering in at the housekeeper's basement room, where the stove stood on its four iron legs, just about the same size as the Snow Man himself.

"What a strange crackling there is inside me!" he cried. "I wonder if I'll ever get in there. That's an innocent wish, and our innocent wishes are sure to be fulfilled. It is my only wish, my biggest wish; it would almost be unfair if it wasn't granted. I must get in and lean against her, even if I have to break a window."

"You'll never get in there," said the Watchdog. "And if you go near that stove you'll melt away! Away!"

"I'm as good as gone, anyway," replied the Snow Man. "I think I'm breaking up."

All day long the Snow Man stood looking in through the window. At twilight the room grew still more inviting; a mild glow came from the stove, not like the moon or the sun either, but just like the glow of a stove when it has been well filled. Every time the room door was opened, the flames leaped out of the stove's mouth; this was a habit it had. The flame fell distinctly on the white face of the Snow Man and glowed ruddy on his breast.

"I can't stand it any longer!" he cried. "How beautiful she looks when she sticks out her tongue!"

The night was very long, but it didn't seem long to the Snow Man; he stood lost in his own pleasant thoughts, and they froze until they crackled.

In the morning the windowpanes of the basement room were covered with ice. They showed the most beautiful ice flowers that any Snow Man could desire, but they hid the stove. The windowpanes wouldn't thaw, so he couldn't see the stove. It creaked, and it crackled.

It was just the sort of weather a Snow Man should most thoroughly enjoy. But he didn't enjoy it; indeed, how could he enjoy anything when he was so stove-sick?

"That's a terrible sickness for a Snow Man," said the Watchdog. "I've also suffered from it myself, but I got over it. Away! Away! There's going to be a change in the weather."

And there was a change in the weather; it began to thaw! The thaw increased, and the Snow Man decreased. He never complained, and that's an infallible sign.

One morning he collapsed. And behold! Where he had stood there was something like a broomstick sticking up from the ground.

It was the pole the boys had built him up around.

"Now I can understand why he had such an intense longing for the stove," said the Watchdog. "The Snow Man has had a stove rake in his body; that's what moved inside him. Now he has gotten over that, too. Away! Away!"

And soon the winter was over, too.

"Away! Away!" barked the Watchdog. But the little girls in the house sang:

> Oh, woodruff, spring up, fresh and proud, round about!
> And, willow tree, hang your woolen mitts out!
> Come, cuckoo and lark, come and sing!
> At February's close we already have spring.
> Tweet-tweet, cuckoo! I am singing with you.
> Come out, dear sun! Come often, skies of blue!

And nobody thought any more about the Snow Man.

THE ICE MAIDEN (1861)

Let us visit Switzerland. Let us take a look at that magnificent land of mountains, where the forests creep up the sides of the steep rocky walls; let us climb to the dazzling snowfields above, and descend again to the green valleys below, where the rivers and streams rush along as if afraid they will be too late to reach the ocean and disappear. The burning rays of the sun shine in the deep dales and also on the heavy masses of snow above, so that the ice blocks which have been piling for years melt and turn to thundering avalanches or heaped-up glaciers.

Two such glaciers lie in the broad ravines under the Schreckhorn and the Wetterhorn, near the little mountain town of Grindelwald. They are strange to look at, and for that reason, in summertime many travelers come here from all parts of the world. They cross the lofty, snow-capped hills, and they come through the deep valleys; then they have to climb for several hours, and as they ascend, the valleys seem to become deeper and deeper, until they look as if they are being viewed from a balloon. Often the clouds hang around the towering peaks like thick curtains of smoke, while down in the valley dotted with brown wooden houses, a ray of the sun may be shining brightly, throwing into sharp relief a brilliant patch of green, until it seems transparent. The water foams and roars and rushes along below, but up above the water murmurs and tinkles; it looks as if silver ribbons were streaming down over the rocks.

On both sides of the ascending road are wooden houses. Each house has its little potato garden, and this is a real necessity; for within those doors are many hungry mouths—there are many children, and children are often wasteful with food. From all the cottages they swarm out and besiege travelers, whether these be on foot or in carriages. All the children are little merchants; they offer for sale charming toy wooden houses, replicas of those that are built here in the mountains.

Some twenty years ago there often stood here, but always somewhat apart from the other children, a little boy who was also eager to do some business. He would stand there with an earnest, grave expression, holding his chip-box tightly with both hands, as if afraid of losing it; but it was this seriousness and the fact that he was so small that caused him to be noticed and called forward, so that he often sold more than all the others—he didn't exactly know why himself.

His grandfather lived high up on the mountain, where he carved out the neat, pretty little houses. In a room up there he had an old chest full of all sorts of carved things—nutcrackers, knives, forks, boxes with cleverly carved scrollwork, and leaping chamois—everything that would please a child's eye. But little Rudy, as he was called, gazed with greater interest and longing at the old gun that hung under the beams of the roof. "He shall have it someday," his grandfather had said, "but not until he's big and strong enough to use it."

Small as the boy was, he took care of the goats. If knowing how to climb along with the goats meant that he was a good goatherd, then Rudy certainly was an excellent goatherd; he could even go higher than the goats, for he loved to search for birds' nests high up in the tops of the trees. He was bold and daring. No one ever saw him smile, except when he stood near the roaring waterfall or heard the rolling of an avalanche.

He never played with the other children; in fact, he never went near them except when his grandfather sent him down to sell the things he had carved. And Rudy didn't care much for that; he would much rather climb about in the mountains or sit home with his grandfather and hear him tell stories of ancient times and of the people at nearby Meiringen, where he was born. This race, he said, had not always lived there; they were wanderers from other lands; they had come from the far north, where their people still lived, and were called "Swedes." This was a good deal for Rudy to learn, but he learned still more from other teachers—the animals that lived in the house. There was a big dog, Ajola, which had belonged to Rudy's father, and there was a tomcat. Rudy had much to thank the tomcat for—the Cat had taught him to climb.

"Come on out on the roof with me!" the Cat had said one day, very distinctly and intelligibly, too. For to a little child who can hardly speak, the language of hens and ducks, cats and dogs, is almost as easily understood as that of fathers and mothers. But you must be very young indeed then; those are the days when Grandpa's stick neighs and turns into a horse, with head, legs, and tail.

Some children keep these thoughts longer than others, and people say that these are exceedingly backward and remain children too long. But people say so much!

"Come on out on the roof with me, little Rudy!" was one of the first things the Cat said, and Rudy could understand him.

"It's all imagination to think you'll fall; you won't fall unless you're afraid! Come on! Put one of your paws here, and another there, and then feel your way with your forepaws. Use your eyes and be very active in your limbs. If there's a hole, jump over it the way I do."

And that's what little Rudy did. Very often he sat on the sloping roof of the house with the Cat, and often in the tops of the trees, and even high up among the towering rocks, where the Cat never went.

"Higher! Higher!" the trees and bushes said. "Can't you see how we climb—how high we go, and how tightly we hold on, even on the narrowest ledge of rock?"

And often Rudy reached the top of the hill even before the sun; there he took his morning draught of fresh, strengthening mountain air, that drink which only our Lord can prepare, and which human beings call the early fragrance from the mountain herbs and the wild thyme and mint in the valley. Everything that is heavy in the air is absorbed by the overhanging clouds and carried by the winds over the pine woods, while the essence of fragrance becomes light and fresh air—and this was Rudy's morning draught.

Sunbeams, daughters of the sun who bring his blessings with them, kissed his cheeks. Dizziness stood nearby watching, but dared not approach him. The swallows from his grandfather's house below (there were at least seven nests) flew up toward him and the goats, singing, "We and you, and you and we!" They brought greetings from his home, even from the two hens, who were the only birds in the house; however, Rudy had never been very intimate with them.

Young as he was he had traveled, and quite a good deal for such a little fellow. He was born in Canton Valais and brought from there over the hills. He had recently traveled on foot to the nearby Staubbach, that seems to flutter like a silver veil before the snow-clad, glittering white Jungfrau. And he had been to the great glaciers near Grindelwald, but there was a sad story connected with that trip; his mother had met her death there, and it was there, as his grandfather used to say, that "little Rudy had lost all his childish happiness." When he was less than a year old he laughed more than he cried, as his mother had written; but from the time he fell into the crevasse his whole nature had changed. His grandfather didn't talk about this very much, but it was known all over the mountain.

Rudy's father had been a coach driver, and the big dog that now shared the boy's home had always gone with him on his journeys over the Simplon down to Lake Geneva. Rudy's relatives on his father's side lived in the Rhone valley, in Canton Valais, where his uncle was a celebrated chamois hunter and a famous Alpine guide. Rudy was only a year old when he lost his father and his mother decided to return with the child to her own family in the Berner Oberland. Her father lived a few hours' journey from Grindelwald; he was a woodcarver, and his trade enabled him to live comfortably.

With her infant in her arms she set out toward home in June, accompanied by two chamois hunters, over the Gemmi toward Grindelwald. They had made the greater part of the journey, had climbed the highest ridges to the snowfields and could already see her native valley with the familiar scattered cottages; they now had only to cross the upper part of one great glacier. The newly fallen snow concealed a crevasse, not deep enough to reach the abyss below where the water rushed along, but deeper than a man's height.

As she was carrying her child the young woman suddenly slipped, sank down, and instantly disappeared. Not a shriek or groan was heard, only the wailing of a little child. It was over an hour before her two companions could obtain ropes and poles from the nearest house to pull her out; and after tremendous labor they brought from the crevasse what they thought were two dead bodies. Every means of restoring life was tried, and at last they managed to save the child, but not the mother. Thus the old grandfather received in his house not a daughter, but a daughter's son, the little one who laughed more than he cried. But a change seemed to have come over him since his terrible experience in the glacier crevasse—that cold, strange ice world, where the Swiss peasant believes the souls of the damned are imprisoned till doomsday.

The glacier lies like a rushing stream, frozen and pressed into blocks of green crystal, one huge mass of ice balanced on another; the swelling stream of ice and snow tears along in the depths beneath, while within it yawn deep hollows, immense crevasses. It is a wondrous palace of crystal, and in its dwells the Ice Maiden, queen of the glaciers. She, the slayer, the crusher, is half the mighty ruler of the rivers, half a child of the air. Thus it is that she can soar to the loftiest haunts of the chamois, to the towering summits of the snow-covered hills, where the boldest mountaineer has to cut footrests for himself in the ice; she sails on a light pine twig over the foaming river below and leaps lightly from one rock to another, with her long, snow-white hair fluttering about her and her blue-green robe glistening like the water in the deep Swiss lakes.

"To crush! To hold fast! That is my power!" she says. "And yet a beautiful boy was snatched from me—one whom I had kissed, but not yet kissed to death! He is again among human beings—he tends his goats on the mountain peaks; he is always climbing higher and still higher, far, far from other humans, but never from me! He is mine! I will fetch him!"

So she commanded Dizziness to undertake the mission; it was in the summertime and too hot for the Ice Maiden in the valley where the green mint grew; so Dizziness mounted and dived. Now Dizziness has a flock of sisters—first one came, then three of them—and the Ice Maiden selected the strongest of those who wield their power indoors and out. They perch on the banisters of steep staircases and the guard rails of lofty towers; they run like squirrels along the mountain ridges and, leaping away from them, tread the air as a swimmer treads water, luring a victim onward to the abyss beneath.

Dizziness and the Ice Maiden both reach out for mankind, as the polypus reaches after whatever comes near it. The mission of Dizziness was to seize Rudy.

"Seize him, you say!" said Dizziness. "I can't do it. That wretched Cat has taught him its skill. That human child has a power within himself that keeps me away. I can't touch the little fellow when he hangs from branches out over the abyss, or I'd be glad to tickle his feet and send him flying down through the air. I can't do it!"

"We can seize him!" said the Ice Maiden. "Either you or I! I will! I will!"

"No! No!" A whisper, a song, broke upon the air like the echo of church bells pealing; it was the harmonious tones of a chorus of other spirits of Nature, the mild, soft, and loving daughters of the rays of the sun. Every evening they encircle the mountain peaks and spread their rosy wings, which, as the sun sinks, become redder and redder until the lofty Alps seem blazing. Mountaineers call this the Alpine glow. When the sun has set, they retire into the white snow on the peaks and sleep there until they appear again at sunrise. Greatly do they love flowers and butterflies and mankind, and they had taken a great fancy to little Rudy.

"You shall not catch him! You shall not have him!" they sang.

"I have caught greater and stronger ones than he!" said the Ice Maiden.

Then the daughters of the sun sang of the traveler whose cap was torn from his head by the whirlwind and carried away in stormy flight. The wind had power to take his cap, but not the man himself. "You can seize him, but you cannot hold him, you children of strength. The human race is stronger and more divine even than we are; they alone can mount higher than our mother the sun. They know the magic words that can compel the wind and waves to obey and serve them. Once the heavy, dragging weight of the body is loosened, it soars upward."

Thus sounded the glorious bell-like chorus.

And every morning the sun's rays shone on the sleeping child through the one tiny window of the old man's house. The daughters of the sun kissed the boy; they tried to thaw, to wipe out the ice kiss given him by the queen of the glaciers when, in his dead mother's arms, he lay in the deep ice crevasse from which he had only been rescued as if by a miracle.

THE JOURNEY TO THE NEW HOME

Now Rudy was eight years old. His uncle, who lived in the Rhone valley on the other side of the mountain, wanted to take the boy, so that he could have a better education and be taught to take care of himself. The grandfather thought this would be better for the boy, so agreed to part with him.

As the time for Rudy's departure drew near, there were many others besides Grandfather to take leave of. First there was Ajola, the old dog.

"Your father was the coachman, and I was the coachman's dog," said Ajola. "We often traveled back and forth, and I know both dogs and men on the other side of the mountains. I never had the habit of speaking very much, but now that we have so little time to talk to each other, I'll say a little more than I usually do and tell you a story that I've been thinking about for a long time. I can't understand it, and you can't either, but that doesn't matter. I have learned this: the good things of this world aren't dealt out equally either to dogs or to men; not everyone is born to lie in someone's lap or to drink milk. I've never been accustomed to such luxury. But I've often seen a puppy dog traveling inside a post carriage, taking up a human being's seat, while the lady to whom he belonged, or rather who belonged to him, carried a bottle of milk from which she fed him. She also offered him sweet candy, but he wouldn't bother to eat it; he just sniffed at it, so she ate it herself. I was running in the mud beside the carriage, about as hungry as a dog could be, but I had only my own bitter thoughts to chew on. Things weren't quite as they ought to be, but then there is much that is not! I hope you get to ride inside carriages, and ride softly, but you can't make all that happen by yourself. I never could either by barking or yawning."

That was Ajola's lecture, and Rudy threw his arms around the dog's neck and kissed his wet nose. Then he took the Cat in his arms, but he struggled to be free, and cried, "You're getting much too strong for me, but I won't use my claws against you. Climb away over the mountains—I've taught you how to climb. Never think about falling, but hold tightly; don't be afraid, and you'll be safe enough."

Then the Cat ran off, for he didn't want Rudy to see how sorry he was.

The hens were hopping about the floor. One of them had lost its tail, for a traveler, who thought himself a sportsman, had shot it off, mistaking the poor hen for a game bird.

"Rudy is going over the mountains," said one of the hens.

"He's in a hurry," said the other, "and I don't like farewells." So they both hopped away.

And the goats also said their farewells. "Maeh! Maeh!" they bleated; it sounded so sad.

Just at that time there happened to be two experienced guides about to cross the mountains; they planned to descend the other side of the Gemmi, and Rudy would go with them on foot. It was a hard trip for such a little fellow, but he had considerable strength, and was untiring and courageous.

The swallows accompanied him a little way, and sang to him, "We and you, and you and we."

The travelers' route led across the foaming Lütschine, which falls in many small rivulets from the dark clefts of the Grindelwald glaciers. Fallen tree trunks made bridges, and pieces of rock served here as steppingstones. Soon they had passed the alder thicket and began to climb the mountain near where the glaciers had loosened themselves from the cliff. They went around the glacier and over the blocks of ice.

Rudy crept and walked. His eyes sparkled with joy as he firmly placed his iron-tipped mountain shoes; it seemed as if he wished to leave behind him an impression of each footstep. The patches of black earth, tossed onto the glacier by the mountain torrents, gave it a burned look, but still the blue-green, glassy ice shone through. They had to circle the little pools that seemed dammed up by detached masses of ice. On this route they approached a huge stone which was balanced on the edge of an ice crevasse. Suddenly the rock lost its balance and toppled into the crevasse; the echo of its thunderous fall resounded faintly from the deep abyss of the glacier, far, far below.

Upward, always upward, they climbed; the glacier stretched up like a solid stream of masses of ice piled in wild confusion, wedged between bare and rugged rocks. For a moment Rudy remembered what had been told him, how he had lain in his mother's arms, buried in one of these terrible crevasses. But he soon threw off such gloomy thoughts, and considered the tale as only one of the many stories he had heard. Occasionally, when the guides thought the way was too difficult for a such a little boy, they held out their hands to help him; but he didn't tire, and he crossed the glacier as sure-footedly as a chamois itself.

From time to time they reached rocky ground; they walked between mossless stones, and sometimes between low pine trees or out on the green pastures—always changing, always new. About them towered the lofty, snow-capped peaks, which every child in the country knows by name—the Jungfrau, the Eiger, and the Mönch.

Rudy had never before been up so high, had never before walked on the wide ocean of snow with its frozen billows of ice, from which the wind occasionally swept little clouds of powdery snow as it sweeps the whitecaps from the waves of the sea. Glacier stretched beside glacier, almost as if they were holding hands; and each is a crystal palace of the Ice Maiden, whose joy and in whose power it is to seize and imprison her victims.

The sun shone warmly, and the snow dazzled the eye as if it were covered with the flashing sparks of pale blue diamonds. Countless insects, especially butterflies and bees, lay dead in heaps on the snow; they had winged their way too high, or perhaps the wind had carried them up to the cold regions that to them meant death. Around the Wetterhorn there hung a threatening cloud, like a large mass of very fine dark wool; it sank, bulging with what was concealed within—a foehn, the Alpine south wind that foretells a storm, fearfully violent in its power when it should break loose.

This whole journey—the stops for the nights high up in the mountains, the wild route, the deep crevasses where the water, during countless ages of time, had cut through the solid stone—made an unforgettable impression on little Rudy's mind.

A deserted stone hut, beyond the snowfields, gave them shelter and comfort for the night. Here they found charcoal and pine branches, and a fire was soon kindled. Sleeping quarters were arranged as well as possible, and the men settled near the blazing fire; they smoked their tobacco and drank some of the warm, spiced beverage they had prepared—and they didn't forget to give Rudy some.

The talk turned to the mysterious creatures who haunt the high Alps: the huge, strange snakes in the deep lakes—the night riders—the spectral host that carry sleepers through the air to the wonderful, floating city of Venice—the wild herdsman, who drives his black sheep over the green pastures: these had never been seen, although men had heard the sound of their bells and the frightful noise of the phantom herd.

Rudy listened to these superstitious tales with intense interest, but with no fear, for that he had never known; yet while he listened he imagined he could hear the roar of that wild, spectral herd. Yes! It became more and more distinct, until the men heard it too. They stopped their talking and listened to it, and then they told Rudy that he must not fall asleep.

It was a foehn that had risen—that violent tempest which whirls down from the mountains into the valley below, and in its fury snaps large trees like reeds, and tosses the wooden houses from one bank of a river to the other, as easily as we would move chessmen.

After an hour they told Rudy the wind had died down and he might go to sleep safely; and, weary from his long walk, he followed their instructions and slept.

Early next morning, they set off again. That day the sun shone for Rudy on new mountains, new glaciers, and new snowfields. They had entered Canton Valais, on the other side of the ridge of mountains visible from Grindelwald; but they still had a long way to go to his new home.

More mountain clefts, pastures, woods, and new paths unfolded themselves; then Rudy saw other houses and other people. But what kind of human beings were these? They were misshapen, with frightful, disgusting, fat, yellowish faces, the hideous flesh of their necks hanging down like bags. They were the cretins—miserable, diseased wretches, who dragged themselves along and stared with stupid, dead eyes at the strangers who crossed their path; the women were even more disgusting than the men. Were these the sort of people who lived in his new home?

THE UNCLE

When Rudy arrived in his uncle's house he thanked God to see people such as he was accustomed to. There was only one cretin, a poor imbecile boy, one of those unfortunate beings who, in their poverty, which amounts to utter destitution, always travel about in Canton Valais, visiting different families in turn and staying a month or two in each house. Poor Saperli happened to be living in the house of Rudy's uncle when the boy arrived.

This uncle was a bold hunter and a cooper by trade, while his wife was a lively little person, with a face somewhat like a bird's, eyes like an eagle's, and a long, skinny, fuzz-covered neck.

Everything was strange and new to Rudy—dress, customs, employment, even the language, though his young ear would soon learn to understand that. A comparison between his grandfather's little home and his uncle's domicile greatly favored the latter. The room they lived in was larger; the walls were decorated with chamois heads and brightly polished guns; a painting of the Virgin Mary hung over the door, with fresh Alpine roses and a constantly burning lamp before it.

As you have learned, his uncle was one of the most famous chamois hunters of the canton, and also the most experienced and best guide.

Rudy became the pet of the house, but there was another pet too—a blind, lazy old dog, of not much use any more. But he had been useful once, and his value in former years was remembered, so he now lived as one of the family, with every comfort. Rudy patted him, but the dog didn't like strangers and still considered Rudy one. But the boy did not long remain so, for soon he won his way into everyone's heart.

"Things are not so bad here in Canton Valais," said his uncle. "We have plenty of chamois; they don't die off as fast as the wild goats. Things are much better now than in the old days, however much we praise the olden times. A hole has been burst in the bag, so now we have a little fresh air in our cramped valley. When you do away with out-of-date things you always get something better," he said.

When the uncle became really talkative, he would tell the boy about his own and his father's childhood. "In those days Valais was," he called it, "just a closed bag full of too many sick people—miserable cretins. But the French soldiers came, and they made excellent doctors— they soon killed the disease, and the patients too. They knew how to strike—yes, to strike in many different ways; even their girls knew how to strike!" Then he winked at his wife, who was French by birth, and laughed. "The French knew how to split solid stones if they wanted to. It was they who cut out of solid rock the road over the Simplon Pass—yes, and made such a road that I could tell a three-year-old child to go to Italy! You just have to keep on the highway, and there you are!" Then the uncle sang a French song, and ended by shouting "hurrah!" for Napoleon Bonaparte.

It was the first time Rudy had ever heard of France or of Lyons, that great city on the Rhone which his uncle had visited.

In a few years Rudy would become an expert chamois hunter, for he showed quite a flair for it, said the uncle. He taught the boy to hold, load, and fire a gun; in the hunting season he took him up into the hills and made him drink warm chamois blood to ward off hunter's giddiness; he taught him to know the times when, on different slopes of the mountains, avalanches were likely to fall, in the morning or evening, whenever the sun's rays had the greatest effect. He taught him to observe the movements of the chamois and copy their leaps, so that he might light firmly on his feet. He told him that if there was no footing in the rock crevices, he must support himself by the pressure of his elbows and the muscles, of his thighs and calves; if necessary even the neck could be used.

The chamois is cunning and places sentinels on guard, so the hunter must be still more cunning and scent them out. Sometimes he could cheat them by arranging his hat and coat on his alpine staff, so that the chamois would mistake the dummy for the man. The uncle played this trick one day when he was out hunting with Rudy.

It was a narrow mountain path—indeed, scarcely a path at all; it was nothing more than a slight ledge close to the yawning abyss. The snow there was half thawed, and the rock crumbled away under the pressure of a boot, so that uncle lay down at full length and inched his way forward. Every fragment of rock that crumbled off fell, knocking and bouncing from one side of the wall to the other, until it came to rest in the depths far below. Rudy stood on the edge of the last point of solid rock, about a hundred paces behind his uncle, and from there he suddenly saw, wheeling through the air and hovering just above his uncle, an enormous vulture, which, with one stroke of its tremendous wings, could easily have hurled the creeping form into the abyss beneath, and there feed on his carcass.

The uncle had eyes for nothing but the chamois, which had appeared with its young kid on the other side of the crevasse. But Rudy kept watching the bird, with his hand on his gun to fire the instant it became necessary, for he understood its intention. Suddenly the chamois leaped upward; the uncle fired, and the animal was hit by the deadly bullet; but the kid escaped as skillfully as if it had had a lifelong experience of danger and flight. The huge bird, frightened by the report, wheeled off in another direction; and the uncle was saved from a danger of which he knew nothing until Rudy told him about it later.

As they were making their way homeward in high good humor, the uncle humming an air he remembered from his childhood, they heard a strange noise very close to them. They looked all around, and then upward; and there, on the slope of the mountain high above, the heavy snow covering was lifted up and heaving as a stretched linen sheet heaves when the wind creeps under it. Then the great mass cracked like a marble slab, broke, and changed into a foaming cataract, rushing down on them with a rumbling noise like distant thunder. An avalanche was coming, not directly toward Rudy and his uncle, but close to them—much too close!

"Hang on, Rudy!" he cried. "Hang on with all your might!"

Rudy threw his arms around the trunk of a nearby tree, while his uncle climbed higher and clung to the branches of the tree. The avalanche roared past a little distance away, but the gale of wind that swept behind it, the tail of a hurricane, snapped trees and bushes all around them as if they had been dry rushes and hurled them about in wild confusion. Rudy was flung to the ground, for the trunk of his tree looked as if it had been sawed in two, and the upper part was tossed a great distance. And there, among the shattered branches, Rudy found his poor uncle, with a fractured skull! His hands were still warm, but his face was unrecognizable. Rudy turned pale and trembled, for this was the first real shock of his life, the first terror he had ever experienced.

Late that evening he brought the fatal news to his home—his home, which was now to be the home of grief. The wife stood like a statue, uttering no word, shedding no tear; it was not until the corpse was brought home that her sorrow found utterance. The poor cretin crept into his bed, and was not seen throughout the whole next day. But the following evening he came to Rudy.

"Write a letter for me please!" he said. "Saperli can't write. Saperli can only take letter to post office."

"A letter for you?" Rudy asked. "To whom?"

"To our Lord Christ!"

"What do you mean?"

And the half-wit, as he was called, looked at Rudy with a touching expression, clasped his hands, and said solemnly and reverently, "Jesus

Christ! Saperli would send him a letter to pray him that Saperli lie dead, and not the master of the house here."

And Rudy pressed his hand. "That letter wouldn't reach up there. That letter wouldn't restore him to us."

He found it very difficult to convince Saperli how impossible his request was.

"Now you must be the support of the house," said his aunt. And Rudy became just that.

BABETTE

"Who is the best hunter in Canton Valais?" The chamois knew well. "Beware of Rudy!" they might have said to each other. And, "Who is the handsomest hunter?" "Oh, it's Rudy!" the girls said. But they didn't add, "Beware of Rudy!" And their serious mothers didn't say so either, for he bowed as politely to them as to the young girls.

He was so brave and happy; his cheeks were so brown, his teeth so white, his dark eyes so sparkling! He was a handsome fellow, just twenty years old. The most icy water never seemed too cold for him to go swimming; in fact, he was like a fish in water. He could outclimb anyone else; he could cling as tightly as a snail to the cliffs. There were steel muscles and sinews in him; that was clear whenever he jumped. He had learned how to leap, first from the Cat, and later from the chamois. Rudy was considered the best mountain guide, and he could have made a great deal of money in that vocation. His uncle had also taught him the trade of a cooper, but he had no inclination for that. He was interested in nothing but chamois hunting; that was his greatest pleasure, and it also brought in good money. Everybody said Rudy would be an excellent match, if only he didn't set his sights too high. He was the kind of graceful dancer that the girls dreamed about; and more than one carried him in her thoughts while she was awake.

"He kissed me while we were dancing!" the schoolmaster's daughter, Annette, told her dearest friend; but she shouldn't have told it, even to her dearest friend. Such secrets are seldom kept; they ooze out, like sand from a bag that has holes in it. Consequently, however well-behaved and good Rudy was, the rumor soon spread about that he kissed his dancing partners. And yet he had never kissed the one he really wanted to kiss.

"Watch him!" said an old hunter. "He has kissed Annette. He has begun with A, and he's going to kiss his way through the whole alphabet!"

A kiss in the dance was all the gossips so far could find to bring against Rudy; but he certainly had kissed Annette, and yet she wasn't the real flower of his heart.

Down at Bex, among the great walnut trees near a small rushing mountain stream, there lived a rich miller. His home was a large house, three stories high, with small turrets; it was made of wood and covered with tin plates, which shone both in sunshine and moonlight. On the highest turret was a weather vane, a shining arrow piercing an apple—an allusion to William Tell's famous arrow shot. The mill was prominent and prosperous looking and allowed itself to be sketched and written about, but the miller's daughter did not permit herself to be described in painting or writing, at least so Rudy would have said. Yet her image was engraved on his heart; her eyes sparkled in it so that it was quite on fire. This fire had, like most fires, begun suddenly. The strangest part of it was that the miller's daughter, the lovely Babette, had no suspicion of it, for she and Rudy had never spoken so much as two words to each other.

The miller was rich, and because of his wealth Babette was rather high to hope for. "But nothing is so high," Rudy told himself, "that one may not reach it. You must climb on, and if you have confidence you won't fall." This was how he had been taught as a child.

Now it so happened that Rudy had some business in Bex. It was quite a journey, for in those days there was no railroad. From the Rhone glaciers, at the very foot of the Simplon, the broad valley of Canton Valais stretches among many and often-shifting mountain peaks, with its mighty Rhone River, whose rising waters often overflow its banks, covering fields and roads, destroying everything. Between the towns of Sion and St. Maurice the valley bends sharply like an elbow, and below St. Maurice it narrows until there is room only for the bed of the river and the narrow carriage road. Canton Valais ends here, and an old tower stands on the side of the mountain like the guardian of the canton, commanding a view across the stone bridge to the customhouse on the other side, where Canton Vaud commences. And the closest of the nearby towns is Bex. Fruitfulness and abundance increase here with every step forward; one enters, so to speak, a grove of chestnut and walnut trees. Here and there cypresses and pomegranates peep out; it is as warm here as if one were in Italy.

Rudy reached Bex, and after finishing his business he took a walk about town; but he saw no one belonging to the mill, not even Babette. And that wasn't what he wanted.

Evening came on; the air was heavy with the fragrance of the wild thyme and the blossoming lime trees; a shining veil of sky blue seemed to lie over the wooded green hills; and a stillness was everywhere. It was not the stillness of sleep or of death—no, it was as if nature were holding her breath, as of posing for her image to be photographed on the blue surface of the heavens above. Here and there among the trees in the green field stood poles that carried the telegraph wires through the silent valley. Against one of them there leaned an object, so motionless that it might have been the dead trunk of a tree; it was Rudy, standing there as still as the world around him at that moment. He wasn't sleeping, nor was he dead; but just as great events of the world, or matters of the highest importance to individuals often are transmitted through the telegraph wires without those wires betraying them by the slightest movement or the faintest sound, so there passed through Rudy's mind the one, mighty, overwhelming thought that now constantly occupied him—the thought of his life's happiness. His eyes were fixed on a single point before him—a light that glimmered through the foliage from the parlor of the miller's house, where Babette lived. Rudy stood as still as if he were taking aim at a chamois; but at that moment he was like the chamois itself, which could stand as if chiseled from rock, and in the next instant, if only a stone rolled past, would spring into life and leave the hunter far behind. And so it was with Rudy, for a thought passed through his mind.

"Never give up!" he said. "Visit the mill; say good evening to the miller, and good day to Babette. You won't fall unless you're afraid of falling. If I'm going to be Babette's husband, she'll have to see me sooner or later!"

Then Rudy laughed, and in good spirits, he went to the mill. He knew what he wanted; he wanted Babette!

The river with its yellowish-white water was rolling along, overhung with willows and lime trees. Rudy went along the path, and, as the old nursery rhyme says,

Found to the miller's house his way;
But no one was at home
Except a pussycat at play!

The cat, which was standing on the steps, arched its back and mewed, but Rudy was not inclined to pay my attention to it. He knocked at the door, but no one heard him; no one opened the door. "Meow!" said the cat. If Rudy had still been a little boy, he would have understood the cat's language, and known that it said, "No one is home!" But now he had to go over to the mill to find out; and there he was told that the miller had gone on a long journey to Interlaken—"Inter Lacus, among the lakes," as the highly learned schoolmaster, Annette's father, had explained the name. There was going to be a great shooting match held there, to begin the next morning and last for eight days. The Swiss from all the German cantons were assembling there, and the miller and Babette had gone, too.

"Poor Rudy," we may well say. It wasn't a lucky time for him to have come to Bex. He could only go home again, which he did, taking the road over St. Maurice and Sion to his own valley, his own mountains. But he wasn't disheartened. The next morning when the sun rose he was in good spirits, for they had never been really depressed.

"Babette is in Interlaken, a good many days' journey from here," he said to himself. "It's a long way if you follow the highway, but not so far if you cut across the mountain, and that's the best way for a chamois hunter. I've traveled that route before; over there is my first home, where I lived with my grandfather when I was a little boy. And there are shooting matches at Interlaken; I'll show I'm the best one there, and I'll be with Babette there too, after I've made her acquaintance."

With his musket and gamebag and his light knapsack packed with his Sunday best, Rudy went up the mountain; it was the shortest way, though still fairly long. But the shooting matches would only begin that day, and were to last more than a week. During all that time, he had been told, the miller and Babette would be staying with their relatives at Interlaken. So Rudy crossed the Gemmi; he planned to descend near Grindelwald.

Happily and in good health he walked along, enjoying the fresh, pure, invigorating mountain air. The valley sank below him; the horizon widened, showing here one snow-capped summit, there another, until the whole of the bright shining Alpine range was visible. Rudy well knew every snow-covered mountain peak. He was now approaching the Schreckhorn, which pointed its white, powdered stone finger high toward the blue vault above.

At last he had crossed the highest mountain ridge. Now the pasture lands sloped down to the valley that was his old home. The air was light, and his thoughts were light; mountain and valley were blooming with flowers and foliage, and his heart was blooming with the bright dreams of youth. He felt as if old age and death would never approach him; life, power, and enjoyment would be before him always. Free as a bird, light as a bird was Rudy; and as the swallows flew past him they sang as in the days of his childhood, "We and you, and you and we!" Everything was light and happy.

Down below lay the green-velvet meadows, dotted with brown wooden houses; and the river Lütschine murmured and rolled along. He could see the glacier, with its edges like green glass bordering the dirty snow, and looking down into the deep crevasses, he saw both the upper and lower glacier. The pealing of the church bells came to his ears, as if they were welcoming him to his old home. His heart beat faster, and so many old memories filled his mind that for a moment he almost forgot Babette.

He was again passing along the same road where, as a little boy, he had stood with the other children to sell the carved wooden toy houses. His grandfather's house still stood over above the pine trees, but strangers lived there now. As in the olden days, the children came running to sell their wares. One of them offered him an Alpine rose, and Rudy took it as a good omen, thinking of Babette. Soon he came to the bridge where the two Lütschines unite; here the foliage was heavier and the walnut trees gave grateful shade. Then he could make out waving flags, the white cross on the red ground—the standard of Switzerland as of Denmark—and before him lay Interlaken.

To Rudy it certainly seemed like a wonderful town—a Swiss town in its Sunday dress. Unlike other market towns, it was not a heap of heavy stone buildings, stiff, cold, foreign looking. No, it looked as if the wooden chalets from the hills above had moved down into the green valley below, with its clear stream rushing swiftly as an arrow, and had ranged themselves in rows, somewhat unevenly, to be sure, to form a street. And most beautiful of all, the streets, which had been built since Rudy had last been there as a child, seemed to be made up of all the prettiest wooden houses his grandfather had carved and that had filled the cupboard at home. They seemed to have transplanted themselves down here and to have grown very much in size, as the old chestnut trees had done.

Every house was a so-called hotel, with carved wooden grillwork around the windows and balconies and with projecting roofs; they were very neat and dainty. Between each house and the wide, hard-surfaced highway was a flower garden. Near these houses, though on only one side of the road, there stood other houses; if they had formed a double row, they would have cut off from view the fresh green meadows where cattle grazed, their bells jingling as in the high Alpine pastures. The valley was surrounded by high mountains, with a little break on one side that revealed the glittering, snow-white Jungfrau, in form the most beautiful of all the Swiss mountains.

What a multitude of gayly dressed ladies and gentlemen from foreign countries! What crowds of country people from the nearby cantons! The marksmen carried the number of their posts in a garland round their hats. There were shouting and racket and music of all kinds, from singing to hand organs and wind instruments. The houses and bridges decorated with flags and verses. Banners waved, and shot after shot was being fired; to Rudy's ears that was the best music. In all this excitement he almost forgot Babette, though it was for her sake alone that he had gone there.

The marksmen were crowding around the targets. Rudy quickly joined them, and he was the best shot of them all, for he always made a bull's-eye.

"Who's that strange fellow, that very young marksman?" people asked. "He speaks the French of Canton Valais; but he can also express himself fluently in our German," said some.

"He is supposed to have lived in the valley, near Grindelwald, when he was a child," someone explained.

The lad was full of life; his eyes sparkled; his aim and his arm were steady, so his shots were always perfect. Good luck brings courage, and Rudy always had courage. Soon a whole circle of admirers was around him; they showed him their esteem and honored him. Babette had almost disappeared from his thoughts. But suddenly a heavy hand was laid on his shoulder, and a deep voice spoke to him in French.

"You're from Canton Valais?"

Rudy turned and saw a fat man with a jolly face. It was the rich miller from Bex, his broad body hiding the slender, lovely Babette; however, she soon came forward, her dark eyes sparkling brightly. The rich miller was very proud that it was a marksman from his own canton who proved to be the best shot and was so much admired and praised. Rudy was truly the child of good fortune; that which he had traveled so far to find, but had nearly forgotten since his arrival, now sought him out.

When in a far land one meets people from his own part of the country, it is easy to make friends, and people speak as if they were well acquainted. Rudy was the foremost at the shooting matches, as the miller was foremost at Bex, because of his money and his fine mill. So, though they had never met before, the two men shook hands warmly. Babette, too, gave the young man her hand frankly, and he pressed it and gazed at her in such a way that it made her blush.

The miller spoke of the long trip they had made and of the many large towns they had seen; it had been quite a journey, for they had traveled partly by railroad and partly by post.

"I came the shorter way," said Rudy. "I came over the mountains. There's no road so high that you can't try it."

"But you can also break your neck," said the miller. "And you look as if you probably *will* break your neck someday; you're so daring."

"One never falls so long as one doesn't think of it," said Rudy.

The miller's relatives at Interlaken, with whom he and Babette were staying, invited Rudy to visit them, since he came from the same canton as their kinfolk. It was a wonderful invitation for Rudy. Luck was running with him, as it always does with those who are self-reliant and remember that "Our Lord gives nuts to us, but he does not crack them for us!"

And Rudy sat with the miller's relatives, almost like one of the family. They drank a toast in honor of the best marksman; Babette clinked glasses with Rudy too, and he in return thanked them for the toast.

In the evening the whole party walked on the lovely avenue, past the gay-looking hotels under the walnut trees, and there was such a large crowd that Rudy had to give Babette his arm. He explained to her how happy he was to have met people from Canton Vaud, for Vaud and Valais were good neighbors. He expressed himself so cordially about this that Babette could not keep from squeezing his hand. As they walked there, they seemed almost like old friends, and she was such a lively, pretty little person. Rudy was greatly amused at her remarks about the absurd affectations in the dress of some of the foreign ladies and the airs they put on; but she really didn't mean to make fun of them, because there must be some nice people among them—yes, some sweet and lovely people, she was sure, for her godmother was a very superior English lady. Eighteen years before, when Babette was christened, that lady had lived in Bex and had given Babette the valuable brooch she was wearing. Her godmother had written her twice, and this year they were to have met her here at Interlaken, where she was bringing her daughters; they were old maids, almost thirty, said Babette—she herself was just eighteen.

Her pretty little mouth was not still for an instant, and everything she said appeared to Rudy to be of the greatest importance, and he in turn told her all he had to tell, how he had been to Bex, and how well he knew the mill, and how often he had seen her, though, of course, she had never noticed him. He told her he had been too disappointed for words when he found she and her father were far away; but still it wasn't far enough to keep him from climbing the wall that made the road so long.

Yes, he said all this, and a great deal more, too. He told her how fond he was of her, and how it was for her sake, and not because of the shooting matches, that he had come to Interlaken.

Babette became very silent now; all this that he confided to her was almost too much to listen to.

As they walked on, the sun set behind the mighty peaks, and the Jungfrau stood in all her glory, encircled by the dark green woods of the surrounding mountains. The big crowd stopped to gaze at it; even Rudy and Babette enjoyed the magnificent scene.

"Nowhere is it more beautiful than it is here!" said Babette.

"Nowhere!" agreed Rudy, with his eyes fixed on Babette.

"Tomorrow I must leave," he said a little later.

"Come and visit us at Bex," Babette whispered. "My father will be very pleased!"

ON THE WAY HOME

Oh, what a load Rudy had to carry the next day, when he started his return home over the mountains! He had two handsome guns, three silver cups, and a silver coffeepot—this last would be useful when he set up his own home. But these valuable prizes were not the heaviest burden he had to bear; a still weightier load he had to carry—or did it carry him?—across the high mountains.

The weather was dismal, gloomy, and rainy; the clouds hung like a mourning veil over the mountain summits and shrouded the shining peaks. The last stroke of the axe had resounded from the woods, and down the side of the mountain rolled the great tree trunks. From the vast heights above they looked like matchsticks, but were nevertheless as big as masts of ships. The Lütschine River murmured its monotonous song; the wind whistled, and the clouds sailed swiftly by.

Suddenly there appeared next to Rudy a young girl; he had not noticed her until she was quite near him. She also was planning to cross the mountain. Her eyes had a peculiar power that compelled one to look into them; they were so clear and deep—bottomless.

"Do you have a sweetheart?" asked Rudy, whose thoughts were filled with love.

"I have none," she laughed, but it seemed as if she were not speaking the truth. "Let us not take the long way around; let us keep to the left—it is shorter."

"Yes, and easier to fall into some crevasse," said Rudy. "You ought to know the route better if you're going to be the guide."

"I know the way very well," she said, "and I have my thoughts collected. Your thoughts are down there in the valley; but up here you should think of the Ice Maiden. People say she is not friendly to the human race."

"I'm not a bit afraid of her," said Rudy. "She couldn't keep me when I was a child, and she won't catch me now that I'm a grown-up man."

Now it became very dark. First rain fell, then snow, and its whiteness was quite blinding.

"Give me your hand, and I shall help you climb," said the girl, touching him with her icy fingers.

"*You* help me?" said Rudy. "I don't yet need a woman's help in climbing!"

Then he walked on away from her quickly. The falling snow thickened about him like a curtain, the wind moaned, and behind him he could hear the girl laughing and singing. It sounded very strange. Surely it must be a specter in the service of the Ice Maiden; Rudy had heard of these things when, as a little boy, he had spent that night on the mountain, during his trip across the mountains.

The snow no longer fell so thickly, and the clouds lay far below him. He looked back, but there was no one to be seen; he could only hear laughing and jeering that did not seem to come from a human being.

When at last he reached the highest part of the mountain, where the path led down into the Rhone valley, he saw in the clear blue heaven, toward Chamonix, two glittering stars. They shone brightly; and he thought of Babette, of himself, and of his good fortune. And these thoughts made him warm.

THE VISIT TO THE MILL

"What grand prizes you have brought home," said his old foster mother. And her strange, birdlike eyes sparkled, as she twisted her thin, wrinkled neck even more strangely and faster than usual. "You carry good luck with you, Rudy. I must kiss you, my dear boy!"

Rudy allowed himself to be kissed, but one could read in his face that he did not enjoy this affectionate greeting.

"How handsome you are, Rudy!" said the old woman.

"Oh, stop your flattery," Rudy laughed; but still the compliment pleased him.

"I repeat it," said the old woman. "And fortune smiles on you."

"Yes, I think you're right there," he said, thinking of Babette. Never before had he longed so for the deep valley.

"They must have come home by now," he told himself. "It's more than two days past the day they intended to return. I must go to Bex!"

So to Bex he went, and the miller and his daughter were home. He was received in friendly fashion, and many messages of remembrance were given him from the family at Interlaken. Babette spoke very little; she had become quite silent, but her eyes spoke, and that was enough for Rudy. The miller, who usually had plenty to say, and was accustomed to making jokes and having them laughed at, for he was "the rich miller," seemed to prefer listening to Rudy's adventures—hearing him tell of the hardships and risks that the chamois hunters had to undergo on the mountain heights, how they had to crawl along the treacherous snowy cornices on the edges of cliffs, attached to the rocks only by the force of wind and weather, and cross the frail bridges cast by the snowstorms over deep ravines.

Rudy looked very handsome, and his eyes flashed as he described the life of a hunter, the cunning of the chamois and the wonderful leaps they made, the powerful foehn, and the rolling avalanche. He noticed that every new description held the miller's interest more and more, and that he was particularly fascinated by the youth's account of the vulture and the great royal eagle.

Not far from there, in Canton Valais, there was an eagle's nest, built cleverly under a projecting platform of rock, in the face of a cliff; and in it there was an eaglet, but it was impossible to get at it.

A few days before an Englishman had offered Rudy a whole handful of gold if he would bring him the eaglet alive.

"But there is a limit to everything," said Rudy. "You can't get at that eaglet up there; it would be madness to try."

As the wine flowed freely and the conversation flowed just as freely, Rudy thought the evening was much too short, although it was past midnight when he left the miller's house after this, his first visit.

For a little while the lights shone through the windows and through the green branches of the trees, while out from the open skylight on the roof crept the Parlor Cat, and along the drainpipe the Kitchen Cat came to meet her.

"Is there any news at the mill?" said the Parlor Cat. "There's some secret lovemaking in this house! The father doesn't know anything about it yet. Rudy and Babette have been stepping on each other's paws under the table all evening. They trod on me twice, but I didn't mew; that would have aroused suspicion.

"Well, *I* would have mewed," said the Kitchen Cat.

"What would go in the kitchen wouldn't do in the parlor," said the Parlor Cat. "I certainly would like to know what the miller will say when he hears about this engagement."

Yes, what would the miller say? That Rudy also was most anxious to know; and he couldn't make himself wait very long. Before many days had passed, when the omnibus crossed the bridge between Cantons Valais and Vaud, Rudy sat in it, with his usual self- confidence and happy thoughts of the favorable answer he would hear that evening.

And later that evening, when the omnibus was driving back along the same road, Rudy was sitting in it again, going home, while the Parlor Cat was running over to the mill with the news.

"Look here, you kitchen fellow, the miller knows everything now. The affair has come to a fine end. Rudy came here toward evening, and he and Babette found a great deal to whisper about, as they stood in the hallway outside the miller's room. I lay at their feet, but they had neither eyes nor thoughts for me.

"'I'll go straight to your father,' said Rudy. 'My proposal is perfectly honorable.'

"'Do you want me to go with you?' said Babette, 'to give you courage?'

"'I have enough courage,' said Rudy, 'but if you're with me, he'll have to be friendly, whether he likes it or not.'

"So they went in. Rudy stepped hard on my tail—he's awfully clumsy. I mewed, but neither he nor Babette had any ears for me. They opened the door, and went in together, and I, too. I jumped up on the back of a chair, for I didn't know if Rudy would kick me. But it was the miller who kicked—and what a kick! Out of the door and back up to the mountains and the chamois! Rudy could take care of them, but not of our little Babette!"

"But what was said?" asked the Kitchen Cat.

"Said? Oh, they said everything that people say when they're wooing! 'I love her, and she loves me; and if there's milk in the can for one, there's milk in the can for two.'

"'But she's much above you,' said the miller. 'She sits on heaps of grain, golden grain—as you know. You can't reach up to her!'

"'There's nothing so high that one can't reach it, if one has the will to do it!' said Rudy, for he is a determined fellow.

"'But you said a little while ago that you couldn't reach the eaglet in its nest! Babette is still higher than that.'

"'I'll take them both,' said Rudy.

"'Yes,' said the miller. 'I'll give her to you when you bring me the eaglet alive!'" Then he laughed until the tears stood in his eyes. 'But now, thank you for your visit, Rudy. Come again tomorrow; then you'll find nobody home! Good-bye, Rudy!'

"Then Babette said farewell too, as meekly as a little kitten that can't see its mother.

"'A promise is a promise, and a man's a man!' said Rudy. 'Don't cry, Babette. I'll bring the eaglet.'

"'I hope you break your neck!' said the miller. 'And then we'll be spared your visits here!' That's what I call kicking him out! Now Rudy's gone, and Babette just sits and cries; but the miller sings German songs he learned in his travels. I'm not going to worry myself about the matter; it wouldn't do any good."

"But it would look better if you pretended," said the Kitchen Cat.

THE EAGLE'S NEST

From the mountain path there sounded lively yodeling that meant good humor and gay courage. The yodeler was Rudy; he was going to see his friend Vesinand.

"You must help me," he said. "We'll take Ragli with us. I have to capture the eaglet up there on the top of the cliff!"

"Better try to capture the moon first. That would be about as easy a job," said Vesinand. "I see you're in good spirits."

"Yes; I'm thinking about marrying. But now, seriously, you must know how things stand with me."

And soon Vesinand and Ragli knew what Rudy wanted.

"You're a daring fellow," they said. "But you won't make it. You'll break your neck."

"One doesn't fall, so long as one doesn't think of it!" said Rudy.

They set out about midnight, with poles, ladders, and ropes. The road led through brushwood and over loose stones, up, always up, up through the dark night. The water roared below, and the water trickled down from above; damp clouds swept heavily along. At last the hunters reached the edge of the precipice, where it was even darker, for the rock walls almost met, and the sky could only be seen through the narrow opening above. Close by was a deep abyss, with the hoarsely roaring water far beneath them.

All three sat quite still. They had to await daybreak, for when the parent eagle flew out, they would have to shoot it if they were to have any hopes of capturing the young one. Rudy was as still as if he were a part of the rock on which he was sitting. He held his gun ready; his eyes were fixed steadily on the highest part of the cleft, where the eagle's nest was hidden under the projecting rock. The three hunters had a long time to wait.

But at last they suddenly heard high above them a crashing, whirring sound, and the air was darkened by a huge object. Two guns took aim at the enormous eagle the moment it left the nest. A shot blazed out; for an instant the outspread wings fluttered, and then the bird slowly began to sink. It seemed that with its tremendous size and wingspread it would fill the whole chasm, and in its fall drag the hunters down with it. The eagle disappeared in the abyss below; the hunters could hear the crashing of trees and bushes, crushed by the fall of the bird.

And now the men began to get busy. Three of the longest ladders were tied tightly together. They were supposed to reach the last stepping place on the margin of the abyss, but they did not reach far enough; and the perpendicular rock side was smooth as a brick wall on up to where the nest was hidden under the highest projecting rock overhang. After some discussion they agreed that the only thing to do was to tie two more ladders together, let them down into the chasm from above, and attach these to the three already raised. With immense difficulty they dragged the two ladders up, binding them with ropes to the top; they were then let out over the rock and hung there swaying in the air over the bottomless abyss. Rudy was already seated on the lowest rung. It was an icy-cold morning, and the mist was rising heavily from the dark chasm below. Rudy was like a fly sitting on some bit of a straw that a bird, while building its nest, might have dropped on the edge of a tall factory chimney; but the insect could fly if the straw gave way, while Rudy could only break his neck. The wind howled about him, while far below in the abyss the gushing water roared out from the melting glacier—the palace of the Ice Maiden.

He then made the ladder swing to and fro, like the spider swings its body when it wants to catch anything in its slender thread; and when he, for the fourth time touched the top of the ladders set up from below, he got a good hold on them, and bound them together with sure and skillful hands, though they swayed as if they hung on worn-out hinges.

The five long ladders, which now reached the nest, seemed like a swaying reed knocking against the perpendicular cliff. And now the most dangerous part of the job was to be done, for he had to climb as a cat climbs. But Rudy could do that, for a cat had taught him. He never noticed the presence of Dizziness, who floated in the air behind him and stretched forth her embracing arms toward him. At last he reached the last step of the highest ladder, and then he found that he was still not high enough even to see into the nest. He would have to use his hands to raise himself up to it; he tried the lowest part of the thick, interwoven branches, forming the base of the nest, to learn if it was sufficiently strong; then having secured a firm hold on a heavy, strong branch, he swung himself up from the ladder until his head and chest were level with the nest. Then there swept over him a horrible stench of carrion, for putrefied lambs, chamois, and birds littered the nest.

Dizziness, who had little power over him, blew the poisonous odor into his face to make him faint, while down below, on the dank, foaming waters of the yawning ravine, sat the Ice Maiden herself, with her long pale-green hair, staring at him with eyes as deadly as two gun barrels. "Now I will catch you!"

In a corner of the nest Rudy could see the eaglet sitting—a big powerful bird, even though it could not yet fly. Staring straight at it, Rudy somehow held on with one hand, while with the other he cast a noose around the bird. Thus it was captured alive; its legs were held by the tightened cord, and Rudy flung the noose over his shoulder, so that the bird hung a good distance below him. Then he held onto a rope, flung out to help him, until his toes at last touched the highest rung of the ladder.

"Hold tightly; don't be afraid of falling and you won't fall!" That was his early training, and Rudy acted on it. He held tightly, climbed down, and believing he couldn't fall, he didn't fall.

Then there arose loud and joyous yodeling. He stood safely on the firm rocky ledge, with his eaglet.

WHAT NEWS THE PARLOR CAT HAD TO TELL

"Here's what you asked for!" said Rudy, as he entered the miller's house at Bex and placed a large basket on the floor. When he took the lid off two yellow eyes surrounded by dark rings glared out, eyes so flashing, so fierce, that they looked as though they would burn or blast anything they saw. The neck was red and downy; the short strong beak opened to bite.

"The eaglet!" cried the miller. Babette screamed and sprang back, but could not tear her eyes from Rudy and the eaglet.

"Nothing frightens you!" said the miller to Rudy.

"And you always keep your word," said Rudy. "Everyone has his principles."

"But how did it happen that you didn't break your neck?" asked the miller.

"Because I held tightly," said Rudy. "And so I'm doing now—holding tightly to Babette."

"Better wait till you get her!" laughed the miller; and Babette knew that was a good sign.

"Let's take the eaglet out of the basket; it's horrible to see its eyes glaring. How did you manage to capture it?"

And Rudy had to describe his adventure. As he talked the miller's eyes opened wider and wider.

"With your courage and good luck you could take care of three wives!" said the miller.

"Thank you! Thank you!" cried Rudy.

"But you won't get Babette just yet!" said the miller, slapping the young hunter good-humoredly on the shoulder.

"Do you know the latest news at the mill?" said the Parlor Cat to the Kitchen Cat. "Rudy has brought us the eaglet and takes Babette in exchange. They have actually kissed each other, and her father saw it! That's as good as an engagement! The old man didn't make any fuss at all; he kept his claws pulled in, took his afternoon nap, and left the two of them to sit and spoon. They have so much to tell each other that they won't have finished until Christmas!"

And they hadn't finished by Christmas, either. The wind shook down the yellow leaves; the snow drifted up in the valleys as well as on the high mountains; the Ice Maiden sat in her stately palace, which grew larger during the winter. The cliffs were covered with sleet, and icicles, big and heavy as elephants, hung down. Where in summer the mountain streams poured down, there were now enormous masses of icy tapestry; fantastic garlands of crystal ice hung over the snow-covered pine trees. Over the deepest valleys the Ice Maiden rode the howling wind. The carpet of snow spread down as far as Bex, so she could go there and see Rudy in the house where he spent so much time with Babette. The wedding was to take place the following summer; and their ears often tingled, for their friends often talked about it.

Then everything was sunny, and the most beautiful Alpine rose bloomed. The lovely, laughing Babette was as charming as the early spring itself—the spring which makes all the birds sing of the summertime and weddings.

"How those two do sit and drool over each other!" said the Parlor Cat. "I'm tired of their mewing now!"

THE ICE MAIDEN

Spring has unfolded her fresh green garlands of walnut and chestnut trees which burst into bloom, especially in the country extending from the bridge at St. Maurice to Lake Geneva and along the banks of the Rhone. With wild speed the river rushes from its sources beneath the green glaciers—the Ice Palace, home of the Ice Maiden, from where she allows herself to be carried on the biting wind up to the highest fields of snow, there to recline on their drifting masses in the warm sunshine. Here she sat and gazed down into the deep valleys below, where she could see human beings busily bustling about, like ants on a sunlit stone.

"'Mental giants,' the children of the sun call you," said the Ice Maiden. "You are only vermin! One rolling snowball, and your houses and villages are crushed, wiped out!" Then she raised her proud head still higher and stared with death-threatening eyes about and below her. Then from the valley there arose a strange sound; it was the blasting of rocks—the labors of men—the building of roadbeds and tunnels for the coming of the railroad.

"They work like moles," she said, "digging passages in the rocks, and therefore are heard these sounds like the reports of guns. If I move my palaces, the noise is stronger than the roar of thunder itself."

Then up from the valley there arose thick smoke—moving forward like a fluttering veil, a waving plume—from the locomotive which on the new railway was drawing a train, carriage linked to carriage, looking like a winding serpent. It shot past with the speed of an arrow.

"They think they're the masters down there, these 'mental giants!'" said the Ice Maiden. "But the powers of nature are still the real rulers!"

And she laughed and sang, and it made the valley tremble.

"It's an avalanche!" the people down there said.

But the children of the sun sang still more loudly of the power of mankind's thought. It commands all, it yokes the wide ocean, levels mountains, fills valleys; the power of thought makes mankind lord over the powers of nature.

At that moment a party of climbers crossed the snowfield where the Ice Maiden sat; they had roped themselves together, to form one large body on the slippery ice, near the deep abyss.

"Vermin!" she said. "*You* the lords of the powers of nature!" And she turned from them and gazed scornfully into the deep valley, where the railway train was rushing along.

"There they sit, those thoughts! But they are in the power of nature's force. I see every one of them! One sits alone like a king, others sit in a group, and half of them are asleep! And when the steam dragon stops, they climb out and go their way. Then the thoughts go out into the world!" And she laughed.

"There's another avalanche!" said the people in the valley.

"It won't reach us!" said two who sat together in the train—"two minds with but a single thought," as we say. They were Rudy and Babette, and the miller was going with them.

"Like baggage," he said. "I'm along with them as sort of extra baggage!"

"There sit those two!" said the Ice Maiden. "Many a chamois have I crushed, millions of Alpine flowers have I snapped and broken, leaving no root behind—I destroy them all! Thoughts! 'Mental giants,' indeed!" Again she laughed.

"That's another avalanche!" said those down in the valley.

THE GODMOTHER

At Montreux, one of the nearby towns which, with Clarens, Bernex, and Crin, encircle the northeast shore of Lake Geneva, lived Babette's godmother, the highborn English lady, with her daughters and a young relative. They had been there only a short while, but the miller had already visited them, announced Babette's engagement, and told them about Rudy and the visit to Interlaken and the young eagle—in short, the whole story. It had pleased them greatly, and they felt very kindly toward Rudy and Babette, and even the miller himself. They insisted upon all three of them coming to Montreux, and that's why they went. Babette wanted to see her godmother, and her godmother wanted to see her.

At the little village of Villeneuve, at the end of Lake Geneva, lay the steamboat which, in a voyage of half an hour, went from there to Bernex, a little below Montreux. That coast has often been celebrated by poets in song and story. There, under the walnut trees, beside the deep, blue-green lake, Byron sat and wrote his melodious verses about the prisoner in the dark, mountain Castle of Chillon. There, where Clarens is reflected amid weeping willows in the clear water, Rousseau wandered, dreaming of his Héloïse. The Rhone River glides beneath the lofty, snow-capped hills of Savoy, and near its mouth there is a small island, so tiny that from the shore it looks as if it were a ship floating in the water. It is just a patch of rocky ground, which a century before a lady had walled around and covered with earth, where three acacia trees were planted that now overshadowed the whole island. Babette was enchanted with this little spot; to her it was the loveliest place to be seen on the whole trip. She said they ought to land there—they must land there—it would be so charming under those beautiful trees. But the steamer passed by and did not stop until it reached Vernex.

The little party passed up among the white sunlit walls that surrounded the vineyards before the little mountain town of Montreux, where the peasants' cottages are shaded by fig trees and laurels and cypresses grow in the gardens. Halfway up the mountain was the hotel where the godmother lived.

The meeting was very cordial. The godmother was a stout, pleasant-looking woman with a smiling, round face. As a child she must certainly have resembled one of Raphael's cherubs; it was still an angel's head, but older, with silver-white hair. The daughters were tall and slender, well dressed and elegant looking. The young cousin with them, who had enough golden hair and golden whiskers for three gentlemen, was dressed in white from head to foot, and promptly began to pay devoted attention to little Babette.

Beautifully bound books and music and drawings were on the large table. The balcony door was open, and from the balcony, there was a lovely view of the calm lake, so bright and clear that the villages, woods, and snow-peaks of Savoy were reflected in it.

Rudy, who was generally so lively and gay, found himself very ill at ease. He moved about as if he were walking on peas over a slippery floor. How slowly the time passed—it was like being in a treadmill! And now they had to go out for a walk! And that was just as tiresome. Rudy had to take two steps forward and one back to keep abreast of the others. They went down to Chillon, the gloomy old castle on the island, to look at dungeons and instruments of torture, rusty chains hanging from rocky walls, stone benches for those condemned to death, trap doors through which the doomed were hurled down onto iron spikes amid the surge. They called it a pleasure to look at these things! It was a dreadful place of execution, elevated by Byron's verse into the world of poetry—but to Rudy still only a place of execution. He leaned out of one of the great windows and gazed down into the blue-green water, and over to the lonely little island with the three acacias. How he longed to be there, free from the whole chattering party!

But Babette was very happy. She had had a wonderful time, she said later; and the cousin she thought was perfect!

"Yes, perfectly flippant!" said Rudy; and that was the first time he had ever said anything to her that did not please her.

The Englishman had given her a little book as s souvenir of Chillon; it was Byron's poem, *The Prisoner of Chillon*, translated into French so that she could read it.

"The book may be all right," said Rudy, "but the finely combed fellow who gave it to you didn't make a hit with me."

"He looks like a flour sack without any flour!" said the miller, laughing at his own wit.

Rudy laughed too, and said that he was exactly right.

THE COUSIN

When Rudy went to visit the mill a couple of days later, he found the young Englishman there. Babette had just set a plate of boiled trout before him, which she herself had decorated with parsley, to make it look appetizing, no doubt. Rudy thought that was entirely unnecessary. What did he want there? What was his business? To be served and pampered by Babette? Rudy was jealous, and that pleased Babette. It amused her to see revealed all the feelings of his heart—the weak as well as the strong.

Love was still an amusement to her, and she played with Rudy's heart; but it must be said that he was still the center of all her thoughts, the dearest and most cherished in the world. Still, the gloomier he looked the more merrily she laughed at him with her eyes. She would even have kissed the blond Englishman with the golden whiskers if it would have made Rudy rush out in a fury, for it would have shown her how much he loved her.

This was not the fair nor the wise thing for little Babette to do, but she was only nineteen. She had no intention of being unkind to Rudy; still less did she think how her conduct would appear to the young Englishman, or how light and improper it was for the miller's modest, newly betrothed daughter.

Where the road from Bex passes beneath the snow-clad peaks, which in the language of the country are called *diablerets*, the mill stood, near a rushing, grayish-white mountain stream that looked as if it were covered with soapsuds. It wasn't that stream that turned the mill wheel, but a smaller one which came tumbling down the rocks on the other side of river. It ran through a reservoir dammed up by stones in the road beneath, and forced itself up with violence and speed into an enclosed wooden basin formed by a wide dam across the rushing river, where it turned the large mill wheel. When the water had piled up behind the dam it overflowed and made the path so wet and slippery that it was difficult for anyone who wanted to take this short cut to the mill to do so without falling into the water. However, the young Englishman thought he would try it.

Dressed in white like a mill worker, he was climbing the path one evening, following the light that shone from Babette's window. He had never learned to climb, and so almost went head first into the stream, but escaped with wet arms and spattered trousers. Soaking wet and covered with mud, he arrived beneath Babette's window, climbed the old linden tree, and there began to make a noise like an owl, which was the only bird he could even try to imitate. Babette heard it and peeped out through the thin curtains, but when she saw the man in white and realized who he was, her little heart pounded with fright, but also with anger. Quickly she put out her light, made sure the window was securely fastened, and then left him to his hooting and howling.

How terrible it would be, she thought, if Rudy were now at the mill! But Rudy wasn't at the mill—no, it was much worse—he was standing right under the tree. Loud words were spoken—angry words—they might come to blows, or even murder!

Babette hurried to open her window and called down to Rudy to go away, adding that she couldn't let him stay there.

"You won't let me stay here!" he cried. "Then this is an appointment! You're expecting some good friend—someone you'd rather see than me! Shame on you, Babette!"

"You are very nasty!" said Babette, and started to cry. "I hate you! Go away! Go away!"

"I haven't deserved anything like this," said Rudy as he went away, his cheeks burning, his heart on fire.

Babette threw herself on her bed and cried. "And you can think that of me, Rudy, of me who loves you so!"

She was angry, very angry, and that was good for her, for otherwise she would have been deeply hurt. As it was, she could fall asleep and enjoy youth's refreshing slumber.

EVIL POWERS

Rudy left Bex and started homeward, following the mountain path, with its cold fresh air, and where the snow is deep and the Ice Maiden reigns. The trees with their thick foliage were so far below him that they looked like potato tops; the pines and bushes became smaller; the Alpine roses were blanketed with snow, which lay in isolated patches like linen put out to be bleached. A single blue gentian stood in his path, and he crushed it with the butt of his gun. Higher up two chamois became visible, and Rudy's eyes sparkled as his thoughts turned into another course, but he wasn't near enough for a good shot. Still higher he climbed, to where only a few blades of grass grew between the rocks. The chamois passed calmly over the snowfields as Rudy pressed on.

The thick mists enshrouded him, and suddenly he found himself on the brink of a steep rock precipice. Then the rain began to fall in torrents. He felt a burning thirst; his head was hot, and his limbs were cold. He reached for his hunting flask, but found it was empty; he had not given it a thought when he rushed away, up the mountain. He had never been sick in his life, but now he suddenly felt that he was ill. He felt exhausted, and wanted only to lie down and sleep; but the rain was streaming down around him. He tried to pull himself out of it, but every object seemed to dance strangely before his eyes.

Suddenly he became aware of something he had never before seen in that place—a small, newly built hut leaning against the rock; and in the doorway stood a young girl. First he thought she was the schoolmaster's daughter, Annette, whom he had once kissed while dancing with her; but she wasn't Annette. But he was sure he had seen her before, perhaps near Grindelwald the evening he went home from the Interlaken shooting matches.

"How did you get here?" he asked.

"I'm home," she said. "Watching my flocks."

"Your flocks! Where do they find grass? There's nothing here but snow and rocks!"

"You know a lot about it!" she said and laughed. "A little way down behind here is a very nice pasture, where my goats go. I take good care of them, and never lose one. What's mine is mine!"

"You're very brave," said Rudy.

"And so are you," she answered.

"If you have any milk, please give me some; I have a terrible thirst."

"I have something much better than milk," she replied, "and you may have some. Yesterday some travelers came here with guides and left half a flask of wine behind them, such wine as you have never tasted. They won't come back for it, and I don't drink it, so you may have it."

She brought the wine, poured some into a wooden goblet, and gave it to Rudy.

"That's fine!" he said. "I have never tasted a wine so warming and reviving!" His eyes sparkled with life; a glowing thrill of happiness swept over him, as if every sorrow and vexation had vanished from his mind; a carefree feeling awoke in him.

"But surely you are Annette, the schoolmaster's daughter!" he exclaimed. "Give me a kiss!"

"Yes, but first give me that pretty ring you're wearing on your finger!"

"My engagement ring?"

"Yes, just that ring," said the girl, then refilling the goblet, she held it to his lips, and he drank again. A feeling of joy seemed to flow through his blood. The whole world was his, he seemed to think, so why torture himself! Everything is created for our pleasure and enjoyment. The stream of life is the stream of happiness; let yourself be carried away on it—that is joy. He looked at the young girl. She was Annette, and yet *not* Annette; but still less was she the magical phantom, as he had called the one he had met near Grindelwald. This girl on the mountain was fresh as newly fallen snow, as blooming as an Alpine rose, as lively as a young lamb; yet still she was formed from Adam's rib, a human being like Rudy himself.

He flung his arms about her and gazed into her marvelously clear eyes. It was only for a second, but how can that second be expressed or described in words? Was it the life of the soul or the life of death that took possessions of his being? Was he carried up high, or did he sink down into the deep and deathly icy crevasse, deeper, always deeper?

He beheld the ice walls shining like blue-green glass; bottomless crevasses yawned about him; the waters dripped, sounding like the chimes of bells, and were as clear as a pearl glowing with pale blue flames. Then the Ice Maiden kissed him—a kiss that sent an icy shiver through his whole body. He gave a cry of pain, tore himself away from her, stumbled, and fell; all went dark before his eyes, but he opened them again. The powers of evil had played their game.

The Alpine girl was gone, and the sheltering hut was gone; water streamed down on the bare rocks, and snow lay everywhere. Rudy was shivering with cold, soaked through to the skin, and his ring was gone—the engagement ring Babette had given him. His gun lay on the snow beside him, but when he took it up and tried to fire it as a signal, it misfired. Damp clouds filled the chasm like thick masses of snow. Dizziness sat there, glaring at her helpless prey, while there rang through the deep crevasse beneath her a sound as if a mass of rock had fallen and was crushing and carrying away everything that obstructed its course.

Back at the miller's Babette sat and wept. It was six days since Rudy had been there—Rudy, who had been in the wrong, and should ask her pardon, for she loved him with all her heart.

AT THE MILLER'S HOUSE

"It's lot of nonsense with those people!" said the Parlor Cat to the Kitchen Cat. "It's all off now between Babette and Rudy. She just sits and cries, and he doesn't think about her any more."

"I don't like that," said the Kitchen Cat.

"I don't either," said the Parlor Cat. "But I'm not going to mourn about it. Babette can take golden whiskers for her sweetheart. He hasn't been here since the night he tried to climb onto the roof!"

The powers of evil carry out their purposes around us and within us. Rudy understood this, and thought about it. What was it that had gone on about him and inside him up there on the mountain? Was it sin or just a feverish dream? He had never known illness or fever before. While he blamed Babette, he also searched his own heart. He remembered the wild tornado, the hot whirlwind that had broken loose in there. Could he confess everything to Babette—every thought which in that hour of temptation almost brought about his action? He had lost her ring, and by that very loss she had won him back. Would she be able to confess to him? When his thoughts turned to her, so many memories crowded his mind that he felt that his heart was breaking. He saw her as a laughing, happy child, full of life; the many loving words she had addressed to him from the fullness of her heart gladdened his soul like a ray of light, and soon there was only sunshine there for Babette.

However, she would have to confess to him, and he would see that she did so.

So he went to the mill, and there was a confession; it began with a kiss, and ended with Rudy's being the sinner. His great fault was that he could have doubted for one moment Babette's faithfulness—*that* was very wicked of him! Such distrust, such violence, might bring misery to both of them. Yes, that was very true! Babette preached him a little sermon, which pleased her greatly and which was very becoming to her. But Rudy was right about one thing—the godmother's nephew was a babbler. She'd burn the book he had given her, and wouldn't keep the slightest thing that would remind her of him.

"Now that's all over with," said the Parlor Cat. "Rudy's back again, and they've made up; and they say that's the greatest of happiness."

"Last night," said the Kitchen Cat, "I heard the rats saying that their greatest happiness was to eat candle grease and have plenty of tainted bacon. Which of them should we believe, the lovers or the rats?"

"Neither of them," said the Parlor Cat. "That's always the safest."

Rudy's and Babette's greatest happiness was drawing near, the most beautiful day, as they call it, was coming—their wedding day!

But the wedding was not to take place in the church at Bex, nor in the miller's house; the godmother had asked that the party be held at her house, and that the ceremony be performed in the pretty little church at Montreux. And the miller was very insistent that they should agree to this arrangement, for he alone knew what the godmother intended giving the young couple—her wedding gift would be well worth such a small concession to her wishes. The day was agreed upon. They would go to Villeneuve the evening before, then proceed to Montreux by boat the next morning, so that the godmother's daughters would have time to dress the bride.

"I suppose there'll be a second ceremony in this house," said the Parlor Cat. "Or else I know I wouldn't give a mew for the whole business."

"There's going to be a feast here, too," said the Kitchen Cat. "The ducks have been killed, the pigeons plucked, and a whole deer is hanging on the wall. My mouth waters when I look at all the food. Tomorrow they start their journey."

Yes, tomorrow! That evening Rudy and Babette sat in the miller's house for the last time as an engaged couple. Outside, the evening glow was on the Alps; the vesper bells were chiming; and the daughters of the sun sang, "That which is best shall come to pass!"

VISIONS IN THE NIGHT

The sun had gone down, and the clouds lay low in the valley of the Rhone between the tall mountains; the wind blew from the south, an African wind; it suddenly sprang up over the high summits like a foehn, which swept the clouds away; and when the wind had fallen everything for a moment was perfectly still. The scattered clouds hung in fantastic shapes between the wooded hills skirting the rushing Rhone; they hung in the shapes of sea monsters of the prehistoric world, of eagles hovering in the air, of frogs leaping in a marsh; they settled down on the swift river and seemed to sail on it, yet they were floating in the air. The current swept along an uprooted pine tree, with the water making circles around it. It was Dizziness and some of her sisters dancing in circles on the foaming stream. The moon lighted up the snow-covered mountain peaks, the dark woods, and the strange white clouds—those visions of the night that seemed to be the powers of nature. The mountain peasant saw them through his window; they sailed past in great numbers before the Ice Maiden, who had come from her glacier palace. She was sitting on a frail boat, the uprooted pine, as the waters from the glacier carried her down the river to the open lake.

"The wedding guests are coming!" was sung and murmured in the air and in the water.

There were visions outside and visions inside. And Babette had a very strange dream.

It seemed to her that she had been married to Rudy for many years. He had gone chamois hunting, leaving her at home; and the young Englishman with the golden whiskers was sitting beside her. His eyes were passionate—his words seemed to have a magic power in them. He held out his hand to her, and she was obliged to follow him; they walked away from her home, always downward. And Babette felt a weight in her heart that became heavier every moment. She was committing a sin against Rudy—a sin against God Himself. And suddenly she found herself alone; her dress had been torn to pieces by thorns, and her hair had turned gray. In deep grief she looked upward, and saw Rudy on the edge of a mountainous ridge. She stretched up her arms to him, but dared neither pray nor call out to him; and neither would have been of any avail, for she soon discovered it was not Rudy, but only his cap and shooting jacket hanging on an alpenstock, as hunters often place them to deceive the chamois. In miserable grief Babette cried, "Oh, if I had only died on my wedding day—the happiest day of my life! Oh, Lord, my God, that would have been a blessing! That would have been the best thing that could have happened for me and Rudy. No one knows his future!" Then in godless despair she hurled herself down into the deep chasm. A thread seemed to break, and the echo of sorrowful tones was heard.

Babette awoke; the dream was ended, and although partly forgotten she knew it had been a frightful one and that she had dreamed about the young Englishman whom she had not seen or thought of for several months. She wondered if he still was at Montreux, and if she would see him at the wedding. A faint shadow passed over Babette's pretty mouth—her brows knitted; but soon there came a smile, and the sparkle returned to her eye. The sun was shining brightly outside, and tomorrow was her and Rudy's wedding day!

When she came down he was already in the parlor, and soon they set off for Villeneuve. They were both so happy, and so was the miller. He laughed and joked, and was in excellent humor, for he was a kind father and an honest soul.

"Now we are the masters of the house," said the Parlor Cat.

THE CONCLUSION

It was not yet evening when the three happy people reached Villeneuve and sat down to dinner. The miller settled himself in a comfortable armchair with his pipe and had a little nap. The young bridal couple went out of the town arm in arm, along the highway, under the wooded hills by the side of the deep blue-green lake. The clear water reflected the gray walls and heavy towers of gloomy-looking Chillon. The little island with its three acacias seemed quite close, looking like a bouquet lying on the lake.

"How lovely it must be over there!" said Babette, who again felt a great desire to go to the island; and her desire could be satisfied at once, for a boat was lying near the bank, and it was easy to undo the rope securing it. There was no one around of whom they could ask permission, so they got into the boat anyway.

Rudy knew how to use the oars. Like the fins of a fish, the oars divided the water, so pliant and yet so powerful, with a back for carrying and a mouth for swallowing—gentle, smiling, calmness itself, yet terrible and mighty in destruction. Foamy wake stretched out behind the boat, and in a few minutes they arrived at the little island, where they landed. There was just room for the two of them to dance.

Rudy whirled Babette around two or three times. Then they sat on the little bench under the drooping acacia and held each other's hands and looked deep into each other's eyes, while the last rays of the setting sun streamed about them. The pine forests on the mountains took on a purplish-red tint like that of blooming heather, and where the trees stopped and the bare rocks began, they glowed as if the mountain itself were transparent. The clouds in the sky glowed a brilliant crimson; the whole lake was like a fresh, blushing rose petal. As the shades of evening gathered, the snow-capped mountains of Savoy turned a dark blue, but the highest summits still shone like red lava and for a moment reflected their light on the mountains before the vast masses were lost in darkness. It was the Alpine glow, and Rudy and Babette thought they had never before seen so magnificent a sight. The snow-covered Dent du Midi glistened like the disk of the full moon when it rises above the horizon.

"Oh, what beauty! What happiness!" both of them said.

"Earth can give me no more," said Rudy. "An evening like this is like a whole life. How often have I realized my good fortune, as I realize it now, and thought that if everything ended for me at once now I have still had a happy life! What a blessed world this is! One day passes, and a new one, even more beautiful than the other, begins. Our Lord is infinitely good, Babette!"

"I'm so happy!" she said.

"Earth can give me no more," exclaimed Rudy. Then the vesper bells sounded from the Savoy mountains and the mountains of Switzerland. The dark-blue Jura stood up in golden splendor in the west.

"God give you all that is brightest and best!" exclaimed Babette.

"He will," said Rudy. "Tomorrow I shall have that wish. Tomorrow you'll be wholly mine—my own lovely, little wife!"

"The boat!" Babette suddenly cried.

For the boat that was to take them back had broken loose and was drifting away from the island.

"I'll get it!" said Rudy, and he stripped off his coat and boots, plunged into the lake, and swam with vigorous strokes after the boat.

The clear blue-green water from the mountain glacier was icy and deep. Rudy looked down into the depths; he took only a single glance, and yet, he thought he saw a gold ring trembling, glittering, wavering there! He thought of his lost engagement ring, and the ring became larger and spread out into a glittering circle, within which appeared the clear glacier. Endless deep chasms yawned about it, and the dropping water tinkled like the sound of bells and glowed with pale blue flames. In a second he beheld what will take us many long words to describe!

Young hunters and young girls, men and women who had once fallen into the glacier's crevasses, stood there as in life, with open eyes and smiling lips, while far below them arose from buried villages the chimes of church bells. The congregation knelt beneath the church roofs; icicles made the organ pipes, and the mountain torrents furnished the music. And the Ice Maiden sat on the clear, transparent ground. She stretched herself up toward Rudy and kissed his feet, and there shot through his limbs a deadly chill like an electric shock—ice and fire, one could not be distinguished from the other in that brief touch.

"Mine! Mine!" sounded around him and within him. "I kissed you when you were little—kissed you on the mouth! Now I kiss you on your toes and your heels—now you belong to me!"

And he disappeared in the clear blue water.

All was still. The church bells had ceased their ringing; their last tones had died away with the glow on the red clouds above.

"You are mine!" sounded from the depths below. "You are mine!" resounded from beyond the heights—from infinity itself!

How wonderful to pass from love to love, from Earth to Heaven!

A thread seemed to break, and sorrowful tones echoed around. The icy kiss of death had conquered what was mortal; the prelude to the drama of life had ended before the play itself had begun. And discord had resolved itself into harmony.

Do you call this a sad story?

Poor Babette! For her it was the hour of anguish. The boat drifted farther and farther away. No one on the mainland knew that the bridal couple had crossed over to the little island. Evening came on, the clouds gathered, and darkness settled down. Alone, despairing and crying, she stood there. A storm broke out; lightning flashed over the Jura mountains and over the peaks of Savoy and Switzerland; from all sides came flash after flash, while one peal of thunder followed the other for minutes at a time. One instant the lightning was so vivid that the surroundings were bright as day—every single vine stem was as distinct as at high noon—and in the next instant everything was plunged back into the blackest darkness. The lightning formed circles and zigzagged, then darted into the lake; and the increasing noise of the rolling thunder echoed from the surrounding mountains. On the mainland the boats had been drawn far up the beach, while all living things sought shelter. And now the rain poured down in torrents.

"Where can Rudy and Babette be in this terrible storm?" said the miller.

Babette sat with folded hands, her head in her lap, utterly worn out by grief, tears, and screams for help.

"In the deep water," she said to herself, "far down there as if under a glacier, *he* lies!"

Then she thought of what Rudy had told her about his mother's death, and of his escape, how he was lifted up out of the cleft of the glacier almost dead. "The Ice Maiden has him again!"

Then there came a flash of lightning as dazzling as the rays of the sun on white snow. Babette jumped up; at that moment the lake rose like a shining glacier; there stood the Ice Maiden, majestic, bluish, pale, glittering, with Rudy's corpse at her feet.

"Mine!" she said, and again everything was darkness and torrential rain.

"Horrible!" groaned Babette. "Ah, why should he die when our day of happiness was so near? Dear God, make me understand; shed light into my heart! I cannot understand the ways of your almighty power and wisdom!"

And God enlightened her heart. A memory—a ray of mercy—her dream of the night before—all rushed vividly through her mind. She remembered the words she had spoken, the wish for the best for herself and Rudy.

"Pity me! Was it the seed of sin in my heart? Was my dream, a glimpse into the future, whose course had to be violently changed to save me from guilt? How miserable I am!"

In the pitch-black night she sat weeping. And now in the deep stillness around her she seemed to hear the last words he had spoken here, "Earth can give me no more." They had been spoken in the fullest of joy; they echoed in the depths of great sorrow.

A few years have passed since that night. The lake smiles; its shores are smiling; the vines yield luscious grapes; steamboats with waving pennants glide swiftly by; pleasure boats with their two sails unfurled skim like white butterflies over the mirrored water; the railway beyond Chillon is open now, leading far into the valley of the Rhone. At every station strangers get out, studying in their little red guidebooks what sights they should see. They visit Chillon, see the little island with the three acacias, and read in their books about a bridal couple who in 1856 rowed over to it one evening—how not until the next morning could the bride's despairing cries be heard on the mainland.

But the guidebooks tell nothing about Babette's quiet life in her father's house—not at the mill, for strangers live there now—in the pretty house near the railway station, where many an evening she gazes from her window beyond the chestnut trees to the snowy mountains over which Rudy had loved to range. In the evening hours she can see the Alpine glow—up there where the daughters of the sun settle down, and sing again their song about the traveler whose coat the whirlwind snatched off, taking it, but not the man himself.

There is a rosy glow upon the mountain's snowfields; there is a rosy tint in every heart in which lives the thought, "God wills what is best for us!" But it is not always revealed to us as it was revealed to Babette in her dream.

THE SNAIL AND
THE ROSEBUSH (1861)

Around the garden ran a hedge of hazelnut bushes, and beyond it lay fields and meadows with cows and sheep; but in the middle of the garden stood a blooming Rosebush, and under it sat a Snail, who had a lot inside his shell—namely, himself.

"Wait till my time comes," it said. "I'll do a great deal more than grow roses; more than bear nuts; or give milk, like cows and the sheep!"

"I expect a great deal from you," said the Rosebush. "May I dare ask when this is going to happen?"

"I'll take my time," said the Snail. "You're always in such a hurry! That does not arouse expectations!"

Next year the Snail lay in almost the same spot, in the sunshine beneath the Rose Tree, which was budding and bearing roses as fresh and as new as ever. And the Snail crept halfway out of its shell, stretched out its horns and drew them back in again.

"Everything looks just as it did last year. No progress at all; the Rose Tree sticks to its roses, and that's as far as it gets."

The summer passed; the autumn came. The Rose Tree still bore buds and roses till the snow fell. The weather became raw and wet, and the Rose Tree bent down toward the ground. The Snail crept into the ground.

Then a new year began, and the roses came out again, and the Snail did, too.

"You're an old Rosebush now," the Snail said. "You must hurry up and die, because you've given the world all that's in you. Whether it has meant anything is a question that I haven't had time to think about, but this much is clear enough—you've done nothing at all for your inner development, or you would certainly have produced something else. How can you answer that? You'll soon be nothing but a stick. Can you understand what I'm saying?"

"You frighten me!" said the Rosebush. "I never thought about that at all."

"No, you have never taken the trouble to think of anything. Have you ever considered yourself, why you bloomed, and how it happens, why just in that way and in no other?"

"No," said the Rosebush. "I was just happy to blossom because I couldn't do anything else. The sun was warm and the air so refreshing. I drank of the clear dew and the strong rain; I breathed, I lived. A power rose in me from out of the Earth; a strength came down from up above; I felt an increasing happiness, always new, always great, so I had to blossom over and over again. That was my life; I couldn't do anything else."

"You have led a very easy life," said the Snail.

"Certainly. Everything was given to me," said the Rosebush. "But still more was granted to you. You're one of those with a deep, thoughtful nature, one of those highly gifted minds that will astonish the world."

"I've no intention of doing anything of the sort!" said the Snail. "The world means nothing to me. What do I have to do with the world? I have enough to do with myself and within myself."

"But shouldn't all of us on Earth give the best we have to others and offer whatever is in our power? Yes, I've only been able to give roses. But you? You who are so richly gifted—what have you given to the world? What do you intend to give?"

"What have I given? What do I intend to give? I spit at the world. It's no good! It has nothing to do with me. Keep giving your roses; that's all you can do! Let the hazel bush bear nuts, let the cows and sheep give milk. They each have their public; but I have mine inside myself. I retire within myself, and there I shall stay. The world means nothing to me." And so the Snail withdrew into his house and closed up the entrance behind him.

"That's so sad," said the Rose Tree. "I can't creep into myself, no matter how much I want to; I must go on bearing roses. Their petals fall off and are blown away by the wind, although once I saw one of the roses laid in a mother's hymnbook, and one of my own roses was placed on the breast of a lovely young girl, and another was kissed by a child in the first happiness of life. It did me good; it was a true blessing. Those are my recollections—my life!"

So the Rose Tree bloomed on in innocence, and the Snail loafed in his house—the world meant nothing to him.

And years rolled by.

The Snail had turned to earth in the Earth, and the Rose Tree had turned to earth in the Earth. Even the rose of memory in the hymnbook was withered, but in the garden new rosebushes bloomed, and new snails crept into their houses and spat at the world, for it meant nothing to them.

Shall we read this story all over again? It'll never be different.

THE TEAPOT *(1863)*

There was a proud Teapot, proud of being made of porcelain, proud of its long spout and its broad handle. It had something in front of it and behind it; the spout was in front, and the handle behind, and that was what it talked about. But it didn't mention its lid, for it was cracked and it was riveted and full of defects, and we don't talk about our defects—other people do that. The cups, the cream pitcher, the sugar bowl—in fact, the whole tea service—thought much more about the defects in the lid and talked more about it than about the sound handle and the distinguished spout. The Teapot knew this.

"I know them," it told itself. "And I also know my imperfections, and I realize that in that very knowledge is my humility and my modesty. We all have many defects, but then we also have virtues. The cups have a handle, the sugar bowl has a lid, but of course I have both, and one thing more, one thing they can never have; I have a spout, and that makes me the queen of the tea table. The sugar bowl and the cream pitcher are permitted to be serving maids of delicacies, but I am the one who gives forth, the adviser. I spread blessings abroad among thirsty mankind. Inside of me the Chinese leaves give flavor to boiling, tasteless water."

This was the way the Teapot talked in its fresh young life. It stood on the table that was prepared for tea and it was lifted up by the most delicate hand. But that most delicate hand was very awkward. The Teapot was dropped; the spout broke off, and the handle broke off; the lid is not worth talking about; enough has been said about that. The Teapot lay in a faint on the floor, while the boiling water ran out of it. It was a great shock it got, but the worst thing of all was that the others laughed at it—and not at the awkward hand.

"I'll never be able to forget that!" said the Teapot, when later on it talked to itself about its past life. "They called me an invalid, and stood me in a corner, and the next day gave me to a woman who was begging for food. I fell into poverty, and was speechless both outside and inside, but as I stood there my better life began. One is one thing and then becomes quite another. They put earth in me, and for a Teapot that's the same as being buried, but in that earth they planted a flower bulb. Who put it there and gave it to me, I don't know; but it was planted there, a substitution for the Chinese leaves and the boiling water, the broken handle and spout. And the bulb lay in the earth, inside of me, and it became my heart, my living heart, a thing I never had before. There was life in me; there were power and might; my pulse beat. The bulb put out sprouts; thoughts and feeling sprang up and burst forth into flower. I saw it, I bore it, and I forgot myself in its beauty. It is a blessing to forget oneself in others!

"It didn't thank me, it didn't even think of me—everybody admired it and praised it. It made me very happy; how much more happy it must have made it!

"One day I heard them say it deserved a better pot. They broke me in two—that really hurt—and the flower was put into a better pot; then they threw me out into the yard, where I lie as an old potsherd. But I have my memory; that I can never lose!"

THE STORM SHIFTS THE SIGNBOARDS (1865)

In olden days, when Grandfather was just a little boy and wore red trousers, a red jacket, a sash around his waist, and a feather in his cap—for that's the way little boys dressed in his childhood when they wore their best clothes—so many things were different from nowadays. There were often street pageants, which we don't see now, for they have been done away with, because they became old-fashioned; but it's fun to hear Grandfather tell about them.

It must have been quite a show to see the shoemakers move their signboard when they changed to a new guild hall. A big boot and a two-headed eagle were painted on their waving silken banner; the youngest journeymen carried the welcome cup and the guild chest, and had red and white ribbons dangling from their shirt sleeves; the older ones wore naked swords with lemons stuck on the points. They had a full band, and the best of their instruments was "The Bird," as Grandfather called the long pole with the half moon and all sorts of sounding dingle-dangle things on it—real Turkish music. It was lifted up and swung, and it was dazzling to the eyes when the sun shone on all that polished gold and silver and brass.

In front of the procession ran a Harlequin in clothes made of many-colored patches, with a black face and with bells on his head, like a sleigh horse. He struck the people with his wand, which made a noise without hurting, and the people pushed against each other to move back and forth; little boys and girls fell over their own feet right into the gutters; old women elbowed their way along, looking sour and scolding. Some people laughed and some people chatted; there were spectators on the steps and in the windows, and, yes, even on the roofs. The sun shone; a little rain fell on the people now and then, but that was a good thing for the farmers; and when finally they became wet through, that was a real blessing to the country.

Ah, what stories Grandfather could tell! When he was a little boy he had seen all that grand show at the height of its splendor. The oldest guild journeyman made a speech from the scaffold where the signboard was hung; it was in verse, just like poetry—which, indeed, it was. There had been three of them working on it, and before writing it they had drunk a whole bowl of punch, so that it would be really good. And the people cheered the speech, but still more they cheered the Harlequin when he appeared on the scaffold and mocked the speaker. The clown cut his capers so gaily, and drank punch out of schnapps glasses, which he then threw out among the people, who caught them in the air. Grandfather had one of them, which the plasterer had caught and presented to him. Yes, it was fun. And at last the signboard hung, decked with flowers and wreaths, on the new guild hall.

You never forget a sight like that, no matter how old you grow, Grandfather said. He himself never forgot it, though afterward he saw many things of pomp and splendor and could tell about them; but the funniest thing of all was when he told about the moving of the signboards in the big town.

Grandfather had gone there with his parents when he was a little boy, and that was the first time he had seen the largest town in the country.

There were so many people in the streets that he thought the signboards were going to be moved; and there were many signboards to move. If these signs had been hung up inside instead of out of doors they would have been filled up hundreds of rooms. There were all kinds of garments painted on the sign at the tailor's; he could change people from uncouth to genteel. There were signboards of tobacconists, with the most cunning little boys smoking cigars, just as in real life; there were signs with butter and salted herrings, minister's ruffs and coffins, and signboards that just carried inscriptions and announcements. Indeed, one could spend a whole day going up and down the streets and looking at the pictures, and at the same time you could learn what sort of people lived inside the houses, for they had hung their own signs outside. That is a very good thing, Grandfather said; in a large town it is instructive to know who lives in all the houses.

But then, something was about to happen to the signboards, just as Grandfather came to town; he has told me about it himself, and there wasn't then any twinkle in his eye, as Mother used to say there was when he was fooling me; he looked quite trustworthy.

That first night he came to the big town, the weather was worse than any we ever have read about in the papers, a storm such as there had never been within man's memory. All the air was full of roof tiles; old wooden fences were blown over; a wheelbarrow even ran for its life by itself along the street. The wind howled in the air; it whistled and it shook everything. It was indeed a terrible storm. The water in the canal ran over the banks, not knowing where it belonged. The storm swept over the town, carrying the chimneys with it; more than one old, proud church tower bent and has never been quite straight since.

A sentry box stood outside the house of the honest old fire chief, whose engine was always the last one at the fire; the storm begrudged him that little box and flung it down the steps and rolled it along the street until, strangely enough, it arose and remained upright before the house of the poor carpenter who had saved the lives of three people at the last fire. But the sentry box didn't give that a thought. The barber's signboard, a large brass dish, was torn off and carried across into the councillor's window. All the neighbors said this seemed almost like malice, for they, like the most intimate lady friends of the family, called the mistress "the Razor"—she was so sharp and knew more about people than they knew about themselves.

A sign with a dried codfish drawn on it flew over to the door of a newspaper writer. That was a pretty poor joke on the part of the storm; it probably didn't remember that a newspaper writer isn't the sort of person to be joked about; he is a king in his own paper and in his own opinions.

The weathercock flew over to the roof of the opposite house, and there it remained—a picture of the darkest wickedness, said the neighbors.

The cooper's barrel was hung just under the sign for "Ladies' Apparel."

The restaurant's menu, which hung in a heavy frame near the door, was placed by the storm just over the entrance to the theater, where nobody ever went. It was a comical program, "Horseradish Soup and Stuffed Cabbage," but it made people go in.

The furrier's foxskin, which was his respectable sign, was hung on the bellpull of the young man who always went to morning church services looking like a folded umbrella, strove for the truth, and was "a model young man," said his aunt.

The sign "Establishment for Higher Education" was moved to the pool hall, and the establishment itself received a board inscribed, "Babies Brought Up Here by the Bottle." This wasn't really witty, only naughty; but the storm did it, and we can't control a storm.

It was a terrible night; and by morning, just think, nearly every signboard in town had been moved! In some cases it was done with so much malice that Grandfather wouldn't talk about it, but he laughed inwardly; I could see that, and it is possible he was up to some mischief.

The poor inhabitants of the big town, especially those who were not familiar with it, were all mixed up figuring out who was who; they couldn't help it when they judged by the signboards. Some people who thought they were coming to a solemn meeting of the town elders, assembled to discuss highly important matters, found themselves instead in a school full of noisy boys just about to jump over their desks.

There were even some people who mistook the church for the theater; and that was really awful!

There has never been such a storm in our days; only Grandfather saw one, and that was when he was a very little boy. Such a storm may never come in our time, but it may in our grandchildren's, and then we must hope and pray that they will keep indoors while the storm shifts the signboards!

AUNTY (1866)

You ought to have known Aunty; she was so lovely. And yet, to be more specific, she wasn't lovely in the usual sense of the word, but she was sweet and charming and funny in her own way—just the type to gossip about when one is in the mood to gossip and be facetious over someone. She should have been put in a play, just because she herself simply lived for the theater and everything that goes on in it. She was so very respectable, even if Agent Nob, whom Aunty called Snob, said she was stage-struck.

"The theater is my schoolroom," she said, "my fountain of knowledge. There I have brushed up on my old Biblical history. Take *Moses*, for instance, or *Joseph and His Brethren*—they're operas now. It is from the theater that I've gained my knowledge of world history, geography, and human nature. I've learned about Parisian life from French farces—it's naughty, but very interesting. How I have cried over *The Riquebourg Family*—to think that the husband had to drink himself to death just so his wife could get her young sweetheart! Ah, yes, many's the tear I've shed in the fifty years I've been going to the theater!"

Aunty knew every play, every piece of scenery, every actor who came on or ever had come on. She really only lived during the nine months of the theatrical season. A summer without a summer stock company was enough to age her, while an evening at the theater that lasted till past midnight prolonged her life. She didn't say, as people did, "Now we will have spring; the stork has come!" or, "There's an item in the paper about the early strawberries!" Instead, she announced the coming of autumn; "Have you seen that the box office is open? They'll begin the performances soon!"

She reckoned the value of a house and its location by its distance from the theater. She was heartbroken to have to leave the narrow alley behind the theater and move to a wide street a little farther away, and live in a house where there were no neighbors opposite her.

"At home my window must be my box at the theater. You can't sit by yourself without ever seeing people. But where I live now, it seems as if I've moved way out into the country. If I want to see people, I have to go into the kitchen and climb up onto the sink. That's the only way I can see my neighbors. Now, in that old alley of mine I could look right into the linen dealer's, and then I was only three steps from the theater; now I am three thousand steps away—a guardsman's steps, at that!"

Aunty might sometimes be ill, but however badly she happened to feel, she never missed the theater. One evening her doctor ordered her to put her feet in sourdough poultices; she did as he told her, but rode off to the theater and sat there with her feet in sourdough. If she had died there it would have pleased her. Thorvaldsen died in the theater; and she called that "a blessed death."

She could not imagine Heaven if there were no theater there; indeed, it was never promised to us, but it surely was conceivable that the many great actors and actresses who had gone on before would want to continue their work.

Aunty had her own private wire from the theater to her room; and the "telegram" came every Sunday for coffee. Her private wire was Mr. Sivertsen of the stage-setting department. It was he who gave the signal for the raising and lowering of the curtain, the setting or striking of the scenery.

From him she received a brief, expressive report of each of the plays. Shakespeare's *Tempest* he called "detestable stuff—there's so much to set up! Why, it begins with water down to the first side drop!" That is to say, the rolling billows extended far forward on the stage. On the other hand, if a play could go through five acts in one and the same set, he said it was sensible and well written; it was a play of rest that could play itself, without all that setting up to do.

In the earlier days, Aunty recalled, meaning some thirty-odd years back, when she and Mr. Sivertsen were indeed much younger, he was then already in the mechanical department, and, as she called him, her "benefactor." At that time it was customary at the town's big and only theater to admit spectators into the cockloft; every stage carpenter had one or two places to dispose of. It was often filled to capacity, and with a very select company; it was said the wives of generals and councilmen had been there, because it was so interesting to look down behind the scenes and see how the performers stood and moved when the curtain was down.

Aunty had been there several times, to tragedies and ballets, for the productions requiring the largest casts were the most interesting to watch from the loft. You sat up there in almost complete darkness, and most people brought their suppers with them. But once three apples and a package of sandwiches filled with sausage fell straight down into the prison where Ugolino was about to die of hunger! The sausage produced a tremendous effect. The audience laughed and cheered, and the sausage was one of the main reasons why the management decided to forbid admission to the cockloft.

"But still I've been there thirty-seven times," said Aunty. "And for that I shall always be grateful to Mr. Sivertsen."

On the last evening that the cockloft was open to the public, they were giving *The Judgment of Solomon*. Aunty could remember it so well, for from her benefactor, Mr. Sivertsen, she had obtained a ticket for Agent Nob. Not that he deserved it, for he always made fun of the theater and teased her about it, but still she had got him a seat in the cockloft. He wanted to look at the goings-on in the theater upside down. "Those were his very words, and just like him," said Aunty.

And so he saw *The Judgment of Solomon* from above, and fell asleep. One would surely have thought that he had come from a big dinner and had drunk many toasts. He slept until after the theater was locked up and had to spend the whole dark night up in the loft. He had a story to tell of his waking up, but Aunty didn't believe a word of it. *The Judgment of Solomon* was played out, the lights were out, and all the people were out, above and below; but then began the epilogue, the real comedy, the best thing of all, according to the agent. Then life came into the properties, and it wasn't *The Judgment of Solomon* that was given now; no, it was *Judgment Day at the Theater.* All this Agent Nob impudently tried to cram into Aunty; that was her thanks for getting him into the cockloft.

The story the agent told was amusing enough to hear, but there were mockery and spite behind it.

"It was very dark up there," said the agent, "but then the witchery began, the great spectacle, *Judgment Day at the Theater.* Ticket takers were at the doors, and every spectator had to show his spiritual testimonial, to decide whether he could enter free or handcuffed, and with or without a muzzle. Fine society people who came too late, after the performance had begun, and young fellows who wasted their time were hitched outside. There they were muzzled, and had felt soles put under their shoes, to walk in on in time for the beginning of the next scene. And then they began *Judgment Day at the Theater.*"

"Purely wickedness," said Aunty, "which our Lord knows nothing about!"

Had the scene painter wanted to get into Heaven he would have had to climb up some stairs he had painted himself but which were too steep for anybody to use. That, of course, was because of his sin against perspective. The stage carpenter who had placed the plants and buildings in lands where they didn't belong had to move them into their proper places before cockcrowing time, if he expected to go to Heaven. Mr. Nob would have to watch his own chances of getting there! And to hear what he said about the actors, both in comedy and tragedy, or in song and dance—why, it was shameful of Mr. Nob! Mr. Nob! He never deserved his place in the cockloft! Aunty didn't believe a word of what he said. He had written it all out, he said—the snob!—and would have it printed, but not until he was dead and buried, since he had no wish to be skinned alive.

Only once had Aunty known terror and anguish in her own temple of happiness, the theater. It was one of those gray winter days when we have only two hours of foggy daylight; it was cold and snowing, but Aunty was bound for the theater. They were giving *Hermann von Unna*, besides a little opera and a grand ballet, with prologue and epilogue—it would last well into the night. Aunty had to be there; her lodger had lent her a pair of sleigh boots, shaggy both outside and inside, that reached all the way up her legs.

Aunty arrived at the theater and was seated in a box; the boots felt warm, so she kept them on. Suddenly there arose the cry of "Fire!" as smoke rolled from one of the wings and down from the cockloft! There was a fearful panic, and people stormed out. Aunty was sitting farthest from the door—"second tier, left-hand side; from there the decorations look best," she said. "They always arrange them so they will look the prettiest from the king's side of the house." Now she wanted to get out of there, but the excited people in front of her thoughtlessly slammed and jammed the door shut. There was Aunty, with no way out and no way in, for the partitions between the boxes were too high. She called for help, but nobody heard her. When she looked over at the tier beneath, she saw it was empty; the balustrade was low; and the drop wasn't very far. Her fright made her feel young and active, so she prepared to jump. She got one foot on the seat and the other over the railing; there she sat astride, well draped in her flowered skirt, with one long leg dangling below, a leg in a huge sleigh boot. That was a sight to see! And it was seen, when finally her cries were heard; and then she was easily rescued, for the fire didn't amount to much.

That was the most memorable evening of her life, she said, and she was glad she hadn't seen herself, for she would have died of shame!

Her benefactor in the mechanical department, Mr. Sivertsen, came to see her regularly every Sunday. But it was a long time between Sundays. So in later years, in the middle of the week, a small child would come to her for the "leavings"; that is, to get her supper from the remains of Aunty's dinner.

This little child was a member of the ballet who really needed the food. She played the roles of a page or a fairy, but her hardest part was the hind legs of the lion in Mozart's *Magic Flute*. She eventually grew up to become the front legs, but for this she was paid only three marks, while as the hind legs she had received one rix-dollar. She had had to creep about as the hind legs, stooping, panting for fresh air. This was very interesting to know, thought Aunty.

Aunty deserved to have lived as long as the theater itself, but she couldn't hold out that long; nor did she die in the theater, but quietly and decently in her own bed. Her dying words were full of significance; she asked, "What are they playing tomorrow?"

She must have left about five hundred rix-dollars; we came to that conclusion from the yearly rental, which amounted to twenty rix-dollars. The money was left by Aunty as a legacy for some deserving old spinster who had no family. It was to be used for a seat in the second tier, left side, every Saturday, for that was when they gave the best plays. There was only one condition imposed on the legatee. As she sat in the theater every Saturday, she was to think of Aunty lying in her grave.

This was Aunty's religion.

THE RAGS (1868)

Outside the paper mill, masses of rags lay piled in high stacks; they had been gathered from far and wide. Every rag had a tale to tell, and told it, too; but we can't listen to all of them. Some of the rags were native; others came from foreign countries.

Now here lay a Danish rag beside a rag from Norway; one was decidedly Danish, the other decidedly Norse, and that was the amusing part about the two, as any good Dane or Norwegian could tell you. They could understand each other well enough, though the two languages were as different, according to the Norwegian, as French and Hebrew. "We go to the hills for our language, and there get it pure and firsthand, while the Dane cooks up some sort of a suckling-sweet lingo!"

So the rags talked—and a rag is a rag in every land the world over; they are considered of no value except in the rag heap.

"I am Norse!" said the Norwegian. "And when I've said I'm Norse I guess I've said enough. I'm firm of fiber, like the ancient granite rocks of old Norway. The land up there has a constitution, like the free United States. It makes my fibers tingle to think what I am and to sound out my thoughts in words of granite!"

"But we have literature," said the Danish rag. "Do you understand what that is?"

"Understand?" repeated the Norwegian. "Lowland creature! Shall I give him a shove uphill and show him a northern light, rag that he is? When the sun of Norway has thawed the ice, then Danish fruit barges come up to us with butter and cheese—an eatable cargo, I grant you—but by way of ballast they bring Danish literature, too! We don't need the stuff. You don't need stale beer where fresh springs spout, and up there is a natural well that has never been tapped or been made known to Europeans by the cackling of newspapers, jobbers, and traveling authors in foreign countries. I speak freely from the bottom of my lungs, and the Dane must get used to a free voice. And so he will someday, when as a fellow Scandinavian he wants to cling to our proud mountain country, the summit of the world!"

"Now a Danish rag could never talk like that—never!" said the Dane. "It's not in our nature. I know myself, and all the other rags are like me. We're too good-natured, too unassuming; we think too little of ourselves. Not that we gain much by our modesty, but I like it; I think it's quite charming. Incidentally, I'm perfectly aware of my own good values, I assure you, but I don't talk about them; nobody can ever accuse me of that. I'm soft and easygoing; bear everything patiently, envy nobody, and speak good of everybody—though there isn't much good to be said of most other people, but that's their business. I can afford to smile at them; I know I'm so gifted."

"Don't speak to me in that lowland, pasteboard language—it makes me sick!" said the Norwegian, as he caught a puff of wind and fluttered away from his own heap to another.

They both became paper; and, as it turned out, the Norwegian rag became a sheet on which a Norwegian wrote a love letter to a Danish girl, while the Danish rag became the manuscript for a Danish poem praising Norway's beauty and strength.

So something good may come even of rags when they have once come out of the rag heap and the change has been made into truth and beauty; they keep up understanding relations between us, and in that there is a blessing.

That is the story. It's rather amusing and offends no one but the rags.

WHAT ONE CAN INVENT (1869)

There was once a young man who studied to become a poet. He wanted to be a poet by next Easter, so that he could marry and earn his living from poetry, which he knew was just a matter of making things up. But he had no imagination. He firmly believed he had been born too late. Every subject had been used up before he had a chance at it, and there was nothing in the world left to write about.

"How happy were the people born a thousand years ago," he sighed. "Then it was an easy thing to be immortal. Even those who were born a hundred years ago were lucky compared with me. They still had things left to make poems about. But now every subject is worn out, and it's no use for me to try my pen on such threadbare stuff."

He thought about it, and worried about it, until he grew very thin and woebegone, the poor fellow. No doctor could help him, but there was one person who would know just the remedy he needed to set him right. She was a little old lady, wonderfully wise, who lived in a tiny gatehouse in the turnpike. She opened and closed the toll gate for everyone who rode by, but she was learned in the ways of the world. She was a clever woman who could do more than open a gate, and she knew far more than the doctor who drives in his own carriage and pays taxes.

"I must go to her," the young man said. He found her house small and tidy, but most uninteresting. Not a tree, not a flower, grew anywhere near it. There was a beehive by her door—very useful; there was a potato patch—very useful; and over the ditch a blackthorn bush had flowered, and now bore fruit—very sour berries that puckered your mouth if you tasted them before they were ripened by frost.

The young man thought to himself, "What a perfect picture this is of the commonplace times we live in." But at least it had set him thinking. He had found the flash of an idea at the old lady's doorway.

"Write it down," she told him. "Crumbs are the same stuff that bread is made of. I know why you have come. You have no imagination, but you want to be a poet by Easter."

"Everything has been written before I was born," he sighed. "Our times are not like the old days."

"Indeed they aren't," the little old lady agreed. "In the old days women like me, who knew dark secrets and how to cure by the use of strange herbs, were burned alive. In the old days poets went about with empty stomachs, and their clothes ragged and patched. Ours are excellent times, the best times of all. But your lack of imagination comes from not using your eyes, and not using your ears, and not saying your prayers at night. There are things all around you to write about, if you only knew how. You can find poetry in the earth, where it grows and flourishes. Whether you dip into the water of a running stream or a stagnant pool, you will find poetry. But first you must understand how to find it. You must learn how to catch the sunlight as it falls. Just try on my spectacles, listen through my ear trumpet, say your prayers, and please, for once in your life, stop thinking about yourself."

That last request was asking almost too much of him. It was more than any woman, however wise and wonderful, should demand of a poet.

When he put on her spectacles and ear trumpet, she turned him out into the potato patch, where she gave him a large potato to hold in his hands.

What did the potato find to tell him about? It told about itself and its forefathers, about the coming of the potato to Europe; about how unjustly it was suspected and abused before anyone realized that potatoes were far more valuable than any lump of gold.

"By the king's own order, we were distributed from the town hall of each city and village. A manifesto was issued to proclaim our great value and merits, but nobody believed it. No one had the least notion of how to plant us. One man dug a hole and emptied his whole bushel of potatoes in it. Another stuck them in the ground, far apart from each other, and waited for the potatoes to grow into trees, so one could shake them off the branches. They saw us grow buds and flowers and watery fruit, but it all withered away. No one thought to look for our real fruit, the potatoes that lay out of sight in the ground. Ah yes, we suffered many abuses—at least our forefathers did—but it was all for the best. Now you know our story."

"That will do," the old lady said. "Come and look at the blackthorn bush."

"We, too," said the blackthorn, "have many relations in the land from which the potatoes came, further north than where they grew. A party of bold Norsemen steered westerly from Norway through fogs and storms, till they came to an unknown land. Here, buried under snow and ice, they found grass and shrubs, and a bush with dark blue berries like the grapes that grow on the vine. These were blackthorn berries that ripen in the frost, the same as ours, so the country was called 'Vineland,' or 'Greenland,' and sometimes 'Blackthorn Land.'"

"What a romantic story!" the young man said.

"Now follow me," the little old lady told him, and she led him to the beehive. It seethed with life. When he looked inside it he saw bees stationed in all the hallways, moving their wings like fans so that the air would be fresh in every part of this great honey mill. That was their business. Other bees came in from the sunshine and flowers. Those bees were born with baskets on their legs. They brought flower dust and emptied it out of their little leg-baskets, to be sorted and made into honey or wax. There was much going and coming. The queen of the hive wanted to try her wings, but when she flies all the other bees have to fly with her. Though the time for this swarming had not yet come, she was bent upon flight. So the bees bit off her majesty's wings to keep her from flying away, and she had to stay right where she belonged.

"Now climb to the top of the ditch, where you have a view of the high road," said the little old lady.

"My goodness! What swarms of people I see," said the young man. "What endless stories I seem to hear in all that buzzing, droning, and confusion. I feel dizzy! I shall fall!"

"Don't!" said the old lady. "Don't fall backward. Go straight forward, right in among the people. Have eyes for all you see, ears for all you hear, and above all throw your whole heart into it. Soon you will find that you do have imagination, and you'll have many thoughts to write down. But before you go, you must give back my spectacles and ear trumpet." She took them from him.

"Now I can't see anything," the young man said. "I can't even hear anything."

"In that case, you won't be a poet by Easter," the little old lady told him.

"Then when shall I be one?" he asked her.

"Neither by Easter, nor yet by Whitsuntide. You have no knack for imagination."

"But how then shall I ever make my living from poetry?"

"That you can do even before Lent. Write about those who write. To criticize their writing is to criticize them, but don't let that trouble you. The more critically you write, the more you'll earn, and you and your wife will eat cake every day."

"How she does imagine things," the young man thought, as he thanked her and said goodbye. But he did just as she told him. Since he could not be a poet himself—since he could not imagine—he took to writing criticism of all those who were poets. And he handled them with no light hand.

All this was told me by the little old lady who knows what one may imagine.

THE GARDENER AND THE NOBLE FAMILY (1872)

About four miles from the city stood an old manor house with thick walls, towers, and pointed gables. Here lived, but only in the summer season, a rich and noble family. Of all the different estates they owned, this was the best and the most beautiful; on the outside it looked as if it had just been cast in a foundry, and the inside was made for comfort and ease. The family coat of arms was carved in stone over the gate; beautiful roses climbed about the arms and the balconies; the courtyard was covered with grass; there were red thorn and whitethorn, and many rare flowers even outside the greenhouse.

The owners of the manor house also had a very skillful gardener. It was a pleasure to see the flower garden, the orchard, and the vegetable garden. A part of the manor's original old garden was still there, consisting of a few boxtree hedges cut so that they formed crowns and pyramids. Behind these stood two old, mighty trees, almost always without leaves, and one might easily think that a storm or a waterspout had scattered great lumps of dirt on their branches, but each lump was a bird's nest. Here, from time immemorial, a screaming swarm of crows and rooks had built their nests; it was a regular bird town, and the birds were the owners, the manor's oldest family—the real lordship! The people below meant nothing to them; they tolerated these crawling creatures, even if every now and then they shot with their guns, making the birds' backbones shiver, so that every bird flew up in fear and cried, "Rak! Rak!"

The gardener often spoke to the noble family about cutting down the old trees; they did not look well, and by taking them away, they might also get rid of the shrieking birds, which then would probably look for another place. But the family did not want to give up either the trees or the swarm of birds; that was something the manor could not lose, something from the olden times, which should never be forgotten.

"Why, those trees are the birds' heritage by this time, so let them keep them, my good Larsen!" Larsen was the gardener's name, but that is of very little consequence to this story.

"Haven't you space enough to work in, little Larsen? Have you not the flower garden, the greenhouse, the orchard, and the vegetable garden?"

Yes, those he had, and he cared for them; he kept them in order and cultivated them with affection and ability, and that the noble family knew; but they did not conceal from him that they often saw flowers and tasted fruits in other people's homes that surpassed what they had in their garden, and that made the gardener sad, for he always wished to do his best and really did his best. He was goodhearted and a good and faithful worker.

One day the noble family sent for him and told him, very kindly, that the day before, at some distinguished friend's home, they had eaten apples and pears that were so juicy and so well flavored that they and all the other guests had expressed their admiration. It was doubtful if the fruits were native, but they ought to be imported and grown here, provided the climate would permit it. It was known that they had been bought from the finest fruit dealer in the city, and it was decided that the gardener was to go there and find out where these apples and pears came from and then order some slips for grafting. The gardener knew the fruit dealer well, because he was the very person to whom he sold the superfluous fruit that grew in the manor garden.

And the gardener went to town and asked the dealer where he got those highly praised apples and pears. "Why, they are from your own garden," said the fruit dealer, and showed him both the apples and pears, which he recognized immediately.

How happy the gardener felt! He hurried back to the family and told them that both the apples and the pears were from their own garden. That they couldn't believe! "That's not possible, Larsen! Can you get a written guarantee to that effect from the fruit dealer?"

Yes, that he could, and a written guarantee he brought.

"That certainly is remarkable!" said the noble family.

Now every day great dishes filled with wonderful apples and pears from their own garden were set on the table. Bushels and barrels of these fruits were sent to friends in the city and outside the city; yes, even to foreign lands. This afforded great pleasure; yet the family added that the last two summers had, of course, been remarkably good for tree fruits and these had done very well all over the country.

Some time passed. The family were dinner guests at court. The next day they sent for the gardener. At the royal table they had eaten melons, very juicy and wonderfully flavored, from their majesties' greenhouse.

"You must go to the court gardener, my good Larsen, and let him give you some seeds of those precious melons."

"But the court gardener got his melon seeds from us!" said the gardener, very pleased.

"Then that man knows how to bring the fruit to a higher perfection!" answered the family. "Each melon was splendid."

"Well, then, I really can feel proud!" said the gardener. "I must tell your lordship that the court gardener had had bad luck with his melons this year, and when he saw how beautiful ours looked, and then tasted them, he ordered three of them for the castle."

"Larsen, don't try to tell us that those were melons from our garden."

"I really believe so," said the gardener.

And he went to the court gardener, from whom he got a written guarantee to the effect that the melons on the royal table were from the manor. This was really a big surprise to the family, and they did not keep the story to themselves; the written guarantee was displayed, and melon seeds were sent far and wide, as grafting slips had been earlier.

These slips, the family learned, had taken and begun to bear fruit of an excellent kind. This was named after the family manor, and the name became known in English, German, and French. This, no one had expected. "Let's hope the gardener won't get big ideas about himself," said the family.

But he took it in a different way; he would strive now to be known as one of the best gardeners in the country and to produce something superior out of all sorts of garden stuff every year. And that he did. But often he was told that the very first fruits he brought out, the apples and the pears, were, after all, the best, that all later variations were very inferior to these. The melons were very good, to be sure, though, of course, they belonged to another species; his strawberries might be called delicious, but no better than those grown by other gardeners, and when one year his radishes did not turn out very well, they spoke only of the unsuccessful radishes and not about all the other fine products he had developed.

It almost seemed as if the family felt a relief in saying, "It didn't go well this year, little Larsen!" Yes, they seemed quite happy when they said, "It didn't go well this year!"

Twice a week the gardener brought fresh flowers up to their drawing room, always arranged with such taste and artistry that the colors seemed to appear even brighter.

"You have good taste, Larsen," said the noble family, "but that is a gift from our Lord, not from yourself!"

One day the gardener brought a large crystal bowl; in it floated a water-lily leaf upon which was laid a beautiful blue flower as big as a sunflower.

"The lotus of Hindustan!" exclaimed the family.

They had never seen a lotus flower before. In the daytime it was placed in the sunlight and in the evening under artificial light. Everyone who saw it found it remarkably beautiful and unusual; yes, even the most highborn young lady in the country, the wise and kindhearted princess, said so. The family considered it an honor to present her with the flower, and the princess took it with her to the castle. Then they went down to their garden to pick another flower of the same kind, but none was to be found. So they sent for the gardener and asked him where he got the blue lotus flower.

"We have been looking for it in vain," they said. "We have been in the greenhouses and round about the flower garden!"

"Oh, no, it's not there," said the gardener. "It is only a common flower from the vegetable garden; but, look, isn't it beautiful! It looks like a blue cactus, and yet it is only the flower of the artichoke!"

"You should have told us that immediately!" said the noble family. "Naturally, we supposed it was a rare, foreign flower. You have ridiculed us to the young princess! She saw the flower in our house and thought it was beautiful; she didn't know the flower, although she knows her botany well, but then, of course, that science has nothing to do with kitchen herbs. How could you do it, Larsen! To place such a flower in our drawing room is enough to make us ridiculous!"

And the gorgeous blue flower from the vegetable garden was taken out of the drawing room, where it didn't belong; yes, and the noble family apologized to the princess and told her that the flower was only a kitchen herb that the gardener had had the idea of exhibiting, and that he had been severely reprimanded for it.

"That was a shame, and very unfair," said the princess. "He has really opened our eyes to a magnificent flower we otherwise would have paid no attention to; he has shown us beauty where we didn't expect to find it. As long as the artichoke is in bloom, our court gardener shall daily bring one of them up to my private room!"

And this was done.

The noble family told the gardener that he could again bring them a fresh artichoke flower.

"It is really beautiful!" they said. "Highly remarkable!" And the gardener was praised.

"Larsen likes that," said the noble family. "He is like a spoiled child."

In the autumn there was a terrific storm. During the night it increased so violently that many of the large trees in the outskirts of the wood were torn up by the roots, and to the great grief of the noble family—yes, they called it grief—but to the gardener's delight, the two big trees with all the birds' nests blew down. Through the storm one could hear the screaming of the crows and the rooks as they beat their wings against the manor windows.

"Now, of course, you are happy, Larsen!" said the noble family. "The storm has felled the trees, and the birds have gone off into the forest. There is nothing from olden times left to see here; every sign and reference has disappeared; it makes us very sad!"

The gardener said nothing, but he thought of what he had long had in his mind, how he could make use of that wonderful, sunny spot, now at his disposal; it could become the pride of the garden and the joy of the family.

The large trees, in falling, had crushed the very old boxtree hedges with all their fancy trimmings. Here he put in a multitude of plants, native plants from the fields and the woods. What no other gardener had ever thought of planting in a manor garden, he planted, giving each its appropriate soil, and sunlight or shadow, according to what the individual plant required. He gave them loving care, and everything grew magnificently.

The juniper tree from the heaths of Jutland rose in shape and color like the Italian cypress; the shiny, thorny Christ's-thorn, evergreen, in the cold of winter and the sun of summer, was beautiful to behold. In the foreground grew ferns of various species; some of them looked as if they were children of the palm tree, others as if they were parents of the pretty plant we call Venushair. Here stood the neglected burdock, so pretty in its freshness that it can be outstanding in a bouquet. The burdock stood in a dry place, but further down, in the moist soil, grew the coltsfoot, also a neglected plant and yet very picturesque with its enormous leaf and its tall stem. Six feet tall, with flower after flower, like an enormous, many-armed candelabra, rose the mullein, just a mere field plant. Here grew the woodruff, the primrose, and the lily of the valley, the wild calla and the fine three-leaved wood sorrel. It was all wonderful to see.

In the front, in rows, grew very tiny pear trees from French soil, fastened to steel wires; by getting plenty of sun and good care they soon bore fruit as large and juicy as in their own country. In place of the two old leafless trees was set a tall flagpole from which Dannebrog—the flag of Denmark—proudly flew; and close by stood another pole, around which the hop tendril twisted and wound its fragrant flower cones in the summer and at harvesttime, but on which in the winter, according to an old custom, oat sheaves were hung, so that the birds could have a good meal during the happy Christmastime.

"Our good Larsen is getting sentimental in his old age," said the family, "but he is true and faithful to us!"

At New Year's, one of the city illustrated papers published a picture of the old manor; it showed the flagpole and the oat sheaves for the birds at the happy Christmastime, and the paper commented that it was a beautiful thought to uphold and honor this old custom, so appropriate to the old manor.

"Anything that Larsen does," said the noble family, "they beat the drum for. He is a lucky man. We should almost be proud to have him!"

But they were not a bit proud of it; they knew they were the masters of the manor, and they could dismiss Larsen, but that they wouldn't do. They were good people, and there are many good people of their kind in the world—and that is fortunate for all the Larsens.

Yes, that is the story of the gardener and the noble family. Now you may think about it!

THE CRIPPLE (1872)

There was an old manor house where a young, splendid family lived. They had riches and many blessings; they liked to enjoy themselves, and yet they did a lot of good. They wanted to make everybody happy, as happy as they themselves were.

On Christmas Eve a beautifully decorated Christmas tree stood in the large old hall, where fire burned in the fireplaces and fir branches were hung around the old paintings. Here gathered the family and their guests; here they sang and danced.

The Christmas festivities had already been well under way earlier in the evening in the servants' quarters. Here also stood a large fir tree, with lighted red and white candles, small Danish flags, swans and fishing nets cut out of colored paper and filled with candies and other sweets. The poor children from the parish had been invited, and each had its mother along. The mothers didn't pay much attention to the Christmas tree, but looked rather at the Christmas table, where there lay woolen and linen cloths for dresses and trousers. Yes, the mothers and the older children looked at this; only the smallest children stretched out their hands toward the candles, the tinsel, and the flags. This whole gathering had come early in the afternoon; they had been served Christmas porridge and roasted goose with red cabbage. Then when the Christmas tree had been looked over and the gifts distributed, each got a small glass of punch and apple-filled *æbleskiver*.

When they returned to their own humble rooms, they talked about the "good living," by which they meant the good food they had had, and the presents were again thoroughly inspected.

Now, among these folks were Garden-Kirsten and Garden-Ole. They were married, and earned their lodging and their daily bread by weeding and digging in the manor house garden. At every Christmas party they received a goodly share of the gifts, but then they had five children, and all five of them were clothed by the wealthy family.

"Our masters are generous people," they said. "But then they can afford it, and they get pleasure out of it."

"The four children received some good clothing to wear," said Garden-Ole, "but why is there nothing here for the Cripple? They always used to think of him, too, even if he wasn't at the party."

It was the eldest of the children they called the Cripple, although his name was Hans. When little, he had been the most able and the liveliest child, but all of a sudden he had become "loose in the legs," as they called it. He could neither walk nor stand, and now he had been lying in bed for nearly five years.

"Yes, I got something for him, too," said the mother. "But it's nothing much; it is only a book for him to read!"

"That won't make him fat!" said the father.

But Hans was happy for it. He was a very bright boy who enjoyed reading, but who also used his time for working, doing as much as he, who always had to lie bedridden, could, to be of some benefit. He was useful with his hands, knitted woolen stockings, and, yes, even whole bedcovers. The lady at the manor house had praised him and bought them. It was a book of fairy tales Hans had received; in it there was much to read and much to think about.

"It is of no use here in this house," said the parents, "but let him read, for it passes the time, and he can't always be knitting stockings."

Spring came; green leaves and flowers began to sprout, and the weeds, too, as one may call the nettles, even if the psalm speaks so nicely about them:

If every king, with power and might,
Marched forth in stately row,
They could not make the smallest leaf
Upon a nettle grow.

There was much to do in the manor house garden, not only for the gardener and his apprentices, but also for Garden-Kirsten and Garden-Ole.

"It's a lot of hard work," they said. "No sooner have we raked the walks, and made them look nice, than they are stepped on again. There is such a run of visitors at the manor house. How much it must cost! But the owners are rich people!"

"Things are strangely divided," said Ole. "We are our Lord's children, says the pastor. Why such a difference, then?"

"That comes from the fall of man!" said Kirsten.

In the evening they talked about it again, while Cripple-Hans was reading his book of fairy tales. Hard times, work, and toil had made the parents not only hard in the hands but also hard in their judgment and opinion.

They couldn't understand, and consequently couldn't explain, the matter clearly, and as they talked they became more peevish and angry.

"Some people are prosperous and happy; others live in poverty. Why should we suffer because of our first parents' curiosity and disobedience! We would not have behaved as those two did!"

"Yes, we would!" said Cripple-Hans all of a sudden. "It is all here in this book!"

"What's in the book?" asked the parents.

And Hans read for them the old fairy tale about the woodcutter and his wife. They, too, argued about Adam's and Eve's curiosity, which was the cause of their misfortune also. The king of the country then came by. "Follow me home," he said, "and you shall be as well off as I, with a seven-course dinner and a course for display. That course is in a closed tureen, and you must not touch it, for if you do, your days of leisure are over!" "What can there be in the tureen?" said the wife. "That's none of our business," said the husband. "Well, I'm not inquisitive," said the woman, "but I would like to know why we don't dare lift the lid; it must be something delicious!" "I only hope there is nothing mechanical about it," said the man, "such as a pistol shot, which goes off and awakens the whole house!" "Oh, my!" said the woman, and she didn't touch the tureen. But during the night she dreamed that the lid lifted itself, and from the tureen came an odor of the most wonderful punch, such as is served at weddings and funerals. In it lay a large silver coin bearing the following inscription, "If you drink of this punch, you will become the two richest people in the world, and all other people will become beggars!" Just then the woman awoke and told her husband about her dream. "You think too much about that thing," he said. "We could lift it gently," said the woman. "Gently," said the man. And the woman lifted the lid very, very gently. Then two small, sprightly mice sprang out and disappeared into a mousehole. "Good night," said the king. "Now you can go home and lie in your own bed. Don't blame Adam and Eve anymore; you two have been just as inquisitive and ungrateful!"

"Where has that story in the book come from?" said Garden-Ole. "It sounds as if it were meant for us. It is something to think about."

The next day they went to work again, and they were roasted by the sun and soaked to the skin by the rain. Within them were grumbling thoughts as they pondered over the story.

The evening was still light at home after they had eaten their milk porridge.

"Read the story about the woodcutter to us again," said Garden-Ole.

"But there are so many other beautiful stories in this book," said Hans, "so many you don't know."

"Yes, but those I don't care about!" said Garden-Ole. "I want to hear the one I know!"

And he and his wife heard it again.

More than one evening they returned to that story.

"It doesn't quite make everything clear to me," said Garden-Ole. "It's the same with people as it is with sweet milk when it sours; some becomes fine cheese, and the other, only the thin, watery whey; so it is with people; some are lucky in everything they do, live high all their lives, and know no sorrow or want."

This Cripple-Hans heard. His legs were weak, but his mind was bright. He read for them from his book of fairy tales, read about "The Man without Sorrow and Want." Yes, where could he be found, for found he must be! The king lay on his sickbed and could not be cured unless he wore the shirt that had belonged to, and been worn on the body of, a man who could truthfully say that he had never known sorrow or want. A command was sent to every country in the world, to all castles and manors, to all prosperous and happy people. But upon thorough questioning, every one of them was found to have known sorrow and want. "I haven't!" said the swineherd, who sat laughing and singing on the edge of the ditch. "I'm the happiest person!" "Then give us your shirt," said the messengers. "You will be paid for it with half of a kingdom." But he had no shirt at all, and yet he called himself the happiest person!

"He was a fine fellow!" shouted Garden-Ole, and he and his wife laughed as they hadn't laughed for years.

Then the schoolmaster came by.

"How pleased you are!" he said. "That is unusual in this house. Have you won a prize in the lottery?"

"No, it isn't that sort of pleasure," said Garden-Ole. "It is because Hans has been reading to us from his book of fairy tales; he read about

'The Man without Sorrow and Want,' and that fellow had no shirt. Your eyes get moist when you hear such things, and from a printed book, at that! Everyone has a load to carry; one is not alone in that. That, at least, is a comfort!"

"Where did you get that book?" asked the schoolmaster.

"Our Hans got it at Christmastime over a year ago. The manor house family gave it to him. They know he likes reading and, of course, that he is a cripple. At the time, we would rather have seen him get two linen shirts. But that book is unusual; it can almost answer one's thoughts."

The schoolmaster took the book and opened it.

"Let's have the same story again," said Garden-Ole. "I don't quite get it yet. And then he must also read the one about the woodcutter."

These two stories were enough for Ole. They were like two sunbeams pouring into that humble room, into the oppressed thoughts that had made them cross and grumbly. Hans had read the whole book, read it many times. The fairy tales carried him out into the world, where he, of course, could not go because his legs would not carry him. The schoolmaster sat beside his bed; they talked together, and both of them enjoyed it.

From that day on, the schoolmaster visited Hans often when his parents were at work, and every time he came it was a great treat for the boy. How attentively he listened to what the old man told him—about the size of the world and about its many countries, and that the sun was nearly half a million times larger than Earth and so far away that a cannon ball in its course would take twenty-five years to travel from the sun to Earth, while the light beams could reach Earth in eight minutes. Of course, every studious schoolboy knew all that, but to Hans this was all new, and even more wonderful than what he had read in the book of fairy tales.

Two or three times a year the schoolmaster dined with the manor house family, and on one of these occasions he told of how important the book of fairy tales was in the poor house, how alone two stories in it had been the means of spiritual awakening and blessing, that the sickly, clever little boy had, through his reading, brought meditation and joy into the house. When the schoolmaster departed from the manor house, the lady pressed two shiny silver dollars in his hand for little Hans.

"Father and Mother must have them," said the boy, when the schoolmaster brought him the money.

And Garden-Ole and Garden-Kirsten both said, "Cripple-Hans, after all, is also a profit and a blessing to us!"

A couple of days later, when the parents were away at work at the manor house, the owners' carriage stopped outside; it was the kindhearted lady who came, happy that her Christmas gift had afforded so much comfort and pleasure to the boy and his parents. She brought fine bread, fruit, and a bottle of sweet syrup, but what was still more wonderful, she brought him, in a gilded cage, a little blackbird which whistled quite charmingly. The bird cage was placed on the old cabinet close by the boy's bed; there he could see and hear the bird; yes, and people way out on the highway could hear it sing.

Garden-Ole and Garden-Kirsten didn't return home until after the lady had driven away. Even though they saw how happy Hans was, they thought there would only be trouble with the present he had received.

"Rich people don't think very clearly," they said. "Now we have that to look after. Cripple-Hans can't do it. In the end, the cat will get it!"

Eight days went by, and still another eight days. During that time the cat was often in the room without frightening the bird, to say nothing of not harming it.

Then one day a great event occurred. It was in the afternoon, while the parents and the other children were at work, and Hans was quite alone. He had the book of fairy tales in his hand and was reading about the fisherman's wife who got her wishes fulfilled; she wished to be king, and that she became; she wished to be emperor, and that, too, she became; but then she wished to be the good Lord—and thereupon she again sat in the muddy ditch she had come from.

Now that story had nothing whatsoever to do with the bird or the cat, but it happened to be the story he was reading when this occurrence took place; he always remembered that afterward.

The cage stood on the cabinet, and the cat stood on the floor and stared, with its yellow-green eyes, at the bird. There was something in the cat's look that seemed to say, "How beautiful you are! I'd like to eat you!" That Hans understood; he could read it in the cat's face.

"Get away, cat!" he shouted. "You get out of this room!"

It looked as if the cat were getting ready to leap. Hans couldn't reach it and had nothing to throw at it but his greatest treasure, the book of fairy tales. This he threw, but the cover was loose and flew to one side, while the book itself, with all its leaves, flew to the other side. The cat slowly stepped backward in the room and looked at Hans as if to say, "Don't get yourself mixed up in this matter, little Hans! I can walk and I can jump. You can do neither."

Hans was greatly worried and kept his eyes on the cat, while the bird also became uneasy. There wasn't a person he could call; it seemed as if the cat knew that, and it prepared itself to jump again. Hans shook his bedcover at it—he could, remember, use his hands—but the cat paid no attention to the bedcover. And after Hans had thrown it without avail, the cat leaped up onto the chair and onto the sill; there it was closer to the bird.

Hans could feel his own warm blood rushing through his body, but that he didn't think of; he thought only about the cat and the bird. The boy could not get out of bed without help; nor, of course, could he stand on his legs, much less walk. It was as if his heart turned inside him when he saw the cat leap straight from the window onto the cabinet and push the cage so that it overturned. The bird fluttered about bewilderedly in the cage.

Hans screamed; a great shock went through him. And without thinking about it, he sprang out of bed, moved toward the cabinet, chased the cat down, and got hold of the cage, where the bird was flying about in great fear. Holding the cage in his hand, he ran out of the door, onto the road. Then tears streamed from his eyes, and joyously he shouted, "I can walk! I can walk!" He had recovered the use of his limbs. Such a thing can happen, and it had indeed happened to Hans.

The schoolmaster lived nearby, and to him he ran on his bare feet, clad only in his shirt and jacket, and with the bird in the cage.

"I can walk!" he shouted. "Oh, Lord, my God!" And he cried out of sheer joy.

And there was joy in the house of Garden-Ole and Garden-Kirsten. "We shall never live to see a happier day," said both of them.

Hans was called to the manor house. He had not walked that road for many years. The trees and the nut bushes, which he knew so well, seemed to nod to him and say, "Good day, Hans! Welcome back out here!" The sun shone on his face and right into his heart.

The owners of the manor house, that young, blessed couple, let him sit with them, and looked as happy as if he were one of their own family. But the happiest of the two was the lady, for she had given him the book of fairy tales and the little songbird. The bird was now dead, having died of fright, but it had been the means of getting his health back. And the book had brought the awakening to him and his parents; he still had it, and he wanted to keep it and read it, no matter how old he became. Now he also could be of help to his family. He wanted to learn a trade; most of all he wanted to be a bookbinder, "because," he said, "then I can get all the new books to read!"

Later in the afternoon the lady called both his parents up to her. She and her husband had talked about Hans—he was a fine and clever boy, with a keen appreciation of reading and a capacity for learning. Our Lord always rewards the good.

That evening the parents were really happy when they returned home from the manor house, especially Kirsten.

But the following week she cried, for then little Hans went away. He was dressed in good, new clothes. He was a good boy, but now he must travel far away across the sea, go to school, and learn Latin. And many years would pass before they would see him again.

The book of fairy tales he did not take with him, because his parents wanted to keep that in remembrance. And the father often read from it, but only the two stories, for those he understood.

And they had letters from Hans, each one happier than the last. He lived with nice people, in good circumstances. But best of all, he liked to go to school; there was so much to learn and to know. He only wished to live to be a hundred years old, and eventually to become a schoolmaster.

"If we could only live to see it!" said the parents, and held each other's hands.

"Just think of what has happened to Hans!" said Ole. "Our Lord thinks also of the poor man's child! And to think that this should have happened to the Cripple! Isn't it as if Hans might have read it for us from the book of fairy tales!"

AUNTY TOOTHACHE (1872)

Where did we get this story? Would you like to know?

We got it from the basket that the wastepaper is thrown into.

Many a good and rare book has been taken to the delicatessen store and the grocer's, not to be read, but to be used as wrapping paper for starch and coffee, beans, for salted herring, butter, and cheese. Used writing paper has also been found suitable.

Frequently one throws into the wastepaper basket what ought not to go there.

I know a grocer's assistant, the son of a delicatessen store owner. He has worked his way up from serving in the cellar to serving in the front shop; he is a well-read person, his reading consisting of the printed and written matter to be found on the paper used for wrapping. He has an interesting collection, consisting of several important official documents from the wastepaper baskets of busy and absent-minded officials, a few confidential letters from one lady friend to another— reports of scandal which were not to go further, not to be mentioned by a soul. He is a living salvage institution for more than a little of our literature, and his collection covers a wide field. He has the run of his parents' shop and that of his present master and has there saved many a book, or leaves of a book, well worth reading twice.

He has shown me his collection of printed and written matter from the wastepaper basket, the most valued items of which have come from the delicatessen store. A couple of leaves from a large composition book lay among the collection; the unusually clear and neat handwriting attracted my attention at once.

"This was written by the student," he said, "the student who lived opposite here and died about a month ago. He suffered terribly from toothache, as one can see. It is quite amusing to read. This is only a small part of what he wrote; there was a whole book and more besides. My parents gave the student's landlady half a pound of green soap for it. This is what I have been able to save of it."

I borrowed it, I read it, and now I tell it.

The title was:

AUNTY TOOTHACHE

I

Aunty gave me sweets when I was little. My teeth could stand it then; it didn't hurt them. Now I am older, am a student, and still she goes on spoiling me with sweets. She says I am a poet.

I have something of the poet in me, but not enough. Often when I go walking along the city streets, it seems to me as if I am walking in a big library; the houses are the bookshelves; and every floor is a shelf with books. There stands a story of everyday life; next to it is a good old comedy, and there are works of all scientific branches, bad literature, and good reading. I can dream and philosophize among all this literature.

There is something of the poet in me, but not enough. No doubt many people have just as much of it in them as I, though they do not carry a sign or a necktie with the word "Poet" on it. They and I have been given a divine gift, a blessing great enough to satisfy oneself, but altogether too little to be portioned out again to others. It comes like a ray of sunlight and fills one's soul and thoughts; it comes like the fragrance of a flower, like a melody that one knows and yet cannot remember from where.

The other evening I sat in my room and felt an urge to read, but I had no book, no paper. Just then a leaf, fresh and green, fell from the lime tree, and the breeze carried it in through the window to me. I examined the many veins in it; a little insect was crawling across them, as if it were making a thorough study of the leaf. This made me think of man's wisdom: we also crawl about on a leaf; our knowledge is limited to that only, and yet we unhesitatingly deliver a lecture on the whole big tree—the root, the trunk, and the crown—the great tree comprised of God, the world, and immortality—and of all this we know only a little leaf!

As I was sitting there, I received a visit from Aunty Mille. I showed her the leaf with the insect and told her of my thoughts in connection with these. And her eyes lit up.

"You are a poet!" she said. "Perhaps the greatest we have. If I should live to see this, I would go to my grave gladly. Ever since the brewer Rasmussen's funeral, you have amazed me with your powerful imagination."

So said Aunty Mille, and she then kissed me.

Who was Aunty Mille, and who was Rasmussen the brewer?

II

We children always called our mother's aunt "Aunty"; we had no other name for her.

She gave us jam and sweets, although they were very injurious to our teeth; but the dear children were her weakness, she said. It was cruel to deny them a few sweets, when they were so fond of them. And that's why we loved Aunty so much.

She was an old maid; as far back as I can remember, she was always old. Her age never seemed to change.

In earlier years she had suffered a great deal from toothache, and she always spoke about it; and so it happened that her friend, the brewer Rasmussen, who was a great wit, called her Aunty Toothache.

He had retired from the brewing business some years before and was then living on the interest of his money. He frequently visited Aunty; he was older than she. He had no teeth at all—only a few black stumps. When a child, he had eaten too much sugar, he told us children, and that's how he came to look as he did.

Aunty could surely never have eaten sugar in her childhood, for she had the most beautiful white teeth. She took great care of them, and she did not sleep with them at night!—said Rasmussen the brewer. We children knew that this was said in malice, but Aunty said he did not mean anything by it.

One morning, at the breakfast table, she told us of a terrible dream she had had during the night, in which one of her teeth had fallen out.

"That means," she said, "that I shall lose a true friend!"

"Was it a false tooth?" asked the brewer with a chuckle. "If so, it can only mean that you will lose a false friend!"

"You are an insolent old man!" said Aunty, angrier than I had seen her before or ever have since.

She later told us that her old friend had only been teasing her; he was the finest man on Earth, and when he died he would become one of God's little angels in Heaven.

I thought a good deal of this transformation and wondered if I would be able to recognize him in this new character.

When Aunty and he had been young, he had proposed to her. She had settled down to think it over, had thought too long, and had become an old maid, but always remained his true friend.

And then Brewer Rasmussen died. He was taken to his grave in the most expensive hearse and was followed by a great number of folks, including people with orders and in uniform.

Aunty stood dressed in mourning by the window, together with all of us children, except our little brother, whom the stork had brought a week before. When the hearse and the procession had passed and the street was empty, Aunty wanted to go away from the window, but I did not want to; I was waiting for the angel, Rasmussen the brewer; surely he had by now become one of God's bewinged little children and would appear.

"Aunty," I said, "don't you think that he will come now? Or that when the stork again brings us a little brother, he'll then bring us the angel Rasmussen?"

Aunty was quite overwhelmed by my imagination, and said, "That child will become a great poet!" And this she kept repeating all the time I went to school, and even after my confirmation and, yes, still does now that I am a student.

She was, and is, to me the most sympathetic of friends, both in my poetical troubles and dental troubles, for I have attacks of both.

"Just write down all your thoughts," she said, "and put them in the table drawer! That's what Jean Paul did; he became a great poet, though I don't admire him; he does not excite one. You must be exciting! Yes, you will be exciting!"

The night after she said this, I lay awake, full of longings and anguish, with anxiety and fond hopes to become the great poet that Aunty saw and perceived in me; I went through all the pains of a poet! But there is an even greater pain—toothache—and it was grinding and crushing me; I became a writhing worm, with a bag of herbs and a mustard plaster.

"I know all about it," said Aunty. There was a sorrowful smile on her lips, and her white teeth glistened.

But I must begin a new chapter in my own and my aunt's story.

III

I had moved to a new flat and had been living there a month. I was telling Aunty about it.

"I live with a quiet family; they pay no attention to me, even if I ring three times. Besides, it is a noisy house, full of sounds and disturbances caused by the weather, the wind, and the people. I live just above the street gate; every carriage that drives out or in makes the pictures on the walls move about. The gate bangs and shakes the house as if there were an earthquake. If I am in bed, the shocks go right through all my limbs, but that is said to be strengthening to the nerves. If the wind blows, and it is always blowing in this country, the long window hooks outside swing to and fro, and strike against the wall. The bell on the gate to the neighbor's yard rings with every gust of wind.

"The people who live in the house come home at all hours, from late in the evening until far into the night; the lodger just above me, who in the daytime gives lessons on the trombone, comes home the latest and does not go to bed before he has taken a little midnight promenade with heavy steps and in iron-heeled shoes.

"There are no double windows. There is a broken pane in my room, over which the landlady has pasted some paper, but the wind blows through the crack despite that and produces a sound similar to that of a buzzing wasp. It is like the sort of music that makes one go to sleep. If at last I fall asleep, I am soon awakened by the crowing of the cocks. From the cellarman's hen coop, the cocks and hens announce that it will soon be morning. The small ponies, which have no stable, but are tied up in the storeroom under the staircase, kick against the door and the paneling as they move about.

"The day dawns. The porter, who lives with his family in the attic, comes thundering down the stairs; his wooden shoes clatter; the gate bangs and the house shakes. And when all this is over, the lodger above begins to occupy himself with gymnastic exercises; he lifts a heavy iron ball in each hand, but he is not able to hold onto them, and they are continually falling on the floor, while at the same time the young folks in the house, who are going to school, come screaming with all their might. I go to the window and open it to get some fresh air, and it is most refreshing—when I can get it, and when the young woman in the back building is not washing gloves in soapsuds, by which she earns her livelihood. Otherwise it is a pleasant house, and I live with a quiet family!"

This was the report I gave Aunty about my flat, though it was livelier at the time, for the spoken word has a fresher sound than the written.

"You are a poet!" cried Aunty. "Just write down all you have said, and you will be as good as Dickens! Indeed, to me, you are much more interesting. You paint when you speak. You describe your house so that one can see it. It makes one shudder. Go on with your poetry. Put some living beings into it—people, charming people, especially unhappy ones."

I wrote down my description of the house as it stands, with all its sounds, its noises, but included only myself. There was no plot in it. That came later.

IV

It was during wintertime, late at night, after theater hours; it was terrible weather; a snowstorm raged so that one could hardly move along.

Aunty had gone to the theater, and I went there to take her home; it was difficult for one to get anywhere, to say nothing of helping another. All the hiring carriages were engaged. Aunty lived in a distant section of the town, while my dwelling was close to the theater. Had this not been the case, we would have had to take refuge in a sentry box for a while.

We trudged along in the deep snow while the snowflakes whirled around us. I had to lift her, hold onto her, and push her along. Only twice did we fall, but we fell on the soft snow.

We reached my gate, where we shook some of the snow from ourselves. On the stairs, too, we shook some off, and yet there was still enough almost to cover the floor of the anteroom.

We took off our overcoats and boots and what other clothes might be removed. The landlady lent Aunty dry stockings and a nightcap; this she would need, said the landlady, and added that it would be impossible for my aunt to get home that night, which was true. Then she asked Aunty to make use of her parlor, where she would prepare a bed for her on the sofa, in front of the door that led into my room and that was always kept locked. And so she stayed.

The fire burned in my stove, the tea urn was placed on the table, and the little room became cozy, if not as cozy as Aunty's own room, where in the wintertime there are heavy curtains before the door, heavy curtains before the windows, and double carpets on the floor, with three layers of thick paper underneath. One sits there as if in a well-corked bottle, full of warm air; still, as I have said, it was also cozy at my place, while outside the wind was whistling.

Aunty talked and reminisced; she recalled the days of her youth; the brewer came back; many old memories were revived.

She could remember the time I got my first tooth, and the family's delight over it. My first tooth! The tooth of innocence, shining like a little drop of milk—the milk tooth!

When one had come, several more came, a whole rank of them, side by side, appearing both above and below—the finest of children's teeth, though these were only the "vanguard," not the real teeth, which have to last one's whole lifetime.

Then those also appeared, and the wisdom teeth as well, the flank men of each rank, born in pain and great tribulation.

They disappear, too, sometimes every one of them; they disappear before their time of service is up, and when the very last one goes, that is far from a happy day; it is a day for mourning. And so then one considers himself old, even if he feels young.

Such thoughts and talk are not pleasant. Yet we came to talk about all this; we went back to the days of my childhood and talked and talked. It was twelve o'clock before Aunty went to rest in the room nearby.

"Good night, my sweet child," she called. "I shall now sleep as if I were in my own bed."

And she slept peacefully; but otherwise there was no peace either in the house or outside. The storm rattled the windows, struck the long, dangling iron hooks against the house, and rang the neighbor's backyard bell. The lodger upstairs had come home. He was still taking his little nightly tour up and down the room; he then kicked off his boots and went to bed and to sleep; but he snores so that anyone with good ears can hear him through the ceiling.

I found no rest, no peace. The weather did not rest, either; it was lively. The wind howled and sang in its own way; my teeth also began to be lively, and they hummed and sang in their way. An awful toothache was coming on.

There was a draft from the window. The moon shone in upon the floor; the light came and went as the clouds came and went in the stormy weather. There was a restless change of light and shadow, but at last the shadow on the floor began to take shape. I stared at the moving form and felt an icy-cold wind against my face.

On the floor sat a figure, thin and long, like something a child would draw with a pencil on a slate, something supposed to look like a person, a single thin line forming the body, another two lines the arms, each leg being but a single line, and the head having a polygonal shape.

The figure soon became more distinct; it had a very thin, very fine sort of cloth draped around it, clearly showing that the figure was that of a female.

I heard a buzzing sound. Was it she or the wind which was buzzing like a hornet through the crack in the pane?

No, it was she, Madam Toothache herself! Her terrible highness, *Satania Infernalis*! God deliver and preserve us from her!

"It is good to be here!" she buzzed. "These are nice quarters—mossy ground, fenny ground! Gnats have been buzzing around here, with poison in their stings; and now I am here with such a sting. It must be sharpened on human teeth. Those belonging to the fellow in bed here shine so brightly. They have defied sweet and sour things, heat and cold, nutshells and plum stones; but I shall shake them, make them quake, feed their roots with drafty winds, and give them cold feet!"

That was a frightening speech! She was a terrible visitor!

"So you are a poet!" she said. "Well, I'll make you well versed in all the poetry of toothache! I'll thrust iron and steel into your body! I'll seize all the fibers of your nerves!"

I then felt as if a red-hot awl were being driven into my jawbone; I writhed and twisted.

"A splendid set of teeth," she said, "just like an organ to play upon! We shall have a grand concert, with jew's-harps, kettledrums, and trumpets, piccolo-flute, and a trombone in the wisdom tooth! Grand poet, grand music!"

And then she started to play; she looked terrible, even if one did not see more of her than her hand, the shadowy, gray, ice-cold hand, with the long, thin, pointed fingers; each of them was an instrument of torture; the thumb and the forefinger were the pincers and wrench; the middle finger ended in a pointed awl; the ring finger was a drill, and the little finger squirted gnat's poison.

"I am going to teach you meter!" she said. "A great poet must have a great toothache, a little poet a little toothache!"

"Oh, let me be a little poet!" I begged. "Let me be nothing at all! And I am not a poet; I have only fits of poetry, like fits of toothache. Go away, go away!"

"Will you acknowledge, then, that I am mightier than poetry, philosophy, mathematics, and all the music?" she said. "Mightier than all those notions that are painted on canvas or carved in marble? I am older than every one of them. I was born close to the Garden of Paradise, just outside, where the wind blew and the wet toadstools grew. It was I who made Eve wear clothes in the cold weather, and Adam also. Believe me, there was power in the first toothache!"

"I believe it all," I said. "But go away, go away!"

"Yes, if you will give up being a poet, never put verse on paper, slate, or any sort of writing material, then I will let you off; but I'll come again if you write poetry!"

"I swear!" I said; "only let me never see or feel you any more!"

"See me you shall, but in a more substantial shape, in a shape more dear to you than I am now. You shall see me as Aunty Mille, and I shall say, 'Write poetry, my sweet boy! You are a great poet, perhaps the greatest we have!' But if you believe me and begin to write poetry, then I will set music to your verses and play them on your mouth harp. You sweet child! Remember me when you see Aunty Mille!"

Then she disappeared.

At our parting I received a thrust through my jawbone like that of a red-hot awl; but it soon subsided, and then I felt as if I were gliding along the smooth water; I saw the white water lilies, with their large green leaves, bending and sinking down under me; they withered and dissolved, and I sank, too, and dissolved into peace and rest.

"To die, and melt away like snow!" resounded in the water. "To evaporate into air, to drift away like the clouds!"

Great, glowing names and inscriptions on waving banners of victory, the letters patent of immortality, written on the wing of an ephemera, shone down to me through the water.

The sleep was deep, a sleep now without dreams. I did not hear the whistling wind, the banging gate, the ringing of the neighbor's gate bell, or the lodger's strenuous gymnastics.

What happiness!

Then came a gust of wind so strong that the locked door to Aunty's room burst open. Aunty jumped up, put on her shoes, got dressed, and came into my room. I was sleeping like one of God's angels, she said, and she had not the heart to awaken me.

I later awoke by myself and opened my eyes. I had completely forgotten that Aunty was in the house, but I soon remembered it and then remembered my toothache vision. Dream and reality were blended.

"I suppose you did not write anything last night after we said good night?" she said. "I wish you had; you are my poet and shall always be!"

It seemed to me that she smiled rather slyly. I did not know if it was the kindly Aunty Mille, who loved me, or the terrible one to whom I had made the promise the night before.

"Have you written any poetry, sweet child?"

"No, no!" I shouted. "You are Aunty Mille, aren't you?"

"Who else?" she said. And it *was* Aunty Mille.

She kissed me, got into a carriage, and drove home.

I wrote down what is written here. It is not in verse, and it will never be printed.

Yes, here ended the manuscript.

My young friend, the grocer's assistant, could not find the missing sheets; they had gone out into the world like the papers around the salted herring, the butter, and the green soap; they had fulfilled their destiny!

The brewer is dead; Aunty is dead; the student is dead, he whose sparks of genius went into the basket. This is the end of the story—the story of Aunty Toothache.

WHAT OLD JOHANNE TOLD (1872)

The wind whistles in the old willow tree. It is as if one were hearing a song; the wind sings it; the tree tells it. If you do not understand it, then ask old Johanne in the poorhouse; she knows about it; she was born here in the parish.

Many years ago, when the King's Highway still lay along here, the tree was already large and conspicuous. It stood, as it still stands, in front of the tailor's whitewashed timber house, close to the ditch, which then was so large that the cattle could be watered there, and where in the summertime the little peasant boys used to run about naked and paddle in the water. Underneath the tree stood a stone milepost cut from a big rock; now it is overturned, and a bramblebush grows over it.

The new King's Highway was built on the other side of the rich farmer's manor house; the old one became a field path; the ditch became a puddle overgrown with duckweed; if a frog tumbled down into it, the greenery was parted, and one saw the black water; all around it grew, and still grow, "muskedonnere," buckbean, and yellow iris.

The tailor's house was old and crooked; the roof was a hotbed for moss and houseleek. The dovecote had collapsed, and starlings built their nests there. The swallows hung nest after nest on the house gable and all along beneath the roof; it was just as if luck itself lived there.

And once it had; now, however, this was a lonely and silent place. Here in solitude lived weak-willed "Poor Rasmus," as they called him. He had been born here; he had played here, had leaped across meadow and over hedge, had splashed, as a child, in the ditch, and had climbed up the old tree. The tree would raise its big branches with pride and beauty, just as it raises them yet, but storms had already bent the trunk a little, and time had given it a crack. Wind and weather have since lodged earth in the crack, and there grow grass and greenery; yes, and even a little serviceberry has planted itself there.

When in spring the swallows came, they flew about the tree and the roof and plastered and patched their old nests, while Poor Rasmus let his nest stand or fall as it liked. His motto was, "What good will it do?"—and it had been his father's, too.

He stayed in his home. The swallows flew away, but they always came back, the faithful creatures! The starling flew away, but it returned, too, and whistled its song again. Once Rasmus had known how, but now he neither whistled nor sang.

The wind whistled in the old willow tree then, just as it now whistles; indeed, it is as if one were hearing a song; the wind sings it; the tree tells it. And if you do not understand it, then ask old Johanne in the poorhouse; she knows about it; she knows about everything of old; she is like a book of chronicles, with inscriptions and old recollections.

At the time the house was new and good, the country tailor, Ivar Ölse, and his wife, Maren, moved into it—industrious, honest folk, both of them. Old Johanne was then a child; she was the daughter of a wooden-shoemaker—one of the poorest in the parish. Many a good sandwich did she receive from Maren, who was in no want of food. The lady of the manor house liked Maren, who was always laughing and happy and never downhearted. She used her tongue a good deal, but her hands also. She could sew as fast as she could use her mouth, and, moreover, she cared for her house and children; there were nearly a dozen children—eleven altogether; the twelfth never made its appearance.

"Poor people always have a nest full of youngsters," growled the master of the manor house. "If one could drown them like kittens and keep only one or two of the strongest, it would be less of a misfortune!"

"God have mercy!" said the tailor's wife. "Children are a blessing from God; they are such a delight in the house. Every child is one more Lord's prayer. If times are bad, and one has many mouths to feed, why, then a man works all the harder and finds out ways and means honestly; our Lord fails not when we do not fail."

The lady of the manor house agreed with her; she nodded kindly and patted Maren's cheek; she had often done so, yes, and had kissed her as well, but that had been when the lady was a little child and Maren her nursemaid. The two were fond of each other, and this feeling did not wane.

Each year at Christmastime winter provisions would arrive at the tailor's house from the manor house—a barrel of meal, a pig, two geese, a tub of butter, cheese, and apples. That was indeed an asset to the larder. Ivar Ölse looked quite pleased, too, but soon came out with his old motto, "What good will it do?"

The house was clean and tidy, with curtains in the windows, and flowers as well, both carnations and balsams. A sampler hung in a picture frame, and close by hung a love letter in rhyme, which Maren Ölse herself had written; she knew how to put rhymes together. She was almost a little proud of the family name Ölse; it was the only word in the Danish language that rhymed with *pölse* (sausage). "At least that's an advantage to have over other people," she said, and laughed. She always kept her good humor, and never said, like her husband, "What good will it do?" Her motto was, "Depend on yourself and on our Lord." So she did, and that kept them all together. The children thrived, grew out over the nest, went out into the world, and prospered well.

Rasmus was the smallest; he was such a pretty child that one of the great portrait painters in the capital had borrowed him to paint from, and in the picture he was as naked as when he had come into this world. That picture was now hanging in the king's palace. The lady of the manor house saw it, and recognized little Rasmus, though he had no clothes on.

But now came hard times. The tailor had rheumatism in both hands, on which great lumps appeared. No doctor could help him—not even the wise Stine, who herself did some "doctoring."

"One must not be downhearted," said Maren. "It never helps to hang the head. Now that we no longer have father's two hands to help us, I must try to use mine all the faster. Little Rasmus, too, can use the needle." He was already sitting on the sewing table, whistling and singing. He was a happy boy. "But he should not sit there the whole day long," said the mother; "that would be a shame for the child. He should play and jump about, too."

The shoemaker's Johanne was his favorite playmate. Her folks were still poorer than Rasmus'. She was not pretty. She went about barefooted, and her clothes hung in rags, for she had no one to mend them, and to do it herself did not occur to her—she was a child, and as happy as a bird in our Lord's sunshine.

By the stone milepost, under the large willow tree, Rasmus and Johanne played. He had ambitious thoughts; he would one day become a fine tailor and live in the city, where there were master tailors who had ten workmen at the table; this he had heard from his father. There he would be an apprentice, and there he would become a master tailor, and then Johanne could come to visit him; and if by that time she knew how to cook, she could prepare the meals for all of them and have a large apartment of her own. Johanne dared not expect that, but Rasmus believed it could happen. They sat beneath the old tree, and the wind whistled in the branches and leaves; it seemed as if the wind were singing and the tree talking.

In the autumn every single leaf fell off; rain dripped from the bare branches. "They will be green again," said Mother Ölse.

"What good will it do?" said her husband. "New year, new worries about our livelihood."

"The larder is full," said the wife. "We can thank our good lady for that. I am healthy and have plenty of strength. It is sinful for us to complain."

The master and lady of the manor house remained there in the country over Christmas, but the week after the new year, they were to go to the city, where they would spend the winter in festivity and amusement. They would even go to a reception and ball given by the king himself. The lady had bought two rich dresses from France; they were of such material, of such fashion, and so well sewn that the tailor's Maren had never seen such magnificence. She asked the lady if she might come up to the house with her husband, so that he could see the dresses as well. Such things had surely never been seen by a country tailor, she said. He saw them and had not a word to say until he returned home, and what he did say was only what he always said, "What good will it do?" And this time he spoke the truth.

The master and lady of the manor house went to the city, and the balls and merrymaking began. But amid all the splendor the old gentleman died, and the lady then, after all, did not wear her grand dresses. She was so sorrowful and was dressed from head to foot in heavy black mourning. Not so much as a white tucker was to be seen.

All the servants were in black; even the state coach was covered with fine black cloth.

It was an icy-cold night; the snow glistened and the stars twinkled. The heavy hearse brought the body from the city to the country church, where it was to be laid in the family vault. The steward and the parish bailiff were waiting on horseback, with torches, in front of the cemetery gate. The church was lighted up, and the pastor stood in the open church door to receive the body. The coffin was carried up into the chancel; the whole congregation followed. The pastor spoke, and a psalm was sung. The lady was present in the church; she had been driven there in the black-draped state coach, which was black inside as well as outside; such a carriage had never before been seen in the parish.

Throughout the winter, people talked about this impressive display of grief; it was indeed a "nobleman's funeral."

"One could well see how important the man was," said the village folk. "He was nobly born and he was nobly buried."

"What good will it do him?" said the tailor. "Now he has neither life nor goods. At least we have one of these."

"Don't speak such words!" said Maren. "He has everlasting life in the Kingdom of Heaven."

"Who told you that, Maren?" said the tailor. "A dead man is good manure, but this man was too highborn to even do the soil any good; he must lie in a church vault."

"Don't speak so impiously!" said Maren. "I tell you again he has everlasting life!"

"Who told you that, Maren?" repeated the tailor. And Maren threw her apron over little Rasmus; he must not hear that kind of talk. She carried him off into the peathouse and wept.

"The words you heard over there, little Rasmus, were not your father's; it was the evil one who was passing through the room and took your father's voice. Say your Lord's Prayer. We'll both say it." She folded the child's hands. "Now I am happy again," she said. "Have faith in yourself and in our Lord."

The year of mourning came to an end. The widow lady dressed in half mourning, but she had whole happiness in her heart. It was rumored that she had a suitor and was already thinking of marriage. Maren knew something about it, and the pastor knew a little more.

On Palm Sunday, after the sermon, the banns of marriage for the widow lady and her betrothed were to be published. He was a woodcarver or a sculptor; just what the name of his profession was, people did not know; at that time not many had heard of Thorvaldsen and his art. The future master of the manor was not a nobleman, but still he was a very stately man. His was one profession that people did not understand, they said; he cut out images, was clever in his work and young and handsome. "What good will it do?" said Tailor Ölse.

On Palm Sunday the banns were read from the pulpit; then followed a psalm and Communion. The tailor, his wife, and little Rasmus were in church; the parents received Communion while Rasmus sat in the pew, for he was not yet confirmed. Of late there had been a shortage of clothes in the tailor's house; the old ones had been turned, and turned again, stitched and patched. Now they were all three dressed in new clothes, but of black material—as at a funeral. They were dressed in the drapery from the funeral coach. The man had a jacket and trousers of it; Maren, a high-necked dress; and Rasmus, a whole suit to grow in until confirmation time. Both the outside and inside cloth from the funeral carriage had been used. No one needed to know what it had been used for before, but people soon got to know.

The wise woman, Stine, and a couple of other equally wise women, who did not live on their wisdom, said that the clothes would bring sickness and disease into the household. "One cannot dress oneself in cloth from a funeral carriage without riding to the grave." The wooden-shoemaker's Johanne cried when she heard this talk. And it so happened that the tailor became more and more ill from that day on, until it seemed apparent who was going to suffer that fate. And it proved to be so.

On the first Sunday after Trinity, Tailor Ölse died, leaving Maren alone to keep things together. She did, keeping faith in herself and in our Lord.

The following year Rasmus was confirmed. He was then ready to go to the city as an apprentice to a master tailor—not, after all, one with ten assistants at the table, but with one; little Rasmus might be counted as a half. He was happy, and he looked delighted indeed, but Johanne wept; she was fonder of him than she had realized. The tailor's wife remained in the old house and carried on the business.

It was at that time that the new King's Highway was opened, and the old one, by the willow tree and the tailor's, became a field path, with duckweed growing over the water left in the ditch there; the milepost tumbled over, for it had nothing to stand for, but the tree kept itself strong and beautiful, the wind whistling among its branches and leaves.

The swallows flew away, and the starlings flew away, but they came again in the spring. And when they came back the fourth time, Rasmus, too, came back to his home. He had served his apprenticeship, and was a handsome but slim youth. Now he would buckle up his knapsack and see foreign countries; that was what he longed for. But his mother clung to him; home was the best place! All the other children were scattered about; he was the youngest, and the house would be his. He could get plenty of work if he would go about the neighborhood—be a traveling tailor and sew for a fortnight at this farm and a fortnight at that. That would be traveling, too. And Rasmus followed his mother's advice.

So again he slept beneath the roof of his birthplace. Again he sat under the old willow tree and heard it whistle. He was indeed good-looking, and he could whistle like a bird and sing new and old songs.

He was well liked at the big farms, especially at Klaus Hansen's, the second richest farmer in the parish. Else, the daughter, was like the loveliest flower to look at, and she was always laughing. There were people who were unkind enough to say that she laughed simply to show her pretty teeth. She was happy indeed, and always in the humor for playing tricks; everything suited her.

She was fond of Rasmus, and he was fond of her, but neither of them said a word about it. So he went about being gloomy; he had more of his father's disposition than his mother's. He was in a good humor only when Else was present; then they both laughed, joked, and played tricks; but although there was many a good opportunity, he did not say a single word about his love. "What good will it do?" was his thought. "Her parents look for profitable marriage for her, and that I cannot give her. The wisest thing for me to do would be to leave." But he could not leave. It was as if Else had a string fastened to him; he was like a trained bird with her; he sang and whistled for her pleasure and at her will.

Johanne, the shoemaker's daughter, was a servant girl at the farm, employed for common work. She drove the milk cart in the meadow, where she and the other girls milked the cows; yes, and she even had to cart manure when it was necessary. She never came into the sitting room and didn't see much of Rasmus or Else, but she heard that the two were as good as engaged.

"Now Rasmus will be well off," she said. "I cannot begrudge him that." And her eyes became quite wet. But there was really nothing to cry about.

There was a market in the town. Klaus Hansen drove there, and Rasmus went along; he sat beside Else, both going there and coming home. He was numb from love, but he didn't say a word about it.

"He ought to say something to me about the matter," thought the girl, and there she was right. "If he won't talk, I'll have to frighten him into it."

And soon there was talk at the farm that the richest farmer in the parish had proposed to Else; and so he had, but no one knew what answer she had given.

Thoughts buzzed around in Rasmus' head.

One evening Else put a gold ring on her finger and then asked Rasmus what that signified.

"Betrothal," he said.

"And with whom do you think?" she asked.

"With the rich farmer?" he said.

"There, you have hit it," she said, nodding, and then slipped away.

But he slipped away, too; he went home to his mother's house like a bewildered man and packed his knapsack. He wanted to go out into the wide world; even his mother's tears couldn't stop him.

He cut himself a stick from the old willow and whistled as if he were in a good humor; he was on his way to see the beauty of the whole world.

"This is a great grief to me," said the mother. "But I suppose it is wisest and best for you to go away, so I shall have to put up with it. Have faith in yourself and in our Lord; then I shall have you back again merry and happy."

He walked along the new highway, and there he saw Johanne come driving with a load of rubbish; she had not noticed him, and he did not wish to be seen by her, so he sat down behind the hedge; there he was hidden—and Johanne drove by.

Out into the world he went; no one knew where. His mother thought, "He will surely come home again before a year passes. Now he will see new things and have new things to think about, but then he will fall back into the old folds; they cannot be ironed out with any iron. He has a little too much of his father's disposition; I would rather he had mine, poor child! But he will surely come home again; he cannot forget either me or the house."

The mother would wait a year and a day. Else waited only a month and then she secretly went to the wise woman, Stine Madsdatter, who, besides knowing something about "doctoring," could tell fortunes in cards and coffee and knew more than her Lord's Prayer. She, of course, knew where Rasmus was; she read it in the coffee grounds. He was in a foreign town, but she couldn't read the name of it. In this town there were soldiers and beautiful ladies. He was thinking of either becoming a soldier or marrying one of the young ladies.

This Else could not bear to hear. She would willingly give her savings to buy him back, but no one must know that it was she.

And old Stine promised that he would come back; she knew of a charm, a dangerous charm for him; it would work; it was the ultimate remedy. She would set the pot boiling for him, and then, wherever in all the world he was, he would have to come home where the pot was boiling and his beloved was waiting for him. Months might pass before he came, but come he must if he was still alive. Without peace or rest night and day, he would be forced to return, over sea and mountain, whether the weather were mild or rough, and even if his feet were ever so tired. He would come home; he had to come home.

The moon was in the first quarter; it had to be for the charm to work, said old Stine. It was stormy weather, and the old willow tree creaked. Stine, cut a twig from it and tied it in a knot. That would surely help to draw Rasmus home to his mother's house. Moss and houseleek were taken from the roof and put in the pot, which was set upon the fire. Else had to tear a leaf out of the psalmbook; she tore out the last leaf by chance, that on which the list of errata appeared. "That will do just as well," said Stine, and threw it into the pot.

Many sorts of things went into the stew, which had to boil and boil steadily until Rasmus came home. The black cock in old Stine's room had to lose its red comb, which went into the pot. Else's heavy gold ring went in with it, and that she would never get again, Stine told her beforehand. She was so wise, Stine. Many things that we are unable to name went into the pot, which stood constantly over the flame or on glowing embers or hot ashes. Only she and Else knew about it.

Whenever the moon was new or the moon was on the wane, Else would come to her and ask, "Can't you see him coming?"

"Much do I know," said Stine, "and much do I see, but the length of the way before him I cannot see. Now he is over the first mountains; now he is on the sea in bad weather. The road is long, through large forests; he has blisters on his feet, and he has fever in his bones, but he must go on."

"No, no!" said Else. "I feel so sorry for him."

"He cannot be stopped now, for if we stop him, he will drop dead in the road!"

A year and a day had gone. The moon shone round and big, and the wind whistled in the old tree. A rainbow appeared across the sky in the bright moonlight.

"That is a sign to prove what I say," said Stine. "Now Rasmus is coming."

But still he did not come.

"The waiting time is long," said Stine.

"Now I am tired of this," said Else. She seldom visited Stine now and brought her no more gifts. Her mind became easier, and one fine morning they all knew in the parish that Else had said "yes" to the rich farmer. She went over to look at the house and grounds, the cattle, and the household belongings. All was in good order, and there was no reason to wait with the wedding.

It was celebrated with a great party lasting three days. There was dancing to the clarinet and violins. No one in the parish was forgotten in the invitations. Mother Ölse was there, too, and when the party came to an end, and the hosts had thanked the guests, and the trumpets had blown, she went home with the leavings from the feast.

She had fastened the door only with a peg; it had been taken out, the door stood open, and in the room sat Rasmus. He had returned home—come that very hour. Lord God, how he looked! He was only skin and bone; he was pale and yellow.

"Rasmus!" said his mother. "Is it you I see? How badly you look! But I am so happy in my heart to have you back."

And she gave him the good food she had brought home from the party, a piece of the roast and of the wedding cake.

He had lately, he said, often thought of his mother, his home, and the old willow tree; it was strange how often in his dreams he had seen the tree and the little barefooted Johanne. He did not mention Else at all. He was ill and had to go to bed.

But we do not believe that the pot was the cause of this, or that it had exercised any power over him. Only old Stine and Else believed that, but they did not talk about it.

Rasmus lay with a fever—an infectious one. For that reason no one came to the tailor's house, except Johanne, the shoemaker's daughter. She cried when she saw how miserable Rasmus was.

The doctor wrote a prescription for him to have filled at the pharmacy. He would not take the medicine. "What good will it do?" he said.

"You will get well again then," said his mother. "Have faith in yourself and in our Lord! If I could only see you get flesh on your body again, hear you whistle and sing; for that I would willingly lay down my life."

And Rasmus was cured of his illness, but his mother contracted it. Our Lord summoned her, and not him.

It was lonely in the house; he became poorer and poorer. "He is worn out," they said in the parish. "Poor Rasmus." He had led a wild life on his travels; that, and not the black pot that had boiled, had sucked out his marrow and given him pain in his body. His hair became thin and gray. He was too lazy to work. "What good will it do?" he said. He would rather visit the tavern than the church.

One autumn evening he was staggering through rain and wind along the muddy road from the tavern to his house; his mother had long since gone and been laid in her grave. The swallows and starlings were also gone, faithful as they were. Johanne, the shoemaker's daughter, was not gone; she overtook him on the road and then followed him a little way.

"Pull yourself together, Rasmus."

"What good will it do?" he said.

"That is an awful saying that you have," said she. "Remember your mother's words, 'Have faith in yourself and in our Lord.' You do not, Rasmus, but you must, and you shall. Never say, 'What good will it do?' for then you pull up the root of all your doings."

She followed him to the door of his house, and there she left him. He did not stay inside; he wandered out under the old willow tree and sat on a stone from the overturned milepost.

The wind whistled in the tree's branches; it was like a song: it was like talk.

Rasmus answered it; he spoke aloud but no one heard him except the tree and the whistling wind.

"I am getting so cold. It is time to go to bed. Sleep, sleep!"

And he walked away, not toward the house, but over to the ditch, where he tottered and fell. Rain poured down, and the wind was icy cold, but he didn't feel this. When the sun rose, and the crows flew over the bulrushes, he awoke, deathly ill. Had he laid his head where he put his feet, he would never have arisen; the green duckweed would have been his burial sheet.

Later in the day Johanne came to the tailor's house. She helped him; she managed to get him to the hospital.

"We have known each other since we were little," she said. "Your mother gave me both ale and food; for that I can never repay her. You will regain your health; you will be a man with a will to live!"

And our Lord willed that he should live. But he had his ups and downs, both in health and mind.

The swallows and the starlings returned, and flew away, and returned again. Rasmus became older than his years. He sat alone in his house, which deteriorated more and more. He was poor, poorer now than Johanne.

"You have no faith," she said, "and if we do not believe in God, what have we? You should go to Communion," she said; "you haven't been since your confirmation."

"What good will it do?" he said.

"If you say that and believe it, then let it be; the Master does not want an unwilling guest at his table. But think of your mother and your childhood. Once you were a good, pious boy. Let me read a psalm to you."

"What good will it do?" he said.

"It always comforts me," she answered.

"Johanne, you have surely become one of the saints." And he looked at her with dull, weary eyes.

And Johanne read the psalm, but not from a book, for she had none; she knew it by heart.

"Those were beautiful words," he said, "but I could not follow you altogether. My head feels so heavy."

Rasmus had become an old man. But Else, if we may mention her, was no longer young, either; Rasmus never mentioned her. She was a grandmother. Her granddaughter was an impudent little girl.

The little one was playing with the other children in the village. Rasmus came along, supporting himself on his stick. He stopped, watched the children play, and smiled to them, old times were in his thoughts. Else's granddaughter pointed at him. "Poor Rasmus!" she shouted. The other little girls followed her example. "Poor Rasmus!" they shouted, and pursued the old man with shrieks. It was a gray, gloomy day, and many others followed. But after gray and gloomy days, there comes a sunshiny day.

It was a beautiful Whitsunday morning. The church was decorated with green birch branches; there was a scent of the woods within it, and the sun shone on the church pews. The large altar candles were lighted, and Communion was being held. Johanne was among the kneeling, but Rasmus was not among them. That very morning the Lord had called him.

In God are grace and mercy.

Many years have since passed. The tailor's house still stands there, but no one lives in it. It might fall the first stormy night. The ditch is overgrown with bulrush and buck bean. The wind whistles in the old tree; it is as if one were hearing a song; the wind sings it; the tree tells it. If you do not understand it, ask old Johanne in the poorhouse.

She still lives there; she sings her psalm, the one she read for Rasmus. She thinks of him, prays to our Lord for him—she, the faithful soul. She can tell of bygone times, of memories that whistle in the old willow tree.

Word Cloud Classics

12 Years a Slave

A Christmas Carol and Other Holiday Treasures

Adventures of Huckleberry Finn

The Adventures of Sherlock Holmes

Aesop's Fables

The Age of Innocence

Anna Karenina

Anne of Green Gables

The Art of War

Black Beauty

The Brothers Grimm 101 Fairy Tales

The Brothers Grimm Volume II: 110 Grimmer Fairy Tales

Common Sense and Selected Works of Thomas Paine

The Count of Monte Cristo

Don Quixote

Dracula

Emma

Frankenstein

Great Expectations

Hans Christian Andersen Tales

Inferno

Jane Eyre

The Jungle Book

Lady Chatterley's Lover

Leaves of Grass

Les Misérables

Word Cloud Classics

Little Women

Madame Bovary

Moby-Dick

*Narrative of the Life
of Frederick Douglass
and Other Works*

Persuasion

Peter Pan

The Picture of Dorian Gray

*The Poetry of Emily
Dickinson*

Pride and Prejudice

*The Prince and
Other Writings*

*The Red Badge of Courage
and Other Stories*

The Romantic Poets

The Scarlet Letter

The Secret Garden

Sense and Sensibility

*Strange Case of
Dr. Jekyll and Mr. Hyde
& Other Stories*

The Three Musketeers

Treasure Island

*Twenty Thousand Leagues
Under the Sea*

*Uncle Tom's Cabin, or
Life Among the Lowly*

*The U.S. Constitution
and Other Key
American Writings*

*Walden and Civil
Disobedience*

The Wizard of Oz